P9-CCQ-613

Promises to Keep

Other Books by the Author

The Presence
The Maestro

Promises to Keep

T. DAVIS BUNN

BETHANY HOUSE PUBLISHERS
MINNEAPOLIS, MINNESOTA 55438

It is important to note that, except as specifically mentioned within the Acknowledgments section, this particular story is entirely a creation of the author's imagination. No parallel between any persons, living or dead, is intended.

Unless otherwise credited, scripture quotations are taken from the Holy Bible, New International Version. Copyright © 1973, 1978, International Bible Society. Used by permission of Zondervan Bible Publishers.

Copyright © 1991
T. Davis Bunn
All Rights Reserved

Published by Bethany House Publishers
A Ministry of Bethany Fellowship, Inc.
6820 Auto Club Road, Minneapolis, Minnesota 55438

Printed in the United States of America

Library of Congress Cataloging-in-Publication Data

Bunn, T. Davis, 1952–
    Promises to keep / T. Davis Bunn.
      p. cm.

    I. Title.
PS3552.U4718P76   1991
813'.54—dc20   91–25561
ISBN 1–55661–213–3   CIP

To all children everywhere
searching for a way home.

"There are only two lasting bequests we can hope to give our children. One of these is roots, the other, wings."

Hodding Carter

T. DAVIS BUNN, a native of North Carolina, is the director of an investment consulting group in Dusseldorf, Germany. After completing graduate studies in economics and international finance, Davis worked first as a university professor and then as marketing manager for a Swiss firm. His career has taken him to over forty countries in Europe, Africa, and the Middle East. Davis draws on this experience and the Holy Spirit's inspiration in crafting his stories. He shares his life and his work on the writing with his wife, Isabella.

*"He has given us his very great
and precious promises, so that
through them you may
participate in the divine nature
and escape the corruption in
the world caused by evil
desires."*

2 PETER 1:4

"When hearings are being held in Congress on issues of significance to the family, you can be sure the American Civil Liberties Union will be there. The National Organization of Women will be there. Gay rights activists will be there. The National Abortion Rights Action League will be there. And Norman Lear's People for the American Way will be there. But where are *our* troops? Well, they're taking care of business back home in Indiana or Texas or Pennsylvania. Chances are they won't even know the issues are being discussed unless some lonely crier spreads the word."

Dr. James Dobson and Gary L. Bauer
*Children At Risk: The Battle for
the Hearts and Minds of Our Kids*

CHAPTER
1

Duncan Wyeth's office was in one of the cheaper mini-center developments outside the city limits of Columbia, Maryland, not far from Owen Mill. Orange aluminum siding disguised the remnants of a Westward Ho steakhouse; the interior had mock walnut paneling and a tricolor shag rug. To his left was a chiropractor who specialized in young female clients. On his right was an overweight dear in baubles and flowery dresses who read palms and swore she was a true Armenian gypsy. Duncan decided she was a recent Jersey import after hearing her roast a guy in a souped-up Firebird who scooped out her rear fender.

Duncan drove a battered Lincoln Continental, one of the last cars made in the style of a chrome-plated tank. The motor was large enough to push a fair-sized tugboat against the tide, and drank an embarrassing amount of oil. But he was attached to it. He had bought it with his daughter on his thirty-sixth and her fourteenth birthday, the last birthday he had ever celebrated. Nowadays, on that one day of the year, he steered clear of the garage and the memories.

Duncan rarely bothered to wash the car, as it only accentuated the scars of a hard life. But he had the habit of rubbing the dust off the bumper sticker every day or so. Otherwise the long drive down his dirt driveway would leave the words as cloudy as his license plate. The sticker read, *Life Is Uncertain: Eat Dessert First.*

Duncan had rented the office during the last stages of his

marriage, when he had wanted more than anything else in life just to be away. Where had not mattered, the going was what had been important. The office had been as good a place as any for meeting the constant stream of developers and contractors and real estate magnates who had wanted to relieve him of his land. Their pitches had all been different, their eyes all the same—greedy and hard. The days between his daughter's disappearance and his wife's departure had been the only times when he had really given their offers any notice. If he had had someplace else to go, Duncan would have probably agreed to sell.

It was in the seventh month of looking for his daughter that he was approached by one of the local builders, whose own son had gone missing after a rock concert. The police had done as much for the builder as they had for Duncan, which was to take a report and put the name on the computer and show steadily declining interest as the days turned to weeks and the weeks to months. The man and his wife came to Duncan as their last hope.

By sheer coincidence Duncan was meandering through the mass hysteria of a heavy metal concert, looking for someone who might know where the builder's son had gone, and he literally walked into the boy. Without thinking he snared the boy's wrist in a panic-grasp and headed for the nearest exit. The boy's friends were too stoned or too caught up in the manic scene to notice his departure; the only battle Duncan faced was with him.

After getting his eye blackened and his ear nearly wrenched off, Duncan wrestled the boy over to his car, opened the trunk, pulled out a towrope, bound him from shoulders to knees, and tossed him in the backseat. Only later, when Duncan was sitting on his front porch still shaking from the experience, did he begin to wonder why a fifteen-year-old boy had fought so hard, and why he had only started fighting after Duncan had told him he was there to take him home.

After that Duncan grew more careful, checking out the family situation with various neighbors before taking the child anywhere. The things he learned surprised him almost as much as the fact that he always found the child. Always, that is, except for his own daughter.

At nights on the farmhouse's lonely front porch, he mused whether one of his forefathers had perhaps been a famous Indian scout, the kind able to spot the broken cattail at a hundred paces, touch the footprint and tell how long ago a fellow passed and what he had eaten for breakfast. Good genes was the only explanation Duncan had for his success. It certainly wasn't training.

The police became accustomed to his face, liked the fact that Duncan only charged expenses, and only when the family could pay. They assumed he was on some kind of religious kick, and Duncan did not feel a need to correct them. Few even knew he had a daughter who had never come home.

The police liked his success rate, liked his careful skepticism toward new inquiries. They started turning business his way, cases from decent families that were threatening to come apart from the strain of not knowing where a son or daughter was sleeping—or if the child would ever wake again.

As the number of cases grew, so did the importance of his office. By the time his fourth year of searching was drawing to a close, Duncan Wyeth could barely remember another existence. Having this office was his way of separating his home life from the sorrow these people brought with them. He liked to think that the only pain he kept up at the farmhouse was his own.

Today the people were already there when he arrived, their two cars taking up the spots directly in front of his office. One was a beat-up Oldsmobile, the other a brand-new pewter-colored Cadillac. Two people sat in each car, heads staring straight ahead, not speaking to anyone, not moving. Duncan guessed the Olds belonged to the neighbors of Detective Bryan Larson. Larson was an old friend on the DC force, one of his greatest sources and the first cop to really go out of his way to help Duncan gather information. Duncan glided into a parking space, turned off the ignition, reached in his pocket for the little notebook, checked the names again.

Larson's neighbors were called Sambini. The guy was the runaway's stepfather, lived in Bethesda, worked for the local milk company. Straight-up people, according to Larson, loved their kids and did well by them; that was not always the case with a stepparent.

According to Larson, the runaway was called Arlene and was a constant trial, especially to her stepfather. The detective wondered privately if maybe the family wasn't better off without her. The other three kids—one like Arlene by Mrs. Sambini's first husband and the other two from the current marriage—were nothing like her. They were happy and well-adjusted and totally in love with their dad.

About the other family Larson knew almost nothing, except their name was Biggs and their daughter was also missing. The two girls had hung around together a lot. Nice girl, according to Larson's wife, who saw her occasionally. Maybe a case of being led astray, maybe some trouble at home—the girl appeared overly quiet, too shy to be healthy. It was the Sambini's who had begged Larson for help, and he had thought of Duncan.

Duncan Wyeth had the sort of shaggy hair that reminded people of a large friendly dog. In earlier years the gray-green eyes had greeted the world with wide-eyed expectancy. The eyes were still wide, but nowadays it was a case of not daring to close them, on account of the memories that tended to appear. That day he wore his grade-two attire; rumpled chinos, denim shirt with coffee-stained tie, cord jacket with mismatched buttons and a permanent case of wrinkles. Grade-three was everything with a hole in it, stuff worn around the farm until the dirt got so heavy he couldn't bear to put them on again. Grade-one consisted of two fairly decent suits he saved for the court appearances, which he had to endure whenever the situation in a runaway's home was so bad as to warrant applying for foster care.

He hated these first interviews, hated the grief and the pain and the fear mixed with hope. They clung to him as to a lifeline. Duncan was not comfortable with the role of hero. He opened his door, slid out of the car, and gave his jacket a futile tug. He walked over to introduce himself, and ushered the two couples into his office.

"I never knew time could drag on for so long," Mr. Sambini said, wiping his face again with the dirty handkerchief. "It's been agony."

"Do you have a picture of your daughter?" Duncan asked.

"Here, I do, sir." Mrs. Sambini opened a voluminous black purse, dug frantically around, came up with what clearly was a school-book class picture.

"How recent is this?" Duncan inspected a fresh-faced girl of about fifteen. It was always hard for him to tell how old a teenage girl was. If they grew up fast they could have nineteen-year-old bodies guided by twelve-year-old minds.

This particular face showed one feature he had seen too often since beginning the present work—eyes much older and much harder and much more experienced than what he would have expected in a girl of this age. It always gave him a pang, seeing eyes like that. He felt the silent accusations of his own daughter staring out of the page.

"It came the day she disappeared," Mrs. Sambini replied, stumbling a little over the last word. "That's why I brought it, it's the most recent one of her. I found one of Jessica Biggs as well, in Arlene's drawer."

Duncan accepted the second picture, wondered why Mrs. Sambini was the one to offer a picture of the other couple's daughter. He saw a very attractive auburn-haired girl with elfin features and eyes that looked as though they never smiled.

"I wish there was something more we could do," Mrs. Sambini said, her fingers a sweaty tangle in her lap.

"There is," Duncan said firmly, looking up from the photographs. His attitude had come with practice. The first time he had been approached, he had felt all thumbs and empty words. Now he understood how important these first words could be. "Go home and raise your family, Mrs. Sambini. Your children need you."

"But Arlene—"

"Arlene is the one who ran away from you, Mrs. Sambini, not the other way around. There are three others who wanted to stay at home, who love you, and whose future is still in your hands."

Duncan leaned across his desk, gave his words all the weight he knew how. "There's something very important I need to tell you. Mr. Sambini, this applies to you even more than to your wife. My own daughter ran away, and it broke up my marriage. We were too busy worrying and feeling sorry for ourselves and arguing over whose fault it was to realize that our love was dying."

He stopped himself there, corrected silently, what love there was left. He went on. "It is perfectly natural to feel grief, Mrs. Sambini, and anger. But remember that it is Arlene who you're angry with, not your husband, not your family. It was Arlene who rejected you, and Arlene who has caused you so much pain. Not your family. You need to keep this very clear in your mind and heart over the coming days, because your first reaction will be to lash out at whoever is nearby. Do that, and you're not only going to hurt those closest to you, you're going to run the risk of losing your other three children as well."

Mr. Sambini was much darker than his red-haired wife, a small balding man with the deeply etched wrinkles of a hard life. He reached over, took her hands in one of his, gave her a look of deep compassion. She leaned her head on his shoulder, worked at maintaining control.

Duncan asked, "How was your relationship with your stepdaughter, Mr. Sambini?"

"Pretty bad." Mr. Sambini looked up reluctantly. "Arlene didn't like to do what she was told."

"Was there ever any physical violence? Any whippings or anything? Excuse me for asking, but I—"

"Yeah, I know. I hear what goes on in some houses." He started to cast a glance toward the Biggs seated next to him, caught himself in time. "No, I never touched the girl. Wanted to a couple of times, but Doris wouldn't let me. Maybe if I had, all this wouldn't have happened."

"Don't start that again." Mrs. Sambini tried to pull her hands away, but he wouldn't let go.

"Arlene was too big for her britches, always trying to show she was boss," Mr. Sambini finished. "But I never touched her."

There was the ring of simple truth to the man's words, and it meshed with what Detective Larson had told him over the phone. "Did she have any special friends at school, a boyfriend maybe, who might know where she went?"

"Not at school. But, yeah, there was a boyfriend, if you want to call him that." Mr. Sambini's face took on a hard cast. "You want my opinion, you find that Chico fellow, you'll find Arlene."

"I take it you don't think a lot of Chico."

"What's to like? The man's twenty-five years old and a drifter. Worked at a garage fixing fancy foreign cars. Had more money than was good for him, met Arlene at that lousy cafe she worked at. I kept telling her, if she stayed around that cafe she was gonna get herself into some deep trouble. I ask you, what would you think of your fifteen-year-old daughter seeing a man twenty-five years old?"

"Pierre was twenty-eight," Mrs. Sambini murmured.

"Pierre, this was Jessica's friend?"

"Friend." Mr. Sambini spat the word. "That was the one time I put my foot down. I wouldn't let either of those two jerks in my house."

"That was why they left," Mrs. Sambini said to her lap. There was no accusation left in her voice, only sorrow. "We told her to stop seeing that man."

Duncan looked up from his notes, asked, "Has anyone been by the garage where Chico worked?"

"Me and the police both," Mr. Sambini said. "I went by the day after Arlene didn't come home, the police the day after that, and then Doris and me, we've both been over again this morning. There's no sign of the jerk."

"Do you have a last name for either? What about a picture?"

"No pics. The police asked, too, and Doris searched Arlene's room from top to bottom. Nothing. Chico's last name is Jones, if you want to believe what he told the garage. Chico Jones. I only met him once. It was enough." He said to his wife, "You better describe him."

"I didn't see him that much more than you," she said. She took a breath, went on. "Very fair complexion. Not at all Latin looking, like you might think from his name. He has the sort of skin that shows freckles rather than tans. Blond hair, an off shade, and wavy. Cut short. Even features, very small ears. His ears were the first thing I noticed about him. Small and close to his head."

"What about his eyes?"

"Grayish green," Mrs. Sambini replied. "I believe that's right."

"Small and mean," Mr. Sambini added. "The man looks like he hurts people for fun. Got the eyes of a snake."

Duncan scribbled furiously, asked, "Can you tell me anything about this Pierre? What about his last name?"

"Matisse." Mrs. Biggs spoke for the first time. "His name is Pierre Matisse."

Duncan did what he had been avoiding up until then, which was give Mrs. Biggs a closer examination. It was not a pleasant sight. Her face had not just been lifted. The skin was stretched so tight that Duncan could not look at it without thinking of some plastic surgeon cranking the chair back, walking around behind her, grabbing two fistsfull of cheeks and yanking back with all his might. The woman looked as if she never smiled, which was a good thing; if she had her face might have snapped up like an overwound window shade.

It was strange how quiet that pair was. Wyeth's meager experience with Washington socialites told him that they would normally dominate in whatever scene they found themselves. Clearly they were uncomfortable with the light this new problem cast on their lives.

Mrs. Biggs had dyed hair sprayed into place like a solid-gold helmet. Her thin mouth was framed with an angry line of painted red, her eyes burdened with fake lashes a good half-inch long. She chain-smoked skinny cigarettes pulled from some fancy hard-paper box stamped with the crest of a famous European jewelry company. Her fingers and wrists were as bony as years of dedicated dieting could make them, and covered with jewels so big they looked like rhinestones.

Mrs. Biggs stared at some point above and beyond Duncan's head. Her arms stayed crossed in front of her chest, one hand raising languidly to bring the cigarette to her mouth. Duncan decided the arm had to have more muscle than it looked if the woman could keep hefting all those diamonds without getting out of breath. Her clothes would have looked fine on somebody half her age; on her they hung like rags on a showroom mannequin.

Duncan could not look at Harvey Biggs without feeling a little ball of tension develop in his gut. Harvey Biggs jittered constantly; he sat on the edge of his chair, his eyes scattering bird shot all over the far wall. The only time his gaze focused was when he looked at his watch. Duncan stifled a desire to play his pen like a microphone, give the airhead's call from another era—Earth to Harvey Biggs, come in, Biggs. But the man looked like the type to rip the pen away and eat it, then go for the hand.

Harvey Biggs wore a European-cut double-breasted suit. French cuffs jutted out the proper three-quarters of an inch beyond his coat sleeves, weighted down with gold cuff links that matched the gold Rolex he kept glancing at.

Duncan decided it was time to reel in this Harvey Biggs a little. "What is your profession, Mr. Biggs?"

"I'm a lobbyist."

"My husband is head of public policy for the American Libertarian United Movement," Mrs. Biggs said.

"Have either of you noticed any recent change in your daughter's behavior?"

"What's to notice?" Biggs leveled beady dark eyes on him. "The girl's got the personality of mashed potatoes."

"What a nice thing to say about your own daughter." Mrs.

Biggs gave him a brief sideways glance.

"What's the matter with the truth? The guy asked if I noticed anything about my daughter. The answer is no. Not now, not before. No."

"What about you, Mrs. Biggs?"

"Come to think of it, yes, I have noticed a difference. Jessica has been seeing far too much of this man Pierre. Frankly, it has disturbed me greatly. I told her countless times she would simply have to stop associating with him and find a friend more her own age."

Harvey Biggs snorted. "You told her to lay off when your friends at the club started giving you a hard time."

"What a horrible thing to say." Mrs. Biggs had a voice as emotionless as her face. "You know perfectly well that's not the truth. I would like an apology."

"Excuse me." Duncan raised a weary hand for peace. "What was this about the club?"

"Pierre worked as a lifeguard at the club," Harvey Biggs replied.

"Which club is that?"

"The Sherbrook Country Club. It's in Chevy Chase."

Duncan made notes, asked, "Has anybody been over to check on this guy Pierre?"

"I called, yeah, but they said it was nearing end of season and a lot of their guards took off around then. Look, we've been through all this with the cops, I don't see why—"

"Just a couple more minutes, Mr. Biggs, and you can go." Duncan caught sight of the look Mr. and Mrs. Sambini were giving the pair, decided he agreed with them. "Can you give me a description of this Pierre?"

"Tall, dark-haired, blue eyes, good tan. Quite attractive," Mrs. Biggs answered in her toneless voice. "He was always most courteous to me at the club. I can't imagine why such a nice young man would want to become involved with a teenager like Jessica."

"That's easy. Because he isn't a nice young man," Mr. Biggs replied, rising to his feet. He was at least a head shorter than his wife and but built like a caged bull. "Like I said, Mister, ah . . ."

"Wyeth," Duncan offered.

"Yeah, right. Like I said, we told the cops all this. The girl's probably out playing house with this Pierre guy. She'll show up when she gets tired of him. She'll take it for a couple of weeks, wake up one morning and tell herself the guy's a jerk, come home with her tail between her legs. I've got a very important meeting that started half an hour ago, so if you'll excuse me—" He turned to his wife. "Gladys, you want to take a taxi?"

"You'll have to excuse my husband," Mrs. Biggs said, preparing to leave. "He's not the world's most diplomatic man."

"Diplomatics don't get the results," Harvey Biggs replied. "Call my secretary if you need anything else." Without another word, the two left the office.

When the door closed behind them Mrs. Sambini said softly, "You should see the daughter, Mr. Wyeth. Such a nice, quiet, respectful girl. Attractive too, much more than the picture. Soft and shy; it makes you want to take her in your arms and hold her close."

"It's the truth, what Doris is telling you," Mr. Sambini agreed. "A quiet little angel. Being raised in that icebox of a house, it makes you wonder, don't it? I mean, sometimes I'd see that look on her face when she left our house, and I could tell she didn't want to go home. Really wished we had given her a place to stay. Nice girl like that, there's no telling what the street is gonna do to her."

"Or to Arlene." Mrs. Sambini crumpled her handkerchief at her lips. "What on earth is going to happen to my little girl?"

◆　◆　◆

Senator Richard Atterly, a member of Congress for over twenty years, did what his schedule seldom allowed, which was indulge his enjoyment of Washington's tourist attractions. A morning meeting with Treasury Department officials had ended earlier than expected, and a call to his office had revealed that his luncheon appointment was canceled. Senator Atterly decided to lunch at a nearby favorite place.

The Old Post Office Building was a turn-of-the-century monument to federal-style architecture that had been saved at the last minute from the wrecking ball of progress. The restored structure housed a variety of restaurants and bars and nightspots and curio shops. The senator pushed his way through the entrance doors, walked down the narrow foyer, and paused at the vending machines to fill his arms with a variety of newspapers. Then he stepped into the large high-ceilinged atrium. From long habit he ignored the stares of tourists who vaguely recognized his face, and slowly circled the four-story central atrium with its graceful iron balustrades and old-style marble checkerboard flooring.

He eased through the swinging doors of an Italian restaurant whose wall booths promised a modicum of privacy, was shown to a seat, ordered a salad, and gave himself over to the pleasure of reading without time pressure breathing down his neck.

Atterly was studying the various front pages when his attention was caught by the conversation going on behind him. He was not the type of man to eavesdrop, but a name came up twice that triggered a reaction far below the surface of his consciousness. The name was Harvey Biggs.

"The last time I went up to Biggs' place, he takes the last curve at about sixty miles an hour," the man behind him was saying. "All the time jamming his thumb down on this little black box, you know, like the ones that open garage doors. So we whiz through the intersection and take the corner, and I just about crawl into the backseat, because we're headed right for these metal gates about fifteen feet high. You know the kind, like a buncha spears welded together, right? So they're cranking out of the way at a snail's pace, and this guy, he wheels through the opening with about an inch to spare on either side. When I finally got my heart back out of my throat, I asked him what he'd do if the motor broke down and the gates didn't open. Know what he said? Make pewter hamburger. Can you believe that? Pewter hamburger. The guy's got nerves of dry ice."

Harvey Biggs was a name well known in Washington political circles. As Director of Public Policy for the American Libertarian United Movement, he packed a powerful punch with both Congress and the press.

"What kind of car does he drive?" The second man had a sort of bored New England drawl, the kind that affects an upper crust British accent that fools no one who has ever traveled.

"One of those sporty Cadillac things. A Cimarron, I think. Nice. Real classy car."

"Seems to be quite a lot of money for a policy type to be spending on his car."

"Like I said, Laney, his wife's got the dough. Her father was some big wheel in glass, owned a couple dozen factories all over the place. Left her this trust fund that'd choke an elephant. You ought to see their house."

"Indeed."

Atterly kept his eyes on his papers while filtering the neighboring conversation from the restaurant's lunchtime clamor. Harvey Biggs' name had come up numerous times over the past few weeks, beginning with the death of a close friend and colleague of his, Senator Wayne Oakes of Kentucky. Since then two members of his morning study group, lawyers with the Justice Department's Criminal Division, had mentioned him on several occasions as they sought to have Atterly take up the cause that had resulted in Senator Oakes' death.

"Yeah, Harv's got this stone-and-wood manor that he calls the morgue and his wife calls necessary. It buys her way into the club, Harvey says. That and these garden parties she puts on. Man, you wouldn't believe it. They cost more than a three-week trip to the Bahamas for forty of their closest friends. The house has got this living room about the size of RFK stadium. In marble, of course. Like the pool. And the kitchen. And the four downstairs bathrooms. Harv put his foot down over the study, though. If you ever wonder where all the redwoods went, go take a look at the floor in there. A couple of Persian carpets for effect, a three-hundred-year-old desk big enough to sail the Atlantic, lead-paned windows, the works. Makes me green just to walk in there."

"I take it this means that your associate can't be bought."

"Harv?" The man laughed. "Not as long as Gladys is around. I don't think Harv cares about the stuff anyway. He likes it because of what other people think, but Harv's not for sale. He's in this for the ride."

"I'm not sure I understand."

"Sure you do, Laney. Harv's a fighter. He loves it bloody." The booth's back shook against Atterly as the man slid himself out. "Here he comes now."

Atterly took the words as a warning and ducked his head down low over his papers. From behind he heard the first voice say, "Harvey, I'd like you to meet Gregory Lannerton of Venus Enterprises. Mr. Lannerton, this is Harvey Biggs."

Atterly searched his mind, tried to recall where he had heard that name before. Then it came to him. Gregory P. Lannerton, President and CEO of Venus Enterprises, key witness with his battery of lawyers at the Senate hearings on mob connections to the pornographic industry. They had taken place amid a blaze of publicity, and amounted to nothing more than a cloud of noisy smoke. Lannerton had sat in stone-faced silence as his lawyers fielded question after question. He staunchly refused to reply to allegations that his porn movies were used to launder drug money, that his video arcades took in as much as twenty thousand dollars a week in untraceable quarters, that his stars were often underage and violently coerced to perform. In the end the evidence remained both contradictory and inconclusive.

"Hey, Roy. Sorry to make you guys wait like that," Harvey Biggs said. "I got held up. Been some trouble with my daughter."

"Nothing serious, I hope, Mr. Biggs."

"Nah. My wife gets a kick out of letting things bend her out of shape. The girl's fine."

"Glad to hear it."

"I was just telling Mr. Lannerton here about your car," Roy said.

"Indeed. The epitome of understated elegance, from the sounds of it."

"I don't have any problem with elegant," Harvey Biggs replied. "Understated is out, though. Understated is for wimps. Come on, everybody sit down. Who else wants a drink?"

"The last time Harvey was over on the West Coast," Roy went on, "he bought himself a bumper sticker that reads, 'Love can't buy you money.' "

"I wasn't so sure about it at first, sticking this blue bumper sticker with orange lettering on my Caddy," Biggs said. "But I can't count the times I've had waves from people pulling up beside me at traffic lights. I finally decided it fits the car just fine."

"Indeed. Perhaps we can get down to business, Mr. Biggs. My plane leaves in less than an hour. That is, if you are certain this is a suitable place for us to discuss matters."

"What's not to discuss? Everything we're involved in here is perfectly legitimate."

"Of course it is. I simply would rather not run into a Heritage Foundation official, or some right-wing senator who enjoys support from the Moral Majority."

"Relax, Mr. Lannerton," Roy said. This place is full of GS–9's on their lunch break. Even if they heard us, they wouldn't have a clue what we were talking about."

"Their biggest concern in life is worrying over when the next pay period ends," Harvey agreed.

"Or IRS flunkies from across the street," Roy added. "The heavy-hitters wouldn't be caught dead lunching this far from Capitol Hill."

"Well, then. Perhaps we might move on to the matter at hand."

"Sure. You want to know about the Per Se bill, is that right?" asked Biggs. He pronounced the words correctly, *per-say*.

"That is correct. I'm not entirely sure what this legislation entails, but my lawyers tell me that if it were to pass, it would virtually outlaw my industry."

"Yeah, well, you can tell your lawyers to stick their heads back in their little shells because the bill doesn't stand a chance."

"Lighten up, Harv," Roy warned. "Laney, the Per Se bill is supposed to redefine obscenity. See, as it is now every court determines what's obscene and what's not on a case-by-case basis. The Per Se bill would set a nationwide standard."[1]

"Which is why it won't fly," Biggs said.

"Right. Like Harv says, it's one thing for a city council or a state legislature to get hammered by pressure from the churches and the local interest groups, but it just can't happen here on the federal level. We're too removed from the little people, and there are too many liberals in Congress who support a broader interpretation of the First Amendment."

"There was a chance it would have passed in the Senate," Biggs added. "But with that Oakes guy outta the way, that's not so likely anymore. And even if it did get through there, we've got the House sewn up tight."

"I'm certainly relieved to hear this," Lannerton said doubtfully.

"Relax, Laney. If Harv says it's a cinch, you can bank on it."

"It's just a ploy," Harvey Biggs said, exuding confidence. "Some of these guys want a piece of paper they can take back to the local conservatives and wave it in their faces, you know,

---

[1]"Per Se" is a Latin term used in the law to mean "in and of itself." Per Se legislation is an objective definition of obscenity that would make commercial distribution of all hard-core pornography *per se* illegal. For further explanation, see the note on page 385.

say look at what a great job I'm doing. But they know it doesn't stand a chance of passing."

"As you say, Mr. Biggs, I was informed that a major proponent of this legislation has recently passed away," Lannerton said.

The waitress chose that moment to bring over Atterly's salad. He did not trust himself to raise his head, for fear of blazing out the anger brought on by his neighbors' casual attitudes.

Senator Wayne Oakes had been a participant first in TJ Case's and then Atterly's prayer meetings, and as fierce an opponent of pornography as Atterly had ever met. Wayne Oakes had been a burly ex-football jock with a broad jaw and an utterly determined expression. He had championed the anti-pornography cause through a variety of administrations, and weathered the resulting storm of abuse and backstabbing with a strength that awed his foes. The battle he had waged with the American Libertarian United Movement, or ALUM, had been long and persistent.

But when Oakes had put forth his latest bill, a Per Se law that would have outlawed the distribution, production, and ownership of virtually all kinds of hard-core pornography, the ALUM had wheeled the big guns from their caves and blasted Wayne Oakes right out of the water.

The ALUM sent its leading shark, one Harvey Biggs, down to Oakes' district in Kentucky to orchestrate a nonstop hate campaign. The ALUM's thickset Director of Public Policy was a no-holds-barred gutter-warrior, trained in tactics that gave lip service to the truth and showed no concern whatsoever for the welfare of his opponents. The attacks became so vitriolic, with the press so eager to print everything the ALUM threw out as bait, that Senator Oakes found himself losing support at an alarming rate. He began making trips back to his district every weekend, working four fourteen-hour days in Washington followed by three eighteen-hour days back home shoring up the walls of his constituency. In the end the strain proved too much, and during one of the countless speeches where he was forced to shout down the ALUM backers with their megaphones accusing him of defiling the First Amendment with his Nazi-type stance, Wayne Oakes had a heart attack and died.

Atterly heard later that the ALUM held victory celebrations in every field office across the nation.

"Yeah, old Oakes couldn't take the heat," Biggs replied easily. "Wish I could have been there to see that tree fall."

"Something like this, it'll make everybody else take a step back and rethink their position," Roy predicted. "You just watch. Support for this Per Se thing is gonna evaporate like a snowball on a hot stove."

"My associates inform me that you were responsible for the senator's untimely demise," Lannerton said.

"Yeah, well, I didn't pull the trigger," Biggs replied, not even trying to hide his satisfaction. "But afterward I started wondering if maybe I ought to start stamping those decals on the side of my car, you know, like a hot fighter pilot."

Once again the booth's back shook to the movement of men sliding out. "Well, if you'll excuse me, I have a plane to catch. I am in the midst of filming my most expensive venture ever, and have another one scheduled to begin in just over two weeks. With something of this magnitude, I find it best to remain close at hand throughout the process."

Lannerton stood where a bent-down Atterly could see his polished shoes, said, "You and your organization can count on our continued financial support, Mr. Biggs. It is most reassuring to know that we have such allies in Washington."

When the man's footsteps had died away, Harvey Biggs said to Roy, "A guy making skin-flicks, I thought he'd have this heavy-duty Bronx accent, flash pinky rings and six gold chains, wear a yellow polyester shirt and floral tie. Something like that."

"Harv, wake up. This is the nineties. The guy's just another successful businessman. This movie he just mentioned? I hear it's got a budget of over five mil."

"Sure, sure. It just wasn't what I was expecting, that's all."

"And he's just about our biggest contributor, don't forget that. Between those guys and the Playboy Foundation, we're pretty much set for life."

Senator Richard Atterly slid from his seat and walked swiftly toward the cashier. His back to the wall of booths, he paid his check and left the restaurant. He needed to call the lawyers at the Justice Department and see if they would meet with him tomorrow. It would mean staying in Washington through Saturday, but his next week was already booked solid, and this was something he could no longer put off.

◆   ◆   ◆

The man was half-hidden in the doorway shadows. Jeremy Hughes thought that was why he could not tell the man's age or the color of his skin. The man was not panhandling, which was a bad sign. When the begging stopped they were usually beyond help. The man was sitting in utter stillness, which was even worse. But his eyes were open, because Jeremy could see the streetlight glint in them as he passed, which was good, because the man was at least alive. Only later did Jeremy wonder why only the man's eyes caught the light.

"Howya doin', friend?" Jeremy leaned over to inspect the face, but still could see little besides shadows. The shadows, and the eyes. "Mind if I join you?"

In reply the man moved one foot over slightly, granting Jeremy the farthest corner of the lower step. Jeremy eased himself down.

"Know a place not far from here," he told the silent stranger. "Most nights it's got hot food and a clean bed for you. All full up tonight, though. Don't know why I'm still walkin' the streets. Habit, I guess. You hungry, friend?"

"Yes." The man's voice was soft, but surprisingly strong.

"Reckon I'll have to take you home with me, then. House is fulla old ladies, though, so you'll have to sleep in the cellar."

The man watched him with unblinking eyes. Jeremy couldn't decide which was more unsettling, the man's silence or his gaze.

"There's gonna be a chill tonight, friend. October the first, clear sky, cold wind, and dew before dawn." Jeremy wondered if the man even heard him. "Seems to me you might oughtta think on stayin' with me tonight, lookin' in on that shelter tomorrow."

Jeremy stood, offered a hand. "Whattaya say, friend? How 'bout a hot meal?"

The man refused the hand, eased himself to his feet. Jeremy looked closely, saw a rail-thin body in shabby clothes, and relaxed. This was not the face of a killer. Or the eyes. The eyes had the open clarity of a child's. Jeremy tried to recall ever seeing such eyes on another of the street people.

The man walked without stumbling—a good sign. Jeremy led him the short distance to his truck, said, "Got us a bottle of cold well water and a thermos of half-warm coffee. You want something to drink, friend?"

"The water of life," the man said softly. "With all God's people."

Jeremy moved back into the yellow pool of light cast by the nearest streetlamp. "Say what, friend?"

"How many children do you have now, Jeremy Hughes?" The eyes searched deep, very deep.

Jeremy squinted his eyes. "How'd you know my name?"

"There is talk of you out there," the man said simply, waving his hand toward the night. "How often is there a need for a man like you, Jeremy Hughes? How can we give hope to the little ones?"

Jeremy swept a trembling hand through the slate-gray lock that fell down on his forehead. "I'm not sure I understand, friend."

"Here comes another," the man replied, and focused his attention on an approaching car.

The low-slung sedan glided up and stopped at the traffic signal, placing it directly in the lamplight in front of Jeremy. The man stood in utter stillness, directing Jeremy with his concentrated sorrow to pay attention to the car and not to him.

It was an old-model Jaguar in mint condition, and by some trick of the light the only face Jeremy could see was that of a girl in the passenger seat. She turned partially toward him, but did not focus on the pair of men. Her features were captured in that miraculous moment of blossoming, the heartbeat of time when a young girl is transformed into womanhood.

The young girl's eyes were wells of aching loneliness. They spoke to him of yearnings so long unanswered that hope had drained away. Her delicate face glowed with a radiant promise, a promise totally absent from her eyes. They gazed into the night with a hopeless vulnerability that tore at Jeremy's heart.

The light changed; the car glided away. The man gave Jeremy a long look, then turned and walked silently into the darkness.

CHAPTER
2

Duncan Wyeth dropped off three boxes of clothes at the Community of Hope, a relief organization in the Adams-Morgan district of Washington, D.C. He then followed the receptionist's directions over to the construction site for homeless-family housing where Reverend Tom Nees was working. Duncan had no real need to speak with the man; he just liked the feeling he had after even the briefest talk. Tom Nees carried strength and conviction in the face of great sadness, something Duncan often wished he could find for himself.

As luck would have it, he got lost, asked directions from a partially reformed drunk, got even more lost than before, and spent twenty minutes retracing his steps back to the Community of Hope's headquarters. By then he was going more out of determination than any desire to talk to the man. He finally found the house five minutes after Tom had left for lunch.

Duncan decided to rest a moment on the site's front stairs and get his blood pressure down to a manageable level. Voices laughed and rang through the partially finished lower level, but he didn't turn around.

"Howdy, son. This seat taken?"

"Help yourself."

"Thanks." A pair of paint-spattered work boots walked down one step, and a dusty work-roughened hand stuck itself into Duncan's face. "Name's Jeremy Hughes."

He accepted it reluctantly. The man's strength surprised him. "Duncan Wyeth."

"Nice to meet you, Duncan. Always like a little fresh air with my meals. Company's just an extra bonus." The big-boned man unrolled his paper sack, pulled out a Coke and set it to one side, brought out a sandwich, said, "Woman who runs my boardin' house always puts enough in here for two. You like a sandwich, help yourself. I'd get it out for you, but you might not care for grit with your BLT."

"No, I'm—" Duncan looked over, caught sight of the two blue-grey eyes peering at him through a shock of graying hair, and forgot what he was going to say.

With the man's lowered forehead and half-hidden eyes, Duncan expected to find fury, a battle-ready look from someone whose life had taught him to meet anything new with anger. Instead he found only ethereal light and kindness. The face was caked in dust and deeply lined, but the eyes, Duncan had never seen eyes glow like that. They regarded him steadily, seemingly willing to wait there all day.

He realized he was staring, came up with, "Haven't I seen you before?"

"I can't rightly say, son, but it's doubtful. I don't get around much these days."

"Sorry. Thought I knew you."

"Anything's possible. You got something to do with the Community of Hope?"

"No, I just bring down a collection of old clothes once a month or so."

"Well now, ain't that nice. Lotsa folks down here probably wish they had the chance to thank you themselves." Jeremy took a bite, asked, "What do you do for a livin'?"

"I've got a farm not too far from here. It's near Columbia, Maryland. Ever heard of it?"

"No, can't say as I have."

"It's one of those planned communities, you know, where they go in and build everything from the ground up. It's up between Washington and Baltimore, used to be nothing but farmland. Now the place probably has two hundred thousand inhabitants. My grandfather's old place fronts the northern limits. I sell off bits and pieces, mostly for houses but a couple of times for part interests in new developments." Duncan hesitated, went on, "For the past six years, I've spent most of my time looking for lost children."

The dusty old man stopped in mid-chew, and the light in

those strange blue-gray eyes grew even keener. "You don't say."

"Runaways, mostly. Teenagers who take off and leave their families in a total panic."

Carefully Jeremy wrapped the wax paper back around his sandwich, set it down on the bag, took a swig of his Coke. Slowly, deliberately, he asked, "You wouldn't be lookin' for a little girl right now, would you?"

Duncan couldn't help but gape. "How did you know that?"

"I didn't, son. Just a lucky guess." The gray-haired man was silent for a moment, then seemed to reach a decision. "Say, how'd you like to let me buy you dinner tonight? I found this down-home restaurant not far from here, got some great food."

Duncan took in the tattered coveralls, the sweat-stained shirt, the old shoelaces cracked and held together with half a dozen knots, said, "Sure, but you gotta let me invite you."

"Tell you what. We'll stuff our faces, then see who's got the energy to pick up the check. Country cookin' tends to take the brakes off my mouth."

"Sounds familiar." Duncan thought of his next appointment, asked, "You interested in runaways?"

Again there was that breath of hesitation, as though the rough-edged old man with the deeply carved face and lanterns for eyes wanted to say something else. "I've been spendin' time with kids all my life. Got a special place in my heart for the little ones in need. Always have."

"Well, I've got a meeting set up with a friend on the D.C. police force. Thought maybe he could help get a handle on the kids I'm after. You want to tag along?"

Jeremy Hughes stood as though pulled erect. "Anything to get me out of an afternoon's work sounds good from where I'm sittin'. Got a change of clothes in my truck. Just give me a second to scrape off the top layer."

The truck was a Ford pickup, designed for hauling and hard work and bought by men who didn't give a whit that the same body style had been used for over twenty years. It was painted a sort of washed-out blue; the tires were new white-walls, the chrome polished, the back end fitted with a hand-crafted solid-oak toolbox and a big galvanized lock. A couple of piles of carefully folded burlap bags were crowded in each corner, seats for kids who'd get a kick out of riding with their hair tousled by the wind.

The North Carolina license plate was customized and read

"1-WAY." The bumper sticker read, "If you were arrested for being a Christian today, would there be enough evidence to convict you?"

Duncan said to Jeremy, "Don't leave much room for doubt, do you?"

"That's the idea." Jeremy unlocked his door, said, "I take it from the way you're dressed that I don't need a tie."

Duncan looked down at his aloha shirt, drawstring pants, rope-sole shoes, asked, "What's the matter with my clothes?"

"Not a thing in this world. I like a man who knows how to be comfortable."

"Ties are for people who need something to hold their heads on," Duncan said.

"Now that's a pure-bred fact," Jeremy agreed. "Ties are for putting on when you want to play pretend."

"A man doesn't have to think as hard when he's got a tie on," Duncan said. "It's like he's hanging a sign around his neck that says, hey, what you got here is one smart dude."

"Kinda strange how everybody believes it, though, ain't it?" Jeremy finished buttoning up his shirt, seated himself behind the wheel, started the motor, said, "Where to, son?"

Duncan climbed in the passenger side, pointed a lazy finger out the front windshield. "Why don't you just start off in that general direction, and I'll say when."

Jeremy turned sideways, swiped the hair out of his eyes for a better look. "You know what? That's the first time in nine solid months somebody's given me directions I could understand."

Beefeaters, a cafe-restaurant across from Ford's Theater on Tenth Street, was nothing more than a narrow hall filled with booths. All the seats wore tired orange vinyl covers. The tables were covered in formica and trimmed with aluminum strips.

Detective Bryan Larson was halfway through an overstuffed roast beef sandwich on a Kaiser roll. He nodded to Duncan Wyeth, said in greeting, "The waitress I got? She's been here since before the war. I remember her from when my pop used to bring me here. No joke." He caught sight of Jeremy and frowned. "What're you doing here, Hughes?"

"Just taggin' along," Jeremy replied. "Nice to see you again, Detective."

Duncan slid into the booth, said, "You two know each other?"

"Yeah, we know. I asked what you were doing here, Hughes."

"I invited him. How do you—"

"I investigated a crime your Mister Hughes got himself involved in. How long ago was that? Six months? Seven? Deal almost cost me my badge."

A waitress in an orange rayon uniform with white apron, tired eyes, scuffed hospital shoes, and a slightly skewed name tag reading "Betty" came up. "What'll it be today, hon?" she said in a tired voice.

Detective Larson said, "Oughtta try the french fries, Hughes. They soak 'em in gravy."

Jeremy smiled at the waitress, said, "That sounds nice, ma'am. And a root beer if it's in season."

"Just coffee, thanks," Duncan said. "I can't get over you two knowing each other."

"Detective Larson took over a case once the secret service types got through with me," Jeremy said. "Lotsa embassies and such like where we lived. That bomb went off, I mean to tell you those men in gray suits came swarmin' in like ants at a picnic."

Duncan gaped at Jeremy. "Bomb?"

"Somebody decided to redecorate the back end of the Hughes residence," Larson said. "Murdered two people in the process. We never found out who it was. Found slivers of plastic explosives, so we know it was a bomb and not just some faulty heater or something. Man, did that ever raise a stink with the press."

Duncan closed his mouth far enough to ask, "Murder?"

"Senior White House staffer blown up with his wife in the middle of Embassy Row, nobody saw anything, police found a total of zip for clues. You don't think the downtown office wasn't out for blood? I'm lucky I still got my head."

"White House?" Duncan asked Jeremy. "Embassy Row?"

"Long story, son," Jeremy said.

"Your man Hughes here is full of surprises." Detective Larson screwed the napkin around his fingers to work off the remains of his sandwich. "You two can get acquainted on your own time. I checked on the guy you told me about, looks like we hit paydirt."

Duncan forced his mind back to matters at hand. "I can't

thank you enough for taking the time, Bryan. I know how busy you are."

"It's crazy," Larson said. "All the stuff on my desk, and I haven't been able to get this outta my mind. I told my wife about it. Big mistake. What does she do but go blab about it to our kids. Now they won't stop. What if this, what about that, can't I do something, man, those three women're about ready to drive me off the deep end."

"Two daughters," Jeremy said. "That's nice, Detective. How old are they?"

"Fifteen and sixteen, about the same as these two girls. I tell you something, though, a little do-gooder deed really gives me a lift."

"Job's pretty bad, huh?"

"Stinks from here to Hawaii. It's been real nice, workin' on something like this. Kinda puts it all in perspective, you know, coupla kids in trouble, coupla small-time jerks. Helps me remember I'm supposed to be here serving the people and all that."

"Really do appreciate your help on this, Bryan."

"Yeah, well, like I said, I checked this guy out. Pierre Matisse, can you believe it? It's not his real name, by the way. Surprise, surprise. He's been using it for a while, though. Five, six years, maybe more. Even got a Pennsylvania driver's license under that name."

Larson tossed down the rest of his drink. "Those guys up there in Philly's motor vehicle department, they're screwy enough to do anything. One dude comes in for a license, got himself a bona-fide birth certificate in the name of Kareem Abduhl Mohammed Buuheeem. So the next guy calls himself Pierre Matisse, no big deal, right?"

Duncan asked, "So he's from Pennsylvania?"

"Who knows? Maybe he sprouted full grown from the slime pit. Farthest back the records go is a summer job in Massachusetts, eight years ago. They think it's him, anyway. Positive identification of the pictures, same scam at work, looks like. Called himself Peter Mearey, back then. Maybe that's his real name, but nobody's got a lead on where he's from."

Duncan made furious notes, said, "So this wasn't his first time up to bat."

"Mighta been, but I'd give it the same chance as my waitress smiling at a nickel tip. Maybe less. Looks to me like our friend

Pierre's been at this game quite a while. Couple of arrests on nothing charges, looks like stuff cooked up to keep him on ice for a couple of days. No convictions. Nothing down on paper."

"Just the smell."

"Like the backside of a fish restaurant after Saturday night. So do I stick to what the arrest record shows, which is a big fat egg, or do I pass out the gas masks and tell you what I think?"

"Your opinion is worth its weight in gold," Duncan said.

"Okay. This guy is a grade-A lizard. Takes a different life-guard job every summer, right? Never works the same town twice, never the same state two years running. It's an old story. Good-looking stud, likes 'em young, right? Then at the end of the summer he takes off with one or two cities, and carries 'em out of state someplace."

Larson reached into his coat, came out with an envelope. "Got a couple of pics for you. Just copies off the machine, but they still give you a pretty good idea. Nice looking lizard, I gotta say that much for him."

Duncan opened the manila envelope, drew out two pictures of a man with sharp features and jet-black hair. "And he just goes on doing this year after year."

"Why not? Lifeguarding is the kind of job where they don't check references so close. They'll look for a valid Red-Cross certificate, make one telephone call to somewhere outta state if they're really diligent. He's bound to have somebody some-where who'll swear he's legit. They decide, yeah, okay, he looks alert and he's got good manners, so they give him a try. Summer help aren't usually known for their brains, if you know what I mean. And they find out the guy is neat as a pin and can keep all the machines running and change light bulbs on those high towers without dropping a hammer on somebody's head. So what if he's getting a little on the side? That's what being a lifeguard is all about, right?"

"And they've never been able to hang anything on this guy."

"Lots of rumors. Stuff adds up after a while. When the end of summer comes, the guy just disappears. And always about the same time, one or two of the local bimbettes who have been friendly with the guy, they vanish too."

"And they never hear from the, what did you call them, bimbettes?"

"Yeah, you know, a baby bimbo. Not as far as the records show. Except for these rumors. You know, about how the girls turn up later in magazines that don't carry a lot of class ads, and movies that aren't real strong on dialogue."

Duncan turned to Jeremy, explained, "He means pornography."

"Thank you, son, I sorta thought so." Jeremy turned toward the detective, said, "But we're talkin' about a couple of children here."

"Fifteen's not a child in the pornography trade," Duncan replied, suddenly very weary.

"Maybe they are when they start, Hughes," Detective Larson said. "Kids, I mean. But they don't stay that way for long."

"The proper term nowadays is juvenile," Duncan told him. "Child pornographers generally work with kids a lot younger than fifteen."

"There's less hassle in the picture trade than in pimping," Detective Larson said, blind to the effect his words were having on Jeremy. "He doesn't have to battle the locals for a piece of the turf. Probably tells the cuties they got what it takes to, you know, model. Modeling swimsuits, that's how it usually starts. Be a fashion model, get famous, have everybody see you in the magazines."

"Why does he keep going after new ones?" Duncan asked. "I mean, it seems like he'd get a lot more out of working the ones who've already been taught the ropes."

"A lot more what? Money? You think this guy is in it just for the dough? Maybe he is, but seems to me there oughtta be other professions for a good-looking guy to get into besides a talent scout for the girlie magazines. Who knows what a guy like this thinks? Maybe he just likes fresh meat."

Jeremy uttered a broken-winded sigh, pushed his plate and glass toward the center of the table.

Detective Larson gave Jeremy a tight, bitter-eyed smile. He said to Duncan, "You got pics of the cuties?"

Duncan reached into his shirt pocket, handed him photographs of Jessica and Arlene. Larson studied them, grunted his approval.

"Not bad. Word was this Pierre guy went for the ripe ones." He passed them back, said, "Sure. A little makeup, right camera angle, who's to say these two aren't eighteen years old?"

Jeremy reached for the pictures, swiveled them around, bent over far enough for his hair to fall like a curtain before his face.

Larson reached back into his pocket, tossed over another picture, said, "All I could get on your Chico character is off his Maryland license. Clean as he is, my guess'd be he's just hooked up with Pierre, gone along for the ride."

Duncan examined the picture, saw a tight-featured young man whose mass of freckles stood out even on a poor quality photocopy. "This guy has got the eyes of a snake."

"Scum of the earth, every last one of 'em," Larson said. "Oughtta be dumped in some dark hole and left to rot."

"You have any idea where this Matisse might have taken the two girls?"

"Nah, but I can tell you where he's not." Larson scooted over and started to rise. "The guy's out of the D.C.-Maryland area, I'd stake my badge on that. He's picked up his new prey, see. Time to head for higher ground."

"Thanks, Bryan." Duncan offered him his hand. "You've been a big help."

"Sure would like to get my hands on this guy." Larson looked at his watch, swore under his breath. "This is good work you're doing here, Duncan. Don't let anybody tell you different."

Larson looked toward where Jeremy was still bent over the pictures. "You're starting at the top, Hughes. Duncan here's got himself quite a reputation for results. Found every one he's ever gone after."

"Except one," Duncan said, subdued now.

"Yeah, well, that was different. You two make a pair, that's for sure. I envy you, you know that? I'd love to take off after this guy. It's crazy to even think like that, with all I got on my desk. You let me know what's going on, okay?"

"Sure, Bryan. Thanks."

"No problem." He adjusted his tie, buttoned the sport coat over his protruding belly, said, "You want some advice?"

"Always."

"Talk to the Feds. The FBI building's only a couple of blocks from here. Nobody'll see you today, but I'll try and set something up for next week. Maybe they got something on this guy I don't know about. And if you're gonna be crossing state lines, they might be more willing to help out, you know, if you be open with 'em up front. The least they can do is put your girls in the national computer, what's it called. . . ."

"The NCIC," Duncan offered.

"Right. You guys take off across country looking for a couple of bimbettes, you're probably gonna need all the help you can get."

◆   ◆   ◆

Senator Atterly was ushered into the bare-walled Justice Department conference room where the two Criminal Division lawyers rose to greet him. The subject at hand was one of great political sensitivity. Over the years, efforts to limit pornography were blasted by powerful lobbying groups and assaulted by a liberal press. The issue's political appeal dwindled as the opposition gained strength and the chances for success dwindled. Nonetheless, there were some who felt strongly enough about the cause to throw caution to the wind; two of these were the lawyers seated across from Atterly this Saturday morning.

Edith Gaines, a member of the prayer group that Atterly had taken over after TJ Case's demise last spring, was made of equal parts grandmotherly concern and fire-hardened steel. No issue could strip away and reveal the iron beneath her soft veneer faster than the advocacy of "adult films." Her associate, Bart Mills, was a mild-mannered balding man with a permanently pained expression. He shook Senator Atterly's hand and sank into a chair two or three seats apart from the others. Both lawyers listened in blank-faced silence as Atterly described the conversation he had overheard the day before.

"It's a perfect example as to why we need your help," Edith Gaines replied, her voice echoing through the empty chamber. She was acknowledged as one of the most brilliant lawyers on the staff of the Justice Department's Criminal Division. "Simply putting your name to a piece of paper this time won't be enough."

"It never is," Atterly replied. "I asked for this meeting because I thought you should be aware of what I overheard. But let me tell you right now, I simply do not have the time to push another cause this session. My staff are dropping in their tracks already."

"You may be interested to know that this was exactly what Senator Oakes said to us the first time we met," Edith Gaines said. "And I'll tell you the same thing I told him—if that's the attitude you're going to take, then we're lost."

"Then you'd be lost with me too," Atterly countered.

"Not necessarily," Bart Mills said. "The sponsors of this legislation in both the Senate and the House are Southern Democrats. To have another sponsor from the Republican side, and a northerner to boot, might just turn this around."

"You don't seem to understand that it's not just your vote we're after." She looked toward Bart Mills. "Why don't you get started?"

Mills partially unwound himself from the seat and said to Atterly, "You have historically focused your attention on matters pertaining to children. The obscenities portion of the latest Crime Bill was passed largely due to your own efforts."

Atterly nodded agreement. This was no secret. Any politician learned soon enough that there simply was not sufficient time to champion every worthy cause. Atterly had focused his efforts on children since his early days as a freshman politician in the Rhode Island House of Representatives, feeling with an urge that went beyond any logical definition that this was where his heart and soul resided.

Many politicians offered vocal support to such causes during election time, as a kind word about children went a long way toward softening the hardest voter's heart. Yet the plain truth was, children didn't vote. And for the professional politician, that often became the bottom line as to which matters required their unequivocal support, and which could be used as bargaining chips. Atterly had seen the gap during his first years as an elected official, and gained a name nationwide for backing local, national and international relief efforts for children.

Several years ago, Attorney General Edwin Meese chaired a Commission on Pornography. Despite tremendous opposition, the findings resulted in anti-child pornography legislation being included in that year's omnibus crime bill. The measure passed, but only barely.

The ALUM was a strong advocate for granting total freedom to the porn industry, including the purveyors of child porn. The campaign it drummed up against the crime bill's passage, because of this anti-porn provision, made headlines across the nation.

But even before this, the Meese Commission had suffered mightily under the ALUM's hand—their efforts spearheaded by none other than Harvey Biggs. He and his staff had traveled to each city where hearings were scheduled and generated up opposition long before the commission ever arrived. The commission was placed on the defensive from the very first moment, portrayed in the liberal press as both biased and anti-porn before they even opened their mouths.

It proved a most effective campaign. The liberal press had thousands of quotes supplied to them by the ALUM that they used to demonstrate widespread support for dumping the commission's findings. All the commission's hearings could then be dismissed as the ramblings of a biased and prejudiced group; all support for future laws based on the commission's report were undermined before the legislative process was even begun. In the end, it did not matter that the commission came down overwhelmingly against pornography in all its myriad of forms. By the time the report was issued, nobody in power was listening anymore. The liberal press had made it clear that they could not afford to.

Up to this point, Atterly had simply granted all anti-porn legislation his qualified support, which meant he could be counted on to vote in favor, but not to go out and beat the bushes. The one exception was when the ALUM took its lobbying power into the White House in an attempt to have the President veto that particular crime bill, the one including the anti-child porn provision. Harvey Biggs organized support from all fifty states in the form of hate mail and legal threats and virulent attacks in the liberal press.

The newly elected President hesitated signing the bill into law. Atterly pressed the President to meet with numerous advocates of the bill, including the Justice Department's Criminal Division. It was not enough, the bill's advocates told anyone who would listen, but it was a step in the right direction. The President agreed to give them a hearing, and was so moved by their testimony that he not only signed the bill, but went before the press and gave the anti-child porn amendment his unqualified support.

"As a practical matter, everyone in the legal system from police to prosecutors is pressed to allocate resources," Bart Mills went on. "We have fought against this attitude within the Justice Department, but the fact remains that under the current laws we are fighting to hold back an incoming tide. The law states unequivocally that anyone under eighteen is still a child in the eyes of the law. As a practical matter, however, the upsurge in problems with the really young is continually pushing us to concentrate on those who do not have the power of reason.

"But it goes further than this. When I was working as a district attorney in New York, it was hard to find a prosecutor willing to take on a sexual offense case where the victim was over the age of fourteen, because the juries would not be sympathetic. I worked especially hard on child sex-rings because I disagreed with this attitude. But according to current thinking, in cases involving adolescents you have a teenager who no one else cares about, and the perpetrator is oftentimes a businessman—maybe someone who's married, possibly a respected professional. Why should a jury convict someone and subject him to harsh penalties for engaging in an act with a streetwise kid? Some would argue that the kid knew what he or she was doing, appeared to be of age, and was very willing.

"I personally think that this ties into society's lie that prostitution is a victimless crime. From dealing with the children and young women and seeing the circumstances from which they came, I *know* these were not people with a whole range of opportunities."

Atterly felt himself foundering. The conversation had moved to a level where he had nothing to hold on to. "You've lost me," he said. "It seems to me that any of these girls could just say no."

"Take it from the top," Edith Gaines suggested.

"Right. Okay." Bart Mills made an effort to change mental gears. "First of all, you've got to understand that kids getting involved in this stuff don't normally come from happy families. Some, of course, are problem kids who have rebelled since their first breath and have always been looking for a way out. But they're a minority. So you've got a kid from a broken or a dysfunctional home, maybe there's been some abuse, whatever. She's not happy, and doesn't have much hope of ever finding happiness at home.

"Nowadays there are professional pimps for the film trade who are constantly on the look-out for kids like this. Video arcades are a great place to meet the kids and pick them up. In the trade, arcades or soda fountains or public swimming pools are called gateways.

"So a girl gets picked up by somebody who starts off as her boyfriend and pretty soon becomes her pimp. Most of the young girls in our experience seem to like this lifestyle for the first year. They get small amounts of drugs, good clothes, and some liberty during nonworking hours. The bad stuff takes five min-

utes at a time, a couple of hours max each day, and so they try
not to think about what is really going on. They're out of the
house, away from the parental abuse, and most of them are
enjoying everything except the job itself."

Atterly felt as if he were reeling from a series of body blows.
The clinical detachment with which Mills was speaking was
mirrored in Edith Gaines' eyes. He looked at her, asked, "How
on earth do you put up with this?"

She allowed a trace of weariness to surface. "Richard, this
isn't even the tip of the iceberg."

"She told me to steer around the hard stuff," Mills agreed.

"All we're discussing is the outset," Edith Gaines went on.
"How they get involved. What happens later on is the stuff that
just breaks your heart."

"I don't want to hear," Atterly said flatly.

"I know you don't," she replied. "We're trying to limit this
to the essentials, just enough to show you how crucial it is to
get this law passed."

Atterly set his face in grim lines. "All right."

"What it boils down to," Mills went on, "is that by the time
these young girls are out on the street, they're easy prey. They
like this new freedom from whatever it was they left behind.
They usually come from some background of submission, some
paternal reliance. At that age, they are still looking for some
of that. There is still a need for a strong male figure. That is
where the pimp comes in. He does a lot of things that a father
would. He provides for the girls. The girls don't keep the money
they earn. They take the money and give it all to the pimp.
Like I said, these girls are still looking for that home life, some
twisted form of love, the best they can find or expect to find.

"There's a change going on with the young girls, though,
and it's making our job a lot tougher. They're being moved off
the street and into houses. Now they work out of what are called
dating rooms. If it's nice the place might have a gurney with a
mattress on top. Sometimes the johns work out the deal there,
sometimes they get it all done with the people downstairs before
they go up. The younger the girl, the less freedom she has.

"This is happening for two reasons. First of all, the money
is so good with young girls, especially if they're put into the
films, that a pimp usually works just one at a time. This means
he's got more time to keep this little girl trapped in invisible
chains.

"Plus, now that it's off the streets and sort of hidden, a sort of detente is coming out between the police and the pimps. The major reason for arrests comes from citizen complaints. If the people aren't seen, then there's less need for the police to apply limited resources to fighting prostitution. They can save it for rape and incest and stuff that is more broadly condemned by the public. For most of our police and prosecutors across the nation, you see, prostitution and pornography come from the same part of their budget as child molestation, rape, incest, and so on. If you are facing a shortfall of resources, as most police departments are, something has to give. So the decision makers, the people who rely on votes for their offices and decide how budgets are spent, say forget the girls and boys over thirteen unless somebody kicks up a fuss. It's as simple as that."

"So now these poor little girls and boys just disappear forever," Edith Gaines murmured. "And we're not talking about just a few isolated cases either."

"Last year," Mills said. "Over a million kids under the age of eighteen ran away from home long enough to be registered with the authorities. On any given night, there are thirty thousand kids sleeping on the streets in Los Angeles alone."

"Not only is the number growing, but the kids are also growing younger," Edith added. "Two Los Angeles shelters are now working exclusively with female prostitutes under the age of fourteen."

"These kids have got to make enough money to pay for whatever habits they might have picked up," Mills went on. "Prostitution and porn films are always there, just waiting for them."

"This is the disposable culture taken to its worst extreme," Edith Gaines concluded. "A girl is used up and thrown away. There are only so many sexual positions you can take, so many acts you can do. So the only thing that's new, the only reason to buy another film, is to see another girl."

"We all like that new suit that's just come off the rack," Bart Mills agreed. "What you've got here is our best asset, our children, being treated with the same unemotional callousness as any other article for sale."

"But they're so young," Atterly murmured.

Mills shrugged a sad shoulder. "Look around yourself, Senator. Advertising in America is constantly shouting out one theme above all else: *Youth sells*. These people at the top of the porn industry are in it for the money, and if they can make more money with a young girl and be fairly sure they can stay out of jail, hey, that's fine with them. So they insist on fake ID's and phoney birth certificates, shield themselves with a battery of the best lawyers money can buy, and enlist the support of groups like the ALUM."

"What the films don't show is what we are too often faced with," Edith Gaines continued. "After you've been in the business for two years, you're not going to have a young, fresh face. You've had maybe two or three thousand guys. You've become at least a casual drug user, because you have to have some way of escaping. After the initial excitement has worn off, all prostitutes will tell you the same thing—that this is not fun. They need an out. They need a way to escape from their conscience. So they use drugs more and more. Then after a while the girl is told, hey, don't come home tonight. I've got another young thing who hasn't got the used look that you've picked up. She's pushed aside. What is there to keep this girl from going off the deep end?"

It took all Atterly's strength to keep his voice level. "So what you're telling me is that the child pornography section of the last crime bill is not enough."

"So long as there is a legal pornography industry in America," Edith Gaines replied, "these merchants of filth are going to find ways to lower the age of the girls and boys they use. So the answer is no. Until the industry itself is outlawed, our nation's children stand at risk of being drawn in and destroyed."

◆ ◆ ◆

Jeremy and Duncan decided to swing back by the Community of Hope for Duncan's car so he could head home straight from the restaurant after dinner. Jeremy's reaction to the Lincoln was, "Is there a car there under all that dirt?"

"I'll have you know I washed it three years ago."

"That car would make a dump truck green with envy."

"If you'd rather, I've got a Harley parked back in my garage, we can take that."

"Is that one of them motorbikes?"

Duncan nodded. "I haven't started it since last spring, but I imagine it still runs."

Jeremy walked toward his truck. "No thank you, son. They got a word to describe somebody who'll sit himself down on two gallons of gasoline and set a spark to it."

"It's perfectly safe."

"That may very well be, but I'll pass on it just the same. Never seen someone climb off one of those suckers with a smile on their face. Makes a body wonder what all the fuss is about." Jeremy started his motor, said, "If we get separated I'll just pull over and look for the dust cloud on the horizon."

The restaurant was in a tiny Falls Church shopping center on Lee Highway in Virginia. The outside was simple brick, like a thousand other mini-centers across the nation. The sign was unremarkable and read simply, The Black Eyed Pea. Inside, the place was straight from another world.

The floors were hardwood, the tables big and simple, the walls lined with booths, the crowd simply dressed and noisy. And happy.

A wiry well-muscled man with graying hair came up to Jeremy, wiped his hand on worn jeans before offering it. Jeremy turned to Duncan, said, "Like you to meet the owner of the finest establishment north of the Carolina border."

The man's grip was hard as his eyes. "Thought maybe the iced tea and lemonade crowd oughtta have a chance to eat without battling their way through a frond forest."

Duncan worked at not wincing over the man's grip, said, "I feel like I've stepped into a time machine."

The man did not disagree. "Nowadays these restaurants, they gotta go buy out a coupla florists, make up some awful brown goop they pour over everything, print up these wine lists in old Gothic can't nobody even read. Which is what they're after, 'cause then they can serve up some Chateau La Seventy-Nine Fifty and pay for their sons to go to Princeton."

"What ever happened to a place where you could go in, sit down, have a decent meal, and not have to hock your socks to get out?" Jeremy agreed.

"What's your line of work?" the man asked Duncan.

Jeremy answered for him. "The man hunts for runaways."

He grunted. "Don't think I could stand the heartache myself. Glad there's somebody out there doing it, though."

Once they were seated Jeremy said to Duncan, "This and church are about the only places around here that keep me sane."

Duncan nodded, decided the time had come to ask this raw-boned man a few straight-out questions. "You sure did look at those pictures a long time this afternoon."

A fleeting look came to Jeremy's solid face and then departed so fast Duncan was uncertain of what he had seen. It wasn't fear, and it wasn't anger, and it wasn't bad. What it most brought to Duncan's mind was *awe*.

But all the gray-haired man said was, "Thought maybe I'd seen one of those girls before."

"Yeah? Where?"

"Doesn't matter, son. Just one of those coincidences of life." Jeremy leaned across the table, asked, "Mind if I ask you a question?"

"Shoot."

"Do you know what it means to be saved?"

"You mean like religion? No."

Jeremy clearly expected the answer. "Had this feelin' all day that you'd not heeded when you heard the call. Can't say why. Something down around gut level that my head never figured out."

"What, you're one of these religious people, thinks he's got all the answers?"

Jeremy shook his head. "I don't have any answers, son. But I know Someone who does."

"I tried God once. We didn't fit."

Jeremy smiled with a tenderness that did not match his work-roughened features at all. "Maybe He's just waitin' for you to give Him another try, did you ever think of that?"

With anybody else, Duncan would have been all over them by now, playing the third degree, pushing hard for answers, hoping he could catch them at an obvious discrepancy. It was usually necessary to call them out before getting down to essentials. People *lied* so much.

But there was something different here, something that left him wondering if there was any real need to question this strange man with his luminous gaze. He had told Duncan almost nothing, yet gave the impression of holding nothing back.

Jeremy laid down his fork, asked, "The food to your likin'?"

"It's great, thanks."

"That Detective Larson is one hard man."

"He's in a tough business."

"Maybe the work took him farther down the road, but I do believe that man was hard to start with."

"Gave us some good advice, though."

"That he did. Was it true what he said 'bout you always bringin' the children back?"

"They're not children, Jeremy. You've got to stop thinking of them in those terms."

"Fifteen's still a child in my book."

"What happens to them on the road, plus what they've already gone through to get them out there in the first place, pretty much kills every last little bit of child there is in them."

Jeremy slid his plate to one side. "Makes it tough, I imagine, havin' them be carted outta state like that."

"It does," Duncan admitted. "I've never had something like this happen before. It changes the whole ball game."

Jeremy bowed his head and grew very still; a quietness spread across the table to touch Duncan as well. He realized the man was praying. Yet there was no discomfort, and that surprised him mightily. He was content to sit and watch the carved features through their curtain of graying hair, and feel a gentle yearning he had not known in years.

When Jeremy raised his head he said, "Tomorrow's Sunday. Why don't you give me a chance to check something out. Then maybe we can meet on Monday. How does that sound?"

"It'll have to be Tuesday. Monday I've got appointments to go talk to people at their school." Then because it came so easily, he asked, "Mind telling me about the bomb?"

"No, son, I don't mind," Jeremy replied.

There was no doubt in Duncan's mind from the very first word that this was the truth he was hearing, no doubt even about TJ Case's letter and the funeral instructions. The strongest voice Duncan heard was the one in his own head, repeating over and over, I can trust this man. It didn't make any sense, and he didn't have enough to go on to make such a sweeping judgment. But that was how he felt.

"After the funeral I came back to see about their affairs and finish up with the police," Jeremy concluded. "The money came through for the Community's projects 'bout then, and those folks got busy as a one-legged man in a hundred-yard dash. So I told myself I'd stay around long enough to get them started. Truth was, though, I didn't have much to go home to. My business is doin' just fine without me, and I don't have much interest in startin' anything new. That's how it's been, see. I'd get some wild idea or another and go racin' off into the wind. Then once it was up and goin' I'd hand it over to somebody who was better at sittin' behind a desk and takin' care of the daily mess, and off I'd go on another wild-goose chase. Only now there ain't a goose left that's worth chasing, far as I'm concerned."

Duncan asked, "What did Bryan say when you told him about Case's letter, you know, with your friends supposedly knowing about their death?"

"Aw, the man just pretended I hadn't said anything. You know what it's like. The Lord's work just didn't set well in his little idea box. He decided it was easier to ignore me than to think maybe there were ideas bigger than what would fit in that size-nine brain of his."

"I'm real sorry to hear about your friends."

"Thank you kindly, son. They're right where they belong. Can't help but get a little hot under the collar, though, about how they left me here on my own."

"So what makes you want to get involved with locating runaways?"

Again there was that *look,* the same look he'd had when he first saw the pictures of the girls. Jeremy focused on Duncan, said, "What say we leave that one for another time? I don't mind being a witness to His power, but I'd just as soon wait 'til you've had a chance to get to know me before I show you just how crazy I really am."

Duncan nodded as though he understood. "Fine with me." The response surprised him, as waiting for anything was not his strong suit.

◆　　◆　　◆

"Hey, fancy lady, what kinda car did Daddy Bucks drive?"

"My name is Jessica," she said quietly. Chico scared her something awful, but she knew enough not to let it show.

They had been driving nine or ten hours each day, keeping to some schedule that only Pierre knew about. They were somewhere in Ohio, Jessica figured. Dusk was gathering and the lights of oncoming traffic were beginning to hurt her eyes, and she wished they would stop. But every time she started to ask Pierre, something held her back. She didn't want to be a complainer, especially not so soon.

"Yeah, that's right." Chico drawled the words, bored and tired and ready to pick on the weakest in the car. "Jessica, what a name. C'mon, honey, let's hear the life story. How old was our little princess the first time?"

Pierre reached his hand over the central console, let the fingertips trace a soft outline around her knee. Jessica settled back and drew strength from him.

Chico jostled the back of her seat with his foot. "I asked you a question, little princess. Whatsa matter, you don't talk to low class?"

"Either lighten up or walk, Chico," Pierre said. He did not raise his voice, did not look around, did not lift his hand from Jessica's knee. But the back seat became silent.

Thirteen, Jessica said to herself, grasping Pierre's hand and settling it in her lap. I was thirteen years old and it was awful. He was nineteen and good looking and made me laugh and wanted it so bad I thought, why not? Daddy was always after it.

She heard about her father every time she went to the club. There goes Jessica, the older women would say, half wanting her to hear their gossipy little chit-chat. Isn't it a shame about how Harvey's all around town like a tomcat, chasing anything in a skirt?

Back then she didn't know what it all meant—the catty glances, the smirks, the highballs at poolside and the gossip they wanted her to hear. She didn't understand it when they said things like, Harvey'd climb in a showroom window if the dummy had nice legs.

I must have seemed awful naive back then, Jessica thought, but not anymore. She lifted Pierre's hand and stroked dark hairs, felt his age and strength and knowledge surround her. She looked at his face, felt a little thrill when he turned to smile at her. She leaned her head against the headrest and let her mind roam back to their first night on the road.

They had checked into a nondescript roadside hotel and had eaten dinner from a fast-food paper bag. Pierre had then lain on the bed and watched her get ready for bed.

She was getting to know Pierre a little bit. When he got that *look* in his eyes, the one he had then, Jessica could say just about anything she wanted. She wasn't sure he listened to everything she said, but that was okay. She had a lot of practice at not being listened to.

The television was murmuring softly, and Pierre lay

stretched out with all the pillows stuffed up behind his head. His shirt was unbuttoned and pulled from his pants, exposing sun-darkened skin. Blue-black hair covered his chest and traced its way down his belly. Whenever Jessica appeared in the bathroom doorway his eyes swiveled from the television to her. He watched her parade across the room to her suitcase and back to the bathroom, observing her with the sparkling eyes and silent ease of a big cat. Jessica liked the feeling of those eyes on her, even though it frightened her a little. It gave her a sense of belonging when he paid this kind of attention to her. She made a lot more trips back and forth through the room than she really needed, partly because she was a little scared and partly so she could feel those eyes on her again.

"It's wild how sure you are your parents won't raise a stink," Pierre drawled in that slow, easy manner.

"I'm sure," she replied, playing at a bright ease she did not feel. "I used to dream a lot, you know, how nice it'd be to have a home where my parents would love me and want to be with me and everything. It's the one dream I remember clearest from when I was little. I'd cover myself up in the bed, get down far enough so my head was all the way under the blankets. Then I'd kinda pull the edges of the covers in around me until I was tucked into this little cocoon. And I'd dream about having this family with a little house and trees and parents who smiled a lot and a couple of brothers and sisters and everything. Then after a while I guess I just stopped dreaming."

She returned to the bathroom but kept the door open. She brushed her hair with swift, hard strokes. Copper-burnished threads fell in gentle cascades. "I used to be *really* jealous of Arlene. She had everything I wanted and hated it all. She was so *mean* to her family. Sometimes I wished I could make a swap. You know, my parents and the money and the house for her family."

Jessica opened the shopping bag with the fancy logo, pulled out the nightgown that Pierre had given her, and draped it in front of her. A little keen pain stabbed somewhere deep inside. There was a ribbon at the neck to hold it together, and no other closure. The fabric was so sheer that she could see the design of her sweater through it. The nightie was just long enough to cover the top of her thighs. There were a pair of panties in there too, made from the same material and laced with the same little ribbon.

Jessica let the nightie fall to the cabinet and gazed deep into eyes on the mirror's other side, eyes that had opened up like wells. She looked beyond the image and saw herself getting ready for bed in her own room, pulling on the long flannel nightgown with the frilly lacework around the neck and wrists, sitting at her own little vanity and brushing her hair. It was a cold room in a cold house, with everything as neat and proper as a full-time maid could keep it. But it was *safe*.

She blinked back the burning in her eyes, fought against the fear that made her legs go weak. Questions she had no answers for clamored for attention. What was she doing here?

"Jessica?" The voice shocked her alert, brought her back to the sink and the bathroom and the nightie and Pierre with a jerk. There was an instant of indecision, a moment of considering a rush for the door, leaving her clothes and the suitcase and Pierre, just fleeing as hard as her legs would take her.

Flee to what? Idly she raised the nightie and dragged the fabric through her fingers. Flee back to the morgue? That was what her father called their home. He had let it slip often enough for her to know that it wasn't just an occasional joke. What would her parents say? She could hear her mother now, talking about how Jessica had made her the laughingstock of the club and how all the women were saying she wasn't much of a mother, asking Jessica how she could be so heartless as to just up and run away.

"Jessica?" Pierre stuck his head in the doorway, saw her fingering the nightie, gave her that look. "Like it?"

"Uh-huh, it's real nice." Where did she have to run to?

"Put it on and come to bed."

"All right." The same reasons that had driven her away were all still there, staring back in the reflection's sadness.

When the door closed she took off her clothes and put on the nightie, avoiding her reflection now, not wanting to have to see what was happening. She had been with Pierre, but never for a whole night, never in a hotel, never in a place where she had felt so isolated and alone, never with any guy like that. The fabric felt cold, or maybe it was her skin that was clammy. She folded her clothes neatly, let her hair fall down between her eyes and the mirror, saw how her fingers would not stop trembling.

CHAPTER
3

It was unseasonably hot for an early autumn day. Jeremy took his accustomed seat toward the church's back left corner, the only white face in the congregation. He exchanged nods and smiles with familiar folks, sat, opened his Bible, reached in his side pocket for his handkerchief and wiped his brow.

It had been hard returning to the church after his friends' death. TJ and Catherine Case had been the tie binding him to the church and the congregation, or so he thought. But after he had missed the two Sunday services that followed the funeral, a steady stream of visitors had begun to appear at the Community of Hope where he worked, asking after him, politely hoping that all was well, quietly wondering when he would be returning to church. After two weeks of this treatment Jeremy had gathered his courage and returned, to be greeted with the same gentle murmurs that had marked his time among them—nothing loud or forced or false or overly friendly, just warm looks and strong handshakes and quietly spoken words to let him know that this was his home, too.

Washington did not hold him as it did before the bomb exploded and killed his two best friends. But the Community of Hope project was a consuming work, and one which suited his own background in construction and project development. They could probably have handled the three contracts for subsistence-level housing without him, but it would have been tough.

So Jeremy Hughes remained on to finish the work his friend TJ Case had begun.

Sunlight streamed through the eastern wall's four stained-glass windows, bathing the hall in a rainbow of colors. Jeremy looked up to where Reverend Wilkins was seated at the podium's high-backed chair. The man was already giving his hand towel a workout, and he had not even started speaking.

Reverend James Thaddeus Wilkins was named after his granddaddy. The eldest son of six, he grew up in Alabama chopping cotton on his daddy's land. But he knew from an early age he had a call on his life, one that would take him far from home and the life he knew. Much as he loved the black dirt between his fingers and the smell of the cows in the neighboring pasture when the wind blew east, much as he loved seeing the little seeds that he'd planted with his own two hands grow up into tall thick cotton, James Thaddeus Wilkins knew that he had to leave.

World War II brought him that one-way ticket out of Alabama. The army sent him to Europe with an all-black regiment stationed in southern France. He never could pronounce the names of where he'd been, and soon all those sad little places with their bombed-out roofs and broken-in doors and bullet-spattered walls and tank-rutted roads began to look and feel and smell the same to him.

The war gave him a chance to see that dirt was dirt, whether on this side or that side of the ocean. He saw that blood was blood, whether spilled from black skin or white skin, American skin or French skin, German skin or Jew skin. He learned that God is God, whether man believed in Him or walked his own way in the hell of man-made blindness.

After the war, his regiment came home *proud* men. They weren't just hard-working boys anymore. They risked their lives, which was just about all they had to give, and they were happy to do it. Yessir, happy. They'd proven for the first time, to themselves and to everybody else in the whole wide world, that America was *their* country, too. The freedom they had fought for, in another land and for another people, was a freedom they wanted for themselves.

James Thaddeus Wilkins landed in Washington, D.C. because his best buddy in the regiment lived there. He found himself a job working for the post office delivering mail in northwest Washington. The job was a piece of cake to him. After

waking up at five-thirty every morning, slopping the hogs, taking the cows to pasture, drawing water, and chopping the wood,
walking up and down the streets all day with a little bitty
leather bag on his shoulder sounded pretty good to him.

But when a man walks all day he has a lot of time, a lot of
space, for God to speak. His calling, the one that had started
so long ago, now had a chance to develop. James Thaddeus
Wilkins walked the streets of Adams-Morgan and prayed.
These prayers of his reached deep down inside and they
cleansed him. They opened his eyes, they opened his heart, they
taught him a new way to look and to see and to feel.

He came home at night and opened his Bible and felt the
words echo down deep where the prayers had been that day,
filling him up with a power and a glory and a love and a light
that just *awed* him. James Thaddeus Wilkins heard those words
speak to his soul. And he knew that God had a work for him, a
service that needed his strong shoulder, a cross that he alone
was meant to bear. One night James Thaddeus Wilkins woke
up from a deep sleep to feel as though *he* were the Lord's seed,
that *he* had been planted, that *he* was bearing fruit, that *he*
was there for others to reach to and take from and grow with.

He went from Sunday-school teacher to trustee to deacon;
it took twenty years to learn how to serve, being taught by the
Master the only way the Master taught, from within. And then
the time came.

James Thaddeus Wilkins was called to be a preacher.

With a nod from the reverend, one of the front-row deacons
stood and approached the lower podium with its oversized Bible.
He was a big man, massive, with hands like skillets and a round
solemn face. Over the PA system his deep voice had a barrel-
like quality.

"We will read today first from the eighty-second psalm, and
then from the ninth chapter of Mark, verse 42:

"How long will you defend the unjust and show partiality
to the wicked? Defend the cause of the weak and needy;
deliver them from the hand of the wicked. They know nothing, they understand nothing. They walk about in darkness; all the foundations of the earth are shaken.

"And if anyone causes one of these little ones who believe

in me to sin, it would be better for him to be thrown into the sea with a large millstone tied around his neck."

Reverend Wilkins appeared reluctant to rise and face the congregation. He sat rigid and erect, his eyes closed, his face set in lines of carved ebony. Twice he grasped the arms of the chair as though preparing to stand, then remained where he was.

At last he moved to the podium, fumbled among the folds of his robe, and came up with a crumpled piece of paper.

"Got me a letter here," he said softly. "Wasn't what I wanted to talk with you about this morning, but I can't seem to get it off my mind. Had it slipped under my door night 'fore last. Don't know how many times I read it. Even dreamed about it last night. Don't know if I can say it, it hurts me so bad. But if it's His will, the Lord will see me through."

He looked over his half-moon spectacles at the crowd, but did not seem to see them. "Late last night a blessed sister gave me the answer I'd been searchin' high and low for. Only thing I can do is pray. Pray it ain't too late. Pray our Lord will show this boy what to do. Pray the power of our Savior is enough to show this boy the way home."

Jeremy had never seen the church so quiet. The congregation sat in frozen silence, every eye fastened upon the pastor. The world began and ended there upon the podium.

"This ain't long. Only a few sentences." A badly shaking hand reached up to touch the glasses, thought better of it, meandered back down to support the reverend's weight once more.

"Y'all know Bobby, Sister Lee's son," Reverend Wilkins said, and was stopped by a chorus of moans that rose from the congregation.

"Bobby's a real nice young man, real polite. Boy graduated from eighth grade last year, family gave him a real nice party. Somebody asked him what he wanted to be when he grew up. Boy answered with one word. Alive. That's all he said. That's all the hope this world would give a fourteen-year-old boy.

"Most of y'all know the boy's been missin' almost a month now. Sister Lee's been takin' it real hard. Real hard. Needs your prayers, 'specially now. She was the one who told me to read it today, told me to ask y'all to pray. Only reason I got the strength to stand up here with this is on account of what Sister Lee said to me last night. There's one thing that can save my boy now, Sister Lee told me. Gotta get the whole world to pray for my boy. Gotta light a candle in everybody's hearts so bright it shines through my boy's darkness. Gotta take it to the Lord on bended knee, that poor sister said. Gotta ask for the miracle of healing. Gotta pray. Tell them if they love Jesus, they gotta pray. That's what Sister Lee said to me last night. And if the sister's got the strength left to ask me to do it, after all she's been through, well, then I gotta do it."

Reverend Wilkins took a shaky breath, kneaded the towel with the fingers of one hand, did not bother to wipe his dripping face.

"All right. Here's what the boy writes me. Give me strength, Lord. Give me strength.

"Dear Reverend Wilkins,

"I dreamed about my family last night, and in it my mother was searching for me and calling my name. I can't write her and tell her I'm all right, so I'm writing you and you can tell her what you want. I'm hooked on crack. I tried it at a party seven weeks ago, and now I can't stop. I got a job directing runners someplace near here, but I can't tell you where. They need me because I'm older and know how to write more than my name. We make a lot of money, but I spend most of mine on drugs. I don't know if I'm going to send this, but I was real worried after the dream. Just tell my mother that I can't come home right now."

Then Reverend Wilkins raised his head, nodded slowly, said in a very soft voice, "All right, I've told his mother. Told her and watched it break her heart." His face took on a look of utter agony. "But what am I gonna tell my Lord? How am I gonna explain this to my Maker? He tells me, right here in His Word, I got a responsibility to His children. Takes precedent over everything in my life 'cept my love of Him. Ain't nothing more important than protectin' His little children, 'cept livin' in His Word. And look what I've gone and done."

More than sweat poured down his cheeks. More than the congregation filled his eyes. "Look what I've done with your most precious gift, Father. Look how I've failed you. You placed me here, called me to your work, said I was to be a shepherd for your flock. And look what I've gone and done. I've lost one of your precious children. I've had to stand and minister to a broken-hearted mother, woman with the soul of a saint, woman who lives for her family. What am I gonna tell her, Father? How can I ease her pain? Boy's so lost he don't even know how to ask for help, writes me a letter just to say he's lost, won't even tell me where. What am I gonna tell her? How can I face that fine lady, tell her that things are gonna be all right?"

The man seated in the pew in front of Jeremy wiped his face with fingers flattened and hardened by a life of toil, cleared his throat, put his arm around the shaking shoulders of the woman beside him.

"Saints, the devil is *busy*. We all got to stay prayed up, walk with our eyes open. You hearin' me out there? We *all* got an enemy. Satan has snatched one of our own. Now how did he do that? Can anybody out there tell me that?"

"Say it, Preacher!" The first voice did not rise, as it did most Sundays, from the front two rows where the deacons and deaconesses sat. It came from high up in the balcony, up near the rafters, and sounded as if it were torn from the man's throat.

"All right. I'll tell you why. He came in right here among the saints 'cause he caught us *nappin'*. Caught us with our eyes closed. Saw we weren't payin' attention and walked right in here and *took* the boy. Stole him away. Pulled him into darkness and despair. Left a hole in Sister Lee's heart and a *wound* in our family."

"Amen, amen, Preacher!"

"Bobby was a good boy. He was smart, obedient too. He came to Sunday school. Bobby was *good* in his books. He *listened*. Now you know it's not every day you find our young people listenin' to their elders."

"Tell the truth, Reverend!"

"But, Church, my heart is burdened today. Quiet as Bobby was, smart as Bobby was, obedient as Bobby was, he never let on that he was strugglin' with sin. Sister Lee had to find out through a letter left under my door in the darkness of a lonely night that Bobby was bein' pushed and pulled and stretched and flattened 'til her Bobby wasn't her Bobby no more."

Silence. Not even a baby dared to whimper.

Reverend Wilkins took his hand towel, mopped his brow with a shaking hand, then held it to his mouth for a long, long time before continuing, "It's tough out in them streets. Our children got to face the devil. Crack, guns, teachers that don't care if they can read or write, and just plain evil people. *Mean* people. We give our children love and hope and strength at home, but they walk through that door in the morning, ain't no tellin' what they're gonna face before they get home at night.

"It's up to us to know in our hearts when something just ain't right with our children. The church shoulda *been* there with Bobby, instead of the crack-heads. When Bobby needed somebody, we shoulda been there beside that boy."

"Hallelujah!"

"But we take for granted that when things look all right on the outside with our children, they're all right on the inside. We don't *want* to see, now, do we? Life's so tough for us out there, we're *burdened*. We got *needs*. We carry pain. But, saints, that's why we need the Holy Spirit."

With visible effort Reverend Wilkins squared his shoulders. He stripped off the glasses, gave his face a long two-handed wipe with the towel. He looked out over his flock with eyes that searched for a boy that was not there.

Reverend Wilkins called out, "Sister Lee, we love you."

The entire congregation sang out their reply.

"We want you to know that you been a good mother and a faithful member. God don't condemn you 'cause your son slipped and fell. He condemns *us*. And why? Because we were too busy bearin' our own burdens to hear the call of your child. We were too caught up in the trials of this world to remember that there's One waitin' to take these problems from us. We were too weary from facin' an uncarin' world on our own to be there when Bobby called."

The gravity of their error lay like shadows upon their faces. They stared forward with eyes turned inward.

"The Lord doesn't condemn you, Sister Lee. Lord knows you're a good momma. But are you gonna condemn us? Do you have the strength in your soul to forgive us after what we've done?"

He lowered a fiery gaze toward the congregation, said, "Sister Johnson, that coulda been your boy."

There was an answering groan from the members. He shook it from him like rain from his coat and went on, "Brother Andrews, it could be your pretty little girl next time. World's got a lotta uses for a pretty young thing like that."

The cry of denial rose from a hundred throats, the fear felt by all.

He slammed his fist onto the podium, and thunder echoed

from the walls. "Enough is enough! We're gonna fight the devil, and we're gonna *win*. God's church is a *big* church, because we serve a *big* God. A *great* God. A *glorious* God.

"Drug pushers, watch out! Pimps, watch out! Devil, you better start runnin'. You took one of our own, and we're comin' after you. We're gonna get him, and all the rest of the little ones you stole.

"Love thy neighbor as thyself. Can anybody tell me who told us that?"

"Jesus!" Five hundred voices spoke the name as one.

"That's right. The Lord himself said it, said it to all of us. Called it the eleventh commandment, didn't He? Yeah. Know who that neighbor is? Well, I'll tell you. It's that child out there sellin' her body on the street. It's the boy breakin' car windows to steal and buy hisself some crack. It's the little one who's run away from parents who hurt him and scare him and make him feel like he ain't nothin' but dirt. Yeah. All those little ones out there shiverin' from more than just the cold, every one of them's our neighbors, strangers lyin' hurt and scared and alone in the streets, wishin' Jesus was more than just some name in a book, wishin' there really was somebody who'd love 'em and help 'em and show 'em a better way."

Wilkins leaned far out over the pulpit and searched the congregation with blazing eyes. "Now who's gonna get out there and help our children come home?"

Gradually understanding dawned, and with it came a rustling, an unsure movement of many heads and bodies. Reverend Wilkins was asking for a commitment. Not just a cry spoken in the thrill of a Sunday service. A *commitment*.

Halfway back a tall reedy black man rose to his feet. He did not shout his words, but rather spoke them with the soft strength of one understanding fully what he was asked to do. "I am, Reverend."

One of the gray-haired deacons followed. "Me too, Reverend. I'm ready."

"Who is gonna heed the cries of their pain?" the reverend called. "Show them that they do truly have a Home and a Father who waits to give them perfect peace?"

A handful of others rose to their feet, carried by the power that swept through the room. A dozen more rose and lifted their voices. A dozen more.

"Who is gonna show this pretty little girl on the street corner that love ain't just something she sells by the hour? Who is gonna help heal their wounds? Who is gonna teach 'em how to *pray*?"

The church was filled with a holy clamor. Reverend Wilkins remained unfazed. He raised his arms and shouted in a mighty voice, "Who is gonna put on their righteous armor and do battle for their Lord?"

It brought the entire congregation to their feet. Reverend Wilkins waited for a moment, raised his hands, asked for silence. They gave it to him reluctantly.

"All right, now. Time's over for sittin' back and takin' things easy. Time's come for action. Deacon Peters, come on up here. All you other deacons and deaconesses, come up to this altar. We're gonna start prayin' right here, right now. Gonna pray, gonna call on the Holy One, gonna call on the Lord our God to come in and save this boy. Gonna start us a prayer circle. Gonna pray us a light to shine out into that boy's darkness, lead him home where he belongs. Gonna pray and keep prayin' right around the clock, each and every one of us, prayin' and searchin' and doin' His will, and we're gonna bring that boy *home*.

"I want every one of you to give as much time as you can. People workin' days, give part of your nights. Mothers with little children, y'all get together, share 'em out. You men with night-time jobs, start plannin' to stop by on your way home from work. Sign-up sheet's gonna be right there when you go out. We're gonna need everybody's help with this. This ain't something we're gonna see solved tomorrow. This is *war*. Gotta outlast the Evil One, gotta snatch this child out of the jaws of eternal death. Yeah. I want all you people to give, help this poor family out the only way we can.

"Another thing. We got us two policemen here in the congregation. Y'all know Brother Thomas and Brother Simmons. Raise your hands, you two, let everybody see where you're at. All right. We're startin' a search party for Bobby. Want all the help we can get. People with a strong stomach, because from the sound of it, what we're gonna be seein' ain't such a pretty sight. It's time to get to work. Everyone who can, I want to see y'all over at my house this afternoon for a plannin' session. Those that can't, want to see your names on the prayer list. All right now, let's all bow our heads and pray for His guidance and strength."

After the service Jeremy stood on the outskirts of the group surrounding Reverend Wilkins and waited to be noticed. The tall man caught sight of Jeremy, reached out a black-robed arm and parted the crowd so Jeremy could come forward.

"Brother Hughes," Reverend Wilkins said, his voice as tired as his face. "Sure do appreciate your bein' willin' to help us out in our time of need."

"Happy to do what I can," Jeremy said. "Matter of fact, though, I got a trouble of my own."

The crowd loosened, relaxed, murmured its sympathy. Sorrow was a tie that bound them all, broke all barriers, opened all doors.

"I'd just like to tell you first of all, what you said up there like to tore me apart."

"Say it, brother," someone responded.

"Strong is all it was," another man agreed. *"Strong."*

"I wasn't interested in strong," Reverend Wilkins replied, his eyes two dark pools of agony. "I wanted all the folks to know just how bad I'd let 'em down."

"Now Reverend, you give me one place on earth that don't have this problem nowadays," Jeremy replied. "It's *everybody's* fault, far as I can see it. Ain't a soul on earth that don't carry some of the guilt for what's happened to Bobby. You burden yourself down like this, you ain't gonna be no good to nobody."

"Man's right, Reverend," a gray-haired elder agreed. "We're all burdened with the guilt here. All gotta turn to the Lord and seek His guidin' hand."

Reverend Wilkins straightened slightly, gave Jeremy a nod, murmured, "Say you got a problem, Brother Hughes?"

"Yessir. Coupla young ladies, 'bout the same age as Bobby, got it in their heads to run away from home. Looks like they've taken off with some men close on twice their age."

"Lord, Lord, their poor mommas," murmured one of the women.

"From what I heard, this fellow's involved in . . ." Jeremy hesitated, then turned to the listening crowd. "Hope you'll excuse me, ladies."

"Go right on, Brother Hughes," Reverend Wilkins said. "Ain't nothin' we haven't all heard before, I'm sorry to say."

"Yessir. Well, it appears he hunts out young women and gets 'em involved in, ah, pictures."

Reverend Wilkins aged visibly. "These girls black?"

"Nossir, both white."

He shook his head, waited for the murmured sorrow to diminish. "Just like you say, Brother Hughes. The problem's with us everywhere, ain't it?"

"Yessir, sure is. What I wanted to ask was, you remember the first Sunday I came here with my friend TJ Case. You told us about sittin' the death watch for a lady who kept prayin' for her son. Don't recall his name. You said he was involved in women and such."

Reverend Wilkins inspected him through narrowed eyes. "You remember a sermon I gave last winter? That's some memory you got there, Brother Hughes."

"Just for the important things in life, Reverend."

"The dearly departed was a Sister Mary. Boy's name is Julius."

"Yessir, that's the one. Julius. What I was wonderin' was, you think maybe I could talk to him? We're gonna try and locate these girls, and we need some help knowin' where to look."

"Ain't much chance of gettin' anything outta Julius," a teenager in the circle replied. "That man is *mean*."

But Reverend Wilkins did not agree. "Easiest way to get to a black man's heart is through his momma, Brother Hughes. Go talk to Mary's sister, Ida. They's twins. Ask if maybe she'll go see Julius with you."

"Thank you, Reverend, that's just what I was lookin' for."

"My wife's over with the other group. She'll introduce you. Tell Ida I thought it was a good idea. Yeah. It'll give Julius something to think about, seein' his aunt again after so long. Oughtta be like seein' his momma's ghost come back to life."

◆   ◆   ◆

"Julius has got himself a real power. That boy is downright handsome too, you know what I mean, Mr. Hughes?"

"Yes, ma'am, and I'd sure appreciate it if you'd call me Jeremy."

"Just pull up and stop right here. And remember, you let me do the talkin' in there."

Logan Circle, a few blocks from Adams-Morgan, was ringed by houses with spectacular architecture. It was run-down and derelict and dangerous, save a scattering of buildings that stuck out from their neighbors like misplaced new pennies. Some years ago a couple of bright-eyed property developers had decided to turn Logan Circle into the next Georgetown. They had bought up a few of the buildings, ones that were going for a song and still had the basics like floors and a roof, and spent a minor fortune fixing them up.

The condominiums were then sold to moneyed folks who decided that until the development really caught hold Logan Circle wasn't safe enough for them to move in their own families. So they rented them out. But the hoped-for renaissance never materialized, and the few people willing to live there who could afford the higher rents weren't exactly what an agent would call ideal tenants. Like Julius.

Ida told Jeremy all this on the way down from church, after first climbing into his truck and ordering him to roll up his window and lock his door. She was a big, no-nonsense sort of woman, dressed in solid black and looking about as mobile as the Jefferson Memorial.

She'd heard him out in utter silence with eyes hard and unmoving and face clamped down tight. But when he was finished she'd made sure her black straw boater with its little collection of glass cherries was set down right, took a two-handed grip on her purse, and said that Julius was probably easiest to find on a Sunday afternoon, so they ought to be moving right along.

Jeremy parked in front of a mansion-sized five-story building of painted brick. It was adorned with fancy scrollwork, turrets, gargoyles, and a series of oval windows across the upper floors. A small, neat little lawn was bordered by a waist-high metal picket fence. It reminded Jeremy of a picture book of France.

To the mansion's left rose a gutted shell of a building that would have looked at home in downtown Beirut. To the right was a weed-choked vacant lot.

"Only building I can see that doesn't wear a coat of graffiti," Jeremy said.

"Oughtta tell you somethin' 'bout what folks think of Julius. Now you hush up and let me do the talkin'."

Ida opened the little gate and walked toward what had once been the mansion's side entrance. Three little steps led from the path to a door that would have better suited a bank; its glass was tinted and looked a full inch thick, and crossed in front were iron bars laced together with wrought-iron leaves.

Ida paused before the first step, took in the door and the

polished marble stoop and the gilded knocker and the matching
door handle. She gathered herself, climbed the stairs, grabbed
the knocker and banged it down hard enough to send shivers
through her hat's lacquered cherries.

The door pushed violently open. A face that would have been
strikingly handsome save for the snarl jutted out. He caught
sight of the woman, and showed a pang of real fear before recognizing her. "Aunt Ida!"

"Hello, Jukey," Ida said quietly. She sounded tired. "How
you?"

"What you doin' in my part of town, Aunt Ida?" Julius
pushed the door wide, made room for her to enter, embraced
the woman and kissed her cheek.

Julius was a tall, powerful man, with a chest and shoulders
that would have appeared comically overdeveloped on most
men. On Julius they just fit. He wore a tight-fitting cashmere
sweater with two gold chains and a diamond pendant hanging
in the V. His hair was straight and slicked back and cut as
neatly as his mustache. His eyes were hard. Dangerous, deadly
eyes. Eyes that showed nothing at all. No fear, no interest, no
concern.

He looked over his aunt's shoulder, caught sight of Jeremy,
and froze.

Ida pulled herself free of the embrace. "Jukey, there's something you need to do for me. And for your mother."

His voice was as flat as his eyes. "What you doin', bringin'
this man here?"

"Jukey, I want you to help this man. His name is Jeremy."

"Why?"

"He's lookin' for two little girls, Jukey. Two little babies only
fifteen years old. Their mommas is goin' plain crazy with
worry."

Julius was not impressed. He said to Jeremy, "What's in it
for you, man?"

Ida answered for him. "He's a good man, Jukey. Been goin'
to our church for best part of a year."

"In a black church?" The eyes glittered. "What you doin' in
my momma's church, man?"

"Jukey," Ida said, her voice eternally weary.

Julius turned to her, said, "What's my family doin', bringin'
this man here? Why you doin' this to me, Aunt Ida?"

Softly she touched his face. "Jukey boy, you know I love you.

Love the sinner, hate the sin, that's one lesson I learned for you. You know I'd never do anything to hurt you, Jukey. You're like my own little boy, always have been. But this man here is on a mission for the Lord. It's what brought him to our church and why I brought him here today. He is God's servant, Jukey, I know that in my *heart*. Just like I know your momma would want you to help him."

She held him with a gaze as soft as her voice. "You know how your momma felt 'bout what you been doin'. You know how she loved the Lord. This is the way, Jukey. You can do something to remember your momma by. You can start gettin' right with the Master."

Julius began to relax and the tension went out of his massive shoulders. He took his aunt's hand from his face, held it, said to them both, "Y'all come on inside."

The living room was ringed by closed lacquered doors and lined with a spotless white carpet. The room was full of expensive things, but in a mishmash of style and taste as though bought simply because of the price tag—a blue leather sofa, an ornate armchair, a marble-top table, a hand-blown crystal lamp, a massive stereo. Big speakers flanked an enormous television set and a whole stack of music machines. Silver CD's were scattered around the floor like oversized gambling chips. The two far corners of the room held waist-high nude statues.

Not letting go of his aunt's hand, he faced Jeremy square on and asked, "What you want from me, man?"

Jeremy forced himself to stare straight back and sketched what he knew. It was hard to concentrate and look into those eyes, hard to keep his gaze steady, hard to believe he was really here asking this man for help. Jeremy was immensely glad when he had said his piece and could retreat into silence. But he didn't lower his gaze. Not even then.

"Always takes his ladies out of state, that right?"

"That's his habit," Jeremy agreed.

Julius thought a moment. "Try Leroy Shell in Chicago, goes by the name of Tip-Toe. Clyde Shaw in Detroit, friends call him See-Through. The ladies really high class? Good-looking?"

"I hear both of them are beautiful, yes."

"Try Gregory Lannerton out in Beverly Hills. Friends call him Laney." He looked down at his aunt, said, "That's all I can do."

She squeezed his hand with both of hers, said, "You done fine, Jukey boy. Thank you."

Ida motioned Jeremy toward the door and started after him. "Jukey, you need to put some weight on, boy. Don't make no sense, a man livin' like you livin' and not eatin' right."

She turned at the door and said, "You call me if you want a good meal, you hear? 'Cause sure as goodness all these women of yours ain't been takin' care of you."

Julius smiled, said nothing, watched them leave. Jeremy nodded to the man and received that same blank stare in return.

As Jeremy held the gate open for Ida, Julius called out, "Aunt Ida?"

She turned back around. "Yes, Jukey?"

"Don't stop prayin'," he said, and let the door slowly pull to. Just before it closed entirely, the shadow-voice said once more, "Don't you dare stop prayin'."

Ida stood there and watched the door a long while before letting Jeremy take her arm and lead her back to the truck.

◆　　◆　　◆

Jeremy clumped up the Community of Hope's central office stairs, waved a greeting to the black woman who handled the front desk on weekends, flung open the doors to what once had been a formal dining parlor and entered Bella Saunders' office.

Weekdays Bella remained a mover and shaker in the Office of Management and Budget, or OMB, and a leader—along with John Nakamishi and Senator Richard Atterly—of the TJ Case Prayer Group. Or one of them. There were now almost a dozen Case prayer groups scattered throughout the city, but the original continued to meet on Monday, Wednesday, and Thursday mornings in the basement cafeteria of the Old Executive Office Building.

Every Saturday and too many evenings for her own good, Bella worked in the project management side of the Community of Hope's new building projects. Jeremy called her the Senior Vice-President of Choke-Holds. They shared a lot of smiles, and found great comfort in each other's company.

Bella had made her mark during her first month at the Community when one of the old women who helped out on occasion came in with a panful of fresh-baked blueberry muffins. They were the best muffins Bella had ever tasted, and she told the old woman just that.

The old woman cackled her delight and said, "When I was

a sweet young thing, all the beaus told me I was good-lookin', sang jes' like an angel, and made the bes' blueberry muffins they was. Now, all that's left is them muffins."

The Pepco boys chose that morning to arrive. Pepco stood for Potomac Electric Power Company, and they had a reputation far and wide for arriving a day late and a dollar short. The law said they had to give approval for all new construction— where to cut, where to drill, how to wire. They made and unmade many a contractor and building project.

Bella heard the receptionist ask why they had not arrived as promised seven weeks before, and received a fairly typical reply. In a moment of inspiration she scooped up the muffin tin, walked into the front hall, and offered it around with a glint in her eye. The Pepco men were ready for another of their daily battles with exasperated builders stretched to the limit by dwindling budgets. The muffins caught them off guard. Bella coaxed and wheedled the group until they were relaxed and smiling, complimenting her and the old woman on the best blueberry muffins any of them had ever put in their mouths.

As they were leaving for the job site Bella told them, whoever comes next time gets a whole basket of muffins. That turned the men around.

For free? they asked, clearly surprised at being offered something for nothing before. Of course for free, she replied. A gift of peace from the giver of all peace.

The next time the Pepco boys were needed the old woman was up long before dawn, proud as a blushing bride to suddenly be so important. The power company truck was there in time for morning coffee and fresh-baked muffins. It was enough of an event to bring Reverend Tom Nees out of his office. Over his third muffin the man let it slip that there had been a near riot in the Pepco office the day before over who was making the call. Yeah, the man said, you're the only people in the district who're guaranteed same-day service for life.

Bella was on the phone, as always. Jeremy plopped himself down in one of the padded chairs, stretched out his legs, and enjoyed the performance.

"Good afternoon, Mr. Mulberry, how are you this beautiful Sunday afternoon? Oh, how nice. I'm so very sorry to be bothering you at home, but we wanted to be the very first to express our condolences."

She listened for a moment, and gave the ceiling an angelic smile. "Who am I? Oh, you don't know me, but I know you, Mr. Mulberry. This is Bella Saunders calling. I'm with the Community of Hope? Yeeess, that's right, the poor people down in Adams-Morgan."

Bella took the phone from her ear long enough to wring it hard in front of her face. She put it back, said, "We are all *soooo* worried about the deep personal tragedy that's struck your company, Mr. Mulberry. As I said, we wouldn't *dream* of bothering you at home, but we just had to call and offer our deepest condolences."

She listened a moment longer, made round eyes at Jeremy. "What? You don't know about any catastrophe? Why, our contract, signed by you and initialled by your legal counsel, specified delivery of chain-link fencing by three o'clock Friday afternoon. You can *imagine* our shock and dismay when the truck never arrived.

"Knowing that nothing short of death or an act of God would keep you from honoring your word, we naturally became *immediately* concerned for your welfare. How are you feeling? Yes? No accidents or strange diseases? Oh, Mr. Mulberry, I'm *soooo* glad for you!"

She smirked at Jeremy. "Oh, Mr. Mulberry, you don't know how *relieved* I am to hear that! And since the crew is all in good health, we can assume they will work around the clock at no extra charge to have the fencing up and completed on time? Yes? Oh, thank you, thank you, Mr. Mulberry. Goodbye."

She hung up the phone and said to Jeremy, "You want to read a modern-day fairy tale, take a look at some of the contracts I've got for this project."

Jeremy said in frank admiration, "Sure am glad I never had to wrangle with you, Bella. That man's been washed and wrung and hung out to dry."

She twisted a strand of hair, said, "This was quite a little think-and-do exercise. Mr. Rogers would have been proud."

"I'd rather wrestle a momma bear for her cub than go up against you on the phone," Jeremy replied.

Bella permitted herself a proud smile. "I could teach you all you need to do this yourself in three easy lessons."

"Now that's where you're wrong. Some folks are wise, and some are otherwise," Jeremy told her. "I don't know nothin' and it's too late to learn."

" 'How to bring a building supply company to their senses,' a weekend course by Bella Saunders. You want to sign up?"

Jeremy shook his head. "Thank you, sister. But I'm busy practicin' bein' lazy. Another couple of years and I oughtta have that art down pat."

She laughed. "You work harder than any three men I know."

"Now that's just plain not so." He pointed at her, asked, "What have you done to your hair?"

"How sweet, you noticed. It's as close as I could get it to my natural color. The hairdresser said they didn't have much call for people wanting to have grey hairs dyed *in*. I told him I was trying to be honest for the first time in twenty years."

Jeremy nodded. "I'll bet you he was some kinda undone."

"He told me not to say it so loud, or I might drive him out of business. Can you imagine? This prissy little fellow bending down real close, waving his hands in my face, asking me whoever in their right mind came into a hair salon looking for honesty. I tried not to laugh at him and said, okay, just dye it the color of my eyebrows. What do you think?"

Jeremy gave her a frank inspection and the honesty she was looking for. "It's the best-looking Bella I've ever laid eyes on." And it was. The autumn coloring softened the hard lines of her face and offset the warmth of her gold-brown eyes.

She thanked him with her gaze, asked, "Did you forget your promise to come to the prayer meeting with me tomorrow?"

"I did, but now that you've reminded me again I'll try and keep it in this sieve of a head."

"It would mean a lot to me and the others."

"Can't see why, a country hick like me mixin' with all them fancy politician people."

"Senator Atterly asks about you at every meeting, Jeremy. And Nak is beginning to wonder if maybe you're mad at him about something."

Jeremy decided there was no future in admitting that he'd been avoiding everything to do with TJ and Catherine Case except for the church. "I'll be there, Bella."

"It'll mean a lot to them. And me." Her voice added warmth to her smile. "Is there anything I can do for you?"

It just popped out then, as if it had been planted in his mouth for him to open and let it go. "How'd you like to have dinner with me on Tuesday evening?"

It clearly startled her as much as it had him. "You mean like a real date?"

Jeremy swallowed his surprise, realized it was too late to turn around. "I suppose I do, Bella."

"Why, I'd love to." She leaned across the desk. "Jeremy Hughes, are you blushing?"

That got him up and out of his chair. "I got three important calls waitin' for me, Bella. What say I come for you at seven?"

A voice in the doorway said, "Bella Saunders, is this man bothering you?"

"Not near as much as I would like," Bella said, her eyes on Jeremy.

Anna, the Community's full-time nurse, walked in and gave Jeremy a strong one-armed hug. "He's tall but he's skinny. He starts making trouble, I do believe we could take him down."

"How're you today, Anna?" Jeremy asked, his voice a tad weak.

"Better than you sound." Anna peered at him more closely. "You're awfully flushed. Are you running a fever?"

"Seven sounds fine," Bella told him softly. "Since you're going to be outside all day, would you like me to make us a reservation?"

Jeremy mumbled something about that being fine, shied away from Anna's round-eyed astonishment, and hustled for the door.

When he was gone, Anna turned moon eyes to Bella. "Girl, you don't mean to *tell* me."

Bella was still watching the door. "You know, I had a funny feeling about this day even before I got out of bed."

Jeremy let himself into an empty office, shut the door behind him, took a deep breath and willed away the jitters. Before he had time to wonder at what he had just done or was just about to do, he walked over to the desk, picked up the phone, and rang for information. He gave the woman the trio of cities and names from Julius. It was an off chance, but he knew of nothing else to do.

Two of the names did not show numbers, but the third, the one for Gregory P. Lannerton in Beverly Hills, was paydirt. Jeremy thanked the operator, set down the phone, bowed his head and prayed as hard as his racing heart would allow. He picked up the phone once more, dialed, and waited.

It was answered on the third ring. "Yeah?"

"Afternoon." Jeremy inspected the page before him, then asked, "Is Laney there?"

"Nah, he's not around." The young male voice spoke with a dullness that sucked his voice dry of all interest, all emotion, all energy. "Have you tried the office?"

"Not yet." Jeremy willed his voice to remain calm and politely interested. "Maybe I should."

"No, wait, I remember now. He's up where they're filming." The words were not really slurred. The young man simply had to search to find the energy to speak. "Who is this?"

"This is Jeremy. Jeremy Hughes. How're you doin' today?"

"Okay, I guess." There were gaps between the sentences, as though the ideas came only with effort. "Do I know you?"

"I don't think so, no." Jeremy searched for something more to say, prayed for guidance, decided to wait.

"You with the film crew? Laney said you guys were supposed to be here yesterday."

"No, I'm calling from Washington, D.C."

"Oh yeah, about the girls. Laney got your pictures. Didn't he talk to you already?"

"Not with me." Jeremy worked at holding the phone steady. "You talkin' about Arlene and Jessica?"

"I dunno the names. They're not supposed to be here for another, ah, I think it's two weeks, is that right?"

"If you say so." He took a breath, asked as casually as he could, "You want to give me that address again?"

"What, the place on Inglewood? You sure Laney didn't tell you all this?"

"Must've been to someone else." Jeremy wrote down the street name with a shaky hand.

"Yeah, I thought Laney said something about talking to a guy with a French-sounding name."

"That must've been Pierre," Jeremy said, and wiped sweat from his forehead. "Pierre Matisse."

"Yeah, Pierre, that's right. I remember now. Like I said, they start shooting in two weeks. Laney'll want the girls here the day before."

"You're sure they won't want the girls to show up any earlier?"

"Nah, not for Laney. He's using that house for this other shoot right now. I coulda sworn he told you all this."

"Maybe he did, but my memory's not what it used to be."

"Hey, tell me about it. Yeah, we're all tied up 'til then, so there's no need to get here earlier. Not for us, anyway."

Jeremy's belly was clenched so tight it hurt. "You be sure and get some rest now, you sound awful tired."

"Yeah, tired. Right." The dead voice was replaced by a long sniff and a sigh. "Where'd you say you're calling from?"

"Washington, D.C."

"Oh yeah, right, I remember now. About the two new girls. Laney said they were perfect. Hey, like how's the weather?"

"Not bad, a little chilly at night. How 'bout with you?"

"Oh, hey, it's righteous. Snows almost every day, man." The dead voice seemed to smile, but no laughter followed. "Yeah, snow in October. Great stuff. You ought to come over and check it out."

CHAPTER
4

"Today's reading comes from the ninety-sixth psalm, verses one through three," Senator Atterly said, and waited for the page rustling to still. He then read:

> "Sing to the Lord a new song; sing to the Lord, all the earth.
> Sing to the Lord, praise his name; proclaim his salvation
> day after day. Declare his glory among the nations, his mar-
> velous deeds among all the peoples."

Jeremy settled back in his seat, glanced around the crowded room. There was a scattering of vaguely familiar faces, people he recognized from the funeral mostly, a few from television and newspaper photographs. John Nakamishi sat up front with the senator, as blank-faced and intent as ever. Bella sat beside him, her presence a comforting touch here in the midst of all this earthly power. Over to the other side of the room sat Congressman John Silverwood. The man did not look at all well.

They were gathered in an austere basement cafeteria, and every seat was taken. Jeremy scanned the room, guessed the number at perhaps seventy or eighty people. A pretty fair turnout for such busy people. And they all seemed so eager. All, that is, save for Congressman Silverwood.

His face was lined, his skin gray, his shoulders stooped. He looked twenty years older than the last time Jeremy had seen him. When was that? He thought back, realized it was just a year before, back during the elections.

When the congressman had spotted Jeremy entering the room he had flinched and turned away. Jeremy inspected the man frankly, wondered if perhaps he blamed himself for TJ and Catherine's death. After all, he was the one who had brought them up to Washington in the first place. No, he decided, there was something else that was troubling the man. Something very big, very heavy. Jeremy felt a twinge of regret at not having contacted the man since the funeral, and decided he would try and speak with him as soon as the prayer meeting was over. Jeremy turned his attention back to the front of the room.

"The psalmist is exhorting the people," the senator continued. His voice was crisp, succinct, as direct as his gaze. "He is telling them to do something they *already know* they should be doing. When I was preparing for this meeting, those words snagged me like a hook on a drag-line. I tried to read on, but I couldn't. So I did what I normally do in such circumstances, which was break the passage down and look for the deeper meaning. It's the way I search for that hidden message, and I'd like to share with you what I found."

Senator Atterly was ramrod straight and tough as they came. His steel-gray eyes pierced whatever they touched. He was not a nervous man, yet there was an air of total impatience with the world's slowness. He gave the impression of having to forcibly restrain himself, slow himself down to the speed of the mortals surrounding him.

"Declare his glory, it reads here. What that says to me is the following: God's people have the responsibility to tell of His marvelous deeds all the time, *all over the world*.

"Now that troubled me. I sat there a while, and saw myself as getting comfortable here. The position and the authority was a little cocoon of work and responsibility. I saw myself as *defined* by these earthly things. I had a place. I was safe from the worry of looking at myself any more deeply because I was always so *busy*. I was safe from facing pain and emptiness and worry and doubt because I remained with the safe and the sure."

Jeremy listened to the words, saw the honesty with which this powerful man inspected himself, and knew the words were meant for him as well. Ever since making that call to Lannerton the day before, he had felt a call in his heart to go to California. He did not want any more strange places and stranger people and new challenges and pushes from the outside to face the aching vulnerability the unknown was bound to cause. It hurt too much. There were too many regrets, too many lost causes, too many absent friends.

"The word for declare in Hebrew is *Safar*," Atterly went on. "It means to *recount* something. To give an example. Now that said to me that I was to tell of the Lord's power through showing what had happened in my own life. But so long as I hold myself back, let my life be defined by what I'm comfortable with, how is the Lord to work His greatest miracles?

"That passage also says to proclaim His salvation. Now the Hebrew word for proclaim is *Basar*, which means to tell good tidings. In olden times it described a person who brought good tidings from the battlefield. Can anyone tell me what this expression was changed to in the New Testament?"

A voice from the crowd replied quietly, "Evangelize."

"That's it. Now in old Greece, an evangelist was a man who brought good news from the battlefield to the king. He carried a laurel on his spear, and wore a wreath on his head, and he was waving a palm frond. The good news was known far and wide even before his opened his mouth.

"I'm not saying that I need to drop everything that I'm doing and go running off to the ends fo the earth," Atterly added. "I don't mean that for myself and I don't mean it for anybody else. What that passage said to me was, don't let the world hold me back. Don't let the world define who I am, or how the Lord is allowed to show himself in my life. When He calls, I must follow. Even if it is into dangerous waters, even if the whole world is going to make fun of me for running up and down the halls of the Senate waving my own palm frond up over my head. I've got to break through those earthly barriers and let Him use me to the fullfest.

"I will close with one example of what that means, something which applies to a new call I feel the Lord placing upon my heart. According to the book of Acts, Barnabas' and Paul's first commission from the Holy Spirit was to leave the church of Antioch and sail for Cyprus. In chapter thirteen we read that when they arrived at the port city of Salamis they preached the Word, and then proceeded across the island to Paphos."

Senator Atterly set one hand upon the podium, moved to the side so that his body was exposed to the crowd. "Now many of you know that I am a student of ancient history. Let me take one moment and tell you a little about this Paphos where Paul and Barnabas arrived. It was the capital of Roman government for the island, which was a senatorial province ruled by a proconsul and an important power center. Besides that, it was the worship center for the cult of Venus.

"Now despite all these pretty pictures you see of what Venus was supposed to look like, let me tell you, this was *not* how the lady got started. Before the Greeks remade her public image, she was known as Aphrodite, and do you know what the people of this island worshiped? Well, I'll tell you. It was a faceless black stone. Not only that, at the time that Paul and Barnabas arrived, *every woman on the island* was expected to submit herself at least once to the rite of temple prostitution. She was forced by her society to reveal herself upon the temple steps and submit to the lusts of whichever sailor or soldier or man of the street happened by. The money was given to the temple, in worship to this faceless black stone."

Senator Atterly waited for the room quieten, then concluded, "The Lord does not call us to go where it is comfortable, nor to preach where it is safe, nor to minister when it suits us. Not if we are intended to glorify Him by service. We are to wave the palm frond in the face of those who will despise us for our beliefs, and why? Because there is always the chance that we shall save a few of the lost ones. How else are they to hear His call if we do not act as His earthly messengers?"

After the concluding prayer Jeremy started toward Congressman Silverwood, only to see him taken aside by Senator Atterly. The two men exchanged a few brief words, then left the room together. Jeremy watched them go and turned back to where Bella was waiting.

"I won't take but a minute of your time," Senator Atterly said, leading Congressman John Silverwood across the hall and into the alcove of an unopened door. With their faces close together and their expressions serious, the barrier they presented to all who might otherwise want to stop and chat was complete.

"Two things, John. The first is that you are not looking good." Atterly's frosty eyes took on a look of deep concern. "I don't know what kind of burden you're suffering under, but I just wanted you to know that I'm here if you ever need a friend."

Silverwood felt the familiar tug at his heart, the answering ache of burdens that threatened to pull him from sanity. He did not trust himself to speak; the shame and the guilt and the humiliation trapped him. It left him with a sense of apathy that only anger pushed away.

He plodded through the hours, lived through an endless series of gray days, found punctuation to his bland existence only in the mindless bursts of fury that had come to be his trademark. His staff had a greater rate of turnover than any other on Capitol Hill, and all who left both swore by Silverwood's intelligence and swore at his uncontrolled outbursts. The man's anger blistered paint at ten paces and left him quaking in his suit, locked inside his inner office, knowing that he was headed for self-destruction unless something changed. But nothing could change, not without exposing a shame that grew bigger by the day. So he sat and he shook and he waited for the axe to fall.

Silverwood ignored the tremor in his gut and the hunger in his heart, clenched his teeth, lowered his eyes, and made do with a single nod.

Senator Atterly turned brisk. "Right. The other item is this Per Se obscenity legislation. I wouldn't approach you here on a political issue, except that you've been attending our little sessions for over half a year now, and I was hoping that this meant I might impose on you."

They were back on familiar territory now. The man was being nice because he wanted something. Silverwood raised his eyes and let a touch of the anger show through.

Atterly recognized the look, forced himself not to back off. "We just don't have enough support in the House, John. It looks like with my help it will pass through the Senate, but unless we move fast the House bill is going to be lost in some paper-making factory called a committee. Tabled and buried. This is too important to let it go without a fight. We need some vocal support inside the House and we need it now. It's the only chance we have of putting a tight lid on this pornography filth during this administration."

"I get it," Congressman Silverwood replied. He had been waiting for this, waiting to hear that these people with their faith and their pious looks were really just the same as everybody else. He looked at the senator with a cynical gaze. "You're after my vote, right? That's what you want. There's no difference here. None at all."

Senator Atterly's eyes turned the color of old ice. He leaned up close and replied with a blast of his own, a clipped voice and reined-in fury that did not need volume to push it home. "That's where you're wrong, John. I'm after your vote because that's the *only* thing you've got to give. You've been sitting through these meetings for almost six months now, dancing on the edge. Never stepping over the line, never committing yourself, never opening the door.

"You certainly won't give the Lord your heart, will you? Of course not. That means taking a *risk*. It means opening up, doesn't it? You can't sit back there behind your walls and watch the world with hate-filled eyes and give of your heart, now, can you? So, yes. I ask for your vote. I ask for what I can get. But the *real* question, John, is whether you're able to hear what *He* is asking of you."

Senator Atterly gave him a cold nod, turned, and strode vigorously down the hall.

♦   ♦   ♦

Duncan Wyeth played at an ease he did not feel, tried to ignore both the assistant principal watching from the door and the clamor rising from the midday high-school cafeteria. He passed the two pictures around the table, watched the trio of teenage girls with their attitudes of practiced boredom exchange little snickers and glances.

The prettiest of the girls handed back Jessica's picture, said, "She was never more than about halfway there, you know what I mean?"

"Not exactly."

"She never *said* anything. She'd kinda stand over to one side like a shadow and not say a *word*. Nothing. You speak to her and she'd get this scared look on her face, it was really weird, like she hadn't even thought you could see her."

"She'd talk to Arlene, though," the other girl said, not looking up from inspecting her nails.

"Yeah, Arlene. Talk about somebody needing help."

"Arlene wasn't a good influence, I take it."

That brought a laugh from the third girl who continually twirled a strand of hair around one finger. "The only time Arlene ever influenced anybody good was when she left town."

"It doesn't look like she was a good influence on Jessica," Duncan agreed.

"Yeah, well, nobody forced her to hang around with Arlene."

"Talking to some of the other kids, I got the impression that Arlene was a sort of leader around here."

The young face turned dark. "Arlene had the guys hanging around her *all* the time. I mean, it was ridiculous the way they'd stand around her with their tongues hanging out."

"No need to wonder why, right?"

Thin shoulders bounced a single time. "Right."

"Jessica seemed to look up to her, though, didn't she?"

"Yeah, I guess so. Poor Jessica. She looked so *sad* all the time. And quiet. You got the feeling sometimes, if you said hello to her she'd jump out of her skin. She got a reputation with the guys, you know, she was really good looking, but talking with her was like talking to a wall. Nothing came back."

"And nobody could get through to her but Arlene."

"Yeah, crazy, isn't it? I mean, the wildest girl in the whole school and the quietest. Who'd have figured it?"

Duncan straightened his stiff back. "Maybe Arlene was the only one who bothered to try to talk with her."

That made the prettiest one angry. "*I* tried. Lots of times. You don't spend a lotta time around somebody who wants to imitate a stone, though."

"Maybe not."

"You didn't know her. Jessica was the quietest person you ever met. Unless a guy had the hots for her, she was just another colorless, odorless gas drifting along the hallways."

Duncan leaned back on the wobbly plastic chair. "So she got around a lot?"

"I dunno. You hear a lot of things, but that doesn't make it true. She was supposed to be easy, but she only went out with older guys, never with somebody from school, so maybe the guys talked about her like that just because they were jealous."

"What did they say?"

Another eloquent shrug. "The usual thing, I guess. How she never talked but she'd do anything you wanted on the first date, that kind of thing."

"She never got asked out a second time," the twirler said to her hair. "Nobody wanted to put up with a vacuum twice in a row. It was either do it the first time or miss out, I guess."

Duncan pretended to make notes. "Did she have a nickname that she went by, something besides her own name?"

The two girls exchanged glances, said in one voice, "Airbag," and broke up laughing.

He wanted to smack them. Hard. "You called her Airbag? Why?"

"Not anymore. This was back before."

"Before what?"

"You know." The twister was exasperated now. "Before she lost weight."

"Jessica used to be overweight?"

Another laugh. "Not just overweight. Fat."

"*Real* fat."

"A regular Vienna sausage."

"Night of the living bubble."

"The Bethesda blimp."

"Miss Biggy goes to class."

He pulled out the picture, looked at it again, trying to imagine this pretty young girl as fat. "That's incredible."

"Yeah, you'd never know it, would you? I mean, she went from the Hot Fudge Sundae Queen to Sleeping Beauty in one easy step. If only she had a personality to match."

♦　♦　♦

He wore scuffed leather hi-tops, a cracked and faded leather jacket, and dirty jeans. His hair was thinning and cut in jagged blond spikes. His face was too lined for the clothes and the hair. His age was a used-up forty, but Jessica didn't know that. All she knew was that he had the creepiest dead eyes and the most dried-up sallow skin she'd ever seen.

Arlene talked brightly and made little jokes, but all Jessica had to do was look at her to know she was nervous too. They were secluded behind a ratty-looking curtain, taking off their street clothes and putting on swimsuits the blond photographer had given them. All the while, Pierre and Chico and the photographer made calm conversation in the studio, as though it was something totally normal, getting undressed so that they could have their pictures taken for some magazine whose name they didn't even know.

In appearance, Jessica was a totally different person than she had been three years ago. So different, in fact, that she wasn't really able to see the person looking back in the mirror. Instead, what she saw was a vastly overweight girl, seven inches shorter and eighty pounds heavier. A real blimp in short socks, was how Arlene once described an old picture.

Jessica had always been overweight. Always. Her baby pictures looked like a white balloon with a toothless smile and eyes folded inside layers of fat with soft curly brown hair on top. Her baby clothes were frilly outfits meant for a child twice her age. Her arms were fat, her legs two puffballs that tottered when other babies ran. Fat and chunky and not the least bit attractive. Her earliest image was of sitting on a doctor's examining table while her mother, rail thin and made up in perfect detail, wrung her hands and went on in horrified detail about how her baby could just *look* at food and put on a couple of pounds.

Some of the doctors would laugh, pick her up, play with her and make her smile. It was incredible how well she could remember them. Especially the looks in their eyes and the feel of their hands—strong hands that did not seem to mind holding her or hugging her or letting her grasp their fingers. She could not have been more then three at the time, but the image of those doctors was as clear as memories from yesterday. Maybe even more so.

Don't worry, was the standard reply. Don't worry, she'll outgrow it. The litany never changed, but the date at which the transformation would take place kept being moved further back. At four years of age, it was, don't worry, it's just a late case of baby fat. Give her a couple of years and she'll outgrow it. At seven it was, when she starts to grow taller over the next year or so you'll see that weight just melt off her. At nine it was, it's only a couple of years until puberty, and then you'll see. Don't worry. There's no need to concern yourself. What is all the worry for? She's a fine little girl who's just a few pounds overweight.

Only she didn't feel like a fine little girl. She felt like an ugly little worm trapped inside a big ugly body. She wished time and again that there was some way she could shrivel up into something really small, a mouse or a mole or a tiny bug, then crawl inside a crack in the floor and hide from everything and everybody.

But Jessica couldn't hide. She kept growing up, and growing bigger. Her size alone shouted at the world that here was someone to pick on and make fun of.

Around the age of nine or ten—she couldn't remember exactly—she stopped speaking unless she absolutely had to. Before this, she had been shy and quiet, but she had been lonely, too. She had wanted to have friends and be a part of things and smile and laugh and have fun. But the only people who would talk with her or be around her were other unhappy people, or ones her parents paid to stay there in the house with her. One day she heard two of her teachers talking about how the name fit her so well, snickering at it when they thought she was gone. One of the teachers had been such a favorite of hers too, a lady who had sought to draw her out and praise her work. Then she had said those awful words to the other teacher, isn't it sad how the Biggs child is so, well, so awfully big? And they laughed and shook their heads, and Jessica stood just outside the door and felt the little worm inside her shrivel up into a ball and melt away.

At age eleven she watched all the other girls begin to transform into women. Nothing happened to her except that she put on another ten pounds. In the space of one school year she went from being the tallest to being the fattest. The other girls were growing up. One by one each was touched by some invisible magic wand and their bodies began to develop. Overnight, it seemed to her, they grew taller and curvier and sleeker and more beautiful. Jessica Biggs simply remained fat.

Her twelfth birthday came and went. A couple of the unhappy guys asked her to school parties, but she wouldn't go. It was too embarrassing. She didn't want to be seen in public. She didn't want to be singled out for ridicule, not while all the other girls were growing up and becoming women and having such a good time.

Then the month before her thirteenth birthday, something happened. A lot of things happened, so much so fast that she wasn't ready. She didn't know what it meant to go through menstruation, and she felt embarrassed and scared and in pain and confused and had no one to turn to, especially not her mother, who had simply decided to ignore her. Gladys Biggs simply could not fathom how Jessica could remain such a horrible little butterball and embarrass her so every time they went out somewhere. No, her mother was the last person Jessica could talk to about this. But there simply wasn't anybody else.

Then by chance she heard a couple of girls discuss it one day after gym class, the things they felt and what they did, and they went into such graphic detail with such calmness that Jessica was able to accept for the first time that everything really was okay, that her body was not breaking down because she was so fat, and that everybody went through it, and that it meant she was growing up.

And then the fat began to disappear.

It wasn't a conscious act. Not at all. Maybe she had a little loss in appetite, but she wasn't really sure. All she knew was that she grew three inches in three months—up, not out—and her mother took her to buy new dresses.

Shopping together was something that they both dreaded, because nothing in the normal stores was big enough to fit Jessica. For svelte and chic Gladys Biggs, in her jewels and fine Paris fashions, to have to take her daughter into Lane Bryant, the shop for "plus sizes," was simply the most loathsome thing she had ever been forced to do in her entire life. She was not someone to suffer in silence, and she would tell Jessica exactly what she thought of having to shop in such a store.

All the shop people in their exactly proper clothes with their oh-so proper expressions would put up with her mother and say nothing except with their eyes. Those eyes followed Jessica in and out of the dressing rooms and made her feel like a worm on some lab table for all of them to poke at. It was just horrible.

But that day when she went in they said the dress her mother had chosen would have to be taken in. It surprised her mother so much that she forgot to do her little tirade on the way home.

Two months and two inches later, they had to go back *again*. This time, Jessica had to choose from the smallest sizes in the store. And for the first time in what seemed like years, her mother actually *smiled* at her.

And that was only the beginning.

Six weeks later Jessica had dropped a grand total of thirty-three pounds, not by anything she had done. Her mother was suddenly rushing about, planning a new wardrobe with the same hand-wringing concern she used to show on their trips to the doctors. One afternoon it was down to the department store for six pairs of shoes, the next to the hairdresser, the next for French makeup, the next to a boutique for the *latest* fashion.

In the space of nine months, although it seemed like only a couple of days, Jessica was standing in her room, in front of a newly installed full-length mirror, looking at a person she did not know and could not recognize.

And then boys started to ask her out.

She wasn't ready for the attention, didn't know how to handle it, couldn't think of any way to respond when they showed in the most graphic ways possible that they not only found her attractive but that they *wanted* her. She may not be much to talk to, one guy told his friend on one of the many double dates, but man, her body just doesn't stop.

Double dates were the best. There were other people in the cars and at the movies and wherever they wound up afterward, and the others could talk among themselves. On double dates there weren't any awkward pauses, because the others simply talked *around* her. Jessica could sit there and pretend to be staring blind-sided out of the front window, when in truth she was soaking it in. What they said, how the other girl responded, what they talked about, how they all dressed and acted and laughed and seemed so comfortable with themselves. And all the while, the little worm inside just kept feeling scared and shriveled up and too unsure of anything to even open her mouth.

Sex was easy. At least, it was easy once she made it through the first couple of times, which were horrible. She was so *scared* at first. She didn't understand anything except that the guy was good-looking and forceful and so sure of himself. Then things got too fast and there was nothing to rely on and no one to turn to, and she just let it happen and tried not to cry.

Jessica met Arlene on a double date, with another of a long line of guys whose names she couldn't remember. Arlene wasn't put off for one minute by Jessica's silence. Once they came to know each other better, Arlene called it the disappearing act, and rode her mercilessly when she tried to run and hide inside herself. That first night, though, Arlene played around it, as though being silent was the most normal thing in the world.

"She doesn't really like us," Arlene told her date in a matter-of-fact tone. "The only reason she's here, see, is because her date with the prince fell through."

Her date didn't have a clue, which was typical for most guys when they were around Arlene. She knew so much more than they did, was so much more sure of herself. Jessica didn't know any of that on their first date, of course. All she knew was here was somebody who always seemed to be in *control*.

Her date said something lame, like, "Yeah, is that right?" Arlene awarded him one of her class-A meat-grinders, as Arlene called those sideways looks of hers that shrank the guy down to bottle-cap size.

"Yeah, that's right," she replied. "It so happens that there's a prince in town, and he met Jessica at the ballet last night, isn't that right, girl?"

For the first time in Jessica's life the words were there waiting for her, the words and the courage to open her inner door that first little crack, with a stranger she'd never set eyes on before. For the first time she *wanted* to play the silly game against these silly boys.

"A Rumanian prince," Jessica replied, in her soft voice, with her eyes never leaving the front windshield.

"You see!" Arlene was triumphant. "This girl's got *class*. Something you jerks don't know anything about. That's why we hang together, Princess Jessica and me. Class. Right, girl?"

"Hey," her date said, finally getting up the nerve to be heard again, "I thought you told me you just showed up in town."

"So? Jessica and me go back a long way. Looooong way. Where was it we met, honey? I forget. London or Paris?"

"The Ritz," Jessica replied, remembering a favorite story. "Paris."

"Yeah, that's right. At the Grand Duke's high tea. Hey, was that guy boring or what?"

Because she knew what was expected, and because there was such a powerful excitement around Arlene all the time, Jessica fed on Arlene's energy and gave her back what Jessica would never in a million years have thought of with anybody else. She said, "Yeah, but he had class."

The two girls broke up laughing, laughing so hard they were down over their knees, Jessica laughing because there was a beautiful girl who wanted to play games with her, Arlene laughing because she was Arlene. And the guys were totally clueless, which made it even better.

Then before the guys could get too angry about being left entirely out in the cold, Arlene bounced back with the story about how she got hired and fired in less than fifteen minutes, a new world record.

"My dad knows this guy, only it's not my real dad, see. My real dad died when I was seven. This is my stepdad. Except he hates for me to call him that, so I only do it when I want to get him mad, right? Anyway, so he knows this guy who's got the health-food and vitamin store in the Northside Mall, and this guy's all up on how laid back he is and how in tune his store is, and he lays all this stuff on me and doesn't hear a word I'm saying, you know the kind? I mean, I could have told him I was heavy into chemicals and week-old dog food and the guy wouldn't have heard a thing. Kinda like you two guys. Full of yourselves, you know."

And the two guys started taunting back, and the atmosphere that had been tense when they went into their major laughing fit was all okay again. She had turned them around, taken the weight off the moment and gotten them feeling as if she were playing for their entertainment. Only she wasn't. Jessica didn't know why she knew, but she knew. Arlene was talking to *her*. This was a story just for *them*, and the two guys were just that—two more faceless guys.

"So he gets me into this little white outfit, you know the kind, one size fits all, and I start unstuffing boxes onto the shelves, real intellectual stuff, let me tell you. Anyway, there I am in my little Miss Nursey outfit and this total nerd comes up to me and asks for some vitamins.

"I look around and there's nobody else free, so I don't panic or anything, I just pretend like, hey, I'm a real expert on all this junk, and I ask him what kind. So he goes into this spiel about this and that, names you never heard of before, and I stand there nodding my head and looking real serious, you know, trying not to break up and tell this guy he's hopeless.

"So he rattles off about thirty-five names, and I spot this bottle up high on the shelf with this name, Ultra-Mega-Vit. Can you imagine? The bottle was so big, it'd take a crane to lift it off the shelf, and it's that half-clear plastic so you can see the pills are about three inches long and weigh maybe half a pound apiece. So I point up there like I know what I'm doing, and say, mister, you've come to the right place 'cause that Ultra-Mega-Vit is just what you need.

"Well, I could tell the guy didn't really want to buy anything. He was just out to impress me with what he knew. And just then this old lady comes by, you know the kind, always got to be in everybody else's business. And she says, oh, yes, those Ultra-Mega-Vit are just wonderful. I've been taking them for two years now and I feel like that. Sooooo much bettah.

"Well the guy catches sight of the price tag, which is something like nine-ninety-nine, ninety-five, and he starts looking a little green around the gills.

"So he turns back to me and says, hey, just because somebody else likes them doesn't mean they're right for me. So I figure I've played around with Supernerd long enough, and I tell him, you know, you're absolutely right. There's no telling what would happen if you swallowed one of those things. And the guy is puffing himself up, like, yeah, I was right all along, this place doesn't have anything good enough for me. So I say, I tell you what, we'll give you a free sample of four, and you stick one up each nostril and one in each ear, and walk around with them until they dissolve. Then if nothing bad happens, you can come back and try one down your throat. How does that sound? And the guy just huffs and puffs his way to the manager and tells him how rude I've been and everything, and two minutes later I'm out of there. Can you imagine? I mean, the guy wasn't going to buy anything in there anyway, why put up with his mess?"

Afterward Arlene insisted that they let her off with Jessica. They hung around outside the house until they both were yawning and shivering from the rising mist, too eager and excited over what was happening to let go easily.

When Arlene asked her to meet at a popular cafe after school the next day, Jessica confessed that she had never been there before, then spent a panic-stricken moment thinking her vulnerability would be trampled on as always.

Instead, Arlene wrapped an arm around her neck, said, "Hey, no problem, we're just the two new girls in town, right? Me because I just got here, and you because you never showed them your stuff before." The arm tightened, the voice lowered and breathed a husky, "Stick with me, kid. We're not even gonna slow down to take names."

Pierre pushed the curtain aside and snapped Jessica's mind back to the studio. He swept his gaze over her with that look in his eyes. "You two gonna hide in here all day?"

He led them into the studio, a high-ceilinged loft with dirty skylights looking out onto a leaded sky. The spiky-haired photographer approached, ran a professional eye over them both, flickered a glance at Pierre.

"What did I tell you?" Pierre said.

"Let's get them under the lights," the photographer said,

not talking to them directly, not looking in their eyes.

Together Jessica and Arlene stepped onto the broadraised platform, its hardwood planking covered with a thin strip of gray-white canvas. Behind the stand hung a white fabric falling in careless folds. A series of lights on metal stands swept around the two sides like a pair of inhuman grasping arms. Two cameras on tripods were set up immediately before the dais.

"You want them together or separate?" Pierre asked.

"Start them together, let them get used to it." With a hand on their arms he brought them close together, facing each other, motioned for them to stay still.

Jessica caught sight of Chico sidling up around the back wall until he was directly behind Arlene and could look at Jessica without being noticed by anyone else. He waited until he was sure she was watching him, then smiled. Jessica felt fear race through her like an icy knife, and dropped her gaze.

The photographer took several measurements with his light-meter, fiddled with a couple of the lights, measured again. He moved back behind his cameras, adjusted one, raised up and spoke directly to them for the first time.

"Girls, I want you to give me your number-one smile, and turn slowly toward me. That's it, real slow, yeah. Try to sway your bodies a little more. Good." The lights flashed brilliantly in time to the shutter's clicking. The automatic winder whirred continually.

"All right now, girls. Raise up your arms, play with your hair, that's it. Smile for me. Great. Arch your back a little more, that's great. Yeah.

"Okay. Slow and easy, now. Show me what you've got."

CHAPTER
5

As he drove to the Community of Hope Tuesday morning, Jeremy turned the radio on low, like a soft-spoken friend who murmured to him gently. The station was one of several that played country music, which was about as close to bluegrass as these citified people ever came. He wasn't paying the music any mind. He was too busy worrying over this strange new direction in his life.

Jeremy was not a traveling man. He preferred to stay in one place and sink down roots for life. The trip to Washington was the farthest he had ever been from the land he called home, and now that the move was made and his work laid out, he was more than reluctant to move again; he was resentful. The thought of picking up and hauling off across America to search for two runaways left him feeling old and stubborn and set in his ways. He was going, though. The need had been set too clearly in his path for him to refuse. But it didn't mean he had to like it.

The song's first strains came on as he pulled up to the light. The sound was so familiar yet so strange in these surroundings that Jeremy thought for a moment his mind was playing tricks on him. He reached over and turned up the volume, and felt a chill that left him deaf to the honking behind him as the light turned green. Then he realized that it wasn't his dead wife's voice after all. It didn't really even sound that much like Ella, save for the fact that the woman was singing from the heart.

Just as Ella always did, especially with this song.

Jeremy pulled through the intersection, stopped in the bus zone, turned the radio up louder still, and let the memories wash over him.

> Take me back to the place where I first saw the light.
> To the sweet sunny South, take me home,
> Where the mockingbirds sing me to sleep in the night,
> Oh why was I tempted to roam?

It had been one of Ella's favorites, and one of the saddest Jeremy had ever heard her sing. She had told him once that it was probably written in the years after the Civil War, but in spirit it was written for every southern boy who ever traveled away from home.

She would sing to him in the sweet languid hour that followed the setting sun. She would sit him down in the old porch rocker, pulled up close to the eaves so he could be surrounded by the smell of the honeysuckle vines that grew up the arbor, and she would sing to him. She would close her eyes and caress the strings of that old guitar her daddy had given her years before, and as she sang, he would know a happiness that filled him to the point of physical pain.

> I think with regret of the dear home I've left,
> Of the warm hearts that sheltered me there,
> Of my darling, my dear ones, of whom I'm bereft,
> And I long for the old place again.
> But yet I'll return to the place of my birth,
> Where my children have played 'round my door,
> Where they gathered white blossoms
> Which garnished the earth,
> Which will echo their footsteps no more.

Memories he had thought buried and gone forever came back on a song. He was not just remembering. He was *transported*. The love he had known with Ella surrounded him, took him beyond the confines of this measly earth and brought him back to the peace he had known in her arms. Jeremy searched his heart, thought at first that he was being called back home. But the feeling was not that. No. The love and the memories and the comfort of his Ella were *here,* in this strange city, at a time when he was being called to venture to the ends of the earth.

He saw it clearly then, as clear as only the honesty of divine love could show. There was no going back. There was no home to return to, not on this earth. That was why she sent him this song, she and her Lord. He could not explain how he knew, but no explanation was necessary in the light of this solid sureness. The only place where his home still existed was in his mind, in his memories of their love and life together.

When the song ended Jeremy turned off the radio, yet the feeling remained; her love and her Lord's protection were with him still. Jeremy leaned back against the headrest, closed his eyes to the scurrying crowds and blank faces, and strained to bring another faintly heard song into his mind and ears and heart. Especially his heart.

What wondrous love is this,
O my soul, O my soul,
What wondrous love is this,
O my soul?
What wondrous love is this,
That calls the Lord of bliss
To bring this perfect peace
To my soul, to my soul,
To bring this perfect peace
To my soul?

It was a song she had kept for those special moments before bedtime, and it filled his swollen heart to remember it. He felt the nighttime breeze gently caress his face again, saw the shadow of where she was sitting there close enough to touch him with her leg, watched the last light of a dying day dim across the star-flecked sky and call them to their bed. Jeremy shifted in his seat and took a ragged sigh and ached for her with all his being.

The music was called Christian Harmony, and was a part of the Shape-Note tradition up New England way. It was designed by Singin' Billy Walker, and although the man had died two centuries before Ella was born, she had always spoken of him as a close personal friend. Each note in the scale had been given a shape, because the rural people for whom he wrote and sang could seldom read or write. So the songs were simple, the words often repeated, and all of them spoke of a joy in knowing their Savior.

Ye winged seraphs fly,
Bear the news, bear the news,
Ye winged seraphs fly,
Bear the news.
Ye winged seraphs fly,
Like comets through the sky,
Fill vast eternity
With the news, with the news,
Fill vast eternity
With the news.

She was here with him, Jeremy knew it. She was here and he was to go to California in search of these little lost girls. His Savior had called and filled him with a love that Jeremy could no more question than he could doubt his own name. He was called, and he would answer the only way he knew how—with an open-hearted yes to his Master's wishes.

And when from death I'm free,
I'll sing on, I'll sing on.
And when from death I'm free
I'll sing on.
And when from death I'm free,
I'll sing in joyful being
And through eternity
I'll sing on.

Reluctantly Jeremy released the sound and the feeling and the presence of his beloved, released it and watched with closed eyes as the sound and the power rose higher and higher, beyond the ability of his mind and heart to follow, beyond all earthly confines, back to the place where they belonged, back to that which knew no bounds.

◆　　◆　　◆

"There's certainly reason for us to concern ourselves, Mr. Wyeth, if in fact a law has been broken." The FBI agent did not even need to inspect his books. "Eighteen-U.S. Code 2423, the White Slave Trafficking Act. It was amended in the eighties to include a section on the transport of minors for illicit purposes. The question is whether there has actually been any wrong-doing."

Duncan kept his face immobile, or so he thought, trying to match the agent's serious, routine manner. "You mean we've got to prove that this guy has actually done what we think he's done."

"The pretext is enough," Agent Williams replied. "But there has to be some concrete evidence that a federal statute has been broken."

He was in the office of Special Agent Donald Williams, Detective Larson's friend on the Washington FBI staff. They sat in a cramped windowless office, two walls covered with plaques and diplomas written in curlicue scrawl. Every hair on the agent's head was in place; his jacket was buttoned, his tie absolutely straight, his fingers motionless on the desk in front of him. Duncan thought the whole thing was made much more chilling, to sit in this sterile office and discuss it in such detached tones.

"The transport of a minor across state lines for sexual purposes is unlawful," Agent Williams went on in his bland voice. "The problem is usually to prove that sex actually took place."

"What about pictures? From what Detective Larson told us, this guy tends to work the photo trade."

"Absolutely." Agent Williams showed increased interest. "Sexually explicit pictures of a minor taken for the purposes of selling are illegal, as is distributing such pictures across state lines. Statute 2251. Both are federal offenses and would require us to become involved."

"Well, thank you for your time." Duncan stood. "I'll be back in touch with you as soon as we have more to go on."

Agent Williams shook his hand. "Watch out for yourself. Any borderline-legal business as big as this one is bound to have mob interests at stake. Those boys play a very mean game of hard ball."

◆　◆　◆

Jeremy had just walked into the Community of Hope's front office when a wide-eyed receptionist waved him over, gave him the phone, said it was the senator's office. Jeremy didn't need to ask which one.

He was put immediately through to Senator Atterly. "Just wanted to say how sorry I was not to be able to chat with you after the prayer meeting yesterday."

"Man as busy as you's got a lot more important things to do than pass the time of day with me, Senator."

"More pressing things, perhaps. Certainly not more important. How are you, Mr. Hughes?"

"Doin' just fine, sir. Hope you're the same."

The senator's voice was crisp, sharp, no-nonsense. Jeremy felt an urge to stand at attention. "Busy trying to remember the Lord's calling in the midst of too many conflicting demands on my time and energy. I'm constantly amazed at how He can reach me through all this confusion."

"Just goes to show, Senator. All you gotta do is hum the tune and God will figure out the rest."

"You sound like the kind of man it would do me good to spend more time with." Atterly paused, went on, "I've been disappointed not to have seen you around before, but I thought you had probably been hit very hard by the loss of your friends."

"I was so low I couldn't find a hope with both hands," Jeremy agreed.

"Well, I can certainly understand that. TJ Case was an exceptional man. I miss him, I don't mind telling you that. I'm facing a few problems right now, and I could certainly use his help. Nak is here on my staff now, I suppose you knew that. He's been a big help."

"Yessir, Nak is a fine young man. Is there anything I can do for you?"

"There might be, as a matter of fact. We have a bill we're trying to place before the Senate and House simultaneously. It's been fashioned to put a choke-hold on pornography once and for all. Hit those filth peddlers just as hard as we can. I have to tell you, Mr. Hughes, there's not much chance of it passing."

"Call me Jeremy, please, Senator. How can I help?"

"Right. Nak thinks we should set up a prayer circle. I don't have much experience with this and don't quite know how to go about it. A few people from our prayer group have agreed to help, and I'll be talking with my pastor tonight. Nak says he knows some other people we should contact. We'd like to have it continue to the day the bill goes up for the vote. That should be in about three weeks. At least, that's what we're shooting for. It's just incredible how lethargic my colleagues are about this menace. I'm trying to drum up some more support, find a few people who can help keep it alive."

"Yessir, I understand." Jeremy thought of the girls, wondering if he should mention them. "There's one man, sir, a Rev-

erend Wilkins. He's the preacher at the church I attend. He was
a friend of TJ's, a real fine man. He's black; I don't suppose
that's a problem."

"Far from it." Enthusiasm made the senator's voice crackle
over the line. "You think he'd be interested in helping out?"

"I can't say for certain without talkin' to him, but I do believe he'd jump at it."

"That's good news, Jeremy. Why don't you speak with him,
have him give Nak a call if he's interested."

"Yessir. You met him too; he spoke at TJ's funeral."

"Of course, I remember him clearly. Tell him I certainly
hope he'll consider giving us his support. And what about you?"

"I'd sure like to, sir, but it looks like I might be makin' a
trip out to California. I've sorta gotten involved in lookin' for a
couple of teenage girls that've run away from home."

"I'm sorry to hear that." Atterly's voice was subdued. "Real
sorry. And you think they might be as far away as California?"

"Looks that way, Senator. Seems they've gotten hooked up
with some folks involved in that same thing you aim on figh-
tin'."

The senator sighed long and hard. "When are people going
to wake up, Jeremy?"

"I surely wish I knew." Jeremy waved as Duncan appeared
in the doorway. "TJ would be awful proud of you, Senator."

"Yes, Nak said the exact same thing. It helps hearing that,
I don't mind telling you. I feel like I'm battling an enemy I can't
even see on this one."

Duncan allowed himself to be ushered into Jeremy's truck
and waited until they were underway before asking, "Where
are you taking me?"

"Thought it was time to show you my boardinghouse, let
the old ladies make a fuss over you." Jeremy handled the truck
like one used to driving heavy equipment, with total concentration and unswerving attention to the road. "Old Mrs. Broyhill runs this place, and I mean to tell you that's exactly what
she does. Eighty-three years old, and the only time she stops is
to pray. Even does that standin' up. She's got four tenants, one
of 'em is blind, one deaf, and the others can't get around too
good anymore. All of 'em over eighty."

"And you," Duncan added.

"Met the old lady back last May when I came out to pick up

a load for the Community. Helped her move some furniture so she could do some spring cleanin', and ended up stayin' for one of the best dinners I'd had in years. Think maybe that was why she let me stay, seein' how I liked to eat."

Duncan settled back for the ride, said, "I've had an interesting couple of days."

"I'm glad to hear that. Feel like tellin' me about it?"

"Not yet. I've got a lot of little bits and pieces floating around in my head. Need a while longer to sort it all out."

"Fair enough. My Monday was pretty normal, just putterin' around the Community and gettin' in the way. My Sunday made up for it, though. Yessir. There's a lotta words I could think of to describe my Sunday, and interestin' is sure one of them."

"Let's hear it, then."

So Jeremy told him about his church and Aunt Ida and Julius and the three names and the telephone call, leaving out nothing.

"I can't believe you just called the guy up," Duncan said.

"Didn't know what else to do. I figured somebody was gonna have to give that phone number a try, so it might as well've been me. I know you don't put much weight on such things, but I kinda felt like I was bein' guided to call. You understand what I'm saying?"

"Not exactly."

"Well, I don't suppose it matters." Jeremy turned off the highway. "And here we are."

The house was one block off a main thouroughfare called Lee Highway, just over the state line in Fairfax, Virginia. The past fifteen years had seen the highway grow from a narrow country road to a six-lane, stoplight-saddled, noisy, cantankerous city street. But one block away was still country. The road was called Maple Lane, and the trees were thick enough to cut the highway's noise down to a dull hum. The birds flittered and sang, the road bumped and rocked and coaxed drivers down to a comfortable crawl. The houses held that timeless quality of country slumber, and when Jeremy pulled up and cut the motor, the loudest noise was that of kids playing in some unseen backyard.

The house was old rough stone, close cut and framed by white-washed wooden slats. The nails that held the slats in place had been untended long enough to stain the wood with rust-colored tears. The sunporch was straight off the farm, with angled glass louvers on three sides so that the walls could be opened or closed according to the breeze and the weather.

The front of the house was lined with a half dozen metal-backed lawn chairs, the grass at their feet yellowed and pressed, legends of daily use. In one of them sat a white-haired lady of incredible years, her head bent forward in a stillness that spoke of deep slumber. The other chairs held the ghosts of summers past, watching over a house grown from the earth and the trees that surrounded it.

Duncan looked at the house, said, "I still don't see why we're here."

Jeremy climbed from the truck, shut his door, spoke through the open window, "Jesus said, apart from me you can do nothing. I thought it was time to see if He could help us out."

Duncan did not move. "What, they've got an open line to the Twilight Zone in there?"

He remained untouched by the man's sarcasm. "You know how they say practice makes perfect? Well, between 'em these ladies have done more than three hundred years of prayin'." Jeremy patted the car roof. "C'mon, son, I promise you they don't bite. And if they do, I promise I'll hide their teeth."

The long sunporch sofas were set with square pillows and old quilts for those afternoons when getting up and walking to the back bedroom was fifteen steps too far. Jeremy led Duncan through the porch and into the living room. It was high-ceilinged and filled with overstuffed horsehair furniture. An upright piano guarded one wall, with hymnals and loose-leafed religious music stacked on its top. The far wall had a framed print of Jesus. It was the only adornment in the room.

A tiny old woman came stumping out of the kitchen, wiping her hands on her apron and peering at the two men through thick-lensed glasses. "That you, Jeremy?"

"Yes, ma'am, Mrs. Broyhill. Like you to meet a friend of mine, Duncan Wyeth."

She came up very close to him, close enough to have to throw her head back in order to peer up into his face. Pale cloud-blue eyes of a very ancient lady peered through the bifocals. "You two gentlemen come right back into the dining room. I've just made a fresh pot of coffee."

Duncan slowed his pace to match hers, followed her down a hall that showed three bedrooms all neat as a pin, the beds decked out in hand-quilted bedspreads, the side-tables covered with crocheted centerpieces.

"Perhaps you ought to pour for us, Jeremy."

"My pleasure, ma'am."

"My hands are real slow on account of this arthritis," she said to Duncan, easing herself down into a chair. "Still get around, though."

"That she does," Jeremy agreed. "Sees to four old ladies better'n any home ever could."

"I used to have nine women here," Mrs. Broyhill said, her voice high and toneless and slightly rasping. "Five have passed on, and I'm not taking on any others. My greatest prayer is that the Lord will take these before my own time comes. I've been doing this for thirty-four years, young man. It's my calling, to help others in this way."

Duncan nodded politely, sipped at the coffee, found himself thinking of evenings with his grandfather, sitting out back with the dog at his feet, watching the sun go down. Strange how he would think of such a thing, here in the dining room of this old house.

"It's hard for old folks to change homes," Mrs. Broyhill was saying. "Harder than young people can understand. They get set in their ways, you see. Everything needs to be just so. I understand that, always have. It's been my calling to help these people know a few good final days, have a home and a friend they know really cares for them."

"There aren't enough people like you around," Duncan replied.

"That's because too many people try to live without faith. Only they can't, because a life without faith isn't a life." She held him with a look of utter assurance that came to some people with age. "Are you a person of faith, young man?"

"I thought about it once," Duncan replied, not needing to consciously decide whether he wanted to tell her the truth. "Then I got caught up in some problems, and it didn't seem like God was there when I needed Him. I guess I just gave up."

She remained silent, clearly content to sit and watch him sip at his coffee. Duncan felt the watchful silence press him to inspect things he had not thought about in years.

"I don't know," he said, turning his gaze down to his cup. "I wanted to do some things with my life, and it seemed like all there was to religion was a lot of *don'ts*. Don't have fun, don't enjoy life, don't try hard, don't expect much out of this life because you'll get it all in the next. It seemed like an excuse for losers to not have to try.

"So I started moving away, I guess. Then I had some problems with my wife, and my daughter, too. And the problems got worse, and I never felt that God did anything but get in the way. No, that's not right. He just didn't really *help* anything. I mean, look at the mess the world's in. God must be asleep or something, right?"

She did not appear to take any more offense than Jeremy. "The Lord is not a bellboy, young man. He's not going to come just because you happen to be in need and decide to call Him. He commands us to live according to His will. If you do that, the joy and the peace that surpasses all understanding are there for you to enjoy."

Mrs. Broyhill bent her head over the neatly starched tablecloth, and folded two arthritic hands together in a careful, deliberate movement. "Young man, just because a person is saved does not mean that he immediately becomes perfect. It simply means that he is *saved*. It means that all is well with his soul. He is then called to *become* perfect, to learn the lesson of living for his Maker. But it is a learning that continues all his life, and some people do not learn the lessons very well, no matter how long they live. The *don'ts* are the least important part of faith as far as I am concerned. Those people who put so much importance on them are the same ones who try and put God in a box. They try to make Him into something they can understand."

She raised her chin up high enough to place him in the correct angle of her spectacles. "Young man, the Lord God is infinite. That is a word many people have a lot of trouble with. Infinite and eternal. He is patient enough to hold His return so that a few more of His children might be saved from the agony of eternal darkness. It is our choice, you see. Yours and mine. The freedom of choice was given us as part of our birthright. We may choose to be part of *His* eternal plan, or we may choose the blind path of selfish desires. The good Lord allows our own self-made pain and suffering to continue a bit longer, so that a few more of *His* beloved children might find their way to the light. He does not hold off His coming for himself, young man. It is important that you understand this. He does it for us. For you. Because once He does come, once all this pain and misery reaches an end, then the Day of Judgment will arrive. And after that it will simply be too late."

"You make it sound like the simplest thing in the world," he replied.

"All eternal truths are simple, young man. It's the only way they can be applied to all mankind."

Duncan turned, saw Jeremy watching him with the gentlest of smiles. Jeremy said to Mrs. Broyhill, "Duncan's caught up in tryin' to locate two runaway girls. Looks like I might go off with him, see if I can lend a hand."

"Those poor lambs," Mrs. Broyhill said, real pain in her voice.

"Yes, ma'am. I was wonderin' if maybe you and the ladies could start a little prayer circle for us," Jeremy said. "We haven't got much more than a thread of hope to go on right now. I thought maybe it might help."

"Of course we can," she replied. The call to action brought her to her feet. "Not only that, but I'm sure I can get some of the people at church to help out. If they won't they'll hear about it from me, I can promise you that."

She looked down at Duncan. "Don't you scoff at the power of prayer, young man. It has healed more broken hearts and homes than any doctor or psychologist could ever hope to."

Mrs. Broyhill turned to Jeremy. "Are these young ladies somewhere in the area?"

"Most likely not, ma'am. Looks like they got themselves taken off a ways, maybe to California."

She gave him a long look. "The Lord's got something in store for you two, I can feel it."

"Yes, ma'am, I feel the same way."

"And how were you planning on traveling?"

"We hadn't really gotten that far yet, Mrs. Broyhill."

"Well, if you'll take the word of an old lady, maybe you should think of taking your car."

Duncan stared at her. "Drive to Los Angeles?"

"You'll do what you think best, I'm sure, young man. But I've come to have quite a bit of faith in the heart's callings. I can hear that still, quiet voice a good deal clearer in my old age. Perhaps it's because I'm moving closer to my homecoming, perhaps because I don't have quite so many desires and concerns and worries cluttering up my heart as I did when I was young. What I do know is that right now this old heart is saying you two can do quite a bit of good if you'll take your time and let the Lord guide your footsteps."

"You mean stop and tell others along the way?"

"I'm sure I don't know, Mr. Hughes. But if the Lord has a

message He wants you to give others, He will make it plain when the time is right."

Jeremy nodded slowly a few times, said to Duncan, "If we're gonna drive, maybe we oughtta think about gettin' started tomorrow."

Duncan searched for a reason to object, found none. "I don't have anything keeping me here."

"I have some relatives up Danville way," Mrs. Broyhill said, pushing herself up from the table on age-twisted hands. "I'll just give them a call and see if they can put you up for the night.

"And rest assured our prayers will be there with you," she added, standing on the front porch and offering Duncan her hand. "You're traveling with a mighty fine man. We'll miss having Mr. Hughes around here."

Duncan wished he had more time to spend with this remarkable old lady. "He can say the hardest things to me, hard to take, I mean. And I'll just stand there and listen. Anybody else, and I'd probably take a poke at them."

"Well, and I'll tell you the reason, young man. It's a very simple fact, too." She looked up at him with eyes that swam behind thick lenses. "Jeremy Hughes has a servant's heart. Now when you understand that, you can pat yourself on the back, because you've come on something that'll carry you a lifetime."

She turned back and stumped to the door. As one withered hand grappled for the latch, she said, "Now you get yourself out there and make your Lord proud, young man. Bring those little girls home."

◆　◆　◆

The restaurant Bella selected for their dinner together was called Tout Va Bien and was located on a cobblestone Georgetown street leading from the C & O Canal. The old-fashioned house had lead-paned windows set in a painted-brick facade, and a door so low Jeremy had to bend over to enter. The restaurant's owner, a thin and energetic Moroccan gentleman in his early fifties, preened as Jeremy straightened up, glanced around the period room, and declared it one truly special place.

Once they were seated, Bella told him, "I was afraid you'd find it too fancy for your tastes."

"Well, I do admit that it's a trifle classy for a poor country boy.

But if they don't mind servin' me, then I guess I don't mind eatin' here." He accepted the menu from the waiter, glanced down the page, asked, "What language you say this is written in?"

"French. Want me to order?"

"Unless you'd rather hang it from the wall over there and let me throw darts at it, I guess you better."

"What kind of fish do you like?"

"Always been partial to the ones that're cooked. Don't think much of the idea of a fish kickin' back when I stick the fork in."

"That mean you don't spend a lot of time in Japanese restaurants?"

"I went once, Bella. They sat me down at this pretty little table and gave me this nice soft towel and smiled and bowed and just made me feel like a king. Then they went and served me something I haven't seen the likes of since I spent time 'round a baby."

She signaled to the waiter and ordered the Dover sole cooked in butter. "I hope you like it."

"I'm sure I will." He fiddled with his hands. "You ever noticed how similar your name is to my former wife's?"

She nodded, played at keeping her face calm. "My real name is Beatrice, but my father said it sounded too fancy. Bella was my grandmother's name—she was Italian. Everybody said I looked like her when I was little, and I liked it more than Beatrice, so it just stuck."

"I like it just fine." Jeremy tasted his water. "Ella's real name was Elizabeth. Don't recall anyone ever usin' it, though. I asked her 'bout it once. She said Ella was a lot more *approachable*."

Bella thought it over and decided she'd like to have it out in the open from the very first moment. "She died some time ago, didn't she?"

"Comin' up on twelve years now."

"You must have loved her very much."

"That I did," he agreed, surprised that the hurt was not there. He thought of Ella seldom and talked of her less because of the ache it caused. Yet here he was, speaking about her as easily as he would the weather. "Don't know many people who knew her and didn't love her. She was just that way."

"You still miss her a lot, don't you?"

"Not the way it used to be. There'll always be that gap in my life, sorta like a leg that's been cut off. But I've learned to live with it. I've adapted to my handicap. As long as the Lord

keeps on makin' gifts of more days, I'm told to praise His name.
Can't carry old grief and new thanksgiving at the same time.
One kinda sours the other."

She nodded. "It's how I feel about TJ. Look at me. I can even
say his name without choking up."

"Time and the Lord, sister. Two best healin' salves I've ever
found, 'specially when they're used together."

"How old were you when you met your wife?"

"I was sixteen and scared to death. But you don't want to
talk about stuff that happened back in prehistoric times."

"Sure I do. Underneath this hard exterior beats the heart
of an old softy. I love a good romance. Did you have a beautiful
old-timey courtship?"

"No, no, and no. It wasn't beautiful, it wasn't old-timey, and
it sure as goodness wasn't no courtship. You sure you want to
hear this?"

She leaned two elbows on the table, cupped her chin in her
palms, said, "I'm going to enjoy this. I can tell it already."

"Well, her daddy owned the local farm supply and feed store.
He was chief deacon in the church, head of the school board,
former mayor, part owner of the biggest bank in town, the
works. My daddy owed him a passel. It's an old story, dirt-poor
farmer bought everything on time 'til the crops came in, then
never had enough to meet his payments, so he just kept gettin'
further and further into debt. My daddy was spendin' one day
a week at their farm to try and work off some of the burden.
For my sixteenth birthday my daddy gave me the duty.

"I thought it was something, man, him trustin' me enough
to let me go up there and work old man Turner's fields. First
time I was up there, Ella came out with this big pitcher of the
best lemonade I ever tasted. After that, I had another reason
for wantin' to help daddy with old man Turner's tobacco.

"I kept goin' up there, and Ella kept comin' out with the
lemonade 'til I finally got up the nerve to ask her to a local
dance. Didn't think my heart could still stay in my chest and
beat so hard. The only woman I ever asked out on a date was
the one who became my wife. Bet a lotta folks these days'd say
I never lived, huh?"

Bella looked down at her plate, said in the old gravelstrewn
voice, "You didn't miss much."

That sobered him. "Shucks, Bella, let's talk about something else, why don't we?"

But the look she gave him was pure warmth. "You can't imagine how much I like hearing this story."

He held her gaze, said, "Come to think of it, this is the first time in years I've been able to talk about her without feeling like somebody's drillin' into my heart. Since before her death, as a matter of fact."

"Don't stop now. I never liked having to fill in the holes myself. It's too much work."

"Well, when my daddy heard I'd asked old man Turner's daughter to the dance, I mean to tell you, he threw a fit that they musta heard in Atlanta. First time I ever stood up to my daddy was when he told me to march back up there and break it off. He said I was bound to make a fool of myself and shame the family before the most important man in the county. I said, nossir, I wasn't gonna do it, I was takin' that little girl and we were gonna have ourselves a *time*. He probably woulda got a piece of stovewood and crippled me right there on the spot, 'cept Momma told him to take his mouth out on the back stoop where it belonged. Momma didn't often speak her mind, but when she did Daddy listened.

"So I got all washed up and put on my only good shirt and my stringy black Sunday tie, polished my best boots with a cold biscuit, and walked the three miles back to the Turner place. I was just about as scared as a body could be, I guarantee you that right now. Daddy didn't help, neither. His mouth followed me down the first half mile or so, callin' out dire warnin's 'bout what was gonna happen if I messed this one up."

"Which you did," Bella guessed, her voice flat but her eyes dancing.

"Like you can't imagine. Turner's place was one of the first homes in the county to have real electric lights. At night you could see it from a mile or so off, 'cause it was the only place around that was so lit up. We didn't have streetlights outside the towns, see. And the moths and night bugs, brother, did they ever have a time. Long as those lights stayed on, they'd come poppin' up against the screened windows, fly around the house in a storm.

"So I come walkin' up to the front porch, swingin' my arms to keep the bugs outta my face, and stopped there to catch my breath and give my hair one more lick. I knocked on the screen door, my heart bangin' loud as a drum. Then this big old shadow appears, and I knew it was old man Turner. All my daddy's words came back, and I straightened up just as tall as I knew how.

"Well, right about then this moth decided my ear hole was just what it was lookin' for, and flew right on in."

Bella gaped at him. "You are kidding me."

"Not jokin' nor jestin'. Sounded like a bomber had landed in my brain. So old man Turner opens up the inside door, and what does he see but this field hand doin' some kinda wild dance on his front stoop, flingin' his arms around and screamin' like a maniac."

Bella worked at keeping a straight face, gave her nose a good rub, asked, "What did he do?"

"What do you think? Slammed the door in my face. Didn't say one word. Just took a look and shut the door and went back inside like I wasn't even worth believin'.

"Then this little shadow comes up alongside the big shadow that was back behind the closed door there, and the big shadow commences to wave his arms around a little. Then out comes Ella, lookin' pretty as a picture. By that time my shirttail was out around my knees and my necktie was strung up sideways like a noose, my hair was down in my face and I was sweatin' something fierce. Instead of tellin' her how nice she looked, I was bent over sideways bangin' my head with one hand and wonderin' if anybody could hear me shout, 'cause all I could hear was the most awful buzzin' you can imagine.

"Ella didn't even bat an eyelid. She just grabbed my arm, led me inside, held my head down next to a light, and danged if that old bug didn't pop out like a jack-in-the-box. Left me standin' there in their nice little sittin' room with my chest heavin', lookin' like a wild man and feelin' like seventeen kinds of a lunatic."

"Your father must have skinned you alive."

"He would have, but I never told him. By the time I walked that girl back to her home after the dance I was just plain in love. Guess he saw that, too, 'cause he never said much more about it."

"There's one good thing about starting off bad like that," Bella said. "Things can only get better."

Jeremy folded his napkin into precise lines, pressed it down flat with a work-hardened hand—very deliberately, very carefully. He did not say a word.

"Oh, come on, Jeremy. You don't mean to say it got worse than that."

"I don't wanna talk about it."

"You can't stop now. It's illegal. If it isn't, it should be. Jeremy Hughes, stop trying to hide behind your hair and look at me. What happened next?"

"What on earth do you want to hear about my goin's-on with another woman for, Bella?"

She cocked her head to one side. "I have no idea. Do I have to have a reason?"

He thought it over. "Guess not."

"Then stop trying to put me off and tell me what happened."

"Okay, but you gotta promise not to laugh."

"Right."

"I mean it, now. This is serious business here."

"Uh-huh."

"Well, after that night you couldn't have kept me off that farm with a team of cross-eyed mules. Didn't have two nickels to rub together, so I couldn't ask the girl out on a real date. I started inventin' things to do around their house. Figured their daddy wouldn't raise too much of a fuss, since he saw me workin' for free.

"It just so happened I'd get there a coupla hours before sunset, work an hour or so, then let Ella invite me up on the stoop for a lemonade and a chat. We had it timed right down to the last second too, I tell you what. When old man Turner's car chugged around the corner, and we saw that plume of dust in the distance, I was up and outta there like a turpentined cat. All he saw from me was the little things I left done around their house and the smile on Ella's face.

"A couple of months later there was a hayride, and Ella said she'd go with me. I tell you the truth, I was so nervous I didn't sleep a wink the night before. I was absolutely dead-set and determined that I wasn't gonna be caught by another bug, nossir, not that time. I walked up her front porch with my hands clapped to my ears, and banged on the door with my shoe. I waited 'til the last moment, when the shadow on the door told me her daddy was standin' there, then dropped my hands and wiped 'em on my pants' legs so old man Turner wouldn't think he was shakin' hands with a used dishrag. Been plagued with sweaty palms all my life, but never worse than that night. Nossir.

"So the old man opened the door, the newspaper danglin' from one hand, and eyed me over those half-moon glasses. He looked at me like I was something that had attached itself to his front fender durin' a moonlight drive. I stepped forward with this grade-A grin and my hand outstretched, and stepped on the family dog."

Bella took a breath, said, "Now you've got to be kidding."

"Wish I was. It was a tiny mutt, been with the family since around the time Ella was born. Looked like a puny gray hairball with legs. I didn't even know which end was up 'til it started barkin' at me. I tell you, that dog wasn't the least bit pleased to have me tread on it. Decided the best way to let me know was to bark up a storm and chew on my cuff. So there I was, tryin' to keep that silly grin on my face and shake old man Turner's hand and not do what I really wanted to, which was to boot that mutt right through the middle of next week.

"Then up came Ella's mom, 'bout the sweetest lady you'd ever care to meet. She was tryin' to lead me into the parlor and help me relax, and I couldn't hardly hear her on account of that mutt tellin' me just as loud as it knew how that we weren't gonna be the best of friends. I let Mrs. Turner take my arm and pull me into the formal parlor, and just as I'm gettin' ready to tell her what a nice home she's got here, that crazy dog grew tired of bein' ignored and sank what felt like six-inch fangs into my ankle."

Bella covered her mouth with one hand and tried to give him a sympathetic look, but her shaking shoulders gave her away.

"Old man Turner had this mantelpiece over the fireplace, stacked from one end to the other with his bowlin' trophies. Well, I mean to tell you I managed to clear up all fifty of 'em with one swipe. Yessir. A clean sweep. Yelled like the dickens and did another one of them little dances I was workin' on the last time out in their front yard, 'cept this time there was a room full of furniture to get in the way.

"I jumped up on top of this pearl-white settee in my dusty shoes, then decided to try the coffee table, only it wasn't built to handle my weight. One of the legs gave way and spilled me onto this little antique cradle they had stuffed with newspapers and magazines. That thing just gave up the ghost. Only I wasn't payin' it much mind right then, on account of that mutt still makin' hamburger outta my ankle.

"Ella came downstairs and pulled that dog away easy as you please. We had a time gettin' me outta there, though. Her daddy was aimin' to attach himself where the dog left off. She finally got him cooled down to the point where he stopped talkin' 'bout bird shot and jail and havin' the sheriff run me outta town. And that was the last time I ever set foot in that house."

CHAPTER
6

Wednesday morning Duncan said in greeting, "It's not too late to back out."

Jeremy climbed from his truck, smiled at an old black gentleman making heavy going of the warped sidewalk, and replied, "Yes it is, son. The ladies at the boarding house told me not to show up there again without those little girls."

"I called up there this morning, they said you'd already left," Duncan said. "I thought I'd come down and meet you, go ahead and get started. If I waited for you to find my farm we wouldn't leave town until next week."

"I know just what you mean. Down home folks'd probably say your farm's easy as pie to find, once you know where it is." Jeremy slammed his door, said, "Where's your dirt-mobile?"

"Around back. Didn't want to give the Community a bad name." Duncan looked the truck over, decided a warning was in order. "If you don't mind my saying so, leaving your truck on this street for three weeks is kinda like giving a rabbit some lettuce to keep for you."

"I already deeded it over to the Community," Jeremy replied. "Told Reverend Tom he could keep the best part of me."

"You're not planning on coming back?"

"I'm tryin' not to plan any more than I have to just now. Whatever happens, though, I kinda got the feelin' that a chapter in my life is through. Deedin' the car over was my way of comin' to grips with that."

Jeremy hefted a weather-beaten canvas carry-all and followed Duncan around back. "I gotta admit," he said as he slung the bag in the trunk, "all of a sudden I'm lookin' forward to this more than I have to anything in a long time."

"Three thousand miles with a total stranger, in a dirty car," Duncan replied. "Think you can handle it?"

Jeremy slammed the trunk closed. "I got myself a little project I'm gonna be workin' on day in and day out. I don't aim on havin' time to fret."

"I've never been much for long-distance road trips, but there's something about this that's got me excited too."

"That's good to hear. Makes my work a lot easier." Jeremy patted him on the back. "Want to come in with me and say goodbye?"

"Might as well. I've got one phone call I need to make before we hit the road."

Duncan closed the door to the empty office, called Detective Bryan Larson, told him what Jeremy had found out. "This guy wants to come along for the ride."

"You asking my opinion or telling me?"

"Both, I guess."

"He's a strange one, and his religion thing's a little hard to take sometimes." Bryan thought it over, decided, "I'd do it anyway. Those were good ideas, talking to the pimp and then calling that guy cold."

"I thought so, too."

"You can't be too careful out there, especially if this guy Pierre's really hooked into the big time. You're bound to have some real nasties hanging around. Might be nice to have a little company."

"You like this guy, don't you?"

"I tell you, I lived in that guy's back pocket for almost six weeks. Thought for a while we had a prime suspect on our hands. I brought him in a couple of times, tried to string him out, the usual. He acted as much at home in the station as he did in that fancy house with the rear end blown to Tennessee. After he left town for the funeral and didn't bother to tell us until he got back, I started bringing him down for questioning like every other day. Didn't mind it a bit. Spent hours trying to convert the drunks and perverts sitting with him out front. I gave up when cops around the precinct station started walking around wearing these thoughtful looks."

"So you're sure he didn't do it?"

"Yeah. The guy was up here working as a servant to that fellow in the White House, TJ Case. You wouldn't believe it, they've got this prayer group named after him now at the White House. A couple more around Capitol Hill."

"How do you know about something like that?"

"You hear a lotta stuff in this job. A couple of the embassy types we're supposed to be guarding have started making it a regular thing."

"You take care of yourself, Bryan. I don't have enough friends to have any of them blown up."

"Look who's talking. Flying off to the city of lost angels, checking out some bimbette playing with the nasties. Anyway, this problem with Case was an exception. We're not so worried about terrorists as a lot of places." Larson paused for a moment. "I got some buddies out on the L.A. force. Haven't seen them in years."

"Think maybe you could give them a call?"

"Why not? Tell them to keep an eye out for a coupla young girls on the game." Larson laughed without humor. "Can't be more than a hundred thousand out there already."

"I made something for you." Bella shut her office door, gave him the shy look of a little girl unsure as to whether she had done the right thing.

"That's awful nice, Bella. But what with everything else you got goin' on, you really shouldn't have."

"I've been working on it ever since the funeral," she said. "It came to mind on the way back to D.C., and just kept coming up every time I thought of you."

Slowly she unwrapped the folds of white tissue paper to reveal a needlepoint design that read:

"May the God of hope fill you with all joy and peace as you trust in him, so that you may overflow with hope by the power of the Holy Spirit."

"My mother taught me to needlepoint when I was a little girl. I haven't done it in, oh, I don't know how long. Not since I moved to Washington, that's for sure. I wasn't even sure I'd remember how." She stroked the surface. "I hope you like it."

"I don't know what to say," Jeremy replied.

"It's from Romans," she told him.

"I know it is. It's one of my favorite passages, something I hoped for and wasn't sure I deserved."

She raised her eyes. "You deserve it, all right. You're just about the best man I know."

"Shows how well you *don't* know me, sayin' something like that."

Bella shook her head. "I knew it even then, back at the funeral. Strange how I could even think such a thing, the state I was in. But I did. TJ was lucky to have you as a friend."

Not trusting his voice, Jeremy took the needlepoint from her, ran a rough hand over the design, felt the hours and hours of work that went into it. "You've made something real beautiful here, Bella. I gotta find a nice frame for this, someplace special to hang it."

Briskly she took it back from him, rolled it up, said, "You just leave all that to me. I was going to do it anyway, but I wanted you to see it before you left and I just finished it last night. It'll be all framed and ready for you to hang when you get back."

Jeremy searched for words. "Thank you, Bella. It's real nice. *Real nice.* Nicest thing anybody's given me in a long time."

She gazed at him with eyes that glowed from down deep. "You take care of yourself out there, Jeremy Hughes. And bring yourself back safe in one piece."

◆　　◆　　◆

In the midst of a typically frantic day Nak ushered Reverend James Thaddeus Wilkins into Senator Atterly's office. Even before the senator had emerged from behind his desk, he knew that here was a man he liked. Reverend Wilkins had the features of another era, and the eyes of another world. He was black as ebony, tall and slightly stoop-shouldered without appearing the slightest bit weak. His was the bent-over stride of a man carrying a heavy burden with determination. The palms of his hands were scarred with the same hard work and harsh winds that had drawn knife-like lines down his cheeks and across his forehead. Yet when the senator looked into the minister's eyes he saw a heart open wide.

"Certainly is nice of you to come by, Reverend."

"It is an honor, Senator. Yessir, it sure is. Lived in Washington nearly all my adult life and never been in these parts."

Senator Atterly motioned him toward a seat. "If that's the case, perhaps you'd like to have a tour of the Capitol."

"Why, that'd be a real treat. Think maybe I might be able to bring my wife?"

"Of course you can. Bring your whole family." He looked a message toward Nak, who gave him a nod in reply.

"Mr. Nakamishi's been tellin' me a little 'bout what you're plannin', Senator."

"Plan may be too strong a word, Reverend. It indicates a certainty of success that we don't have. Nak and I have both felt that we are being led to back this legislation. I wish I could tell you how disappointing a response the sponsors have received, even from people they had assumed would be on their side. There are a whole battery of groups lined up against us, I'm afraid, all decrying our efforts as unconstitutional. The opponents claim that by attempting to make pornography unlawful we are infringing on their freedom of speech."

"The sponsors barely managed to get the legislation before the committee," Nak said in his quiet, unemotional voice. "Now one of the primary backers is dead."

"So you're feelin' called to take up what these other folks're workin' on," Wilkins pressed.

"I feel this need as strongly as I've ever felt anything in my whole life," Senator Atterly replied.

"Me too," Nak said. "I don't know why, there's not been a lightning bolt out of the sky or anything. But there's just no room for questioning it."

Senator Atterly gravely regarded his assistant. "Nak has it much harder than I do. My colleagues are in a sense required by tradition to treat me with a modicum of respect. With Nak they can and do say straight to his face what would only be said behind my back. Nak receives what they can't give to me directly, as it were."

"It doesn't matter," Nak insisted. "I know it sounds hard to believe, but I feel as though I've got a barrier that keeps me from feeling their arrows."

Atterly appeared not to have heard. "We've only been at this for two days, and already the attacks have started. I suppose you know that Nak formerly worked with a friend of yours in the White House."

"TJ Case," Wilkins replied, nodding his head. "May he and

Sister Catherine rest in peace. Yessir, he was a fine brother in our Lord."

"Yes he was. We miss him terribly, especially now. In any event, one little barb is that Nak has shifted over from the White House to the Senate in order to bring me down in flames as well."

"There's no political mileage to be gained by carrying the banner against pornography," Nak said. "Putting together a wholehearted charge like this opens us up to attack from too many different fronts. Since this is the first time the senator has become involved in something this politically volatile, people on Capitol Hill sort of assume that he's been misled by my advice."

"It's nothing short of amazing how many people have approached me over the past twenty-four hours and suggested that I find another assistant," Atterly said. "Almost as though they cannot fathom a reason for taking on something this potentially explosive. Nothing in their political lives, no cause or stand, is as important as the advancement of their careers."

"We've already located some new backers, though," Nak added.

"Yes, we'll possibly have enough support in the Senate to see it through," the senator agreed. "But the numbers in the House are disappointing."

"Most of the supporters on the House side are involved in our prayer group," Nak said.

"We've been trying to continue the work that TJ began," Atterly explained. "Splinter groups have been started in several of the buildings, but many of TJ's regulars still manage to meet three times a week in the cellar of the OEOB."

"That's the Executive Office Building connected to the White House," Nak explained.

"Right. It's remained a sort of focal point. Even though it's not the most practical place for us to come together, it gives us all a very good feeling to pray in the shadow of the White House."

"The senator mentioned in one of his early sessions that he liked the idea of bringing the Holy Spirit into the seat of earthly power at least once a week," Nak said. "It really struck home. I think that's what has kept so many busy people fitting this meeting into their schedules every week."

Reverend Wilkins sat in the intent silence of a practiced

listener. His eyes shifted from speaker to speaker, his face as grave and unmoving as a granite carving. There was no impatience in his being, no need to press or cross-examine or hone in on a specific point. He listened with his ears and with his heart.

"As I mentioned, the anti-pornography legislation was introduced simultaneously in both Houses. That was no small event, let me tell you. There was enough interest to have the bills passed on to committee, but unless we can marshall more support on the House side, it will languish there forever."

"The Senate will probably pass on it once its committee makes a recommendation," Nak explained. "But the House is something else entirely. There's a good chance their committee will table it, which is a method of burying a politically unpopular motion without actually having to go on the record as voting against it."

"We've started working full time on building support," Atterly said. "And on the House side we're getting absolutely nowhere. It is the most frustrating effort I have made in three and a half decades of political life. I have spoken to countless people trying to describe to them how crucial this bill is to the health of our nation. On the House side, to a great extent, I have received the most politely infuriating brush-off imaginable."

"People have already begun avoiding us," Nak said quietly. "Turning away when we walk toward them. Refusing to return our calls."

"We are becoming political pariahs. Tarred with the brush of political extremism. There is no greater terror to a career politician than to be associated with a cause that might lead to his defeat at the next election, and in their eyes this is where I am willfully headed. They do not understand, and do not want to become involved.

"It doesn't matter whether or not the pornography issue in itself draws sufficient opposition to bring me down," Atterly went on. "My more liberal-leaning colleagues have now tagged me as an extremist, someone willing to risk all on an issue that is clearly doomed to failure through lack of support. The majority of my associates see this as nothing short of insane."

"But when we pray we still come out feeling very clearly that this is correct," Nak said.

"Absolutely no room for doubt," Atterly agreed. "Strangest

thing I've ever known. These past few days, the peace I have found in prayer has been a blanket that descends out of no-where and leaves me with no room to maneuver."

"Then we came up with this idea of a prayer circle," Nak said.

"Or rather Nak did," Atterly corrected. "That's why we wanted to meet with you, Reverend. We would like to draw support from a number of different sources, sort of extend our spiritual base outside the avenues of earthly power."

Reverend Wilkins nodded his head slowly a few times, wait-ing to be certain that the pair had said all they wished. He bowed his head for a moment, drew down deep inside himself. Atterly and Nak waited with the patience of people accustomed to watching others pray.

"Sometimes it's hard for me to bring His Word to mind," Reverend Wilkins said in his deep-hoarse voice, his face still downcast. "Times like this, my old heart just wants to fight its way out of my chest, say we got to do this, run after that, win the war in minutes and hours and days that I can measure."

Reverend Wilkins raised a face clenched with iron-clad de-termination. "What I got to remember, gentlemen, is the war is already won. The Lord's already handed us the victory."

Wilkins' dark eyes cast from face to face, searching out a hint of understanding. Senator Atterly fought back the urge to take control, break in, hurry things along. But there was some-thing too important here for him to sweep it away. Nak sat beside him in impassive silence, showing nothing but his nor-mal blank expression.

"Our church is sufferin' 'cause one of our little ones has run away, got himself hooked on crack, lost his body and his mind and his soul out there on the streets.

"The Lord didn't send that boy out there to kill himself day by day. Called to him just as loud as He could, but the boy let the world defeat him. He didn't turn and run to his Lord when the goin' got tough. Decided the answer wasn't there, let the prince of this earth whisper them lies in his ear, lead him into the endless night."

Reverend Wilkins sighed and dropped his head back down. "I haven't been able to go out on the street these past few days without carryin' the pain of that little lost lamb with me. Can't pass a streetwalker, can't walk by a house where the Lord ain't welcome, can't smell the drug smoke or see the empty liquor bottle or hear the curses of a man broken by hopelessness and drink without seein' poor little Bobby's eyes there lookin' back at me. And it ain't just me, gentlemen, it ain't just me. The whole church is burdened. Yessir, Bobby's mother has got saints droppin' by all the blessed day long, huggin' her and lovin' her and lettin' her know she ain't goin' through this alone. The church has got so many people comin' in to pray we've had to move our circle three times. We finally put it up in the choir loft.

"I couldn't sleep last night, got to worryin' 'bout what I could do to help them children more than I was already doin', and I decided to walk over and pray with the saints a little. Musta been close on four o'clock this mornin'. Know what I found? Thirty-seven people in there prayin' and singin' and readin' His Word. At four o'clock in the mornin'. Folks with work waitin' and families gettin' ready to wake up and have breakfast. We even had teenagers in there prayin' for their lost friend. Asked 'em what they were doin', know what they said? Told me they couldn't live with doin' nothin'. Every place they turned around Bobby was there waitin' for 'em, callin' out for help. Like to have broken down right there, it touched me so."

Reverend Wilkins paused and looked up at Senator Atterly. "The victory, gentlemen, is not in reachin' some goal we set out there in front of us. The victory is in *tryin'*. The victory is in callin' out the best we know how. The victory is in makin' sure we reach the end safe in His care.

"You feelin' so strong about this makes it pretty clear to my head that you're workin' His will on this. The foe is on every side, though. He's reachin' out, tryin' to slow you down. Blindin' all the eyes and ears that will let him. We've been given this light for a purpose, gentlemen. A divine purpose. A callin' that leads to glory. So we mustn't falter, mustn't let the lamp drop or go out."

Senator Atterly eased a spine that had become rigidly set in one position. "Reverend Wilkins, you don't know how much your words mean to me."

"I feel like I've been waiting just to hear this," Nak agreed.

"I guess the next question is, Reverend, whether you might be able to help us set up a prayer circle down here on Capitol Hill."

Reverend James Thaddeus Wilkins' voice was as solid as the set of his features. "Gentlemen, there is something here that needs doin'. The Lord's burden has been set on our shoulders for a purpose, drawn us together for a reason. Don't need to wonder over why. Just need to *do*."

Senator Atterly permitted himself a smile. "That's the best news I've heard in quite a while, Reverend. Thank you."

But the minister was not finished. "Have to tell you gentlemen, there's a feelin' buildin' inside me. Sittin' here listenin' to you fine people talk about what you're plannin' and tryin' and workin' on in His name, it came to me strong as anything I've ever felt that there's something more He wants you to do."

It was the senator's turn to be surprised. "More than the legislation?"

Reverend Wilkins shook his head. "More than the prayer circle. Got the feelin' that's not why I'm here. Don't know what it is we're bein' called to look at. But the feelin' I got in my heart is too strong not to at least say it's there."

Atterly and Nak exchanged baffled glances. "What do you think it is?"

"I can't rightly say," Wilkins replied. "So what I'd suggest, gentlemen, is that we just bow our heads and ask the Lord to make His will clear."

♦   ♦   ♦

"The worst part about living alone is racing the food in the fridge," Duncan said.

They were crawling down I–95 toward Richmond, trapped in a snaking line of traffic that filled all eight lanes as far as they could see. Rising car exhaust made the air up and down the curving hillsides shimmer with their drivers' pent-up frustration.

The Lincoln had the roominess of a big sofa, space for even Jeremy to stretch out his legs. He laid one arm across the cracked leather seat-back and began the delicate process of getting to know a stranger. The conversation sort of meandered around to Duncan and the farmhouse and the fact that it hadn't been really cleaned since his last maid quit four months ago. The lady had stood on the front porch and said it was a crying shame to see such a fine old house go to ruin. That's why I need you to stay, Duncan had replied. The lady had retreated down the steps, said, I can't get a bulldozer through the front door and don't know any other way to shift the dirt.

Jeremy nodded. "Know just what you mean. A man livin' alone goes away for a coupla days, he's gotta kinda sneak up on the fridge when he gets back, wear them gloves made for stirrin' acid."

"I hate watching those little black freckles come up on the baloney," Duncan said.

"And havin' to hold your breath before you fling the door open."

"Or prying the lid off those little plastic containers and feeling like there's a hand inside it pulling it back down."

Jeremy nodded and said casually to the side window, "It's a hard thing to do, face a silent home. Man's got nowhere to look but inside. So he keeps searchin' for things to fill up his time, anything to keep him from havin' to go home and face up to how empty he is. Emptier than any home is ever gonna be. All the lies get stripped away, 'til there ain't nothin' left but the loneliness of a life without God."

"I wonder why it is I can hear these things from you without wanting to take a swing."

"Ain't no future in hittin' an old man. Either he falls down and breaks something and sues you and you wind up poor, or he takes his cane and whacks you upside the head."

"You don't use a cane."

"No, but I ain't aimin' on fallin' down neither, so I guess I'd have to hunt around in the trunk for a crowbar."

"Didn't you ever hear of fighting fair?"

"Fair's a place to take your best animals, son. Don't have nothin' to do with somebody takin' a swipe at you."

"What about turnin' the other cheek?"

"Yeah, well, I oughtta work harder on that one. And I'm meanin' to, I truly am. Question is, do you wanna risk findin' yourself up against a cantankerous old man with a shovel 'stead of a meek Christian with a sore cheek?"

They stopped on the other side of Richmond for gas. Duncan emerged from the station to find Jeremy kicking clods and looking downcast. He walked over, asked if something was the matter.

"Wasn't gonna say anything until this evenin'. Didn't want to trouble you right off, but it just won't leave me alone. It don't seem right, startin' off without gettin' this settled."

Duncan leaned against a rusting oil drum, said, "Fire away."

Jeremy kept his eyes on his work-scuffed boots. "I ain't gonna do anything but ask, son. Can't twist a body's arm and have it come to any good. Not about this. But I gotta at least ask. That all right with you?"

Duncan shrugged. "It might be if I knew what you were talking about."

"Son, I know you're not of the believin' sort, but what we got ourselves here is a miracle. Just think about it, now. We've had a detective drop everything and spend goodness only knows how much time chasin' down something that ain't any business of his at all. Then a man walkin' in darkest night comes right out and tells us where we need to look. And then a young man caught in Satan's net tells us where to go and when."

Jeremy shook his head. "The Lord's at work here. We're workin' at something bigger than any of us can understand. Talkin' among ourselves, pretendin' we know what's goin' on, well, it's like two moles tryin' to guess what an eagle overhead is seein'. I know you don't think about such things like I do, but you gotta admit there's a *chance* that His divine hand's at work here."

Jeremy raised his head. When Duncan held his gaze steady and did not object, he went on. "So what I'm gonna ask is that you accept there's a *chance* I'm right. That He is guidin' us. And on account of that chance that you'll join with me in prayer. Twice a day. Dawn and dusk. Ask for His guidance, open our hearts to Him. On account of this *chance*."

Duncan thought it over, decided that the idea appealed to him for reasons he could not put into words. "Anything you say, Jeremy."

"That's fine, son. That's just fine. What say we bow our heads right here and now and have us a little practice session."

"You mean, get down right here on my knees?"

"No, that won't be necessary. We can just bow our heads, and the Lord'll understand. Gotta tell you though, there ain't any place better on this earth than kneelin' before your Lord in prayer."

Duncan inspected the pavement at his feet as though looking for clues. "I haven't done this in years."

Jeremy suppressed a smile, said, "Do tell."

◆　◆　◆

Anna ignored Bella's closed door, walked in, said, "Girl, what on earth are you doing here?"

Bella did not raise her head. Her desk was covered with three layers of forms and documents and half-finished plans. "I took the day off."

"Lemme see if I got this straight." Anna shut the door behind her, strolled over, said, "You take a day off from a job that demands just about everything you got to give, so you can come down here and work on another job. And this other one's for somebody who's not paying you a cent. Now, does my poor old mind have all that right?"

Bella leaned back, rubbed tired eyes. "I'm not getting a lot of work done here, either."

"Um hmmm." Anna strolled around the room, inspected the frayed calendar from the year before last that still hung above the filing cabinets. "Have a nice time last night, did we?"

Bella sighed. "Wonderful."

"How interesting. And did our Mister Hughes leave today?"

"This morning."

"Ummm. Still gallivanting off to Los Angeles?"

"Last I heard he was, yes."

Holding to that same casual voice, Anna asked, "And did we fall in love last night?"

"I'm too old for that."

"Humph. You can just go hawk that down at the other end of the street, girl." Anna walked over, propped herself on the edge of Bella's desk. "Now ain't that one nice man."

Bella looked up at her. "Don't you have somebody sick and dying downstairs in the infirmary?"

"Naw, it's real quiet. Been a cease-fire called this morning. Everybody's out falling in love. 'Cept me." Anna noticed the embossed pamphlet peeking from the side pocket of Bella's purse, pulled it out, said, "What's this?"

Bella looked over, furrowed her brow in thought. "What's that doing in there? I thought I threw it out."

"So what is it?"

"Just another of those seminars. The Government Contract Managers' Association annual meeting, or something like that."

Anna read down the front page, smiled broadly, said, "Girl, you are not going to miss this one."

Bella snorted, turned back to her work. "That's a laugh.

They're about as interesting as their name. GCMA."

"But, honey, did you see where they're meeting?"

Bella did not look up. "Spend a weekend talking about understanding government form CP 35–82 dash 17 slice A yawn
B. Being wined and dined by a load of hungry sharks who're
out to sell the government another load of thousand-dollar ham-
mers. A total snooze. I've successfully missed it twenty-five
years in a row."

"Bella, sweetie, honey-pie, open your eyes. Los Angeles.
They meet in L.A. the week after next."

"What? Gimme that."

"We ain't talkin' forms, child. We're talkin' *romance*."

"But who'll look after my cats?"

"I will. I'll house sit. Where do you live?"

"Oh, would you?" Her eyes grew wide. "I live in the Olym-
pus. It's a condo complex in Alexandria."

"The suburbs. Hmmm. Lotsa nice men out there in the
sticks. The marrying kind. How long you say you'll be gone?"

Bella read swiftly, said, "The convention lasts just over a
day, but I could probably stretch it to a full weekend."

"No problem. I'll have the whole place checked out by then."
She raised her arms and did a little jig. "Mommas, it's ten
o'clock. Do you know where your boys are?"

◆　　◆　　◆

Jessica never even knew where the second photo shoot took
place. While the guys were downstairs checking out of the hotel
that morning, Arlene bounced around with what she declared
was some really great blow. Jessica held back when Arlene
handed over the coke, said that Pierre might not like her doing
it. Arlene laughed at that, replied, who do you think told me
to come over?

Arlene had green eyes that could turn from soulful to ice
and from ice to fire and back to soulful in a heartbeat, and she
used them against the world of men like a weapon. She discon-
certed, dominated, teased, overwhelmed. She liked to tell Jessica that she had a thirty-year-old mind in a fifteen-year-old
body, and nobody knew whether to go for the mind or the body,
so she was always in control. That was what attracted Jessica
to Arlene the most—her sense of control. Jessica had never felt
in control of anything in her life, especially her body.

Arlene had reddish-blond hair the color of a fiery autumn sunset and the features of a Greek statue Jessica had seen once in a book. Everything was balanced and in perfect proportion. Her eyes were large and painted to look huge. Her hair tumbled in careless disarray down to slim sculptured shoulders. Her breasts were far too big for that slender body, her waist looked small enough to wrap two hands around, and her legs stopped traffic. Literally. When Arlene did her strut across the school parking lot, Jessica in reluctant tow, the entire scene held its breath and watched the parade.

She loved to dress in black. Loved it. According to Arlene, black sucked in all colors and *dominated* them. Her favorite outfit was a black off-the-shoulder skin-tight sweater-dress that stopped *way* above mid-thigh, with black stockings and black fold-down Italian boots and a black beret cocked jauntily over to one side. In that outfit, Arlene could get the guys to follow her everywhere.

She knew all the latest hits long before the sounds ever reached the streets. She could dance as though her body was made of elastic and live wires. On a dance floor she turned so wild that a lot of guys would just shrug their shoulders and walk back to the bar. Don't even look their way, she'd tell Jessica as they stopped to pat their faces and shoulders dry. If they give out so fast on the floor think what they'd be like in private.

She didn't ask Jessica if she wanted to learn how to dance. She simply dragged her into the disco and said, let go. As if it were that simple. Arlene told her, all you need is an unwinder, you're too uptight. So they tried booze, but it just made Jessica sick. Grass put her to sleep and turned her dreams awful. Then they got hold of some crank, and Jessica felt as if she were being reborn every time she touched it to her nose.

Crystal methadrine. Meth to the ones in the know. Crank in a rawer form, ice when refined, a stairway to heaven anytime she took it. Jessica didn't have any hesitation about giving it a try. Why should she? Arlene said it was hot stuff, and Arlene knew more about everything important than anybody Jessica had ever met.

The first time it came in a little plastic capsule like her mother's nerve pills. Arlene opened it up very carefully, said, this is something from another age, but it's all I could find tonight. She wet the end of a match, stuck it in and coated it with crystals that looked like raw sugar. She gave it to Jessica.

Stick that in your nose, honey, and get ready to ride.

The disco floor that night was a magic carpet to never-never land. Jessica watched Arlene and yet had no need to see with her eyes. She *felt* what her friend was going to do with the music, and matched her move for move. A little circle of gawking strangers formed around the edge of the floor, watching the two girls with wings.

Under Arlene's care there were suddenly two Jessicas. The little worm who never felt comfortable with anything about herself was still there most of the time, and she watched Arlene fit her out in super-tight blouses and even tighter pants and crazy little underclothes and Italian shoes, and felt that it was happening to another person. On the weekends, this new Jessica was dressed up and taken out and taught another lesson in how to party.

Coke was okay, except it wore off too fast and the guys who had it were usually a drag. They were older and wore clothes that were out of date before Jessica was born and pretended they were cool because they had a full spoon.

Crack was forbidden, just like skin popping and going full on with the needle. Arlene told her all about what happened to girls who fell in love with the needle. They lose control, Arlene told her time after time. We didn't get this far just to turn it over to a pimp with a needle, right? And Jessica would shake her head and agree, thinking that nobody had ever had a friend as great as Arlene. Nobody.

There was never any real worry about whether it was wrong or not. Why should there be? Her mother was always popping one kind of pill or another. Her father's favorite gesture around the house was shaking the martini mixer, his second favorite opening a bottle of wine.

Her mother had been to Los Angeles, Miami, and New York half a dozen times for face-lifts and tummy-tucks and lyposuctions, and had cheeks stretched so tight that her smiles looked like something off the late-night horror show. Her father, when he was home, which wasn't all that much, walked around the house with a drink in one hand and a cigarette in the other. That was the easiest way for Jessica to tell when her father was around, by the trail of cigarette smoke—that and the arguments and the slammed doors and the maid banging pots in the kitchen.

Coming down was a problem for Jessica. Around dawn her

eyeballs would begin to scratch from the inside and her muscles would twitch a little, like there was this little electric current that was going haywire inside her. She never told anybody, but she sort of felt that it was the new Jessica shedding her wings and turning back into the little worm again.

She never took the pink pills Arlene used. She didn't like taking anything that slowed the world down. She felt like her whole world had been lived in slow motion until she met Arlene. So Saturday mornings she would lie in bed and watch the sky lighten into dawn, and finally fall asleep, and wake up in time for breakfast around seven in the evening. Then it was back out again, ready for another night, and another sleep, and then another Sunday night watching TV and laughing with her best friend over the crazy things that the weekend had held, and saying, yeah, school sure was a drag, and thinking how great it would be to walk the halls the next day as Arlene's best friend.

Arlene always wanted to come over to Jessica's house. She hated her own family and said the place was a zoo. Jessica was too shy to reply, but she thought Arlene's family was great. It was the only thing that she was really jealous of about Arlene. All the rest—the clothes, the looks, the way she attracted the guys—she could admire and enjoy being around. But she envied Arlene her noisy, happy family.

Coming from the tombs of her own home to the loud chaos of Arlene's was like stepping into a dream from her own childhood. There were *people* here, and they *smiled* and *laughed* and *talked* to each other. The only people she talked to at home were the string of maids that never stayed longer than a couple of months. Her father was never home, and her mother never came downstairs except to give orders. Then she paraded from room to room like a queen visiting her domain, before walking out to her club or her coffees or her shopping or her theater or her committees.

Arlene originally told Jessica that her father died when she was a little girl, but one afternoon that spring she showed up at Jessica's house crying so hard she could barely walk and cursing her mother and stepfather with words Jessica had never heard from a girl before.

Arlene had a younger brother from her own dad and two half-sisters from her stepfather. That day Arlene told the other children what she remembered about her father, which wasn't a lot, since he had vanished from her life when she was five. But she embroidered the truth with fantasy until the man was nine feet tall and a prince among men, tall and dashing and always smiling and with pockets full of money.

Arlene's mother would probably not have said anything, since Arlene talked constantly about the father who was no longer there. Only this time she had compared her *real* father with her stepfather, and the stepfather had come out way down the totem pole.

The other kids looked up to Arlenea lot, and before long she had all three, who really loved their father, so upset the house was full of their wails.

Then Arlene's mother took her aside and told her straight up what her father had really been. She said it with the fury of a woman who had been holding it in far too long, and had Arlene crying in no time. Arlene stood there letting her mother shake her back and forth with an iron grip fastened to one arm. Her mother hisssed the truth with biting words into Arlene's face. You think your father was a great man? Well, you're wrong. You're wrong and you're shaming me in front of my own family. Your stepfather is a king among men and you, you haughty little child who's grown too big for her pants, you show him nothing. Your father was a *drunk*, do you hear me? I used to have to throw myself at his feet to keep him from beating you when he had been drinking. You could remember that if you tried, the tears I cried over your little body and the pain I suffered and the screams that made the neighbors call the police at least once a week. The only good thing your father gave me were the two children who I love more than my own life. And now I thank the good Lord I was given a man better than I deserved, who has tried with all his heart to make no difference between the children of his own loins and those I saddled him with. The best thing your father ever did was leave, do you hear me? The happiest day of my life was the morning when I finally allowed myself to accept that he had left me forever.

So Arlene arrived at Jessica's in tears, and Jessica had listened with a sense of delicious horror. Her friend was showing a weaker side, and it gave Jessica a tremendous sense of power, sitting there holding her and letting her cry, listening to her tell truths that were pretty bad, really.

Arlene's stepfather was a milkman. Her mother worked

long hours as a seamstress in a local boutique and made more than her husband. Arlene thought that was about the weakest thing she had ever heard. Didn't the man have any pride? Jessica held her peace and thought that Arlene's stepfather was the nicest, kindest man she had ever met.

Jessica loved the Sambini home. She loved the sense of a family that cared for each other. She loved the noise and the carefree chaotic way the older children watched after the young ones while their parents were at work. She loved the television and the games and the kiddie instruments and the cries and the shouts all going on all at once. Arlene hated it. She would scream at everyone and leave the house in a huff. Jessica liked it, though. Once Arlene started working at the cafe that spring, Jessica started going over to Arlene's house in the afternoons by herself and staying as long as she could.

Arlene's mother called Jessica a little angel when she was there alone, but had the good sense never to refer to it or to Jessica's solitary visits when Arlene was around. The little kids all got to love Jessica. Jessica could spend hours with the little ones on the floor, driving trucks loaded with headless dolls and getting lost in the dream world of a younger time. Arlene's mother loved it when she was there. She said the kids were always on their best behavior when Jessica visited. Jessica would go home on those afternoons happier than she could ever remember.

Following that argument with her mother, things grew steadily worse. Arlene started refusing to be known by her stepfather's name, Sambini. She said it was a wimp name for a wimp kinda guy. She called her stepfather Mister Drip behind his back and to his face. Her stepfather took it as long as he could, then exploded with a fury that terrified everyone in the house except Arlene. Arlene's fights with her stepfather became the talk of the whole neighborhood.

Despite the battles, Arlene's mother loved her, and in the arguments always took Arlene's side. Always. It was the one thing that kept her stepfather from going over the edge, knowing that in the crunch her mother would choose to lose her husband before losing her daughter. This was the basis behind Arlene's strategy, and she made no bones about it with Jessica. She was constantly trying to find a way to push her stepfather into uncontrollable fury, so her mother would throw the bum out of her house and they could get on with their lives. On his part, he tried to ignore Arlene whenever possible, which just drove Arlene further around the bend. Jessica sat on the sidelines of these battles and understood that much. Arlene was courted by everybody but her stepfather. She was called attractive by everybody but her stepfather. She was *wanted* by everybody but this stranger in her own home. Arlene responded by hating him.

Arlene did the things she knew would irk him. That spring he said that his fifteen-year-old daughter was to be in by one in the morning. Arlene yelled back that she wasn't his daughter and then *never* came in by one. Her stepfather would wait up for her, and she could always get him angry and they'd start screaming and wake her mother, who would come out and yell at her husband. Arlene would go on to bed and go to sleep and the next morning go off to school and her mother and stepfather would still be arguing with each other. It was great.

◆　　◆　　◆

That spring Arlene took a job at a new cafe, and Jessica could see it was the beginning of the end. Even Arlene said it, though she put it differently. The second day of her new job she told Jessica, I'm making enough money playing up to those jokers that I can leave home anytime I like.

Her stepfather hated the job and was always after her to quit. Her mother didn't like it, but sensed that if she put her foot down Arlene would use it as an excuse to leave home. So she pleaded and played the shield once more, and finally managed to change her husband's mind. At first Arlene was mildly disappointed that the showdown had been put off, but then decided it really didn't matter anymore. Arlene had found a new world to play with, and it was taking up more and more of her time.

The place was called the Amman Bazaar, and had once been a mid-town kiddie carousel. It jutted out at an odd angle from one of the older department stores, and looked like a round metal tent with a peaked roof. For years it had sat rusting and empty, until a gay couple had taken a long-term lease for a song and sunk their life's savings into making it over.

The open spaces between the metal posts were filled with tinted glass cut to fit the roof's stylish arches.The metal pillars and roof were painted a slate gray to match the color of the glass, so that it looked from the outside like a burnished sphere wearing a pointed hat. In the daytime, passers-by could catch glimpses of shadow figures moving through murky depths. At night, gauze-like drapes were lowered so that while the light spread out from the cafe like a beacon, it was almost impossible to make out who was inside.

The cafe appealed to the older artsy crowd—models, journalists, artists, musicians, night-people, gays, swingers, people skirting the fringe of legality. It was smoky and noisy and almost always full. The floor was polished hardwood, the counter marble and brass, the fittings plush, the music the absolute latest. Arlene's eyes would light up with an excitement Jessica had never seen before whenever she spoke about the Amman Bazaar.

Arlene was a hit from her very first night. The idea of a fifteen-year-old flaunting it all in outfits that were absolutely *made* for a tight young body, yet carrying herself with the assuredness of a woman twice her age, was just kinky enough to appeal to almost everyone. One of the clothing designers began to have her model his latest disco fashions, on the agreement that Arlene would only wear his clothes when on duty. Now she had a chance to flaunt the wildest fashions even before they were in the magazines, much less on the streets. It was a dream come true for Arlene.

The coke Pierre had given Arlene was dynamite; by the time they arrived at the photography studio she and Jessica were halfway to the moon. Pierre rarely used drugs of any kind, but clearly didn't mind it if they did. Chico matched them hit for hit, but showed no change except a slight reddening of his eyes. Jessica found herself terrified of those eyes. They tracked her everywhere. She felt as if they were burrowing under her skin.

The studio was another high-ceilinged loft in another dingy building, up another set of creaking wooden stairs. It was big and well fitted and cold—too cold for walking around in their underclothes, which was what the photographer wanted.

He had a raised section about four feet wide and lit from both sides, like a model's runway, and he wanted them to dress in different kinds of underclothes and walk down it. For starters, anyway. Arlene was too blasted to put up with the photographer's petty demanding manner. She spotted a boom-box in the corner beside his camera gear, raced over and switched it on. The latest hit by INXS filled the room.

Arlene clambered up on the runway and began a wild sort of dance-step down its length. The photographer went crazy, trying to set up and act as though he were still in control of everything and shoot her from a dozen different angles at once. She kept calling for Jessica to come up there and join her.

"I can't," she replied. "It's too cold."

"Not after you start moving," Arlene called down, then jumped off and ran over.

Jessica let herself be pulled up on stage. Arlene stripped off Jessica's sweater, unwrapped her arms from around her front, and started dancing a swaying rhythm still holding on to Jessica's hands. The photographer loved it. Jessica found herself warming up, glanced over to find Pierre smiling at her. That was nice. He almost never smiled. Jessica raised her arms and tried to match Arlene's swaying dance, sure that it must be all right if it made Pierre smile.

CHAPTER
7

Jeremy awoke to the sound of birdsong and the faint rustlings of a strange house. He lay with his eyes shut, trying to orient himself, working to remember where he was. Murfreesboro, Tennessee. Yes. It was the fourth morning of their trip. They were making a snail's pace across the country, but there was no need for speed, since the girls they sought were not scheduled to arrive in Los Angeles for another two weeks.

Prior to their departure and then several more times after they had gotten underway, Duncan had spent uncounted hours working with detailed maps and patient long-distance operators. He tried to locate the two other names Julius had given to Jeremy, both inside the cities and in the surrounding suburbs. But he had no success, and calls placed through Detective Larson to the local police had also turned up nothing. So there had been little reason for them to rush anywhere.

The friends of Mrs. Broyhill in Danville had passed them on to friends in Johnson City, Tennessee; they in turn knew of a church family in Murfreesboro who would be happy to take them in for the night. Already this family had called ahead and arranged for them to be hosted tonight by friends of theirs in Poplar Bluff, Missouri. Jeremy stepped around Duncan's indecision by accepting with polite thanks, wondering all the time what hand, if any, was guiding them. Their meandering way took them along the old two-lane highway system, through the hearts of slow-moving towns where the twenty-five-mile-per-hour speed limit gave the pedestrians time to spot their out-of-state license plates and give them gentle waves of greeting.

Jeremy reached for the Bible left on the nightstand the night before, but did not open it. He was not the type of man made for traveling, and this shifting to a different bed every night left him unsettled. Several times a day he found himself wishing he were back in Washington among the newly familiar faces and recently acquired habits. But every time the desire rose to throw in the towel, call it quits on the whole silly business and let Duncan take this mission on alone, memories would arise of the stranger in the night and the impression left in his heart by the two songs.

There she was again, Ella's voice sounding in his mind and heart as clear as a bell. Jeremy set the unopened Bible on his chest, gave in to the feeling of lying in bed on a soft summer Sunday morning, back before his wife had died from cancer. He would lie there stretched out with all the pillows behind his head and a full cup of coffee beside him, the Bible opened and unread in his lap. It was the only time of the week when Jeremy could slow down and not feel guilty. He would sit there and watch the sunlight dance through the leaves outside his window and make speckled patterns on the bedroom's hardwood floor, and listen to Ella make herself ready for church. When she was happy, Ella always kept herself company with song.

It was such a joy to be able to feel her close like this, without the heartache that had burdened his years since her death. He could remember her now with clarity and fondness, and know that here was a gift beyond human understanding. The questions all faded in the light of this simple gift of love.

The song in his mind was replaced by the voices of children awakening to a new day. Jeremy sighed and swung his feet to the floor. He had no idea why he was being called to traipse all the way across this wide nation, or keep this unwashed man company, or take this wandering path that was set before them. The state of his heart left him with no room to doubt.

"It was certainly a pleasure to have you join us, Jeremy. You too, Duncan. My wife and I were talking about it last night. We admire you for what you're doing, that is, the little we know about it."

His wife chimed in with, "All these problems we're facing, it's so easy to just shrug your shoulders and think, well, there's nothing we can do so we might as well not try. Then we see two gentlemen like you, taking off and going after a couple of runaways. It makes us feel like maybe we can do a little something after all."

"Times when I start feelin' like the world's problems are gonna swallow me whole," Jeremy said, slamming the trunk of the car shut, "I like to think about the fourth chapter of Revelation where it says, 'I was taken to the throne room, the seat of power. And it was not empty.' "

Jeremy studied the sidewalk at his feet, thought of his moment of doubt that morning, nodded his head slowly. "All we have to do is to seek out God's power and let Him show us the way to use it. That same chapter in Revelation, the elders take their crowns off and set them before the throne. They recognize, see, that all power, no matter how great, is granted to them by God and for a purpose. It is His power, not ours, and His will that we need to do with it. The first sin of power is to try and keep it. The second is to try and use it for our own purposes."

The man nodded his head slowly. "I've stayed awake most of the night feeling like you were brought here for a purpose. I don't know what it was, maybe just to show us that steps like yours really can make a difference."

"It's hard not to despair sometimes," the woman said, "listening to the news and thinking that this is the world that I'm sending my children out into."

"What saves us is not worryin' nor waverin'," Jeremy said, knowing the words were meant as much for him as for the others.

The man smiled grimly. "That's all there is to it?"

"Didn't say it was easy, now, did I? I just said it was the answer."

Once they had found their way out of town Duncan said to him, "What are you, some kind of super-intelligence?"

Jeremy shook his head. "My IQ's just one step ahead of a grain of salt."

"So how do you know so much of the Bible like that off the top of your head?"

"Simple case of dire need. Only thing that keeps me goin' sometimes is findin' that verse that speaks to my heart."

Duncan gave his passenger a quick glance, asked, "What are you smiling about over there?"

"Oh, nothin' much, son. Nothin' much. Just thinkin' 'bout a little lesson I learned this mornin'."

"You've been grinning like a Cheshire cat ever since we got under way."

"Been thinking 'bout my wife, Ella. Woke up hearin' a song she used to sing on Sundays."

"I didn't know you were married."

"She died almost twelve years ago."

"Oh. I'm sorry to hear that."

"Thank you, son. She was a fine woman. Always felt like God gave me the chance to share a few days with her just so I could know a taste of what His love must surely be."

Duncan found himself thinking of his own wife, and the fights that had scarred their last few years together. He pushed the thoughts aside. "Seems to me like there's not a thing in life you can be sure of."

"Well, I don't know how to say this any way 'cept straight out, but you're wrong. There's two things you can bet your bottom dollar on, son. The first is that Jesus Christ reigns in heaven and wants you there beside Him."

Duncan gave a noncommital nod. "And the second?"

"The second is that you ain't gonna ever hear me sing. Nossir. There's no limit to how loud I can go, but it don't seem to help. When I sing, the paint just peels off the walls. It's a tragic sight, so I try real hard to resist temptation." Jeremy shook his head. "Lord's gonna have some major transformations on His hands before any angelic choir's gonna let me in the back door."

"But your wife used to sing, is that right?"

"Ella had enough talent for both of us. She could make the mockingbirds turn green with envy. Always had this way of putting love into her words, man, she could quiet a room of kids with her voice faster than with a bowl of salt-water taffy."

"What'd she sing?"

"Old-time hymns, mostly." Jeremy leaned his head against the back of the seat, closed his eyes, droned in the voice of a man who could not hold a tune:

"O to grace how great a debtor
Daily I'm constrained to be!
Let thy grace, Lord, like a fetter
Bind my wand'ring heart to thee."

"You must have really been in love," Duncan said.

"That I was, son. That I was. First argument we ever had was the night we got engaged, ain't that just typical? The church was havin' one of them box dinners, you probably never heard of that. Well sir, each of the ladies would fix up this nice little picnic dinner for two, then they got up on the stage and the pastor auctioned them off. Highest bidder got to eat dinner with the lady, and all the money went to charity.

"I was 'bout as broke as a boy could be, so naturally I didn't have any business bein' there. Couldn't help myself, though. By that time I was followin' Ella around like a little puppy dog. She did the best she could, and got away from the fellow who bought her dinner fast as she was able. But I was just a dumb kid and couldn't help myself, I guess. I was so jealous of that other fellow with his deep pockets and nice suit and all I couldn't hardly see straight. So I lit right into Ella."

"Mistake," Duncan guessed.

"Son, you just said a mouthful." Jeremy chuckled at the memory. "That little lady tore a chunk outta my hide so big you could drive a tractor through. Told me if I was gonna make such a fuss over her bein' with other men, then I'd better ask her to marry me and get it over with. Which I proceeded to do. Almost shouted it out."

"Which was exactly what she wanted you to do in the first place," Duncan said.

"Prob'ly. She always told me it took her as much by surprise as it did me, and she was just too mad to back down then. But that was one smart woman, and I always figured she saw me for a stumblin' bumpkin who'd take years to work around to it by myself. Lord only knows what she saw in me, but she'd set her cap and just decided she was gonna have to stir things up a bit. Or so I always figured."

They drove in comfortable silence for a while, then Duncan said, "Praying with you is getting to be easier."

"I'm glad to hear that, I truly am."

"At first it was like all I could do was keep from cringing when you started in. But this morning, I dunno, I thought it was okay. I can't say I'm looking forward to it or anything, you understand. But it was okay."

Jeremy looked at him, a faint smile playing across his face, said, "You know how God sees prayer? It is perfume to His nostrils. Says it right there in the fifth chapter of Revelation. It rests in a golden bowl in the center of His throne room, right there in His presence, and fills His throne room with the fragrance of incense."

Duncan took his time chewing that one over, working with the sensation of something unseen tugging at the doors to his heart. He drove the massive Lincoln around curve after curve; the road was kept to a gentle slope only by having its way blasted through steep-sided hills. Bare rock gleamed white and veined, crowned by untamed crops of ancient pines. Overhead the sky gleamed blue and unending, the sort of sky that drew the gaze up and up and into thoughts as deep as Jeremy's words.

Finally Duncan replied, "It's not that I've got anything against your religion, you know, I don't want to offend you."

"Don't you worry about that," Jeremy replied. "Any man who's willin' to listen to what I say, especially if he don't agree, and give me honesty in return, deserves nothin' less than my full respect."

"I just don't see any need for it. I mean, if that's what you need to see you through the day, hey, go for it. But I'm doing okay on my own."

Jeremy stretched out his long legs. "Life's got a way of handin' out surprises, son. It's an awful good feelin' to know you've got a friend on your side, somebody who can see around the corners and help you deal with what's up ahead."

◆ ◆ ◆

No matter how often he stood before television cameras, Senator Atterly never escaped the clench of nervous tension. Radio did not cause it, nor newspaper reporters, nor the largest crowds. But there was something unrelenting about the fierce halogen lights, the shadowless environment, the cameras positioned to record his every word, his every gesture, his every breath. It was the only time in his political life when Atterly did not feel able to shoot straight from the hip. It was also one of the few times when he knew he could not draw on that still small voice. There wasn't time, there wasn't *space*. The camera's eye watched him relentlessly.

The program director was an old acquaintance, a man who strove to maintain faith as his central theme regardless of the pressures television and fame placed upon him. The program itself was beamed nationwide, one of the most widely viewed Christian programs in the country. Once prayerful study had

assured him that this was what the Lord intended, Senator
Atterly knew that this was the place where the announcement
needed to be made. Much as he disliked television and loathed
being on the air, there was not time to get the message out in
any other way.

The program director was a handsome man, his craggy features marred neither by the makeup nor by the sharp-edged
lights. He showed a carefully relaxed attitude that Senator Atterly greatly admired. Around them was a constant scurrying
of hectic activity as the minutes counted down. In a distant
corner Nak and Reverend Wilkins were bowed with a contin-
gent of people they had brought for prayer support. When not
otherwise occupied, Atterly kept his eyes on them. It helped to
still his nerves and keep him from doubting again.

"Wish you had given us more time on this, Senator," the
program director said, immune to the frantic swirl of voices and
people and lights and cables and cameras. "We could have
worked this into our regular broadcasts as a recurring theme,
drummed up a good deal more support."

"It's all the time we have," Atterly replied briefly. To say more
would open up the floodgates to his own internal worries. He had
gone through that too often and too long to gain anything from
another dose. "If we are going to match this effort with the anti-
pornography legislation, then the timing is crucial."

"I understand," the program director said calmly. "How
many churches did you say are involved?"

"Somewhere over fifty, I'm not quite sure." This had been
handled entirely by Wilkins, who had spent the past four days
and nights drumming up support among the D.C. churches.

The program director gave him a knowing look. "I imagine
a number of them were reluctant to put their name to something thrown together overnight. That's probably why you're
not getting clear responses from some of them."

"That's not exactly been the case." Quite the contrary, as a
matter of fact. Reverend Wilkins had initially made up a list
of only fifteen churches, which was all he thought he could cover
personally in four days. He felt that personal contact would be
crucial with this first effort. To their surprise, all fifteen
churches had jumped at the chance to involve themselves in
the program. All fifteen. It had appeared as though they were
all waiting for the opportunity to do something.

There were friends and acquaintances and organizations

these ministers wanted to tie in, have Nak or the senator or Wilkins contact, or call themselves for support. There were existing in-church ministries who wanted to work with them. There were other ministers who heard of it through a friend or a colleague or someone who knew someone who had heard about it through some discussion, and wanted to know why they hadn't been contacted and what could they do.

All that had helped to strengthen their resolve, and give reassurance to what had seemed so solid and correct in their time of prayer. But it could not lessen the risk they were taking, especially for Senator Atterly. He was too old a hand at the political arena to paper over what this action would probably mean to his career.

"All right, Senator," the program director said, pointing through the control booth glass to the man giving them the high sign. "It seems they're ready for you."

They approached the small podium, and the program director went through it one more time. "I will say just a few words of introduction, apologizing for the break in normal programming, and then hand it over to you. There's a clock right over there beyond the second camera. You're sure you can do this in six minutes?"

"I'm sure." Atterly searched the relative darkness beyond the lights, located the tightly clenched prayer circle, felt reassured.

The camera's ready light came on in time to the second high sign from the control room. The program director gave the camera his professional smile, said, "We interrupt our regularly scheduled broadcast for a special message from the United States senator from Rhode Island, Richard Atterly. I have known Senator Atterly for more than twenty years, and as anyone who has worked with him will attest, he is both a fine Christian and a hard-working member of our government. Senator Atterly has requested this time to speak with you about something of considerable importance to each and every one of us, something of vital concern to our nation as a whole. I ask that you please give him your undivided attention. Ladies and gentlemen, Senator Atterly."

"Thank you." Atterly allowed himself to be ushered in behind the podium, glanced at the notes he knew he would not need, forced himself to stare unblinkingly into the camera's relentless eye, and began.

"For several months a small group of senators and congressmen have been battling for legislation that would virtually out-law pornography in America. We are seeking to eradicate this evil unconditionally, a goal that has never been attempted be-fore. I am here to tell you tonight that if things continue as they are at present, our efforts will fail, and the bill will die on the House floor.

"For that reason, after long and careful prayer, I am coming here before you to ask that we as a nation call for a Solemn Assembly. The reason is simple. How many other evils lurk beneath the depths of this activity—lust, greed, exploitation, depravity? How long will it be before God deals with such evil? It is time for us to take unequivocal action, before the right of action is taken from us.

"We as a nation have bought into the idea that because the church is protected, the nation is protected. My friends, this is simply not true. Nor is it true that we may blur the lines be-tween God's people and Satan's world. We have only to look around us to see the devastating results that arise from closing our eyes to the growth of evil within our society.

"In the book of Joel, the Lord is planning a famine of pun-ishment. Yet He changes His mind, and says instead that a revival will take place. Why? What makes the difference?

"The answer is a Solemn Assembly. The root word means a setting apart, a shutting off. We as the family of God are called to shut off our contact with all our worldly affairs and focus on what God has to say to His people. It is a holy convocation, when His people are called forth to set aside their daily lives and focus upon their Lord and Savior.

"In Israel of old, a man of faith had no choice. When a Sol-emn Assembly was called, *everyone* was ordered to attend. In the second chapter of Joel the Lord instructs a nursing mother to come and bring her child, and a honeymooning couple to come home. They are extreme examples, used to show that no one was exempt from the call, that no excuse was acceptable.

"This cannot be a sideline activity. In the twenty-third chap-ter of Leviticus the Lord says that it is *expected* to cost us to attend a Solemn Assembly. It must be a total involvement of the heart. It is a time to be serious at the deepest possible level.

"Be forewarned, however. This is not to be an experience-centered event. We are not called to come together and be worked to a fever pitch by a high-powered evangelist. This is not a mardi gras celebration. It is a time of prayerfully asking for the Lord to show us, as individuals and as a nation, any darkness in our hearts. We are to be humbled before our God. We are to be impacted with the weight of our own and our nation's sin. And by allowing ourselves to be confronted in this way, by seeing the sin in our lives and in our nation for what it is, we will be *forgiven*. We will truly know His mercy. We will cry out to God, and He will *answer* us.

"The Bible is clear in telling us what will occur if we are sincere in our motives. There will be solemn affirmations, covenants drawn between us and our Lord. There will be Sovereign visitations. When God sees His people gather with a genuine desire to seek His face, does anyone truly believe that He will remain silent? He will give us His abiding Presence. He will be in the midst of us. He will be our Lord, and we will be His people."

Senator Atterly paused to wipe at the sweat trickling down his temples. "The Lord will not endure forever the sins of His church and our nation. We must restore the testimony of Christ. We must place His Son at the center of our lives. We must focus our attention on Him.

"I am therefore calling a Solemn Assembly of our nation to take place in Washington, D.C., two weeks from this coming Thursday. I urge you all to search your hearts, ask yourselves if this is not something that calls you to attend, to return with us to a state of expectation.

"According to the Bible, there are five purposes to a Solemn Assembly, all five of which are important to us now. First of all, it is to be a time of *unity*. We are called to gather together as one body united in faith and desire to release ourselves from the taint of evil.

"Second, it is a time of *corporate confession*. In the ninth chapter of Ezra, we see a nation stained by the sins of the people. There is a stench in the holy of holies by what has been done. We as a nation need to come together and beg forgiveness from our Lord.

"Third, it is a time of *personal repentance*. In the second chapter of Joel, the Lord tells His people not to tear our garments, but rather to rend our hearts. We are to allow ourselves to be broken of pride. We are to recognize the barriers that separate us from our Creator, and repent of them.

"Fourth, we shall seek to *avoid God's judgment*. Time after time we are warned, if we as a nation do not repent of our sins, we shall be destroyed. Our nation will be turned to ashes. We must therefore take the option that He allows, that He *begs* us to take. We are to repent, and we are to receive His forgiveness.

"And finally, there shall be a *spiritual renewal*. This is our Lord's goal. This is why throughout the Scriptures He calls His people to assemble. He *wants* to redeem us. He wants to give us His blessings. If we will only ask, He will be zealous for His land and His people. He will pour out His blessings on us. That is His solemn promise.

"The Solemn Assembly is to begin in seventeen days, at noon, and end on Saturday morning after a city-wide worship service throughout Washington. That will give those of you who travel from distant areas, as I hope and pray you will, time to return home and begin your week on schedule. Thursday is the day Congress is expected to vote on the anti-pornography bill. It is my fervent prayer that by demonstrating before this government the power of faith, the course of our nation will be altered, beginning with this specific legislation.

"The number of churches and civic organizations who have offered their support is growing by the hour. A partial list will be shown at the close of this broadcast. We are working to organize housing for all who would prefer not, or who cannot afford, to stay in hotels. Food will be supplied. Welcome stations will be opened around the city. Organization will be haphazard, as this call has only come to us in the past few days. We will need your help, we will need your prayers.

"It is a time of crucial importance to us, as a nation and as a people seeking to follow our Lord's will. A crossroads has been reached, and our actions will determine the course of our nation for decades to come. This above all else has been the recurring message that has resounded through my mind and heart as I pray through this call. I humbly beg all of you, all my brothers and sisters in Christ, to heed this call, and gather with us for our Solemn Assembly."

◆   ◆   ◆

Jeremy sat still and silent as their host for the night walked over to the television set and video recorder, pressed the eject button, drew the tape from the machine, and labelled it. "I like to record all his shows," he explained to their guests. "There's a lot of things I find I can use in my Sunday school classes."

The family noticed Jeremy's quietness, but being good hosts

they talked around it. Thankfully, Duncan was there to pick up the slack. Jeremy sat and stared at the dark screen, and wondered about what he had seen.

The Senator had clearly been uncomfortable with what he was saying. Jeremy knew enough about politics to know that the Senator's normal demeanor was absent from that speech. Yet there had been such a *power* there. Such an *appeal*. He had been caught up in it, and so had the rest of the room. The others had remained totally silent throughout; even the family's two teenagers had been still as statues.

Jeremy recalled the perspiration that had traced its way down the side of Senator Atterly's face, and realized it was not just nerves over the speech that made it hard for the man to speak. No. It was also that the Senator knew just exactly what reaction he could expect from his colleagues for making such an appeal. Calling for an assembly the likes of which had not been seen for over two thousand years. Playing the Biblical patriarch to a society wrapped in a blanket of self-gratification. The senator could very well have been committing political suicide, and he knew it.

There was a lesson here for Jeremy. He sat, feeling miles away from the talk that swirled around him, and knew that there was something here for him to learn. If the senator was willing to put a lifetime's work on the line, Jeremy should certainly be able to overcome his shyness enough to help spread the word. He knew that was what he was being called to do— as much as he hated being in front of people, as aware as he was of his own shortcomings and lack of education. It was what he was called to do.

Yet what was he to say? The instant the question appeared in his mind, the answer was there waiting. Tell a story. That was all. Instead of weaving his tale for a few close friends, he would tell it for the family of God, with whomever he was brought into contact.

Jeremy turned to face his hosts, and the conversation died around him. "Seems to me we might ought to tell you the whole story of what's got us chasin' across the country, instead of just a couple of little bits and pieces," he said. He began telling the story of their hunt for Jessica and Arlene. He told it from the beginning, right from the moment he met the stranger on the streets.

And he told it well.

CHAPTER
8

"The divorce thing is going to hurt us this election," Mark Zimmerman said. "And TJ Case isn't here to help us out this time."

"My divorce should be finalized before things start heating up," Silverwood replied. He sat in his office with Bobby, his number-one assistant, and Zimmerman, his campaign manager. It was thirteen months to the next election—congressmen must be reelected every two years—and time for the first strategy meeting.

"Doesn't matter," Zimmerman replied. "It'll still be fresh in the voters' minds. And if it isn't, your opponent's gonna try his dead-level best to put it there."

Zimmerman was in his early thirties, the owner of a regional public relations firm and a professed addict of the campaign fervor. He had kinky blond hair, pale blue eyes, and a narrow face that still bore the marks of adolescent acne. He was an energetic man, sitting while other people lay down, standing while others remained seated, running while others walked. His perpetual accessory was a battered leather briefcase that he called his Pandora's Box and always kept close to his side.

Zimmerman glanced over his shoulder to make sure the door was closed, but paid Bobby no mind. In Zimmerman's presence Bobby remained the silent shadow, there to do Silverwood's bidding, never offering a single word or gesture or even facial expression to show his sentiments. Silverwood knew from half-spoken asides that his assistant did not care for Zimmerman at all. But Bobby was loyal to his boss, and if Silverwood chose to remain with the man who had brought him successfully through the first campaign battle, then Bobby would live with it.

Zimmerman leaned forward and said in what friends and foes alike called his cloak-and-dagger voice, "Good thing we've got big money backing you this time. We're going to need it."

The reason for those funds brought up a feeling of revulsion in Silverwood. "Do we have to be going over this stuff already?"

"Already?" Zimmerman reached inside his briefcase and brought out a stack of heavy cardboard advertising mock-ups. "We can't do this often enough. C'mon, John, rule number one in politics—the campaign is never over."

Silverwood clenched his jaw muscles, willed himself to pay attention. It was hard, though. Hard to accept the financial assistance, harder every day to care at all.

He had been framed soon after his arrival in Washington. He had essentially traded his integrity for a seat on the Ways and Means Committee, the most powerful in Congress. At the time it had seemed an offer impossible to refuse, a reward of untold power to a freshman congressman in return for simply looking the other way. But as time went on the hold he had granted these men with their hidden agendas tightened like a noose around his political aspirations, until now it was hard to remember ever wanting anything as badly as he had desired entry into Washington politics.

"These are the latest ads from Madison Avenue," Zimmerman said, spreading out the mock-ups on Silverwood's desk like a card-shark dealing his deck. "I think they've done a fine job. We're targeting these for the Sunday supplements in all the local papers."

"Looks good," Silverwood murmured, having trouble focusing on his own smiling image.

"We'll run them every other week starting next summer, and continue right up to election day." Zimmerman leaned back, clearly proud of his work. "We're lucky this primary is a nonissue. What, some retired pharmacist from Selma, isn't that right? Served six terms on the school board, now he's got the hots for the big time. Not a chance."

Silverwood nodded agreement, said, "I'd like to keep that primary as friendly as possible."

"Friendly?" Zimmerman was shocked. "Sure, if all we had to worry about was the Republicans. You're the one with the party backing, and the bucks. This guy's out in Siberia. But don't forget, it's the primary that sets the stage for the contest in November. You've already given the Democrats a big stick with this divorce. They need to see that you can hit back hard before the battle's even started."

Silverwood noticed Bobby watching him and wondered if his assistant could see the struggle he was having not to sweep the mock-ups off his desk and throw Zimmerman out of the room. It was all so meaningless, his power reduced to a charade of empty motions, and it was his own fault.

It did not matter how he raged at the fate that had trapped him inside the chains of another group's ambitions. Nor did it matter that the group had not requested his help or even asked to meet with him since the first incident had been settled seven months ago. No matter how much freedom they allowed him, no matter how much time elapsed between their calls, he knew that someday, sometime the call would come for him to render another service. The weight of waiting for that day threatened to send him crashing to the earth, immobile under its burden.

"The party's sure been generous this year," Zimmerman went on. "Looks like they've got big plans in store for Congressman Silverwood."

It wasn't party funds. Silverwood knew that. It was funds from his invisible backers, paid out in a stream they diverted from shady dealings that he himself had helped to perpetuate.

This financial assistance carried a price tag, one which he would continue to pay so long as he stayed in office. Worrying about his reelection only served to show how trapped he was, how powerless, how alone.

Zimmerman rose from his chair, gathered the mock-ups and stowed them away in his case. "And the really good news is we're gonna have a budget for television shots. A full two months leading up to the election. Gonna get the boys in New York working on that right after Christmas."

He stuck out his hand. "Sure is nice working for a candidate with a bottomless pocket."

Silverwood watched Bobby usher Zimmerman out, motioned for his assistant to close the door and leave him alone. He leaned his head back on his seat, closed his eyes, wondered how he could be so exhausted at ten o'clock in the morning.

He had a sudden vision of an endless treadmill, a lifetime of shaking hands, smiling for photo opportunities, mouthing words to a television camera, and speaking at chicken dinners. It was so empty now, so futile, so void of meaning.

The thought struck him with a power strong enough to eject him from his chair. He reached for the telephone, dialed a number, said, "This is John Silverwood. Is Senator Atterly available?"

"No, sir, I'm sorry, Congressman," his secretary replied. "He's just left to sit in on a Judiciary Subcommittee hearing over in Dirksen."

Silverwood searched his Daily Record, asked, "Would that be the one on S–1422?"

"The Per Se Anti-Porn bill, yessir. Today's the final hearing, and the senator wanted to make an appearance, since he's decided to back it."

Silverwood thanked her, hung up, moved for the door. If he hurried perhaps he could speak with him before the hearing started.

The Dirksen Senate Office Building was linked to the Hart building, where Atterly's offices were located, by a hallway in continuous transition. Hart was new and white marble and spartan and modern and had a three-story atrium that gave an impression of a luxury hotel lobby; walking the connecting hallway always gave Atterly the feeling of passing from one Hollywood movie set to another. Where Hart was cool and smooth and airy and light-filled, Dirksen was saggy and dull. Linoleum-lined hallways were adorned with brown wooden doors and dim yellow lights and drably painted walls. It carried the weight of years with visible fatigue.

It was very unusual for a senior senator, with so many obligations and committee assignments of his own, to attend a hearing for which he had no direct responsibility. There was no need for Atterly to make an official statement. His appearance alone would be sufficient to announce in unequivocal terms his full backing of this measure.

Through the double doors Atterly saw that the hearing had not started on time. People milled around the semi-circular rows of wooden seats, clustering at the clerk's desk, reaching for documents related to the hearing, talking softly among themselves. Toward the back a television crew was putting a camera in place.

"Senator Atterly," a voice called from back down the hall. Atterly turned to see Silverwood hurrying toward him. The closer he came, the more clearly his face bore the burden of some internal struggle.

Atterly felt a sudden urge to rush the man over to one side and shake some sense into him. Instead he said in greeting, "John, you look like death."

"I was wondering if I could talk to you."

"What about?"

For a moment the man looked uncertain, almost fearful, before his resolve strengthened. "I've been thinking about what you said to me the other day."

Atterly inspected his face a moment, and the coldness evaporated. "I'm supposed to catch a plane back to Providence for a series of meetings just as soon as this hearing is over. If you can't wait until I get back tomorrow, though, I'll put the trip off."

"I can wait."

"You sure? I wouldn't want to have anything this important on my conscience."

"What time?"

"Seven o'clock tomorrow evening, my office?"

"I'll be there." Silverwood turned and walked down the hall on legs that seemed barely able to support his weight. Atterly watched until the man had disappeared around the corner, then turned and entered the hearing room.

As the nervously eager aide led him to his seat, Atterly spotted Harvey Biggs speaking in low urgent tones with a man he did not know. It was the first time he had seen Biggs since overhearing his conversation in the restaurant; the sight of the man left his body cold.

He sat, nodded his thanks to the obsequious aide, noticing the excited reaction his appearance was causing at the press table. He pointedly ignored the whispers and stares and focused on the committee dais as the chairman introduced the first speaker. It was the man he had seen talking to Harvey Biggs; he was identified by the committee chairman as the legislative counsel to the ACLU, the American Civil Liberties Union. Atterly leaned forward in his seat and concentrated on the man's speech:

Mr. Chairman and Members of the Subcommittee:
    The American Civil Liberties Union is a national, nonpartisan membership organization with approximately

250,000 members dedicated to the preservation and enhancement of the principles embodied in the Bill of Rights of our Constitution.

It is no secret that the American Civil Liberties Union is opposed to "obscenity laws," believing that such efforts to carve out an exception to the First Amendment for certain sexually oriented communications are damaging to the concept of free expression. . . .

Although it is true that not every use of words or pictures triggers the protection of the First Amendment, only in the area of "sexual speech" (pornography is nothing more than speech—words and pictures—about sex) has the Supreme Court permitted legislatures to suppress material on the basis of "offensiveness" to the majority or its lack of "serious" value. Is the Supreme Court right? To the ACLU, the answer is clearly "no". . . .

The underlying presupposition that there is a difference between sexually oriented speech and all other kinds of speech is completely unwarranted. In fact, sexually explicit material fulfills the traditional functions of speech: transmitting ideas, promoting self-realization, and serving as a "safety valve" for both the speaker and the audience. It is also clearly considered socially useful by many consumers (who spend billions of dollars each year on the material), although it should be repeated that the element of social utility is not a requirement, in other contexts, for First Amendment protection of expression.

That sexually explicit speech transmits ideas can hardly be doubted. Indeed, the messages of pornography are often far from subtle. To the extent that pornography depicts sexual activity in nearly clinical detail, it can be educational. It shows what people can do and how to do it. It can also suggest that the kind of sexual activity depicted is worth doing, or at least worth watching. Even with regard to less frequently practiced sexual activities, pornography sometimes portrays as contextually desirable those activities which, when considered more abstractly, might seem unpleasant.

Pornography may also have as its purpose or effect the promotion of a political or ideological viewpoint. Those feminists who criticize pornography as sex discrimination because it legitimizes or eroticizes sexual inequality are accurately perceiving the message of some pornographic material. Surely much pornography does represent male anger toward women and seeks to humiliate women by portraying them as submissive and unprotected. That kind of message is quintessentially political and concerns the distribution and use of power in social relationships. . . .

Although the prevalence of this idea is unfortunate, the political nature of this message, and pornography's allegedly effective role in conveying it, would at least undercut any argument that pornography does not express important political ideas. . . .

In addition to transmitting messages, pornography also fulfills a second function that is often asserted as a justification for freedom of speech. This function is sometimes characterized as "the achievement of self-realization," the "fostering of individual self-expression," or "self-fulfillment." It represents an urge to create, validate or respond to one's feelings even if this is not intended to have any persuasive effect on others. This function has a dual value, serving not only the speaker, but also the viewer, reader, or listener. Indeed, it is important to recall that the First Amendment is designed to protect both those seeking to communicate and those wishing to receive information and ideas. . . .

The social message of certain sexually explicit material may be viewed by some people, particularly those in sexual minorities, as beneficial to their self-identity and self-understanding. . . . Acknowledgment of the sexual diversity of our society can be an important step toward a healthier overall understanding of human sexuality. . . .

A third function of free expression that pornography may sometimes fulfill, just as other speech does, can be described as a "safety valve" role. An audience may find some material useful as a cathartic substitute for antisocial activity. . . .

[You] have stemmed the possibility of any real marketplace of sexual ideas and images from emerging, by having governmental regulation link arms with moral mob rule to change 'apetites' by coercion, not choice . . .

The First Amendment works because it works for everyone and everything. As soon as a hierarchy of ideas is postulated—some to be protected more than others—grave damage has been done. . . .[1]

[1]These are verbatim excerpts from: (A) U.S. Senate Committee on the Judiciary, Hearing on S. 703 and S. 2033, child Protection and Obscenity Enforcement Act, and Pornography Victims Protection Act of 1987, statements by Barry Lynn of the American Civil Liberties Union, pp. 167, 168, 170; and (B) Lynn, Barry. "Polluting the Censorship Debate—A Summary and Critique of the Final Report of the Attorney General's Commission on Pornography." *American Civil Liberties Union Public Policy Report*, July, 1986, pp. 29–37, pp. 109–110.

Atterly pulled out a pen and used an envelope from his coat
pocket to make terse notes in a spiked illegible scrawl. The
committee chairman thanked the ACLU legislative counsel,
then invited a woman Atterly had never heard of before to come
forward. He raised his head and saw a stirring among the staffers lining the wall behind the committee members. There was
a sense of rising anticipation, especially among the conservative senators and their aides. Something big was coming here,
something intentionally set as a direct rebuttal to the ACLU's
position. Atterly leaned forward as the woman began to speak:

We hear so often that pornography is a victimless crime.
Perhaps my story will help to convince some of these people
who may believe this that it is not true. The fact is, pornography has many victims. It not only victimizes those
who are caught in the sordid world of murder, rape, drugs
and prostitution, but it victimizes the innocent children and
those of us who feel that our lives will never be touched by
these people who are part of a world that we do not know
and have never been associated with.

The unfortunate facts are, however, that we are not safe
from these people. At some point in your life, you or a loved
one, a special friend or acquaintance will most likely become a victim. This is why we have to convince those who
say pornography is a victimless crime that it is not so. Let
me tell you about a beautiful 22-year-old college student
who had her whole life ahead—my daughter, Linda Dan-
iels.

Linda was a petite 5-foot, 2-inch blue-eyed natural
blond. From the time she was just a little girl she loved to
read and go to school, listen to music, and she loved cats.
Linda was very bright and was identified in school as gifted
and talented. She was above average and capable of doing
anything she set her mind to do. She was a varsity cheerleader for three years in high school, carried a 4.0 grade
point average, and had earned three college credits before
graduating from high school.

Linda attended Colorado State University for two years
before transferring to the University of New Mexico in Albuquerque in January 1985, where she wanted to major in
anthropology. She was extremely happy at UNM and had
made many friends; she met a wonderful boyfriend and
planned to be married after graduation.

Linda had been home for Christmas just three weeks

before her abduction. We had a great time at Christmas. She had spent a week at home and was anxious to get back to Albuquerque to her boyfriend so she could spend New Year's Eve with him. I will always remember seeing her in line at the airport waiting to get on the plane. She was happy and smiling and everything was great. That was the last time I saw her alive.

I had talked to Linda a couple of times after she returned to Albuquerque. Then I got the call on Sunday, January 12, 1986, about 11:30 P.M., telling me that they thought Linda had been kidnapped. I could not believe it. This could not be happening, but it was true. And we arrived in Albuquerque from Denver the following morning.

Linda was abducted from the driveway of her boyfriend's parents' house after coming home from grocery shopping in a very nice section of Albuquerque. The whole incident occurred because one perverted sick man, aged 44, wanted a girl, or a "product," as he referred to them, preferably a blond, to be used in a pornographic movie.

The four men involved in this horrendous crime were caught and brought to trial, and they are currently serving sentences. According to testimony at the trial, the 44-year-old, named John Zinn, told three young acquaintances of his that if they would find him a "product" for a pornographic movie, he would give them $1,500. He told them to tell the girl that she would be taken to Farmington, NM, where she'd live in a large place, she would have all the clothes and drugs she wanted, and she would be driven around in limousines. This information was given at the trial by two girls who had been approached by Zinn to be in pornographic movies, and they had refused. One girl who testified was 16 years old.

The three men roamed the streets day and night prior to Linda's abduction, looking for a willing participant to be in a pornographic movie. When they could not find anyone willing to do what they asked, which included among other things performing sexual acts with animals . . . Zinn ordered the three guys to "grab someone off the street."

By this time, it was Sunday, January 12. The three men gathered the necessary items—TV wire to tie her up, bandannas for a blindfold, a Polaroid camera for pictures, a syringe, and a bottle of pills. They set out driving around the city. They spotted one lady and followed her to her home. Fortunately, she had a garage door opener and drove straight into her garage.

They also had spotted a 12-year-old girl walking down the street, but they were not able to grab her in time.

So they went back to a grocery store parking lot where they were just waiting to see someone. When one of the guys saw Linda drive in, they saw her long blond hair and they said, "There, that is the one we want. The boss likes blonds." They waited for her to finish her shopping, and when she didn't come out when they thought she should, one actually went in and looked for her and then followed her out of the grocery store. She came out, got in her car, and they followed her back to her boyfriend's house. She drove in the driveway, and they went to the end of the street and turned around and came back where she was unloading her groceries, and two of the three guys jumped out of the car and grabbed her and pulled her into the car.

From there they took Linda to the motel where they gave her drugs and alcohol, raped her repeatedly and took pornographic pictures of each one raping her. This continued all night long.

The next morning, it was in the newspapers that Linda was missing. Because John Zinn knew Linda could identify them, he ordered his three partners to "get rid of her." So they drove her to the mountains, and while she pleaded for her life, one of them shot her in the head.

Why did this happen? Because one perverted sick man wanted a "product" for a pornographic movie. You always think something like this is never going to happen to your family. Pornography and drugs and the crime that goes on all the time only happens to the "low-lifers," or people who "ask for it" by the way they live, people like drug users, prostitutes, alcoholics. This was not the case at all. Ours was the all-American family. Linda was the all-American girl. She had something to offer society, and yet her life was taken by animals that roam day and night looking for victims.

When something like this happens to you, it is like the light has been turned on. You start finding out that pornography does affect all of us. And as you read the daily newspapers, you generally can find an article about child molestation, sexual abuse, rape, et cetera; and in most cases some form of pornography or child pornography has been involved. Before it happens to you, you think, "Oh, that is terrible," and you just turn to the next page of your newspaper. After it happens to you, your heart is broken and you know the pain that the child and that family is suffering. And they are suffering because no one has taken the time to care and rid our society of pornography.

All I know is that my daughter would be alive today if it were not for a sick mind wanting a "product" for a pornographic movie. The unfortunate fact is that we need more people to care and more people to take a stand.

Criminals seem to have more rights now than the victims. We must remember we have rights, too, and we must fight to keep our rights. Linda had a right to live. I had a right not to have those animals take my daughter away. It is our right to live in a society that is not overrun with pornographers, rapists and murderers.

We must protect our children. If we do not, who will? It is too late for my daughter, but it is not too late for yours.[2]

Atterly found himself unable to rise from his seat without supporting his weight with his arms. He forced himself up, nodded to the committee chairman, wondered if his own face looked as pale and strained as the chairman's.

Around the room press rose with him, gathering toward the exit, clogging his way. Atterly lowered his head and moved insistently through the group and out the door. In the hallway he stopped and fought for composure, which was all the time the press required. When he felt centered enough to look up, he found a battery of microphones and tape machines thrust toward him.

A reporter asked, "Was there any particular reason for your attendance today, Senator Atterly?"

"Yes. I have decided to come out in favor of this legislation, and I felt it best to attend the segment of committee hearings which my schedule would allow."

The voices were very insistent, very urgent, barely waiting for him to stop speaking before pressing forward with the next question. "What is your reaction to the hearings?"

Atterly did not need his notes to reply, "To summarize the ACLU position, they feel that pornography is good and justifiable since it allows deviants to feel better about themselves because they can see that there are other deviants out there engaging in the same acts which excite them. I disagree."

---

[2]This is a verbatim excerpt from: U.S. Senate Committee on the Judiciary Hearing on S. 703 and S. 2033, Child Protection and Obscenity Enforcement Act and Pornography Victims Protection Act of 1987, June 8, 1988. Statement of Dixie L. Gallery, Denver, Colo., pp. 388–390. U.S. Government Printing Office, Washington: 1990.

He held up a hand to stop the next question before it was asked. "Furthermore, he referred to 'mob rule' as something which is always to be opposed. I must remind the gentleman that democracy is also mob rule, so long as the 'mob' is in the majority.

"The ACLU position is based upon a desire to 'protect' the Constitution and the Bill of Rights above and beyond the wishes of anyone, including a possible majority of both Congress and the people, if this majority happens to disagree with them. Anyone who knows the Bible will recall that this same devotion to law was severely criticized in ages past. To paraphrase a great man who placed people above the law and considered their welfare more important than upholding legal principles, the Constitution was made for man, not man for the Constitution."

His forward progress was stopped by an insistent voice demanding, "What about the woman's testimony? Do you have any comment?"

"Yes, I do." Atterly paused to swallow. "I am sorry."

◆　◆　◆

When Jeremy saw Duncan head for the passenger side of the car the next morning, he said, "I guess that means my turn's up."

"I hope you're not going to surprise me," Duncan replied. "Come up with something like, I haven't had but thirty-six accidents since last month."

Jeremy shut his door, waved to the woman and two teenagers standing at the front door. "I know how much stock you put in this car. I'll be careful."

"Just remember you have to sort of lean it around the corners, and you'll do fine."

"I know all about takin' curves in oversized boats. Now where was it that fine lady said she'd gotten a place for us to sleep tonight?"

"Someplace called Carthage, Missouri. I sure hope that's in the direction of California."

"You got the map there in the glove box, better get busy." Jeremy backed out of the driveway, gave the family a final wave, headed off. "From where I sit, goin' to California is just one step away from goin' to the moon."

"You mean to say you're not what they called well traveled?"

"If you count the miles I clocked up goin' to outside conveniences, I suppose I am." He squinted at a street sign, nodded that he had it right. "Far as gettin' up and out is concerned, I'd planned to stay right there at home from womb to tomb. Never did hear of anything worth packin' up and searchin' for."

Duncan played at sunrise. "Broadway? The Eiffel Tower? What about the Alps?"

"Let's see. Broadway's a street, and I got one of them outside my front door. The Eiffel Tower's that spaghetti of steel the French plugged together, ain't that right? Seems an awful long way to go to see a buildin' they never got around to stickin' the walls on."

"You're making fun of me now."

"Only a little bit. Tell me something, son. Do folks from Carolina need a passport to go to California?"

"Last time I looked we were all still part of the same union. Of course, Californians don't always check back with the home office before doing what they feel is best. They'll get a message through their crystal balls or read it in their astrology charts or hear it from the neighborhood medium, and they crank up their brooms and fly away."

Jeremy gave him a sideways look. "Now who's the one makin' fun?"

"They're Americans, Jeremy. Just like you and me. The air's a little different over there and it makes them think a little weird sometimes, but basically they're just people." They put some miles behind them before Duncan broke the silence with, "That was some speech you gave last night."

"Thank you. I've never been one for public speakin', only done it once before, and that was in church. But it came to me last night while we were listenin' to the senator's speech that we've got a story to tell."

"I don't know about that 'we' bit, but I found myself getting a little choked up while you were talking, and I've been in on it from the start." He hesitated, added, "And that beginning. Part of me wanted to laugh out loud when you talked about that beggar and seeing Jessica on the street. I don't know how to describe it, but I didn't believe it and I *wanted* to believe it at the same time."

"All I did was tell 'em what's happened."

"It really was like you said? With the guy knowing your name and wanting whatever it was you said?"

"The water of life. Yessir. The man stood there beside me and said he wanted to drink the water of life. Had more chills runnin' up and down my spine than a fellow takin' his true love on a roller-coaster ride."

"Didn't it worry you that those people back there might not believe you?"

"Tried not to think about it. I felt the urge to tell my story and didn't want any earthly doubts gettin' in the way. It was hard enough as it was to talk about myself."

"Did you see the lady over there sniffing back tears?"

"Not but one quick glance. I was afraid if I looked again she'd start me off."

"What I still don't get, though, is why you wanted to tell them."

"It's like this. I got a strong feeling sittin' there listenin' to the senator speak that maybe I could make his message a little more alive for those good people if they could hear about one little girl who's gettin' eaten up by the very thing he's out to stop."

"That's why you took the video tape of the speech?"

Jeremy nodded. "Seems to me like there's a lot of people out here who might want to hear about it."

"I liked the way you stressed that this wasn't necessarily the parents' fault. Sure, a lot of times they just do awful jobs, shouldn't have ever had kids in the first place. But others, they really loved those kids, gave them the best home they knew how. Either the kids got taken in by the lure of the street or were just bad apples from the start. You ought to see them, Jeremy, those parents come into my office absolutely crippled by their grief and their worry. I wish there was something I say to help them stop feeling so *guilty*."

"Seems simple enough to me, son. Tell 'em that our Father in heaven is the perfect parent, and even His first two turned out wrong as wrong can be."

Duncan inspected the lanky gray-haired man. "When you talk like that, all cut and dried and laid out flat, it reminds me of my grandfather. He was religious in a quiet sort of way, or at least I think he was. He never said much about it, but there was just this feeling about him." He turned his eyes back to the windshield. "Sometimes I wish a little more of it had worn off."

"It's time you faced the facts of life, son. There isn't any family plan in heaven. There's never been a grandchild of God, and He's not aimin' on startin' with you. You're either in His hands or you're not. In a world of nothing but gray, this is one black and white choice you can count on. And believe you me, your life depends on what you decide."

"So you say," Duncan countered. "Seems to me you're awfully sure about something you can't see or feel or touch." He looked over at Jeremy. "I'm taking you at your word, you know, like you said yesterday. That you won't turn red in the face and say I'm headed for the flames or anything."

"My job's not to doom you," Jeremy replied easily. "Go ahead, son. Speak your mind."

"Well, from where I'm sitting, all this religion stuff makes about as much sense as the emperor walking down the street dressed in invisible clothes."

Jeremy drove for a while in a comfortable silence before saying, "I had a friend once, real security-conscious kinda guy. Went up on the roof to clean the leaves outta the gutter, and before he climbed up he tied one end of a rope around his waist and the other end to the bumper of his car. He was workin' 'round back, see, so if he slipped and fell the rope'd keep him from fallin' the story and a half to the ground. Or so he thought.

"Problem was, though, his wife came out to go to the supermarket, and didn't see him since he was over on the other side of the house. Didn't think about the rope snaking up the front of the house and over the roof, since her husband was always doin' something 'round their home. So she got in the car, started it up, and drove off. Dragged her husband up one side of the roof, down the other, pulled him off the house, and landed him in the bushes. She was commencin' to cart him down the driveway and out into the street when she finally noticed that there was somebody screamin' bloody murder back behind her car somewheres."

"Wait, I get it. You're gonna tell me not to put my faith in things of this world, right?"

"That's not a bad thought, son. Guess I was, either that or if you're gonna clean the gutters like my friend did, be sure and hide the car keys real good."

"I've never met anybody who turned religion into something they laughed about."

"My wife used to say that most men walk around with a little bit of the boy in 'em," Jeremy replied. "The Lord Jesus said if we wanted to get to heaven we needed to learn how to let this child part of us out into the light of day. And if my time around kids has taught me anything, it's that one thing a child loves to do more than anything else in this whole wide world is laugh."

"I don't see too much reason for fun and games in this world."

"That's 'cause you ain't lookin'. You wouldn't know a laugh if it walked up and bit you on the leg." Jeremy paused long enough to barrel his way around a slow-moving truck. "You gotta lighten up on life before it can give you *reasons* to laugh. All you're seein' right now is your burden. Gotta learn to set that burden down, turn it over to a stronger set of shoulders. Then you'll find laughter there just waitin' for you."

Duncan shook his head. "I don't understand it. I mean, you've got this way of talking that really takes all the fight out of me."

"A lot of life depends on how we look at it," Jeremy persisted. "Everybody has troubles. Some people get better, others get bitter. What you seek in life is what you're gonna find. Things could always be worse than they are."

Duncan did not laugh. "Not always."

Jeremy sobered. "No, that's right. Some things are just too much for a body to bear. And that's when you need your Lord the most."

◆　◆　◆

The next shoot wasn't for another couple of days. That was the only explanation Pierre offered. The money was good, and the practice before an audience would be helpful. Jessica pleaded as hard as she could, but avoided saying what she knew would lead to an explosion. She concentrated on the smaller worry, the one she knew would not drive Pierre over the deep end—that she was afraid of dancing in front of people. Pierre gave her that strange smile of his, and said, "Don't worry, it's all taken care of. And besides, after the first night it'll be a breeze."

In the gray light of an overcast Kansas City afternoon the club looked very tired, very sad, much in need of a new paint job, and enormous. The cinder blocks with their faded white-wash were decorated by strings of unlit colored lights and cracked plastic lettering that named it The Boardroom. A massive sign loomed beside the highway, shouting in faded paint and streams of unlit bulbs that inside were Girls, Girls, Girls!

Inside the walls were covered with red velvet, the floors with stained dark carpeting. Much of the vast room was taken up with a stage and three runways that angled out like long fingers. Tables and seats sprouted out from each of the runways, and two bars with stools extended the length of the back wall. The air stank of old smoke and spilled drinks and cheap cleanser and lust.

The owner was a dark little man with rail-thin features and slicked-back hair and eyes like brown pebbles. He cast a glance over Jessica that made her skin crawl, and said to Pierre, "You got ID's for the pair?"

"Of course, two for each girl."

"I don't want no trouble with any cops," the man said, his gaze lingering on Arlene.

"What's for trouble," Pierre said. "They're both eighteen."

The man's shoulders gave one slight bounce before he replied, "Long as you got the two ID's."

Pierre fished them out of a pocket and handed them over. "Take a look for yourself."

The man inspected them minutely, handed them back, asked, "They dance as good as the photographer, what's his name, Jerry, yeah, they dance as good as Jerry says?"

"Absolutely," Pierre replied. "They'll bring the house down."

"They better," the man replied, "for what you're getting paid."

"Don't worry," Pierre said, "these girls deliver."

The rest of the afternoon Jessica spent with Pierre in the nameless motor lodge that felt manufactured from the same line that had produced all the others they had stayed in. Pierre held her close, kept the fears away with his smooth voice and gentle hands and reassuring words that she, only she, was his girl. But there were moments, like when he and Chico drove somewhere for their dinner, that the murmurs of doubts became voices that clawed at her, calling for her to look and see and remember.

For the final three months of school, Jessica had alternated her time between Arlene's home and the Amman Bazaar cafe. With summer came the country club, and for the first time going to the pool was not an ordeal. At least, it was not an ordeal like all previous summers, when she would have to sit in utter isolation and pretend not to care that the other kids were laughing and talking and running around.

It was always hard entering the pool and seeing the stares and enduring the snickers whenever she came out in her bathing suit, big and balloon-like and looking an utter freak in the fancy-cut high-fashion suits her mother made her wear to *the* club. But anything was better than lying around at home. The house was big and cavernous and so quiet it made her skin crawl. Jessica's only companions at home were on the other side of the television screen.

This summer was different, though, starting with the fact that instead of wearing a double-overcoat of blubber, Jessica was now growing into a *figure*. And to make matters infinitely better, there was Arlene to be with, laugh with, talk with, keep the loneliness at bay, show her the ropes to this strange arena called growing up.

Arlene had taken her down to one of the boutiques where Jessica's mother always shopped, with the oh-so skinny mannequins in the window and the price tags that were just incredible. But her mother didn't complain about how much they were spending on Jessica's outfits. No, nowadays Jessica's mother was complaining because Jessica wouldn't become more *involved* in her group and their activities. That was one of her mother's favorite expressions these days, *involve*. Jessica needed to *involve* herself with the right group. She needed to get *involved* with a nice boy who would stay around for more than just one date. She ought to let her mother introduce her to some of the committees that could *involve* her in some plays or music or something where she would meet the right people.

The biggest surprise of all over this changing relationship with her mother was when Jessica came home one afternoon to find *Arlene* and her *mother* having *coffee* together. It shocked her so bad all she could do was stand in the arched entranceway and gawk. There they sat, the two of them all chummy with their heads together and both talking at once. Her mother was even *smiling*. After that, there was no worry about Arlene taking over the shopping with Jessica. Her mother even went so far as to allow Arlene to use the charge accounts.

Arlene loved going into those stores where Jessica's mother had her charge accounts. They treated the two girls like queens, letting Arlene try on the most outrageous outfits and paying them both the most ridiculous compliments.

One day that spring they went to pick out bathing suits, and they came out of the dressing rooms in designs of barely nothing. Two young business types in suits and horn-rimmed glasses stared so hard that Jessica started blushing and Arlene began her little swaying dance, giving the guys a real show.

The guys just stood there, all ideas of business and buying and what they came in there for totally out of their heads. For the first time Jessica saw what it meant to be able to use her body for *control*.

The salesgirls saw it and played up to them like old friends, pretending the guys weren't even there. Everybody knew who the show was for, but they acted as if they were alone, saying how nice it was to have a *real* body to put inside one of their outfits, instead of the old bags who lied about their dress size and then needed a can of oil and a trowel to get inside. When the guys finally stumbled for the door, everybody had a good laugh, and Jessica didn't even put up a fuss when Arlene told her to buy the two most outrageous bikinis they had seen.

She bought them, but she never wore them except when Arlene was there. She was afraid to be seen in them when she was by herself, afraid to even take them out and look at them. Only when Arlene was there could she hide behind her best friend's confidence and class and style. Then Jessica didn't mind putting on the little bits of nothing and turning heads as far away as the clubhouse on the other side of the pool.

Otherwise she stuck to her one-piece suits, especially when she went for her morning swims. That was one real solid bit of advice Arlene gave her about her body. You've still got those little love-handles, don't you, Arlene said back during one of their springtime shopping sprees. All you got to do is swim twenty laps every morning, and by the end of the summer they'll be gone. Jessica did forty.

It was hard at first, so hard she thought she wouldn't have the strength to pull herself out of the pool when it was all over. But it got easier. And she grew to like coming out in the quiet morning air when she had the entire pool to herself. The lifeguards came to know her by sight, smiling and making little comments about the weather and the day and how many laps she would do. And then one of them, the number-two lifeguard and one of the best-looking guys Jessica had ever seen, started coming in and doing laps with her.

The pool was very clear and blue and empty in the mornings, all the chairs lined up neatly and the place all washed-down and clean, the lifeguards looking muscular and clean-cut and friendly. There were none of the catty glances from matrons who whispered about her or her parents behind her back, none of the screaming kids, none of the guys her age with their groping hands and awkward moves. All the lifeguards were college-age or older, all of them smiling at her and giving her looks that from most other people would have her blushing. But there was something about them, a genuineness that left her feeling more relaxed. It was almost as if they had seen enough and done enough that a lot of the dumb games she hated were gone forever. It left her able to smile a shy hello and sometimes even say a few words to them when they wished her good morning or talked about how nice the water looked in the early morning sunshine, or how she had to be a real good girl to be able to get up so early and swim so far, or how they were going to leave her their phone numbers so she could call them when she grew beyond being jail bait.

Jessica knew about the number-two lifeguard long before he started swimming with her. The whole club did. The head lifeguard was a fat and balding guy who had been around as long as anyone could remember. He stayed in his office mostly, the only person at the club who would still be white at the end of summer. He drank a lot, so the word was. That was why he hired a good number two, because the guy was either going to do all the work or the club would fire them both. Jessica lay on her club chair in the early summer days, her eyes hidden behind opaque glasses, and heard the gossip circulate that next year the number-one position was Pierre's for the asking.

Pierre was dark even before the summer began. He had that sort of leather-bronzed complexion that remained tanned all year long. His hair was jet black, so black it looked blue in the sunlight. He was fairly tall, but appeared much taller than he was, with his erect stance and broad shoulders and flat belly and strong legs. His face was a series of sharply chiseled lines, his eyes such a deep blue that they looked almost violet. He was twenty-eight years old and the darling of the poolside set.

Arlene tried to flirt with him early on; he reacted with the same polite detachment he showed to all the other women. It was the last thing Arlene expected, and it threw her hard, left her unsure of how to act around him. She became one of the few girls at the pool who did not even look his way. Instead she pushed Jessica to try for him.

Look at the way he follows you around the pool with his eyes, she said a dozen times, so often that Jessica began wondering if it might be true. She had never spoken to him except to say hello in the mornings, and he did not seem to pay her any more attention than he did the others, but it could be true. Maybe. He did seem to track her progress around the pool with his eyes. She began watching him and imagining them together, watching his slow pirouettes in the pool before all the catty eyes, dreaming schoolgirl dreams where she and Pierre were a thing, wishing she had the nerve to say more than hello.

Then one morning in the third week he was swimming beside her, taking it easy, speaking in a smooth languid voice, talking about nothing, making her feel more comfortable than she had ever been with a guy before. The first day it happened, she could scarcely believe it, and decided to pass it off as just a guard doing some laps before the day began. But it continued, through the third week and into the fourth, until the morning she overslept after a really late night with Arlene and arrived to find that he was waiting for her. For *her*.

Days at the pool were normally spent lying around, working on a tan, dozing in the sun, getting ready for another night somewhere with Arlene and whomever she picked up at her cafe. That day, though, it was different. Jessica lay safe and snug behind her sunglasses, trying to come to grips with the incredible truth. Pierre had waited for *her*.

The next morning she made no move to leave the pool after her laps. It was hard to stay there in the water, Pierre's closeness and the morning chill making her shiver a little, not knowing what to say or do with a guy that old and that good-looking. But she stayed just the same. And then she almost lost it when he asked her out.

The real surprise was Arlene's reaction. When Jessica told her, she got real quiet, real cool. He asked you out, huh? Like that. No big deal, nothing to get excited over, even though Arlene was the one who had talked her into making a play for him. Then she kind of spun away to talk about a new dress and somebody that had come into the cafe, and all of a sudden Jessica realized that her friend was jealous. Of *her*.

Pierre's apartment wasn't at all what Jessica expected. It was a two-room walk-up, full of bare walls and a plastic table and plywood bookshelves and dime-store lamps and cheap canvas chairs. I rent it furnished, was what he said. I don't know how long I'm going to be here, so there's no point in bringing in all my own gear.

It's fine, she replied, and meant it. She was nervous, but not as much as she had feared. He was so calm, so in control, it was as though he gave her the assurance and the ease she had always wanted—sort of like what Arlene did for her, but stronger. *Much* stronger.

They couldn't go out in public, he told her, in a way that made her feel as if he knew she'd understand. He said everything as if he was sharing some dark, hidden secret, letting her in on something that no one else would ever know. We can't go out because all the people at the club would just love to have something else to talk about, he said.

She nodded, and *did* understand. I hate the people at the club, she replied.

He turned to her with a smile, the look in those violet eyes making her shiver a little. Wouldn't it be nice if we could have the club and the pool just for us, he told her. Nobody making fun of us behind our back, making us follow rules that don't make any sense, smiling out one side of their mouths and spitting poison out the other. The way he said it and the way he looked at her left her feeling as if he could really read her mind.

All it took was that one first night. Jessica felt as though all her dreams had been brought to life. He was so gentle, and so sure of himself, and knew so *much*. He kept telling her how beautiful she was, long after she had made it clear he was going to get whatever he wanted. Pierre didn't say these things because he needed to. He didn't make them sound like some broken record that played over and over all night. He stroked her as she'd always dreamed of being touched, and whispered things she'd wanted to hear so badly that she'd never really put them into words—how much he cared for her; how special she was; how soft and smooth and pure and beautiful and right for him. He wanted to take care of her and make her his own special girl. Jessica lay in his arms and listened to his deep-throated whispers and decided she had never heard anything so beautiful in all her life.

Her nights out with Arlene stopped right then. Pierre could not see her more than two or three times a week; he had other responsibilities than running the club and had to rest and needed time alone. He explained all these things their third night together, back at his apartment in front of the television, but she had already decided that there wasn't anything else that really mattered. He made her *happy*. She could think of moments when she had known happiness before, good times with Arlene and nights at the disco, but never something that made her happy just to think about it. So she saw him when he wanted and stayed as long as he let her, and lived in her dreams and her memories until their next time together.

Those first weeks, Pierre never let her stay past eleven. It did not matter what she said about her parents not caring, or how she pleaded, he always had her dressed and in his rusty car and back home before eleven o'clock. We've got time for all that, he would say when she asked him why. Right now it's important that nobody have any reason to get down on either of us.

Arlene sensed the change and drifted off to her cafe and her new crowd without a backward glance. Maybe Arlene spread it around, or maybe it was one of the other lifeguards. Maybe it was a careless kiss in the early morning water when they thought the pool was still empty. However it happened, by the end of July the whole club knew. Nobody said anything, but they knew. Jessica could see it in their eyes when she walked by. The girls her age started *talking* to her, never saying anything outright, just making those little snide comments that put her teeth on edge. But they knew. And so did the matrons. Their gossip stopped being about her father and started being about her. Jessica started walking around with her Walkman plugged into her ears and her eyes on the sidewalk ahead of her—or on Pierre. And she hoped all the while that he would not catch on, not get worried and break it off, not do anything that would take away from the nights they had in his apartment.

The distance between Jessica and Arlene lasted all through the rest of July and into August. Then Arlene met Chico, and there wasn't any need for her to be jealous of Jessica any more.

At night The Boardroom, the place where Pierre had booked them to dance, looked entirely different. The acres of parking spaces were full to the brim, the lights were flashing, the letters stood out boldly under the spotlights, and the building thumped to the sound of very loud music. Pierre led them around to the back of the club, their footsteps scrunching on the gravel. He pounded on the locked metal door until a rheumy-eyed old man opened it to scowl at Pierre and leer at the girls.

There was a fuss when the old man wouldn't let Pierre enter, but he and Chico backed down when the old man turned and called into the interior for somebody named Jack. The man who swiftly appeared loomed high and fearsome and said in a booming voice that nobody but the girls were allowed in back. Pierre pressed something into Jessica's hand and said they would be waiting for them out front when it was over.

The music was much louder inside, and the lighting was so bad that Arlene almost tripped over a mop and bucket. They followed the bouncer down a narrow hallway that circled behind the stage. Girls in heavy makeup and smelly shawls and skimpy outfits watched their arrival with empty expressions. They sat on a long wooden bench and smoked and chewed gum and shouted gossip back and forth over the grinding music that was much too loud for the hallway's grimy confines.

A trio of girls sheened in perspiration danced through the opening at stage-side and immediately dropped their smiles. A man with glittering eyes whistled loudly and pointed at the bench. Cigarettes were ground out, shawls discarded, hair patted, sequined straps pulled tight, and a new trio pasted on the smiles that the other girls had discarded. The roar of the crowd hovered over them like a hungry bird of prey.

The bouncer pointed Jessica and Arlene toward a door at the far end of the hall marked *Ladies*. Beside it were double doors leading out to the club proper. Jessica followed Arlene inside, stopped at the sight of the three dancers toweling off in the cramped space before the mirrors.

The trio looked them over with blank, tired eyes. One asked "How old are you two?"

Without blinking an eye Arlene snapped back, "Eighteen, how old are you?"

The trio exchanged smirks and head-shakes, and the girl told them, "Don't leave anything here that's worth stealing. You do and you'll never see it again."

The ladies' restroom was a tight squeeze for the five of them. Arlene motioned Jessica into the corner by the toilets and whispered, "This is the dressing room?"

The trio heard them and laughed. Another girl spoke in a husky, sand-paper growl, "What, you honeys're used to finer digs?"

Another slipped a sweater over her head, said in an eternally bored voice, "Welcome to the real world, ladies."

Arlene and Jessica made themselves small and waited for them to finish dressing and leave.

The noise of booming music and the roaring crowd echoed in the empty restroom. Clothes were laid in carefully spaced piles under the sinks. The shelves below the mirrors were cluttered with lipstick and spilled powder and bobby pins and hair spray and hairbrushes and eyeliners and soiled tissues. The single trash container spilled its contents onto the floor. Around it lay torn stockings, shoes with broken heels, tattered women's magazines, bags from fast-food restaurants, and wrappers from everything under the sun. The floor and wall tiles were cracked and stained and dirty. The air was fetid.

"What did Pierre slip you?" Arlene asked.

Jessica opened her hand and found a tiny wedge of carefully folded paper.

Arlene smiled for the first time that night. "Just the thing to get us through."

Jessica felt panic mounting, pleaded, "Can't we just skip it?"

Arlene started unfolding the paper. "What you've got to do is learn how to hold your breath. You know, just switch off and pretend like it's not really happening. Then it'll all be over before you know, and we can go back to the good times." She offered Jessica the powder. "Here, take a hit and you'll see."

By the time they were signaled up to the stage entrance, Jessica's heart was zinging along at about three times normal speed. The music was suddenly bearable, and Arlene was there beside her, so the crowd's roar wasn't as frightening as before. As they stood beside the opening in the stage curtain, the man with glittering eyes draped a wandering hand across Arlene's bare shoulder, then showed no reaction when she angrily pushed him off. He bent down and shouted above the noise, "I want you to stay up on the stage. Don't try to get down on the runways—these animals'll eat you two alive!" Then with a push he sent them out under the lights.

CHAPTER
9

The old-timey farmhouse outside Carthage, Missouri, was full of early morning light as the hardware store manager and his family lingered over a big country breakfast, clearly reluctant to have Jeremy and Duncan depart.

"I can't tell you how much I was moved by your story last night," the lady said, straightening the lace tablecloth with nervous fingers. "I couldn't get to sleep until nearly dawn."

"Sure wish there was something more we could do," her husband agreed.

"Y'all can do more for us than you'll ever know," Jeremy replied.

"Wish you'd tell us how," the man said.

"More for us and more for them little girls, too," Jeremy went on. He planted his elbows on the table and leaned far over, giving the words all the emphasis he could. "Y'all can *pray*. Help us with that divine power. Call His attention to the needs of the families and the needs of them little girls."

"That doesn't sound like anything," the wife replied.

"It don't sound like anything because all you been concentratin' on is what you can see. You don't feel like you're doin' anything worthwhile unless you're gettin' your hands dirty. I'll tell you something, ma'am. Nothin' can help those little girls out there right now much as prayer. What are we gonna tell them when we find 'em? *If* we find 'em, that is. What kinda words are gonna put their world back together again? What

they need to hear are the words that touch their *hearts,* and
the only way you can power up words like that is when the Lord
is with you, Him and all His saints."

"Then maybe we ought to start now, don't you think?"

They prayed right there at the table. Even Duncan. He felt
strong about it, strong and strengthened by the act and *right.*

When they finished, the wife turned to her husband and
said, "We're gonna get together a prayer group."

He responded as if he had been expecting it. "Ought to see
if we can't get our Bible group together once a week. Or why
not twice?"

"Why not every night? We could have them meet here on
Mondays, then try and get the group together every night at
somebody else's house, see if we can't get them all praying about
it."

"One hour a day, seven days a week, praying for those girls."

"Pray for them girls and all the other girls and boys."

"And their families," Jeremy offered.

"Maybe we ought to try and get a group together to go to
Washington for that meeting—what did the Senator call it?"

"A Solemn Assembly," Jeremy offered. "Sounds like a fine
move to me."

Then Duncan spoke up, just as naturally as though he were
into this every day of the week. "And pray for the country," he
said. "Man, the whole country's sick with this."

"He's right," the wife said. "It's a filthy disease."

"The only way to cleanse ourselves is if we ask the Lord to
do it for us," Jeremy agreed. "We gotta ask the Divine Healer
to cleanse our wounds, heal our nation, turn back the hand of
destruction and show us the sin of our ways."

The man rose to his feet and started pacing. "I gotta make
a list of people, see if I can't get some other churches around
here involved. There have to be a few other people who'll take
this seriously."

"Everybody takes it seriously," Duncan said. "The problem
is finding people who take it serious enough to want to do something about it."

"That's part of the problem," Jeremy agreed. "Too many
people tellin' the government, this is a problem, y'all go out
there and do something. But the only healin' that's gonna make
a difference here is if the Lord does the healing. We gotta pe-
tition the Lord on behalf of our land."

"Amen," the man said. "Y'all gotta excuse me, I got places to go and people to see."

The drives had settled into long comfortable silences, interspersed with discussions about the people they were leaving and where they might end up next. There were times for stories from Jeremy, times for reflections internally. Jeremy made occasional remarks on faith and left them sitting out there like little gifts for Duncan to accept or reject. When Duncan refused to comment, Jeremy refused to push. It became the basis for their growing friendship, these times of shared quiet.

They stopped for lunch in a roadside diner after crossing the Nebraska state line. Jeremy leaned back in the booth and asked Duncan to tell about himself. "I've got no idea where you're comin' from, and it troubles me."

"I've told you twice. Born and raised in Richmond, Virginia."

"That don't tell me a thing. I know less about you than I do about a coon back there in the woods. At least I know the coon's habits."

"So what do you want, my life story?" Duncan played at being casual, glanced around the half-empty diner. It was built in an old arched-roof barn. The floor was still patterned with posts and planks which marked the old animal stalls. Expanses of glass had been set into the outside walls, giving the room a light and airy feel. Sunlight made streaming patterns across the high-ceiling room, writhing and drifting and sharpening back into focus in time with wind-swept clouds overhead.

"Naw, give it to me in little dribs and drabs. I'm a storyteller, and I've got a storyteller's love of detail. Big pictures are like somebody tellin' you in five minutes about a book it took 'em all summer to read." Jeremy leaned across the booth. "Tell you what. How 'bout you tellin' me the time when you felt you really grew up."

He laughed at that. "You don't want to know."

"Sure I do. If I didn't, I wouldn't have asked."

"Believe me, Jeremy. You do *not* want to know."

"Listen here, son. You think maybe I'm gonna get scared and run off into the sunset? I've already decided you're a good man. I just wanna to know what built this man into who he is, besides the hand of God."

"I might have seen God that summer, but I doubt it was

because God's hand was guiding me."

Jeremy settled back in his seat. "There you go. What you've just done is the hardest part to a storyteller's job. You've hooked me. I haven't got the slightest idea where you're gonna take me, but I'm hooked and rarin' to go."

"My family and I never really got along," Duncan told him. "They were real middle-class America, and I was the neighborhood rebel. The word my father most often used to describe me was embarrassment. I don't even remember when he started saying that, it must have been when I was still pretty young. By the time I was a teenager any excuse was good enough if it got me out of the house."

Duncan started slowly, not really sure that Jeremy was as interested as he said. But as he spoke Jeremy listened with an intensity bordering on hunger.

"My father was a dentist and my mother worked in his office. It seemed to me that all their time was spent on show—the right club and the right friends and the right neighborhood and the right restaurant on Saturday nights and the right school for the kids. It made me sick. My sister and my brother ate it up, though. My parents were always sticking it in my face, pointing at them and asking why I couldn't grow up and behave more like them. Now my sister is married to a banker and my brother is a dentist in my father's old practice, and their lives are just as big a fake to me as my parents'. Every time I go into their homes I feel like I'm going to choke to death for lack of air."

Jeremy sat back and fastened those luminous eyes on Duncan's face and said *nothing*. He was clearly too busy absorbing it all to respond. He heard what was said and gave Duncan the impression of understanding clearly what was *not* said as well.

"The only place I really felt at home was my grandfather's farm. I'd been going there ever since I was a baby. My brother and sister hated the place, which made it even better as far as I was concerned. My grandmother had died before I was born, and my grandfather just held on to the old life and sort of ignored all the stuff that was going on in the outside world. He never really said much, but every time I showed up he gave the impression that he had been expecting me and that I belonged. That was real important to me, this feeling that I belonged somewhere.

"About a mile and a half away these developers had built

an entire city called Columbia, Maryland. The only time my grandfather ever talked about it was when people would drive up and try to buy the farm. He called the town a people factory, and said it was the worst excuse for a place to raise kids that he'd ever seen. Where is the soul to a place like that, he'd yell at those real-estate brokers, and sooner or later they'd drive away. It was the only time I ever heard him raise his voice.

"By the time I turned eighteen my hair was so long I could reach up from behind and grab a fistful. I wore it held back by an Indian silver and turquoise clasp that some girl had given me. My grandfather was getting old, and most of the time I wasn't even sure he was seeing me, like he was looking at me and remembering the little kid I used to be. But sometimes I'd catch him staring at me with a little smile on his face, like he could see right through the jeans and the hair and the tie-dyed t-shirts, and it didn't mean a thing to him. Times like that, I'd think I could never love anybody as much as I loved that old man.

"I'd try and help out around the farm, coming up on weekends and going back late, skipping a lot of Monday classes that last year in high school. I had been accepted to the University of Maryland, so there wasn't a lot the school could do to me as long as I didn't flunk out. My family was getting *real* glad to see me go, and even gladder that my grandfather was able to keep me in line. Only he wasn't. I played at being a good kid as long as I was on the farm, and I never brought any of my friends up there, but right over the horizon was Columbia, Maryland. And no matter what my grandfather thought of the place, for a kid who saw himself as a rebel without a cause, Columbia was *happening*."

A deep stillness enveloped their table. Jeremy sat and listened. There was no judgment in the man, no barriers of unspoken criticism or condemnation. Duncan felt as if he were seeing back through Jeremy's listening spirit into a time he thought lost and gone forever. He talked, and as he spoke the events and experiences and memories took on a totally different light. He remembered, and in placing the memories into words, he brought them into a sharper focus than they had ever had while it was all taking place.

There were three places in Columbia where Duncan used to go a *lot*: the lake, the mall, and the Merriweather Post Pavilion. It was best to go to the lake at night. It was a man-made lake near the commercial center, and had a long pier that went out to the middle. At the end of the pier was an open-framed structure that had a beautiful, kind of spooky feel to it. It was very quiet out there at night. Very dark.

The pier was a *great* place to go and get high.

Right before the platform, back on the shore, there was an enormous fountain. It was actually possible to walk inside the fountain. From within this water-walled cavern, all that could be seen was fancy stonework and the shimmering gold-lit waterfall.

The fountain was a great place to go and *be* high.

From the parking lot beside the lake ran a pedestrian bridge that went over the street to the mall. On two stories with about seventy-five shops, the mall was very contemporary for its time, with lots of wood and tile and angular skylights. It was a place to shop and a place to hang out. For Duncan and his friends, the mall was also a *great* place to pick up girls who were shopping. But the most unique feature of the mall was on the second floor, the product of some forward-thinking urban planner. It was called simply, Your Store.

It was nothing more than an empty shop reserved for teenagers. Outside there was a big mural painted in blue and gray and white enamel that read, Your Store. Underneath were larger-than-life silhouettes of kids standing shoulder to shoulder. Inside, the place was carpeted and brightly lit. There were lots of floor cushions to lounge on. One large wall was whitewashed and left bare for graffiti.

Your Store was the place to meet and hang out and leave messages. Duncan remembered thinking at the time how wild it was that management would give up the space for kids, especially for a group that was not classed as real high spenders. It was only some time later that cynicism set in and he decided that they were basically trying to collect all the riffraff and limit their pranks to one corner of the mall. That way the kids wouldn't stand in the big spenders' way.

Almost all of the Columbia kids came from broken families. The kid whose two original parents still lived together was odd enough to be talked about. The kid whose parents still loved each other and showed love to the kid just didn't exist.

These kids carried the scars of their home life like badges of courage, proud of the fact that they knew no love at home and had learned to live without it. They were the survivors of the modern material world.

The real Mecca in Columbia was not the shopping center, however; it was the Merriweather Post Pavilion. During the summer months there would be daily pilgrimages from a tri-state area and the District of Columbia. The list of performers read like a Who's Who of rock and roll. During that era of Duncan's awakening there was a concert almost every night—The Who, Rolling Stones, Led Zeppelin, The Byrds, Johnny Winter and White Trash, Santana, Pink Floyd, Black Sabbath. That summer he saw them all.

For Duncan, those months were a time of transition. Before him stretched a lifetime of suits, short hair, responsibilities, and grubbing for money. The best time he ever had was running with the wind that summer. He drank his fill of everything, tanked up for all the hard times to come, felt and tasted it all.

Marcie was still in high school, a year younger and a world apart in attitude and lifestyle. She'd never tried drugs, never wanted to, and never would agree to marry him until he'd straightened out. It was okay. He knew the life of that summer couldn't last.

His generation was already filled with blown-out cases, the ones who hadn't let go of the high life in time. He and his friends used to call them crispy fritters, the ones with minds burned to ashes in the bowls of their hash-pipes. No, he never planned to stay with it long. All he wanted was one last fling before the men in gray suits fitted him with a straitjacket for life.

The Merriweather Post Pavilion was located in the middle of a large park with green rolling hills and lots of trees. The area looked a lot like what it once had been—a cow pasture. Two dollars bought a lawn seat. For five ninety-five the more well-off went inside, where seats descended down in amphitheater fashion to the stage. People would arrive hours early because the lawn was one big party.

Nearly everyone would arrive high already, then would complete their psychedelic experience with their drug of choice. *Everything* was available—freely, easily, and at competitive prices. The pre-concert party was sort of a large stoned picnic. Nobody was really eating; they were sort of feasting on each other and the *power* generated by such a collective high.

There was very little alcohol, except for Yago Sangria, Boone's Farm Apple Wine, and—if somebody was already making big bucks—Mateus Rosé. Because of crowd control problems, there were gate checks for alcohol, and a lot of it was confiscated. There were scattered hassles by people who didn't like getting ripped off by the guards, but most really didn't care. There was too much available inside to worry about a couple of bottles at the gate.

People would bring sleeping bags or blankets, and sit out and talk and laugh and get high. The drug peddlers were usually men in their early to mid-twenties. They wore long hair and beards, and strolled from blanket to blanket announcing what they had to sell.

The peddlers were like gypsies in an old marketplace, shadows that drifted far outside the law. A dealer would walk past and say, "Mesc, coke, 'shrooms, windowpane, blotter, sunshine, mister natural, weed, Lebanese?" He would then raise his eyebrows, and if he did not get a reaction, just keep walking. If he heard or saw that the people were interested, he would sit down on the blanket and transact business.

As the afternoon wore on, the light carnival atmosphere would slide into a strong tension. Part of the tension was the anticipation of the show. Most of the tension, though, arose from the collective consciousness of a group whose inhibitions were lowered and whose paranoia was heightened by a variety of chemicals.

Violence was inevitable. At the very least there would be a scuffle between gate crashers and guards. At the extreme, police cars were set on fire, concession stands were stormed, tear gas thrown, and heads were smashed. Such riot-like conditions were not at all easy to take by those who were desperately seeking in their drug-induced darkness for some fragile handhold on control.

Once the performance started, tension was heightened by the ever-present phenomenon of rushing the stage. As the sun went down and the concert started and the revelers on the lawn became absorbed in the music, they would all want to get closer to the center of *power*.

The orchestra pit at the edge of the stage was the best place to be. Those on the lawn would push past barriers and ushers to join those from the inside seats, and all would rush as one toward the pit.

The music was loudest there. The listeners moved in time with everybody else moving around them. They breathed with one breath. And the air was filled with the odor of marijuana, sustaining their high well into the night.

Then, as the night slid quietly into a dawn that seemed both unreal and unwelcome to the revelers, Duncan would separate himself from that which no longer held any life, and go home to sleep and prepare to do it all again the next night.

Duncan listened to himself tell the story, and saw the light in Jeremy's eyes not fade, but somehow *deepen* as the tale wore on. What amazed Duncan the most, beyond the surprise he felt over being so open with someone who would never have known that side of life, was the effect it had on how he himself saw it all.

He looked into those eyes across the table and saw the crowds and the lights and the smiles and the bands and the flashes of sanity in the nights of drug-induced journeys into altered states, and he found himself rethinking it all. One part of him was caught up in the telling, in the sharing of that summer that had marked his move into manhood and solitude and rejection of so much that his own family held as lifelong ideals. And all the while, another part of him kept saying, in words that barely seemed to register in his conscious mind, where did I go wrong? How did something that seemed so right at the time take me so far from where I wanted to wind up?

In the silence that greeted the end of his story, Duncan leaned back on his side of the booth and watched the afternoon sunlight dapple the inside of the diner with flecks of brilliant color, and he thought of all that had come after. For the first time in his life, he admitted to himself that maybe, just maybe all the pain and disappointment, the trauma and bitterness and frustration—the sheer, utter *futility* of it all—had been planted deep in his being during that strange summer and all those lost, purple-hazed days.

◆ ◆ ◆

Congressman John Silverwood arrived at Senator Atterly's office just a few minutes shy of seven o'clock in the evening.

Little of the desire that had pushed him to ask for this meeting remained. He stood before the outer door in a state of acute indecision, embarrassed and angry and yet drawn to enter. He opened the door with a decision to pay polite attention and leave as quickly as he could.

He walked into barely suppressed bedlam.

At first glance there appeared to be four different conferences going on, or at least four that he could see. A black man with a strong, deeply seamed face was holding court in the outer office; three of the seven gentlemen gathered around him and talking all at once wore clergymen's collars. Through a series of open doors he could see another group constructing a vast flow-chart against an office's back wall, while in front of them four or five young people were on their knees chattering excitedly and sorting papers on the floor. Three women sat around the desk of Atterly's private secretary talking on cordless phones and taking frantic notes. Through yet another door Silverwood caught glimpses of the senator pacing while several other people talked in quietly urgent tones.

The senator spotted Silverwood, and walked out to him with a hand extended in greeting. "How long have you been standing out here, John?"

"Just a few minutes." He ignored the score of faces turned his way, asked, "This have something to do with the bill you're working on?"

"Sort of." Atterly grasped his arm and led him into the inner sanctum. To the group gathered there, he said, "I believe you all know the congressman."

Silverwood murmured greetings, held the surprise off his face. The dozen men and women crammed into the senator's office represented an amazing spectrum of Washington's power cliques. They were all known faces, Democrat and Republican congressmen and senators, and one senior White House official who was reputed to loathe the congresswoman seated beside him. There was also a television newswoman whom Silverwood remembered vaguely from a couple of Atterly's prayer meetings, two top officials from a major think-tank, and the well-known head of a Christian family organization. They all looked tense and tired.

"I need the keys to somebody's office, please," Atterly said to the room. "John and I have something important to discuss in private."

One of the senators, a brusque middle-aged lady with an air that Silverwood had always found abrasive, fished in her purse and came up with a set of keys. "I don't need to tell you that the place is a mess."

"If it wasn't, I'd be worried," Atterly replied. "Let's go, John."

They walked down the silent hall, only a few lights glimmering from under the doors which they passed. Silverwood asked, "Are all of them working on that bill with you?"

"Sort of. We're involved in a public prayer meeting, and it's grown a lot bigger than we thought it would." Atterly squinted at a door, fumbled with the keys, opened it, and turned on the lights. "After you, John."

"Looks to me like your support for the legislation is growing."

"Yes and no. There is quite a groundswell rising up around the country, but we need more support from elected officials."

"That's where I come in, is that it?"

"Not tonight." Atterly sat in the outer office's single armchair, waved Silverwood to the lumpy-looking sofa. "You said you had something you wanted to discuss with me."

"Yes, I suppose I did." Silverwood seated himself on the unyielding couch, wondered how he could get out of this as quickly as possible. "I don't like taking you away from that conference, though."

"Nonsense." Atterly rubbed a tired hand across his forehead. The man was showing his age. "John, if it was anybody else but you I would have put them off, suggested they call someone with more time. But you've been on my mind ever since TJ's funeral. I don't mean every once in a while, either. I've been praying for you more often than I have for anybody else outside my own family."

Silverwood adjusted his tie. "To what do I owe this honor?"

"Because you're in pain," Atterly snapped. "I have neither the time nor the patience to play games with you, John. Anybody with eyes and an interest in looking beneath the surface would know it. You've got a burden that's eating away at you, and you need help."

"I've done all right on my own so far."

Eyes the color of sunlit ice bore down on him. "That's why you came over and found me, to say that you're doing fine on your own?"

"I don't even know myself why I did it."

"Yes you do." Atterly leaned back and shut his eyes for a moment. "This is wrong. All wrong. I should be showing you peace and brotherly love, and instead I'm trying to take your head off."

"Like I said, maybe I should wait and talk to you another time."

"Maybe so." The senator looked utterly drained. "Are you

sure there's nothing you'd like to talk with me about right now, John?"

"Not that I can think of."

Atterly nodded once. "Well, I've failed at my duty, and I'm sorry."

"I can't think why you would say that. I'm perfectly—"

The senator waved it aside. "Would you let me give you a piece of advice?"

"Sure." Silverwood settled back, feeling himself tighten up as though expecting a blow.

"The one good thing that's come out of this evening, John, is that you didn't deny being in pain. It's a big step, and I know it must have cost you to come this far. I'm only sorry that I wasn't in the right frame of mind to be able to help you."

Atterly stopped Silverwood's protest with, "No, no, hear me out, John. This won't take long. It would have been nice if I could have been a better listener, and shown you a sympathetic heart and mind. But in truth the person you really need to learn to talk with is Jesus Christ. Talking with me is only important if I can point you in that direction. Don't see my own imperfections as a barrier to making that step, John. Please don't make that error. Please. Discover what it means to have an eternal friend who is truly on your side.

"The key here is forgiveness. Confess your sins and accept forgiveness. This is the central purpose behind Christ's ultimate sacrifice. He has died in order to create an eternal bridge between imperfect, sinful man and the perfect loving Father. To cross that bridge, you must confess your sins and accept Him as your Savior. Period. There is no other way."

Atterly waited to see if he would respond. Silverwood remained motionless. "Would you like to pray with me, John?"

He managed a shake of his head. "You go ahead."

The prayer seemed interminable. Silverwood sat with bowed head, barely breathing, wondering if Atterly could hear his heart. For the life of him he could not recall why he had wanted to speak with the man, why there had been this urge to unearth past mistakes. His whole body felt clammy with nervous sweat. Turn it over to Jesus. What a joke. He had gotten himself into this mess and he was going to have to find a way out. There had to be something. There had to be.

CHAPTER
10

Senator Atterly strode vigorously toward the front of the room, wished the crowded hall a brisk good morning, set down his Bible, patted his notes into a neat block of pages, and asked Nak to lead them in prayer. John Silverwood bowed his head, wondered if Atterly's averted gaze was intentional.

Silverwood's concern was dispelled with the man's first words. Although spoken to the other side of the room, there was no question as to whom Atterly addressed. "I had not intended to give the lesson this morning. Most of you are well aware of what is happening, or at least *appears* to be happening, with our Solemn Assembly. Like the poll-taker before elections, however, I must be careful not to count the votes until the day has arrived.

"But last night I was approached by a friend in need, and I answered him out of my lack rather than from the Lord's eternal bounty. I sought to give him from my own meager share rather than assist him in finding the eternal Source for himself. I owe this man my deepest apology, as well as my gratitude for joining us once again this morning. I therefore dedicate this lesson to this dear brother and his search, and ask that he please look beyond my own human frailty and see the One who never, ever lets our pleas go unanswered."

Atterly searched an inside coat pocket, brought out his rimless half-moon spectacles, set them in place, and went on, "Our first reading comes from the seventh chapter of Second Corinthians, verse ten and the first part of eleven:

> "Godly sorrow brings repentance that leads to salvation and leaves no regret, but worldly sorrow brings death. See what this godly sorrow has produced in you: what earnestness, what eagerness to clear yourselves, what indignation, what alarm, what longing, what concern, what readiness to see justice done."

Senator Atterly stripped the glasses off as though this admission of weakness embarrassed him. "Now to my mind, the pivotal word in this passage is *repentance*. It is what differentiates constructive regret, or godly sorrow as it is called here, from the useless meanderings of worldly sorrow. Repentance is the beginning step for a Christian, and the second step, and the step that we must continue to make every day of our lives."

Atterly laid one arm on the podium, clearly not needing his notes for this, and let the spectacles dangle from his fingers. "To truly repent, we must begin by seeing God as the righteous being. We must set aside all the lies we have used to keep Him out of our lives, and recognize Him as the All in All, the *only* way to salvation. Repentance is the first step. We turn away from one thing and turn toward another."

He slipped his spectacles back on, turned pages, then looked out over the lenses. "The Bible is very clear about what we are to turn *away* from. Paul calls them dead works, and says they are the product of our sinful nature. Galatians 5:19–21 says:

> "The acts of the sinful nature are obvious: sexual immorality, impurity and debauchery, idolatry and witchcraft; hatred, discord, jealousy, fits of rage, selfish ambition, dissensions, factions and envy; drunkenness, orgies, and the like. I warn you, as I did before, that those who live like this will not inherit the kingdom of God."

He went on. "These acts are *obvious*. Even people who lack the first vestige of conscience are aware that they are doing wrong in the eyes of somebody else. They *hide* the act. Now this hiding may come in two different ways. They can hide it from the world, do it in the dark, act it out behind closed doors and only with people who share the same lusts. Or they can flaunt it before the world and hide it from themselves. They hide the sinfulness of their natures behind barriers of rage and guilt and pain and hate. It keeps them from being forced to see their acts and their lusts for what they are. It holds them back from recognizing their need for repentance, and their need for Jesus."

Atterly continued speaking, but Silverwood's mind fixed on one of the words the senator had read. *Selfish ambition,* the man had said. The words struck at him, a hammer ringing through the innermost chord of his being. *Selfish ambition.* That was where it had all begun.

For the first time that day Atterly allowed his gaze to rest momentarily on Silverwood. The thrust of those piercing eyes remained a long time after the senator's attention had turned elsewhere.

"I would like to close today with a special message intended for my searching friend. I know you are beset by doubts, just as we all are from time to time. I beg you not to allow this to be a barrier to your search. Make the step of repentance. Reach out in prayer and prayerful study of the Bible, and allow yourself to feel the wonderful peace that comes with knowing—not believing, mind you, but *knowing*—that this gift of love and light and reassurance was truly meant for you."

Slowly, deliberately, Atterly closed his Bible and said, "Let us pray." When all heads were bowed save two, he allowed his eyes to turn toward Silverwood, who remained erect and watchful. The habitual ice in Atterly's eyes melted away, and he took a moment to look in silent appeal at the man he called his friend.

◆ ◆ ◆

After breakfast the next morning Duncan made a beeline for the passenger side. Jeremy slid behind the wheel. "Let'ssee, how far do we have to go today?"

"Not far, I hope." Duncan shut his door. "I didn't have what you'd call a restful night."

"Smile and wave," Jeremy said, putting the car in reverse. "We got a whole passel of folks watchin'."

"The wave I can probably manage," Duncan said. "You're gonna have to smile for both of us, though."

At the first stoplight, Jeremy fished the handwritten directions from his shirt pocket, held them far enough away to be able to focus, said, "Says here we got dinner waitin' for us in Greeley, Colorado. It oughtta to take us about five hours. Think you can hold out?"

"Long as I don't have to do anything useful."

Jeremy cast a knowing glance his way, eased through the intersection. "Sure has been nice, drivin' cross-country like this with you. You make for good company."

"I haven't taken a road trip since my college days," Duncan said, settling down so he could prop his head on the neck rest.

"You know, the Bible talks about the big things clear as day, even to an old fool like me. But sometimes you gotta read between the lines to see how the littler stuff fits in. Like there was this one time, Jesus and the disciples walked to Jericho after a big argumentation in Jerusalem."

"Argumentation?" Duncan gave the road ahead a tired smile. "Sounds like something a plumber'd say about your washing machine when he's getting ready to hit you with the bill. Yeah, sorry ma'am. All that argumentation meant I had to replace the fly whinger and reshore up the frame bolts. Comes to six hundred and ninety-eight fifty."

"As I was sayin'," Jeremy resumed, "Jesus walked to Jericho. That's quite a ways from Jerusalem. You gotta ask yourself, now, what did they do with all that time? Way I look at it, they took some time off and they *healed*. They walked and they talked and they mighta stopped and fished a while—had to eat something. They slept under the stars, maybe they sang around a campfire."

"You're saying I need to heal, is that it?"

Jeremy eased the massive car around a narrow bend in the road. "Ain't nothin' special 'bout you, son. We all do. You want to make a real difference in God's plan, you gotta take time out to take care of yourself. Ain't nobody else gonna do it for you. It's one of those responsibilities God gave each and every one of us."

"Seems to me I've had more free time than most."

"It's not just havin' time, any more than standin' in the corner and talkin' to the wall is prayin'. The key is what you do with what you've got."

The next curve brought the morning glare into view. Duncan squinted. "So what am I supposed to be doing that I'm not?"

"Well, to start off, you need to forgive whoever's hurt you— forgive 'em so completely it feels like it never even happened."

Duncan shut his eyes to the thought. "If anything ever sounded impossible, that's it."

" 'Course it does. And it'll stay that way, long as you try to do it yourself. Only way you'll ever understand that it's possible is by lettin' the Spirit show you, and the only way that can happen is by askin' Him in. Gotta see this from the inside, son, by gettin' yourself outta the way and lettin' the wonders be worked in you, for you. Then you'll see the miracle firsthand, when the Lord shows you what it means to *really* forgive. The Master tells us, forgive others like we want to be forgiven ourselves. And that's just what He's gonna do, son. I *know* that's the truth."

Duncan thought that one over. "So that's what you think they did on the road, talked about forgiving people?"

Jeremy shook his head. "No, I doubt they were able to remember much about wrong done 'em, standin' as close to the Savior as they were. Nossir, I figure what He did in those lazy days was show His friends what they'd need to help others come to see the light. And to tell you the plain truth, I believe He's still doin' it. Every time we slow down enough to let Him speak to our hearts, His message is still comin' through."

"You mean, you think you can hear God talk to you?"

"No, I'm not that gifted. It's more like He uses the trials I'm facin' to help me see things I might otherwise spend my whole life just runnin' away from." Jeremy kneaded the steering wheel with work-hardened hands. "Sometimes we don't want to give up pain because it sorta defines who we are."

Duncan's voice grew very small. "I guess I never thought about it like that."

"And when a man gets ready to unburden himself, it might mean he's ready to look for a new meaning to life. You see, son, there's only one thing on heaven and earth that can really give a life meaning, and that's the Lord Jesus. All I can offer you is a listenin' heart. But the Lord, why son, He'll offer you *freedom*."

"My wife's family used to talk about freedom in Jesus," Duncan recalled, his eyes on the road ahead. "I never could understand what the fuss was all about, though."

"Did you do all that wild livin' you told me about with your wife?"

He shook his head. "My wife couldn't have been any more different from me. I think that's maybe one reason why I found her so appealing. She had just about everything I didn't as a kid."

"How so?"

"Marcie practically grew up in a Norman Rockwell painting. I never felt like I was good enough for that family. When I was with them I'd get this feeling that everything I did was an act. Like there was some kind of dirt inside me that only showed up when I was sitting in their living room, this big glass of iced tea in my hand, watching them laugh over something the dog did or talk about how some kid down the block had this cough that just wouldn't go away.

"I didn't really envy them. Whenever I went to their house I felt like I was in some Disney dreamland, completely set apart from the world I knew. But at the same time I wished I could fit in and be a part of it myself.

"It was really hard sometimes, really hard. I'd talk to Marcie before we went over about how bored I was going to be, and make like it was this really big issue, whether we should go or not. But that wasn't the truth. I really *liked* those people. I just didn't understand how they could be so nice, and so kind and so, I don't know, *protected*.

"Around dinnertime Marcie's dad would open up this huge Bible. He had a ritual he went through every night. He'd call to his wife to come out, and she'd always say she was in the middle of dinner, and then she'd come and stand in the doorway to the kitchen. He'd read three or four verses, and stop for a moment, and look out into the distance, and say, that reminds me of something that happened. Always the same words. Then he'd have this story about some guy he knew or something that happened earlier, or something he read in the paper, totally calm and incredibly naive."

Duncan shook his head. "I wanted to stand up sometimes and shout, 'Hey, there's people getting blown to smithereens all over the world, how can you sit there looking so doggone smug?'

"Only I never did. I don't know why. Maybe because of how much Marcie enjoyed it all. She'd sit there with her arms wrapped around her legs and her chin on her knees and just *drink* it in. I used to think she was just reliving something from her childhood, but when I kept finding her on her knees all the time when our marriage was falling apart and our daughter didn't come home, I started wondering if maybe it was something different."

Duncan's voice trailed off, his eyes shadowed with pain. Jeremy glanced his way and understood enough to hold his tongue, letting the only voice that spoke be the one of his heart, lifting wings heavenward for the healing of his new friend.

The previous night had proven very difficult for Duncan

Wyeth. Their hosts' open friendliness had pointed accusing fingers at his own unresolved pain. Duncan had felt an unexplained need to avoid their eyes and those of their two teenage girls. The clear demonstration of love between parents and children had acted as a mirror to his own mistakes.

The after-dinner meeting with several dozen couples at a local church was almost more than he could bear. Instead of hearing Jeremy speak of the two runaways, Duncan listened to a silent inner voice and reheard the telling of his own tale.

All that evening the voice inside his head and heart droned on about an aimless life led in pursuit of pleasure that meant almost nothing once it was gained. About a husband who refused to accept the importance of his family, for fear of being forced to change.

He listened to the voice and knew that instead of loving his family as he should, he treated it all as a casual addition to his walk down easy street. His wife learned to ask little of him, for it was all he was willing to give.

Jeremy's talk gave way to the video, and still Duncan's internal monologue continued, its honesty a relentless fist pounding at the barriers of his heart. Even after his child was born, his life's unspoken rule remained that self-sacrifice was for the suckers of this earth. Everybody was out for happiness, he figured, but they let themselves be sidetracked by things like commitment and responsibility and status. All those things did for you was turn you old. Suck you into this giant machine called society and squeeze you dry.

The way he saw it was, the first step to eternal defeat was caring for anyone or anything too much. The key was to just take what came, free and easy and all in stride. Don't let anybody clamp that steel collar around the throat, because sooner or later they'll start tightening the screws.

His daughter learned the lesson well. Too well. When the free-swinging older crowd noticed the blossoming new teenager, they swept her up like a hawk falling on a mouse. One minute she was Daddy's little girl, the next she was wearing too-tight clothes and too much makeup and staying out until dawn.

And then she was gone.

After the evening's video ended, there were a few questions directed at Jeremy; the big raw-boned man answered with words that Duncan could not hear. A woman somewhere nearby started to sniff the way somebody does who is fighting a losing battle with tears; *that* sound cut through the fog of his inward search like a scalpel. Who was crying for his daughter tonight? Who wept tears for his wife? He had not spoken to Marcie in almost five years. Did she still wake up in the middle of the night and lock herself in the bathroom and sob so hard she could scarcely catch her breath?

He sat and pretended to listen to Jeremy and remembered a recurring dream from those early weeks after his daughter's disappearance—stumbling through endless dark corridors and screaming his daughter's name until there came an instant of terrifying realization that he too was now lost, alone in an end-less maze of empty corridors, and would never find his way out. Never.

Duncan let out a ragged sigh, said to the front window, "Is there really such a thing as hope?"

"There is indeed," Jeremy said, as firmly as he knew how. "And it's called the Lord Jesus Christ."

"Part of me really wants to believe you, man. But there's this other part that says it's just bunk."

"I hear what you're sayin'," Jeremy replied easily. "Down home they say the voices of this world call to you the loudest just when you're ready to turn. That reminds me of a story. You mind if I ramble on a while?"

"Go right ahead," Duncan said, his head lolling back. "I'm pretty much talked out."

"My wife's daddy was a big man," Jeremy began. "Big man in business, big man in the right clubs, big man in the city government. His wife was this little frail wisp of a woman. She never stood up to that man, far as I know, except one time when I told 'em I was aimin' on marryin' their daughter. The old man was settin' on takin' after me with his twelve-gauge. But she stood up to him right proper, gave him fifteen kinds of what-not, and danged if he didn't just fold up like a wet newspaper. That woman's had a special place in my prayers ever since.

"Anyway, we were all down at the ocean fishin' one weekend, at a place called Oregon Inlet. Oregon Inlet connected Nags Head to Hatteras, see, and when the tide was risin' that inlet had a current run through there faster'n a flooded river.

"In the autumn the bluefish used to run in there against the tide, goin' after all them minnows that lived in the marsh is-

lands crowdin' the waterway borders, eatin' whatever minnows
eat and growin' fat and sassy. At low tide, this spit of land stuck
out almost halfway across the inlet, real solid sand. At high
tide there wasn't nothin' there at all. Not that you could see,
anyway. Whole thing just disappeared under that fast-runnin'
water.

"Anyway, we were out there one Saturday just havin' ourselves a *time*. There musta been seventy, eighty cars pulled up
on that spit of hard-packed sand, at least three hundred people
out there catchin' fish 'til they could scarcely stand up. The
blues were so hungry they'd bite anything. I mean *anything*.
The tide was risin', and there wasn't that much time left 'fore
we'd have to be gettin' outta there. We were catchin' fish that
we'd dress and freeze and fry up all winter long, see, so to save
time we stopped botherin' to bait our hooks. Them blues were
bitin' so crazy that day they'd hit a bare hook just because it
was shiny.

"So there stood the four of us, me and my wife and her
momma and daddy, haulin' those blues in and castin' back out
so hard and fast our arms were near 'bout rubber, and all the
time the water was creepin' higher up that spit of land. We'd
cast and wait and haul another fish in and take another step
back, 'til we were standin' flush up against the car doors and
the water wasn't more'n ten, twelve inches from our feet.

"We started throwin' these glances over toward where my
daddy-in-law was standin', but that man wasn't stoppin' for
nothin'. That was always his problem, see. The man didn't know
when to let go of a good thing. Finally I asked him for the car
keys, so I could haul the car back a ways.

" 'You just leave that car where it is,' old man Turner told
me. 'We'll be outta here 'fore it starts gettin' high.'

" 'Course by then the water was lickin' against the tires and
Ella and her mom were wearin' these real worried expressions.
But we stood there real quiet-like 'til the water got up so far it
was lappin' over the top of our ankles and touchin' the tire rims,
and I figured it was about time to do a little more pleadin'.

"Old man Turner turned around to snap at me, and he
caught sight of the fact that every other car on that whole spit
of land was long gone. Yessir, we were the last ones out. And
between us and the main island was this little lake growin'
bigger by the minute, 'til there was only this thin little strip of
dry land over to one side that looked like it was goin' under
with the next big wave.

"Well, sir, you ain't never seen four people move so fast in all your born days. I came flyin' 'round the side of the car with that icebox full of blues and knocked Ella's momma clear into next week. Just mowed her down. And then we couldn't find her. She'd slipped and fallen into the water and the tide just picked her up and carried her off. I was down on all fours scramblin' and snortin' that water up my nose and scared half to death.

"Then she popped up on the other side of the car, and we didn't need any more urgin' to get in the car and outta there. 'Course, I don't need to tell you what happened next."

Duncan guessed, "The car wouldn't start."

"Battery was as dead as last autumn's leaves. Wouldn't even grunt. So we're sittin' there, wonderin' which one of us was gonna have to tell the old man it's time to ditch the car and run for the hills, when the sweetest sound this side of glory came waftin' in with the breeze.

"I looked out the window and spotted this big old tractor chuggin' toward us, the one they used for pullin' in the nets at the wharf across the street. That tractor came drivin' up on them high wheels, stopped about thirty feet away, and this old geezer yelled out, 'It's gonna cost you three hundred bucks for me to pull you out.'

"Now you gotta understand, Ella's daddy didn't get where he was without bein' hard on a nickel. That man was so tight if a quarter dropped in Richmond he'd be down on all fours in Raleigh. He knew how to pinch a penny until it screamed. And three hundred dollars was a lotta money back then."

"Lotta money now," Duncan said.

"Not like then. Back then there was a lotta folks raisin' families on paychecks that size. But that man and his tractor had us where it mattered, and he knew it, and he was dead set on givin' old man Turner a good squeeze.

"But Ella's daddy wasn't one to give in easy, so he jumped out of the car and screamed at the man, 'Three hundred dollars!'

"The old fellow on the tractor was busy with a wad of chewin' tobacco, so he took time to squirt out some juice. Made a right good job of it too, pretty near cleared the distance between the tractor and the car. The fellow eyed the car and said, 'Price's just gone up to three-fifty.'

"Well, old man Turner got real mad then, and said some things I don't believe I'm gonna repeat here. Only thing that stopped him was his wife callin' from inside the car that there was a bluefish swimmin' 'round her feet. He looked over at the man and said, 'I'll give you two hundred, and that's my last offer.'

" 'Price is five hundred now,' the fellow kinda drawled out, just as relaxed and happy as a cat in a sunny window. 'And you open your mouth again, mister, and I'm gonna drive back over there and watch you float away. Might take your wife with me, but I sure don't have no room up here for you.'

"I do believe old man Turner ground a good half inch off his molars on that ride back. Didn't help any to see the whole dog-gone road up ahead lined with people laughin' and pointin' and takin' pictures and wavin' at us. Ella and I kinda huddled down low in the backseat and didn't look at each other, not one instant, nossir. Wasn't no time to get into a gigglin' fit.

"So after he'd shelled out another coupla hundred on top of the five for them to clean up his motor and fit in a new battery, we started back home. You don't think that was a long ride. I mean to tell you what's the truth, I've seen more smilin' faces at a cemetery.

"But here's the secret, son. Them dollars didn't even begin to make a dent in old man Turner's pocket. If truth be known, that money wasn't even worth countin'. Nossir, what that man was so angry about payin' out was his *pride*.

"It's just like a lot of us, when the good Lord's called our name and we're standin' there scared and mad and hurtin' and wishin' there was some way we could get outta this mess with our pride intact. And our pain. We get awful attached to our burdens, awful attached to the lie that we can handle this alone, find our way free without help. Pride, pure pride. We know the price we're gonna pay ain't really that high. But man oh man, do we ever have trouble wrestlin' with our pride."

Duncan sat for a long time in absolute silence, contending with forces only he could see. Then, in a hesitant voice, he asked, "You think maybe we could pray together?"

It was as though Jeremy had been waiting for the words all along. In one smooth motion he signaled and braked and swung onto the shoulder, saying as he did, "Son, there ain't a single solitary thing in this whole wide world that'd make me happier."

CHAPTER
11

Congressman John Silverwood was leaving committee chambers the next morning when Harvey Biggs rushed up and grabbed his elbow. "Wonder if I might have a quiet word with you somewhere, Congressman."

"Let go of my arm."

Biggs dropped his hand to his side, gave a smile that meant nothing to either of them. "A certain lobbyist who is a mutual friend of ours suggested I speak with you."

"He is not a friend," Silverwood replied.

"Whatever. He assured me I would find a listening ear."

Silverwood allowed himself to be led into a nearby alcove, pretended to listen as Biggs outlined the upcoming anti-porn legislation bill. "I have been asked to inform you that it would be in the best interests of everyone concerned for this bill to die a quiet death on the floor, Congressman."

Feeling a rise of pure dread at the words, Silverwood worked at keeping his gaze level and his face blank. The feared summons had come once again. He had never felt so helpless in his entire life.

Harvey Biggs mistook his silence for refusal, flickered light from a solid gold cuff link into Silverwood's eyes as he raised his hand and patted his sparse black hair. He used the motion to glance up and down the hall, ensuring that no one was close enough to overhear him. In a lower voice he said, "I was told to tell you that specific interests are extremely concerned about this, Congressman. They urgently require your assistance in killing the anti-porn measure. I am quoting them exactly."

"I don't control the House," Silverwood replied.

"No, but your word goes a long way, in there as everywhere else. The freshman congressman who everyone has marked as a highflier, the first to be given a seat on the Ways and Means—"

"I'll let you know," Silverwood said, spinning away and putting as much distance between him and Biggs as he could without running.

Once he was back in his office he called Senator Atterly's office, insisted on being put on hold while the senator completed a meeting. Fifteen minutes later the familiar bark said, "Great to hear from you, John. What can I do for you?"

Silverwood recapped the discussion with Biggs. "They're going to put the pressure on me."

"Of course they are. Why should you be any different?"

He hesitated, confessed, "They have some things on me that could make this a career decision."

"I see." Atterly was quiet for a moment, then asked, "Does this have anything to do with what you've been needing to get off your chest?"

"Yes." It was no longer enough to hold it inside, keep it bottled up, run from what he could never leave behind, hide in overwork and fury and drink. "Yes it does."

"Have you tried praying about it, John? Not about this Biggs and company. I mean about the problem."

"Last night," Silverwood said, having to struggle with the words.

"Well, it sounds to me like it's come time for you to choose sides, John. I've found that the Lord has a way of bringing people to these crucial junctures. You can't remain in a situation where you're forced to accede to wishes you know are wrong, and find comfort in His forgiveness. You've got to make a choice."

"Even if it means giving up my political career?"

"It all comes down to that, does it?" Atterly's voice was very grave. "Well, it has for me too, John. I'm sorry to hear that it's the case, but for what it's worth, you're not losing that much. No, hear me out. I've spent more than half my life defining my very existence by the political title I happened to be wearing at the time. And now that I'm losing it, I find that it really isn't much more than an extra suit of clothes. I take them off, and the real me is still there. The *real* me, John. The one fashioned by my faith. The only one that matters, because it's the only one that lasts.

"Now I can't tell you what to do about this situation, but I want you to think about what I've just said. And while you do, go look at yourself in the mirror. It seems to me, you've become a man who doesn't feel right in his own skin. Maybe the Lord is pushing you in this way because it's the only chance for you to find a little peace in this life, to discover that misery is just another burden you've got to learn to set down."

◆ ◆ ◆

Senator Richard Atterly rose from his chair to shake the newspaper reporter's hand. He nodded his thanks to Nak, waved the reporter to a chair. The man was young and fresh-faced and extremely earnest. Atterly settled himself back, knowing that there was little chance of focusing this interview upon the issues at hand.

Over the past few days attacks upon him and the anti-pornography bill had begun to surface. The appeal for a Solemn Assembly had only added fuel to the fire. The worst broadsides had come from the American Libertarian United Movement, the ALUM, who had gone so far as to actually call the senator deranged. The Per Se bill, according to the latest attack, was a perfect example of how religious radicals sought to constrict the freedom of the American people under the banner of religious principle.

Senator Atterly inspected the man seated across from him. The newspaper reporter was still new enough to his job to show a trace of nerves. The assignment had come to him, the senator knew from experience, because none of the senior staff wanted to touch it. There was still too much mystery attached to a senior politician calling for some biblical assembly that no one had ever heard of before. But the ALUM's attacks had become so noisy and constant that a response from the senator was called for.

The reporter leaned forward in his chair and asked, "Senator Atterly, would it be fair to treat the ALUM as your nemesis on this issue?"

"I wouldn't like to paint anyone as my nemesis, because

then they would never see me as anything else. If that were to happen, then I would be going directly against the teachings of Jesus Christ."

The reporter visibly winced, covered it by scribbling busily. Senator Atterly permitted himself a hint of a smile. There was no chance of the reporter being allowed to use a quote that mentioned Jesus Christ by name. No chance at all.

Taking pity on the man's position, he added, "If I were ever wrongly imprisoned, I would hope and pray that the ALUM would take up my case. But insofar as this particular issue is concerned, I think they are wrong as wrong can be."

"Why is that?"

"They approach the pornography issue from the standpoint of Constitutional law. I approach it from the standpoint of harm to the victim. Taking my own personal view to its logical conclusion means that I want to *prevent* the individual from *becoming* a victim. It is a question of protecting legal principles versus protecting citizens."

The reporter took careful notes, but was clearly not satisfied with the reaction. Well-thought-out sentences were not as interesting to the press as a furious retaliation.

The reporter asked, "Do you have a reaction to their attacks on the religious nature of your call for this new law?"

Senator Atterly realized that his response would most likely be shortened to the negative only, but if for nothing more than his own sake he needed to state both sides. He began, "First of all, it is essential to commend the ALUM for their extremely worthy efforts on behalf of the nation's downtrodden. They do much good in the name of humanistic activity, helping the little man who otherwise would very likely go without any legal representation whatsoever.

"But in every instance where Christianity is involved, they stand in direct opposition. The foremost evidence of this fact is that in the ALUM charter they champion every single element of the Bill of Rights *except* freedom of religion. They leave this out *entirely*."

"This would appear to indicate that they are your opponents when it comes to religion," the reporter persisted.

Senator Atterly leaned back in his chair. He had known from the beginning that this would be the direction sought by the interviewer. He repeated, "I feel that the ALUM should be highly commended for their efforts to assist the downtrodden.

But yes, I also believe that they are against organized religion and God Almighty's directives."

The reporter did not attempt to mask his delight. This was the quotation that would elevate his byline to the newspaper's front page. "Could you tell me why?"

"They are a wolf in sheep's clothing," Senator Atterly replied bluntly. "Their greatest danger comes by virtue of the public's ignorance. The ALUM masks their stance on religiously related issues because there would otherwise be too great a risk of a unified backlash. Yet they champion the humanistic cause at the cost of the Christian faith."

"You have used that word humanism before. Could you tell me what it means to you?"

"Humanism in this specific instance is the call to attack social ills. That in itself is a fine ideal, and is why I feel that so much of the ALUM's efforts are laudable. What creates the difficulty is the basis upon which this call to service is founded.

"Secular humanism believes in the fundamental good of humanity, and in the ability for man to heal himself and make himself better or whole or complete. I believe the term currently in vogue is self-actualized. It holds that mankind is capable of achieving this goal alone, calling upon nothing more than his own higher intelligence and willpower.

"Christians, on the other hand, believe that man alone is incapable of correcting either his own personal ills or those of any society which he has created. To a Christian, the state of our world speaks for itself. People cannot find their way any more easily today, in this era of self-generated power and unlimited opportunity, than they ever could before. There are still wars, there is still famine, there is still oppression and conflict and disease.

"The humanists look for self-serving remedies, bringing up whatever policy or belief or new religion best suits their current mentality. They choose what is most comfortable for the moment, and ignore the fact that the same ills refuse to be healed. Communism is a perfect example of what happens when mankind attempts to replace God's law with man's law. No matter how fine and noble the precepts of this new belief structure may sound, the result is the same. In the end, self-centeredness and greed and personal ambition will corrupt the system, and turn the ends toward evil."

"You are saying, then," the reporter pressed, "that the situation is hopeless. And since there is no chance to better the circumstances, why try?"

"Not at all," Senator Atterly replied sharply. "The Lord has granted us very clear precepts by which we are instructed to rule both our lives and our nation. We are ordered to follow them. Please note the word I used here. God did not come to Moses on Mount Sinai and give him the Ten Suggestions. Those precepts by which we are to shape our lives are *commandments*. And when His Son walked this earth and fulfilled the law, He too issued us further commandments. Love thy neighbor as thyself. Do no harm to children. Serve those in need, and do so with love in His name. We are commanded to obey His instructions to the very best of our ability. We fail, yes, we all fall short of His commands. That is predetermined by our very nature. But we must still *try*."

"Yet no matter how valid you consider your own position to be," the reporter persisted, "the ALUM enjoys a considerable amount of support. Since we are living in a democracy, wouldn't you say that these people who disagree with your position also have a right to their own views?"

"Of course they have," Atterly replied. "And your question is a valid one. But there are three very essential alliances which the ALUM has forged, partly in secret and partly in the open, which have magnified their influence far beyond anything justified by the number of people who either belong to their organization or agree with their policies.

"The first of these alliances is with Congress. The ALUM has become an expert at lobbying and at applying backroom pressure to promote their aims. As a result, Congress has recently passed several laws offering federal financing to some of the ALUM cases. Through their tax dollars, people who often totally disagree with ALUM positions are now *forced* to pay for ALUM-selected court cases out of their own pockets.

"The second alliance has been with lawyers. The Academy of Trial Lawyers, which operates in every state of the nation, is very closely tied to the ALUM. Why? The reason here is very logical—money.

"Literally thousands of lawsuits, in every city and county in the nation, are ALUM-generated. But the ALUM itself, you see, does not have many lawyers on its own staff—certainly not enough to handle even one-half of the lawsuits that it brings to court every year. They farm out a *tremendous* amount of legal business, and their allies reap the benefits. For some major law firms, the ALUM is one of their largest sources of business.

"Here the issue of secrecy arises once again. Most Christians are not aware of this alliance, you see. Once it did become public knowledge, they could conceivably refuse to work with any law firm that does business with the ALUM. It would force these firms to publicly declare their colors. If Christian businesses and households across the nation were to take such a concerted action, the result would be catastrophic as far as the ALUM is concerned. So they seek to keep such alliances in the dark.

"The third alliance is the most unholy of all, the alliance with the more liberal portions of our nation's press. The reason to me is obvious. The ALUM says, number one, freedom of everything. Freedom of speech, of press, of everything. They attack any infringement whatsoever."

The reporter interrupted. "Can you give me a specific example of this?"

"Of the alliance or of their policy to attack on any infringement on freedom?"

The reporter shrugged. "Both, I guess."

"Certainly. The ALUM believes in protecting any kind of pornography whatsoever. The use of it, the production of it, the dissemination of it, regardless of whether it is child or adult pornography. In child pornography, they make the defense that once the abuse has taken place, then repression of the resulting films or photographs will accomplish nothing. It should therefore be freely available and distributed. Over the airways, over the press, in your local supermarket. Regardless of the harm that may result or how some customers may feel about it.

"To put this in general terms, I believe that I should have the legal right to swing my arm until just before it connects with your nose. At that instant, just before the contact is made, my freedom ends. The ALUM's position is that they should have the right to swing their arm *regardless* of who might be hurt— even if the person who is damaged for life by their so-called freedom is a little child.

"Horrible as the repercussions clearly are, this same attitude of total freedom links them with the liberal press. The press, of course, wants absolute freedom. They don't want to answer to anyone for what they say or print. They don't wish to face libel or slander charges from anybody. They don't want to have anyone exercising any control whatsoever over their actions. They want total freedom to say whatever they wish, to hold whatever policy they feel is correct, to attack whomever they want. And this is exactly the position of the ALUM."

The reporter had already stopped writing and put away his pad. As soon as Atterly paused to draw breath, the newsman was on his feet with hand outstretched. "Thank you very much for your time, Senator. I believe I've already gotten everything I came for."

"Just one moment." His stern tone stopped the reporter. "I cannot make you put this in your article, young man, but I am going to ask you to make note of one more point. Will you grant me that courtesy?"

Reluctantly the reporter took out his pen and notebook. "Sure, Senator. Anything you say."

"Historically and constitutionally, our nation has existed on the basis of separating the *institutions* of church and state. Nowadays, however, the ALUM and other humanism-oriented organizations seek to separate our government and our legal system from the *principles* of faith. Despite what the ALUM would have you believe, this is not what the Constitution was written to protect. In fact, nothing on earth could be further from the truth. The very first document our nation created as a nation, the Declaration of Independence, clearly states our loyalty to God Almighty. Our nation's very motto shouts out where our first loyalty lies—In God We Trust.

"And yet now these self-proclaimed protectors of our Bill of Rights and our Constitution seek to *destroy* this loyalty, and to *divorce* our government from any explicit allegiance to a higher power. Why? Because this very same higher power tells us where and how to limit our freedoms."

Senator Atterly leaned across his desk and shot a finger at the reporter. "Now you go out there and find an answer to this question: What do they intend to install in the place of our Lord God? What guiding principles will dictate the path our nation is to take? Ask yourself that, young man. Dwell on it night and day until the answer is clear. Ponder it as though your country's very future depended upon it. Because it does."

◆　◆　◆

Lou Ann Walker set the coffeepot down on the living room table just as the front doorbell rang. She hurried to greet the neighborhood women, all of them carrying Bibles and note-books and study guides. There was the normal friendly chatter as everyone settled, the habitual joking when her next-door neighbor arrived last and breathless as usual.

As was their custom, they went around the circle discussing special needs for themselves and their families before the prayer time. There were also quite a few happy moments, when the women shared prayers that had been answered. This sharing and praying normally took up to half of the Bible study period, but no one complained. There had been too many incidents that couldn't be chalked up to coincidence for them to consider it time ill spent.

Lou Ann waited until all the others had spoken, taking notes as she usually did so that she could remember the new prayer needs throughout the week. When it came her time she closed her notebook, leaned over and picked up the video she had set under the coffee table, and said she had something special to share.

"Last night Vic and I were invited over to friends for dinner. They had a couple of guests staying with them from Washington, D.C. They showed us a talk made by a United States senator, I forget his name. If it's all right I'd like to take the time to show it to you."

There was the sort of politely curious response that she expected. Lou Ann smiled her thanks, then said, "I wanted to show it as a part of our sharing because we all have children, and I think it's something we may all want to include in our prayers. These two men are traveling across the country searching for a couple of teenage girls who have run away. They say that it looks like they've become involved—"

Suddenly Lou Ann was crying so hard she could hardly breathe. She waved aside the concerned hands and murmurs, struggled for control, managed to say, "This is *important*. We've got to *do* something. We've *got* to get involved."

◆　◆　◆

At the lunch break Stan gathered with his buddies at the back end of the larger stamping machine. It was a dark-colored behemoth, rising up so high the company had built a special thirty-foot ceiling and then dug a square pit through the six-inch concrete floor and sunk the machine down another fifteen feet just to get it under the crane. It generated almost one hundred tons of pressure and could bend metal plates up to one and a half inches thick. Stan was one of the three men trained to operate it, under the management's program of duplicating every shop-floor skill at least twice, but his main job was overseeing the CNC-operated milling and grinding machines. Stan was a highly skilled machinist and an active Christian, and the group that gathered with him at the back of the shop floor were all part of a Bible study group he had organized a couple of years ago. It had grown from a trio of men who went to the same church to over fifteen guys, with two of the management getting down at least twice a week to sit with them and pray and talk through the lunch hour.

The talk that day was about a discussion his church was having. Three days before, he told the group, there had been a special evening service where a visitor had spoken.

"The big guy, I forget his name, he was straight off the farm. Hands that'd make fists the size of my six-pound hammer, hair that was always getting in the way, an accent you could cut with a knife. The other guy, he didn't say much, just sat there and kinda watched this big fellow make his spiel."

Stan took a bite from his sandwich. "Couldn't for the life of me figure out what I was doing there at first. I mean, these guys are chasing across the country for a couple of girls who've got themselves hooked up with some real sleazy types.

"Then they showed this video of a speech from the senator, what's his name, the guy from Rhode Island or someplace back east that's on all the big committees and everything."

"Senator Atterly," one of the management offered.

"Yeah, that's the one. It was a tape of a speech he gave a while back, talking about some big meeting he wants to get together in Washington."

"That Solemn Assembly thing," another man offered. "Yeah, my wife saw that. She's been talking about it for over a week. That guy musta really poured it on."

"Nah, it wasn't anything like that," Stan replied. "The senator looked nervous as a guy his first day on the job. It was something else. I can't put my finger on it. I tell you something, though. I couldn't get it out of my mind. Spent almost all night sitting downstairs thinking about what he said."

"I'd like to see that," the manager said.

"The pastor said he was gonna make some copies and let

people borrow them. I'll give him a call tonight and see if I can get my hands on one."

"Get two, why don't you?" a buddy said. "I wouldn't mind seeing that myself."

Stan nodded and wiped his hands on the empty wax paper. Come to think of it, he had a couple of other friends at church who ought to see the tape and hear the story about these two kids that pair were chasing. Yeah, and maybe the pastor at the church across town, too. Stan closed his lunch box, set it aside, and pulled out his little pocket Bible for the reading. Something important was going on here. No doubt about it.

◆   ◆   ◆

It was a simple sterile motel room somewhere on the outskirts of Las Vegas. The carpet wore a tired checked pattern and smelled vaguely of disinfectant. The bed was slightly bowed in the middle, the bedspread patterned to match the carpet and stained at one corner with something dark. Light came from a bedside lamp and a hanging globe set over the cheap wooden counter and the television. The drapes that shut out the streetlights were plastic and almost matched the rug. The two chairs looked very uncomfortable.

Jessica waited there alone because Pierre had ordered her to. It was not often she heard the threat in his voice, but it had been there today. Don't let the pleading in your eyes go any further, his tone had said, the unspoken warning very clear. Scared as she had been, she had held down tight on the fear and the dread and the sickness and the trembling, at least as long as he had been in the room.

But once he was gone and she was truly alone, more alone than she had ever been in her life, she let the shivers rise up and consume her slender frame. Her mind scampered like a frantic little animal, seeking escape in all the hidden corners. When no refuge was found, it turned in on itself and replayed the one and only time she had defied the threat in Pierre's voice and told him no.

Pierre's favorite hobby was photography, and all that summer his favorite model was Jessica. He started her out in a most gentle fashion, showing her his cameras, speaking to her in that smooth voice, describing how great and glamorous it was to be a model. Jessica listened because it was Pierre who was talking, and only slowly did it dawn on her that he meant it for *her,* that *she* could become a model. Even when he said it outright, she refused to believe he meant it. I don't like having people look at me, she said.

He nodded his understanding, replied, this is the great thing about being a model, see? You can have thousands of people looking at you and envying you and wishing they were you, but you're separated from seeing them or knowing them or hearing anything bad they might say because all they see is the page or the movie. And she nodded and listened and *wanted* to believe because he made it all sound really nice, and because it was Pierre who wanted it for her.

Like everything else of Pierre's, his camera gear was always packed away when it wasn't being used. It surprised her how all his clothes were kept in a large stand-up case with special little drawers. His stereo was very compact; the speakers connected back to the sides, and all the cassettes and CD's were kept neatly in their own little cases. Even his books had their own suitcase, turned up on one end to act as knee-high shelves. The camera case was special white aluminum, and the gear was packed into form-fitted foam rubber. There were two camera bodies and three lenses and two light attachments and a compact tripod.

The first night he showed it to her, Pierre carefully explained what everything was for, the close-up lenses and the strobe with toning filters and the hand-held secondary lamp. He was gentle and patient and so very caring, stroking her and answering her questions in the greatest possible detail, taking pains to put her at ease and make her feel a *part* of it all.

It's such an incredible energy, he said to her time after time. There's such an amazing bonding force between photographer and model. The life is so great; imagine, you're paid real money to get up in the morning, make yourself just as beautiful as you can, and then go in and show off your body. Isn't that incredible? She nodded and looked up at him and agreed that it really was incredible, almost as incredible as how he cared for her.

She felt very self-conscious the first few times she posed in front of the camera, but it meant a lot to him, and she wanted to do what would please him. It was important that he be pleased.

But she balked when he asked her to pose in her underclothes. "I can't do it," she told him. "I'm scared."

"Fine," he replied, and immediately froze up inside.

The change and the suddenness scared her more than anything she had known in their relationship. One moment he was all gentle coaxing, the next the room was filled with a tension that terrified her. It was the suddenness as much as the force that frightened her, as though there was this little voice inside her head saying, see, this is the way it is, you don't do what he says, he's going to dump you just this fast.

She was all over him in an instant, pleading with him not to be mad, feeling the incredibly tensed muscles under his clothes, begging for him to turn around and look at her. There was a fury in his eyes and in his tightly clenched face that seemed just barely under control. It frightened her to stay draped all over that much anger, but not as much as having him leave her.

Jessica fought off losing her own control and asked him to lighten up a little, *please*. But he wouldn't respond, and after a couple more minutes insisted on taking her home. Ignoring her tears and her pleading, he just dropped her at the base of the driveway and roared off into the night, leaving her there to sob out a final call for him to stop, please, turn around and come back.

The next morning was the first time in a month that he did not swim with her. She spent over an hour gathering her courage, then followed him into the storeroom and ignored his furious command to get out of his way. She struggled not to break down again and said in a rush what she had spent the whole night thinking over—that she was sorry she got him so angry; she didn't know it was so important to him. He cut her off with a chop of his arm, saying in that hateful cold voice that she had it wrong, *nothing* was important to him. She stifled the instinct to jump away from his hand and away from the power in his fury, but she couldn't keep the tears back anymore as she pushed on, desperate to hold on to him, desperate to make him understand. It was just that it was all real new, Jessica told him around her sobs. She would do what he wanted, just let her come over and see him tonight, okay? Pierre gathered up a double armful of cushions and pushed past as though she wasn't even there.

That night she went by anyway, terrified that if she didn't she would lose him for sure, hoping she'd somehow get him to listen to her. But when she arrived at his apartment Pierre was all gentleness and smiles, saying that he was really glad to see her, really sorry for how upset he had been. He had a bad temper that just exploded sometimes, especially when something like this was so important to him.

We have this great way to be together, Pierre told her, something really special, and here you are acting like a *child*. If you want it to be a great relationship, something special and lasting, you're going to have to drop a lot of these stupid meaningless rules and open up to me. All the while he was talking, he held her and stroked her hair and spoke in that slow gentle way that made her feel as if she were melting.

He had offered her joints before, but she had always refused because of the bad dreams that the smoke brought. Tonight, though, she could refuse him nothing. He lit it and passed it and said, it will help you relax. She nodded and took it and tried not to cough when the smoke burned her throat. He smoked with her, and watched her with that dark hidden gaze, and stroked her face, and told her over and over how much he really cared.

This time, when he brought out the camera case, she did not wait to be asked; she simply started taking off her clothes. He responded by returning to the sofa for another long hug and more words that touched her heart, and then by rising and putting on some soft music.

The smoke did help, it really did. She was somehow more numb and more sensitive at the same time. Jessica sat on the sofa and watched him set up his camera and let him stretch her out into a pose, and decided that maybe he was right after all. It did feel nice, now that the drug helped reduce her fear, having him direct her and fashion her position and tell her how to look and then stand back and take his pictures and return and start all over again. She felt bonded to him, just like he said.

The camera and the poses and the pictures and the smoke became a part of the routine every time Jessica came over. And the more she did it, the easier it became. Things she would not have thought possible early on became almost natural by the sixth or seventh time.

Sometimes when she was away from him she thought about how excited he got when she posed like he told her to, and she felt a little shiver of fear. He seemed so close to the edge at those times, just barely in control. She felt as though there was an animal inside him she could catch little glimpses of from time to time. She didn't understand it exactly, but this photography thing was a part of it. Taking her pictures like this *excited* him. It *pleased* him. At those times the invisible something below Pierre's dark silent surface threatened to rise up like a roaring beast free of invisible chains. She felt as if she were standing at the edge of a chasm sometimes when she posed for him as he wanted. But she did it anyway because he wanted it so, and she tried not to think of what lay behind the burning hunger in those dark violet eyes.

She was brought back to the present with a start when the door to the motel room opened and a man walked in. Jessica stood up quickly, glanced one time, then cowered with hunched shoulders and fingers laced in terror in front of her body.

He was a man of large dimensions and solid power. His hair was swept back and perfectly trimmed and dyed as brown as his eyes. A faint trace of gray touched the edges of his sideburns, like the markings on a rich lady's fox fur. His suit was cut to hide his bulk and fitted him like a glove.

It was a broad face. A wide forehead jutted above eyes encased in heavy folds, ones that leaned downward with his cheeks and jowls and mouth. His whole face frowned mightily.

Jessica kept her eyes down, fastened on the toes of his polished shoes, and fought to control her trembling. He didn't say a word as he stood in front of her. She could hear his breath whistling in and out of his nostrils as he reached up with meaty fingers and twirled a strand of her hair. She had never heard anything in her life that sounded as horrible as his breathing.

When he planted a hand around the side of her neck, she allowed the pressure in her heart to rise up and swamp her. Jessica did not even try to hold back her sobs.

CHAPTER
12

A companionable pair arrived in Los Angeles that bright sunny afternoon four days later. Through constant contact, Jeremy and Duncan had come to know each other quite well, and found to their surprise that they not only got along but actually liked each other. They were glad to have the cross-country trip behind them, happy to be getting on with the search, glad to be together.

The sky of Los Angeles was a strained milky blue, as though the clouds had condensed and fallen and been trapped close to earth; their imprisonment had wrung the sky of moisture and left it laden with dirt. The air was dry and flat and smelled of too much industry and too many cars. The hills were brown and arid and void of charm. Hillside housing developments scratched rude furrows in the scarred earth and left the countryside with an unfinished look, as though the money had run out before the landscaping could be completed.

And the freeways were a nightmare come to life.

"Hey, you with the map. You got any idea where we are?"

Jeremy turned the map up on its end, squinted through the windshield at another road sign, shook his head. "Son, I'm as lost as last Tuesday."

The freeway was six lanes in each direction and packed solid. Duncan struggled to keep his speed from being raised by the aggressive tactics surrounding him on all four sides. He was constantly passed by heavy trucks pushing eighty. There was nothing easy to this drive. The freeway ducked its way up and down a series of steep hills and blind curves before entering into the chaos of Los Angeles proper.

"I know we've got to go straight through town to get to Santa Monica. At least, that's what the guy told us last night."

Jeremy pointed ahead, said, "Will you just look at that."

Duncan saw an enormous billboard posted to the side of a hotel that read *Have your next affair here.* He laughed. "Welcome to California."

"There's a sign for Santa Monica, son. Work your way over to the left lane."

"How?" Duncan swiveled, searched, found no opening. "This is worse than bumper cars."

A sixteen-wheeler blasted by them, its back doors emblazoned with an enormous decal of a skull and crossbones and the words *No Mercy.* Duncan hunched his shoulders, held his breath, and swooped into an invisible air pocket behind the truck. The car behind him greeted his move with a thirty-second blare of his horn.

"Good going, son. Just three more lanes to go."

Duncan glanced into his rearview mirror. "I think somebody's trying to climb inside my trunk." He switched off his turn signal since nobody was paying it any mind. "A couple weeks of this and I'd probably decide an automatic weapon under the dash was as necessary as a steering wheel."

They had spent the evening before in Visalia, a farming community in the California Central Valley, one of the most productive agricultural regions in the world, four hours inland and north from Los Angeles. Their host had an aunt who had retired to a joint apartment/hotel in Santa Monica, a town that had sort of melted into its bigger neighbor until it was little more than a Los Angeles-by-the-sea. She explained that the hotel stood between Wilshire and Santa Monica boulevards, was a straight shot into the city, and more pleasant than staying downtown.

The freeway grew progressively more congested as they passed signs for downtown Los Angeles, then Hollywood, West Hollywood, Beverly Hills, Century City, and finally Venice and Santa Monica and the Pacific Coast Highway. They took the Thirteenth Street off-ramp because they were trapped in the exit lane and would have needed either a tank or a bazooka to work their way over. It was just as well. Progress along the local streets was slower, but a lot more pleasant.

They stopped at a red light; Jeremy caught a glimpse of someone out of the corner of his eye. The man was tall and good-looking and wore slick shorts, new shoes, spiked dark hair, a face with a perpetual sneer, and a t-shirt that read *How do you spell love? M-O-N-E-Y.*

Duncan followed his gaze, said, "That's what clothes are for out here, I guess. Advertise your attitude."

"Store-bought cynicism," Jeremy agreed. "How can a body be proud about bein' so cynical?"

"It's the style of the nineties. Nobody can take advantage of you if you don't show any heart."

"Appears to me all that pain'd be awful hard to bear."

"What pain?"

"The pain that the cynicism is restin' on," Jeremy replied.

The hotel on Santa Monica's Ocean Boulevard was right out of another age. It was dwarfed by newer structures to either side, but its whitewashed art-deco finery shone like a polished gem. A broad veranda fronted the street and was lined with comfortable looking settees. The double doors were frosted glass with brass insets in the form of prancing flamingos. Tiny balconies of fluted ironwork adorned the upstairs windows. The building's corners were decorated with the same lavish carvings as the edges of the roof, all white-on-white and freshly painted. Beside the mirrored surfaces of the more modern structures, the hotel held an understated elegance that put its neighbors to shame.

Six white-haired matrons sat on the veranda and gossiped as Jeremy and Duncan pulled up. The pair was greeted with bright-eyed curiosity and the silence of people who from experience were not sure if the men would even look their way. When Jeremy gave them a little half bow and murmured a good afternoon, they positively beamed.

Duncan gave the lobby a brief once-over, took in the large plate-glass windows and art-deco chandeliers and grand piano and high ceiling and leather furniture, and said to Jeremy in a low voice, "Maybe we ought to sleep somewhere else."

"What's the matter, you bothered by all these old folks?"

"I'm bothered by what the price is going to be. I don't think you can afford this place."

"Don't give it another thought."

Duncan caught up and stopped him with a hand on his arm.

"Listen, I've had more experience with big-city hotels than you have. This place has expensive written all over it. If you look carefully through that window over there, see that little sparkle of blue? That's the Pacific Ocean. That means this place is not cheap. Not by a long shot."

"We got friends of friends expectin' us here. No reason to disappoint them."

"And there's no reason why we can't stay a couple of blocks inland and come visit. Look, Jeremy, one of the families I'm working for is as close to poor as you can get and still be doing okay. I'm not going to be able to bill them for this hotel."

"But you can afford to stay here, can't you?"

"Well, sure. But we're not talking about me."

Jeremy sighed and turned to stare out the window. "I guess our talk back in Washington didn't sink in."

"What talk?"

"I suppose you could say I was right well off."

"You mean, as in rich?"

"Well, that might be stretchin' things a bit. Let's just say that it ain't gonna burn a hole in my wallet to bed down here for a while."

Duncan stared at him a moment longer, asked, "Is there anything else I ought to know about you? I mean, now that it's confession time and all. You don't own a fleet of Lear jets or anything, right?"

"I thought all that was cleared up before we left, I really did."

"So have I been traveling all this time with another Howard Hughes? A hobo with a billion bucks buried in his backyard?"

"It ain't a billion, and it ain't buried. Well, it is sort of, I suppose. Like I told you, I build things. And own some of them, or parts anyway. Shopping centers, a couple of buildings, and a farm."

His voice flat, Duncan asked, "How big a farm?"

"Oh, just a piddlin' little thing compared to what folks've got in Texas. But it's about more than I can handle."

"How large, Jeremy."

"Little over ten thousand acres. Used to be this swamp, see, and I—"

"Okay, which one of you is Jeremy Hughes?"

They looked down on a silver-haired dowager dressed in purple shorts, blue suede sneakers, and a pink t-shirt that read

You're never too old to hear the Good News.

"I am, ma'am. How you doin' this afternoon?"

"Not bad. Could be better, if you find some way I can shed forty years." The eyes were bright, the gaze friendly. "My name is Mavis, Mavis Talmadge. My nephew says you're out here looking for two runaways. That right?"

"Yes, ma'am. At least, my friend Duncan is. I'm just sort of along for the ride."

"Not what I hear. My nephew says that story of yours packs quite a punch, and my nephew is nobody's fool. I've told a few of the ladies around here what you're up to, hope you don't mind. We want to know what we can do to help."

"Pray," Jeremy replied. "Can't think of anything that could help us more."

"That we'll do." There was an air of no-nonsense about her. "Anything else?"

"Only thing I can think of now is where we might find a church that's tryin' to help the runaways."

"I'll have to check on that one. Now why don't you gentlemen go ahead and check in, and I'll do a little calling around."

Their room turned out to be a two-bedroom apartment. Thanks to Mavis and a friend behind the desk, for the price of two singles they were given an apartment with two bedrooms, a spacious kitchen, high ceilings, and a view out over the Pacific. The ocean was quite a ways off; across the four-lane road was a slender park, and beyond that cliffs which fell to the Pacific Coast Highway. Figures on the broad white-sand beach were indistinct, shimmering shadows at that distance, and the water looked pure and inviting. Duncan decided against telling Jeremy of recent pollution problems in the Santa Monica Bay that had made the national news.

The carpet and furniture were new, but little else had been altered since the twenties. The closets were massive walk-in affairs, the bathroom adorned with ceramic taps and hand-painted tiles and a vast tub supported by clawed feet. The windows were lead-framed and opened on hinges that squeaked with age, and every time its motor started, the refrigerator shuddered hard enough to shake the entire apartment.

"This place is funky," Duncan declared, walking into Jeremy's room and plopping down on a split-cane chair.

"Don't know about that, but I would say it's got its share of down-home charm."

"This is L.A., Jeremy. Down home doesn't make it this side of the Rockies. People need dictionaries to understand Southern here. We're going to have to teach you some Californese."

"Not much chance of that. My attention span is about as long as it takes to finish my coffee and have the phone ring and hear a buddy tell me the fish are biting." Jeremy eased open a window and took a deep breath. "We're talking mighty high cotton here for a simple Carolina country boy."

"After what you told me downstairs, I wonder how much is simple and how much is a put-on."

"It's always better for the other fellow to think too little of you than too much. If he learns something new and has to adjust his thinkin' upward, he stays impressed with you a mighty long time. But if he decides that you're not everything he thought you were at first, he'll carry that bad taste in his mouth to his grave. It's a strange thing about human nature, son. Nobody likes to be disappointed, especially by people close to them."

"But that's not why you didn't tell me more about your business."

"No, it wasn't." Jeremy turned from the window, met him with a level gaze. "Up to now you've been talkin' with me on this one level, see, and we're makin' progress and talkin' faith and gettin' to be friends. I just didn't want anything like business to muddy up the waters."

"Mind if I ask you something?"

"Fire away."

"Why is it that you always call me son?"

Jeremy hesitated, said, "I don't rightly know why I started it. But if you want to get right down to it, I suppose if I had ever had a son, I'd have wished him to be a lot like you."

Duncan hid his reaction. "A cynic like me?"

Jeremy shook his head. "You try real hard, but you just don't quite make it. You're too honest to be a cynic. A *real* cynic's gotta be able to lie so good he can get even himself to believe he doesn't care about anything, and doesn't need hope to live."

Duncan thought about that. "Well, aimless then."

"Wrong again, son. You're saved from idleness by carin' too much for these poor little lost ones."

"Agnostic. You can't argue with that one."

"Sure I can. Who's been prayin' so hard with me the past four days his eyes stay all scrunched up after we finish?" Jeremy waited for a reply, and when none came, he went on. "Ever since that first day on the road, I've been admirin' how you'd bow your head to a God you don't know just because a stranger asked you. That says a lot about what kinda person I've been travelin' with."

"It's a lot easier listening to somebody talk about faith when I don't feel like they're going to jump down my throat every time I step out of line." Duncan scuffed the carpet at his feet. "Come to think of it, I've never thanked you for praying with me."

"No need to thank a servant for doin' as his Master says."

"Yeah, well, I'm grateful that you'd take this time with me. I always thought of myself as pretty much a lost cause."

Jeremy stretched out on the bed, laced his fingers behind his head. "I'm what you'd call your basic optimist. I'd go out after Moby Dick in a rowboat and carry tartar sauce with me."

Dusk was painting the world with softer lines when Duncan emerged from the hotel's front doors. A gentle sea breeze washed the air with salty perfume, making the day's dry harshness retreat into a vague memory, one out of place with the evening's beauty. A constant stream of people paraded by on the sidewalk fronting the hotel—old people making slow going and talking among themselves in low tones, street people with filthy clothes and matted hair, freshly groomed yuppies with glowing skin and shining eyes and excited chatter and sweaters tossed over their shoulders like badges of office.

Jeremy sat in one corner, so intent on the Book in his lap that he did not even notice Duncan's approach. "Your first night in California, and you're gonna sit here reading the Bible? Say it isn't so."

Jeremy looked up and smiled a greeting. "Sometimes His savin' grace is about the only thing that makes any sense to me."

Duncan looked down at the gnarled and knotted hands resting on the Bible, wondered at what those hands had done. "You read the Book a lot, don't you?"

"I suppose I've read the Bible as much as some preachers. It just never did me as much good. Some Sundays I'll be sittin' down there listenin' to a lesson I've heard six dozen times before, noddin' my head like, sure, I know that. Then it'll strike me just how far it is between *knowin'* and *doin'*."

Duncan pointed toward the street. "What say we head down

to Third Street and see what we can find?"

"No thanks, you go on ahead, though. I been in some bars. Whatever it is they put in them little glasses, it ain't smiles. Besides, I've never been partial to the nightly entertainment you find in a lot of those places."

Duncan sat down beside him. "Jazz?"

"Naw. Fights."

"Come on, Jeremy. You don't really think all night spots are like that."

"No, I guess you're right. The real problem with nightlife is it starts too dang late. If they had themselves an afternoon matinee, they might have to worry about me." He looked momentarily uncomfortable, went on. "Matter of fact, it looks like my dance card's gonna be filled up the next couple of nights."

"How's that?"

"Oh, I called back to the Community of Hope, wanted to see if any of my roofs'd fallen in since I left. Turns out a lady I work with is gonna be out this way for a two-day seminar, wants to see me for dinner. Maybe you've seen her around, she's the fine-lookin' red-haired lady, name of Bella."

"Don't think so." Duncan stood, stretched. "I guess I'll be off, then. You know what they say. You can't take it with you."

"I've heard that one, and I'm here to tell you there's something I'll be carryin' along. Yessir, when they start on my hole in the ground, they're gonna have to dig it three feet deeper. Gotta have room for all my memories of love. That's one thing I'm takin' with me, all the love people've given me. That and the smiles I've seen. Gonna take 'em and lay 'em at the feet of my Maker and say, 'I've been savin' these for you.' " Jeremy raised his Bible again, said, "You have yourself a good time, son. I'll keep the light on for you."

Duncan hesitated on the top step, decided to ask what had been on his mind for several days. "Jeremy, do you think God is punishing me?"

Jeremy gave him a long look before replying, "No, son. I think you're punishing yourself. It's man's most common way of runnin' from his need for forgiveness."

♦　♦　♦

Senator Richard Atterly pushed through his outer office door, so tired that the door felt as if it were pushing back, holding him out, telling him to go home. The silence that greeted him was a big enough surprise to help him force the fatigue away. Then he smelled the familiar fragrance, expensive smoke, and understood. Atterly straightened his shoulders and walked through the darkened secretary's office to his own private chamber.

The only light burning was the antique glass lamp on his side table, the one his wife had given him on their last Christmas together, before she had passed from this world and his life seven years ago. Its honey-colored hand-blown globe painted the room with warm tones, casting a veil of shadows across everything that was not directly in its light.

The man seated behind Atterly's desk was leaning back so that half his face was lit in ruddy tones and the other half lost in shadows. The cigar tip glowed fiercely as he drew deeply, illuminating hidden features and showing the sardonic amusement glittering in his coal-black eyes.

He removed the cigar from his mouth far enough to say, "I shoved them all out, Dick. Told them to go home and get some rest. Whole lot of them looked about half dead and in desperate need of some R and R. Hope you don't mind."

"If I do it's too late to change anything, so why bother?"

"That's Dick Atterly for you. Even when he's busy digging his own grave, he greets the world with the honesty of a scalpel."

"Is that what you came here for? To warn me off this fight?"

John Jakes "Mover" Mattherson waved the senator to one of his own visitor's chairs. The nickname "Mover," as in "mover and shaker," referred to the clout Mattherson held in Rhode Island politics. He was a man in his early sixties, more or less the same age as Atterly. But a fondness for rich food and single malts and Havana leaf—combined with an outspoken aversion to anything resembling exercise—had blurred the edges and added fifty pounds and three jowls to an already massive frame.

"Take a load off, Dick. No, I'm not here to talk issues. I've never had time for lost causes, and I know what you're like when you've got your teeth in something."

Atterly remained standing. "Then what brings you to Washington?"

Mover Mattherson reared back far enough to make Atterly's chair complain loudly, and plopped two size-fourteen double-E's on the edge of Atterly's wormwood desk. "I've come down to pay my respects, that's all. We've been through a lot, you and I. It seemed like the only decent thing to do."

Atterly's impatient rigidity contrasted with Mover's sloppy ease. "I'm not through yet."

"No, you're not." Mover made a vague search for an ashtray, found none, waved his cigar in the direction of the wastebasket and watched the ashes fall like dirty snow on Atterly's carpet. "But you will be before this is over. Dead, I mean. Dead and buried. And I've never had much time for corpses either, Dick. Especially the corpse of a dearly departed friend. So I thought I'd mosey on down here before the big guns come out and waste you away. Take one last look at the man I intend on remembering. Strong. Virile. Dedicated servant of the people. A man possessing a rare balance of strong moral fiber and common sense."

Mover Mattherson's gaze turned hard as marble. "Until now."

"What big guns?" Atterly demanded.

The relaxed grin surfaced and almost reached Mover's eyes. "Aw, c'mon, Dick. Let's be reasonable. We're old friends—I've known you since you were a green city councilman strutting the halls like a new deputy sheriff with his shiny tin badge. How long's that been? Thirty-six, thirty-seven years, isn't that right?"

"Somewhere around there."

"Long enough for you to know what's going to hit you, here and back home both. The ALUM and all those liberal vultures are going to unwrap the guns they've had in storage since Viet Nam and the Chicago riots. The hunt they're gonna make for your hide is gonna make McCarthy's last days look like a backwoods turkey shoot."

Atterly refused to sit down, refused to let this man put him in a subservient position. "You've heard something from Rhode Island?"

"Not much so far. Nothing negative, I mean. I guess most people are still having trouble believing that the state's all-time favorite politician has gone off the deep end. Some of the religious cable stations have made your speech a sort of nightly pablum, about what you'd expect. Hear there's been some of that all over the nation." The hard-eyed look returned. "Guess you could call it an alarm clock, telling the giant it's time to wake up and come out and eat you, bones and all."

Mover Mattherson took time to draw on his cigar. He released a stream of smoke toward the ceiling, then went on. "A few regular stations picked it up, but kinda quiet-like. They brought out the acid bath only a couple of times, sorta reluctant to scald their favorite son. Left it for those Sunday afternoon talk shows nobody bothers with except when they're flipping the dial searching for the ball game. The papers, now, they did you up proud. They put you on the front page and gave the nasties equal time in the op-ed section. All in good fun, sort of waiting for their man in Washington to come to his senses and call the whole thing off." The eyes glinted hard again. "Before he finds himself knocked cold and thrown from the ring."

"I take it you don't think I've got a fighting chance."

"About as much as I would against Mohammed Ali in his prime."

"What if I told you we're gaining support from every state in the nation?"

Mover Mattherson inspected him through the cigar smoke. "Support for your anti-porn bill or for your two-thousand-year-old carnival?"

"Both. Not to mention a fairly solid chance of seeing the bill pass the full Senate unscathed."

"Then I'd say you're gonna draw the biggest funeral crowd in history. Make no mistake, Dick. These ALUM boys are gonna be out for blood, soon as they pick their jaws off the floor and get it through their tiny minds that you mean business."

"I realize that."

" 'Course you do. And anybody fool enough to plug a stick into a cave where he *knows* a bear's sleeping deserves just exactly what he's gonna get. Which is a mauling." Mover Mattherson dropped his feet to the floor with a thud. "But you're too street smart not to already know this, so I'm not gonna change your mind with anything I say, now, am I?"

"No, not this time."

"Didn't think so." Mover Mattherson rose to his feet with a sigh. "Only thing you've got on your side is speed, Dick. I hear you're pushing to have the bills placed before both Houses before the end of next week. That right?"

"It's what we're trying for, yes."

"Isn't that about the same time you're gonna try and turn this city into an Old Testament prayer meeting?"

"That's why we're pushing so hard for the votes to go ahead on schedule."

"Well, you've sure caught everybody by surprise. I'd go for it hard as I could if I were you. Keep them off balance."

"I aim to do so."

"Thought you would," Mover said, waving his cigar toward the wastebasket once more. "Even so, you're hanging by this one tiny silver thread, and the ALUM boys've got this big old knife they keep sharp for morally committed conservatives like you."

Atterly decided there was nothing he could say to that, and so remained silent.

Mover Mattherson smiled slightly and nodded. "Well, I don't suppose we'll be seeing each other again, Dick. Doubt if the pressures at home will allow me another trip down here until the bloodbath's over and the dust settles. I'd wish you luck, but anybody out to do himself in has moved beyond luck. No, don't bother, Dick. I know my own way out."

Mover Mattherson walked through the secretary's office, paused with his hand on the outer door, and turned back to the motionless Senator Atterly. "You know what I'm going to say when people start talking about you."

"That you don't know me," Atterly replied, not bothering to look around.

"That's it on the nose, old buddy. I'm going to put a distance between you and me that even Einstein couldn't figure out." He opened the door, said, "I'd say something like, be seeing you around, but I'm not going to end our friendship with a lie."

After the door closed behind Mattherson, Atterly stood in silence for a very long time. He watched the tendrils of cigar smoke drift in the soft golden light, lost in thoughts that left his eyes looking cavernous.

◆ ◆ ◆

Congressman John Silverwood returned to his office after the evening reception; over the past four days he had developed a habit of returning to the office before going home, no matter what the hour, to pray. Mornings he prayed at home, and was comforted during these predawn times of stillness. Evenings, when he prayed here, he had the sense of being seated at the eye of a hurricane.

Silverwood did not know if he believed in God, did not try to reason out to whom he was praying. He had grown immensely attached to these twice-daily prayers in a short span of time, partly because he had laid the groundwork through more than eight months of struggling with the concept, partly because the storm was rising and there was no other lifeline to which he could cling.

Added to the normal pressures of his office was now the demand to take a visible stand against this anti-porn bill. The bill looked to be passed virtually unchanged by the Senate Judiciary Committee, and would be coming up for a final vote in the next day or so. The House Committee, far more conservative-leaning than the entire chamber, was expected to pass on it tomorrow.

ALUM made the proper noises at committee hearings. But they counted heads on the Senate side and knew that a nay vote was next to impossible. That body had a strong conservative bent to it, and Atterly's endorsement had swung a lot of the maybe's behind the bill's passage. A liberal cause was almost a write-off.

On the House side, though, things looked very different. Even some of the Republicans were Law-Review types, who felt more comfortable with a legal principle and a trail of footnotes than they did with the concept of serving the people. Stories of the street remained nothing more than stories to them. The people involved were not from families or neighborhoods they knew, and so in their minds were as far from reality and importance as the goings-on in some Third World nation.

So it was on the House side that the ALUM focused its efforts. The count looked very good—if not for outright rejection of the bill, then for burdening it with so many amendments and additions that not even a whale could swallow it.

There were two ways for the bill to make it to the President's desk. The first way was for both Houses to pass the measure in identical form. Sometimes, mostly on exceedingly unimportant or uncontroversial matters, this happened. Usually, however, because of differences either in the initial bill or through a myriad of subsequent amendments, the legislation passed respectively by each house was dramatically different. It would then be sent to Conference Committee—a joint House/Senate group—which would hammer out the differences and vote out a compromise bill for the further consideration of both Houses of Congress. If no compromise could be reached, the bill would die a silent and lonely death. This was the ALUM's last-ditch intention.

Thus even if the impossible happened and the anti-pornography legislation passed by both chambers, the versions would be different and have to go to Conference Committee, supposedly to have the differences ironed out but in reality to be killed. The ALUM had a well-earned reputation for smothering bills that were sent to a joint committee. They made it a point of knowing exactly who the committee players were and bearing down hard on them.

The Senate's vote on this legislation would be monitored, of course. Offensive strikes would be planned for later against those who actively backed the bill, in order to minimize the risk of further inroads against ALUM-supported policy. But on the House side they would push as hard as possible. And contingency plans would be made to pressure the Conference Committee from every possible angle.

Silverwood picked up the pile of documents that had been delivered to his door earlier that evening, unlocked the outer door, entered, and dropped the stack on his secretary's desk. Absentmindedly he opened the top document, and saw that it was a transcript of Congressional committee hearings on the Per Se bill. He took the transcript with him as he walked into his office, sank down into his chair, and started scanning. But the words would not let him maintain his normal distance; their strength was too great, their appeal too strong. His reading grew slower, his expression grimmer, the hold on his heart ever stronger.

> Many of the performers in pornographic films report being runaways, and then throwaways as child prostitutes slowly descend into the world of pornography where self-esteem and dignity have long since lost their meaning. Obscenity is sexual exploitation, prostitution and rape in pictures and in progress—in other words, crimes in process with many direct and indirect victims. Child pornography is simply a permanent record of child sexual abuse, which claims hundreds of thousands of child victims each year.

As he read, he felt his body grow cold. His trembling fingers burned from the pages he held.

Witnesses of juvenile pornography reported being coerced into pornographic performance, bound and beaten in direct imitation of pornography, and forcibly imprisoned for the purpose of manufacturing pornography. Others told of being shown pornography as children as part of the sexual seduction process and then being coerced into sexual acts.

His mouth was dry. He clenched and unclenched his jaw, feeling the muscles tighten down his neck and across his shoulders and wrapping his chest in unyielding metal bands.

Recent studies of rapists reveal a correlation between pornography and rape. A 1983 study ... of inmates of Canada's Kingston Penitentiary who were convicted of rape indicates that 86% of those studied admitted regular use of pornography, with 57% admitting actual imitation of pornographic scenes in the commission of sex crimes. And a 20-year Michigan state police study ... reveals that 41% of all sexually violent crimes in that state involved hard-core pornography either during the commission of the crime or immediately preceding it.

The atmosphere in his office grew horribly oppressive. Voices rose from the words on the page, took on form, and began leaning over his shoulders and whispering into his ears. He read, and as he read he felt the presence of unseen children gather in his office until there was barely room left for him to draw breath. They cried to him with voices that tore at his heart, telling stories that tied lead weights to his soul and sent it plunging into darkness.

Pornography's connection to organized crime is well-documented ... Organized crime controls 85–90% of the estimated $7–10 billion obscenity industry. . . .

Some of the crimes that are linked to the obscenity industry include murder, narcotics distribution, money laundering, tax violations, copyright violations, and fraud. . . .

In Cincinnati, Ohio, over a 5-year period, the County Prosecutor closed down the pornographic outlets from a certain downtown neighborhood. At the end of that 5 years, with all the pornographic outlets closed, the major offense crime rate in that neighborhood had declined by 83%. These major offenses included robbery, theft, aggravated assault, rape and murder.[1]

He pulled his pen out of the desk holder and started stabbing the tip into the blotter as he read. He glanced up and looked at the mahogany bookcases lining the far walls, filled to overflowing with bound copies of U.S. laws—hundreds of volumes, and yet none of those laws succeeded in stemming this problem, stopping this pain, ceasing this outrage, curing this cancer that ate at his nation's bones.

He looked to the side wall, covered with plaques and certificates and honors and awards. He was an outstanding statesman in the eyes of the world. What had he ever done that would hold value once he was gone? Why was he holding on to something that had lost all value long ago?

He folded his hands in his lap, bent over slightly, and stared at the report without seeing it any longer.

He had decided.

◆　　◆　　◆

Jessica had never been as sure of anything as Pierre seemed to be about every part of his life. She liked him as much for his certainty as she did for the looks or the things he said or the things he did—more, sometimes. His sureness made her feel protected, even when the things he pushed her into began to get more and more uncomfortable, then scary, then painful. She kept holding on to the way he talked to her, and the way he looked at her when they were alone and he was showing that she had done it all right. He was so *sure* of what he was telling her to do. So *sure*.

Only one time did he talk openly to her, without holding back anything—the night after they arrived in Los Angeles. They were in another nondescript motel, cut from the same mold as so many others in their meandering trek across the country. Only this time the people she met in the hall looked at her with eyes that said they knew what her game was, knew what she was there for, knew more about her and where she

---

[1]These excerpts were taken verbatim from: (A) Hearing before the Committee on the Judiciary, United States Senate, Child Protection and Obscenity Enforcement Act and Pornography Victims Protection Act of 1987, and (B) Final Report of the Attorney General's Commission on Pornography, July, 1986.

was going than Jessica did herself.

Pierre usually went out when they hit a new town, leaving her either alone with the television or alone with Arlene, but always alone—never taking her with him, never offering an explanation, never wondering that she might feel afraid and abandoned in a new place on her own. And she never asked.

She had learned long before, long before even meeting Pierre, that men close to her did not offer explanations, did not feel her needs were important enough to merit discussion. She had never been able to talk freely with a girl either, until Arlene, and the hole that Arlene had left in her life when she had avoided her that previous summer had been the only dark cloud in those first heavenly days with Pierre.

Jessica lay on the lonely L.A. hotel-room bed and recalled how, after three weeks of almost total silence, Arlene had reappeared. She had entered the country club one mid-August morning, plopped her stuff down beside Jessica's chair, sprawled out, stretched her body like a lynx, and said in greeting, "Your post-modern girlfriend is totally in lust."

That was all it took for the frozen chill to melt away, for the lonely days to be wiped clean. They were friends again. All was made well because Arlene didn't have any reason to be jealous any more.

Jessica said in reply, more because Arlene expected it than because she wanted to know, "Tell me everything and don't leave out the juicy bits." What she really wanted to say was, I missed you.

"He's the chillest guy," Arlene replied, making her body writhe as she settled into the chaise lounge. Arlene pretended she didn't notice the reaction of guys near enough to watch the show and told Jessica, "I met him the other night at the cafe and finally had to come up for air. I'm so beat I could sleep a week. My mom was past borderline. Way past. Over the edge and off the cliff."

Jessica asked, "You didn't come home last night?"

Arlene smiled at her. "Not last night or the night before or the night before that. Didn't want to leave a good thing," Arlene said. "Too good. And you should have seen my step-dad. I had Chico walk me up to the door this morning, that's his name, Chico. My step-dad had the door open even before I was out of the car. You could see he was getting ready to jump all over me, then he caught sight of Chico. Stopped him cold. Chico's not a big guy, but it doesn't matter. All it takes is one look to know you don't want to mess with the *man*."

Arlene gave a long sigh of pure satisfaction, said, "He sure shut the old man up, but good."

"I bet he didn't stay shut up," Jessica told her.

"It doesn't matter," Arlene said. "Not anymore. The old man's met his match, and I've met my ticket out of here."

That raised Jessica up. "You're going to leave? When?"

"Soon as he's got some money saved up. Chico's a specialist at servicing these really fancy old cars. Makes more an hour than a lot of doctors. He's got a name and can get a job anywhere he wants. We're gonna travel around the country, maybe go down to Mexico for a while."

Jessica fought down the rising swell of loneliness. "All this after just three nights?"

Arlene turned her head so as to face her friend. The dark glasses gave her smile a disembodied air. She said, "All this after three hours, little girl."

Jessica made her face smile back, said, "So when do I meet the man of your dreams?"

"Chico's taking me dancing tonight," Arlene said. "Wanna come?"

It was the first time Jessica asked Pierre to take her anywhere, but for some reason she didn't want to go meet Arlene and her new friend alone. It wasn't that she was scared or anything. It was just that she wanted Arlene to see that Pierre wasn't afraid to be out with her. To be with her. That had never bothered Jessica before, but now that she was about to meet the guy who was going to steal her best friend away from her for good, she wanted to go in prepared. She wanted it bad enough to ask Pierre to come. She knew the instant she asked him that he didn't want to do it. But he agreed. It gave her a tremendous lift, hearing him say he'd come even when he didn't want to.

So they met outside the place, and Arlene couldn't keep her hands off the guy. In Jessica's eyes Chico was really not all that great. He was extremely good-looking in a sleazy sort of way, with small solid-looking muscles and slicked-back blond hair and a strong jaw that came down to a nice-looking chin. But his ears were tiny and pressed so flat to his head that they looked glued down. Having his hair brushed back made them look even worse, as if he'd been born with ears that size and they'd never grown up with the rest of him. And his eyes were the color of dirty glass, a sort of grayish nothing that had no life to them at all. He just sort of stood there, smirking a little with these thin colorless lips whenever Arlene wrapped herself around him, and raked Jessica with a gaze that gave nothing away.

Chico looked at Pierre, and the look went on a long time, long enough for both the girls to get a little nervous. Then the smirk actually turned into a smile, showing tiny well-set teeth, and Chico stuck out a hand. Pierre took it, still wearing his mask, and gripped it hard enough to make the muscles on his forearm writhe. Chico just grinned a little bigger and said, "Hey, all right, nice to meet you, man."

Arlene laughed a little nervous sound and said, "Great, now we're all gonna go in and be friends, right?"

But Chico was already fishing around in his pocket. "Sure, but first we gotta go back to the car and try out this blow."

Jessica looked to Pierre for guidance, who kept his eyes on Chico and said, "A peace pipe without the pipe." She didn't understand, but was glad enough to join in the laughter with everybody else.

Chico's car was a little two-seater foreign job, an old car by some company Jessica had never heard of before. They couldn't sit in it but had to go by and inspect it anyway. Then they stood around while he went into this long drawn-out explanation to Pierre of what he'd done to get it back on the road. Arlene started getting impatient, which wasn't a surprise; it usually took Arlene about fifteen seconds to get irate when she wasn't the center of attention. She kind of whined out something about, "Hey, are we gonna get inside before dawn or what?"

Chico stopped mid-sentence and turned to look at her, his features hardening into this look like a knife, all the strength and concentration just centering down into this silence that seemed to reach out and slap Arlene. Hard. Arlene wilted under his gaze, which shocked Jessica more than anything else that night, seeing her friend disintegrate before her eyes.

Arlene flowed over to Chico and wrapped her arms around him and said, "I was just kidding, really, everything's cool, isn't it? I mean, we're all gonna have a great time tonight, aren't we?"

Chico spoke to her for the first time that night, the words

bland and totally lacking in the force that still held his body tensed up like a coiled snake. "I'll be with you in a minute," he said.

She backed off from him as from a hot stove, and sort of played at being cheerful as she walked around the car to where Jessica was standing. Arlene's back was to the men, so she didn't see Pierre look down at Chico and give a little half smile.

They finally made it over to Pierre's car, a rusty Chevy Impala with dirty blankets thrown over the back seats. Chico said something to Pierre, "Yeah, like I always say, if you can't have class, go for useful."

What Pierre said then came as a total shock to Jessica. "I've got a eighty-eight Jag XJ6 with only twenty thousand on the clock, but I don't like to drive it in the summer." And while Chico stood there trying to decide whether to believe him or not, Jessica was looking at this man she was with and wondering what else she didn't know about him.

They all climbed into the car and tooted up some lines while Pierre answered Chico's questions in a calm drawl, everything under control, clearly not caring too much whether the guy believed him or not. Jessica sat in her normal utter stillness, listening and watching and learning something new every time Pierre opened his mouth. Pierre told Chico how he traveled the country during the off-season, hitting the major cities like New York, Chicago, Denver, Dallas, naming them with the ease of somebody who was out there a lot, answering questions about the places that Chico knew with such casual ease that the skepticism gradually gave way to the eagerness of a kindred spirit.

Chico asked what he did on the road, and all Pierre would say was, "Make money."

"Yeah," Chico said, "like how much money?"

Pierre dipped his head toward the mirror, took in a line big enough to make for good sledding, said, "Enough to pay my way, not so much as to get in the way of a good time."

Chico smiled at that, his skin stretching out tight and his little ears easing their way up either side of his head. "Hey, I like this man's attitude."

As they walked toward the club Jessica tuned out Arlene's aimless chatter and tried to think about what she had just heard. But the coke made her thoughts scatter like snowflakes blowing in a light breeze. Each idea was caught by her mind for a fleeting instant, held up to the light and inspected with a clarity that she only knew in the first flush of a new high, and then was lost, swirling away as the next thought took its place.

She'd been afraid to ask Pierre about what he did in the winter. She didn't want to hear of anything that might mean he would leave her, or worse. Yet what could be worse than losing Pierre? Suddenly she was overwhelmed by a sense of dread, and then could not find the reason why. She had glimpsed the answer to a question she had been afraid to ask, felt it there at the back of her mind, then watched it swirl away before she could put the feelings into words.

Then the drug swept her away, and she forgot that she had even been looking for the thought, or that it had ever been there at all. She returned to the knowledge, the utter solid assurance that there was nothing worse than losing this man, and in that instant knew that if he asked her to go with him, she would. And if he didn't, she would beg him to take her anyway. And just before they got to the entrance she hoped with a force that squeezed her heart tight that he would, he would ask her, he would want her to go, and that she would not have to beg.

That night she danced as she never before, so wild and wanton that even Arlene stopped at one point and gave her a sort of hand-on-the-hip, head-cocked grin as if to say, look at the little girl go. But she wasn't doing it for Arlene. And she did it in spite of the eyes that tracked her across the floor. The only eyes that mattered to her were Pierre's, and he watched her with the same heavy-lidded intensity he had when he was in that certain mood. If this was what he wanted, then she would give it to him. She wasn't sure she liked it, but he did, so that made it all right, made it *important*. She had to do it so that he'd want to take her, want to ask her to come along on this adventure across the country to cities that for her were only names.

Between those dark-eyed looks at her, she watched him talk to Chico. She danced and wished she could hear what he said. Whatever it was, it was enough to make Arlene's new friend drop his jaw in surprise, then grin bigger than he had all night. He leaned forward and pumped Pierre for more with questions that he had to shout out over the noise, forgetting about the dance floor and the people and the drink at his elbow, forgetting about everything until he threw his head up and laughed out loud, then turned to where Arlene and she were dancing and threw them both a double-arm kiss.

The next evening Pierre sat her down in a solemn way she hadn't seen since the first time he asked her to let him take her picture, and she almost had to sit on her hands to make them still. He reached over, caressed her cheek, touched her hair, told her a couple of times how special she was to him. He said the words that in the hours when she was alone she would run over and over and over in her mind, the dreams of her childhood come to life.

He wanted to take care of her, Pierre told her. He loved her too much to let her go. He wanted to tell her the secrets of his life, but only if she promised not to tell anyone. It would be just their secret, and she was round-eyed and solemn and so nervous she could barely swallow.

"I'm a talent scout," Pierre told her. "I find a special sort of girl and help to launch her career. That was why I wanted to take those pictures of you, because there are some really big names that would pay a lot of money to have you as their model.

"What I'm asking," Pierre said in that soft soothing voice, "is if you wouldn't like to come with me and let me build you a career as a special model. I'd give you the kind of life that most girls would only dream of. Nice clothes, great hotels, the finest food. We'd travel to all the big cities, go to the best clubs, have your picture taken by the really class photographers."

He stroked her cheek with one finger and said, "Would you like that?"

Then she was in his arms, holding him close, so close, and so excited that he had asked her, wanted her to come and liked her enough to want to give her all these things and travel with her and take care of her. Her heart felt like a frantic little bird that threatened to break free of her chest and fly away.

That first night in Los Angeles, Pierre came back unexpectedly after leaving her alone for less than an hour. He pulled out what he said was some really great dope. California sinsemilla, he told her, the best there was.

Sinsemilla came from plants selected for their quality and their sex, since only the female marijuana plants had the THC drug in any quantity. Given no chance to cross-pollinate, the plants gave all their strength to producing more and more of the drug. The result was a bud a *thousand* times as potent as grass from the seventies.

Pierre kept handing her the smoldering joints long after she had lost all interest in smoking more. The television was tuned to MTV and turned down low, and the higher she grew the more realistic became the flickering music images with their five-minute stories and songs. Jessica clung to Pierre's silent strength and the television's repetitive messages to keep from floating out so far away she might not be able to return.

They were sprawled across the bed, Pierre upright against the headboard and Jessica leaning against his chest, listening to his heart, wishing there were some way to keep from having to face what he had already told her was coming the day after tomorrow. He ground the last third of his joint into the ashtray, asked her if she didn't think it was the greatest stuff she'd ever had.

"It was great," she agreed, wishing she had the strength to ask him, beg him, not to make her do it.

He looked down at her. "What's on your mind, baby?"

But she couldn't ask. She sighed, nestled closer, wondering if there was any way to make the moment last forever, keep the nightmare from coming back again. All she said was, "I was just wondering what made you so sure of yourself all the time."

He chuckled, his voice made hoarse by the smoke. "Tell you a secret."

"What?" She lifted her head.

"I've got the magic in my mind." He reached to the side table for another joint. "All I got to do is think something, and it happens. Poof. It's there."

She inspected his face, wondered if it was something she should smile at, but his expression remained heavy-lidded and flat and calm.

He lit another joint, took a long hit, and said with the smoke, "Yeah, there's not any power on earth like that. So many people walk around wishing all the time, don't have any idea what it means to have *power*. They never figure it out. They think you gotta get it from somewhere outside, see? But it's really all there, all you got to do is learn how to focus."

"Focus," she repeated, having no idea what he was talking about.

"Find out what it is you want, and then want it *totally*. Don't let anything get in your way, don't think about anybody outside, no blocks or *anything*. You gotta learn how to look at it and see it and want it with everything inside you, see?" He dragged deep. "Want it bad enough and it's yours."

I want the bad things to stop, Jessica said to herself, clinging to him, wishing she could say it. *More than anything I've ever wanted in my life, I want it to stop.*

"Like one thing I discovered," Pierre went on. "Was how I've been through all this stuff before. Most people, see, they're always busy learning how to make it go right. They keep learning the same things again and again starting over from scratch, see?"

She nodded, liking him opening up to her, yet disturbed by how little she understood of what he said.

He draped an arm around her. "One thing this focusing does, see, it opens up doors inside you. Doors most people don't even know are there. All kinds of doors. And one of them, it's all about how I've been down here and through it all before. Lots of times before."

"You mean, like in a different body?"

He looked at her with eyes that were gleaming dark slits. "You ever heard of a French guy called Matisse?"

"I don't know. Maybe."

"Really famous painter. That was me." Just like that, so casual and matter-of-fact in the way he said it that Jessica was almost positive now he was serious. "Yeah, that's why I took the name, see, 'cause it helps me draw on that power. Keeps me solid in tune with all I learned that go-round. Makes it easier to focus."

"Have you ever seen his pictures?" Jessica asked, and instantly knew she had said the wrong thing.

"Whattaya mean, *his?*" His tone sharpened as much as the drug would allow. "They're *mine.* So how come I need to go see 'em hanging on somebody else's wall? I *painted* them. They're all right here, see? I'm tapped into the flow, and all that stuff from way back, it's here. Now."

"I guess I understand," she assured him, sensing that she shouldn't ask why he wasn't painting now. She kept her eyes on him, watched him float out into drug-colored clouds of his own, knowing it was a good time to lie still and silent. She would focus as hard as she could, and wish she had the kind of strength Pierre took so much for granted.

CHAPTER

13

Senator Richard Atterly's secretary buzzed him. "You're scheduled to make your remarks in fifteen minutes, Senator."

"Thank you." He raised his head from where it had been bent over his folded hands. He rose from his desk, took in the room around him. The arched ceilings of the Senate Minority Whip's office in the Capitol Building were embellished with green and gold designs and capped with a multi-tiered crystal chandelier. A large gilt-framed mirror adorned the marble fireplace. Everywhere there were souvenirs and mementos and plaques and photographs and trophies, gathered from a lifetime spent building his political career—a career he now threatened to dismantle.

Atterly exited his office, turned left, and walked down the marble-floored corridor. He passed the old Senate Chamber, the Senate Conference Room, and entered through the Senators' Private Lobby with its gilded archways and ornate gold-leaf crown moldings and antique desks.

Normally when he entered the lobby someone was immediately at his elbow seeking advice, asking how a vote was lining up, feeling him out on an issue, pressing him for assistance, requesting that he make a speech, inviting him to lunch. Today, however, he walked through the lobby alone. To be sure, he was accorded respectful nods and smiles. But word had spread about his stand on faith and the assembly, and how both applied in his mind to the anti-pornography legislation. It was clear no one wanted to be seen with him.

He entered the Senate Chamber through the double doors and walked with head erect to his seat in the front row. His desk was finely oiled mahogany, darkened with age, shaped like an oversized old-fashioned schoolboy's desk. His name appeared on a small brass plaque in the upper right-hand corner. The top of the desk was hinged, and on the inside cover colleagues who had preceded him had followed the time-honored tradition of carving their names into the wood. He sat facing the rostrum—in the Senate, Republicans sat to the left of the rostrum, Democrats to the right—from which the Vice-President of the United States presided as head, or President, of the Senate. The rostrum itself was trimmed in the same black marble that stood in column-like design around the chamber itself. The room had a high coved ceiling, with a Visitor's Gallery encircling its perimeter.

This was a down-time, with no bills crucial to the current administration up for a vote; the Vice-President was not present. His place was taken by the President Pro Tem, a stately older gentleman known for his kindly visage and an ability to rule without ever raising his voice. The chamber itself was less than a third full, with no one paying strict attention as a colleague read several statements into the Congressional Record.

Most Senate speeches were motivated by the desire to create an impressive-looking reprint from the Record, which could then be dispersed among the constituents back home. The voters would never know that the speech was mumbled to a handful of senators preoccupied with other business, if spoken at all. Remarks intended for the Record did not even need to be stated; it often happened that a senator would simply request that the following "extensions of remarks" be included. The Congressional Record was printed each night, ready for mailing and distribution by early the next morning.

In the mind of the American public, the legislator's job was to sit in the House or Senate Chamber and pass bills into laws. This was simply not the case. Unless there was a joint session or consideration of an enormously important bill, viewing the Houses of Congress in session could be a disappointing experience.

The crowded chambers, the impassioned speeches, the senators straining forward in their chairs, the pounding gavels—these things did not often happen. Most work was done outside the actual chambers, and most representatives knew how they were going to vote before the actual floor debate began. The real work was done out of sight—in tedious committee hearings, in private discussions, in hurried conversations with lobbyists and constituents and legal counsel and staffers and trusted allies and Administration arm-twisters.

In reality, the Senate Chamber almost always looked as if it were waiting for something else to happen. This was one of the controversies about filming House and Senate sessions; the politicians were not keen on being pictured chatting or dozing or preoccupied with matters other than those transpiring on the floor—or even worse, not to be seen at all.

On the other hand, because the sessions were televised, a congressman could monitor developments on the C-Span network while attending to more pressing matters in his or her office. Nowadays the television provided a continual background noise to the harried activities of a congressional office.

While the senator completed his remarks, those who were present conferred quietly with their colleagues in small clusters around the room, reviewed files and correspondence, read hometown newspapers, worked on speeches of their own, came and went with smiles and greetings for those around them. Atterly sat enclosed within a bubble of isolation, surrounded by a million reasons why it was not necessary to make his intended remarks, yet knowing that in truth he had no choice.

As the speaker returned to his place, the President Pro Tem thanked him, consulted a sheet of paper, and said, "Now Senator Atterly would like to make a few remarks."

That was all. His speech was introduced with the same informality given someone inserting birthday greetings or a favorite menu into the Record—both of which had occurred on more than one occasion. The only reason the President Pro Tem accorded him the honor of being formally recognized was because of his position as Minority Whip. Otherwise senators might, and often did, simply line up at a microphone and talk about whatever concerned them that day.

This was not the initial debate marking the Per Se bill's return from committee to the Senate floor. That had been done the day before, during the afternoon session. His own remarks at that time had been very brief and very guarded. There had been no need for anything more. The bill's supporters had taken an initial head-count; with Atterly's support the legislation's passage was virtually assured.

But that night he could not sleep. In the darkness of his midnight vigil he recognized that his reluctance to speak out was founded on more than just a desire to remain in consensus with the other backers of this legislation. He did not speak out because he was afraid.

Atterly could not explain, even to himself, how he was so sure there was more that needed to be said. But this lack of logical explanation did not change his conviction to speak out. He was called by some deep urging to make a public declaration, and the silent voice that called to him was one he could not deny. He could not. No matter how worried he was over the repercussions of this second immense step away from political logic and into the realm of what others would describe as religious extremism, he could not turn away.

"Thank you, Mr. President," Senator Atterly began. "Colleagues, ladies and gentlemen, I have felt compelled to come before you today to urge your open-hearted consideration of S–1422, known as the Per Se Anti-Pornography Bill. If you gain nothing more from my remarks today, I sincerely hope that you will carry away with you a sense of the urgency which this bill carries."

Very few people were listening intently. Here and there a head turned his way, most especially among the younger senators who were not yet sure of their power base. This was, after all, the Minority Whip. Two or three colleagues resumed their seats, several others folded up their papers, a few moved away from the clusters of discussion to stand and listen in silence. Atterly focused upon them, and sought to ignore those who paid him no mind.

"Ladies and gentlemen of the Senate, if my thirty-seven years of service to this fine nation have taught me anything, it is to never introduce a bill to this house on the basis that it combats evil. Some of you don't even believe it exists, I am sad to say, and others complain that if we start trying to combat evil we'll have to bury the whole country under six feet of government forms.

"But evil is not just some personal interpretation of another's actions, much as the humanists would have us believe. And service to this country cannot, for me at least, pander to the personal philosophies that eat away at the heart of this great nation. Despite what many may think, ladies and gentlemen of the Senate, evil exists. And one such manifestation of this evil which I ask you to act against today is pornography."

A head popped out of the Senate Private Lobby, heard enough to duck back out of sight and then reappear followed by a half-dozen other senators; they spread out around the back of the chamber. Gradually the other clusters began to unravel, as one by one the senators fastened their attention upon Atterly.

"Pornography fits all the descriptions of a drug. It is injected through the eyes. It gives a warped high, a totally unnatural adrenaline rush. It requires greater and more powerful doses. It alters the perspective the user has to the outside world. And for those who become habitual users, coming off this drug has emotionally painful and lingering side effects.

"Pornography has taken our consumerist mentality and transformed it into something depraved. It has made million-aires out of people who care absolutely nothing for their fellow-man, who emotionally and physically flay a young woman and then cast her aside. It has created a well-heeled but ill-inten-tioned sales force who flood the country with their wares of flesh.

"I will not describe case histories of individuals whose lives have been destroyed by this insidious evil. There is no need to burden you with the nightmares that have plagued my nights since taking up this cause. I am aware that many of you are both attracted and repelled by pornography, and feel extremely uncomfortable attempting to play moral policeman to a nation. But we must, I beg you, look beyond our established positions and examine this deeply. We *must*.

"In just fifty years our nation has passed through a meta-morphosis of liberality toward pornography that would be un-believable were it not for the evidence which surrounds us. Be-fore the Second World War, all that anyone could legally buy were poorly printed magazines of women in two-piece swim-suits. The most provocative movie scene was of a couple rolling around in the surf. Today, you can go into two dozen shops in this very city and have anything. *Anything.* I do not mean some-thing that you might find vaguely acceptable by any moral scale. I mean *anything*. Sodomy. Bestiality. Sadomasichism. Girls and boys who are clearly still children doing the most horrid of acts.

"This, ladies and gentlemen, is glaring proof that we have failed in our duty to protect this nation. We must pause and think about this, I beg you. We must put an end to this evil, this darkness that even seeps into our homes and steals our young ones. And we must put a stop to it now. Today. Close the door on this nightmare and banish it from legal existence.

"Up until now, we have permitted local councils and state legislatures to determine what is and is not obscene. While this may sound right and proper on paper, it has proven to be wholly inadequate; and this inadequacy, I submit to you, was both anticipated by the proponents of pornography and was one reason why they permitted this federal directive to local communities to be enacted.

"My colleagues, the truth of the matter is that our courts have tied up virtually every one of the local communities' attempts to pass anti-pornography laws. We have preferred to turn away from this evil rather than confront it head-on. And by taking this attitude, we are playing directly into the hands of those who wish to perpetuate this evil.

"We, by our silent inactivity, are as guilty as the governor of old, who washed his hands of the affair and turned his back on innocence.

"What we require, and what I am proposing, is to establish a single standard for the entire nation. This bill which is now before you is such a law. I am convinced of that one hundred percent. It is a Per Se law that defines the legally acceptable limit of obscenity. It slams the door shut against anyone who would either make, distribute, finance, sell, advertise, possess, pander to or act in pornography. It spells out very clearly that the harshest penalties are reserved for the distributors and financiers and producers. We are after the big men, ladies and gentlemen. We are after the top players. We want to shut this game down once and for all.

"For myself, I am obliged to do this. I have no choice. I must either cast aside the cloak of silence or give up my faith. I must seek to rebuke these wrongdoers, and eliminate their contemptible behavior.

"I ask you, my friends, my fellow servants of this great country, to help me heal this wound. Help me right this nation's course. Help those who have no voice. Help those who are being tormented in the name of freedom and commerce. Help us shape a better tomorrow for our children and for our children's children. Vote for the passage of this bill. Please. In the name of your own inner needs and the needs of our nation, vote for this bill."

◆ ◆ ◆

Mavis Talmadge stopped them on their way out of the hotel the next morning with a bright-eyed smile. "They grow all you southern boys this big, Mr. Hughes?"

"Shucks, ma'am, back where I come from I'd be called the runt of the litter."

The old lady was dressed against the morning chill in a white long-sleeved college cardigan that almost reached her blue-suede sneakers. She had it tied around her middle with a beaded Indian cord. The sleeves were rolled up half a dozen times but still slid down to cover her hands every time she moved. "I found the church you were asking for."

"Did not. I found it and told you about it." Mavis was joined by a woman dressed in a checkerboard pattern from head to toe—checkerboard pants, sweater, and tam-o'shanter as big as a skillet with a bright red pompon that bobbed up and down as she walked. Underneath the massive headgear was the most wrinkled face either man had ever seen.

Mavis gave the lady an exasperated look. "The gentlemen don't have time for details, Agnes."

"Hmph. Don't seem in that much of a hurry to me."

"All right, you tell it then."

The seamed face stretched into an expression that probably passed for a smile. Duncan had a fleeting mental image of ancient pulleys straining against the weight of years to lift the withered cheeks. "My grandson works with the street people in Hollywood in his spare time. He's a big television producer, so there's not all that much free time, not with two young children to worry about. You probably wouldn't guess it, but I'm a great-grandmother six times over."

"The gentlemen aren't after your family history, Agnes. They were asking about a church."

"And I'm just going to tell them, if a certain somebody will remember her manners and stop interrupting." The unsteady smile returned. "As I was saying, I spoke to my grandson last night, and he told me that you needed to contact the First Presbyterian Church in Hollywood. Here, I wrote down the address for you."

Jeremy accepted the paper, squinted, tried to read the cramped handwriting. "That's awfully kind of you, ma'am."

"It was a pleasure. Those other addresses are for some of

the organizations in Hollywood who work with runaways. He said you'd do yourself a favor if you went by and talked with all of them. They're all so busy, what you'll need is to find one who takes a special interest in your case. It doesn't matter which one, as far as he's concerned. They're all doing a good job." She gave them an encouraging look. "I hope that's helpful."

"Yes, ma'am, it surely is," Jeremy said. "Tell the truth, just about anything we receive looks like a miracle at this point. Please tell your grandson thank you kindly."

The old face beamed. "Where are you off to this morning?"

"Don't pry, Agnes," Mavis said crossly.

"Nonsense. We're praying for these gentlemen, aren't we? It would help to know what they're up to."

"Honestly," Mavis said. "Sometimes you are such an old busybody."

"It's all right, ma'am," Jeremy said. "We've got an appointment with the Beverly Hills police."

The two old ladies made round eyes. "Oh, how exciting," Mavis said. "It's like being inside one of those horrible detective stories you're always reading."

Agnes arched her neck. "Who's always reading?"

"Don't be petty."

Duncan waited until they were in the parking lot to ask, "How old do you figure that Agnes is?"

"Old enough to look baptized in pickle juice, and that's the truth." Jeremy headed for the passenger side. "What say you drive, son? I don't believe I've got the hang of this city yet."

The early Friday traffic was heavy. Stoplights stretched out in front of them as far as they could see, disappearing into the vague haze that already obscured the morning. They continued down Wilshire Boulevard through the mirrored high-rise jungle of Century City, then got thoroughly lost where their street joined several others at the Beverly Hills city limits. They were straightened out by a giant with surfer's shoulders and blond dreadlocks. His t-shirt bore a toppled cocktail glass with a stain draped around the words *Lifestyles of the Young and Aimless*.

The Beverly Hills Police Station was part of the newly completed city administration complex on Santa Monica Boulevard. It and all the other buildings were designed in the stucco-clad Spanish mission style, washed a brilliant white by the morning sunshine.

Duncan was visibly nervous as they gave their names to the officer manning the front desk. When he turned to call upstairs, Duncan told Jeremy, "Two men he doesn't know, coming by and taking his time because of some cop three thousand miles away he met at a conference a couple of years ago. He's going to inspect us with a microscope. We need to make an impression or he's gonna have us out on our ears."

"I understand what you're sayin'," Jeremy agreed. "Gotta walk in there like a man with a purpose."

"And discreet. We can't be propping our boots on his desk. Think you can handle discreet?"

"Don't you worry your head none. I'll be discreet as a foam-rubber door-knocker."

The entrance hall of the new Beverly Hills Police Department was open and high and carpeted and curved. The officer set down the phone, and told them to take the stairs up to Juvenile on the third floor.

The whole building smelled faintly of fresh paint. There were tell-tale signs of recent construction—stray cuttings of carpet in various corners, streaks of paint on the concrete stair-wells where painters brushed by carelessly, open wires dangling next to unfinished ceiling fixtures.

In the third-floor's front hall a swarthy man stood waiting for them. He was a couple of inches under six feet and looked solid as a wall. His skin was a rich golden hue, his hair jet black. The eyes behind the black spectacles were dark and hard as his grip. He shook their hands briefly, introduced himself as Jaime Allende, left them with the impression that he had memorized everything skin-level about them in his ten-second glance.

Allende listened to their story in unblinking silence, inspected the affidavits and letters of authority from the girls' parents, asked for their identification, and disappeared.

"Gone to make a few calls," Duncan guessed.

"That man's got professional written all over him in ten-foot letters," Jeremy said.

"Wouldn't want to be in here on the bad side of the law," Duncan agreed.

The conference room was utterly bare. The windowless white stucco walls and gray carpet were unadorned. The table was cheap and wobbly, the chairs of the folding metal variety. With the door shut the place held the silence of a prison. It sucked the conversation from them.

They waited fifteen silent minutes for Detective Allende to return. When he did, there was only a brief, "Okay, you guys check out. What do you have?"

Duncan told him of Jeremy's visit to the pimp and his calls, then gave the address of the house.

There was a flash of humor in those dark eyes. "You just called this guy up, got somebody on the phone, and they gave you the street name and told you this guy—what's his name again?"

"Pierre Matisse," Duncan replied. "Or at least that's what he goes by."

"Matisse, yeah, they told you this guy's gonna show up with your girls?"

"He didn't say which girls they were," Duncan said.

Allende's eyes did not leave Jeremy. "Man, you want a job?"

"No offense, officer," Jeremy said. "But I do believe I'd rather be mugged every Saturday night than do your work."

"Can't say I blame you." Allende made a couple of notes. "Yeah, this is enough to start. Why don't you leave it with me a couple of days, let me see what I can dig up."

"Mind if I ask what you'll be doing?"

"Routine check. See if there's any likely looking house along that stretch of road, run a check on any that might fit the bill." Allende finished with his notes and looked up. "This is border-line Hollywood, but we're on good terms with the L.A.P.D. when it comes to kiddie crimes. They won't mind us checking it out."

"What are you looking for, if you don't mind me asking."

Allende settled back, fiddled with his pen. "Can't say for sure, of course, but there are usually some signals for this sort of thing. Needs to be a house surrounded by a high wall, set so the neighbors can't see in. A big place, probably, if they're doing a major production and don't want to be seen bringing people in and out all the time. Maybe we'll see a grocery delivery truck, ask if they've caught sight of any funny business inside. Could be there's some muscle hanging around. There's usually a swimming pool, but around that area they build swimming pools like some people buy neckties."

"Status," Duncan guessed.

"Gives the rich something to talk about besides the lousy trade-in they got on their Rolls," Allende agreed.

Jeremy wondered if his voice sounded as flat as theirs.

"What can you do if you find a house that looks likely?"

"Quite a bit, especially if it's got kids involved. You'd be surprised how helpful even the toughest nut can be when it comes to somebody fooling around with kids. We'll try and learn who owns the house and if it's rented out. Talk to the gas and telephone companies, see who's paying the bills. Check if they've got a California driver's license, maybe a record. Won't take long. Where are you staying?"

"Santa Monica. Place down on Ocean Boulevard."

"Nice area. Yeah, give me a couple of days, I'll be back in touch." He looked up. "Are you guys gonna be willing to testify about this in court?"

"Absolutely," Duncan replied for them both.

Detective Allende gave them another hard look, seemed to reach a decision, opened up a little further. "Pornography is not a crime. You gotta understand that from the very beginning. I could drive you around this place, show you a dozen houses that've been used for filming. Major productions, I'm talking about. Million-dollar budgets. And I couldn't even begin to talk about the over-nighters. Those guys shoot with a couple of hand-held video cameras and some portable lights, got a budget that wouldn't pay the lunch ticket on the big ones. They try to be in and out in forty-eight hours.

"These biggies, though, they go in and rent a house, swimming pool, tennis court, the works. You ought to see the stuff they use for the filming. Big sun screens just like the regular pictures, tons of lights, cables running around thick as your arm, makeup people, the works. Sounds like this is gonna be one of that kind, and that's great as far as we're concerned. Always gives us a thrill to have an angle to bust one of the big boys.

"So they choose a house that can't be seen from up above, you know, the grounds outside are private, too. They rent it for a couple of months, get some nut-case to write them a script short on dialogue and long on action. They spend over a million bucks on the filming and the music and the marketing. All legit and above board."

"Not if they're using underage kids," Duncan said.

"That's the thing. The guys down in L.A.P.D., they've got a whole section in their Juvenile Division that does nothing but sexual exploitation. The problem is, though, there's so much kiddy stuff they don't have time to work with the older victims.

A teenager at least has got the chance to choose right from wrong—supposedly, anyway. They're old enough to maybe know if something's really coming down and it's time to run. A little kid, though, how's he gonna know if anybody hasn't told him?"

"Doesn't it make you sick?" Duncan asked.

"Yeah, there's some real low-life scum out there." Allende plucked off his dark-rimmed glasses, breathed on them, began cleaning the lenses with his tie. "If you've only got so many men and so much time, you gotta go for the worst cases, if you see what I mean. That's why it's not a bad thing, having this come up here and not in Los Angeles. Down there, they may have time to check it out, or they may be up to their eyeballs with fifteen custody fights over sexually abused kids, with a dozen lockers full of videos and kiddie porn."

Jeremy shifted in his seat. "Maybe I oughtta go out and wait in the hall, let you gentlemen finish this off on your own."

Detective Allende gave him a look of bitter humor. "Your name's Hughes, that right? Yeah, sorry, Hughes. You forget sometimes how people don't know what's going down in the house on the other side of town."

"It just tears me apart, Officer, hearin' about them little ones."

"Yeah, me too." He slid his glasses back on, said, "Okay, about these kids. If they're really being taken up to a house off Mulholland, especially one that was booked in advance like this, chances are it's a big production. That's good—good for us, I mean. Means a major bust if we can prove they're using these juveniles in a film."

"Seems a crazy chance to take with a big film like this. I mean, if they can get all the people they need who are over eighteen, why take the risk?"

"Youth sells in America." Allende replied. "You don't believe it, just turn on your television. Drink this cola and you'll be so young and alive you're jumping out of your skin. Eat this candy bar and you're guaranteed a love life that makes Marilyn Monroe look like a nun. These guys don't get involved in porn just for kicks. It's all money. And what sells best is the young ones, the younger the better.

"So the guy who's bringing them in will fix them up with a fake ID, maybe even a birth certificate. Los Angeles Juvenile's got a couple of lockers full of fakes. It'll cost maybe four, five hundred bucks. When the girls go in and meet Mister Big, all he wants to know is whether his backside is covered if the heat comes on. So he looks at them and he looks at these ID's, and he asks himself, 'Is my lawyer gonna be able to keep me high and dry on this?' And what pushes him on is how great a shoot he's gonna be able to make with these *young* girls. You gotta understand, these big guys, they don't see nothing wrong with what they're doing. They're just businessmen. This is just another deal. Using a young girl just means a couple of extra bucks."

Jeremy's features wrinkled in confusion. "Officer, don't you ever get the least little bit sick over all this?"

The bitter smile returned. "Can't let it get to you, Hughes. Not if you're gonna survive."

"I'm not sure I could survive, not and stay sane."

Detective Allende stood, reached across the table to shake their hands, said, "Lemme ask you something, Hughes. If we don't do this work, who's gonna hold back the tide?"

◆　　◆　　◆

At two-thirty Friday afternoon Silverwood was finally able to track down Senator Atterly. "I have a favor to ask of you."

"Let's hear it."

"I know you don't think much of me, but so help me God I'm playing it straight this time."

"Don't be so quick to draw yourself in a bad light, John," Atterly replied. "Especially in my eyes. Besides, it's nice to hear you call for God's help."

"It's the anti-porn bill that's up before the Senate Tuesday for a vote. There are six amendments I've been thinking about. I was wondering if you could get them included on the Senate bill before it's passed."

Atterly's voice turned skeptical. "What amendments might those be?"

"If you really looked at the House package, you'd see that they'd just be working for conformity."

Atterly's mind clicked ahead like a chess master tracking out his next move. Conformity meant making one House's bill look just like the other House's bill. Even in a case like this one, where identical bills were introduced in both Houses simultaneously, amendments and attachments usually altered them until they were too different to be enacted into one single law. There were then two ways that the bill could be adjusted. Either the bill would be sent to Conference Committee to be reworked and then voted on by both Houses again, or it would be amended on the floor of one or both Houses to introduce a factor of conformity.

"Conformity to your bill on the House side?" Atterly asked.

"That's right."

"And there's no catfish amendment here?" He referred to an amendment designed to kill an unpopular bill. The provision looked totally innocuous to the untrained eye—it might not even appear to change anything of importance—but in truth it made the resulting law illegal. Attaching a catfish amendment was one of the ALUM's favorite tactics. It allowed the fight to be taken from the limelight of the Congressional floor, and left it to the relative obscurity of the courtroom to render the law void. The name came from the fisherman's tactic of calming a struggling fish, getting it to hold still long enough to be gutted. That was the aim of a catfish amendment, to gut a bill by making it unconstitutional.

"I assure you, Senator, this is totally above board," Silverwood replied.

Atterly thought a moment. "So let's say we can get these amendments accepted on the Senate side. Your crew over in the House is just going to rewrite the bill anyway. That bill's going to be strung up like a Christmas tree by the time your liberal faction finishes hanging on amendments."

"Senator, I can understand your concern. But you've got to trust me on this one. If all goes well, I'm going to push this legislation through without any further alterations." Silverwood replied. "I'll send the proposed amendments over by confidential courier. This needs to be done with a measure of subtlety. But with your role as Whip for the party, I don't think too many eyebrows will be raised."

"Tell you what I'll do," Atterly decided. "I'm going to trust you on this one. There's a line in the Book, 'We walk by faith, not by sight.' I'm afraid if I looked at this one too long, I wouldn't be able to grant the favor. Send me the documents."

Atterly hesitated, then continued, "The amendments shouldn't pose too much of a problem, but it it won't be as easy as it would have been two weeks ago. I knew the chance I was taking when I went public with the assembly call and the pornography issue, and my fears have proven correct. I have difficulty figuring out just how much influence I still have left."

"You're still Minority Whip," Silverwood said.

"Yes, and that's probably enough to push it through. But I'm getting more than just a few raised eyebrows nowadays as I walk through the halls. My colleagues are beginning to avoid me outright." Atterly's tone sharpened back into focus. "But that's neither here nor there. I'll get those amendments through for you, John. Count on it."

"I appreciate that, Senator. Thank you."

"Call me Richard. All my friends do. Your assistance on this is an answer to a prayer. I've been wondering how in this world I'd have time to lend my weight to the House effort. Our Solemn Assembly has grown into something almost beyond belief."

"I've heard." Silverwood replied. "It's incredible to see what an effect your speech had."

"It's not my speech at work here. No speech on earth could be bringing these people together. It's God's Spirit, the same Spirit who's at work in your life." Atterly paused, then went on. "I can't tell you how I am pleased to hear that you've made this step, John."

"I don't know how to put it into words yet," Silverwood confessed. "It's all too new."

"I'm not talking about this legislation."

"I know," Silverwood said. "I can't thank you enough for all you've done for me."

"I was just trying to do as I was told," Atterly replied. "Same as you are on this bill."

"Well, I just wanted you to know that I appreciate it."

"You're welcome. Oh, one more thing. I don't know if it is of any use to you, but I've heard through some contacts with the religious networks that *Sixty Minutes* is planning to cover our assembly."

Silverwood brightened immensely. "You don't say."

"Yes. They did a program on child pornography back in the seventies. It seems that this sequel has been in the works for some time, and the assembly is the reason they've been looking for to push it forward. From what I've heard, they intend to dramatize how the situation has continued to worsen, and despite the visible concern of middle America, Congress has failed to do anything about it. Mind you, this is all just rumor. I've not been able to confirm it."

"I'm scheduled to speak at the National Press Club tomorrow night. I'll dig around, see if there's any possibility of confirming it." Silverwood's mind was racing. "If it's true, it could be just the lever I was working for."

"Well then, I hope the news is correct. And John, good luck on this issue. If you start to falter, just remember that you'll have the largest prayer group in two thousand years on your side."

◆　◆　◆

When they were back in the car, Duncan said, "We've still got two days until the girls're supposed to show up. Any ideas?"

"I wouldn't mind moseyin' around that street, what's its name?"

"Inglewood," Duncan said. "Something tells me Allende's not going to be real pleased to hear we went straight from his office out to snoop around on our own."

"No, you're most likely right on that score. Best we keep that one to ourselves." Jeremy stretched out long legs. "How'd you like to take a little tour of the city before we head out?"

Duncan played at shock. "You mean, cruise the streets of Hollywood?"

"This is my first time west of West Virginia, and I've been hearin' about this city all my life. Might as well see what all the fuss is about."

"You're in for a surprise, Jeremy." Duncan started the car and eased forward. "Be sure to lock your door."

They stayed on Santa Monica Boulevard through the remainder of palm-lined Beverly Hills, then were greeted at the city limits by a pothole the size of a small canal. Hollywood was a transformation from wealth to glitz, from chic to sleazy. In the space of one block the world crumbled, then tacked on vast billboards and flashing lights to mask the decline. The buildings took on a tired gray look; the grass medians grew mottled and unkempt; the palms lining the road looked diseased. People did not parade the sidewalks as they did in Beverly Hills; here they either slouched and slid from shadow to shadow, or strutted with aggressive tension evident in the snapping heels and the upturned collars and super-tight jeans and ultra-dark wrap-around shades. Hairstyles ranged from purple and spiked to long and unkempt to fifties bee-hives to elaborate ducktails to no hair at all.

Business suits were rare enough to attract their attention. The Rolls and Jags and Mercedes of Beverly Hills gave way to two very distinct automotive categories—either they were rust-mobiles or cars meant to shout status. Jeremy counted *two* Ferrari and *four* Porsche and *eleven* antique car dealerships in a fifteen-block stretch.

The farther toward downtown they traveled, the more slum-like the neighborhoods grew, and the quieter the two of them became. After a four-block stretch of cratered streets and littered sidewalks and bookstores specializing in smut, Jeremy sighed and said, "I do believe I've seen just about enough of this for one day."

Duncan made a sweeping U-turn in the relatively empty street. "And this is a main thoroughfare. Just think what it must be like a couple of blocks away."

"I'd rather not," Jeremy said, searching the glove box for the city map. "Might as well take a look around Inglewood for that house."

They turned over to Sunset Boulevard, which ran parallel to Santa Monica, and retraced their path toward Beverly Hills until Jeremy spotted a road that would take them up to Mulholland—the street that curved its way around the high ridge up and to their right, where Inglewood Drive originated.

The connecting road was steep and narrow and lined with thick vegetation. Houses near Sunset reminded Jeremy of backwoods dwellings in North Carolina, with overgrown yards and yawning open windows and sagging porches and crumbled foundations.

The road scrambled around curves so steep and tight their progress was slowed to a crawl, and the higher they climbed the flashier the houses became. Within a dozen blocks the homes were palatial and the yards manicured. One driveway they passed was crammed with seven Rolls-Royces. Seven.

Mulholland Drive rode the crest of a narrow ledge too high to be called a rise and too lonely to deserve the title of mountain. It offered a breathtaking view of Los Angeles on one side and Burbank on the other. Beyond Burbank spread Studio City and Universal City, replete with the Disney and Paramount buildings and the studio sprawl. Still farther away rose the San Gabriel mountains, dry and brown and uninviting in the midday heat. A smoky gray-blue haze hung over the lowlands like a brooding menace. Through it sunlight reflected back from faceless buildings, their mirrored windows glittering like distant jewels.

The area held an artificial quietness, an eerie stillness. It was not a tranquility; it was a vacuum. All the beautiful houses with blank windows and empty decks and untouched pools were utterly still—perfectly groomed as a corpse, and just as devoid of life.

There were for-sale signs everywhere, and a lot of other signs as well. *No parking. Armed guard response. Electronic alarms. Continual surveillance. Trained attack dogs on premises.*

Closed entrance-ways with iron bars and windowless walls fronted the streets. High barriers of stucco or concrete or bamboo or cedar jutted over the last possible inch of space, with ornate steel or brass or solid-wood fortress-like doors and electronically controlled gates.

What yards they could see were pristine and ornate. There was a mish-mash of desert foliage and cactus and cedar and eucalyptus and pepper trees and blooming mountain laurel and bamboo and vast clutches of tropical flowers.

Mulholland remained fairly level as it snaked around a series of gentle curves. To their right a new hill grew and took on form, a second mini-mountain covered with ultra-expensive houses.

Duncan was keeping his speed low enough to rubberneck at the surroundings, when Jeremy told him to stop a minute. Gingerly he pulled over to the narrow shoulder that separated the road from a thousand-foot drop. "What's the matter?"

"Nothing." Jeremy slid forward, squinted through the fron windshield. "That's a sign for a filling station over on the other side of that far curve."

"So?"

Jeremy leaned back. "Just gave me an idea, is all. Okay, son. You can drive on now."

Duncan started up, only to stop again and point out the front windshield. "Will you just look at that."

High on the hillside above their road rose an octagonal house of glass and steel. It sat like a landed UFO on a single massive concrete pillar. Steel girders ran out from the base like a series of aggressive jaws, supporting a vast patio that encircled the house. A miniature cog rail ran from the road up to the base of the pillar.

"Whoever built that wasn't countin' pennies," Jeremy said.

"They were out to make a statement, not build a home," Duncan agreed.

The sign for Inglewood appeared. The street was not long, but was even narrower and steeper than the drive up to Mulholland. If they met head-on traffic they would have to back down the slope; there was no way anyone could pass them. But there was little chance of that. Isolation closed in around them like a tightly clenched fist.

Two houses on Inglewood fit the characteristics given by Detective Allende. But the first was near the corner, and they wondered if it might not attract too much attention. The second was set in its own private circular alcove, and what they could see of the house was constructed in a thirties Spanish style. The curved walls had the look of a two-story stucco fortress. The only windows fronting the street were of heavy glass bricks that allowed in light but revealed nothing from within, not even shadows.

The house was built on the property's higher end. The entrance drive was guarded by a solid-steel gate and a gatehouse built as a miniature replica of the main residence. The houses were joined by a ten-foot high seamless stucco wall that appeared to run the entire way around the property. The wall at the slope's lower end was granted further privacy by a carefully cultivated forest of massive bamboo. Not a person was in sight. The only sound they heard through the car's open windows was that of their own engine and the distant barking of a dog.

Duncan drove up to the end of the street, turned laboriously in the narrow cul-de-sac, and drove by the house again as slowly as he dared. "You'd kind of expect to see a dark cloud hanging over it, wouldn't you?"

"The first thing to remember about evil is that it lies," Jeremy replied, not taking his eyes from the house. "The Bible says that even Satan disguises himself as an angel of light."

◆　　◆　　◆

They were somewhere on a street called Sunset Boulevard, Jessica knew that because she had seen the street sign as they entered the bar. It was like a lot of the bars she had come to know, full of dark corners and flashing lights and over-loud music and men who looked at her with knowing eyes. She kept her eyes on her drink, copied Arlene's stance of sulking silence, wished they could get out of here and go somewhere else. Anywhere, it didn't matter to her, just so long as she didn't have to be reminded of what was going to start soon. In this place, every time she raised her eyes she saw her coming day reflected in the flat blankness of the men's gazes.

Pierre was talking intently to a very dangerous man, in tones too low for her to hear. Chico was standing close enough to listen in, every once in a while giving a little jerking nod of agreement. The man made no move at all, except to raise his head and look at Jessica with a gaze that stripped her bare.

A horror-flick death's head was stitched in rainbow threads onto the back of the man's satin jacket. On most men the puffy sleeves and padded shoulders would have looked a little swish; on him they fit just fine. He wore single-strap sandals over white tobi socks. His black sweatpants had some Japanese or Chinese characters printed on the sides. His sideburns were cut into long knifelike lines that reached almost to his mustache. His pigtail fell between his shoulder blades and had black leather thongs woven into the hair. The nose was hawk-like, the lips full, the skin pocked, the eyes hard and cruel. Jessica thought he probably did karate because he enjoyed hitting people and making them hurt.

The conversation ended by Pierre turning and draining his drink and grabbing for her arm. There was no goodbye to the man, at least none that she could hear. She didn't care. They were leaving, getting away from that strange man with his hard empty eyes. It was enough.

They made their way down a sidewalk crowded with young people. Cars cruised slowly down the nearby lanes with windows opened wide; men leaned out to search with eyes that said they knew who she was. They did not need to know her name, did not care where she came from or where she was going; they knew who she was.

A girl separated herself from the night shadows and came walking toward them. She teetered on spiked heels, her walk restricted by a skin-tight leather mini-skirt. Her hair was teased to the extreme in a kinky bouffant, and the makeup was caked to her face. Jessica decided she either looked sixteen or fifty, depending on whether you watched her body or her eyes.

"Hey, Pierre, how's it going?" She stopped as close as she dared. The look she gave him was desperate. "It's Cindy, remember me?"

"Better get back in position—Mickey's around here somewhere," Pierre said, his voice a flat drone. He did not even glance her way.

Cindy tossed a frightened look over her shoulder, turned back to Pierre, and worked at a tiny smile. "I sure miss the good times we had, don't you?"

"There he is, right across the street. He's looking this way, too."

The false bravado dropped; Cindy became a panic-stricken little girl. "Please, Pierre, you gotta take me back. Please. I'll do anything you tell me. I don't mind working the streets. I'm good at it. Ask anybody. You can keep it all. Please, c'mon, Pierre, look at me."

"He's headed this way," Pierre said, still looking out over the girl's head.

Cindy broke down completely. "I'm scared, Pierre. Mickey's mean. *Real* mean. He's always threatening to burn me or cut me." The words were barely making it out around the tears and the trembling. "There's nobody around anymore to take care of me, Pierre. Please, you *gotta* take me back."

"Here he comes," Pierre droned.

Terror stretched her face taut. She took time to shoot Jessica a look of pure venom, then turned and raced back to the corner.

A black man stepped up on the curb near Pierre, shouted toward Cindy, "Girl, what you doin', talkin' to that man?"

In the distance Cindy forced out, "Oh, hi, Mickey. Just talking to an old friend. That's okay, isn't it? Pierre's your friend too, isn't he?"

"Hey, you askin' for it, you know that?" Mickey turned smoldering eyes toward Pierre, said, "We got us a deal, man. You leave my girls alone."

"Didn't say a thing to her," Pierre said, his eyes still fastened on some distant point. "This is your turf, not mine."

"Yeah, well, don't you go gettin' any ideas, they's bad for your health," Mickey said, and turned to stalk toward the girls.

Jessica watched the fear paint their faces, saw how they huddled down like terrified puppies at his approach, knew for certain she was going to have to find a way out while there was still time.

CHAPTER

14

The next morning Jeremy entered the breakfast room with a frown of pure disgust. He said to Duncan, "You're not gonna believe what just happened to me."

"Thanks for asking, I slept just fine," Duncan replied. "How about some coffee?"

"Walked around the corner to buy me a paper, and what do I see but nine vending machines lined up one after the other. Nine. Wondered how on earth a body could get anything done and still have time to read two papers, much less nine. And they weren't just any old vending machines neither. Nossir. Got these solid steel pillars sunk down in the sidewalk, faces on 'em that'd look more at home on a bank vault. Never seen the like. So I bend over to look through what I figured was prob'ly bulletproof glass and guess what I found."

"I don't need to," Duncan replied.

"Eight of 'em got the awfullest filth I ever *hope* to see. Shoulda known, I guess, but it's hard for me to think real clear before coffee. I tell you what, though. I sure to goodness was awake before I finally found a *real* paper. Yessir. Had no idea folks'd take as divine a gift as sex and twist it into something so evil."

"That's why we're out here," Duncan replied.

"Don't remind me, son," Jeremy said, opening his paper with a resounding snap. "I had a flash of them two little girls bein' advertised like so much supermarket meat, and I couldn't hardly make it back to the front door."

Duncan searched for another subject. "Your girlfriend is coming in this afternoon, isn't she?"

It took Jeremy halfway through his second cup of coffee before he could reply, "Yes, I suppose she is at that."

"I thought you hadn't heard me."

"I heard you all right. Just had to let go of the mess I'd picked up on the street." Jeremy set down his paper. "Took me a while on top of that to swallow the idea she was my girl-friend."

Duncan hid his smile behind his cup. "Well, hey, it's no big deal, right? Just a little weekend fling, take your mind off your troubles, show the lady a few local hot spots, that's all. I mean, we're not talking bells and rice and rings now, are we?"

"You've spilled coffee on your lap there."

"Hey, did I? Guess I was too shook up over the thought of breaking up our team." He lifted the pot. "More coffee?"

"No thank you, son. Two cups is my limit. Any more and I'd probably leap tall buildings with a single bound." Jeremy buttered a last piece of toast. "Where are you off to?"

"Thought I'd make the rounds of the Hollywood runaway shelters, ask a few questions, pass out a few photos. You?"

"Oh, had me a little idea last night. Thought maybe I'd mosey back on up to Inglewood. You mind if I take the car?"

"Guess I could take a taxi. You're not planning on just knocking on the door and asking if they're making a skin-flick with a couple of runaways, are you?"

"Not exactly, no."

Duncan gave him a hard look. "I'd just as soon keep my partner alive a little longer, Jeremy."

"I don't aim on leavin' this world just yet. Don't worry, I'll be careful."

It took Jeremy almost two hours to retrace the fifteen miles from Santa Monica to Inglewood Drive. He used the time while stalled in traffic to study the map and maintain his bearings.

As he wound his way up the steep connecting road, he decided he was comfortable enough to turn on the radio. He flipped the dial past two stations that concentrated on chain saws and loud drums, then heard a traffic reporter say in that flat, perpetually tired California tone, "Bad traffic today in L.A. Too many cars out there. Let's hear something new, right? I'm not naming the streets because it'd take me through the middle of next week to work through them all. Just figure on taking a long time to get wherever it is you're going." Jeremy clicked the radio off.

At the point where hills began rising up from Mulholland's right side, Jeremy pulled over to the shoulder and turned off the motor. He sat and waited and watched, searching with the patience of a man who had often listened to nothing more than the falling of a country dusk. What struck him the hardest was the utter lack of birdsong. He restarted the car, drove slowly on and found that he could not get it off his mind. He spotted the rainbow mist from several sprinklers, as well as lush tropical growth in many gardens, so water was not a problem. There was plentiful foliage—thick bushes and eucalyptus and desert pine. But no birds. Their absence added to the highland's eerie quality.

Jeremy followed the winding ridge road on beyond the turnoff for Inglewood. The filling station was half hidden behind a rocky rise where cactus and mountain laurel competed for space. Jeremy pulled in by the pump, close to a young man washing a vintage roadster. He swiveled in his seat, enormously pleased to find his guess correct—he had an uninterrupted view of the estate's front gates.

The station attendant dropped his sponges in the bucket, walked over, and did a slow circle around the car. He was dressed in a sleeveless t-shirt, cut-off jeans, and grimy sneakers.

He walked around to Jeremy's open window, worked busily at a mouthful of gum, said, "Why'd you have to come here?"

"Like something out of a nightmare, ain't it?" Jeremy agreed.

"I can't tell which is dirt and which is car." He walked back around to the front. "When did you last wash this, mister?"

"Fellow who owns it is allergic to soap," Jeremy said.

"We're gonna have to work out something special here," the guy said. "Like maybe charge you by the day."

"It's a lost cause," Jeremy said, stepping from the car. "I just wanted to ask a couple of questions."

"This isn't just a joke? You really didn't bring this in for a wash?"

"Just a little information is all. Might as well fill 'er up while you're at it."

"No problem." The guy fitted the nozzle in Jeremy's tank, asked, "You a cop?"

"Not even close. Just curious is all."

"About what?"

Jeremy straightened his back. The air smelled of pine and sweet-scented sage and dry heat. "You ever wondered why there aren't any birds around here?"

The guy shrugged a bored shoulder. "Dunno, mister. Never thought about it. Maybe they just got better sense."

Jeremy pointed to the walled enclosure across the way. "You ever seen anything comin' or goin' out of that house up yonder?"

The kid bounced his gum a couple of times. "They pay me not to see anything around here."

Jeremy took a moment to inspect the pavement at his feet, sighed, reached into his pants, pulled out a bill, popped it straight, slipped it into the kid's pocket. "And I'm payin' for a little rememberin'."

The kid lowered his chin, eyed his pocket, said, "Five bucks don't buy much of anything in these parts, mister. 'Specially not a lot of memory."

"You just start talkin', sport. We'll see if there's anything there worth buyin'."

The kid topped off the tank, slammed the nozzle back into the pump, and came back to where Jeremy was waiting. "Yeah, they stop in here sometimes. Tony doesn't like 'em, though. He'd just as soon not have their business, and he doesn't make any bones about it. Kinda crazy, if you ask me, talking like he does to guys that big."

"Tony's your boss?"

"The owner, yeah. Says he's seen some of 'em standing around the front drive up there, weren't much more than kids. No matter what they call themselves, Children of Venus or whatever, anybody who plays around with kids' minds has gotta be twisted. That's what Tony says."

"Sounds like your boss has a lot on the ball," Jeremy said. "He around?"

"Nah, his wife's sick. Won't be back for a coupla days."

Jeremy nodded. "The kids ever come in here?"

"You kidding? Most folks haven't ever seen the kids at all. They don't hardly ever come out. One time a carload came through, one of those mini-vans, right? The back was full, all of them dressed up, sitting real straight, not saying a word, just sitting there."

"How old were they?"

"I dunno. Fourteen, fifteen, maybe sixteen, maybe twelve, it's hard to tell, you know?"

"They just gassed up and headed out, huh."

"Two of the biggest men I ever saw to cart around a busload of kids, they get out and give me this look, right? Didn't say two words the whole time, no, they said three—fill it up. The kids all sat there like they were made of stone, these two gorillas hiding behind their mirror shades, standing beside the van waiting for me to finish. Made my skin crawl."

"You ever heard anybody say what they might be doin' up there?"

"Nah. Don't take a genius to know something funny's going down, though." The kid shook his head. "Crazy system, ain't it?"

"What's that, sport?"

"Well, you know. These guys, all you gotta do is look at them and you know they play rough. But who're the ones the system's gonna protect, them or the kids?"

Jeremy reached forward, patted the kid's pocket that held the money, said, "And who's made it the way it is, sport? Ask yourself that sometime."

Jeremy found Mavis Talmadge sunning herself on the hotel's front porch, wearing a pink jump suit and purple suede sneakers.

"Afternoon, Mrs. Talmadge." Jeremy said, "How you gettin' on?"

The wrinkled old face smiled up at him. "Found those girls yet, Mr. Hughes?"

"I'm workin' on it, ma'am. You seen my friend around?"

"No, not since this morning. Why, were you expecting him?"

"Can't say for certain. Don't rightly know where he is. Say, ma'am, where can I buy me a decent suit around here?"

"That depends. Are you interested in a place that sells monogrammed underwear for eighty dollars a pair?"

"Now, you know it's not nice to pull a fellow's leg like that."

"I guess that means no. Try Broadway over in the mall at the end of Third Street—you know, the walking street where the yuppies hug one side and the druggies the other. It's not Rodeo Drive, that mall, but they'll fit you up with some nice clothes." She looked him up and down. "I'll bet you look fine in a suit, Mr. Hughes."

"Thank you, ma'am. I haven't ever given much thought to clothes, none at all since my wife died."

"Get yourself a dark gray, that's my advice, It'll suit your hair and your eyes just fine. You're a tall man, so the single-breasted will make you look distinguished. And a light blue shirt with a long collar. Don't let them sell you any Italian foppery. You're too old and stately a gentleman for that."

"That sounds like good advice, ma'am. Thank you."

"And a simple club tie. My husband, bless his soul, was an elegant dresser, and it was because he had the sense to buy clothes that suited him. You're a classic-looking gentleman, Mr. Hughes. You'll do well to remember that in your choice of clothes." She leaned forward, added, "And if you'll take the advice of an old woman, you wouldn't do yourself any harm having a haircut while you're over there."

After purchasing a new suit and having his hair trimmed, Jeremy walked down the Third Street pedestrian walkway feeling trapped inside somebody else's clothes. He fought the urge to hunch his shoulders, pull at his collar, tug on his sleeves, wipe the faces of his shiny new shoes on his pant legs.

He passed a black man seated at the base of a modern sculpture dipping his forefingers in a jar of peanut butter and shoveling the globs into his mouth. He was dressed in a denim vest, no shirt, and pants too dirty to tell the color.

"How's it goin', friend?"

The man gave Jeremy a confused squint, surprised by the friendly voice. "Pretty good, man, how 'bout wich you?"

"Can't complain," Jeremy replied, and held out the change that came out of his pocket with his hand.

The man took it, inspected his grimy palm, laughed a phlegm-filled cough. "Seventy-five cents? Whatchew wan' I should do with this, man? Seventy-five cents don' buy no high in this town."

Jeremy fished out another fifty cents, said, "Wouldn't want you drinkin' with my money anyway, friend."

"Shoot. Cup change is all it is," the man muttered, his eyes on his hand. "Can't get me a hit a' nuthin' with no cup change."

The car dealership was exactly where he'd remembered it, just after Santa Monica Boulevard entered West Hollywood. The sign outside offered any car on the premises for short- or long-term lease. Jeremy paid off his taxi, entered the double glass doors, and skirted a car built so low to the ground he wondered whether they might have a couple of mattresses in there instead of seats.

A trio of salesmen were gathered around the far desk while several tourists walked the floor and gawked unabashedly at the automobiles. Jeremy spotted the car he was after and walked over.

"A gentleman who knows what he wants, how nice." A young man with lacquered hair and one hand cocked at half mast strolled over. "I take it you're not in here to escape the heat."

"Not today. This here's one of them British royalty cars, ain't it?"

"How quaint." The young man graced him with a tiny smirk. "Now let me guess. You're the fellow from Arkansas who just did the remake of 'Bikers From Mars,' am I right?"

"Sorry, you musta got me mistook for somebody else. I—"

"No, no, don't tell me. I know, you're one of those good old boys from Texas who was plowing his field to plant hay—or whatever it is they stick in the ground—and struck oil." The young man clapped his hands. "How positively thrilling."

"Do I need to sit down before I ask how much this car is, sir?"

"That depends on the state of your heart, sir. We also have a doctor on call day and night, if that would make you feel any better. Or we can ice down a bottle of champagne and administer a little nerve-medicine ourselves, if you're as afraid of the men in white coats as I am."

"Why don't you just tell me what it is I'm lookin' at, kinda ease me through this thing."

"Certainly, sir. This here thaing, as you call it, is a Rolls-Royce Corniche Convertible, one of the last few automobiles on earth that is made completely by hand. The body is constructed by laying sheets of special-alloy steel along a frame and beating it into place. The exterior color is our very popular Sovereign Blue, and the interior is Magnolia Yellow with blue piping. Leather, of course. A truly fine automobile."

"And you'll let me rent it?"

"Sir, we'll let you pick it up and stick it under one of those brawny arms and carry it home if that's what the gentleman prefers."

"I won't need it but for a coupla days." Jeremy fished for his wallet, extracted plastic, and handed it over. "Come to think of it, don't even tell me how much it costs. I been feelin' a little weak lately, and the strain might do me in."

The young man looked down at the card. "Just like that? You don't want to hear about our famous lay-away plan? The trunk? The motor? You're going to let me waste those *months* of training they put me through to learn how all the icky little bits and pieces are stuck together?"

"Not today, thank you. There's this young lady waitin' for me to—"

The salesman held up his hand. "Say no more, sir, I understand perfectly. The call of the wild. I take it you want full coverage and all the little extras?"

"Dot all the i's and cross all the t's," Jeremy agreed. "And go easy on that credit card. It ain't never bore such a strain before."

The young man walked off, saying over his shoulder, "Sir, when I get through, I seriously doubt there will be anything left but a smoldering little puddle."

◆ ◆ ◆

They were picked up that afternoon by two very big men driving a gray mini-van. There was no greeting from the men, no comments from either Pierre or Chico. Jessica followed them out to the van, climbed in the back, clamped her hands between her knees to hide the trembling.

They drove for what seemed like hours, climbing in air-conditioned comfort up above the Saturday Hollywood din, rising to a level where the world below was turned ghostly and distant by the unmoving layer of hazy smog. They took a long, winding road along a high ridge, turned onto a narrow street, then turned again into a stubby driveway. The tall white-metal gates stood silent and blank in front of them. To their right was a second white door, this one leading to what appeared to be a windowless gatehouse.

The taller man in the front passenger seat swiveled around. His muscles stretched the fancy knit shirt into broad ridges. "You two sports gotta get out here."

For once Chico had nothing to say. Jessica felt Pierre clench her hand tightly, and knew without being told that she was going to be left alone. A different kind of fear filtered in.

"We stay with the girls," Pierre said.

"That so?" The guy was not impressed. He turned to his companion, said, "Turn off the car, Joey."

The dark-haired man cut the motor. "Service with a smile."

His companion gave a one-shoulder bounce, a laugh that did not touch his mouth. "Here we are, beautiful uptown Babylon. You guys are lucky. We got space in the gatehouse for you. Otherwise we'd have dumped you down on Sunset where you belong."

"If we go, the girls go with us," Pierre said, his voice flat.

"Yeah? Hey, you know, I'd really like to accommodate you two gentlemen, but we got our orders, right, Joey?"

"Yeah, life's hard, ain't it? Just when we were gettin' to be such friends and all."

The shoulders bounced once more. "We were told to let the two ladies into the compound. No mention was made of any personal bodyguards or anything."

"We stay with the girls," Pierre repeated.

"No, buddy, that's where you're wrong." The voice was quiet and cool and as flat as the eyes. "Hey, listen, I really wish we could sit around here and talk with you guys, but we gotta get to work. That's about all the time we got for chit-chat, right, Joey?"

"Ten seconds and counting."

"Yeah, see, if you guys wanna leave with all your arms and legs in one piece, maybe you oughtta be saying your goodbyes to the little ladies and climbing on out."

Joey opened the driver's door, climbed out, pulled his shirt straight in a pumping motion of both arms. He walked around to the other side, slid back the van's central door, and gestured with his free hand. "You guys wanna walk outta there, do it now."

"That's what we call Joey's last and final warning," his companion explained. "You don't wanna have him help you out. You really don't."

Pierre surrendered with a silent slackening of his muscles. He slid from the seat without a backward glance.

"Chico, where you going?" Arlene's hand reached out and grasped empty air as he followed Pierre from the van.

Jessica managed, "Pierre, please don't leave—"

The door slid back shut. Joey walked back around, climbed in, shut his door.

The taller man pointed Pierre and Chico toward the gatehouse door, waited until they had walked in, and closed the door behind them. He then flipped down his sun visor, punched a button on a little black box, and the tall white gate slid silently to one side. He asked his companion, "Did you hear that? Chico and Pierre."

"Sounds like a couple of those little rug-rat dogs," Joey said.

Once more the shoulders bounced. The man turned around and said, "Don't worry, girls. You got no need for the two bodyguards anymore. There's not much market for damaged goods, right, Joey?"

"You get treated like fresh-laid eggs," Joey agreed.

The van started up and passed through the open gates and onto the gravel drive beyond. Jessica heard a sound so strange she thought at first she must have imagined it. She turned her head and saw frantic green eyes staring blindly ahead. Arlene was just as afraid as she was.

◆　◆　◆

Jeremy Hughes pulled up in front of the Hotel Bonaventure in downtown Los Angeles. The hotel's five copper-colored cylindrical columns jutted up into the dusky evening sky like mirrored fingers. He glided the Rolls to a stop, wondered if anything could make him feel more uncomfortable than the dozen people who stopped to stand and gawk as he got out.

The parking attendant came around, said, "Nice car, sir."

Jeremy gave him the expected bill, asked, "You mind if I just leave it here out front? I won't be long."

The young man pocketed the bill in a well-practiced motion, said, "Hey, no problem, sir. Car like this, you can leave it here all night far as I'm concerned."

Jeremy entered the red-carpeted lobby and called Bella's room from the courtesy phone. He was both nervous and excited about the coming evening.

"Jeremy Hughes in a suit?" Bella came up wearing a simple yet elegant dress of smoky-blue wool. The color accented her eyes, while the cut drew out the lines of her erect carriage and treated her years with gentle respect.

"It's sort of an occasion," Jeremy said, taking in the single strand of pearls, the matching suede shoes, the warm smile. "You look wonderful, Bella."

"You say that to all the girls," she said.

"Yes, ma'am, every girl I've ever taken out in Los Angeles."

"The suit looks very nice on you, Jeremy. You should try it more often."

They stepped through the doors and Jeremy led her toward the Rolls. He did his best to ignore the heads turning their way, said, "There's something I've been meanin' to tell you."

She made no effort to hide her surprise. "Oh my."

"This ain't my car."

"That's all right." She allowed him to open her door, sat down, adjusted her dress, ran one hand over the smooth leather upholstery. "How on earth do they get this to feel like butter?"

Jeremy shut her door, asked, "Do you want me to put up the top?"

"Don't you dare. I want all the world to see me and wonder which aging movie star I am. I might even have a scarf in my purse for my hair."

Jeremy walked around to his side. "I just rented it for a couple of days, that's all."

"All, the man says." Bella took in the hand-finished burl dashboard, the silver-plated framework, the ebony knobs, the polished rosewood steering wheel. "Can you imagine driving this to the supermarket every day?"

Jeremy started the motor. As the car slid forward, all heads followed him out. The heavy traffic paused to give him passage. "It's like partin' the Red Sea."

"You're talking a language people understand around here, money and power." She nestled down farther in the soft seat. "It really is like driving on a cloud, just like they say."

They drove in companionable silence all the way down Santa Monica Boulevard to where it made a fashionable dead-end on Ocean Boulevard. There were faster ways to get to the coast, especially now that evening was thinning the freeway's frenetic pace. But they were not after speed, and the silence between them was that of old friends long accustomed to each other's company, or new lovers too grateful for the moment of shared ease to risk destroying it with careless words.

The warm air drifting above their heads took on the ocean's perfume as they turned down the ramp by California Street and entered the Pacific Coast Highway. Jeremy powered them toward Malibu in leather-lined luxury, grateful for the opportunity to place his worries and concerns aside for a brief moment and enjoy the company of a woman he was learning to truly care for.

They pulled into the Chart House Restaurant parking lot and caused a stir that only fame or fortune could bring in Southern California. Jeremy felt like apologizing for not being somebody famous as he walked Bella toward the entrance.

They ordered from menus carved on wooden planks. When the waiter departed Bella started to ask Jeremy something, only to be stopped by his upraised hand.

"What's the matter?"

"Last time I did all the talking. Tonight it's your turn."

"I don't know what to say."

"Beginnings are always the hardest part of any job. Let's see if I can give you a hand. Where are you from, Bella?"

"Buffalo, New York. Have you ever been there?"

"Can't say I've had the pleasure."

"Pleasure." She gave her throaty chuckle. "Honey, Buffalo's one of the best places on earth to be coming *from*."

"Do I hear you sayin' it's not a garden spot?"

"It's a very industrial town. We all lived and breathed Bethlehem Steel. When I was a little girl, I used to think that was very special, being a part of the steel company. It was a cold place, very hard place. It's what they call a blue-collar town nowadays. The only white collars you'd see were the ones the priests wore. And there were lots of those. What with all the Irish and Polish and Italian immigrants, every street in Buffalo had a bar and a church."

Jeremy did not need to say anything for her to know that he was truly interested, truly *open* to what she was telling him. There was a genuine caring in those shining eyes, a real sense of digging under the words, hearing what she wanted to tell him. It was a remarkable feeling to her, having someone who listened for what she was trying to say, rather than for what he wanted to hear.

"The bars were doing the better business," Bella went on. "My grandfather, my father's father, came over from Ireland during the potato famine. He died long before I was born—from hard work or whiskey, I'm not sure which. My father married an Italian girl, my mother. I'm sure she was beautiful when she was young. I don't remember her ever being young, though.

I just remember her looking more and more tired.

"My father worked as a truck driver for Bethlehem Steel. It was hard work, but the pay was good. He used to have to get up very early in the morning, when it was still dark and very cold outside. His shift began at six o'clock. By the time I was getting up for school he was already gone. I remember a couple of times the unions went on strike. My father would stay at home, and he would seem so worried. But I thought it was wonderful to see him at home with us. I couldn't understand why he was so upset.

"By the time he retired he was earning sixty dollars a week. That was big money in the fifties. I still lived at home, and I worked in the personnel department at Sattler's, the most chic store in all of Buffalo. That's not saying a lot, mind you. Buffalo is not a chic place. You know how some cities are worldly? Buffalo is inwardly."

"I like that," Jeremy murmured, nodding his head and smiling. "An inwardly city. That's good, Bella. Real good. It makes me feel like I know the place."

"Traveling abroad meant going to see Niagara Falls from the Canadian side," Bella said. "Most people's horizons didn't stretch farther than the smokestacks on the outskirts of town. So there I was, working for Sattler's, and one day my manager told me that he was going to take something called a Government Civil Service Exam. It was given in every city in America on the same day. Even in Buffalo. He suggested that I should take it also."

Bella paused and watched Jeremy smile his thanks at the waiter as their plates were set down—mesquite broiled salmon for them both. It was nice to have this chance to look at him when he was not watching, to study the unearthly mixture of strength and hard lines and gentle voice and shining eyes. They were such open, beckoning eyes.

"We've got a hard choice to make here," Jeremy told her. "We can either let the food grow cold, or we can wait and finish your story after dinner. I can't do them both justice at the same time."

The silence returned and kept them company as they ate. There were smiles over little things, murmurs about the excellence of the meal, an occasional remark just to show that their attention never strayed very far from the other.

When he was finished Jeremy leaned back, said, "Time for the main course."

"I can't even remember where I was."

"Don't worry yourself. That's the listener's job. You were just going in for the exam."

"That's right, I was. Well, I took it, and I did well. Very well, in fact. So well that I was offered a job in Washington. I took the train down to Union Station and arrived with little more than a good head for numbers and a fair dose of Irish-Italian feistiness.

"No one knew me, so I could be anybody I wanted. And I wanted to be tough. I wanted to make it in the nation's capital. Back in sixty-two I started as a GS–4, a cost analyst for the General Accounting Office. My head for numbers and my toughness put me where I am."

Bella dropped her eyes, wanting to have her feelings out in the open but unable to look at him. "If I had to do it all over again, yes, I would have left Buffalo. Would I have done anything different? No, but I wish I had *been* different. I wish I could have known this softness of faith and shown it to others.

"I understood hardship and I understood struggle. I understood how it felt to be the outsider. But I could not understand compassion or love or joy until TJ introduced me to Jesus Christ. I could only sneer at those things and guard my position all the more closely.

"To me, life was always a zero-sum game. There was only so much to be had, and if I gave away anything, I would have less. Why should anybody else profit at my expense—that was my attitude. And that is one of the most amazing things about faith to me. The balance sheet goes right out the window. I've come to realize that the more I give, the more I have."

She kept her gaze turned downward, fearful now that judgment would stand as a barrier between them. But when she raised her eyes all she saw was that same gentle brightness, that light-filled gaze from a man who was happy just sitting and listening—without judgment, without condemnation. Bella felt a sudden urge to rush around the table and enfold him in her arms.

"You have a gift with words," Jeremy said.

She smiled at that. "You have a gift of listening."

"Do you ever go back to Buffalo?"

"I used to go back from time to time. The place was always the same, only older. The people were the same too, only more tired and more lined and more gray. Buffalo made the word deindustrialization real to me. Sattler's was boarded up, blocks upon blocks of houses were condemned, the place was just a shell of its former self. I haven't been back since my parents died. That was over ten years ago. It's strange, I've found myself thinking about it now, wondering if maybe I should try to go up there and do something. I've prayed about it, but there's never been any feeling that I'm called to go there."

"There's work to be done just about everywhere," Jeremy said.

"All that time I spent trying to put the misery of a decaying city behind me. And here I am, spending my spare time working in the middle of a Washington slum, and you know what? I'm happier than I've ever been in my entire life."

"It shows," Jeremy said quietly.

"I'm not doing it for myself anymore. At least, that's the way it feels. Sure, there's still a lot of selfishness in me, and a lot of other things I don't like. A *lot*. But where I live and what I do, these things I've fought so hard to get, I've learned what it means to find life's direction through faith."

"It sure changes things, doesn't it?"

"New and improved," Bella agreed. "I never knew life could be so, well, *rich*."

Jeremy gazed at her a long time, then shook his head slowly. "You're one special lady, Bella."

Bella hid her feelings, declined the waiter's offer of dessert, decided that there would never be a better time. She forced her hands to stop fidgeting, took a breath, and said, "Just tell me one thing, one time, and I'll never ask you again. Are you really free of your first wife? Is there really any chance of starting over?"

Jeremy became utterly still, his eyes on her face, his hands motionless on the table before him. "I tell you what it's like, Bella. The pain and the loss just about drove me 'round the bend there at the start. But life goes on, and after a while it got so I could manage, like a man who learns to make his way on one leg. It never stopped hurtin', and I never stopped missin' her. But it got so the ache and that empty hole in my heart became more or less normal. After a while, I'd lived with it so long I stopped payin' it much mind. It was just there. The only time it really pushed hard at me was when something reminded me of her kinda unexpectedly, and I learned to sidestep places and things that might've poked at my wound.

"Something's happened, though. I don't know when, don't know how, don't even know if it's temporary or permanent. All I can tell you is for this day, this moment, the pain's gone. It's just plain not there. I can think back over the times we had and feel that warm glow in me, or talk about her now here with you, and not need to get up and race for some dark corner. It doesn't hurt me inside anymore.

"It's so strange, I'm almost afraid to think much about it. I've carried that weight around for so long I feel, well, it's almost like I feel *guilty* about it not bein' there."

He stopped and looked down at hands that suddenly seemed too big for his body. "I don't guess I've done much in the way of answerin' your question, have I?"

Bella reached over and clasped his rough hand in both of hers. "No, I think you did just fine."

"Times like these, I can't help wishin' I was a better man."

"I know what you mean. I feel that way every time I wonder what on earth I'm meant to *do* with my life."

"Ella used to say that a woman's first duty was to keep her man first in her life. And a man's first duty was to *deserve* it."

"Ella scares me silly sometimes."

"No need. She's not here, Bella."

"Yes she is."

"No, excuse me for sayin' it, but you're wrong. Her *absence* is here. I'll carry the *lack* of her with me 'til the day I die. But she's not here, Bella. No, ma'am. You are."

◆　　◆　　◆

It was almost one o'clock in the morning when Duncan started down Sunset Boulevard, trying hard not to flinch over what he saw. He accompanied a seminary student named Brent who worked at the way-in center, the Salvation Army's runaway shelter. Brent was tall and dark-haired and a bit overweight, but that fact was only noticeable when he was standing still, which was seldom. He carried himself with the bouncing light-footed gait of someone trained to keep the pace up all night long. As they walked Brent talked about his world in matter-of-fact tones.

"When I first started down here, oh, I guess it must be eighteen months ago now, it seemed like every parked car I passed had some john sitting behind the wheel with his little toy. But all that's changed, thanks to stiffer jail terms for the pimps and some of the pros who get a reputation for showing up in the court dockets a little too often."

Brent carried himself in a slight crouch, as though ready to jump aside from danger only he could see. His face was a mixture of concrete-hard inspection and warm concern, the same mixture Duncan had found in shelter supervisors thoughout his day's tour.

"The younger they are nowadays, the harder it is to get to them. They're holed up somewhere, with prices pushed up high enough for the pimps to live off one, maybe two girls. He doesn't leave them alone very often, and before he does he'll tell them in no uncertain terms what he'll do if he catches them taking one step out of the house."

Duncan had made the rounds as the old lady at the hotel had suggested, going by seven or eight shelters, working his way continually farther toward downtown L.A. Everyone distrusted him until they had inspected the affidavits, and made some calls. Then they accepted him into the fold, listened to his story, searched and dissected and analyzed, photocopied his photos of Jessica and Arlene, posted them, and passed them around. But the Salvation Army had offered him the warmest welcome, including an invitation to prowl the streets with a leader of their Outreach Program.

"These kids are so young," Brent went on, "and so scared of the pimp in the first place, they don't dare breathe without getting permission first. Then by the time the cops find out about the house or somebody alerts a shelter or a neighbor spots something fishy, the kid's too far gone to be saved."

Duncan tried to match Brent's resigned, casual tone and asked, "How do they let themselves get involved?"

"Sometimes they don't. Let themselves, I mean. A girl can be tricking for a pimp who just tells her she's gonna do it. If she doesn't like it, the pimp can come down heavy on her, but more than likely she'll know that one way or the other she is gonna have to do what the pimp wants her to do. So she'll just grin and bear it."

"Without the grin," Duncan said.

"Yeah, you don't see a lot of smiles out there, that's for sure." He paused and shook his head. "Other girls are enticed. They don't have a lot of skills, and they're not of legal age, so the jobs they get offered are the pits. A girl can either work at

McDonalds and smell like hamburger grease and get minimum wage, or she can do what the pimp wants and dress real fine and have a lot of people chase after her and hear promises of becoming a *star*."

Brent was continually pausing and ducking into dark entranceways, waving to kids, weaving his way through gawking tourists out for a late-night fling. It did not interrupt his flow. "When you meet a kid involved with prostitution or porn, it's really hard to get her to talk about the tricks, how nasty it is and how awful she feels sometimes, and how the pimp really doesn't love her forever like he says. She wants it to be true, you see what I mean? They all want so bad to have their nothing lives turned into some dream off the pages of a magazine. They *want* to believe it. So they retreat into a make-believe life in their minds, and they shut out everything about the street that doesn't fit the dream world they've made up."

As Duncan walked he was reminded of a children's party he had attended when his daughter had been very young. For some reason all the parents had left the room except him, and he had been stuck away in a tiny alcove where the kids could not see him. The noise level had risen by staggering proportions in a very brief span of time, as though the children were stretching their wings, trying to see just how far they could reach with their voices now that there was nobody around to tell them to behave. The noise had battered at him, and amid the general chaos, high-pitched squeals and shrieks had plunged into his eardrums like daggers. The laughter had been shrill and without joy, fed on an excitement of abandon.

That was how it sounded on the street, but amplified beyond anything he could have imagined possible.

The curses were meaningless, little bits of flotsam stuck inside every available crack and cranny of the conversation. The kids cursed with the ease of people who had forgotten what the words ever meant. They were simply punctuation marks to a verbal street game.

"I don't hear any real street jive," Duncan remarked, trying to sound as casual as Brent acted. "You know, like in the movies when the kids talk this language that an adult can't understand without an interpreter."

"First of all, these kids come from almost every state in the nation," Brent replied. "If they started off with that kind of talk they'd be left out in the cold. And second, most of these kids haven't ever really *belonged* anywhere long enough to develop a language of their own. That's what it's all about, belonging. You got a throw-away kid who's never belonged anywhere, he doesn't have the confidence in himself to play artist with the language. A lot of these kids never learned to communicate beyond the level of basic need, and even there it's warped. For instance, you'll never hear a kid out here say he's lonely. Know why? Because you've got to have something to compare it to before you can understand what it means. For these kids, loneliness is as basic a part of their existence as breathing."

He stopped Duncan's forward progress with a warning hand. Ahead of them a black kid was pushing a white kid down the pavement, screaming at him to get out of his face. The white kid seemed to crumble up inside, then turned and ran. Taunting laughter echoed down the street behind him.

"The black kid saw through the white kid's act because his hair was neat and his clothes intact," Brent said. "Not clean, but intact. He hasn't been on the streets long enough to know what's for real and what's just a game. So the black kid pushed him around and raised his own status with the group."

"Can't you do anything?"

"Sure." Brent watched the gathering disperse with a weathered eye. "I've talked to the white kid four or five times. His name's Larry, he's just turned sixteen, and he's from Colorado. He'll go nurse his wounds for a while, or if he's got enough money, spring for a cup of coffee. Then in an hour or so he'll come back out here and pretend like nothing's happened. He doesn't have any choice. The street's his home. Only he'll still be shook up inside, and there's a chance that he'll let me talk to him, shake him up in a different way. Maybe he'll listen when I say it's dangerous out here and sooner or later if he stays he's going to die. Maybe he'll let me take him into a shelter, get him cleaned up, give him a hot meal, talk with him awhile, put him to bed, hope that he'll still be around the next morning and still be willing to listen. There's not much chance, but it's all I've got. It's what keeps me out here, hoping for those little chances."

They returned to the car and continued down Sunset, past a decrepit warehouse converted into a mammoth strip-tease bar, past a row of restaurants interspersed with boutiques specializing in chains and leathers and shades of black, past the first of several bars catering to the homosexual trade, to where the traffic lane closest to the sidewalks slowed to a walking-paced crawl. Brent parked the car and led Duncan through on foot.

He stopped on the next street corner and called out to a young boy, "Hey, Fancy, how's it going?"

"Don't stand too near, man." The kid spoke with a distinctive lisp. "You'll scare the trade."

A car almost stalled as its driver leaned across the passenger seat and out the open side window for a better view. Fancy did an exaggerated hip-swinging walk toward the car, one hand propped on his lower ribs, asked, "You looking for a good time?" The driver replied by gunning the motor and driving away. The kid made a gesture at the car, then turned and walked back toward them.

"You eaten today, Fancy?" Brent asked.

The kid pulled a cigarette from his pocket, lit up, and dragged with a force that belied his fifteen years. Maybe sixteen. He was dressed in skin-tight jeans and a woman's white blouse with the collar turned straight up and the sleeves rolled beyond his elbows. He wore eyeliner, and a tiny gold chain on each wrist. "Let's see. What day is it?"

"Two-thirty Sunday morning."

"No, not today, then. Had a sandwich yesterday. I think it was yesterday."

"Fancy is trying to keep himself from growing up," Brent explained.

"All the johns want is *young*," Fancy said to the passing cars. "The younger the better."

"Maybe it's time for you to get off the streets, then. What do you say? How about sleeping in a nice clean bed tonight?"

"Hey, I sleep in nice beds all the time. Silk sheets even."

"I said *sleep*, Fancy," Brent said. "No danger, no pain, nobody hitting on you."

"What do you call what you're doing right now?" Fancy spotted an interested face, dropped his cigarette and started off on his vampish walk. "Sorry, fellas. Duty calls."

"He's been out here about a year now," Brent pressed. "We got him into a shelter once, oh, maybe a week after he arrived. His nightmares kept the whole house awake. Turns out his old man passed him around to all his friends before the kid finally wised up and left."

Duncan watched the kid open the car's passenger door and

climb in. "So there's no hope for him?"

"There's always hope," Brent replied. "It just gets a little bit smaller every day he's out here. A lot of the shelters say a kid won't come in if he's been on the streets for more than two weeks. After that he or she's been hit on too much, seen too many bad things, been hurt too many times, to ever trust an adult again. I think that's pessimistic. I'd give them three weeks, maybe even a month if the street treats them easy."

A very young girl with an overdeveloped body strolled by, spotted Brent, gave him a little wave before turning back to the passing cars. Duncan felt the girl's raw sexuality like an all-pervading scent. He tried to guess her age, settling on fourteen. She danced along the sidewalk on heels five inches high, her tight-knit skirt swaying provocatively with each step.

"There aren't many girls down here on Sunset," Brent said. "Tina likes it because the pimps don't hang out around the gays, and she's trying to keep from getting involved with a pimp again."

"You know all the kids this well?"

"A lot of them," Brent admitted. "Especially the ones who have been out here awhile. Tina's special, though. She's what we call a recidivist. She's been in and out of shelters since she was eleven. She'll get trapped by a pimp who treats her like a queen for a while, then when he gets mean she'll slip into hiding, usually with Children of the Night. They specialize in working with under-fourteen prostitutes."

"She started when she was eleven?"

Brent looked at him with weary humor. "Nine years old is not uncommon. Not anymore. The problem nowadays is that the really young ones have been driven off the street by increased police vigilance. They're mostly out in homes, kept by some pimp or maybe a gang out in the Valley."

"So what about Tina?" He watched her strut and sway and smile at each passing car with what from that distance looked like childlike eagerness.

"She'll probably wind up in a house if she's not careful. For a while, anyway. A year or so more under those conditions and she'll be too old for a lot of the places out there. They'll put her on some kind of circuit or maybe in a bar, it depends on how well she holds up."

Tina was clearly becoming restless with the lack of interest. She pasted on the friendly smile and walked over toward them.

"Looks like everybody's out for something I don't have."

"How are you doing, Tina?"

She looked Duncan over with a practiced eye, stripping away all the false veneer and exposing his own carnal curiosity for what it was. Then she dismissed him. "You got a smoke?"

"No, sorry, I don't use," Brent replied.

"Hang on a sec."

She trotted over to where a couple of gay boys were playing the street, no mean feat on her heels. They joked with her for a while, handed over a cigarette and lit it, then she turned and walked back. Up close the hard life showed clearly, like heavy varnish applied to fresh wood. Her copper-colored hair was held in its bouncy little pose by so much hair spray that under the streetlight it looked shellacked. The knit dress was so tight that in a couple of places the side seams were unraveling. Perhaps that was why she preferred to stand or walk or strut with her arms kept close to her sides.

"Where're you sleeping these days?"

"Who's got time to sleep?" She blew out the smoke with practiced ease. "Mostly I hang out at the squat off La Brea."

"The condemned building where they found that kid last month?"

"They found a kid there?" Despite the pale bottle-green color of her eyes, they seemed dark, void of light. "Really? What happened?"

"Same as could happen to you," Brent said. "He got unlucky."

For a brief moment the hard facade crumbled, and a scared little girl showed through. Instead of the sexy vampish figure, now there was only a fourteen-year-old who did not know where to turn. She dragged on her cigarette and watched the passing cars. "I saw Jackson the other night."

"Your old pimp? Where?"

"At a bar on Hollywood. I was real careful. Soon as I spotted him I was out the door, whoosh. I'm pretty sure he didn't see me."

Brent shook his head. "This is the same guy who promised to cut you after you left him for the shelter, right? Don't you think you ought to get off the streets for a while?"

"I've been off the streets." She struggled with the facade, managed to fit it back in place, turned a hard eye toward him. "It's boring."

"Life in the fast lane eats you up," Brent warned.

That was clearly a topic she didn't want to carry further. "There's some new stuff on the street," she said.

"Yeah? What kind?"

"Windowpane." She fished in her ratty purse, came up with a crumpled tissue, unfolded it, showed him a trio of what looked like tiny stars of photographic negative film. "Three bucks a hit, supposed to keep you up for two days. I'm saving it for after work."

"Why?" Brent pressed. "Business hasn't been so good? You haven't eaten for a while?"

She ignored him. "The bikers brought it down from Berkeley. I walked down Hollywood a while ago, they're up at the usual place. Teeter says it's really good stuff."

"Yeah, well, Teeter ought to know, seeing as how he'd put anything into his mouth or arm or nose that he thought'd maybe make him high."

"Yeah, right." She folded the tissue and put it away. "I saw a couple of new faces last night up at Kramers."

"On Highland? They been around tonight?"

"Not yet. Still too early, probably. A guy and a girl. About my age, I guess. Maybe younger. I heard they squatted under the bridge last night. Maybe you could still catch them."

"I'll give it a try, thanks." Brent allowed the concern to show through. "Why don't you give it a rest for a while, Tina? Do yourself a favor, let us take you to see your friends at the shelter."

There was an instant of pain, of indecision and longing, and the little girl appeared in her face again. Then the child was gone, so quick a flash that it was hard to believe she had ever appeared. "I'll be all right."

"No you won't," Brent replied.

"Catch you later," she said, and did her swaying walk back to where the traffic crawled and searched and hunted for prey.

Duncan watched the sexuality return to her being with the practiced turn-on of a neon sign. "She told you about some new kids? Just like that?"

Brent's voice retained a trace of pain over the one that walked away. "That's something you see over and over with the kids who trust you out here. They won't do anything for themselves, and if you ask they'll keep telling you how great it is living on the streets. But soon as they spot a fresh face, they'll tell you in an instant. They may think they themselves are too far over the edge to save, but they hope maybe we can still do something about the new ones." He turned away. "Come on, I want to check out the tunnel."

"Hearing about windowpane acid on the streets kinda takes me back to the sixties," Duncan confessed, hurrying to keep up with Brent's practiced strides.

"Yes and no," Brent replied. "Most of the stuff nowadays is made up in labs around the Berkeley campus. Acid heads who graduated with degrees in physics or chemistry or didn't bother to graduate at all hold down a normal job in the daytime and cook up all kinds of designer drugs at night. The stuff we get here on the street is mass-produced, cheap, and about a thousand times more powerful than it was twenty years ago. Tina wasn't kidding when she said it would keep her up for two days. Two days is probably a little on the conservative side, either that or the stuff is second-rate. Three dollars is kinda cheap for a dose, now that I think of it. Five is the more normal price. Five bucks for a high that'll keep you tripping out of your head for three, sometimes four days."

"What was that she said about the bikers?"

"The Hell's Angels are responsible for most of the drugs and a lot of the gang-related prostitution around here. You'll see them parked either on their bikes or on these little garden chairs they cart around, usually up around Hollywood and Vine, starting around one, maybe two in the morning. They sell the kids their dope, try to string along any of the good-looking younger girls they might be able to draw into one of their houses. It's getting tougher for them, though. Word is out that if a girl goes into one of their houses, she doesn't come out—not alive, anyway. So they mostly just sell their dope around here and work the bus stations and freeways, picking up their fresh meat before the girls learn who to stay away from."

Up ahead drummed the irrepressible thunder of another freeway. The closer they came to the bridge that carried Sunset above the frenetic traffic, the more littered became the sidewalk. Mostly it was refuse from countless burger runs—hundreds of orange styrofoam cartons. Here and there were trademarks of a twisted life—torn underclothes, a bent needle attached to a broken plastic syringe, used plastic vials for poppers or crack, a broken switchblade, liquor bottles, comic books, a filthy doll. Everywhere there were cigarette butts. Thousands and thousands and thousands of butts.

Brent scooted down a narrow dirt path that from above appeared to drop precariously onto the freeway. Duncan hesitated and leaned farther out, saw there was a narrow strip of mud held in place by a concrete barrier wall and a chain-link fence. He followed Brent down and almost lost his footing on the slimy path, racing the last twenty feet and slamming into the fence.

"Gotta watch that drop, man," a young-old voice said from the shadows to his left. "Someday that old fence is gonna give and there's gonna be something more than squirrel for the boys to scrape off the pavement."

"Yeah, right." Duncan watched a young man in a tattered t-shirt and three-day beard emerge from the tunnel made by the Sunset Boulevard overpass. "How's it going?"

"Can't complain, man. Got a smoke?"

"No, sorry."

"How about a hit. You got any extra?"

"Sorry, I don't use."

Duncan heard a metallic click, saw a glint in the young kid's hand, felt his blood go cold. "How 'bout some jack, man? You spare twenty bucks? I need a hit bad."

The kid took a step forward, backing Duncan up against the fence and the fifty-foot drop and the drumming freeway traffic. He searched the darkness behind the kid, saw no glimpse of Brent. He started to yell for help, saw the knife weave upward, knew there wasn't time.

Duncan felt the words in his heart long before his mind could form them, a silent scream of a prayer, the call of a lost and frightened man to a God he did not know.

"You always need something," a phlegm-filled voice said from the tunnel's shadows. A large slatternly woman in a filthy wrap-around print dress walked up. Her heavy legs were bare to the night's chill, her feet slapping and sliding inside what once had been quilted bedroom slippers. She laid an elephantine hand on the kid's arm, said in an immensely casual voice, "You need a smoke, Blue? Here, I got one. The man'd help you, but like he said, he don't use."

The tension faded, the blade disappeared, the kid's eyes lost their pinpoint focus. "Yeah, I could use a smoke."

"Sure you could." She lit a cigarette, pulled it from her mouth with a flamboyant gesture that made the fat on her arm shiver. "You the fellow with Brent?"

"Yes," Duncan said, his voice very shaky.

"They call me Mom. I kinda take care of the place, keep the kids in order." She spoke with evident pride. "We've never had a bust down here, and that's really something, lemme tell you. Eleven months in a place without a bust. The cops know me, know the kids stay in line, and they leave us alone." She pointed back into the tunnel's darkness. "Brent's waiting for you. Looks like he might need your help."

Duncan stumbled past the kid, on legs made rubbery by fear. The tunnel yawned before him like a gaping misshapen mouth. Along the freeway side was a wall of unfinished concrete, set at a steep angle up and over the drumming traffic. The other side was a dirt hillock that scrambled up to meet with the bridge pilings. The floor was muddy and slick and grimy. The walls were stuffed with bedrolls and duffel bags and battered boom boxes and sodden cardboard boxes. The beds themselves were set to either side of the tunnel and built on odds and ends of crates and bricks and rotting wood so that they were raised to waist level, high enough to escape the filth underneath.

Duncan could only see three beds back into the darkness, and they were all occupied with filthy blankets and stinking mattresses and bodies that slurred groans and curses at no one in particular.

When he stepped into the darkness, he had a sensation of being *enveloped*. It was more than the smell and the lack of light: there was an oppressive energy to the place, a force strong enough to leave him wanting to turn, to flee, to race up the hill and out of the miasma of unspoken horror that closed in on him.

As he walked and slid his way down the tunnel's gloomy depths, Duncan had a fleeting thought of the kid with his knife as a sentry to a world where he did not belong, a world which objected to his presence and wanted to see him either gone or dead.

"Duncan, is that you?" Brent pointed toward him with a bright-beamed flashlight. "Come over here and give me a hand."

He clambered toward Brent, who crouched over a softly moaning form. He bent down and saw that it was a young girl. "What's the matter?"

"Little too much acid." Mom's unexpected voice made him

jump. "They was jumping all over the place a while back, screaming about stuff coming through the walls for 'em, all kinds of junk. Waylon fed 'em both a coupla pills, quieted 'em down. That's my bed she's in."

"Where's the boy? I heard there were two of them," Brent said.

"Under the bed," Mom said, with a laugh that slurred into a rasping cough. "Got tired of trying to keep him outta the dirt. Every time we'd pick him up he'd crawl back under there, screaming about some demon coming down outta the ceiling."

Brent leaned over and shone the light beneath the bed's sodden frame. He spotted a blanket-covered heap curled up against the tunnel wall, shivering and whining softly. He dropped to his knees, handed the light up over his shoulder, said, "Try to keep this on me, will you?"

"Just a little too much junk in his system," Mom repeated. "He'll be all right in a coupla hours or so."

As Brent grabbed the boy's shoulders the kid came out of his stupor enough to struggle feebly, straining toward the tunnel wall with a clawed hand. Brent soothed and gentled and crooned comforting words, pulled him out and raised him up high enough to pat his body for weapons and sling one limply waving arm around his shoulders.

"Think you can manage the girl?" he asked Duncan.

"Sure."

"Here," Mom said, her gap-toothed grin never slipping. "Lemme hold the light for you."

Together they staggered back toward the tunnel entrance, set the girl gently down, and with Mom lighting their way, climbed up the steep slippery slope with the boy. Then back down again, and a second time up with the girl, breathing hard by the time they arrived on top. The boy was comatose, huddled into his fetal position, blind to all but his own internal shivering struggle.

"You stay here with them while I go call an ambulance." Brent said.

"Well, I guess you've got it all under control," Mom said. In the better light Duncan saw that grime blackened her hands almost to her elbows, and her feet and ankles and shins as well. "Hey, you guys think you could maybe spare the light? It'd sure come in handy down there."

Brent waved at her; he was already trotting toward the

nearest neon sign. Mom gave a smile large enough to reveal that she only had three teeth in her head. She gave a vague gesture with the flashlight and then disappeared into the ever-thundering traffic.

Duncan crouched over his two moaning charges, their inert bodies shaken occasionally by invisible winds. He did not think it out, did not logically come to a carefully drawn conclusion; the action, rather, came from somewhere beyond himself. He rested a hand on each of them, bowed his head, and prayed with a strength and a conviction and a love that was his only because he sought to give it to another.

CHAPTER
15

The Sunday morning streets were quiet save for late-night revelers straggling home and hustlers looking to score a drink, a snort, a hit, a toke, or a trick. For them it was just another day.

They drove the Lincoln to church. Duncan had given the Rolls a long look that morning, said to Jeremy, "This is supposed to be an insult, is that it?"

"I just got myself an idea, is all," Jeremy replied. "What say we drive your car?"

"My baby brings us all the way across the country, and the first thing you do when we get here is go out and buy a car that costs more than Ecuador."

"I didn't buy it, and there's nothin' the matter with your car that a wire brush and a coupla hundred gallons of soapy water won't solve." Jeremy opened the passenger door. "You stand around here much longer and we'll be late for church."

Duncan started for the car. "If I didn't know you, I'd guess you were hot after some sweet young thing."

"I'm hot all right, but it's on account of this wind smellin' like something out of the tail pipe of a dump truck." He climbed in and slammed his door. "And she's not a sweet young thing."

Jeremy was so quiet on their way to church that Duncan finally asked him what was the matter. He answered with a sigh, "Had me a thought this morning over coffee. Those little girls should've arrived yesterday, isn't that right?"

"You know it is."

"Wonder how they're spendin' their Lord's day," Jeremy said, turning his head toward the side window.

"Don't let it bother you, Jeremy."

"Bother me? Son, this is tearin' me up something awful."

"Weren't you the one who told me I had to stop trying to carry these burdens on my own?"

Jeremy eyed Duncan, said, "You been listenin'."

"I gotta tell you, Jeremy. Some of that stuff has made more sense than just about anything I've heard in a long time."

Jeremy turned his head back toward the front windshield. "All right, son. Take us to church. I'm ready to worship Him now."

They took the left off Sunset Boulevard by Hollywood High School and drove up Highland until the street was overshadowed by the seven-story Church of Scientology Hospitality Center. The white monstrosity loomed over the neighborhood like a tombstone to truth. Its mammoth proportions completely dwarfed the nearby red brick church, making it appear much smaller than it truly was.

The First Presbyterian Church of Hollywood was surrounded on all sides by rubble and refuse, yet stood proud and stately upon an island of pristine calm. They were directed down two long blocks to a shaded corner of the church's fourth parking lot. Duncan cut the motor, climbed out, leaned and looked upward at the Scientology Center, said, "Shouldn't we go to the place with the bigger vote?"

"One plus God is a majority, son. Don't ever forget that."

The red-brick exterior gave way to massive close-cut stone in the church foyer. They entered the sanctuary, sat, and took in their surroundings. The ceiling was the upside-down belly of an ark, with massive reinforced oak beams that streaked across the heavens like wood-stained rainbows. The entire altar, choir, vestry and pulpit were of hand-carved wood, as was the ornate balcony running along all three sides. Morning sunlight played through beautiful stained-glass windows and illuminated a congregation drawn from every race on earth.

"It certainly is nice to see so many people here this morning," the pastor began. "Even with the number of our services cut from three to one, I was afraid that so many of you had decided to travel to Washington that I would be speaking to an empty house."

Duncan shot Jeremy a look, could not get the man's attention. He was lost in his own little world, his whole being focused on something only he could see.

"In our moment of silent prayer this morning, I think it would be a good idea for each of us to offer a special word for the gathering that is scheduled to begin in Washington on Thursday of this week. It is a monumental undertaking, and I was moved to see how many of us were willing to set aside their daily lives and travel over with our associate pastor. Six full busloads left this morning, I am happy to report. Please be sure and remember them in your prayers, and ask that His glory will reach throughout this nation as a result."

The minister appeared to be in his early fifties, with the refined features of a television actor. His movements were smooth and fluid, his graying hair set in perfect lines, his smile constant and practiced. Duncan found it difficult to set the man's elegant attractiveness aside, wished he could achieve the single-minded concentration that surrounded Jeremy like a blanket of stillness.

"Today I'm going to talk about nine of the most dangerous words in the English language," the minister began. "They are, 'I have got to get control of my life.'

Duncan had the impression that he was being drawn toward this soft-spoken gentleman preacher, and given the sort of loving advice that can only come from a trusted friend.

"The whole story of the Bible, all the problems of mankind, come down to one issue: *Control*. Who is in charge here? How important is your darkness to you? Have you never wanted to know the presence of unchanging guidance? Have you never thirsted for a peace that is not dependent on external things?

"If control is an issue in your life, then there is one thing for certain—your God is too small and your Christ too constricted.

"You can never know His power until you let go and let God, then see through your own personal experience what it means to have Him guide your footsteps. Your life is one divine gift, your free will another. What do you choose to do with these precious gifts? Will you continue to seek control for yourself, and cover your lack of it with cynicism and hopelessness and anger and emptiness? Trying to control your own life is like painting your own portrait in the dark. You remain blind by insisting on sitting in a self-imposed prison, and are afraid of moving into the light because it would illuminate the lie of a life seeking self-control.

"The same power that raised the dead is there to assist you if only you will step out of the darkness and turn control over to the One who made you and is calling you home. If only you can find the strength to overcome your past pains and future fears. If only you can stop the internal arguments that call you to remain in the darkness of self-direction. If only you can move from *believing* in His power to *knowing* His guiding hand. If only you can turn to Him in prayer and say, 'I will strive for self-control no more.'

"God's work, done by God's power in God's way, demonstrates God's presence to all the world, and transforms us into living beacons. It grants us the opportunity to speak to the world of the *experience* of Christ, the *freedom* of Christ, the *peace* that comes through relinquishing control to Him."

The pastor announced the final hymn, then raised his hands and invited anyone who wished to join him at the altar for prayer. Duncan stood, holding the hymnal in numb fingers and feeeling an overwhelming urge to move forward with the others. But he was fearful and ashamed to be singled out before all those strange eyes.

He turned to find Jeremy's luminous gaze on him. Jeremy asked quietly, "Think maybe you'd like to keep me company up front?"

Not trusting his voice, Duncan nodded and followed his friend out of the pew's safety and down the aisle, down to the very front where he knelt in the ever-growing circle. He shook his head at the elder's offer to have someone pray with him, wondering if the whole church could hear his pounding heart and see his shaking frame.

The only words he heard of the final prayer were the last ones the pastor spoke: "Help me, Father, to leave here today with you in control."

Duncan did not rise with the others. The flame in his heart was too strong to let him go just yet. There were other words waiting to be said, other needs which had not been met through someone else's prayer. Duncan kept his head bowed and his hands clasped and his body clenched in concentration, and felt the heart-flame rise up and give voice.

After he and Jeremy had left the church, Duncan found the

strength to say, "Thanks for helping me walk up front."

Jeremy gave him a careful look. "I didn't do it for you, son. Not just for you anyway."

"That pastor really touched me."

Jeremy shook his head. "No he didn't, son. Christ did."

Traffic that Sunday afternoon was immobile for the cars headed from downtown L.A. toward the coast. But for Jeremy, as he travelled inland to the Hollywood Hills, the lanes were almost empty.

Jeremy drove the Rolls past Inglewood on Mulholland, made sure the service station was closed, then pulled in and cut off the motor. He got out and adjusted his suit coat, started a leisurely walk up the road that ran parallel to Inglewood—just a tall gray-haired fellow, alien enough to the California way of life to be wearing a suit on Sunday, out for an afternoon stroll.

He climbed up the steeply sloping street, searching for a cranny where he could look down on Inglewood. The world was quiet and hot and empty. Nobody was around. A dog barked from miles away, a ghostly sound in the still air.

Jeremy found a brief concrete passageway between two houses. He debated for a moment, wiped his palms and walked the path. Looking down on the Inglewood house, he saw a flat roof and tree tops, and between silver-green needles glimpsed a sparkling hint of swimming-pool blue; the property was all covered from the top as well. He turned and retraced his steps to the service station.

Back at the car Jeremy stripped off his coat and got busy under the hood. It took him forever to find the radiator's release valve. Any place else he would have been laughing, enjoying the fancy motor with the foreign configuration; as it was he kept fighting a fear that somebody from the house would drive by and see him. He waited in the oppressive heat while almost all the water drained from the cooling system, then slammed the hood and slid behind the wheel with a sigh. He was committed.

The key to his scheme was to drive far enough to build up a visible head of steam without getting so far from the house that the car would conk out where it couldn't be seen. They had to see the Rolls, had to take him for an innocent, or it just wouldn't work.

After ten minutes of driving with the air conditioner turned on full, making tight little circles that ended three blocks to either side of Inglewood, white smoke began to spew from under the hood.

He steered back toward Inglewood, and just as the gate-house came into view, the car began to make some agreeably awful sounds. Wheezes, grinds, rumbles that shuddered the entire frame announced his arrival as he turned into the stub of a driveway. Jeremy wiped at his mouth, cleared the sweat from his forehead, switched off the motor, and sat through a couple of final gasps from the severely aggravated motor.

He almost lost it as the gatehouse door opened to reveal a hard, suspicious face set upon a short but equally hard frame. The man was dressed in California casual—slacks of some shiny expensive-looking material and a knit shirt stretched by a broad expanse of muscle.

Jeremy stepped from the car and waved at the steam still drifting in thick white clouds from the hood. "Afternoon, friend. How you doin'?"

"Move the car, Jack." The man crossed his arms, solid and threatening as a mountain.

"I'd sure like to, friend, but I do believe I could cook an egg on that thing. You mind lettin' me have a little water?"

"I said move the car, Jack. This ain't no service station."

"Ah, lighten up, Joey." An equally hard-looking man, taller than the first, walked from the gatehouse shadows and gave Jeremy an empty smile. "How's it going, man?"

"Doin' fine, thank you kindly," Jeremy said, and thought to himself, that smile don't mean nothing to nobody, friend. "Wish I could say the same for my car."

"Yeah, that's one hot little number. Nice, though. Always did like a Rolls. You're a long way from home, aincha?"

Worlds, Jeremy agreed. "North Carolina, yessir, right the way across the nation. Over here visitin' friends, thought maybe I'd take me a little Sunday afternoon drive, have a look at these parts."

"Yeah, it's nice up here in the hills, if you can afford it. You got some kinda ID I could see?"

"Sure thing," Jeremy said, treating it as the most normal request in the world. He reached for his wallet and handed over his driver's license.

"North Carolina, just like the man said. Only way plastic can get all cracked up like that is if it's been worn in a back pocket for a couple of years." The bigger man handed back the license and turned to his associate. "Go get the nice man a bucket of water."

"Laney said—"

"I know what Laney said, and I'm telling you to get a bucket of water. Now." He turned back to Jeremy, asked in a casual tone, "You thinking about moving out here?"

"Not permanent-like, but maybe for a while. I—" Jeremy felt his whole body clench as a face appeared from the gatehouse's murky depths. He did not need a second glance to know it was the man who had taken off with Jessica's friend, Arlene. For one panic-stricken moment he was afraid he might be recognized, then realized the blond-haired man with strange tiny ears had never laid eyes on him before.

Jeremy could not for the life of him remember what he was going to say. He turned his back to the pair, looked out over the valley to the mountains beyond, said, "I ain't never seen anything like this in my whole life."

"You hear that, Chico? They don't got hills like that back in North Carolina."

Chico. Yes. That's what Duncan said the man was called. Chico. Jeremy forced himself back to calmness, turned and gave them the best smile he could manage. "Maybe I could borrow a cloth too, friend, if you've got one that wouldn't be hurt by a little grease. Keep me from burnin' my hand on the motor."

"Well, shoot, we'all cain't have no Kentucky-fried fingers 'round here, can we?" The big man said, mimicking Jeremy's accent. To Chico he said, "Grab a towel outta the bathroom."

The shorter man appeared bearing a sloshing plastic bucket and a deep scowl. He set the bucket down hard enough for water to splash all over Jeremy's pant legs.

"Thank you kindly, friend."

"Aw hey, Joey, look what you did, got water all over the nice man's shoes." The big man was clearly enjoying himself.

"Don't matter, friend. It'll dry." Jeremy accepted the towel from Chico, felt his skin crawl at the man's touch. He turned and hit the hood release, was gratified to be greeted with another realistic cloud of smoke.

"Laney is gonna—"

"Laney is gonna do nothing at all," the constantly smirking taller one replied. "Whoever heard of the heat driving a Rolls?"

"Watch your mouth," the shorter man hissed.

"What, you think this back-woods boy's got idea-one what we're talking about?"

Jeremy used the towel to open the scalding radiator, tipped the bucket, and was immediately enveloped in a new cloud.

"Man, that is one hot car. What'd you do, buddy, race it up the hill?"

"Not so you'd notice, friend." Jeremy emptied the bucket, and handed back both the bucket and the towel, holding on to his casual pose with a death's grip. "Can't thank you enough for the kindness."

"Hey, like, what are neighbor's for, right?" The man gave him a final smirk, waved to the two other men, said, "Party's over, boys. Back inside."

Jeremy endured the tall man's unswerving gaze, climbed behind the wheel and started the engine. He gave a silent sigh as it caught and purred and gave no hint of the noises he had heard a few minutes ago. Jeremy put it into gear, backed from the drive, gave a final nod and wave. The tall man stood with arms crossed and made no answering move at all.

Jeremy forced himself to drive along Mulholland to the first connecting street leading back downhill, then pulled into an empty driveway and gave himself over to a good case of the shakes.

♦   ♦   ♦

Duncan was quiet and withdrawn while preparing for the evening. He had not talked of the night before, but there was a hunted look to his eyes and a troubled frown on his features that deepened as the night approached. Jeremy gave him room while they were dressing, held his own comments to a minimum, decided to keep his news to himself for the time being.

He had not been able to locate Detective Allende. No one on shift that slack Sunday afternoon knew where the detective could be found—at least, that's what they told Jeremy. They were clearly used to panic-stricken callers, and saw no need to interrupt standard Sunday procedure for a man they didn't know.

Once in the lobby, Duncan seemed reluctant to be on his way. Jeremy struggled to put his own worries behind him, pointed toward the ceiling, asked, "That the stuff they call muzak?"

Duncan lifted his head in surprise. "I didn't even hear it. Guess I'm just so used to it I can tune it out. Yeah, that's muzak all right. Also known as elevator music. Or cream of strings. Boneless Blues. Graveyard of the musicians. Lawrence wept."

"Back home, the only time I used to hear that stuff was when I'd come into the big city to get my teeth fixed. I'd be sittin' in the front room, listenin' to a cheery little tune, and in the background there was a kid just screamin' his head off. And on top of it was that whinin' noise, like the doc was in there drillin' for the center of the earth."

As they walked out onto the veranda, Jeremy went on, "You know what I love most about doctors? It don't matter how much you're hurtin', they still wanna grab the painful part and give it a good poke. That's one. The second is they keep their stethoscopes in ice buckets."

Duncan sighed his way down to a seat and gave his friend a small smile. "It's been hard for me this time," he said. "Harder than it ever has before. And it seems like the prayers have only made it worse. Like I've been stripped of my defenses, and now everything hits me a lot deeper than it used to."

Jeremy was silent long enough to be sure Duncan was through, then asked, "Do you wish you hadn't started prayin'?"

"No." His voice sounded caught somewhere inside."No, I guess not. I've been thinking about that, and I guess it's part of the package. If I'm going to feel the good, maybe I've got to start feeling the bad too."

Jeremy said nothing, just nodded silently.

"I've finally had the strength to face some things in my life that I've spent years running away from," Duncan said.

"Sometimes faith gives you a mirror," Jeremy agreed. "The Savior's love is the clearest surface you'll ever find for inspectin' yourself, measurin' out what's real."

Duncan nodded. "I feel like I've sort of coasted through the eighties. You know how little towns used to have these main drags, all the businesses built up and down the strip, twenty-five-mile-per-hour signs so the people could walk around safe, stop when they liked and greet friends."

"Son, you're talkin' about my kinda town."

"Mine, too. There were a lot of those around my grandfather's farm when I was a kid. Then along came this new development, and they built these big new thoroughfares, and all the businesses along the old main road kinda shriveled up.

They'd been bypassed. Maybe they didn't die, but they got all dusty and the paint chipped off and the lights went out and weren't ever replaced, and before too long they were all kinda seedy and old-fashioned. A hundred yards away you could see the traffic speeding by, but the world had taken another direction and didn't touch the old places anymore."

Duncan watched a couple of derelicts stumble by, arguing over a bottle, totally oblivious to the warm night and fresh sea breeze and everything else but the hunger that drove them forward. He went on, "That's the way it feels with my life. I missed opportunities, I made mistakes, I didn't grow up. There were things I needed to change, but I just ignored them. I pretended they didn't exist, pretended there wasn't any reason to change. On the outside I stayed in the same clothes I wore in college, put a new motor in my old car and kept driving it until it couldn't pass inspection any more. I still listened to the Grateful Dead and watched *Leave It to Beaver* reruns.

"Now I feel like I chose to sleep through ten years of my life in this little bypass I made for myself. I understand why, too. Change never had any appeal for me. Change into what? Another corporate clone? What for? So I could buy more things I already knew weren't going to make me happy?"

Duncan turned to Jeremy. "Now I feel like there's something to change toward. When I pray, when I read the Bible, I feel this comfort and this peace, but I also feel this *challenge*. It hurts, though. Man, sometimes it hurts so much to think of all the time I've wasted, all the people I've hurt, all the things I've left undone."

"One of the biggest steps to learning the lesson of forgiveness is learnin' to forgive yourself," Jeremy said. "The prophet Joel promised us that the Lord will replace the years the locusts have eaten. I can't think of a better way to describe time wasted livin' without the Savior. It's not lost, son. Not once you've faced up to your sins, asked His forgiveness, and then accepted it."

Duncan stared at the floor by his feet. "I had a *lot* of trouble ever accepting that my daughter was growing up. I kept wanting to see her as this little kid, this little baby girl, when she was already in her teens and sprouting a figure and going out with guys. The truth is, I couldn't see her as a growing-up teenager because I still saw *myself* as a kid. Accepting the responsibility of a maturing teenager meant accepting that I was growing up too, growing *old,* and I just wasn't ready to face that. So the problems with my wife and my daughter just kept getting bigger and bigger, and finally I ran them both off."

Jeremy sighed for the hurt in his friend's voice. "I don't know, son. I can't crawl inside your skin and say why it's taken this long, why your loved ones had to suffer with you. Maybe the only reason you'll ever know on this earth is that back then you weren't ready to listen, and now you are. Maybe there's more, but that's something for the Lord to show you directly, in His own time, in His own way. As far as I'm concerned, what's most important is that the lesson's learned *now*."

Duncan told him about walking the streets, going into the tunnel, finding the boy and girl. He finished with, "So there I was, kneeling over these two kids that were as far gone as last year, praying from the heart for the very first time in my life. Then Brent came racing back, and just like it was the most natural thing in the world, he dropped down beside me and joined right in. He didn't even ask what I was doing, just popped down in the mud and puts his hands on the kids and goes at it until the ambulance arrives.

"There wasn't room in the ambulance for both of us, so I saw them off and came back home, and you know what? Just as I was getting into my car I had this feeling—no, it was more than that—this *certainty* that the kids were going to be all right. Not necessarily going home or anything like that. Just all right. Safe and healthy. And there was this feeling of being *surrounded* by love, and peace, like I was going to be all right, too.

"And then right there on Hollywood Boulevard at five in the morning, I was suddenly bawling my eyes out."

Duncan turned his eyes to the night beyond the hotel lights. "I realized that part of what made me cry was facing a hope I had always pushed away before, that maybe the Lord would guide me to find my lost little girl. Only she wouldn't be so little anymore—twenty-one, almost twenty-two. And it hurt so bad to hope. So *bad*. All those cases, all that searching, all this time looking for other people's kids, when deep down inside I was really just looking for Steffy. And at the same time I cried because I was finally accepting that she was gone."

Duncan held down tight on his emotions, forcing them back under control. He took a ragged breath and went on, "I don't understand it. I don't understand how both of them could feel so *right*. I mean, not even God could give Steffy back to me and finally force me to accept that she's lost and gone forever."

Jeremy looked at him with a gaze that came from somewhere far beyond the gentle sea breeze and the warm night and the soft sounds of traffic and passers-by. "I don't know, son," he finally said. "It's hard to know what the Lord intends sometimes. I *do* know that He will make all things clear if you ask Him and wait upon His reply.

"The only way these things I have to say are of any importance, son, is if they strike an answering chord in your own heart. Advice is only good if it's something that you've already discovered in prayer, seems to me, but just haven't gotten around to puttin' into words yet.

"Part of acceptin' the Lord Jesus' good grace is bein' broken. Only your own heart and mind can tell if that's what you were goin' through out there in the car, but it sure does sound like that to me.

"As to that paradox of yours, I can't rightly say. Maybe, though—and it's just a thought, mind you—maybe what the Lord intends is for you to have another blessed child to take your little daughter's place. Maybe there's another little girl out there who's never known a daddy who cares, never had a momma who'll rock her when she's hurtin'. Maybe there's a little girl who needs to know the touch of a man who's been touched by Christ.

"Seems to me that might be your answer, son, but it's up to the good Lord to tell you for sure. You just keep prayin'. The Lord'll show you what He has in mind."

◆　　◆　　◆

The restaurant where Jeremy took Bella was on Olivera Street, a center of Los Angeles' Hispanic life. The pedestrian street lined with souvenir shops and filled with vivacious dark-haired women in starchy blouses with ruffles and long colorful skirts. They talked virtually nonstop in Spanish, smiling a lot and showing gold teeth. Their men looked worn down from work, slow and short and beefy. They talked mostly to other men in voices that were rarely audible to anyone but the listener, murmurs that seemed to match the fatigue that lined their dark round faces. They wore short-sleeved cotton shirts that hung loose over dark pants, and sandals with socks. Their only ornaments were heavy gold wristwatches.

Jeremy and Bella chose an outside table at the only Mexican restaurant that did not sport an off-key mariachi band. The air retained a taste of dry daytime warmth, and they sat in companionable ease and watched the colorful parade pass by.

"I want to hear more about this mystery woman," Jeremy said once they had placed their orders.

"There's no mystery."

"Yes there is. You're a fascinating person, and there's an awful lot I don't know about you. Makes for a lot of mysteries."

"Like how come a nice girl like me hasn't ever settled down?"

Jeremy settled back in his chair. "Perfect."

"Well, actually I came close to getting married once. No, that's not exactly right. I *thought* I came close to getting married." She hesitated. "Are you sure you want to hear this?"

"I'm sure," he said, giving her the seriousness she needed. "It's an important part of what's made you who you are, Bella, I can feel it in my heart."

"It's not a pretty story, I'm afraid."

"No, I didn't think it would be. That's the sad part of our poor world. We're bruised by the bad times, and don't learn the lesson of how to heal."

Bella let her gaze rest comfortably on his. "I was pretty new in Washington, and had a week-long seminar on a most fascinating topic—Cost Accounting Under Defense Acquisition Regulations. Doesn't that just take your breath away?"

Jeremy shook his head. "I'd need a month just to figure out what it means."

"It was five days long, given down in the Navy Yard Annex. Do you know that place?"

"Can't say as I do."

"It's in the bowels of southeast Washington. Anyway, I showed up for class and in walks the personification of a dashing young officer. You know what they say about a woman being a sucker for a man in uniform? Well, it's true.

"He was very crisp, very polished, gold stripes here and there, little tags of different colors on his lapel. Clifford Jameson was his name. Jameson like the whiskey, he introduced himself. I suppose what he had to talk about was quite dull, but I found it fascinating. He seemed to know everything about contract administration and I was still trying to figure out which was the buff copy and which the canary yellow.

"At lunch breaks he would sit at my table, along with four or five other co-workers, and we would talk the usual Washington talk—bureaucracy and politics and weather. Anyway, on the last day, as I was taking my tray back toward the kitchen, he followed me and said that he wished he could flunk me so that I would have to come back for another course."

Their food arrived, and as the waiter started to say something Jeremy warned him off with a frown. Bella had not even seen him. She was staring off into space, caught up in the act of remembering and confessing to someone whom she truly could trust—trust not to judge, not to condemn, not to feel threatened, not to back away. The words came in the steady stream of someone glad to finally have the chance to share this with one who would feel for her and with her.

"Then he said, I've got to pick up some documents at the Pension Building next week, that's right across the street from your office. I know a great place down G Street in Chinatown, so why don't we grab a bite to eat?"

Bella was quiet for a moment, locked in memories. Than she went on. "So that's how it started. He was on special assignment to the Pentagon, he told me, and had to travel a lot. He kept a furnished apartment in Arlington, but he'd be gone for weeks at a time. And of course I couldn't call him and he couldn't call me—strategic reasons, he said, he knew I'd understand. Of course I said I did, because Washington is the kind of city where you don't ever let anyone know when you don't understand. So we would see each other when he was back in town, and we became intimate, as they used to say in those days.

"About eight months passed, and we met discretely here and there. Discretion is required, strategic reasons, he'd say, and I told him I understood. He was gone for Christmas, came back in early February, and was leaving again three days later. I really missed him when he was gone. I missed not being able to communicate with him. And I was very much in love.

"So before he left again I wrote a long letter, full of how I felt about him, the first time in my life that I had opened myself up like that. I told him all about my hopes for the future and for us.

"I made dinner for him that night at his place. I was too embarrassed to give him the letter, but I wanted him to take it with him. So I planned to put it in the drawer with the socks and the t-shirts I knew he'd be packing. And when I opened the drawer I saw a gold ring.

"My heart really fluttered. It was two days before Valentine's Day, the perfect time for him to propose. He wanted to surprise me, I thought.

"Then I picked up the ring, and suddenly I felt as if all the veins in my body had been tied into one big knot at the bottom of my stomach. That was *his* ring. That was his wedding band.

"It turned out that home was really a military base somewhere outside of Las Vegas, and that Washington was the special assignment. He had a wife and two kids halfway across the country, waiting for him every time he left. And I could never talk to him for strategic reasons. Of course his wife could never call Washington either. For strategic reasons."

They lingered over coffee as long as they could. Their silence lasted through the check's arrival, remained untouched by the loud banter at nearby tables, kept them leaning close together long after Jeremy's change had been returned and the waiter's good-night accepted.

Bella finally straightened and said, "I guess I'd better be getting back to the hotel. My wake-up call is going to be coming almost as soon as I hit the bed."

But Jeremy did not move. "Sure has been nice to have you over here, Bella. More than nice, but I don't know the words to tell you exactly what I mean."

She settled back in her chair. "I didn't come over here for the conference," she confessed.

"I kinda figured that. It means more than I can say, havin' you travel all this distance to let me have this time with you. Especially now."

"It's been hard on you, hasn't it, searching for these girls."

"Hardest thing I've ever done, and that's a fact."

Jeremy let one of his fingers bashfully trace a line across the back of her wrist. "Not just the search, you understand, but being put so close up to all that pain. It hardly seems like a day's passed when I haven't learned something new about our children's pain."

"I've been a little afraid of asking you about your work here," she admitted.

"I don't mind tellin' you about it—matter of fact, I want to. Just give me a while to let the skin grow back where my hide's been worn raw."

"That's a part of why I need to be getting back," Bella said. "I mean, one of the reasons why this Solemn Assembly thing got started was Atterly's desire to do away with this evil of pornography once and for all."

She recapped the work Atterly had been doing since Jeremy's departure, ending with, "It's not going to be possible to tell how much an effect the gathering will have on the legislative process, if any. That is, as far as the vote goes. It's already had an effect in other important areas. A lot of churches have become involved in setting up conferences and seminars and meetings to deal with problems related to the family, all of them taking place during the Assembly."

She fingered her empty coffee cup, let her worries show through. "It's also brought out the heavy hitters, and that worries me. Atterly's staff says it was inevitable, and so we shouldn't give it any thought. But they've been really vicious. Especially the ALUM. Have you ever heard of them?"

Jeremy nodded. "Matter of fact, one of the girls we're looking for is the daughter of some big-wig in that organization."

Bella's jaw dropped. "One of these runaways? One of the girls you're over here tracking down?"

"Duncan told me about his meeting with her parents. Sounded awful poor in the spirit, awful poor. You ought to see a picture of their little girl, Bella. Little angel of a darlin' with eyes that just make you want to weep."

She scrambled through her purse for a pen and a piece of paper. "This could be something really important, Jeremy. You don't happen to recall her last name, do you?"

"Biggs," he replied immediately. "Jessica Biggs."

She stopped her search. "The daughter of Harvey Biggs, ALUM's Director of Public Policy?"

"That I wouldn't know."

"Does he know what his girl's up to?"

"Not as far as I know. Matter of fact, Duncan said he'd tried a dozen or so times to get through to the man before takin' off with me. Never got anybody to return his calls. He finally just dropped him a note, sayin' he was headed for California, but I don't recall him mentionin' the picture stuff. Not a thing you'd want to tell a parent unless you were absolutely sure."

"But you're sure now."

He didn't have to hesitate. "Sure as can be. 'Specially after today."

She was already up on her feet. "C'mon, you've got to drive me back to the hotel. This can't wait until tomorrow. Maybe somebody's still in the senator's office."

He snagged her arm with an iron grip. "Bella, I don't want to end our evening with talk about the girl." His voice dropped and his face reddened. "I'd really like to come calling when I get back, Bella."

Bella dropped her purse, grabbed his face with two impatient hands, gave him a kiss loud enough to draw glances and smirks from surrounding tables. She eased her head back far enough to smile down on his lantern-lit features. "You dear sweet man. Nothing would make me happier. Now come on and take me back. This is big news, Jeremy. Big news."

◆　◆　◆

The filming was different from anything Jessica had ever had to do before. When she endured those bad things before, part of her kept saying, it can't get any worse than this. Whenever she thought she couldn't take it, she did as Arlene said and held herself inside, like she was going down for a long deep dive and if only she could hold her breath a little longer it would all be over and she could go back to just being Pierre's girl.

But now it was different. It felt as though everything had been leading up to this. Pierre wasn't there anymore. And the stuff they had her doing just went on and on.

Finally they stopped for the evening, and after a cold, plastic-tasting dinner they locked her and Arlene in a stuffy little room with four mattresses on the floor. "Don't get any ideas," the man said, " 'cause there'll be somebody on guard out here all night."

A little brown-haired girl lay down on the mattress in the corner, pulled the blanket up over her face, and rolled up in a ball like a little baby. The other kid in there with them was probably about sixteen, but he looked a lot younger because he was so small. The three of them gathered together away from the silent girl. They huddled and whispered and tried to put a little human warmth in this totally frightening scene.

The guy didn't need much encouragement to tell his story, such as it was. His folks had divorced when he was a little kid, and his mother had married this man who beat on him a lot. He'd finally gotten tired of having other kids stare at his bruises when he undressed for gym, tired of having the teachers give him pitying looks and try to get him to talk over something they couldn't do anything about, tired of having to wear long-sleeved shirts buttoned up to the collar, tired of everything about his home. So he ran away. He didn't have any money or anywhere to go, and got picked up by a trucker who liked little boys and offered to trade him a meal and a place to sleep for his body.

The kid spent three months working his way across the States, living in these really rough trucker hotels, not much more than concrete boxes with a mattress and maybe a black-and-white TV and a bar up front. There were lots of drugs—lots of speed for the thirty-six-hour runs and downers for the rest stops at the end. Lots of crazies with wild red-rimmed eyes who'd do just about anything after amping on a long haul for a couple of days. The kid learned to avoid the ones who laughed insanely and shouted words that didn't connect, knowing that they promised only pain.

He also avoided the really quiet ones, the calm ones with concerned eyes and quiet voices and Bibles; they tried to talk with him, just talk, just get him to tell what he was doing and where he was going. But sooner or later these nice ones would turn on the blinking red light in the kid's brain by asking where his folks were and didn't he want them to give a call and didn't he think they'd be worried sick. He knew he had to flee them, no matter how much he liked the kindness in their eyes. Sometimes he'd carry a memory of them for a day or so, wishing he could somehow make everything over so that one of those guys could have been his dad.

When he finally made it to Los Angeles, he was standing out in front of the central bus station wondering where he could get something to eat when these two guys walked over. They had real smooth voices and real cold eyes, and they asked him if he was hungry and if he needed a place to crash. He knew what they wanted but he went anyway, he was so hungry. It was pretty bad, but not as bad as some of the nights in the trucker's hotels. Nothing would ever be as bad as that.

After the kid finally gave in to nervous exhaustion, Arlene kept sitting as she had all that night, her legs clenched up tight to her chest and her chin resting on her knees. They sat there a long time, Jessica wondering about Pierre and trying not to think about what they might have to do the next day, when suddenly her best friend, the one who never was bothered by anything, was crying and unfolding and crawling over so that she could be held by Jessica.

Jessica was too startled by the breaking down of Arlene's rock-solid barriers to react for a moment. Then she rocked her and held her close and they slid under the covers together and lay there drawing comfort from each other. Arlene started whispering to her, telling about her father.

"I really do remember him," she whispered, her voice very soft and very shaky. "I don't remember what he looks like or anything, I was only five when he left us. But I remember waking up a couple of times and hearing him shouting at Mom and her sobbing and screaming back, and I would burrow down under the covers and pretend that it was all just a dream. He was really good to me when he wasn't drinking. Really. I'm not making that up.

"I didn't like to think about what he was like when he started on the bottle. I could see the way my mother looked at us when he wasn't home on time, and how she would put us to bed all together in the far room, and bar the end of the hallway with this big dresser. I can still remember the way it scraped across the floor in little jerky motions that made the whole room shudder, like it was as scared as Mom was.

"Once I had to get up and go to the bathroom in the middle of the night, and it was on a night when my father had been drinking and there had been a fight, and I had to squeeze my way around the dresser, and I saw my mother laid out on the floor in front of the dresser, like she was still guarding the room where we slept, only she wasn't moving, she was just lying there real still, and I got scared that maybe all the bad thoughts wouldn't just stay in my nightmares, and maybe it would become real, so I went back and ended up wetting the bed. Strange how I can remember that so clearly, and all this time I've been trying to forget it."

Arlene was crying very hard by then, and Jessica didn't know what to do but hold her. All Jessica could see of her were the tears on Arlene's face. They made shimmering little lines in the dim sliver of light that creeped in under the door.

"I remember him," Arlene whispered. "I remember him but I never wanted to let him out of my nightmares. When he left I thought it was all going to be okay, and I would be able to keep it all boxed up like that, but I needed something to take its place, and I knew it couldn't be my step-dad. I remember the first time he came home with my mother, he looked at me and my brother like we didn't belong, like we weren't supposed to be there in that house, and I hated him. I know he's tried to be good to us, but I never could forget that first look he gave me, and how it always felt like he wished we weren't around. So when I couldn't use him I made up another father, somebody that my mother should have married in the first place. And I figured if I could say it loud enough and long enough then all this other stuff would stay in the box and just go away."

The next morning Arlene was off in another world. Not drugs this time, there weren't any drugs around as far as she could see—at least none for them. No, Arlene was just gone. Her body was there, but the fire was out. Jessica sidled up to her in the little dressing area and asked, hey, are you all right? Arlene didn't even show she had heard, just undressed a little faster and took the dead look and the rest of her out back under the lights.

The movie was about them being in a school for problem kids, the director said, going on and on in this voice that was twice as big as he was, all of them just standing there wishing they could be somewhere else. They hid their nervousness as best they could with eyes fastened on the wall or the window or the floor at their feet. But there was nothing they could do about the eyes that fed on them, nor about the thoughts behind those eyes.

Suddenly the thought was with her once more, the same she had on the street that last night with Pierre. It came to her with a power that sharpened her perception of everything around her, forced her to look at it all in focus, and see it all for what it was, one lie built on another and another and another right up straight to the roof. *I've got to get out of here,* she thought, and wondered for a moment how it could happen.

Then there wasn't room for thought anymore. Not if she wanted to stay sane. She had to curl her mind up inside that little safe space, way back inside where it didn't really see what was happening to her outside, and hold it there very tight, not letting it out, holding it there longer than she ever had before. Because the bad stuff just kept going on all day long.

CHAPTER
16

At eight-thirty Monday morning Silverwood picked up the phone and placed a call to the Speaker of the House. He had spent the better part of the weekend mapping out his strategy and marveling at the new-found clarity of vision granted him by prayer. For this to work, he had realized early on, it would all have to happen quickly, and with as little noise as possible.

Surprises in the Washington political arena were very rare. The few that did filter up unexpectedly usually came by someone doing something totally out of character. Something unpredictable. Such people and such circumstances were the source of nightmares for those who played the chess game of political intrigue.

Speaker of the House James Mullins was a Democrat from Colorado. Although they were from different parties, he and Silverwood had fought several noteworthy battles together from the same ideological ground. Mullins was one of the few truly conservative Democrats not from the Deep South, and continued to be elected despite yearly struggles from within his more liberal-leaning local party to oust him.

The Speaker didn't much like Silverwood. He had risen too far too fast, and there was the taint of switching allegiances on a couple of key issues when logic and background would have insisted that he go another way. Still, they met quite often; Mullins saw him as an informal pipeline into the thinking of young Republican members of the House. And as a member of the Ways and Means Committee, Silverwood was too powerful to be ignored.

When Mullins' secretary came on the line, Silverwood introduced himself and asked, "How does your boss's schedule look this morning?"

"About the same as always, sir. He's on his way to Hart in about fifteen minutes. You might be able to catch him when he leaves his chambers here at the Capitol."

Silverwood thought a moment. The Hart Senate Office Building was a ten-minute walk from the Capitol. "It's a nice day. Tell him I'll walk over with him."

On mornings like this, Washington looked like a picture postcard. The sky was an artificial blue, and the white marble buildings looked like cut-outs pasted onto the horizon. It wasn't often that the muggy city enjoyed an Indian summer day, but when one arrived, the only place to be was outdoors.

"Let's take the high ground," said Mullins, waving his arm toward the Independence Avenue exit. The high ground meant walking outside; the low ground meant winding their way through miles of tunnels that connected the Capitol with all of the Congressional office buildings.

"I gave a speech at the National Press Club Satuday on transportation funding," Silverwood remarked, keeping his voice casual. "I caught wind of something I thought you should know about. It seems that *Sixty Minutes* is planning an hour-long special on the plight of juvenile runaways and their growing connection with the pornography industry. It's partly a follow-up to a piece they did on child pornography in the late seventies, and partly in response to what they see as a rising problem within society. They plan to use footage from this week's vote on the Per Se Bill to show how irresponsible Congress is in failing to enact protective legislation."

Mullins gave his chin a tug. "Seems to me we should give them as little footage as possible."

"Just what I was thinking, Jimmy," agreed Silverwood. "Something like that could make all of us look bad."

"Right," Mullins nodded thoughtfully. "So what do you propose?"

"I think it's time for a little railroading. Get that anti-porn bill on the floor and off the floor as quickly as possible. Put a rule out against any further amendments. Limit the floor debate."

"Sounds good," said Mullins. "I can work that out. Of course, Humboldt is going to have to make a few remarks. After all, it's his bill."

The principal sponsor of the House bill, Congressman Humboldt, was a staunchly conservative Bible-belt Democrat. But being from Mullins' own party, the Speaker would have little problem limiting the man's time at the podium.

"Then we'd need a rebuttal," Mullins went on, and elbowed Silverwood in the ribs. "Now there's a job for you, my boy."

Silverwood examined the horizon. "I would have thought you'd want a Democrat imploring the cause of Constitutional freedom."

"Right," Mullins said. "But with those cameras rolling, I'd just as soon it be a Republican."

"Well, you should be aware, Jimmy, that I've been giving this issue a lot of thought—"

"I know exactly where you stand on this issue," Mullins cut him off. "And I know exactly how much you want to be seen as a vocal opponent on camera, which is not at all. But just let me remind you that if anyone owes anybody in this game, I've got a few chips to collect from you, my boy. And I'm cashing them in right here, right now. All of them, if need be."

Silverwood started to say something further, but Mullins cut him off with, "Wait just a minute. There's another good reason for you to be the one. If I start talking to some of our colleagues and the press gets wind of this, *Sixty Minutes* might do a special on how we try to manipulate congressional matters to avoid looking bad in front of prime-time America. That's exactly the sort of publicity we're trying to avoid here, aren't we?"

"I guess you're right," Silverwood agreed, masking his own feelings.

"Come on, John," Mullins said. "You're a master at this. You've got the information. You keep it close to your chest, and you use it. Think of the political mileage it'll give you on both sides of the fence when this is over. A Republican who stands up for the Constitution. We're talking national coverage, my friend."

"This is true," Silverwood said.

"*Sixty Minutes* is going to be looking for some liberal cloud-hanger who goes into a tirade about lofty Constitution principles, right? Then they'll cut over to some ten-year-old junkie on the streets of L.A. selling herself for the next fix. I need a level-headed ally, John. Somebody I can trust to stand up and soft peddle this issue, leave *Sixty Minutes* with nothing but a yawn and maybe a few old transcripts to work off of."

Mullins stopped and faced Silverwood head-on. "I'm not taking no for an answer on this one, John. Look at it this way. I can't say I'll owe you one, but maybe you'll owe me one less."

◆ ◆ ◆

The chairs lining the entrance to the Beverly Hills Police Juvenile Division were extremely uncomfortable. They were the plastic and metal kind made for ten-year-olds; anybody weighing over eighty pounds threatened to buckle the backs if he put his weight down. Jeremy sat with elbows on knees for half an hour that Monday morning, waiting for Detective Allende. His bend-over position saved him from facing the hard-eyed stares thrown by every cop coming through the door. He only wished he carried a hat so he could spin the brim through his hands, give himself something to do.

"Lessee, you're Hughes, that right?" Allende was neither glad nor sorry to see him. The eyes watched with a focused intensity that did not leave room for snap feelings.

"Yessir, Officer." Jeremy heaved himself to his feet. "I tried to find you yesterday, but nobody seemed to know where you'd gotten to."

"Crime doesn't take the weekend off," Allende replied. "But policemen do. Sometimes, anyway. What you need?"

"Sorry to bother you, but I decided maybe you'd rather see me too often than hear later that I had something you could use."

"You playing private detective, Hughes?" The eyes ground on him.

"Nossir, just lookin' for a coupla little lost girls."

"You all that sure they want to be found?"

"That's the first question I aim on askin' them, Officer."

Allende gave a fraction of a nod, crossed his arms, said, "Okay, what you got?"

"There's a house up there on Inglewood with a big white wall around it."

"Yeah, number fourteen; we're checking it out. So? Lotta houses got walls out here, Hughes."

"Yessir, that's true. Only this one's got busloads of kids comin' in and out."

A new light surfaced in Allende's dark eyes. "Yeah? Who told you that, the kid at the service station?"

"Yessir."

"How'd you get him to talk to you?"

"Bribed him," Jeremy said. "Hardest five dollars I've ever spent in my whole life."

"You got him to talk to you for five bucks? Don't let the lieutenant hear you say that, Hughes. Five bucks won't even park your car out here, much less get you information. What else did he say?"

"They've got some name they go by, sounds almost religious."

"Children of Venus, yeah, that's the name the rental contract's signed under. You'd think something like that'd ring a few warning bells, right?" The detective shook his head. "The agent said she figured it was some new group she'd missed, on account of her never turning on the TV anymore. Allende looked at him with new respect. "Anything else?"

"Yessir. The fellow told me there were always some real heavy types in the van when it came out. And the kids were always quiet. Too quiet. Never even looked around."

"That's new," Allende said. "You mind if we get a deposition down on tape, Hughes? Sounds like maybe we oughtta go for a search warrant."

"Nossir, I don't mind. But there's a little something more you maybe oughtta know about." Jeremy told him about his afternoon excursion, about the overheated car, about the two men, and about Chico.

Allende was quiet for a moment after Jeremy finished. "A Rolls, no less. Musta cost you a fortune."

"Yessir, probably did. I don't aim on openin' that bill for a long, long time."

"That was a good idea, though." Allende unbent enough to give a grudging smile. "Stay right there a minute, will you? I want the lieutenant to hear this one for himself."

So Jeremy repeated the story from beginning to end for the lieutenant and a couple of others who drifted over, then did the whole thing a third time for the stenographer and what by that time seemed like the entire staff room. Nobody said a lot, but there was now a clear feeling of camaraderie in the room. Of approval. Jeremy looked at the surrounding faces, saw hardness coupled with a sense of purpose, a hard-earned confidence in what they did with their lives. Fatigue, too. Every face in the room looked tired.

"That place up there didn't leave me with a good feelin'," Jeremy concluded. "Not just the house. I mean the whole neighborhood."

There was universal assent. One policeman said, "Tell me what kinda guy's got the bread to buy a piece of land for a million bucks, put a house on it that costs maybe twice that, then never comes home."

"Hollywood Hills is for garbage with money," another voice said.

"Sleazeballs with status. You wouldn't believe some of the things we find around there."

"No, I probably wouldn't," Jeremy agreed, standing and shaking hands all around.

"That guy Chico is totally 51/50," Allende said, leading Jeremy back to the elevators. "I don't need to meet him to know. I've been around too many of that type for too long. Way too long."

Jeremy gave him a sidelong glance. "Are those numbers some kind of police talk?"

"Yeah. Means he's got the IQ of a Snickers bar. Dances on the third-floor stairs in a two-story house."

"I guess you mean crazy."

"Nah, that word doesn't fly in L.A. Crazy gets you a movie contract in this town. Crazy drives a Porsche and gets good tables in all the best restaurants. Crazy buys t-shirts on Rodeo Drive for ninety bucks a pop. What we're talking about here is a guy who's dived into the deep end of an empty pool one time too many. A guy whose brains couldn't be found with an electron microscope. You got the picture?"

"Sounds pretty clear to me, Officer," Jeremy replied.

"This town's full of crazies. You take the crazies out of L.A. and the tumbleweeds'd drift down empty streets at high noon. What we got here is a real certifiable fruitcake."

Allende faced Jeremy as they waited for the elevator to arrive. "This helps us a lot, Hughes. One thing, though. We're probably gonna be going in the next day or so. Maybe sooner. I don't want to see your face around there when we do, you got that?"

"Yessir, Officer. I wouldn't think of gettin' in the way."

"We find your little girls, you'll be hearing from us. But you leave the bust to the pros."

The elevator doors opened; Jeremy stepped inside, turned back and said, "I just want you to know that you'll be goin' in with my prayers, Officer."

"Far as I know they haven't made that against the law yet." He shook Jeremy's hand once more. "You'll be hearing from me."

◆　◆　◆

Late Monday afternoon, Senator Richard Atterly arrived at the Providence airport to be met by his Administrative Assistant, Kevin Stewart. The AA was the highest position of an elected official's regional office. Constituents seeking access to the official usually only got as far as the AA, whose primary responsibility was that of palace guard. He acted as a sort of shadow senator, having overall responsibility for managing both office and staff, and scheduling all of the senator's appointments during his frequent return visits. Yet to the public at large, the AA remained largely invisible. He did the work so that the official might gain the credit. If he was a trusted ally, the AA also played a major role in developing the official's legislative strategy. The best AA's were the ones who thought like their bosses, but who strove to remain two steps ahead.

Kevin Stewart possessed his Scottish ancestors' coloring. Thick red hair was matched by an abundance of freckles. He was of medium height and stocky build, and used Benjamin Franklin glasses because his wife told him that they helped balance out his somewhat uneven features. He wore a yellow Oxford shirt with a button-down collar, a knit tie, khaki pants, navy-blue single-breasted sports coat, and brown loafers. He looked every inch the overaged, overly serious, ambitiously active New England preppie.

Once they were inside the car, Kevin began his favorite mode of fidgeting, which was to twirl his heavy Dartmouth class ring in a never-ending spiral. "All they'd give you was five minutes."

"Five minutes on the six o'clock news is better than an hour any other time," Atterly replied. "What is it they call that segment, *Meet the Press?*"

"*Face the Issues,*" Kevin replied, starting the car. "Your standard intellectual exposé format. To hold the audience they stick it between sports and weather.

"Five minutes is enough," Atterly repeated. "It's the perfect time frame to lay out my position and get it over with."

"You know how these are set up. The Program Director tries to schedule two strong personalities as diametrically opposed on an issue as possible," Kevin explained. "Controversy means solid commercial sponsorship."

"He's certainly got it here. Do you know who will be representing the ALUM?"

"I've heard it's our old friend Harvey Biggs."

"Perfect." Atterly refused to let his habitual case of television nerves show. "I've got to catch the next flight back after the interview, so if there's anything else we need to discuss, let's do it now."

"It doesn't look good," Kevin said, reaching to the backseat. He handed Atterly a manila folder filled with clippings and editorials from papers around the state. "I brought these— thought you should see them before you go on the air."

Atterly flipped through the pages, read such headlines as: "The Northern Flank Of The Bible Belt," "The Holy Roller From Rhode Island," "The Separation Between Church And State: A Reminder To Our Senator," "Atterly Finally Falls Off The Right Wing."

He continued reading. "No one is coming out with anything positive?"

"The religious press, sure. They're holding you up as the beacon they've been praying for. But who reads that stuff anyway?"

The tone of all the clippings was similar; highly structured Constitutional arguments were placed in counterpoint to disdainful references about a man whose faith had gone overboard. The Op-Ed pieces showed outright disgust over Atterly's biblical fervor. There was no mention of the human side to the pornography issue, no discussion of the victimization or the information that he had disseminated on the personal cost involved, few direct quotations from him at all. The ALUM, however, was quoted throughout. Their policy stand was mirrored by the press.

"I can't say as I've ever seen anything like it, Senator," Kevin said. "They're really on the warpath this time, and it's not even an election year. There's something bigger behind all this. There just has to be."

"Yes, there is," Atterly replied. He closed the manila folder and turned his face toward the side window.

"The letters have started coming in, and it looks a little better there. The mail is running two to one in your favor, quite a difference from the press, which as far as I can see is a hundred to nothing against. We've done all we can for damage control, but it looks like a line has been drawn, and people are really either black or white on this issue. The ones that are for you are offering a stronger support than I've ever seen, calling up or writing and promising to back you with everything they've got. The opposition, though, has the press pretty much sewn up, and they're out to nail you."

The television station was a fairly standard regional affair, a two-story modern building with the call letters emblazoned above the entrance. The interior was decorated in the station's colors of pale gray and royal blue. Carpeting was everywhere, crawling up the walls and cut into decorative motifs on the hall ceilings, giving the place a secure yet muffled feeling.

The studio room was cavernous, painted in black and filled with a jungle of cameras, lights, mikes, booms, cables, and scaffolding. In the center was a platform that looked like a slice from someone's living room—three Queen Anne chairs surrounded a low coffee table with a flower arrangement spilling over its center. Behind the chairs rose a fake paneled wall set with a mock fireplace. Above the mantel hung a very bad reproduction of a farming scene by Van Gogh.

Through the glass window in the side wall a young man with a headset and thick spectacles counted off with his fingers, then pointed a rigid forefinger at the announcer separating Richard Atterly from Harvey Biggs.

"Good evening, and welcome to *Face the Issues.*" The announcer's practiced resonance sounded irritatingly artificial close up. "Tonight we address the controversial problem of pornography. Should it be outlawed? Or is it protected by the Bill of Rights of the U.S. Constitution?"

He turned toward Atterly, and the camera swung with him. "We have with us tonight Senator Richard Atterly, a Republican from Providence who is serving his fourth term, and who is also the Minority Whip in the United States Senate. Senator, we are glad to have you with us."

"Glad to be here," Atterly replied, holding still for the camera to sweep in and give a close-up introductory shot.

"Also with us tonight is Mr. Harvey Biggs, Director of Public Policy for the American Libertarian United Movement. Good evening, Mr. Biggs, and welcome."

"Thank you."

The initial few minutes were taken up with a relatively calm exchange of Constitutional views, with the mounting tension between Atterly and Biggs hidden behind polite masks. The announcer showed practiced patience as he smugly waited for the pivotal moment, and then with genuine pleasure dropped his prearranged bomb.

"Let's move away from these lofty legal questions to the personal side of the pornography issue. Mr. Biggs, how would you feel if *your* daughter were to become lured into making pornographic films?"

Biggs jerked back as though slapped from his blind side. "You keep my daughter out of this," he said, stabbing the air with his finger. He stopped, collected himself, went on, "What we're talking about here is the foundation of our government. Atterly wants to repress our freedom. He wants to strangle us in the name of morality. Where does this religious choke-hold of his end?"

The announcer turned to Atterly, making no effort to hide his delight. "Senator?"

It took Atterly a moment to respond. Bella had contacted him prior to his departure from Washington, and told him what they knew and what they suspected about Biggs' daughter. For a moment he was tempted to prod the man's evident weakness, but something held him back. A gentle inward urging kept him to the central theme that needed stating.

"All human civilization and all human dignity rests upon rules," Atterly replied. "You cannot have rights without responsibilities. It is our responsibility both to protect the innocent against exploitation and to uphold the moral fiber of our nation."

"What right do you have to try and impose your way of life on somebody else?" Biggs snapped back. "Americans are entitled to the right of life, liberty, and the pursuit of happiness. Or have you decided to rewrite the Declaration of Independence while you're at it?"

The announcer knew better than to get in the way. He moved back in his seat, clasped his hands before his chest in thoughtful attentiveness, and watched the sparks fly.

"There is no need to rewrite it," Atterly replied. "According to the Declaration, it is our Creator who endows us with these rights. Our Creator, Mr. Biggs, the same Creator who *demands obedience* from His subjects."

"I wish I knew how you could be so *sure*," Biggs snapped back. "Doesn't it ever bother you that you might be wrong? That you might not have the perfect handle on the Almighty's will?"

"Not if it is clearly stated in the Bible. No. Not about this. No."

"Isn't that great." Biggs turned immensely sarcastic. "We've finally got ourselves an infallible man. His connection to God is so clear he feels able to impose this divine plan on everybody else, regardless of how they think or feel. That's right, isn't it? Your personal interpretation of freedom and justice and the will of God are all infallible, and so you're going to *force* an entire nation to bow to your whims. That is some definition of democracy you have worked out for yourself."

"I would be the first to confess my imperfections before God," Atterly replied crisply, holding a tight rein on his anger. "All I can do, therefore, is *try* to follow His instructions, especially on issues where the Bible states the divine position in absolute black-and-white clarity. What we are in truth discussing is the need to follow divine edicts within our own government. This single point is the pivot upon which you and I differ. Our nation must decide whether to return to the principles upon which it was founded or to surrender to the willful humanism that you represent.

"Yes, there were enormous errors made in this nation's inception and in its attempt to follow divine law. Yes, these errors have in some instances continued to plague us even to today. But at least our Founding Fathers *tried*. They *tried* to hold this divine star as their guiding light through the darkness of doubt and human blindness and greed and self-serving ambition. They *tried* to instill a clarity of vision into their founding documents, this Constitution which you and your group now so eagerly claim to defend. They *tried* to institute faith-directed guidelines into the Federalist Papers and the electoral process and the civil foundations upon which our lives are based. They *tried* to include their worship of God as they knew Him in every facet of their lives. They *tried.* And what, may I ask, are *you* trying to do? Where do your loyalties lie? What checks and balances do you have on your own personal ambitions? I for one would prefer to err on the side of faith, to say that I have sought to return this nation's legal course to one based upon biblical doctrine. I for one would like to say that I, too, have *tried.*"

◆　◆　◆

They had just finished with another day's shooting, another day of endlessly being shuffled back and forth from one movie set to another, and being ordered to do things that left Jessica barely able to control the sick rising in her throat. They ended with an affair at the edge of the swimming pool that kept on until long after dark, until it was all she could do not to scream. She held back because that single thread of control was all that kept her from going out of her mind.

Just when they were up and drying off and getting dressed, an enormous blast of sound from somewhere around the front gate rocked the night, and all Jessica could think of was, no, I can't stand it, not something more, not tonight, I'll do anything—

Then three of the big bodyguards, the ones with skin-tight knit shirts and shoulder-holsters and endlessly staring eyes, came running over so fast she could do nothing more than raise her arms and cringe. Two of them literally picked her up and carted her toward the back wall, hustling so hard she didn't even have force enough to draw breath and scream. They lifted her up and yelled with one voice, "Climb!"

She was barely on top when the taller one jumped up and shoved her *hard* so that she fell off the wall and landed in the bushes on the other side.

Jessica rolled out and stumbled to her feet. She barely had time to rub at the scratches on her arm and brush the hair from her face before Arlene appeared with a squawk and tumbled down into the same bushes. Jessica helped her up, started to ask what was going on when over the same wall appeared the young boy from their room. He hit the bushes and scrambled to his feet in one panic-driven motion.

He gave them a bug-eyed look, hissed, "It's the cops!" And was gone.

It was all they needed. Without really understanding why,

Jessica followed Arlene across the manicured lawn, clambered over the little half gate, fled around the silver-lit swimming pool, through the outer door, down the drive and out along the street.

There was a squealing of tires and a flash of headlights. A car roared up and slammed to a stop half on the street and half on the hedge ahead of them. The driver leaned over to throw open the passenger side.

"Get in!" It was a fiery-eyed Chico.

Arlene did not even miss a beat. She raced up and flung herself into the car.

Jessica felt as though a hand reached out of the sky and wrapped itself around her chest and held her fast. She slithered over loose soil and stopped cold.

"C'mon, move it!" Chico screamed at her. "The cops are right behind me!"

Without conscious thought, Jessica turned back up the main road, away from the car, and fled into the night.

◆　◆　◆

Jeremy peered owl-eyed through the taxi's dirty window, but could see nothing that looked interesting to his sleep-addled mind. Duncan's call had awakened him from a slumber so deep it had taken half the conversation just to realize that he had not been dreaming it all. But there had been an urgency to the man's voice that had pushed him to dress and get downstairs and wave for a cab. He gave the sleepily scrawled address to the driver and spent the long ride rubbing his face awake.

Two punkers in full leather-and-chains regalia staggered into view. "Are you sure this is the place?" he asked the driver.

"The Salvation Army headquarters on Hollywood," the man rasped around the remains of a badly mauled cigar butt. "There ain't but one."

Reluctantly Jeremy paid the man and climbed out. "You mind sittin' here long enough for me to get inside?"

The man raised a gravelly laugh. "Tell you what, Mac. For fifty bucks I'll call the cops and tell 'em where to ship your remains."

"Mister, you finally woke me up," Jeremy said. "I suppose I ought to thank you for that."

"Look, you want some cheap thrills, head back up a few

blocks to where the sidewalk's got all those footprints from the stars. Last time I looked, the chicks weren't half bad and the pimps don't let the place get too rough."

Jeremy watched the taxi lumber away, turned and glanced into a tiny sliver of a shop from whose open door blasted heavy metal music. He saw racks of black canvas jackets with spiked silver shoulders and chains around the collars, tight black jeans with little skull-and-crossbone designs down the legs, black t-shirts with demons' heads printed in vivid colors.

He walked past the storefront used as the Salvation Army's adult center, turned in the drive as Duncan had directed, made his way to the series of linked prefab buildings bearing a sign that read: *Teen Way-In Center.*

He found Duncan seated in a side alcove made cozy with low-slung sofas and framed wall-posters. Duncan introduced the two people with him as Brent and Tanya.

"I checked in with Detective Allende earlier this evening," Duncan told him. "He called back an hour or so ago, asked us to stay close to the phone 'til he called again."

"He didn't say why?"

"No, and it didn't sound like he'd tell me if I asked."

"Sounds to me like we better do as the officer says. Mind if I join you?"

Duncan told Jeremy that Brent was the man who had taken charge of his street education. Brent shook Jeremy's hand and gave him a silent inspection with eyes that searched deep. Above his head was a poster that quoted the twenty-seventh psalm: "For my father and mother may abandon me, but the Lord will take care of me."

Tanya was a raven-haired young woman with the ancient eyes of a former runaway. She and a young man moving around in the other room took care of the shelter, while Brent and two others roamed the streets. She rose to take a phone call, and returned to say that the local hospital had just received another two cases of kids on bad trips.

"Lotsa acid on the streets these last couple of days," Brent explained to Jeremy. "I guess your friend mighta already told you that."

"No, he didn't mention it," Jeremy replied, wondering at how casually they took it all.

"Yeah," Brent went on. "Orange microdot and four-way win-dowpane, mostly. Microdot is little orange cylinders about the size of birdseed. Windowpane comes in different shapes, little stars or flakes of varnish or camera film. On a night like this, when you get in a crowd, you feel like you're the one who's seeing the world wrong."

"Like everybody else is seeing reality, and you're the one who's out of it," Tanya agreed, sitting down again.

"That's the way it is on the street," Brent went on. "The drugs hit here in hundred-thousand lots, and all of a sudden everybody you see is on acid or crank or meth or something. You oughtta be here when it's Quaaludes. The whole place moves like it's under water."

"You end up with some really funny scenes because of this constant drug use," Tanya said. "Not funny ha-ha, funny weird-tragic. Have you ever heard of tweaking?"

"I don't think so."

"No, probably not. It's not something that comes up in polite society very often. Tweaking is when a kid's been up on a drug high for two or three or four or maybe even five days straight, and his body starts complaining by going through uncontroll-able twitches. Sometimes it leads to convulsions, sometimes there's a super-intense paranoia, sometimes he can't stop crying, sometimes he can't stop screaming. The really unlucky ones start tweaking while they're still on the drugs, you know, before they come down, and then the mind just takes this new symptom and magnifies it a billion times. The hospitals around here get fairly used to it, kids with their eyeballs rolled up to the roof of their heads and having to be restrained with padded leather straps before they can risk giving them a tranquilizer."

A young man with spiked pink hair appeared in the door-way. He wore the inevitable faded jeans and a t-shirt that read: *Fragile, Handle With Prayer.*

Brent waved a hand, said, "Hey, Sniffles, how's it going?"

"Makin' it, man." The kid grinned back. "Stayin' a little weirder than anybody else, that's all it takes."

"Sniffles is a recent addition to our staff," Tanya said. "One we take special pride in. He ran away when he was twelve, spent two years living on the streets. He finally wised up and came to us. We got him into a good foster home, and now he's a freshman at U.C.L.A. "

Brent offered him the two pictures, said, "You seen either of them around?"

The kid squinted and pointed at Jessica. "Check this Barbie

doll out, man. Tell me she's not in some serious trouble."

"Barbie-doll girls have it really tough out there," Tanya explained. "Nothing in their lives has ever prepared them for what they'll find on the streets."

"Meet Duncan and Jeremy," Brent said. "They've traveled over from Washington looking for them."

"Hey, all right. We need all the help we can get."

"Don't know how much help we can give you folks," Jeremy replied. "I've never felt so out of my depth in my life."

"We all gotta start sometime," Sniffles replied. "First fact of life you gotta learn is, fear rules the streets. Fear. Either you give it or you take it. If you're not making others scared, you're *running* scared. It doesn't take a genius to figure that one out. The place is like a machine, chewing up everybody it can get its hands on. Doesn't even spit out the bones. All you get is hollow bodies with the life sucked out. Yeah. Big monster machine running on fear."

"The streets are really hostile," Tanya agreed. "It's best to remember this when you go out there. If you have an attitude, the street will take it and amp it through the roof."

"A giant runway for kids ready to weird out," Sniffles agreed.

"It's a violent scene," Tanya went on. "Made worse by unemployment, drugs, hopelessness, AIDS, and babies making babies."

"The largest employer of young men in L.A. is drugs," Sniffles added. "Whattaya expect from a culture ruled by drugs and violence and fear?"

"You don't go out on the street looking for miracles on the first night," Brent said. "We're mostly a reality check. A lot of the time it's all they'll let us be."

"We act as a mirror to their own insanity," Tanya added. "All we have to do sometimes is say hello, and they know. You can see it in their eyes. They know."

Brent pointed toward the outer door. "A lot of the kids out there are having a *blast*. There aren't any rules. None at all. The street tells them, look, you can do anything you like, be as crazy as you like. Do as many drugs as you want, have sex with whoever you can find. The street *rewards* weirdness. It's an unhappy kid's wildest dream come true."

"And then we come along," Tanya added. Her voice had a sandpapery sound to it, roughened by years of tough living.

"We tell them hello, offer a sandwich, ask how they are, and it's enough. We're the gentle tug, the reminder that there's another way. And every once in a while some kid wakes up and says, hey, if I stay out here I'm gonna *die*. And then we're there to help, us and the Covenant House and Children of the Night and others. He or she has seen us around and knows we can be trusted. It's great when that happens. Makes up for all the sadness."

"Trust is hard to build with kids like this," Brent went on. "You got to understand, for some kid abused by adults in the system, the wildness of the streets seems a lot more acceptable."

"Too right," Sniffles agreed. "What's their alternative? Rules are set by adults they *know* they can't trust. They've learned that the hard way. Society's got rules set up so these people can *hurt* them. Why should they return, or believe anything the system and the adults tell them?"

These three were truly at ease with themselves and their task. They wore a hardened edge similar to what Jeremy had seen in Detective Allende's staff room, but there was a light in their eyes that set them apart. It permeated the entire building, this feeling that they were not alone, that they worked in a war zone for a higher cause.

He said, "Sounds like I could learn a lot from you folks, long as I could grow me a hide tough as leather."

"You get a different perspective of society, looking at it from down here," Tanya replied. "We talk about it a lot, you know, here in the office and out on the streets at night looking for kids who never learned to cope. Their parents couldn't teach because *they* never learned to cope. These kids come from a long line of non-copers."

"People start to define their lives by where they live and how they dress and who they do business with and what they drive," Brent agreed. "They lose sight of all the essentials that the advertisements forget to mention. Like love. And concern for our neighbors. And giving without expecting something in return. And sticking it out through the tough parts. And being honest. For us out here on the streets, these kids are kind of the tip of the iceberg, the clearest evidence that Advertising America has worn through the varnish and gotten down to eating at its own heart."

"Some of these kids have parents who one day just decided they wanted a human toy," Sniffles said. "Like mine. A new kind of pet they can dress up and take places. Then after a while they decide it's too much trouble, or they decide they don't like what they've bought, so they toss it out. It's a great American sport—have kids, get bored with them, and dump them on the street. The Feds say *seven thousand* American kids are abandoned every year by their parents. Word out here is that the figure is low. Way low."

"The problem is," Tanya said, "whenever there is a major deficit in parental love, the child responds to that deficit by blaming himself or herself. In other words, Mommy and Daddy don't love me because I'm not worth loving. This negative self-image opens them up to exploitation by anyone who is willing to manipulate with lies."

"Which means someone willing to exploit another person's weaknesses in order to satisfy their own selfish hungers," Brent explained.

"If all your experiences are negative, you're in a really deep hole," Tanya said, her gaze turning inward. "It's a tremendous struggle to climb out of that hole."

"That means our work has to come in several stages," Brent said. "First we take the hours and days and weeks and sometimes months necessary to show the kids that we're not like the adults who pushed them out on the street in the first place. Then we try to convince them to come inside, to give life and reality and hope another chance. Once they've been brought in off the street, we try to help them build a positive self-image. We take a lot of our philosophy straight from the Twelve Steps. You ever heard of them?"

"No, I can't say as I have," Jeremy replied.

"They're from Alcoholics Anonymous. The principles apply just about anywhere, though. We're not with most of these kids long enough to work through all of the steps, so we try to concentrate on the first three. Those I can quote from memory. The first step is, I admit that I am powerless over whatever it is that got me out on the street—drugs, alcohol, sex, fear of abuse, hatred, rebellion, whatever—and that my life has become unmanageable."

"It makes my heart ache to imagine a little kid havin' to say those words," Jeremy said.

"Hey, if we can get a street kid this far, man, we're halfway home. Really. Think about it a minute. They've probably never had anyone in their entire lives who's said to them, face up to your problems. Can you imagine? No parent ever taught them the discipline of dealing with the problems of growing up, no one ever showed them what it means to be deep-down honest with themselves."

"And then here we come," Sniffles went on. "And we're saying, look, the only way you're going to be able to put your life together in a healthy manner is if you trust a grown-up. Only you've never had a grown-up worth trusting before, okay? You've got to trust us enough to believe in what we're saying, and *admit* to yourself, no matter how much it hurts, that things have gotten out of control. It takes a strong kid to do that, believe me."

"Then comes step two," Brent said. "That one is, I have come to believe that a Power greater than myself can restore me to sanity."

"I like that one," Duncan said, his voice low. He remained still and settled in his spot, *drinking* the words.

"It's how most of these kids are able to take step one," Brent said. "By beginning to believe that there is someone perfect, someone who's not going to abuse them or see them only for what they can get out of them. That's a big move, coming to believe that there really is someone who will just love them for who they are."

"Man, you want to see some miracles," Sniffles said. "You ought to watch one of these kids come to Christ and know love for the first time in their lives."

"Step three," Brent went on, "is, I have made a decision to turn my will and my life over to the care of God. That is the goal that we're working for here. If we can get kids that far before they leave our care, a professional counselor has a good chance of getting them through the rest and putting them on a solid course for life."

The phone sounded again. The room quieted as Sniffles walked over, answered, and called out for Duncan, "It's the heat."

Not a word was spoken until Duncan returned to the doorway, looked down at Jeremy, said. "They raided the house on Inglewood."

"Something in your face is tellin' me this ain't good news," Jeremy replied.

"The cops caught a couple of the muscle men at the back wall, think maybe they were trying to toss all the under-age kids over, you know, trying to get rid of them. They hunted around, didn't find anything except a couple of trampled bushes. There's all sorts of other evidence to make the charges stick, Allende says. And they caught Pierre Matisse, but it looks like Chico slipped through the net."

"And the girls weren't there," Jeremy said. It wasn't a question.

"Allende says they found some film, got some straight from a couple of the cameras, they're developing it right now. Hopefully we'll have confirmation in a couple of hours that the girls were there." Duncan sighed. "But no, they didn't find them."

"If you want my opinion," Brent said, "from everything I've heard, I'd stake my job on them having been there."

"I think so, too," Jeremy agreed, feeling immensely tired. "But where are they now?"

Brent said nothing, simply turned and pointed out the side window, into the blackness of impenetrable night.

CHAPTER
17

The sky was slowly gathering strength toward a rose-tinted dawn, when Jessica finally made it down the winding road and onto one of the main streets leading into Hollywood.

Several times during the night she had felt her eyelids sinking beneath the burden of exhaustion and fear and worry over where she was going and what she was going to find once she got there. She had crawled under a likely looking shrub, once into a tangled grove of bamboo, and curled up into the smallest ball she could make and simply went away. It was not sleep in the normal sense; there were no dreams, no passage from wakefulness into another state. One minute she was there and the next she was gone. After an uncounted hour or so of giving into the exhaustion, a dog would bark in the distance or a car would squeal its tires as it powered up the slope, and she would start awake with a gasp and sometimes a scream, and be back on her feet and heading downhill again before she really understood that she was awake.

The street she walked gradually changed from surly houses with tiny unkempt lawns to low-slung commercial buildings. Several times she limped around scattered piles of filthy cardboard and newspaper that leaned against a nearby wall or chain-link fence and blocked most of the sidewalk. She was just stumbling back into another walking slumber when the pile ahead of her shifted as though moved by a heavy wind, although the dawn was breathlessly still. Jessica hesitated, not sure what to do, when the pile heaved itself once more and gave a long drawn-out groan. Her exhaustion vanished as a grimy arm erupted from the pile and grasped at the distant sky. She moved to the center of the street and stumbled on.

Three blocks farther a car drove by, and when the male driver turned to look her way she froze, unable to move, unable to draw a decision from her fatigue-addled brain. She drew her hands into a single tight-fisted clench at her stomach, lowered her head so that she was watching the craning face through the curtain of her hair, then gave a couple of sobbing breaths when the car finally speeded up and drove away. She had to get somewhere safe. It was the only thought that made any sense. Find somewhere safe and sleep.

Across the street from where she stood was a one-story fake-adobe house with an enormous billboard perched on its flat roof. The billboard announced that here was the best Tex-Mex restaurant in Los Angeles. Her stomach clenched in a sudden spasm of hunger as she looked at the steaming platter painted across the sky. Then a pair of grimy hands appeared above the adobe wall encircling the roof, grasped one of the billboard's guy wires, and pulled a head with matted hair into view. She started to run, then hesitated. The kid raised himself erect, turned away from her while rubbing his face, stumbled across the roof and half scrambled, half slid down a shaky wooden ladder propped against a side wall.

A second head appeared, and even from that distance she could see that it was another young kid. She watched him drop a collection of what looked like blankets to the unseen roof, reach for a shirt, swing it over his head, and move for the ladder.

She did not really think it out; it was more an instinct that here was safety. After the second boy had made his way down the ladder and stumbled into the distance, Jessica swallowed her fear and forced her legs to carry her across the street and along the wall and up the ladder.

As her head rose above the roof-wall, she saw scattered across the roof perhaps two dozen unmoving forms huddled beneath layers of burlap and rags and filthy blankets. All the faces she could see were dirty and young, some much younger than herself. She willed strength into her rubbery legs and pushed herself up and over the ledge.

Piled against one of the billboard's pillars was a jumbled mass of grimy blankets and strips of cloth, all so dirty as to be colorless. She tiptoed around snoring, coughing, moaning, crying forms and pulled out several coverings. She took them over to as distant a point as she could find from any of the others, wrapped herself up so that she was covered from head to foot, curled up into the little ball once more, and gave herself up to the awaiting blackness.

◆　◆　◆

Tuesday morning the Per Se anti-pornography legislation with its six newly added amendments passed on the Senate floor as though orchestrated by some unseen hand. Atterly left the chambers giving silent thanks, so glad to have it over that the lifted eyebrows and snide whispers that followed his exit touched him not at all.

Two blocks away, the ALUM headquarters was wedged on a main avenue within shouting distance of both the Capitol and the U.S. Supreme Court. It was a white three-story building constructed in the dignified federal style. An elegant double balustrade curved up from the street to the front entrance. Several large ivy-covered trees graced the small front lawn. To the right, there was a beautiful enclosed garden.

The impression of elegance faded quickly, however, upon entering the foyer. The ceilings were very high and painted a dull off-white. The walls were trimmed with a dust-laden Italian gold-leaf design. The wooden floors creaked and were covered with cheap commercial carpet. A brown formica reception desk was placed front and center, unmanned and unused. Behind the desk rose a curved staircase with wooden banisters. Everywhere there was an air of unappreciated stateliness.

At the back of the foyer, double doors led to a large room that probably was once a wealthy statesman's formal gallery; now it was occupied by a jumble of desks and tables and chattering secretaries and ringing phones and hushed conversations. Every level surface was cluttered with stacks of paper—forms, articles, books, newsletters, transcripts, government documents, directories, copies of press releases.

Harvey Biggs, Director of Public Policy for ALUM, had an office on the second floor with a view of both the Capitol dome and the back of the Supreme Court Building. He told visitors that they were his two primary targets, and liked to keep them in sight at all times. Tall sash windows, the old kind with rope pulleys that should have helped balance the window's weight but which now took two strong men to force up and down, stood to either side of his desk; they let in strong sunlight that illuminated dust motes floating across the room's musty air. A boarded-up fireplace was flanked by overflowing bookshelves; back issues of magazines and congressional records were stacked in all four corners of his office, like pillars holding up an invisible ideology that only he and his cohorts could identify.

Biggs' secretary appeared at the door and began to say something, but was cut off by his slapping the newspaper with the back of his hand and shouting, "Have you seen this article in the *Post*? Makes us look like real desperadoes on this handgun bill." He gave her an exasperated look. "I'm all in favor of free speech, so long as they quote me right. But just look at this mess. They've got me saying that no one should be inconvenienced by having to wait seven days before buying a gun. Then we got Brady coming back saying he wished I could see how inconvenient it was to spend seven days in a wheelchair."

He flipped the paper across the desk and leaned back. "Okay, what is it?"

"Roy just called, said he wouldn't be back 'til later this afternoon from BIA."

"BIA?" Biggs slammed his chair down hard. "What is he doing at Indian Affairs?"

The secretary shrugged one tired shoulder. "Something about gambling on the reservations. Said it was important he be there for a briefing session."

"Yeah, yeah, okay. So who's up on the Hill covering S–1422?"

"That Per Se stuff? Roy sent Valerie over there this morning. She should be back any minute."

"No big deal, I guess. Roy told me it looked like we'd have to wait 'til the House vote to kill it. Have her come see me as soon as she gets back."

Fifteen minutes later Valerie knocked on his doorjamb. She was a second-year student at the Georgetown Law Center, working part time as an ALUM research assistant. She was very bright and very east-coast intellectual. She wore her brown hair in a Dutch-boy cut and her wool skirts unfashionably long.

"I just got back from the S–1422 vote," she announced. "Passed by two votes more than we thought. There were also a couple of amendments stuck in at the last moment."

Harvey Biggs remained seated sideways to his desk, his feet up and his lap full of documents. He swung his head around. "What about?"

"Looks mostly procedural to me," she replied. "I'm going to take a look at them right now."

"Yeah, you do that," he said, turning back to his papers. "And give me a side-by-side by the end of the day."

"Right," she said, frowning slightly.

"Hang on a second," Biggs said. "When's the House vote?"

She consulted a small spiral notebook, said, "Looks like Thursday morning."

"The same day all those religious clowns are supposed to roll into town," Biggs said glumly. "Great. Just great."

She returned downstairs to her work space in the conference room's back corner by way of the secretarial station. She chose an older secretary, one too bored and too out of it to use Valerie's lack of knowledge as a weapon. Fingering a couple of books on the shelf, she asked casually over her shoulder, "What do they mean by side-by-side?"

"Side-by-side? Did Harv throw that one at you?"

"Yes."

"That's when you analyze a piece of legislation. List the key provisions on one side of the page and on the other side compare how they're treated by companion legislation in the other House."

"I see," Valerie replied, keeping her eye on the bookshelf. "Do we have a file on S–1422?"

"That anti-pornography thing?" The secretary gave a deep-throated chuckle. "Honey, that's not a file, that's a pile. Wait, isn't that Roy's issue?"

"I guess so, but he's busy with something else."

"Yeah, that's right. He's on the warpath about some Indian issue, isn't he? Well, you can start over there with that bottom drawer, then there's a box full of stuff under the conference table. When you're done, come back to me and I'll find you some more."

♦ ♦ ♦

Jessica was awakened by raucous laughter and shouted

curses and sunlight that heated her coverings into a stinking cauldron. Footsteps drummed by her head; she scrambled upright, slithering back until she rested against the wall, raising her knees up to her chin and crouching down in preparation for a blow that did not come. She uncovered her eyes, peered at a very young girl combing tangles from spiked dyed-blond hair while an even younger boy preened and shuffled in front of her, talking loud and crying out for attention.

He flicked a hand at the girl's hair, said, "It's you and me against the world, right, Tina?"

A slightly older black girl watched the pair from her perch on the billboard's guy wire. "Girl, that boy is out to rob you six ways from Sunday."

The blond looked at her with eyes a lot older than her twelve or thirteen years. "And your pimp was different, right?"

The black girl was dressed in ballerina tights and a tiny flared skirt and scuffed patent-leather pumps. She played at unconcern, said, "I wised up. What you think I'm doin' here?"

The young kid danced between them, said, "Hey, I just wanna take care of you, Tina, make sure the heat don't come messin' around."

She laughed at that, said, "C'mon, a little loser like you?"

"Losers die, man. I ain't never gonna lose." He strutted a quick dance step that made his oversized t-shirt balloon out around him. "I heard you talkin' with Fancy yesterday, tellin' him you thought I was really fly."

"Fly?" She put down her comb. "You?"

"Don't gimme that. I heard it all. He's got a great jaw, that's exactly what you said. His jaw meets you an hour before the rest of him gets there."

Tina stood and picked up a little purse of faded pink satin. She pulled down a miniskirt of some knit fabric that looked sprayed on. Her high-heeled boots were stained and cracked and looked much too big for her slender legs. "Sorry, Spanky. I don't know what you heard, but it sure wasn't about you. Now I gotta go to work. I'm hungry."

Jessica sat as still as she could and watched the rooftop scene from her hunched-over position, trying to concentrate on the people scattered around her, working to figure out this strange new world, struggling to keep her mind off her cramped and empty stomach and what she would have to do to get something to eat.

Their hands were *filthy*. The dirt was ingrained into finger-nails and crevices. Their clothes and their bodies had the look of being dirty so long it had somehow worked its way beneath the skin.

They were always scratching. They huddled under blankets, sprawled on mattresses or sat in corners and stared at nothing. There didn't seem to be any hurry to leave the safety of their blankets unless some desire or hunger hit them, then it was announced in a loud cursing voice, as though preparing for whatever was going to meet them away from the roof's safety as they hunted for drugs or money or food or cigarettes or sex.

Jessica sat and watched and huddled back even tighter when someone looked her way or moved in her direction. Their teeth were awful and their breath stank at ten feet. As they undressed she saw the most awful scabs, especially in the joints and folds of their skin.

Everybody seemed to have a cough. They all sounded as if their lungs were coming up.

They ate like starved animals. They competed to see who could make the grossest move—jamming entire double burgers in their mouths, then laughing as the refuse dribbled all over their fronts, eating with hands that were both filthy and scarred with running sores. As they ate they shouted about the trip that was over and the one that was just about to start, where the money was going to come from, who had made the worst move to get the bread to buy the high. Jessica listened and breathed as quietly as possible and pushed as hard as she could at the hunger that knotted her belly.

Then another head appeared at the ladder, an older one that belonged to a tall overweight body. Jessica tensed, then took a lead from the others on the roof who looked his way and either ignored him or called out something crude. Brent, she heard several voices say. The man scrambling over the ledge was called Brent. He had a friendly smile for everyone, and carried a plastic sack of sandwiches in one hand. Jessica's stomach cried at the sight, and she wondered what he would make her do before he gave her one.

She watched him progress in a meandering circuit around the roof, handing out sandwiches and friendly words. An older boy took one, said something in a low voice and jutted his chin in her direction. Brent turned toward her, patted the boy on the shoulder, and headed over. Jessica felt her heart take flight.

Brent dropped down on his knees before her crouched position. Up close his eyes looked red-rimmed and very tired. But his smile was from the heart as he extended a hand and a sandwich and said, "How's it going this morning? You hungry?"

◆　◆　◆

The Christian television producer hung up the phone to find his chief assistant hovering anxiously in the doorway. "What's up?"

"Two of the people you're scheduled to interview on the show today haven't shown up." There were normally four people on the hour-long talk show, which meant that there was now half an hour of air time left unfilled. A half-hour last-minute gap was a fairly major problem.

The producer rested his head on the back of his chair, thought for a moment. "You try to find substitutes?"

"It's crazy. Everybody I could normally get is either out or tied up in knots."

"Looks like we'll have to pull up something from the archives, then." The producer cast his mind back over the past few weeks. "What about that speech of Atterly's?"

His assistant nodded agreement. "He was really nervous, but there was something to it."

"I know just what you mean. His delivery was uncertain, but I haven't been able to get that talk out of my mind."

"I even dreamed about it the other night," his assistant said.

"Imagine calling a Solemn Assembly in this day and age."

"Maybe so, but you'd be surprised how many calls we've had for copies of that talk."

That was news. "How many?"

"I don't know. I just overheard Shirley down in archives mentioning it to somebody. Seemed like they had over two hundred calls one day last week, all wanting copies."

"Two hundred tapes in one day?"

He shook his head. "Two hundred *calls*. A lot of the people were ordering more than one copy."

"Why wasn't I told about this?"

The assistant shrugged his unconcern. "I guess nobody thought it was that important. Shirley said there was this one guy who wanted five whole boxes, sixty tapes. He was going to give it out to all the churches in his town."

The producer picked up his phone and punched a button. When his secretary answered, he said, "See if you can find Shirley, would you? Ask her to give me a call."

"This was all overheard, you understand," his assistant said. "She was talking to somebody at the next table. But I got the impression it's been like this for over a week."

"Maybe I ought to speak to the senator about this, let him know of the interest he's stirring up," the producer said, ringing his secretary back. "After you find Shirley, please get Senator Atterly's office for me."

"I hear a couple of the networks made mention of it in their news programs," the assistant said.

"I'm not surprised," the producer said, hanging up the phone. "A United States senator calling for the first Solemn Assembly in over two thousand years ought to be worth a couple of seconds' air time. It's a good idea, mind you. Pity he's bound to fail. Something like this would have to take years of planning. The logistics alone would be a nightmare."

"I heard from a friend over on Capitol Hill that they've started calling him Senator Suicide," his assistant agreed. "And that Japanese-American who works in his office? He's been renamed Kamikaze Joe."

"I'm sorry to hear that. I've always had the greatest respect for Atterly. If he's taken on something like this, there's bound to be a good reason for it."

"Maybe so, but all I hear is how he's put his political life on the line for a prayer meeting nobody can figure out and an anti-porn bill that's bound to fail in the House."

"Then that's the position I'll take in my introduction," the producer decided. "Let the people understand just how much this man is sacrificing for his principles. I don't know if it will do any good, but I for one want everybody to hear how much is at stake here."

The producer had just finished writing out his opening remarks when his secretary put her head through the doorway. "Shirley isn't here just now, sir. Her office says she and another colleague have gone out to buy more blank tapes."

"It took two of them to go buy video tapes?"

"I asked the same question. It seems that they wanted to buy so many that they needed two cars. I asked her office what they needed so many tapes for, but they didn't know."

"Well, just leave word for Shirley to come see me as soon as she gets back."

"Yes, sir, I did. And I've tried and tried to get through over at Senator Atterly's office, but all the phones are busy."

The producer tore the notebook pages out and handed them over. "Type these up quickly, please, and let them know I'll want them on the monitor." He stood, checked his appearance in the little mirror attached to his side wall, said, "The senator's probably caught up in some issue or another. Remind me after the show to drop him a line and let him know there's been some interest in what he had to say."

Carl Henrichs was an accountant and loved his work unabashedly. He was also a Christian and a vocal one. Carl wore his conviction and his profession so clearly that an unfriendly co-worker had labeled him "The Nerd for Christ." If Carl minded it, he did not let it show.

That morning, however, Carl's constant grin was not in place. His worried silence attracted attention throughout the office. Believers and nonbelievers alike paused in their morning routine to speak of the dark cloud that hung over Carl Henrichs. They did not realize how much they took his constant good humor for granted until it was not there, until no one spared them the light that was Carl's unspoken trademark.

Carl was blessed with a good boss, a gray-haired matron who truly cared for those in her department. She stopped by Carl's alcove as soon as word worked its way into her office with the morning mail. She found Carl with his head supported in his hands, the heavy black glasses laid to one side.

"Carl, is everything all right?"

He started guiltily, as though caught asleep. It took a moment for his eyes to focus on who it was speaking. "Oh, Mrs. Abbott, I—it's all right. I just had a rough night. I don't think I slept a wink."

She slid into the seat next to his desk. "Is there anything I can do?"

He seemed to be struggling with some internal decision. "I don't know. Maybe. I think I'm going to have to take a few days off. I may need to travel to Washington."

"Of course." There was no need to think. "Is there something wrong? Is it your family?"

"No." He hesitated. "Well, yes, I suppose you could say it is."

A secretary poked her head around the entrance. "Mrs. Abbott, your first appointment is here."

"Thank you, Ruth." She stood and said, "You have several years of unused sick leave. Take as much time as you like, I'll clear it with Personnel."

The woman was a flurry of activity that sunny autumn afternoon, as silent and intent as her husband. Together they loaded the car, pressed by reasons they could not explain to pack extra food and sleeping bags and all three thermoses. When the tailgate was finally closed on the overfilled station wagon, she returned to the front stoop to hug her children one last time. She watched with worried fondness as her husband did the same, then he returned to the car and started the engine.

She said to her mother, much more calmly than she felt, "Thanks again, Mom. We shouldn't be gone more than four or five days. A week at the most."

Her mother wore a deeply worried expression. "But where will you be staying? I heard Ralph in there on the phone—he must have called two dozen hotels. All were full, weren't they? You can't expect to sleep out on the streets, honey. Think of the children. Washington's a dangerous place these days."

"The Lord will provide," she replied, hoping it was true. "We'll call you as soon as we know."

Her mother pressed the children behind her, let her concern grow. "What on earth is going on? Just because that man on television says come doesn't mean you have to. Would you go jump off the Empire State Building if he said fly?"

She hugged her mother with a ferocity that surprised them both. She walked over to the car and opened her door. "It wasn't the man who called us, Mother. We'll be in touch just as soon as we get settled."

◆　　◆　　◆

Congressman John Silverwood returned to his office after lunch and sorted through the pink message slips piled at the center of his desk. His hand stopped when he came across the one saying that Harvey Biggs had telephoned. He decided this call would have to go first.

"Yeah, Congressman," Biggs' fake-hearty tones rolled over the phone. "Thanks a lot for returning my call."

"What can I do for you, Mr. Biggs?"

"Hey, that's a good one, what can you do for me. As if you didn't already know, right?" The tone carried a forced oiliness that left Silverwood wanting to hold the receiver a foot from his ear. "By the way, Congressman, we've got our annual meeting in November. I thought maybe I could pencil you in as our keynote speaker."

Silverwood remained silent. The ALUM annual function was a major political event, with the keynote speaker position normally reserved for an elder statesman with a long record of advancing ALUM-backed causes and a strong power base they could call on in the future.

"It's up in Boston over Veteran's Day weekend," Biggs went on. "Might interest you to hear that the honorarium's been doubled this year, too."

"I'll think about it and let you know," Silverwood replied mildly.

"Yeah, you do that. Oh, one more thing. About the anti-porn legislation. Just wanted to say we sure could use your help in finding a few more like-minded colleagues to strike this thing down."

"How does the vote look to you?" Silverwood hedged.

"Got a chart right here," Biggs said. "Call it my score card. Tells you who might go with us on this if they got a shove from the right man." He reeled off a dozen names.

"I see," Silverwood replied. "So you also have a list of who might vote against you?"

"Count on it," Biggs said. "It's all here. Hey, you want a copy? It might help you decide who to have lunch with tomorrow, right?"

"Yes," Silverwood said thoughtfully. "I think your list could be of great help to me. Why don't you fax it over?"

"Consider it done."

Silverwood settled back in his chair, scraped open the top drawer, fiddled off one shoe and stuck his toes into the recesses. He marveled at how everything was coming together, wondering if this was what it meant to be guided.

CHAPTER

18

Wednesday morning Biggs walked into ALUM headquarters, climbed the stairs to his office, and greeted his secretary with, "Did Valerie leave anything on that anti-porn bill for me?"

The secretary searched through her in-box. "No, I don't see anything here. She was still working when I left at half-past six last night. She's got class this morning, so I can't reach her. She'll probably be in around three."

He ran the hand not carrying his briefcase through his thinning hair. "You want anything done around here, you got to do it yourself."

"Roy called," she went on. "It looks like he's going to stay tied up with that Indian mess all week."

"It's a good thing we've got friends in high places," Biggs said, turning toward his office. "Or else we'd be sunk deeper than the Titanic."

"He wants you to go over this afternoon and take a look at the situation for yourself," his secretary called after him, still searching her desk. "Wait, here's a note from Valerie. She's still working on the side-by-side you requested, and she'll have it ready for you before she leaves the office this evening."

"These kids!" he exclaimed, slapping his hand on the door-jamb. "They got no idea of timing. It's not enough to have the info the day of the vote. I need that stuff when there's still time to use it."

"Maybe I could call the law school," his secretary said doubt-fully.

"Nah, they won't pull her out of class." Biggs entered his office. "I don't guess it matters so much anyway. With the contacts we got, I'm ninety-nine percent sure we got a dead solid lock on this thing in the House."

◆　◆　◆

"They've found one of them," Duncan said, his eyes shining with the excitement that sent him bounding into Jeremy's room.

Jeremy was already up and heading for the door. "Let's go, son. I've heard all I need to hear. You can tell me the rest on the way."

On the drive to Hollywood Duncan filled him in about the rooftop squat and the group and the way Brent had found Jessica. "He left her over at the Covenant House. I asked him why he hadn't taken her back with him to the Salvation Army. He told me that every day there are over thirty thousand runaways living on the streets of Los Angeles, and only thirty-four teen-shelter beds in the entire county. He'll take one wherever he can find it."

"No sign of the other girl?"

"Brent said she wasn't up there. He asked Jessica about her, but couldn't get anything except a shake of the head."

Duncan pulled into the parking lot in front of a nondescript house on Sunset Boulevard. A tiny sign planted beside the cracked sidewalk announced this was the Covenant House. A black security cop stood in the parking lot and watched him with eyes that clearly said this was not a routine job.

Duncan cut the motor, said to Jeremy, "The rent-a-cops are here twenty-four hours a day. A lot of the girls have pimps who would come charging in after them, threaten them with stuff you can't imagine to get them back on the streets."

They climbed out and Duncan said to the cop, "We're here about Jessica Biggs."

"Right through that door," the man replied, his stare unblinking. "You're expected."

"All right if I leave my car here for a couple of hours?"

"Long as you're out of here by midnight, nobody's gonna say a thing," the cop replied. "That's a late-night club," he pointed with his chin, "specializes in S&M."

Duncan eyed the simple clapboard structure. "You're kidding."

"You ought to come back here sometime around three in the morning, see all the fancy cars with out-of-state tags parked there. Place wears a dark cloud all night long."

"C'mon, son," Jeremy called from the Covenant House door. "Time's a' wastin'."

The cramped front parlor was across the entrance hall from a large kitchen-dining area, and did duty as both a receiving station and social room. The Hispanic woman at the small desk wore the same hard-eyed stare as the security cop outside. "Can I help you?"

"We're here about Jessica Biggs," Duncan explained.

"Are you the gentlemen that Brent told us about?"

"From Washington. Yes, ma'am."

"May I see some identification, please?"

They passed their documents over, and Duncan unfolded the affidavits the parents had signed granting him both power of attorney and temporary custody over the two girls. She inspected it all very carefully, compared their names with a handwritten note.

She handed the documents back, saying, "I have also received a call from Inspector Allende, who says that you check out. I will ask Jessica if she wants to speak with you, but I must inform you that it will be entirely her choice. We act here as advocates for the children, sometimes the only ones they have. I must also insist on sitting in on your conversation."

"We understand," Duncan said somberly.

"Wait here, then, and I'll see if she's up to it."

When she was gone Jeremy gave a small smile of greeting to the two girls watching from the low-sprung sofa. As soon as his attention turned their way, they responded with eyes that darted everywhere around the room but at him. He found himself unable to look away. Their bodies rested limply, as though incapable of movement. Their hands were totally motionless. Their faces showed no strength whatsoever, set in a heartbreaking mixture of tragedy and childhood softness. Their eyes looked so very, very sad, defeated by a life that was over before it had begun.

Jeremy realized he was staring, tore his gaze away and fastened on the small poster set above the bricked-up fireplace. It read:

Covenant House Mission Statement

We who recognize God's providence and fidelity to his people are dedicated to living out his covenant among ourselves and those children we serve, with absolute respect and unconditional love. That commitment calls us to serve suffering children of the street, and to protect and safeguard all children. Just as Christ in his humanity is the sign of God's presence among his people, so our efforts together in the covenant community are a visible sign that effects the presence of God, working through the Holy Spirit among ourselves and our kids.

Jeremy turned around and said to Duncan, "I think maybe you ought to meet with her by yourself."

"Why's that?"

"Two strange men might be too much at once, especially since she's probably runnin' scared."

The woman appeared in the entranceway, and ushered forward a slender, attractive girl made even smaller by the voluminous man's shirt she wore over jeans scrubbed to the point of falling apart. Jessica walked with her shoulders stooped and hands wrapped limply around each other, her head down, her hair falling like a golden-brown curtain to hide her face. Jeremy felt a lance slide through his heart, and clamped his jaw down hard.

"Jessica," the woman said softly. "These gentlemen would like to speak with you for a minute. Don't worry, dear, I'll stay right here with you."

"I'll be just across the hall," Jeremy said. He forced his feet to move, entered the large kitchen-dining room, and steadied himself against the wall.

"Smart move, man," a deep voice said. "Getting out of the way like that. Real smart."

Jeremy looked up, focused on a friendly black face seated at the far table chomping heartily on a sandwich.

"Name's Tony Dawson. I'm one of the day counselors here." He lifted the sandwich. "You hungry? We got just about every cold cut you could ask for."

"I don't believe there's anything I want less right now than food," Jeremy said weakly. "Thank you kindly, though."

"Hey, no problem. Strongest thing we got in here is coffee, but that pot's been cooking since about six this morning. Go pour yourself a cup."

Jeremy did as he was told, brought it back over and sat down. He sipped at what he could not taste, saying, "I don't think it really hit me, what I was doin', 'til just then."

"You over here looking for that Biggs kid, right? This your first time hunting a runaway?"

"First and last," Jeremy said firmly.

"I hear you, man. All the same, don't talk too fast. You know how it is, the first time's always the worst. And there's a lot of kids out there who could use a helping hand."

Jeremy scrubbed hard at his face. "They all look so *beaten*."

"Sure do. There's a lot of what you might call the 'I can't' kids out there. They still got one foot in childhood and the other already in adulthood, and life's been busy trying to chop the childhood foot off. The only lesson they've all learned real well is that they're not gonna make it. If they don't get some kind of advocate on their side, you know, somebody who's there to offer them a hand and a caring heart, a lot of them are gonna be deformed for life."

The young man lifted himself easily from his chair, glided back behind the kitchen counter, poured himself a glass of water. "They feel powerless in the adult world because they come from parents who don't have any values. I don't mean right versus wrong values. I mean they just don't have any values at *all*."

He came back around and sat down. "So they wind up on the street just ripe to be used. These little girls come in, they've been with this guy who's pimped her from here to Vegas, stuck her in some really raunchy film work. Now he's gotten so nasty with her one way or another that she's finally run away from him and looked for help, right? So she talks to you and still says stuff like, 'He treats me bad sometimes, yeah, but he cares about me. Really. I can tell.' " The young man shook his head. "What can you do, man? The definition of love they've learned from their parents and other adults is so twisted, they're afraid to expect more than that from life."

"So what do you do?" Jeremy leaned across the table. "How on earth do you keep going?"

"Spend as much time as I can on my knees," the young man responded without having to think. "And I don't work with kids

who have had a chance to turn away from this life, and instead
turn away from the chance. They do that, I got to write them
off my list. I *got* to. If they're not able to go a coupla weeks
without using, if they run back to their pimps the first chance
they get—they'll still call them boyfriends, but these guys,
they're out for the power and the control and the street status
and the money. They're pimps. If they go back to them, or get
back on drugs, start feeding me some stock story and take it
back out on the street, I don't touch 'em. I *can't*. I can't let them
break my heart so bad that I'm not able to help somebody *ready*
to be helped. You understand what I'm saying?"

"I understand," Jeremy said quietly. "It does me a lot of
good, listenin' to what you've got to say, friend."

He looked at Jeremy, a smile in his eyes. "Where you from,
man?"

"North Carolina."

"Long way from home, aren't you."

Jeremy nodded, said quietly, "A long, long way."

Duncan stuck his head into the room. "Jeremy," he said,
"can I talk to you for a minute?"

Jeremy stood. "Sure do thank you, friend."

"Hey, no problem, man. You just remember what I told you.
There's a lot of kids out there who need an open hand and a
good heart. They don't find somebody who cares enough to reach
out and keep reaching, they're gonna wind up our next generation of homeless."

"Jessica's upstairs getting a couple of things," Duncan said
to Jeremy. "She's agreed to come back with us. It seems that
the shelter's badly overcrowded just now."

"Stacked up like sardines," the young man agreed cheerfully. "Got 'em sleeping on roll-out pallets about as soft as old
linoleum. It's better than having them spend another night out
on the street, though."

"This is Tony," Jeremy said. "He's one of the counselors on
duty."

Duncan nodded toward the young man. "It looks like Arlene
escaped with her, then for some reason decided to turn around
and go with Chico again," he said to Jeremy. "I don't understand
it."

"Don't try to, man," Tony replied from his place at the table.
"Concentrate on the one who maybe wants to come home, and

remember that finding one out of two puts you ahead of the game. Way ahead."

"I've got to bring her back for at least three days of counseling," Duncan said to Jeremy. "And the doctor needs to give her a checkup."

"The counselors try to spot the danger points," Tony explained. "We've got experience looking for the things that come up too often on the streets—drug addiction, abusive situations at home, stuff like that. The doctor's gonna be on the lookout for all the bugs they pick up sleeping rough and living rougher."

"I promised her that I would not try to talk her into going home to her parents, and that I would talk to them on her behalf, try to be a buffer," Duncan said. "That seemed to be the turning point."

"That's real important, man," the young man said. "Got to let her know there's somebody who'll help her take those first steps back into the adult world, keep her protected from whatever drove her onto the street in the first place."

"You mind if I move into your room and take that other bed?" Duncan asked Jeremy.

The hard-eyed woman appeared in the doorway, leading Jessica with a gentle hand on her arm. "Here we are, gentlemen. I'll expect you back at eleven o'clock tomorrow on the dot. If you're not here, rest assured I'll be on the phone to the police."

"I think we can trust this pair," the young man said, smiling at Jeremy. "Something tells me they're on our side."

Jeremy waited for Duncan and Jessica to make for the front door, said to the young black man, "You've given me a lot to think on, friend."

"Just keep in mind, we're the bridge builders," Tony told him. "God calls us to assist our young brothers and sisters to find their way. First we build the bridge, then we put splints on their broken spirits and help them walk across. It's a sacred duty, man. If He's called you to it, He'll give you the strength you need."

Duncan kept up a running commentary directed toward the still, silent girl as Jeremy drove them back to the hotel. He did not appear the least bit fazed as Jessica remained utterly silent, utterly unresponsive to his light chatter.

When they arrived back at the hotel, Duncan announced, "Maybe it would be a good idea if I took Jessica down to the mall, help her pick out a few things, maybe get a bite to eat. Would you like that, Jessica?"

There was a longish pause before the auburn head gave a tiny nod, little more than a shiver.

Jeremy walked up to Duncan, rested a hand on his shoulder and said quietly, "I'm so proud of you I could burst, son."

He turned and walked toward the hotel entrance. It was time to make the call to Washington. Bella was waiting to hear from him. She had impressed upon him how important it was to be in touch just as soon as they knew something for sure.

◆　◆　◆

Wednesday morning Silverwood pulled the fax from Biggs out of his pocket, smoothed it on his desk, studied the names one more time. Yes, a final lunch at the Congressional Club, another happy hour at Bullfeathers, and he would have touched base with all the ones who wavered. He buzzed his secretary, asked Marge, "Could you please have Bobby come in here for a minute?"

The young man with his perpetually surprised expression appeared in the doorway. "Morning, boss."

"For starters you can close the door and come in and sit down."

Silverwood watched undisguised pleasure appear on Bobby's face. These were the times the young man lived for, being in the know on something that remained confidential even from other staffers. He knew that Bobby would later fill Marge in—this was part of what kept the rapport between them alive—and she would no sooner impart this confidential knowledge without his prior consent than tell her own true age. He also knew with a pang of guilt that it had been too long since the last time he had invited Bobby in like that. Months, in fact. As long as he had been working to someone else's dictates, no matter how great the material reward, there had been nothing that truly involved him. Nothing worth sharing.

"Can you keep a secret?" Silverwood asked.

"A secret?" Bobby made round eyes, held his hands to his pen-filled breast pocket. "What else do you think keeps me in this crazy place?"

"You know that two-pager you prepared summarizing HR–97?"

"You mean the Per Se porn thing? Sure."

"I want you to pull a clean copy off the computer for me."

"No problem," he said, clearly confused.

"Then I have a couple of things to be photocopied." Silverwood picked up the document that had so captivated him several evenings before. "I've marked some sections here that I think are the hardest-hitting. I want you to lay them out together and run them off."

Bobby flipped through the pages, his confusion growing. "How many copies do you want?"

"One," Silverwood said softly.

Bobby could not keep his questions silent any longer. "If you don't mind my saying so, I thought you didn't like my summary. Didn't you tell me just last week that you were going to vote the Per Se bill down?"

"Let's just say I had a change of heart."

"Great," Bobby said, pleased and uncertain both. "Who's the copy for?"

"Wait," Silverwood said, handing over a second bulletin. "I found this report from the National Network of Runaway and Youth Services. I want you to join up these sections I marked and run me off a copy of them. We need that five-page statistical summary at the back too."

"Just one copy?"

"I'll only need one," Silverwood replied. "But on second thought, why don't you prepare another fifty and hold on to them. Make sure the sources are marked clearly at the top."

"Right," Bobby said, unasked questions clear in his face. "Anything else?"

"Yes," Silverwood replied. "Can you type?"

"I try to keep that confidential," Bobby replied, a little exasperated over not hearing what he was hoping for. "It'd make me overqualified for my job if it got out."

"Good," Silverwood said. "There's an old Remington portable in that corner cabinet."

"Why not the computer?"

"No, I need to have this done right here, right now, just the two of us. I can't trust those disks and backup systems." Silverwood held up his hand. "I know all about your confidential file drawer. I also know that Charlie broke into it three weeks ago, dug out your love letters, and pasted them up on the cafeteria bulletin board."

Bobby lugged the typewriter over to the coffee table, plugged it in, blew the dust off the keyboard. Silverwood handed him a piece of personal stationery. "To Norman Green-baum, Presidential Chief of Staff, the White House," he began. "Re: S–1422 and HR–97, the Per Se Anti-Pornography Act. Date it tomorrow."

"Let's see." Bobby paused long enough to push his glasses back up his nose. "That's Thursday, October 21."

"You will be interested to know," Silverwood dictated, "that the above-referenced legislation has passed both Houses by a substantial margin. The voting record will be sent to you by courier later this afternoon.

"The legislation is a landmark in the effort to outlaw por-nography by clearly defining its standards through a Per Se ruling. This takes the evaluation of what is obscene away from subjective and inconsistent community standards and into readily measurable nationwide criteria.

"In particular, this legislation will protect the thousands of boys and girls under the age of consent who are currently being drawn into commercial pornography rings.

"I have attached a brief on the legislation prepared by my office, samples of testimony presented at the committee hear-ings, and a statistical summary showing that the problem has reached crisis proportions.

"I do not need to remind you, Norm, about my own past record on Constitutional rights, nor that I have voted against laws limiting pornography in the past. However, I have given this matter a great deal of thought, and am now absolutely convinced that this legislation is not only necessary, but con-sistent with our nation's moral foundations.

"I also wanted to alert you to a very important opportunity for the President as this bill reaches his desk next week. *Sixty Minutes* is in the process of completing a major special program on teenage runaways, prostitution, pornography, and other re-lated family issues. No doubt it will also include footage of the Solemn Assembly that is scheduled to begin tomorrow. It occurs to me that the President's signing of this legislation into law would be an outstanding conclusion to the program, and would certainly put our party out front on family values and common decency. If you agree with my thinking, I do not need to tell you how crucial it is that you act on this immediately.

"This is an unprecedented opportunity for an effective so-lution to what has become a disease eating at the very heart of our nation, destroying one of our most cherished assets—our children. I will be waiting for your call, and stand ready to assist you in any way required."

When the typing stopped Silverwood looked over, found Bobby positively beaming at him. His assistant said, "You don't surprise me very often."

"I surprised even myself on this one," Silverwood confessed.

Bobby cranked the memo out of the typewriter, said, "That's not just a change of policy, sir. It's a complete change of heart."

"You've hit the nail right on the head," Silverwood agreed. "Get me those attachments photocopied, then bring it all back in here and lock it in my safe. I'm going to hand you this envelope at the close of voting tomorrow. I want you to get in a taxi, go straight to the White House, and deliver this into Mr. Greenbaum's hands personally. Then come back here and be prepared to give the press those other hand-outs. And plan to stay late. I think we may be a little busy around here tomorrow afternoon."

Bobby gave his bug-eyed nod. "I didn't think this legislation stood a chance in the House."

"It didn't," Silverwood said, signing the document.

"So what made such a difference?"

Silverwood folded the paper carefully. "A miracle," he replied.

♦   ♦   ♦

Detective Bryan Larson, head of the regular police detail covering Washington D.C.'s Embassy Row, stepped into the captain's office and let himself be waved into a chair. The conversation tying up the captain could only have been about one thing, the same item that had moved from being a locker-room joke to a headline-grabbing nightmare in just three days.

"Yes ma'am, I know the road's gotta stay clear, but whattaya expect me to do? I canceled all leave as of the day before yesterday, got everybody including the janitor and my mother-in-law out walking beats, and I still need another thousand men. No, ma'am, I am *not* pulling your leg. A thousand. Yes ma'am. Now how many can I take off of embassy security?"

The captain twisted his face into a heavily creased grimace. "You got to be kidding. Begging your pardon, ma'am, but how do you expect a terrorist to attack anybody with all this going on? He'd need a battalion of tanks just to get through the streets. Yes ma'am, I know the President is concerned. Tell him he's not alone. No, ma'am, that wasn't meant to be disrespectful. Yes ma'am. The roads'll stay open. Yes, ma'am. Goodbye."

The captain smashed the phone down hard enough to make Larson wince, then stood watching it, one hand rubbing the back of his wiry neck. "That was the mayor."

"I kinda thought it mighta been."

"The mayor is concerned."

"A good word, concerned. Strong. Carries a lotta weight with the heavies."

"The mayor wants us to be sure and keep the main roads clear. All of them."

"Now ain't that a coincidence." Larson shifted in his seat. "I was just thinking about that very same thing this morning over breakfast. 'Geraldine,' I said. That's my wife, by the way. 'Geraldine, you know something? We're gonna have to keep the roads clear, so the President can high-tail it outta town if it turns out these seventy-seven zillion religious freakos we got pouring in decide to turn ugly.' "

The captain did not raise his eyes from the telephone. "I asked the mayor if she knew about the cars that stopped for the night along interstate ninety-five last night."

"Let's see. You mean the ones that lined up all the way from here to Richmond? The ones the TV helicopters made to look like one long line stretched maybe two hundred miles?" Larson eased out his legs, played at nonchalance. "What did our great mayor have to say?"

"She said they were meeting about it this morning."

"Hey, that's good news. Did you ask her about the prayer battalions that've turned the airport into a zoo? Not to mention the bus and train stations."

"They're gonna meet about them, too."

"Well, now. I'm real reassured. I guess I won't have to lose any more sleep about it then, will I."

The captain shook his head. "I asked her if maybe we could call out the National Guard. She asked me how I thought it would look to have pictures taken of our men in uniform shoving their guns into the faces of people carrying nothing but Bibles. Know what I told her? Sane. That's what I said. I told her I thought it would be the sanest thing we could do under the circumstances."

"The mayor musta loved that," Larson said.

"Right. Said it would not be possible to fire me under the current situation, but I could rest assured that I would be up for review after this crisis had passed."

"Crisis? Old Ice-For-Blood called this a crisis?" Larson grinned. "Goodness gracious me, I guess we do have ourselves a little problem then, don't we?"

"They'll be meeting in committees from now 'til doomsday."

" 'Course they will," Larson agreed. "Why should this be different from any other problem?"

The captain looked at him for the first time. "I want you to leave one man on detail max. The rest of your people are taking over regular calls from the Adams-Morgan area, and traffic watch on all the major thoroughfares from the Taft Bridge to the Capitol."

Larson nodded his head slowly. "Kinda figured you didn't want me in here to discuss the weather."

"If we don't watch it, there's gonna be major trouble downtown. No, strike that. We got major trouble already. What there's gonna be is an all-time disaster. You thought the Ruskies nuking the White House was bad? Forget it. We're talking a walking, breathing, right-out-of-your-darkest-night kind of disaster."

"I guess that means I don't call down here for backup if, say for instance, the general population of Adams-Morgan decides it's a good day for a riot."

"Sure, you can call down here. While you're at it, call the mayor too. Try the President, if you've got time. At least they'll probably have somebody on hand to answer the phone. There sure won't be anybody here. We're gonna have the telephone operators down handling barricades. Know where they got permission to hold the first prayer service?"

"Not the Mall."

"Yeah, right there between the Washington Monument and the Lincoln Memorial. What is it, four, maybe five hundred acres, right? The last I heard they figure they're gonna fill the whole thing. Right there in the heart of D.C. Why not just open up the White House gates, let them come in for a barbecue in the Rose Garden?" The captain ran a weary hand down his bald head, went back to rubbing his neck. "For one lousy nickel I'd—"

The office door opened. A fresh-faced black uniformed cop stuck his head in, said, "Captain, you're not gonna believe this."

"Not now, Jones. I got enough unbelievables in here already."

"No, really, Captain. You gotta see this." The man was smiling.

The captain gave him a hard-eyed stare. "I always wondered if a rookie's hide would make a good wall covering."

"Captain, I swear this is for real. Take a look."

Larson gave a tired shrug, extricated himself from the chair, and followed the captain out into the main administration center. He had to look twice to believe what his eyes were telling him. Seated at one end of a cramped and crowded room was Harvey Biggs, Director for Public Policy for the ALUM. If every cop in the nation had a chance to draw up their most-wanted list, Harvey Biggs would be no lower than the five slot. Probably higher.

There had to be a hundred cops standing along the walls, slouched on desks, crammed into every available chair, all of them working hard to keep a straight face.

The stuffy air and rising temperature was not the only thing that was making Harvey Biggs sweat. There wasn't a single cop in the room who hadn't lost an arrest to one of the legal appeals championed by Harvey Biggs and his minions at the ALUM. And here he was, the man himself, a sort of friendly grimace stretching his face out of shape, trying to keep his voice from rising into a whine, pretending the only guy in the room was the public safety officer he had come in to see.

The lieutenant was bent over a standard form, writing at a snail's pace. "Let's see now, sir, what was your name again?"

Ignoring the flurry of coughs that broke out around the room, Harvey smiled tightly, said, "Biggs. Two g's."

"Right. Mr. Biggs. Yeah. And you work with the, lessee, what was that group called?"

"ALUM." Harvey fought to keep his voice level. "The mayor's office suggested I talk to you about rescinding the permits issued for this Assembly thing. It's gotten way out of hand."

The lieutenant kept up his laborious writing, droned, "ALUM wants to rescind their right of free speech." He looked up. "Hey, aren't you the guys always out pushing for everybody's right to say whatever they want?"

"It depends on the circumstances." Harvey Biggs was straining hard to keep it cool, play it down. "I mean, you can't keep order in the nation's capital with who knows how many religious fanatics walking the street. All I'm asking is that you rescind their permits."

The cop leaned back, gave his nose a real hard rub before he came back with, "Yeah, well, Mr. ah, hey, I'm sorry, what was your name again?"

"Biggs."

"Right. Biggs. See, Mr. Biggs, those permits didn't come from us. We just rubber-stamped them according to orders from the mayor's office. And what we hear is the mayor got it from a couple of senators and somebody on the President's staff."

"I've been trying for almost a week to get in to see the mayor, but she's always tied up." Biggs' neck was puffed up like a bull's. "Like I said, I received word from her office this morning that I should come down and speak with you."

"Yeah, I mean, yessir, Mr. Biggs. I understand. The mayor's awful busy right now, I guess."

Harvey Biggs leaned his stout body forward and played at a sincere expression. "So all I'm asking is that you act on behalf of the mayor and rescind permits that should have never been issued in the first place."

"Please," the officer replied.

Harvey Biggs backed up a fraction, caught himself. "What's that?"

"You're asking a favor, right?" The officer kept his face stone-cold sober. "It's polite manners to say please."

Harvey Biggs went through a full minute of internal struggle before coming out with a strangled, "Please."

At that point Larson had to step back into the captain's office, but not before he saw a dozen or so faces turn toward the nearest wall.

From the room outside he heard the officer say, "Well, I'll have to talk with a couple of people about this one, you understand."

"But you'll be back to me today, won't you?"

"Hey, I don't know about today. We're kinda busy right now, sir. But I should be able to see to it before next week."

Harvey Biggs exploded from his chair. "The thing is starting tomorrow!"

The lieutenant leaned back in his chair, let his smile finally show through. "Aw, hey, is that right? Well, whattaya know about that."

When Harvey Biggs had packed his final fireworks away

and stomped from the room, the captain returned to his office wearing the first contented expression Larson had seen since the elections. "Remind me to thank the mayor."

"I was thinking maybe we should all get together, take up a collection, send her a little gift," Larson agreed.

The captain eased himself down in his chair with a happy sigh. "I guess we can handle this thing okay after all."

"Absolutely," Larson agreed. "If that bloodsucker's against it, it's got to be worth the trouble."

◆　◆　◆

The Congressional Club was a beige brick building on the Senate side of Capitol Hill. It was probably once an apartment house for gentlemen-politicians who needed a Washington base. Now it housed offices and function rooms and a Members' Only restaurant. Silverwood jumped from his cab and passed under the long white awning leading up to the club entrance. He had never lost the impression that the awning oversold the place and brought up visions of a fancy wood-lined club far removed from the rather shabby rooms within.

Silverwood didn't much like the place, or its dated blue-on-blue decor. He had come here often when he had first arrived in Washington because it was exclusive, and he had hungered for access to the inner circle. Now that the power was his, he avoided the club unless there was some need to seek out the people who would presumably be there at this time of day.

The clique he sought was seated at a back table. "Hey, John," one of them called, waving him over. "Haven't seen you around much. Grab a chair."

The three men shifted around to make room for Silverwood. He shook hands around the table, pulled over a chair and sat down. He declined their invitation for a drink, told the waiter, "I'll just have a chef's salad and an iced tea."

The three Republican congressmen were all elected to national office in the 1982 elections and had maintained that freshman bonding a decade later. Over lunch their conversation ranged from toxic waste clean-up to the S&L crisis, to the way this Solemn Assembly crowd was already clogging up downtown traffic, to federal funding for the Arts Council, to the cost of dry cleaning at the valet on C Street. Silverwood sat and ate in silence, offering polite smiles at the right places, waiting for the moment to pounce.

It came over coffee. Silverwood toyed with his spoon, leaned forward slightly so as to add a note of confidentiality, said, "I've been in contact with the man upstairs."

The group stopped moving, almost stopped breathing. They knew Silverwood's access to the White House was good. He was a master at obtaining information and sharing choice morsels with a chosen few.

"I can't go into much detail right now," Silverwood said. "I'm sure you'll understand. But we must consolidate our position on an important public policy issue. It's going to come up on the floor tomorrow, and I'll need your support. You will know it when you see it."

They waited. When he said nothing more, the heavier of the three men shifted uneasily in his chair, said, "C'mon John, you're not gonna make us walk into this thing blind."

"I can't go into it now," Silverwood said firmly. "It means a major shift in policy, and the press are watching us like a hawk."

He rose from his chair, said to them, "Be there at first bell."

"How many others know about this?"

"We've had to keep it pretty quiet," Silverwood replied.

"So who's in on it?"

"You are," he said, his eyes a warning. "When our position comes out, there's bound to be some rustling among our colleagues who aren't in the know. I'm going to count on you to give them the nod, let them understand it's all planned, keep them in line."

The trio was silent while Silverwood walked from the room. "Looks to me like somebody's dangling a little carrot in front of us," one of them said.

"My thoughts exactly," said his colleague, the one whose hair had been turned prematurely gray by a hard-fought campaign. "Wonder what goodies are in store."

"No, I don't think that's it. It's no coincidence that all three of us have broken party lines on at least half a dozen occasions in the past three months. I'd say this is a warning."

"Or a way to get back into somebody's good graces." The heavy-set man nodded. "You know the administration doesn't like to stick its neck out. My guess is they've sent John over to do a little lobbying. Then if this thing falls flat on its face, they can distance themselves from the failure."

"What do you think the issue is?"

"What have we got coming up tomorrow?"

It hit them simultaneously. They said in unison, "The porn bill."

"This religious group thing must be gathering steam."

"I heard they're expecting a couple of hundred thousand people here for it."

"You heard wrong." The heavy man ponderously rose from the table. "That many showed up last *night*."

The others stood with him. "So how do we handle this?"

"Seems clear to me. The White House wants the element of surprise on their side. Catch the opposition off guard. The warning still stands, far as I'm concerned. I'm going to handle this with a nod and a wink, just like the man said."

"Sure," a colleague agreed. "Besides, there's no harm in letting the old boy have his way on this one. Even if it does pass, the real action is going to be in the Conference Committee. Anything that really gets the opposition's feathers up can just be plucked out later."

◆   ◆   ◆

"This is Sandra Hastings for WBTV News. Here today with me is Senator Richard Atterly, who in recent weeks has made a name for himself by championing what others have referred to as not one but two lost causes. The first is a bill before Congress that would virtually outlaw all forms of pornography. The second is a call for a Solemn Assembly. Senator, could you please tell us just exactly what is a Solemn Assembly?"

"It is a biblical event, found in the books of Joel and Jonah, among others. It is a nationwide gathering for prayer and repentance."

"This is the first time such a call has gone out in quite some time, I believe."

"That is correct. So far as we know this is the first call for a Solemn Assembly in over two thousand years."

"How would you describe the response thus far?"

"Overwhelming. We have had over three hundred churches and religious organizations offer their support in the past twenty-four hours alone."

"But in terms of people attending, what kinds of numbers are we talking about?"

Senator Atterly showed indecision for the first time, then stated, "It would be impossible to estimate. Absolutely impossible."

"Yet is it true that every hotel room within eighty miles of Washington has been booked?"

"That is what we have been told, yes."

Atterly's phone lines were tied up from dawn to dusk, and Reverend Wilkins was camping out at one of his assistant's desks doing nothing but fielding inquiries. The response had baffled all of them except the reverend. He remained their rock amidst the whirlwind of doubt. The calls had risen to the point that people complained of waiting three *hours* just to have a free line into the senator's office. The number of people and organizations offering assistance and demanding to be a part of this rose from the tens to the hundreds and then the thousands. The clamor threatened to overwhelm them all. But Reverend James Thaddeus Wilkins remained unmoved. He was the first to arrive, the last to leave, the one willing to take on the most menial of tasks—from opening the mail, to handling the three extra phone lines when Atterly's staffers fled elsewhere, to saying it was time to stop and close the doors and pray.

That was his answer to everything. That was the one point he hammered home constantly. This isn't us working here, he said whenever someone took time to look his way. This isn't some *human endeavor*. You can sense it, if you'll just stop for a second and listen to your heart. We're here to do something in God's name, and the only way we can be sure we're doing it right is if we stop and turn it over in prayer.

So they did. And in the midst of watching their little idea of a prayer circle grow into something that none of them had even in their wildest dreams imagined could take place, they learned anew the meaning of awe.

Sandra Hastings asked the senator, "Then where are any additional people supposed to sleep?"

"Many local homes and churches have opened their doors and offered us mattresses and sleeping space. It won't be luxurious, but it should be adequate."

"Are you still seeking further assistance?"

"Urgently. Anyone interested in helping out should contact my office or any local church. We would be most grateful for their help."

"But you are not looking for money, I understand."

"That is correct. We need beds, we need hands to help with the mobile kitchens. We need people to help organize the outside prayer meetings and set up awnings in the case of bad weather. But we do not require funds. Numerous organizations have been . . ." Atterly searched for words, "more than generous."

"And when is this Solemn Assembly scheduled to begin?"

"Tomorrow. We have been granted a permit to hold our first prayer meeting on the Mall at ten A.M."

"The latest police estimate suggests that as many as three hundred thousand people may attend. Do you think this is possible?"

The same strange look passed over Atterly's features. "It is hard to say at this point, but we have reason to think so. Yes."

"Thank you, Senator." The camera focused in more tightly on the attractive young woman's face. "Is this a lone and solitary voice calling for an absurdity in modern times, or have we reached a point where the first Solemn Assembly in two thousand years will become reality? Time will tell. This is Sandra Hastings at the Capitol Building for WBTV News."

♦   ♦   ♦

At five o'clock that afternoon Silverwood entered Bullfeathers, a narrow restaurant with a beautiful mahogany bar down one side and small marble-topped tables arranged in the adjoining room. It was the favorite watering hole for just about everyone on Capitol Hill, from summer interns to crusty old power brokers.

As expected, he found Quinn and Peterson holding court at the bar. He knew from the list Biggs had supplied him that their two swing votes were critical to the bill's passage.

"Good evening, gentlemen," he said, leaning toward the bar.

"John, nice to see you out and about. What'll you have?"

"Saving myself, thanks. Just a Perrier. Can I buy you another round?"

"Watch out, Quinn. The man wants a favor."

Silverwood smiled. "Yes, there is something I want to let you know about. I've gotten word from a higher authority about backing a piece of legislation tomorrow. We've all got to get behind this one. I wanted to let you know it was coming."

"The President asked you to come over and talk to us about

it?" Quinn sipped his drink. "I'm honored."

"No, I wouldn't say that. But I'm certain this is the direction our party must take."

"Right you are," Peterson said. "Which bill?"

"You'll know it when you see it," Silverwood replied.

"Cute," Quinn said. "That's what the Justice, old what's-his-name, said about pornography in that Supreme Court decision. You're talking about the anti-porn bill, aren't you."

"A little discretion, gentlemen. If I don't say it, you can't quote me around the halls. This needs to stay under wraps."

"I don't doubt it," Quinn said, smiling his cynical understanding. "The pack of wolves down at ALUM headquarters would be out in force."

"Tear your leg off in an instant," Peterson agreed.

"Pretty clever," Quinn said. "It ties in with this religious demonstration, doesn't it?"

"It took me forty-five minutes to walk the six blocks from my office in Rayburn," Peterson said. "Never seen such crowds."

Silverwood drained his glass, said thoughtfully, "There are more reasons to push this bill through than you can imagine. See you in the morning, gentlemen. Be there bright and early."

CHAPTER
19

His first term in office, Richard Atterly had witnessed a march on Washington where over a hundred thousand people had been *arrested*. As he stood before this new gathering, one which he had a hand in bringing together, he found himself recalling that earlier time, and comparing the two in his mind.

Back in the early seventies there had been a march on Washington against the Viet Nam War, when America's youth had invaded the capital with a fervor that had terrified the establishment. People had come from all over the country, hitchhiking and traveling in vans and overflowing from busses and cars and trains and planes. They had all converged on the Mall area—the Washington Monument grounds—but there had been so many of them that they spilled over everywhere.

Many of the people were in their late teens or early twenties, but Atterly was surprised at the number of older men and women taking part. Most of the younger men had long hair and headbands, and virtually everyone was in blue jeans. It was almost as though they had all taken on a uniform of blue denim. Many brought sleeping bags, and impromptu bands played from a variety of points throughout the center city. The whole arena was fumigated with marijuana smoke.

Thousands of people were there with a genuine desire to protest the war; thousands *more* were there simply to take part in the capital's latest and greatest craze. It was part protest and part carnival, with many coming simply to express a gen-

eral outrage with an establishment and an established way of
life that had cheated them, abused them, fed them what they
had discovered was little more than hollow lies.

Atterly had spent two solid days walking the crowd, to the
amazement of his colleagues—the majority of whom avoided
the marchers as they would plague victims. He stopped and
chatted to those whose eyes were not totally clouded over from
one drug or another. He found himself barraged by anger and
frustration and genuine *fear* from young men who saw their
only way of avoiding a futile jaunt into the land of death as the
life of a fugitive.

He walked through a forest of protest signs reading *Stop
The War, Dump Nixon, Bring The Boys Home, Give Peace A
Chance.* He was awash in acres and acres of voices calling,
shouting, chanting continually. Most of the slogans contained
curses, all of them carried the fury of young and old who *demanded* to be heard.

Police in riot gear lined the streets, with blue paddy wagons
backing them up. Sporadic incidents of violence broke out regularly, causing ripple effects through the gathering. The police
would be taunted to the breaking point, or would endure the
verbal abuse until impatience caused a protester to throw whatever was handy. Then the trained warriors in blue would un-
leash their own rage and *hurl* themselves at the crowd; the
protestors would shriek and run, causing those behind them to
panic and flee, and the effect would continue on through the
mass of humanity until the reason for the shoving and jostling
and running and screaming was left so far behind that those
being bothered would start pushing back.

The local jails were filled to overflowing long before sundown
on the first day. The party continued on through the night, and
on the following morning the march spilled onto the streets and
the steps of various government buildings. In addition to marijuana, there was now a trace of tear gas in the air. Tension
mounted to the point where police began making massive
sweeps of the streets, arresting tens of thousands, ranging in
age from fourteen to eighty-five, including many secretaries
and civil servants who were trying to make their way back from
lunch breaks. There were no longer jail cells available, so the
police herded those arrested into the fenced training fields of
the Redskins football team. And there they remained until the
demonstration was over, and the majority of people began the
long trek home.

The gathering that Atterly now witnessed could not have been more different.

The crowd was not smaller. If anything, it was much larger. Even from his position on the stage—rented from a company that supplied sound equipment to major outdoor rock concerts, and erected by the shell-like structure of the outdoor Sylvan Theater—he could not see an end to the people. They stretched out across the grassy Mall area, surrounded the Washington Monument, and continued down to where the grounds met Fourteenth Street. And even there they did not stop. That far away, they appeared to be a slowly moving stream of colors that parted only to keep the streets clear.

The police were out in force, but there was nothing for them to do. Nothing at all. It was not that their presence was a cautionary menace; the people simply did not pay them any mind except to nod their greetings or ask directions or stop and pass the time of day. On his way up to the stage Atterly had witnessed the impossible—an on-duty policeman smiling and chatting to a group of gray-haired matrons, while beside him three denim-clad youths argued with his sergeant, who was smiling, too.

As he sat on the stage between the Christian television producer and Reverend Wilkins, Atterly looked out to where the turrets of the Old Smithsonian Building rose like a distant red-brick castle. He listened to the constant hum of voices rising up from below him, searched for some thread, some constant tone or atmosphere that would give him a clue to what it was he faced. The only feeling that rose clearly to his elevated place was one of *anticipation*.

Senator Richard Atterly stood and approached the podium. He said into the microphones, "There will be time—"

He had to stop. His voice boomed out of speakers five times his own height, mammoth stacks that rose like black sentinels to either side of the stage. The sound was so loud it pushed against his chest.

Atterly braced himself and went on. "There will be time to discuss specific issues later on. I wish to begin, however, by welcoming you in the Spirit that has brought us together, in a shared desire to commune as one body in the living Christ.

"The last press reports I heard have estimated our numbers at somewhere over one and a half million. When I first heard this, I was enormously impressed. Now, however, I find myself very grateful and very humbled to be a part of this gathering.

"As you know, our initial focus pertained to anti-pornography legislation that is scheduled for a vote today in the House. As we watched our concept of a prayer group being taken and molded to the Lord's will, we also found our own concerns being extended to include *all* problems that affect our homes, our children, and our families. You know as well as I do that even to try to list these issues would take us through the remainder of our time together. So what I would like to request is that each and every one of you take time several times each day to stop and pray for our families. Pray for God's love and light to shield our families from the myriad of temptations and dangers that surround us daily, pray for the sanctity of our own holy Family of God here and throughout the world. And pray for our children. I ask that you accept this responsibility to pray for us, and for those who have yet to learn to pray for themselves."

Atterly turned and nodded to Reverend Wilkins, who rose and joined Atterly at the podium and led the group in an opening prayer.

When Wilkins had finished and returned to his seat, Atterly went on, "Given the definition of a Solemn Assembly as being a time of prayer and repentance, I feel our next act should be a personal confession, a repentance from here on the stage, a witness to the mercy of our Divine Lord.

"This cannot be something done in theory. It is not enough to discuss it in general terms. Confession has meaning only if it is done from the heart, a personal communion between a believer and His Maker. I will therefore begin with a confession of my own, a realization which emerged over the past few weeks and made clear to me only last night."

He opened his Bible, looked up, said to the gathering, "I will now read from the fifteenth chapter of John, verses one through four:

"I am the true vine, and my Father is the gardener. He cuts off every branch in me that bears no fruit, while every branch that does bear fruit he prunes so that it will be even more fruitful. You are already clean because of the word I have spoken to you. Remain in me, and I will remain in you. No branch can bear fruit by itself; it must remain in the vine. Neither can you bear fruit unless you remain in me."

Senator Atterly continued. "Over the past several weeks, I have seen my political career deteriorate dramatically. Those of you who have spent a lifetime building up a name in your profession will understand when I say that it has caused me a tremendous amount of distress. Yet I have felt the Lord calling me to champion a cause that is viewed by most of my colleagues as suicidal. That cause, as you know, is a law that would virtually outlaw the production, the sale, and the ownership of pornography.

"Within a few days after I spoke on behalf of this bill in the Senate and issued the call for this Solemn Assembly, I became ostracized. Access to information and avenues of political power were shut so tightly, so quickly, that it was almost as though they never had existed. Over and over these past three weeks I have watched political associates, some of whom have been friends for over four decades, draw away from me. I have comforted myself with the thought that in seeking to do the Lord's will I am forcing those around me to choose sides as well. Yet this thought has not always been sufficient to hold back the pain."

The crowd was settling. Blankets were appearing and being laid upon the grass, movements were slowing and gradually stopping completely. A *calm* settled upon the gathering. A *peace*.

"Our society teaches us to assume that anything which causes us pain is bad. We are inundated with advertisements and products and programs who tell us repeatedly that pain must be avoided at all cost. No further judgment on our part is required. All pain is bad. Period. In accepting this idea as fact, however, we open ourselves to the condemnation that if we are experiencing pain, we too are bad. We have done something wrong. We should be ashamed of ourselves and our position. This in turn magnifies our pain to a point where for many people it becomes unbearable.

"I do not advocate the seeking of pain. Such masochistic tendencies are both unhealthy and against God's law. But I do say that sometimes, in God's wondrous grace, we arrive at lessons through pain that could perhaps not be learned by any other means.

"Each of us carries with us blocks against certain lessons, areas of fear or doubt or resistance to change where only something that shakes us hard enough to hurt can teach us. We all require this divine pruning of aspects that do not now and will never bring forth proper fruit. For me, one area of my life where this is true is my professional career."

Senator Atterly pressed fingertips into a forehead creased by concentration, as though seeking to reach inside his head and pull the thoughts out. "I have caught a tiny glimpse of a *different* perspective—a perspective that showed how fleeting life was, how hollow the things of this earth, how empty the goals on which we bestow such importance.

"It now seems to me that much of my life was spent *avoiding* this realization. I sought to fill my life with as much activity as I could, so that the discipline of prayer and private worship would *have* to be set aside. I am now convinced that much of what I had called essential was nothing more than an excuse to maintain a hectic lifestyle, a constant need to assure myself that I was important and my contribution worthwhile.

"This was my own failing, one for which I daily must ask forgiveness. I now see that it is not enough for me to seek to work in His service. I must also discipline myself to take time in the midst of this high-pressure life to restore my soul, and to maintain a daily communion with my Maker and His Word. Indeed, this is the only way I can come to know what God's will truly is for me.

"I urge you, brothers and sisters in our Lord, to reconsider your path. Question it prayerfully, and ask if truly you are placing the Lord your God first and foremost in your life. Do not be afraid. His is not a vindictive Spirit. His mercy and goodness are there to comfort you in taking this awesome step, if such a step is called for in your life. He has promised this in His Word, and I stand before you today as a witness to its truth."

◆　◆　◆

Thursday morning Biggs pushed open the ALUM headquarters entrance, calling out at the top of his lungs, "Valerie, you got that memo for me yet?"

Valerie appeared in the conference room doorway. "Yessir, I left it on your desk yesterday evening, just like I promised."

"C'mon, let's go take a look at it." He bounded up the stairs two at a time. Valerie hurried to keep up.

As they hustled through the second-floor secretarial suite he went on, "Yesterday was one for the books. First I had to go play nice-guy with the cops downtown. What a total waste. They don't understand anything they can't beat with their sticks. Then I got caught up in this Indian thing with Roy, thought maybe it'd take me half an hour. I didn't get home 'til close to two this morning, had to fight through the screwiest traffic you've ever seen in your life."

"The religious assembly thing," his secretary said, holding out a handful of letters and faxes and phone messages. "The papers are full of it."

"Not half as full as the streets. You wouldn't believe the battle I had driving in from Chevy Chase this morning."

"Roy called four times already from BIA," his secretary said. "He says he needs you."

"No lie," Biggs said, sorting through the pile with little jerks of his hands, tossing the majority back on his secretary's desk. "It's incredible how far this BIA thing's gotten out of hand. You know up in Canada, the Indians have started shooting at outsiders over stuff like this. Crazy. Roy's over there pulling out what hair he's got left. We're talking major damage control here."

Biggs walked into his office, shuffled through his in-box and pulled out the memo. "So. What've we got here?"

He scanned page after page of wordy background information as Valerie explained, "Well, there were six amendments to the Senate bill, and they were mostly procedural in nature. No surprises, just like I thought. In fact, all the amendments are just like the language we've already seen in the House bill."

Biggs dropped the memo to his desk. "What are you telling me?"

"It's there on the last page."

He flipped over the pages so hard that the last one tore out from the staple. The page's left-hand side was headed *Senate*; there was a series of provisions beginning with the words, "Delete the following language," "Add the following language," "Rewrite paragraph four to read as follows."

On the page's right-hand side was a column headed *House*. Biggs tensed visibly as he read down the column: "Same. Same. Same. Same. Same. Same."

Biggs glared at Valerie. "Are you trying to tell me that the Senate bill they passed Tuesday now looks *exactly* like the House bill that's up for vote *this morning*?"

"Yessir, that's what it seems to be," Valerie replied cheerfully.

He jammed the memo into his briefcase and headed for the door. "I don't like this. Don't like this one bit."

Valerie raced out of the office behind him. "What's the matter?"

"This never happens. Something's up here." He stopped Valerie's progress with a hand that punched the air between them. "No, you're not coming. I want you over at the BIA. Find Roy. Tell him to drop everything and meet me back here. Don't let him put you off. I want you both here five minutes ago."

By the time Biggs reached the Capitol, raced up the stairs, went through Security, and made his way up to the gallery lining the House of Representatives, he was sweating profusely. The security guard held him at the gallery door for a moment, forcing him to collect himself, quiet his breathing, get himself back under control. The guard then pointed him to an empty spot in the front row. Biggs tripped down the steep stairs and jammed his bulky frame into a too-hard and too-narrow seat.

Below him the House floor was fairly quiet. To his seasoned eye all appeared to be business as usual.

The semicircular rows of banked seats looked like dark wooden college desks from above. They faced the Speaker's forum, an enormous oversized desk placed upon a raised dais with flags to either side and a vast seal directly overhead. To either side of the Speaker were lower desks for his staff. Counting the congressmen who stood in small soft-talking clusters, the chamber appeared to be about three-quarters full—considerably more than a normal working day. Perhaps the Solemn Assembly was having an effect on attendance; the gallery was certainly full to the bursting point.

Speaker of the House Mullins leaned into his microphone and said, "The next order of business for today is the consideration of HR–97, the Omnibus Per Se Legislation Redefining Standards, Enforcement, and Prosecution of Pornography."

Like all Speakers, he intoned the day's business with the enthusiasm of a schoolboy assigned to read the phone book from cover to cover. His voice droned on, "Pursuant to earlier consultations, there is a closed vote on this issue, no amendments will be entertained, debate will be limited to one rebuttal after the sponsor's introductory remarks."

Biggs was on his feet, his fists clenching the banister with a force that threatened to tear the rail from its moorings.

The security guard moved up beside him and forcibly shoved him back down in his seat. The guard took in Biggs' wild-eyed expression and mottled complexion and said, "Excuse me, sir. If there's any disturbance of the proceedings, I'm going to have to ask you to leave."

Biggs barely heard him. His attention remained centered upon the Speaker as he said, "I would now like to recognize the honorable congressman from the state of Arkansas, Mr. Humboldt."

Congressman Humboldt was as much an institution as a representative, elected into office by a mostly agricultural constituency that remained solidly and unswervingly loyal. He was now in his eleventh term, and tended toward florid ties and suits that bulged comfortably around his protruding middle. His voice was perpetually loud, designed for the outdoor events that characterized his campaigning, and sounded uncomfortably stentorian in the chamber's confines.

The congressman moved to the aisle microphone and began. "I am honored to come before you today to urge your aye vote on HR–97, known as the Per Se Anti-Pornography Act."

He slipped on a pair of half-moon glasses, and boomed out his remarks. Biggs only half listened, spending the time in a perpetual scan of the floor for anything out of the ordinary. The only point worth noticing was the series of nods and glances thrown by several swing votes toward John Silverwood. Biggs concentrated on the man, saw him nod back, felt his sense of uneasiness grow without understanding why.

"Thank you, Mr. Speaker," Congressman Humboldt concluded. "I now yield the floor."

"Thank you, Mr. Humboldt," Speaker Mullins replied. "I would now like to recognize the honorable congressman from the state of North Carolina, Mr. Silverwood."

Silverwood approached the microphone, scanned the room, took a deep breath, and began. "Thank you, Mr. Speaker, fellow colleagues, ladies and gentlemen.

"My record against any legislation that might impinge upon Constitutional rights, however broadly defined, is well known to you. Indeed, when it comes to the First Amendment, I have advocated a more liberal position than most liberals. I stand before you today to tell you I was wrong."

Heads that had been bent in quiet conversation raised and turned his way. There was a stir around the gallery, and a short man at the edge of Silverwood's vision shot to his feet; the guard was swiftly by his side, and forcibly lowered him to his seat. There was a muffled shout from the man before the guard and the crowd hissed him to silence.

"I was wrong," Silverwood repeated. "And it troubles me deeply to realize there are victims out there who might have been spared the agony of sexual exploitation had I not blocked efforts to protect them."

All eyes in the House were fixed on him. A few congressmen nudged their nearby colleagues, shared astonished looks. The Speaker glanced to one side, signaled with a furious gesture for a staff-member to come and explain what on earth was going on; he received a monumental shrug of noncomprehension in reply.

"We cannot eliminate the evil in man's nature," Silverwood went on. "But we *must* restrain it. We must no longer allow the perpetrators of pornography to hide behind our Constitution and our Bill of Rights. It is not freedom of speech that motivates the pornographer, but rather depravity, greed, and lust.

"We must take a careful look at the testimony of those whose lives have been twisted and deformed by this trade in flesh, and ask ourselves about *their* rights. We must change our reflexive response of turning away from those who suffer degradation and violence as a result of this industry, and understand that here are people who truly need our help.

"The crux of the problem is that existing anti-pornography laws are insufficient, and their interpretation is inconsistent. Pornography flourishes due to underinvestigation, underprosecution, and undersentencing. A Per Se approach to defining hard-core pornography will help the criminal justice system attack this problem more effectively.

"One of the greatest champions of rights in our time, Martin Luther King, Jr., remarked, 'Judicial decrees may not change the heart, but they can restrain the heartless.'" Silverwood paused to sweep the chamber with his gaze, then concluded, "We must act to restrain the heartless. I urge you to pass HR–97, the Per Se Anti-Pornography Act, without any further delay."

The room erupted at the conclusion of Silverwood's remarks. A hundred voices called out at once; the gallery was filled with the clamor of people normally in the know being caught totally unawares.

The Speaker hammered the gavel for silence, then when order was finally restored seemed unable to remember why he had insisted on it. "Er, thank you, Mr. Silverwood. Your remarks were most interesting. The matter will now proceed to a vote."

Silverwood returned to his seat, his head swimming, his heart throbbing loudly in his ears. All the formalities, the announcements, the bells, the voting, swirled around him as though in a dream.

An hour later the final gavel sounded, and the Speaker of the House intoned, "HR-97, the Omnibus Per Se Legislation Redefining Standards, Enforcement, and Prosecution of Pornography, has passed by a vote of 167 to 112."

Silverwood jumped up. He strode toward the Members' Private Lobby. Bobby was straining to see through the little window cut in the doors, remaining poised like a relay runner awaiting the hand-off of the baton.

Silverwood pulled a manila envelope from his briefcase. "Straight to the White House with this one," he said.

"Yes, sir!" Bobby turned on his heels and ran down the marble corridor, clutching the envelope to his chest.

Voices called out to Silverwood as he made his way through the lobby. He rounded the corner into the main hallway, almost collided with a swarm of newspaper reporters surging forward and clamoring for attention. He made a short statement, answered a few questions, invited them to meet back in his office for further information in fifteen minutes. As he separated himself and proceeded down the hallway, Silverwood permitted himself the luxury of a satisfied smile.

◆　◆　◆

Duncan found Jeremy downstairs in the hotel lobby, talking to a wide-eyed Mavis Talmadge. "You think maybe you could relieve me for a while?"

"Sure thing." Jeremy stood up. "Sounds like you've talked yourself hoarse, son."

"Something the counselor said this morning really shook Jessica up," Duncan replied. "Or maybe it's all just coming together. She doesn't talk enough for me to be sure. Anyway, I don't want to leave her alone just now."

"We're all praying for you," Mavis said, her voice quietly insistent.

Duncan thanked her solemnly, said to Jeremy, "I can't explain it, but I get the feeling we're reaching some kind of crisis point here."

Jeremy patted his friend's drooping shoulder. "You go out there and recharge, son. I'll be just fine."

Jeremy found Jessica upstairs in bed, her body curled up and wrapped with her frail-looking arms. Jeremy stalled in the doorway, overwhelmed by the sorrow that pervaded the little form.

He willed himself forward, sat down in the chair still warm from Duncan's presence, said the first thing that came to his mind. "I asked my friend if I might come up and sit with you a little while. Is that all right with you?"

The auburn hair was strewn in a circular sweep that totally covered her face. There was no movement, no sound, no sign that she had even heard. Jeremy resisted the urge to reach out, stroke her hair, touch her arm, show that there was somebody who cared. He had seen enough to know that such a move would be viewed as something totally different than what he meant.

Then a tiny voice, a whisper of sound without strength or emotion, said from beneath the veil of hair, "My life is over."

"Daughter, life ain't over 'til the good Lord says so," Jeremy replied, immensely glad that she had acknowledged his presence this much. "And not even then if you've accepted Him into your heart."

"You don't understand. Nobody does."

"Maybe not. There's a lot about this poor old world I can't understand, and that's a fact." Jeremy kept his tone calmly conversational. "There was once a woman here on this earth I loved more than life itself. She's dead now, God rest her soul, passed on almost twelve years back. She was a lot wiser 'bout a lotta things than me, and times like this I find myself wishin' she was still around to tell me what to say and do."

He slid his long legs out in front of him, paid no mind to Jessica's buried face. "Back before I got to know her well, I was still too shy and too all-fired awkward inside my own skin to tell her how much I loved the little girl in her. But I sure 'nough did. She had this way of laughin', made me think of a five-year-old runnin' through a field of wildflowers under a bright summer sun. So what I did was, I told her how lookin' at her made me wish more grown-ups knew how to cherish the child they used to be. That's when she told me this story, and I want you to know I've never told it to a single solitary soul in the forty-some years since she shared it with me. Always felt like this was her very first way of showin' that she might come to love me, and something that special I decided I could treasure best by keepin' close inside. But I'm sure she'd want me to tell you this, and I'd bet if she could she'd be tellin' it to you herself."

Jeremy saw no change in the tight little form, but he was pretty sure she was listening. "Ella—that's her name, short for Elizabeth—he began, "had a daddy who was a real power back in the town where we came from. When he walked down the street, people'd step aside right smart. The men'd all doff their hats and stare at the sidewalk and kinda mumble something 'bout the morning or the weather or the crops, knowin' all the while that old man Turner wasn't gonna say nothin' back. He never did. Old man Turner was 'bout as quiet as quiet can be, with eyes hard as those black marbles we used to call grannies and not much more alive.

"Seemed like the only time Ella's daddy ever spoke at home was to order her momma around. Had this voice, sounded like some machine talkin', no more feelin' to it than this chair I'm sitting on. Ella's momma was 'bout what you'd expect, gray and used up as an old cleanin' dish-rag. All the life and all the joy'd been wrung outta her long ago. Old man Turner was that way. He took what he wanted and didn't pay much mind to the rest.

"Now you gotta understand, Ella's daddy wasn't a evil man, not even bad in the way you might think. He didn't beat nobody, not so you'd be able to look and say, right here, yessir, this man's been hittin' on a defenseless woman. Nope. It wasn't in his nature to beat with his fists, if you catch my meanin'. He did it with his mind instead, just walloping that woman with his tongue and his words and his brain 'til the light of hope just plain died out. Ella didn't need nobody to tell her that's how it was. All she had to do was look her momma's way to see what it was like to live without hope.

"For her thirteenth birthday Ella's daddy gave her a job. He called it teachin' her the work ethic, but she knew the other side to the gift, and it scared her worse than anything she'd come up against in her short life. Her daddy sent her down to milltown, I guess you never heard that name before, have you? 'Course not.

"Back when I was your age, see, most Carolina cities had themselves a milltown, which was sort of a village inside a village. They were row upon row of cheap little houses that kept threatenin' to fall in a soft breeze, on account of being mostly cardboard and peelin' paint held up with spit and tacks and a lotta prayers. These mill houses circled a big textile mill, and were put up for the workers who let themselves get swallowed up every day so's they'd have something to put on the tables for their babies that night.

"Didn't matter which Carolina city you called home, if you told somebody you lived in milltown you didn't need to say nothin' more. Everybody already knew all there was to know.

"Ella's daddy's bank was part owner of the mill in our town, and it was a mean-spirited place. I can still remember my momma tellin' me when I outgrew whippin' size that if I wasn't good she was gonna send me off to milltown, and boy, lemme tell you, that always straightened me up right quick. I had to walk by there on my way to school, and it always seemed like that ol' place sucked the light right outta the sky.

"It was brick and probably was red once upon a time, but what with all them years of soot and sweat all you could say about it was that it was big. So big it cast a shadow three streets away, with smokestacks that stretched right up to the low-lyin' clouds, or so it seemed to a scared little thirteen-year-old girl named Ella.

"Ella got stuck in what was called the weavin' room, and lemme tell you right here, right now, you ain't never known what noise is 'til you've stood inside a room with seven hundred weavin' machines goin' full tilt. They got these little blades holdin' the threads, see, and they shoot back and forth through these machines like bullets, and every time they pass through there's this sound like a metal fist comin' down, *WHAM*. That was the sound made by this long blade that pressed the thread up tight to the cloth it was weavin'.

"Mind you, that was just one machine. What you gotta do if you wanna understand what was facin' my little darlin' is multiply that by seven hundred times. And then add on the fact that it was over a hundred degrees inside that room, and the ventilation in that place was just plain awful, and dust was everywhere. Dust so thick it clogged up your throat, coated the inside of your mouth, stuck to your skin like a second set of clothes."

Jeremy didn't notice the swipe he gave his eyes, he was so busy remembering. "By the end of that first day Ella was so tired she could hardly stand to make her way outside, and she was more scared than she was tired. She knew if she stayed there all the summer long like her daddy wanted to, why, come autumn she was gonna be washed out just as gray as her momma.

"As she was stumblin' outside she felt an arm go 'round her shoulders and a warm voice say, 'Child, you look just about as tired as I feel.' "

Gradually, no more than an inch at a time, Jessica swung up and around until she was able to watch Jeremy with both of her quiet eyes. Jeremy paused in his story long enough to greet her with the silence of shared sorrow. She did not flinch under his gaze, not this time. Her eyes were encircled by a shadow that came from more than sleeplessness, her stillness a result of more than just fatigue. He sat, looked at her with the aching vulnerability that came through sharing secret hurts, and hoped to God that he was doing the right thing.

"Ella looked up into those eyes," he went on. "And right then and there realized that this woman was *alive*. I don't mean her heart was beatin' and her lungs breathin', nossir, that ain't livin', not in my book anyway. That woman had a light in her eyes that just poured out, bathin' Ella with something so strong the fear she was carryin' just up and disappeared. And what was more, that woman seemed to understand right off the bat what Ella was goin' through.

" 'My name's Rose,' she said, and kinda steered Ella away from the other tired gray women filin' outta the factory. 'You got a moment, there's something I'd like to show you.'

"Far as Ella was concerned, that woman coulda dragged her off to the ends of the earth, long as she showed her what it was that lit up her face like that. So she let her tired feet walk her off the main road and down this little dirt track that led 'round back of the factory and out into some fields where the next row of milltown houses were gonna go.

"Then right there, not two hundred yards farther down that little lane, the whole world just up and changed. Birds were singin' and there was the sweet smell of risin' summer pine sap and bloomin' flowers. 'Stead of the bangin' of those machines she heard cricket song—you prob'ly know the one, kinda hums this long note invitin' you to lay down wherever you are and just drift away.

"Rose took her out behind this stand of young trees to where a little stream meandered through some big boulders and poured itself into a sorta basin carved from the rocks. The sun was flickerin' in and outta the pine boughs overhead, and there was this breath of breeze that made the trees whisper secrets back and forth. She sat Ella down beside the little pool, and said, 'Now why don't you just tell me all about it.'

"So she did, right there, right then. Told her about her momma and her daddy and her birthday present and her fears and everything. Just let it pour out, sittin' there in the peace of that little place, knowin' without needin' to think it out that here was a woman who knew what it meant to listen from the heart.

"Rose heard her out in silence, waited when she stopped 'til she was sure that every last word had been let loose. Then she waited some more, long enough for Ella to wonder if she was maybe upset with something Ella had said. But when my little darlin' looked in the woman's face, all she saw was this woman waitin' for something. Ella didn't know what, but she felt like here was somebody she could trust, so she sat in silence and waited too.

"All of a sudden she found her self noticin' things she hadn't seen before. She watched how the water sparkled under the sunlight, saw it shift and change with the flickerin' light, one moment dark and mysterious, the next lookin' like it was molten gold. She started hearin' the stream's chucklin' little melody, a song that was always changin' and always the same. She heard how all the voices of this green world kinda melted into one bigger voice, singin' something that was never meant for her mind to understand, hummin' a tune of pure comfort to her scared little heart.

" 'This is my little chapel,' Rose finally said. 'When the day's done I come down here to find my Lord again. I got three little ones and a sick man at home, and they all need me. Need more than I got to give in the best of times, and after a day in the mill I don't have enough for even one of them. That's why I come down here, to find my Lord Jesus and let Him fill my heart. 'Cause I know when I am weak, He is gonna be there and be strong for me.'

"Rose turned towards her then, and with eyes that spoke straight to my Ella's heart she said, 'I never brought anybody here before. But the Lord said to me this day, there was another who needed what I'd found. Guide me, Father, I said, and He did. Straight to you. So now I'm gonna tell you a secret, sister. I'm not an educated woman, can't hardly read nor write. But there's a few truths that've come to me one way or the other, and I hold on to 'em just as tight as I can, 'cause I know they've been given to me by the good Lord to see me through to the other side.'

" 'Sister, there's a little child that lives inside you, right in the center of your heart. And the world is gonna try and kill off that child. It's a sad thing, saddest story on earth near 'bout, but it's true. The world is gonna find the best way it can to make you give up on that little child and let it go. You hear what I'm sayin'?'

" 'I hear,' Ella replied, and she sure 'nough did. She knew she'd be able to stand some big hard blow, but to have to stand up to a whole set of blows, comin' on her each and every day like it would in the mill, why, it was gonna kill something precious inside her.

" 'Long as you try to make it on your own,' Rose went on, 'You're lost. Hear what I'm sayin', sister. It ain't just the child's that's gone. It's your way home. Gotta be like a little child to make it to heaven. Gotta know the Master with the trustin' joy of that little child He placed in your heart. You try and stand up to the world alone, and you close the eyes of the child in your heart. You're gonna start thinkin' the only way to make it is with a heart hard as stone, cold and unfeelin', protected from bein' hurt by not carin' much for anything at all.

" 'There's only one way to keep that little child alive and happy, and that's to feed it on the love of the Lord above. Recognize that you can't make it alone, and turn to the One who's there waitin' to help you find a hope that won't ever let you down.'

" 'This is real important,' Ella said to her, feelin' real hope for the first time in a long, long while.

" 'Ain't nothin' more important in the whole wide world,' Rose told her. 'Gotta do like the old song says. Build your world on things eternal, and hold on to God's unchangin' hand.'

"So Ella started goin' down there every day, and 'fore much longer started seein' as how maybe she was not only gonna survive this hateful time, but somehow come outta there a better person. And once she'd worked out that she didn't need to fear so much for herself, see, she was able to look around her and start understandin' other people better.

"What those folks had to realize, Ella decided, was that the child wasn't ever really dead. Nossir. It *can't* die, much as Satan'd like to see it otherwise, 'cause God made it to live *forever*. All that child is, you see, is asleep. And the way we wake that little blessed child up is to go to the Lord in prayer. Yessir. Just turn it over to the Lord and ask Him to wake up that little child in our hearts the only way it can be woken up. And you know how that happens? Well, I'll tell you that too. With love, daughter. It's the only way. And no matter what the world tries to tell you otherwise, there ain't no braver man or woman on earth than the one who's able to love in the face of what the world throws at us. Nossir. That takes *courage*. But you see, once we've been truly cleansed by the blessed Father, once we've stood in His presence and asked His forgiveness and learned to trust in His guidance, why, we *want* to have that little child awake in our hearts again. We *want* to laugh and run and love with the wonder that the Lord planted in each of our hearts."

Jeremy leaned back in his chair, said, "That's what my darlin' Ella told me, and that's what I'm tellin' you. In this dark hour, honey, you've got to hold on to knowin' just how important that little child inside you really is."

CHAPTER
20

Voices continued to bubble from all corners of the House chamber long after Congressman Silverwood's departure. The Speaker pounded his gavel repeatedly, calling for order. Congressmen scrambled to talk with associates, confirm the events, find out if they were the only ones who had not been in the know.

Biggs remained glued to his seat in the gallery, kneading his hands on the railing, working to regain control. His eyes were fixed blankly on Silverwood's empty seat. It was not just that the bill had passed and been steered around the need for a conference committee; he had been duped, and his own weapons turned against him. Scenarios of revenge alternated with frantic worries over how to stop the damage. He needed to check why the vote went this way; no, he had to call his buddy at Justice and ask what they'd been up to over there; no, he needed to discredit this position; no, it was too late for that, he had to go for sabotage. That was it, he decided, rising to his feet. He had to lay a mine in that turncoat's path.

He resisted the urge to go storming into Silverwood's office. The press would be crawling all over that place, and it was not time for a public scene. Not as a loser. Harvey Biggs had made it this far by being the invisible man whenever events did not work his way, never being visible as a loser, never being available unless he was in the winner's circle and had something to crow about. Now was the time for working from the gutters, down where nobody in the press could spot him. There would be time for a public match with Silverwood, but only after the man had been firmly planted in the dust.

Almost an hour later Biggs walked down the halls of the Longworth building toward Silverwood's office. He passed two reporters, but luckily they were scribbling in their notebooks and scurrying toward the elevators to go file their stories and did not notice him. As Biggs approached the doorway, he saw Silverwood calm, poised, handing documents to the last reporter, urging him to read the background information.

When the reporter had departed, Biggs stepped forward aggressively, said, "Mind if I come in?"

"Not at all," Silverwood replied, and waved a hand toward his own office. "Why don't we step back here."

The man's calmness was a jarring note. There was something going on here. The man had been expecting him. Silverwood could only be so easy-going if he had some secret weapon up his sleeve, some unseen power that he thought would keep him protected.

Biggs sat down, leaned as far forward as he could and still stay in the chair. He held his anger in check by clenching the edge of the desk, asked in as casual a tone as he could muster, "What do you think you're up to?"

"Politics is a dirty business," Silverwood replied. "I've wallowed in the trough for too long."

"What do you think this is, a philosophy lesson? Listen, buddy, this betrayal takes the prize. I don't know who's got you on the take, but I can tell you one thing. You're not gonna get away with it."

"I don't expect to," Silverwood replied calmly.

Biggs rode over him. "You think you've got everything figured out, don't you?"

"I can barely see one step ahead," Silverwood told him. "But I feel like I've finally found the right path. For the first time in my life."

"Yeah, well, enjoy it while you can. There's gonna be a rude awakening, Congressman. First we're gonna pull some strings in the White House, get the President to veto this piece of work you cooked up. I could even write the President's veto message myself." Biggs raised one hand and ran it in a sideways motion, as though tracing words off an unseen newsprint. "While I commend Congress for approaching the issue of pornography, I am deeply disturbed that they would do so in such an over-reaching manner. This is clearly inconsistent with our nation's Bill of Rights. I urge Congress to reconsider this matter in the next session, and develop legislation that can pass Constitutional muster."

He dropped his hand. "Once that's done, we're gonna come after you."

"You know where to find me," Silverwood replied.

Biggs stared at him. "What, you think this is just hot air?"

"No," Silverwood said, shaking his head slowly. "I am fully aware of just how low you people can sink."

"Not yet you aren't." Biggs bounded to his feet and started for the door, saying over his shoulder, "But believe me you will be. Wait 'til our mutual friends hear about this one. They're gonna use your hide for shoe leather."

Biggs returned to his office through some of the worst crowds he had ever seen in Washington. Through the fog of frustrated rage he took brief notice of them, wondered at how he could not classify the atmosphere. There was none of the habitual party free-for-all air of a standard protest, none of the insane fervor of a political convention, no badges or banners or buttons declaring their affiliation. But there were smiles everywhere. People stopped and chatted and shook hands and consulted what unbelievably looked like *Bibles.* Harvey leaned over a trio of shoulders to get a better look, then walked on shaking his head in bewilderment.

He passed a gathering of several dozen men and women, young and old, sitting and kneeling and standing together with eyes closed in a sort of ragged circle on the grass. It was the strangest thing he had ever seen in a city that thrived on politically inspired weirdness.

He arrived back at his office and asked his secretary, "Is Roy back?"

"No, Valerie called to say they were in closed session and she couldn't even pass him a note, but that she was camped out at the doors."

"I want to see them as soon as they get in." He entered his office and started calling Congressman Quinn, one of the swing votes and a man with whom he had a long-standing rapport. On the tenth try he was finally put through. "Afternoon, Congressman. Appreciate you taking my call."

"No problem, Harv. Sorry I wasn't available before." Quinn covered the mouthpiece long enough to mutter something at another person in his office. "Where were we? Oh yeah. Hey, looks like you guys took a beating this morning."

"Right." Biggs made an effort to keep his tone easy, although the hand holding the phone was squeezed a bloodless white. "I was wondering if you could tell me what happened down there. I thought we had you in our corner on this one."

"Well," the man's voice gave an unseen shrug. "We got the word on how the vote should go, and that's the way the vote went."

"What word? From Silverwood? Since when does Silverwood have the word?"

"I wondered about that, too. But you know how it is, they probably decided to hand the high-flier a plum. Anyway, he tipped us off earlier this week that the administration was going to go a different way on this."

"He told you that?" Biggs stood, ramming his chair against the back wall. "What administration? C'mon, you know I've got my ear to the ground on this stuff. He told you the White House was behind this?"

"In so many words. He said he had word from a higher authority. Must say, though, his performance today sure surprised a lot of us."

Biggs picked up the phone and began pacing. "Yeah, well, the surprises aren't over yet."

"That's politics," Quinn replied, not understanding. "You never know what's going to happen next." He dropped his voice. "Listen, Harv, I've got some people coming in the door, you know, from this Assembly thing. It feels like half my constituency has shown up all at once. Why don't you give me a call next week when they're out of town, let's get together, okay?"

Biggs hung up the phone and shouted for his secretary. When she arrived in the doorway he asked, "Do you have the voting results yet?"

"The messenger just dropped them off. House or Senate?"

"House, House, House," he barked. "Doesn't anyone understand anything around here?"

"At what we get paid," she said in her eternally flat voice as she left the room, "thinking would be overtime."

When she brought it in he looked down the long column of aye votes, wincing at some of the names he found there. All of his marginal congressmen had gone for it. All of them. There were a number of other surprises. He slammed the paper down, then remembered the scorecard he had faxed to Silverwood. He slapped his hand to his forehead, moaning a curse.

"I gave him a blueprint!" Biggs shouted.

His secretary appeared in the doorway. "You call?"

"No, no." He picked up the phone, chose another name at random from the list, drummed his fingers impatiently until the connection was made.

He had time for three more calls before his secretary reappeared. "They're back."

"It's about time. Get 'em both in here."

Ray and Valerie gathered in his office, and Biggs sketched the situation in short bursts. "We went down in flames. Silverwood did a major end-run. I'm looking at this voting record, and there's no question. None. He pulled all kinds of votes on his side that didn't belong there. How? I'll tell you how. He claimed he was talking to all the swing votes for a higher authority."

"You're kidding," Roy moaned.

"I know it for a fact. A higher authority, those were his words. I've heard it from three different congressmen he put the arm-twist to."

"Did they tell him to?" Roy asked. "The White House, I mean."

"Of course not," Biggs snapped. "You think the White House could make a shift like this without us catching wind of it?"

"Now that you mention it," Roy said, "there might have been something fishy about those Senate amendments. How do you figure they got the exact same wordings as the ones on the House side?"

"That's right." Biggs slammed an open palm down on his desk. "That guy's lied to both Houses. Greenbaum's gonna hit the roof."

"The President hates that stuff," Roy agreed. "We just might have a chance there."

"More than a chance," Biggs replied. "We're gonna blow this sucker out of the sky."

"Right," Valerie said, determined to be heard. "We're really going to have to lobby that conference committee hard."

"Conference committee?" Biggs face reddened. "You know what? I'm gonna send you back to civics class. There isn't any conference committee. The Senate's passed a bill; now the

House's passed the *exact same bill*. What's the committee supposed to confer on, menu selections at the cafeteria? The color
of ink the President's gonna use to sign it into law? This sucker's gonna go straight to the President's desk."

"Unless we stop it," Roy said, smoothing Biggs with his
voice. "This end-run thing gets his blood boiling more than just
about anything else there is. He might just be angry enough to
shoot this one down. We'll need a strong case, though."

"Right. I want you to put all this stuff down in a neat little
package," Biggs told both of them. "Something that'll look good
sitting on the President's desk. Put it in one of those leather
portfolios, stick some of our best arguments on this porn issue
in there as a kind of appendix. I'm going to see Norm Greenbaum before he goes home today and lay the whole thing out."
Biggs started pacing again. "I want this thing dead and nailed
to the door before sundown."

◆　　◆　　◆

If Reverend Wilkins felt any nervousness over facing such
a massive audience, he did not show it. He stood at the stage's
podium and gave the congregation his habitual frown, ignoring
the screen to his right that blew up his features to a visage over
twenty feet high. "There's some of us here today that're lookin'
for somebody to stand up in front of 'em and *shine*. Lookin' for
somebody else to do the work, wantin' to sit there and get all
fired up, hopin' to get something for nothing. Yeah. Then they'll
trot back home and say, yes, Lord, I was *there*. I felt the Spirit
move. But lemme tell you something, brothers and sisters—
anybody who gets comfortable out there listenin' to others
stand before 'em spoutin' out the nice things is gonna go home
a *failure*."

Reverend Wilkins squinted and peered forth, as though
granted some special vision with which he could search out the
lazy, haul them to their feet, get them moving in the right
direction by strength of will alone. "We're not gathered here to
be preached over. Nossir. We're here to confess and repent. Confess our failings and make that great turnin' in our lives Y'all
hear what I'm sayin'? This ain't no time to sit back and be
preached to. All we're doin' up here, mornings and middays and
evenings, is remindin' you of why we're all here. Help point out
the way. Maybe give you something to think on when you're

searchin' out what needs seein' to.

"Y'all better listen to what I'm sayin', now. If you turn away from turnin' within, the biggest loser is the one you'll be carryin' home with you. All these talks and seminars and discussion groups organized 'round town, why, they're just fine, long as you remember the most important work to be done here today is the work you've gotta do *alone with your Lord.*"

He paused for a moment to be sure that the message had struck home, and was answered with a silence so palpable that the air itself seemed to hold its breath. The distant traffic rumbled in a continual comforting hum that only accented the stillness. Reverend Wilkins then opened his Bible and drew out his half-moon reading glasses. "Our midday reading comes from the first chapter of Haggai, verses three through eight:

> "Then the word of the Lord came through the prophet Haggai: 'Is it a time for you yourselves to be living in your paneled houses, while this house remains a ruin?'
>
> "Now this is what the Lord Almighty says: 'Give careful thought to your ways. You have planted much but have harvested little. You eat, but never have enough. You drink, but never have your fill. You put on clothes, but are not warm. You earn wages, only to put them in a purse with holes in it.'
>
> "This is what the Lord Almighty says: 'Give careful thought to your ways. Go up into the mountains and bring down timber and build the house, so that I may take pleasure in it and be honored.'

"I hear that call," Reverend Wilkins told the massed audience. "I heard it deep down in my spirit. I feel the nation's need, just like I see the need in the eyes of my brothers and sisters.

"What holds us from doin' as the good Lord commands? Impurities, that's what. You can take all them problems, all them doubts and fears and wrong deeds and lump 'em all together under this one name. Things we do or think that're barriers between us and God. Debauchery. Doin' things to excess. Idolatry. Look at what Haggai says about that. Look and listen with your hearts. He don't talk about something that fits a people dead over two thousand years. Naw. He's talkin' about *us*. You and me. This nation, here and now. Look at what he says. We've placed our own well-bein' in a higher place than the call of our Lord."

His voice boomed out with a magnitude that shook more than the physical bodies massed beneath the stage. "Just think on that, now. Just think on that, and decide which one of us here today needs to turn to our dear heavenly Father and say, 'Forgive me for bein' weak-willed and self-centered, Lord. Forgive me, give me the strength to go out of here a better man. A stronger man. Able to carry your message of love to the world and make it *live*.'

"If we're gonna love in Christ's name, now, we're gonna love no matter who a person is, what they think, how they look or what they can do for us. Love is more than a feeling. Love is an *action*. Love is a *choice*.

"Now I want all of you brothers and sisters to take this time and search your hearts and find out for yourselves what burdens you're carryin', what darknesses you're hidin' within, what desires you've got on that pedestal of idolatry set up there in the spotlight that oughtta be reserved for your Lord alone. I want you to search out what parts of your lives and minds and hearts still haven't known His healin' touch. And I want you to join with me in confessin' these parts of your lives and minds and hearts to Him, to turn them over and know what it means to be *cleansed*. Yessir. Purified with the only light that shines with love, the only love that heals all wounds, the only healing that is eternal. Amen."

◆　　◆　　◆

"John!" Atterly's voice over the phone carried tremendous joy. "I've been trying to reach you for hours. I can't tell you how excited we all are about what happened."

"Thank you," Silverwood said. "I was just voting my conscience, Richard."

"Voting your conscience. What a beautiful way to put it," Atterly said. "What a wonderful direction for our nation's politics to take in the future."

"Without me, I'm afraid," Silverwood said, facing up to the pain that had shadowed his movements all week. "I'm through."

"I can't tell you how sorry I am to hear that," Atterly said. "Are you sure?"

Silverwood recounted Biggs' threat. "I know I'm done for. I had to accept it before making this step. But I'd hate to see him kill the bill as well. He made it sound like it was a done deal.

I'm afraid it would take a miracle to get the President to sign this legislation."

Atterly became very grave. "It so happens I've been given a little information that up to now I had hoped I would not need to use. But it looks like the Lord's hand is at work here as well."

"I wish I could be as sure as that as you sound."

"Listen to me, John. There has been divine intervention here, a greater hand than ours at work. You know as well as I do that this bill didn't stand a chance of getting anywhere near this far. Our primary task here is to seek His will and do it."

"Well, you've at least succeeded in lifting my spirits," John said.

"Glad I could do that much. Say, an idea's just come to me. The main thrust of this Assembly is personal growth and prayerful introspection, but we have a brief gathering every morning, mid-day, and early evening. I want you to come address it tomorrow."

"I'm not sure enough of my own path to share it with others just yet."

Atterly would not let go so easily. "You've just championed a cause in His name before the entire nation; how public can you get? These people have gathered from all over the country, John, drawn here in part because of this very issue. Now I want you to drop what you're doing and come on over to my office. We'll grab a bite to eat together and talk a little about what you might say. Then I want to introduce you to some of the people that have put our gathering together. There are a few others here who'd like to shake your hand."

Atterly put down his phone and looked up to where Nak was standing in the doorway. "It looks like we're going to have to use Bella's information after all."

"I heard."

He sighed and shook his head. "This pains me no end, I don't have to tell you."

Nak nodded his understanding. "Perhaps it'd be clearer to you after prayer."

Harvey Biggs finally paid off the taxi and got out to walk. The crowds around the White House spilled in undulating waves over the curbs and into the streets. The lanes were jammed with slowly crawling out-of-state cars packed to the gills with waving, shouting, singing people. People everywhere.

Harvey felt as if he were swimming upstream as he struggled forward, the leather portfolio for Presidential Chief-of-Staff Norman Greenbaum clasped grimly under one arm.

The closer he came to the White House, the worse the crowds became. He finally did what no Washingtonian in his right mind would have attempted in normal times; he stepped off the curb and out into the first lane of traffic. The traffic was moving so slowly that he continued to pass cars. He glanced at his watch and moaned an oath; Greenbaum had only reluctantly agreed to see him, and only for ten minutes between two very important international visitors. Who could have imagined that it would take him over three-quarters of an hour to get from his office to the White House?

By the time he crossed Fourteenth Street and entered the little cul-de-sac called Executive Boulevard, Harvey Biggs was sweating mightily. The concrete road barriers and glassed-in guardhouse and black-metal sentry gates that led up the White House entrance loomed in front of him, but he could go no farther. The crowd was simply impassable.

The normal tourist action and homeless tents and anti-whatever demonstrations around Pennsylvania Avenue and Lafayette Square actually faced the rear of the White House; the Presidential residence overlooked the sweeping green lawns that led down to Independence Avenue. Today the wide expanse of green was invisible, covered by more people than Harvey had ever seen gathered in Washington. And all of them were singing.

Above the din Harvey could catch an occasional sound of the White House guard dogs going berserk. Police stood around in uncertain cordons, making no move to break up the gathering or even shift it unless the gates rose and a stretch-limousine passed through. At those moments arms unlinked and people moved aside, waving and smiling and then gaily coming back together as soon as the car was gone.

The sound was like one massive voice singing from one gigantic heart, a vast harmony of song and joy and something else that Harvey Biggs could not understand. He stood uncertainly outside the linked-arm throng, feeling the power of their voices in his chest, drawing close to the nearest group of police for protection against something unseen, something powerful enough to make Harvey Biggs forget both his urgency and his appointment and his purpose.

"Mr. Biggs!" One individual squeezed through the throng separating Harvey from the White House gate and rushed over. The man's Oriental features looked vaguely familiar, but Harvey could not for the life of him remember where he had seen him before. The massed sound of the voices drained him of all power of thought.

"I'm John Nakamishi, on Senator Atterly's staff," the man said, raising his voice to make himself heard above the song. "Your office said I'd find you over here." He reached into his coat pocket, drew out an envelope, handed it over. "Senator Atterly asked me to give you this."

With fingers as numb as his brain, Harvey Biggs fumbled to open the letter, feeling the sound reach out and batter at him with an ever-stronger force.

Dear Mr. Biggs,

I have been informed that your daughter, Jessica, has been found in Los Angeles. She has been in the company of a man whom I believe you know, Gregory Lannerton of Venus Enterprises. That is all I am sure of at this moment, and a letter is certainly no place to speculate on such troubling circumstances.

I am sure this news must be both a relief and a source of grave concern to you and your wife. Please understand that this information will be passed on to no one else; our own differences will in no way impinge upon the utter confidentiality with which this matter will be treated.

Please know that our prayers and heartfelt concern go out to you, your wife, and your daughter. May you and your family find comfort in the embrace of our Lord.

Yours in His service,
Richard Atterly

Harvey Biggs dropped his hand to his side, the letter clasped in fingers that felt nothing at all. The voices and the throng of uplifted faces loomed before him. A wave of revulsion shook his stocky frame as he visualized his daughter in Lannerton's clutches.

He fought down these thoughts, willed himself to concentrate on the issue at hand. He was too experienced a political animal not to read between the lines of Atterly's letter. It did not matter what Atterly said about confidentiality. He knew what he himself would do with anything this explosive. Naturally the senator had not expressed anything that even vaguely sounded like a threat in writing. There was always the risk that Harvey would use the letter to smear the senator further down the line. No, he did not openly threaten because he did not need to. The senator had lied, just as Harvey would have lied in a situation like this had such information fallen into his own grasp.

Harvey understood Atterly's unspoken threat perfectly. Atterly would remain silent only so long as Harvey did exactly as the senator wanted, which was to drop the issue, walk away from the fight, let the Per Se anti-porn bill be signed into law. If he made one step further toward the White House, opened his mouth and said anything at all, the senator would plant this information all over Washington. And as soon as the story came out, as soon as all the implications of this generated the national publicity that it certainly would, Harvey Biggs' career in Washington would be lost and gone forever.

Harvey Biggs made the only move open to him. He turned and walked away.

CHAPTER
21

Congressman John Silverwood was not nervous. He had given too many speeches to have a case of nerves over standing in front of a crowd, even a crowd that stretched so far that he could not make out the edges. No, he was not nervous about speaking. But he was *scared* by the thought of what he was about to say.

He looked out over the *sea* of faces and clothes and colors and noise, and murmured, "What on earth do I tell them?"

The black man with features carved by knife-like slashes, the man Atterly had introduced as Reverend Wilkins, was close enough to hear. "Whatever it is, Congressman, if it comes from you it's *wrong*."

"I've got a speech prepared," Silverwood said. "It seemed fine when I was writing it out, but nothing I've ever prepared has felt as wrong as it does right now."

"What you say up there has gotta come from the Lord," Reverend Wilkins replied. "Gotta be full of His Spirit. Now you just close your eyes and ask the Lord's guidance. Them folks ain't goin' nowhere. They can wait."

Congressman Silverwood bowed his head, felt a heavy hand rest upon his shoulder, heard a soft basso murmuring beside him.

When he raised his head, he straightened his shoulders and looked at the crowd without fear.

Reverend Wilkins watched him approvingly. "The Lord showed you His will."

"I think so, yes."

"Then you just go up there and do it, Congressman. And the Lord be with you. Yessir, the Lord be with you all the way."

He walked to the podium and found the audience watching him, waiting calmly for him, patient and secure in the presence that filled the air to overflowing. It startled him, how content they seemed to wait. Then he realized that it was not John Silverwood that they were waiting for at all. And with that realization came the strength and the assurance and the peace of mind to stand at the front of the stage, to smile for cameras that expanded his every expression into a picture over two stories high, and speak with a calm voice.

"I had prepared a talk for this morning based on the Per Se anti-pornography bill, which the President is expected to sign into law next week. But as I stand before you, I find myself drawn to speak on a passage from the Bible which I came upon last night. It called to my heart very strongly, and I would like to share my feelings with you."

It took him a moment to find the correct page, but eventually he looked up and said, "I would like to read from the one hundred and sixteenth Psalm, verses one through four and eight through twelve:

"I love the Lord, for he heard my voice; He heard my cry for mercy. Because he turned his ear to me, I will call on him as long as I live. The cords of death entangled me. The anguish of the grave came upon me; I was overcome by trouble and sorrow. Then I called on the name of the Lord: 'Oh, Lord, save me!'

"For you, O Lord, have delivered my soul from death. My eyes from tears, my feet from stumbling, that I may walk before the Lord in the land of the living. I believed; therefore I said, 'I am greatly afflicted.' And in my dismay I said, 'All men are liars.' How can I repay the Lord for all his goodness to me?"

John Silverwood looked up from the Book, said to the gathering, "The author had a close encounter with death, that much is clear to me. It was literally staring him in the face. Perhaps it was physical death, but I don't think so. In my own heart I hear him saying, 'I was on the path *toward* death.'

"The author speaks to me, and speaks *for* me when he says, 'I called out from my darkness and my despair, I called out from the depths of my absolute, abject terror.' I, too, have made such a call.

"As long as I could, I fought against the need to find strength or direction from anyone or anything other than myself. In order to remain content with my isolation, I continually lied to myself about the path I was on. I can see now that deep down I realized even then that I was walking toward death. But to admit this, to accept that I had spent so long lying to myself, was the most difficult truth I have ever faced in my life.

"I always argued that I couldn't love or worship someone I couldn't see. To me, God was a figment of somebody else's imagination. He was invisible and unknowable, if He existed at all.

"But the psalmist doesn't say that he has seen the Lord. He says, 'I love Him because I have seen *what He has done.*' I realize now that I don't *need* to see Him. All I need is to be honest enough to recognize what He has done in my life.

"But loving the Lord in itself is not enough. I want to go *deeper* into my personal experience with the Lord. I want to use my life, every day that I have left in this world as a witness to His majesty and a servant to His will. I want to know Him as the one who sticks closer to me than a brother."

John Silverwood placed his hand upon the Bible's open page, and it seemed as though an energy made the paper alive under his touch. He looked down and felt his mind filled with another verse from that same psalm, "I will fulfill my vows to the Lord in the presence of all his people." He read the verse through several times, conscious of the crowd's waiting silence. He did not understand why the stillness that filled his mind and heart was important, but he no longer needed to understand all the mysteries. The act of being still at this moment did not take from his message. It was meant to be.

◆ ◆ ◆

The stream of people that swept around Jeremy as he carried Duncan's bags and followed the two of them into the Los Angeles Airport terminal was endless, impatient, frenetic, and rude. He was immensely pleased to see Jessica respond to the aggressive back-and-forth shunting by lacing both sets of fingers into Duncan's free hand.

Jeremy trailed along as Duncan took Jessica to the gift shop and bought her a miniature teddy bear in top hat and tails, saying that even the bravest grown-up lady needed company on a long trip. Jessica hesitated a long time before accepting the gift, then warmed both their hearts by looking up and giving him the smallest of smiles.

When their flight was called a second time, Duncan turned to Jeremy. "Sure you don't mind driving the car back alone?"

"Not if you don't mind me using it around here for a while first."

Duncan offered a smile of his own. "If I start missing it, I can always have you scrape off a bagful of dirt and mail it to me, right?"

"It's good to see that old sparkle, son. That's the memory I'd like to keep of this goodbye."

"You don't mean to say this is going to be a permanent relocation."

"Not on your life." Jeremy glanced over to where Jessica was seated by the boarding gate, huddled up so tightly that the plastic seat looked oversized. "It still hurts me to look at her, but I do believe there's an improvement."

"I was afraid to admit it to myself until this morning, but I think so too."

"Looks like you're a good influence on her," Jeremy said, patting his friend on the shoulder. "Take good care of her, you hear?"

"I will if she wants me to," he replied. "It's her decision. Arlene's parents have told her in no uncertain terms that she's welcome in their home. I've made it as clear as I know how that she has a place out on the farm with me as long as she wants."

"Just take it day by day," Jeremy agreed. "You're sure there won't be any problems from her parents?"

Duncan shook his head. "I know their type. The first threat of legal action or publicity will have them running for the hills. If they hadn't been so concerned with their social position and careers in the first place this tragedy would never have happened. Publicity of this kind would pull down their world like a house of cards in a hurricane."

Jeremy patted Duncan's shoulder, walked over, took the seat beside Jessica, said softly, "I keep me a boat down on the Carolina coast, did I mention that to you?"

She managed a fleeting glance his way, gave her head a tiny shake.

"I thought maybe I'd forgotten it. Yeah, I have this passel of kids I like to take out when I can. Some friends do it for me when I'm not around. Maybe you and Duncan might like to come down one weekend, let me show you some of the prettiest coastland this side of paradise."

Again there was a fleeting nod, the smallest of motions.

"That's fine. I'll talk to Duncan just as soon as I'm back." Jeremy hesitated, leaned closer and told her, "I work a lot with orphans and kids from broken homes. The only reason I mention it is because there's this one lesson I see 'round me every day, and I want to give it to you as a going-away present. Love isn't something that has to come from family, Jessica. It ought to, but when it doesn't, you can find it in the most wonderful of other places."

Jeremy rested a hand on her arm. "I'll be prayin' for you just as hard as I know how."

The boarding call sounded, and their goodbye could not be put off any longer. Duncan moved up and faced Jeremy. "I can't thank you enough for all you've done."

"Best thanks I could ever have is for you to stay firm upon the Way," Jeremy replied.

"I'll try," Duncan said, and let his hand be engulfed in a rock-solid grip. "Pray for me."

"Every day, son. Every blessed day."

◆　　◆　　◆

That evening Brent was waiting for him when Jeremy pulled up in front of the Way-In Center. "I gotta tell you, Mr. Hughes. There isn't a very big chance we'll find your girl Arlene."

"Call me Jeremy, will you? Tackin' a mister to my name adds on too many years."

"You've got a lot working against you here. This Chico character is an unknown from out of town, nothing established around here, nothing to hold him. He's got every reason in the world to put some miles between himself and the Hollywood Strip."

"I know," Jeremy sighed. "My mind's been tellin' me this all blessed day. But my heart's too busy cryin' for that lost little girl to listen."

Brent eyed him hard. "You can't let it get you down, Jeremy."

"It's too late for that," Jeremy replied. "I spend my nights startin' from sleep, wonderin' if she's not out here somewhere callin' for help."

Brent studied the pavement at his feet and gave a single reluctant nod. "Some nights I hear it too."

"I gotta stay here long enough to be sure," Jeremy said, as much to himself as to Brent. "Gotta know the poor little fallen angel's not out there wishin' somebody was still lookin', still searchin', still believin' she can be found."

Brent reached for the car door. "We might as well get on out there, then."

"Right you are," Jeremy agreed. "The night's waiting."

Explanatory Note on "Per Se" Legislation

By Isabella Bunn

The laws of the United States and almost all fifty states make the sale, distribution, or exhibition of materials defined as "obscene" a criminal offense. The definition of what is obscene, as well as the determination of what is obscene in particular cases, is a matter of constitutional law. The Supreme Court has repeatedly ruled that obscenity is without first amendment protection; in other words, that it is excluded from the right of freedom of speech.

Thus the definition of what is "obscene" takes on special significance, as great care must be taken *not* to restrict materials (including materials dealing with sex) which are entitled to constitutional protection. The 1973 U.S. Supreme Court case of *Miller v. California* (413 U.S. 15) sets forth the current legal test for obscenity. According to the case, material is obscene if *all three* of the following conditions are met:

1. The average person, applying contemporary community standards, would find that the work, taken as a whole, appeals to the prurient interest; and
2. The work depicts or describes, in a patently offensive way, sexual conduct specifically defined by the applicable state (or federal) law; and

3. The work, taken as a whole, lacks serious literary, artistic, political, or scientific value.

Over the years, virtually every word in the Miller test has been the subject of extensive litigation as well as commentary in legal journals. There is a large body of explanations and clarifications of such concepts as "taken as a whole," "prurient interest," "patently offensive," and "contempory community standards." Some legal authorities have noted that this morass of conflicting definitions can discourage prosecutors from bringing obscenity cases to trial. They are also concerned that jurors may become confused, causing deadlocked and hung juries, and acquittals on material that is clearly obscene.

These commentators urge Congress and state legislatures to adopt an objective definition of obscenity that would make commercial distribution of all hard-core pornography *per se illegal*. "Per Se" is a Latin term used in the law to mean "in and of itself."

It is argued that such laws would remove most of the confusion regarding what is legal or illegal, providing a clear definitional line for producers and merchants. Prosecution of violators would become more frequent and efficient.

Supporters of the "Per Se" approach also contend that the bulk of the illegal pornography industry's prostitution-based trade would eventually become unmarketable, and, "like child pornography, retreat into an underground culture far from the general public."

Child pornography statutes are based on a different standard than the obscenity test set forth in the Miller case. In the case of *New York v. Ferber*, the U.S. Supreme court unanimouisly rejected the constitutional protection arguments, and instead applied a "balancing of interests" test. The court held that in rare instances, when the "evil to be restricted so overwhelmingly outweighs the expressive interests, if any, at stake, that no process of case-by-case adjudication is required." In effect, the Court supported a "Per Se" approach to criminalizing the production, sale, exhibition, or distribution of photographs of children engaged in any sexual activity.

Supporters of the "per se" approach to new legislation suggest that the courts apply a similar "balancing of interests" test to hard-core pornography as a whole. This would lead to the conclusion that the "expressive interests" of hard-core pornography, if any, are heavily outweighed by its harmful effects.

Although not an expert on the issue, the author believes that both legislative reform *coupled with greater resources for law enforcement* are needed to address the problem of pornography in America.

Taylor, Bruce A. "Hard-core Pornography: A Proposal for a Per Se Rule." Volume 21, *University of Michigan Journal of Law Reform*, Fall 1987—Winter 1988, pp. 255–282.

ACKNOWLEDGMENTS

Before beginning with the acknowledgments, I need to make several remarks. To begin, I would like to thank our heavenly Father for both granting me this incredible learning experience, and for keeping me safe during the process. I have learned an enormous amount, and hope that my appreciation for the efforts of those on the front line of the battle against juvenile exploitation has come through in this book.

It is important for readers to understand that the relatively large number of organizations working with teens in the Los Angeles area does not signify a duplication of efforts. The "bigger-is-better" mentality is inappropriate to the care and counseling of runaways. A scared, drugged-out, emotionally and spiritually wounded teenager needs to be placed in a shelter that will not overwhelm him or her with its size. There needs to be a homelike environment, with individual attention to particular needs.

The larger the structure, the greater the chance that the individual will feel like a cog in a machine, run through a regimented system that in a few weeks will complete its paper-ridden exercise and deposit him or her back out on the street. The place needs to be a small enough for each teen to feel important. They must understand that the disciplined program is designed to help them with their problems, not to meet bureaucratic guidelines.

What this means is that, notwithstanding its practical appeal, the solution to provide more accommodation for teenage runaways does not lie in larger projects. Rather, multiple small-scale programs responsive to local needs are required.

Readers should also understand that the often-related problems of child abuse, teenage runaways, and juvenile pornography are not limited to our larger metropolitan areas. In fact, these problems affect nearly every community in the nation. Los Angeles was used in this book because of the relatively large number of children who gather there. Yet nearly every child I spoke to—and they numbered over one hundred—came from somewhere else. Most originated from small and mid-sized towns, representing almost every state. My research with the various front-line organizations indicates that this is the norm. No region is immune to this tragic epidemic, and assistance is required everywhere.

The National Coalition Against Pornography, based in Cincinnati, Ohio, has outlined a number of ways that individuals and groups may become involved in ridding their community of this evil. They continually stress that time and personal vigilance are much more important than money.

Most cities now have groups actively working with children seeking to overcome the trauma of an abusive background. If your church cannot help you in making contact, perhaps you might wish to check with your local Rescue Squad or Salvation Army. You may also check through the Covenant House Nine-Line (1–800–999–9999), but this is suggested only as a last resort, as the line is primarily intended for use by the teenagers themselves.

If you are a teen who is either caught up in traumatic circumstances or are burdened by such memories, I beg you in the strongest possible terms to PLEASE SEEK HELP. It has been found that the greatest barriers to overcoming such problems are the shame and guilt associated with them. No matter how bad you think the problem may be, no matter how much pain you might be carrying, no matter how scared you are of ever trusting another person, please know that there is a loving God who seeks to heal your spirit and dry the tears that only you and He can see. A Christian counselor can help you confront the memories and release these burdens while remaining protected within the sheltering love of Christ. Many churches are in contact with local counselors who are both trained in psychotherapy and firmly rooted in faith in our Lord. I urge you to show the courage required to turn to such a person, and be guided toward both a healing and a new start.

Each of my books deepens the working relationship which I have with my wife, Isabella, whom I call by the Polish diminutive of Izia. With *Promises to Keep,* Izia has moved beyond the myriad of her commercial and research responsibilities to begin drafting sections with me. Numerous scenes were developed with her direct assistance. Yet most important to me is the love with which she fills my days, and the friendship which she has brought into my life. I thank God daily for this gift.

This book, as with all my other novels, is filled with the advice and the inspiration of my pastor, Reverend Bill DeLay. Bill and his wife Cathy heeded the mission call ten years ago, gave up the senior ministry of an enormously successful church in Georgia, and moved to Dusseldorf, Germany. I am indeed grateful for their support, and for the prayers and encouragement offered by the congregation of the

International Baptist Church of Dusseldorf.

Lawrence Davis, Chairman of North Carolina's Democratic Party, was extremely helpful in charting the progress of an unpopular bill through the legislative process. For the sake of story development, I have simplified and accelerated much of the Washington political process; I have nonetheless tried to remain true to the pattern and the strategy outlined by Lawrence and others. I am most grateful both for his kind assistance and for his friendship.

The information given by Senator Atterly on ancient Greece came from the second volume of Reverend J. Phillips' *Exploring Acts*. I highly recommend these books to anyone interested in a deeper exploration of that wonderfully complex book of the Bible.

Jim and Marilyn Gray opened up their hearts and homes to me during the early stages of my research, and allowed me to enter into the life of a small North Carolina community. Much of the dialogue and attitudes found in Jeremy are based upon the rich folklore of this area.

The story of Columbia, Maryland, in the early seventies was a gift from a very dear friend who survived those times by the grace of God. I am so very grateful for this insight into experiences that shaped an individual and a part of our culture. The Lord in His mercy has granted this beloved friend the gift of healing. If only our culture would turn around and ask the same of Him.

Laura Boosinger, a very fine singer from Asheville, North Carolina, took time from mixing her latest album to tell me of the Shape Note music heritage. Both of the songs that came to Jeremy during that drive across Washington are to be found on her album.

Jeanette Miller is a counselor who has specialized in working with runaways. She helped tremendously in my initial research on both motivation and perspective.

Mrs. Ruby Broyhill is indeed a fine lady and qualified nurse who runs a home in Fairfax, Virginia, for elderly women. Do not bother to apply. As she has long since left her four-score years behind her, she sees only to the needs of those guests who joined her some time ago.

The story about the man cleaning the gutters who gets dragged halfway to the shopping center is a true one. It comes from my father's own personal testimony. His assistance was also critical to making the ALUM confrontation as realistic as possible; during his long career as a trial lawyer he has had some monumental run-ins with those who hold to the humanist perspective. Thanks, Dad. I hope the message has as much meaning for others as it did for me.

Reuben Blackwell, vice-president of the Raleigh Chamber of Commerce, has been kind enough to help me with black dialogue in all three of my books. He is both a good friend and a patient teacher.

The dawn walk that Jessica took through the streets of Hollywood is based on the true-life experience of Anita Taylor, who was also kind enough to help me with *The Presence*. She is a warm and caring person, who took great time and trouble to assist me in seeing through her eyes.

The concept of the Twelve Steps originally came from Alcoholics Anonymous. The first three steps are currently being used by both the Salvation Army's Way-In Center and the Alpha Teen Center as a basis for their therapy, as was described in this book.

Lieutenant Ed Kreins and Detective Hector Alatorre of the Beverly Hills Police Department gave a considerable amount of time and assistance to my work, opening doors in numerous organizations and offering a great deal of very helpful advice. Although their primary focus is in apprehending law-breakers, these gentlemen—along with those officers of the L.A.P.D. Juvenile Division—must be commended for the compassion and concern they show toward juveniles on the streets.

Brother Phil Mandel, Order of the Salesians, is Director of the Los Angeles Covenant House. Robert Pfeiffer has moved from New York to run their Outreach Program. Trey Baskett and Jana Milhon are two of the individuals who nightly cover the streets of Hollywood, West Hollywood, and Los Angeles in their efforts to assist kids in crises. These fine people gave both thoughtful insight and tremendous assistance, especially in allowing me to accompany them in their endless search of the L.A. streets.

Jim Province of the Stepping Stone shelter in Santa Monica was the first outreach worker with whom I spoke during my research trip to Los Angeles. He was remarkably kind, not only answering my questions but also showing me what questions needed to be considered. Jim is a warm and caring individual who has given his heart as well as his life to serving those in need.

The runaways whom I encountered in the Los Angeles area left me with wounds that still give me nightmares. Most of them are so emotionally burdened by their experiences that they prefer the dangerous freedom of the streets to the potential pain of ever trusting another adult. I must respect their wishes and maintain their anonymity. Yet I would like to mention the first names of two people, in heartfelt appreciation for sharing their stories with me. Frank is a runaway from Chicago, who left behind a traumatically abusive home-life five years ago, and made the streets of Los Angeles his home. Michelle is thirteen years old, and after having been sexually abused by her stepfather and three stepbrothers two years ago, ran away from home. She was well on the way to becoming a prostitute when she hearkened to the call of Jesus Christ and made the incredibly wrenching effort to look for help. I commend them both, and ask that all who read this remember them—and the hundreds of thousands of other fallen angels out there—in your prayers.

Melissa Stanley is a former runaway who is now studying to become a clinical psychologist. Her honest observations and willingness to discuss so many aspects of what clearly were extremely painful experiences helped tremendously in the formation of a proper perspective.

Although I have never met him personally, I would like to thank Zig Ziglar and his staff for the outstanding lecture series, "Raising

Positive Kids In A Negative World," and "Raising Drug-Free Kids In A Drug-Filled World." Both have given important personal guidance, as well as considerable direction during the formation of this story.

Detective Bill Dworin of the Los Angeles Police Department is head of the city's Sexually Exploited Children Unit. Although the area of his work is brutally painful, Bill has managed to maintain both a sense of dedication and a warm and compassionate attitude. He was kind enough to give up his Sunday afternoon to meet with a total stranger and discuss his work and his findings, then host me through a visit to his department the following day. His advice to all newcomers, both volunteers and professionals, is to stay with the work only so long as your heart allows you to give what the kids need, especially the very young ones, with a minimum of bitterness and hatred and anger, and a maximum of love.

Vickie Ballet of Children of the Night stopped in the middle of an incredibly hectic day, created her very own little island of calm, and patiently dealt with all of my questions. The Children of the Night deals specifically with prostitutes under the age of sixteen who are seeking a way out. Like all of these organizations, they have more children seeking help than they have space to give.

Terry Helms, Jack Hart, and Cathy Thompson are counselors working with the Alpha Teen Care center. Their primary focus is on granting emergency care to teenagers in crisis. This is done in conjunction with long-term treatment centers or counseling that would take place either once the teenager returns home or is resettled into foster care.

Phillip Ludwig is a former San Diego policeman who has made it his life's work to locate runaways and either reunite them with family or place them in appropriate foster care. His patient assistance with my book is very much appreciated.

Angel's Flight is a crisis center that works primarily with under-eighteen runaways who have decided that it is time to come in off the streets and begin the painful process of working through whatever it was that took them out there in the first place. I would like to thank Paul Henson and Haydee Sanchez for their help.

The Way-In Center is a teen crisis center operated by the Salvation Army. All my life I have seen their blue-suited bands made fun of, and I have allowed this misconception to hold me back from seeing the truth. I was humbled by the open-hearted honesty with which they face their work and their trials with the street kids. They truly live by prayers, which are filled with meaning by their works. I would like to both thank and commend the following people: Joan Thirkettle, James Stewart, Sabane Robertson, and Scott Brewer.

There was one church that I heard of almost every time I turned around in Los Angeles. It was mentioned by almost every outreach organization with whom I worked. It was mentioned by the kids. Its name is the First Presbyterian Church of Hollywood, and I have tried to remain true to the feeling it left me in this description. The City Dwellers Evangelical Outreach is one part of its program. They were also one of the groups that helped the Covenant House and the Children of the Night get started. They were a wonderful group of people, and I thank them and their Reverend Olgive for letting me be a part of their worship service.

The Oasis Nightclub is an island of relative sanity—although many of the people who work there might disagree with that—in a storm-tossed sea. Located one block off Hollywood Boulevard, it is a well-run outreach program that has seen remarkable success in recent years. A much-needed rebuilding program is now being sponsored by several local churches, a local Christian radio station, and such well-known Christian artists as Bryan Duncan.

One of the hardest conversations I had during the development of this book was with Dean Kaplan, Director of Public Policy for the National Coalition Against Pornography. Dean is the former president of a successful computer company, who gave up his career to follow what he felt was the call placed upon his heart. He has developed an incredible ability to speak with both compassion and distance on some of the most horrific problems I have ever come across. The calm summary of statistics gives way to genuine feeling for the individuals suffering under a lack of the Lord's presence in so many hungering hearts.

Bill Delahoyde, an assistant U.S. district attorney, helped with that most crucial of first steps—determining what questions needed to be asked, and how they should be phrased. Law is an immensely specialized field, and it was by the grace of God that I was brought into contact with a strong believer who knew enough of this field to help me structure my initial work.

I would also like to thank the following organizations located in and around Washington, D.C., for their assistance in gathering source material and legal documentation: Tom Birch, Director of the National Child Abuse Coalition; D'ann Taflan, Director of Public Relations, and Judy Schrader, General Counsel of the National Center for Missing and Exploited Children; and Della Hughes and Phillip Martin of the National Network of Runaway and Youth Services.

The concept of the Solemn Assembly was given to me by Reverend David Horner, who is pastor at the Providence Baptist Church in North Carolina. David's sermon on the assembly struck a note in so many people's hearts one Sunday morning that his evening prayer service filled the main hall to overflowing. A three-hour prayer circle with more than six hundred people left me drained, exhilarated, and absolutely certain that here was an essential point for this book. He and his associate minister, Mike Sparks, have been a great source of guidance and inspiration through the years.

As I continue working with Bethany House Publishers, I find it is no longer possible to single out certain people for special thanks. There are too many people who give selflessly to the creation of a book, and all of them deserve my heartfelt thanks. I would, however, like to mention Dr. Penny Stokes, whose work as consulting editor has added enormously to both this work and to *The Maestro*.

Anyone seeking assistance in matters related to growth in faith are cordially invited to write Reverend Paul McCommon, a very dear friend who has recently returned from work as a missionary pastor in Panama. Paul is a man who continues to grow in both wisdom and in spiritual strength, and whose counsel has meant a tremendous amount to me personally. If anyone is facing what appears to be a blank wall, either in their personal life or in their spiritual walk or in their career, Paul is a very good man to help find the door. He may be contacted by writing Reverend Paul McCommon, % Bethany House Publishers, 6820 Auto Club Road, Minneapolis, MN 55438.

BIBLIOGRAPHY

Books:

Claudia Black, *It Will Never Happen to Me!*, (Denver, Col.: MAC Publishing, 1981).

Szifra Burke and Kathy Mayer, *Private Practice*, (Denver, Col.: MAC Publishing, 1987).

D. Campagna and D. Poffenberger, *Sexual Trafficking in Children*, (Dover, Mass.: Auburn House, 1988).

Ross Campbell, M.D., *How to Really Love Your Teenager*, (Wheaton, Ill.: Victor Books, 1982).

James Dobson and Gary L. Bauer, *Children at Risk*, (Dallas, Tex.: Word Publishing, 1990).

James Dobson, *Preparing for Adolescence*, (Ventura, Calif.: Regal Books, 1989).

Eliana Gil, *Outgrowing the Pain—A Book for and About Adults Abused as Children*, (New York, N.Y.: Dell Publishing, 1983).

George Grant, *Trial and Error—The American Civil Liberties Union and Its Impact on Your Family*, (Brentwood, Tenn.: Wolgemuth & Hyatt Publishers, Inc., 1989).

Mark-David Janus et al, *Adolescent Runaways—Causes and Consequences*, (Lexington, Mass.: Lexington Books, 1987).

Tracy Kidder, *Among Schoolchildren*, (New York, N.Y.: Avon Books, 1989).

M. Scott Peck, M.D., *People of the Lie—The Hope for Curing Human Evil*, (New York, N.Y.: Simon & Schuster, 1983).

Father Bruce Ritter, *Sometimes God Has a Kid's Face.*

Samuel Walker, *In Defense of American Liberties—A History of the ACLU*, (New York, N.Y.: Oxford University Press, 1990).

Terry Williams, *The Cocaine Kids—Inside Story of a Teenage Drug Ring*, (Reading, Mass.: Addison-Wesley Publishing Company, Inc., 1989).

Earl D. Wilson, *You Try Being a Teenager—A Challenge to Parents to Stay in Touch,* (Portland, Ore.: Multnomah Press, 1982).

Phyllis and David York, *Tough Love—A Self-Help Manual for Parents Troubled by Teenage Behavior* (Sellersville, Penn.: Community Service Foundation, 1980).

Materials from Organizations:

Alpha Teen Care
CPC Brea Canyon Hospital
875 North Brea Boulevard
Brea, CA 92621

American Civil Liberties Union
122 Maryland Avenue, NE
Washington, D.C. 20002
  "Civil Liberties in the 101st Congress"
  "Selected News Clips from the Washington Office"
  "Civil Liberties Alert"
  "Polluting the Censorship Debate—A Summary and Critique of the Final Report of the Attorney General's Commission on Pornography," 1986.

Children of the Night
P.O. Box 4343
Hollywood, CA 90078
  Various reports, newspaper clippings from the past decade relating to child prostitution in Los Angeles

Covenant House Administrative Offices
346 West 17th Street
New York, N.Y. 10011–5002

National Center for Missing & Exploited Children
2101 Wilson Blvd. Suite 550
Arlington, VA 22201
  Various reports, including those on child sex rings, child molesters, and youth at risk

National Center for Prosecution of Child Abuse
American Prosecutors Research Institute
1033 North Fairfax Street, Suite 200
Alexandria, VA 22314

National Coalition Against Pornography
800 Compton Road, Suite 9224
Cincinnati, Ohio 45231
  Series of Briefing Papers entitled "Research on Pornography: The Evidence of Harm," covering topics such as rape and sexual aggression toward women, child sexual exploitation and abuse, the nature and content of hard-core pornography, and the relationship of pornography to abnormal sexual behavior/sexual offenders.

National Network of Runaway and Youth Services
1400 Eye Street, NW Suite 330
Washington, D.C. 20005
"To Whom Do They Belong?—Runaway, Homeless and Other
Youth in High-Risk Situations in the 1990's"
Various press releases and newsletters

The Salvation Army
Southern California Divisional Headquarters
900 West Ninth Street
Los Angeles, CA 90015–0899
Materials on "The Way-In" Ministry

United States Capitol Historical Society
200 Maryland Avenue, NE
Washington, D.C. 20002
"We, the People—The Story of the United States Capitol"
"Washington Past and Present"

United States Department of Justice
Washington, D.C. 20530
"Attorney General's Commission on Pornography—Final Report,"
July, 1986.

United States Senate Committee on the Judiciary
Washington, D.C. 20510
Hearing Report on Child Protection and Obscenity Enforcement
Act and Pornography Victims Protection Act of 1987, June 8,
1988. Serial No. J–100–74.

Magazine Articles:

"The New Teens: What Makes Them Different?" *Newsweek*, Special
Edition Summer/Fall 1990.
"Symposium: Civil Liberties vs. Political Agendas." *Society*, January/
February 1991.
"A Primer on the ACLU." *The Wall Street Journal*, October 3, 1988.
"The Unbelievable Beliefs of the ACLU." *Focus on the Family—Citizen*,
March, 1988.
"In Sizzling Demand: A Peep into the Life of a Corporate Call Girl."
Cosmopolitan, April, 1989.
"A Tale of Two Smut Merchants." *Reader's Digest*, February, 1990.
"Church Groups Urged to Join Dirty Battle." *Christianity Today*, April
22, 1988.
"Are You Going to Cry, Father Jackson?" *Christianity Today*, September 22, 1989.
"The Drive to Make America Porn-Free." *U.S. News & World Report*,
February 6, 1989.
"Running Away." *The New York Times Magazine*, October 2, 1988.
"A Fresh Assault on an Ugly Crime—Federal agents enter a sleazy
underworld to track down kiddie-porn customers and child molesters." *Newsweek*, March 14, 1988.

"My Porno-Movie Career." *Cosmopolitan*, April, 1988.

"Somebody Else's Kids—On the streets with our teenage runaways, where the dead end is deadlier than ever." *Newsweek*, April 25, 1988.

"Coming of Age on City Streets—runaway and homeless teens thought crack, prostitution and violent pimps were the worst street life could do to them. That was before AIDS." *Psychology Today*, January, 1988.

"The Runaway Crisis." *McCall's*, January, 1988.

"In the Hands of Strangers—Portrait of a New Kind of Kidnapping." *California Magazine*, May, 1989.

"Portrait of a Runaway." *Seventeen*, March, 1989.

"The True Story of a Remarkable Woman—The Child Finder." *Redbook*, May, 1988.

"Meet the Real Working Girls." *Mademoiselle*, March, 1990.

"Loving a Prostitute." *The Christian Century*, April 19, 1989.

"Children of the Night." *Woman's Day*, March 29, 1988.

"Keeping the Hope Alive—Parents of missing kids must learn to live with 'chronic uncertainty,' " *Newsweek*, November 27, 1989.

"Pornography: An Agenda for the Churches." *The Christian Century*, July 29, 1987.

"The American Civil Liberties Union (ACLU): Wolves in Sheep's Clothing." *Tomorrow*, March 13, 1989.

Phoebe Courtney. "Beware the ACLU!" *Tax Fax No. 224.*

Law Review Articles:

Andrea Dworkin, "Pornography Is a Civil Rights Issue for Women," *University of Michigan Journal of Law Reform*, Vol. 21, Fall 1987-Winter 1988, p. 55.

Bruce A. Taylor, "Hard-Core Pornography: A Proposal for a Per Se Rule," *University of Michigan Journal of Law Reform*, Vol. 21, Fall 1987-Winter 1988, p. 255.

Jefferey J. Kent and Scott D. Truesdell, "Spare the Child: The Constitutionality of Criminalizing Possession of Child Pornography," *University of Oregon Law Review*, Vol. 68, 1989, p. 362.

P9-DKF-399

Steppin'
Into the
Good Life

CHASE BRANCH LIBRARY
17731 W. SEVEN MILE RD.
DETROIT, MI 48235
578-8002

FEB 2011

CH

CHASE BRANCH LIBRARY
17731 W. SEVEN MILE RD.
DETROIT, MI 48235
578-8002

FEB 2011

Tia McCollors

Steppin' Into the Good Life

MOODY PUBLISHERS
CHICAGO

© 2011 by
TIA MCCOLLORS

All rights reserved. No part of this book may be reproduced in any form without permission in writing from the publisher, except in the case of brief quotations embodied in critical articles or reviews.

Published in association with the literary agency of MacGregor Literary, 2727 NW 185th Avenue, Suite 165, Hillsboro, OR 97124.

Edited by Francesca Gray
Interior design: Ragont Design
Cover design: Barb Fisher, LeVan Fisher Design
Interior image: Jupiter Images
Cover photos: Leonard McLane/Digital Vision/Getty Images and
                Andersen Ross/Blend Images/Getty Images
Author photo: Mic Nash

Library of Congress Cataloging-in-Publication Data

McCollors, Tia.
    Steppin' into the good life / Tia McCollors.
       p. cm.
    ISBN 978-0-8024-6291-6
    1. African American women—Fiction. 2. Self-actualization (Psychology) in women—Fiction. I. Title.
PS3613.C365S74 2011
813'.6—dc22

                                                            2010043958

1 3 5 7 9 10 8 6 4 2

Printed in the United States of America

Dedicated to all women who walk by faith
. . . and do it in style!

For we walk by faith, not by sight.
—2 Corinthians 5:7

Chapter I

Ace couldn't have looked better if I'd plucked the perfect six-foot, six-pack, six-figure man out of my dreams. I was finally at the wedding ceremony I'd envisioned. My happily-ever-after. And I was a stunner, too—from my cascading locks to the delicate diamond toe ring on my right foot. Any other day it would be my mission to make every head whip around in admiration—watching me. They'd stare in envy while I soaked up the attention like a drought-starved plant thirsty for water.

But that day I was incognito near the back of the church. Not just because I didn't want to draw attention, but because I wasn't even invited to this lavish wedding affair. I thought—even hoped—that Ace's marriage to Lynette was going to be simple and understated. After all, this was their second time around. But Ace wasn't a mediocre man, so perhaps I should've expected the archway of white roses at the altar and the aisles lined with five-foot-high candelabra.

I should be in that wedding dress, I thought as I accepted the tissue from the woman sitting to my left. I patted the tears streaming down my face, and she did the same to her own bag-rimmed eyes. No doubt the dark streaks framing her eyes weren't from lack of sleep, but from the mounds of purple eye shadow smeared on her eyelids. The tissue she'd given me felt like it had been wadded between her chubby fingers for the entire wedding ceremony. Actually, the program I was holding said it was the "Recommitment Ceremony of Scott and Lynette Bowers." It might as well have been my funeral program because I felt like I could have withered and died. I was convinced that whoever said, "Love doesn't hurt," had never been in love before. Not like this. Not like I was.

Scott was better known as Ace by everyone who knew and loved him. He'd carried the nickname since his infatuation with airplanes as a young boy. What was once a hobby of toy model airplanes was now a full-fledged career as a pilot. There weren't many with skin as brown as his working in the high ranks for major airlines. Ace was a rare catch. And Lynette had caught him, thrown him back, and then caught him again.

After two years in a relationship with the man I thought I was going to marry, he had walked out of my life. Physically. But there were still little pieces of Ace in my heart. Those remnants were ripping away at my heart right then.

This is too much to handle, I thought as Ace gripped Lynette's hands like he needed her to breathe. He hadn't taken his eyes off of her since she had walked down the aisle, preceded by her two teenage daughters. Ace's eyes were on Lynette; mine were on him. I had to grudgingly admit Lynette looked radiant. She glowed. That's what a good man will do for you. And an exceptional father has the same effect on his daughters. Carmen and Jada looked age-appropriate beautiful. I'd never connected with them—through no fault of my own. Ace hadn't believed in involving his girls in our relationship. Now it made me wonder if Ace knew all along that I

8

was his "temporary" woman. At the time we met, the ink on his divorce papers had been dry for two years so I had had no thought about whether I was a rebound woman.

I brushed away a single tear then happened to notice a brother across the aisle checking me out. I'm sure he thought I was caught up in the moment instead of the truth—mourning a lost love. But love lost can always be found again. At least I prayed so. *I might as well take advantage of being inside the four walls of this church.*

This was the perfect time for me to wash the remains of Ace out of my system. I sat up straight, elongating my frame, and tried to pretend I didn't know he was watching.

Ms. Purple Eye Shadow shifted in the pew. She unfolded one of those paper fans that spread out like a colorful peacock, then covered her mouth with it.

"That young thing is checking me out," she whispered to me.

She can't be serious, I thought.

"I'm old enough to be his mama," she said.

She fluttered that fan so fast I thought she'd take flight. In my peripheral vision, I could see her adjust her lilac-colored V-neck blouse. Not up, but down. I guess she wanted her so-called admirer to get a peek at her bountiful blessings.

Why she would think his eyes were on her when they were obviously on me, I'll never know. But I decided to let her live in her dream world.

My admirer was paler than I usually preferred; I'd always loved a man who was at least the shade of a toasted piece of wheat bread. I totally missed something the minister must've said that was funny, because he laughed along with everyone else there. He had a deep dimple in his left cheek and eyebrows so thick they almost met in the middle. He glanced back again, and this time I gave him a smile that said I noticed him, noticing me.

"Ummm. He really must like 'em well-seasoned," the woman beside me said.

Antique was more like it.

I thought about how I could slip him my number without seeming too obvious and without disrupting the ceremony, because by the time Ace and Lynette were pronounced "husband and wife," I'd planned to disappear without a trace.

I had the closure I needed to move on with my life. It had been Cassandra's idea to make this secret appearance so that one of two things would happen. One, I'd realize Ace and Lynette's love was destined and there was nothing I could've done to stop it. Or two, I'd be so angry that Ace walked out of my life the way he did that I wouldn't care what happened with the two of them.

Being here I realized that even if the pregnancy I'd faked in order to try and salvage our relationship had been real, Ace and Lynette would've eventually found their way back to each other. Then not only would I have been alone, but I'd have been alone with the stresses and drama of a being a single mother.

Ms. Purple Eye Shadow was still murmuring things under her breath, but I truthfully didn't know if she was talking to me or having some mental issues.

"God has seen fit to reunite Scott and Lynette," the minister's voice suddenly boomed and brought my attention back to the ceremony. I saw a couple of people in front of me nearly jump out of their seats like he'd shaken them up, too. I think he forgot he was officiating a peaceful ceremony and not preaching a Sunday morning sermon.

"And I tell you, this is like a miracle before my eyes. Nobody can ever tell me that God isn't in the miracle-working business."

I rolled my eyes. There were plenty of miracles I've needed in my life for almost a year, and to date God hasn't worked out a single one. Evidently He hangs out a "Closed for Business" sign when He sees me coming.

Ace slid his arm around Lynette's waist. She looked at him like it was love at first sight and it was the first time they'd met. It was like they'd forgotten they had a church full of spectators.

Two years of your life is a long time to invest in someone and not get your expected rate of return—in this case, the coveted "Mrs." title. The next man I'm with is going to have to know within nine months whether he plans on putting a ring on my finger. If a woman can have a baby in nine months, then surely a man should know if he wants to be married.

Hindsight is twenty-twenty. There had been red flags I'd been too in love to see. Love wasn't only blind, it was stupid. I sighed, and must have done it louder than I thought, because the chubby hand reached over to pat my knee.

"I always knew they'd get back together," the woman said. She wiped her face, leaving light brown makeup on the tissue and small pieces of cotton on her face. "God can restore any marriage if you make Him the head of it." She folded her fan and stuffed it down into the side of her open purse. "And to think Ace had been seeing some other woman for two years when he finally came to his senses. Ain't God good?"

Her comment made my heart patter. I guess I'd been the talk of the family gossip. I'd been reduced to the phrase "some other woman."

This isn't closure, I decided. *This is torture.*

Chapter 2

What had I been thinking coming here? That's the problem: I hadn't been thinking.

Now my pew partner was making it her business to be my personal comforter. I wished I could crawl up in her lap, lay my head on the mountains across her chest, and cry a river. She'd rock me to sleep and promise me that a knight in shining armor would come to my rescue soon. And then I'd wake up and clean the purple eye shadow off my Donna Karan blouse.

If I didn't have at least a few wits left about me, I would've thought she'd read my mind.

She patted me again. This time on my ringless left hand.

"Your day will come. There's somebody out there for everybody," she whispered. She leaned closer to me and brought the smell of some kind of fruity candy on her breath. "I'm married to my third husband. I buried the first one at the graveyard and the second one at the courthouse." She fanned out the fingers on her left hand, then wiggled her ring finger. "Custom made with a ruby instead of a diamond," she boasted. "That's my name. Ruby."

I wonder what Ruby's third husband would've thought of his wife's flirtatious flaunting.

Ruby—and her purple eye shadow—was starting to work my nerves. I wasn't interested in hearing another peep from her. I wanted one husband, and one husband only. 'Til death do we part.

I crossed my legs and shifted my body so that I was slightly turned away from her. She didn't get the hint.

"What's your name?" she whispered.

"She —" I reeled in the truth and threw out a lie. "Cheryl." I could almost see how she would've stood up in protest if I'd told her I was Sheila Rushmore. I had no way of knowing if my name had been tossed around in the family gossip, and I wasn't about to be dragged out of the sanctuary in a headlock.

"My best friend's name was Cheryl growing up," she whispered and flipped that fan out again. "I thought we'd be connected at the hip forever. Some things are only for a season, you know? People are in your life for a reason, a season, or a lifetime."

I knew that all too well.

I pretended to look for something in my purse so she'd stop talking. A few people had already glared over their shoulders at us. So much for being incognito. I looked behind me at the exit doors, but there were two burly men standing in front of them like they were guarding Fort Knox. I needed to plan a perfect moment to escape. From this ceremony. From Ruby.

"We're not going to ask if there is anyone here who objects," the minister was saying. "As Lynette's uncle and their pastor, I think I speak for both of them and say that we don't care what anyone else thinks."

I think I was the only person in the congregation who didn't laugh.

Ace looked over his shoulder at the congregation and winked at someone on the first pew. I craned my neck to see who he was looking at. A regal-looking woman with a wide, dentured smile was sitting straight as a peacock, like she knew all eyes were on her. I assumed it was his beloved Grandma Toot, the woman who'd raised him and whom I'd never had the pleasure of meeting. That was one of those red flags.

I adjusted the brim of the hat that swooped down over the right side of my face. At first I thought it might be overkill and that it would draw attention, but there were a handful of southern belles in the congregation who didn't disappoint so I fit right in.

I'd been so lost in my own thoughts that I didn't realize that Ace and Lynette had turned to face the congregation. I shifted quietly in the pew so that I could hide safely behind a woman with a bleached-blonde Afro.

"What you're looking at is a result of prayer," the minister said.

I wasn't. I was looking at the woman in front of me who needed to touch up her roots.

Ruby waved her hands like she was at some sort of revival. "Amen to that."

I thought about the lonely sesame seed bagel that I had left in Cassandra's refrigerator, and my grumbling stomach announced it to everyone on my pew.

"You're not the only one," Ruby whispered. "I hope they have some real food at the reception and not that finger food stuff or some fancy appetizers. I'm starting a new diet tomorrow. Give me some of that stuffed chicken with some rice or potatoes."

The only person paying me attention in this entire church slid out of his pew and out the back door. He looked even better standing up than he did sitting down. I picked up my purse and tucked it under my arm, so that I could pull my disappearing act at the perfect time. Maybe it was God, and not Cassandra, who'd led me here. Maybe the man of my dreams was actually waiting outside the church doors and I'd had to go through all of the drama with Ace in order to get to him. Maybe Ace and I would cross paths again. At the family reunion.

Ruby rambled on and so did the minister. Ace and Lynette were still facing the congregation.

"If there is anyone here today that doesn't know the God that reunited this beautiful couple, Lynette and Scott wanted me to offer *you* a gift on this day of *their* celebration. The free gift of salvation is available for anyone who wants to accept Christ into their heart."

Ruby swayed. "Yes, Lord. Do a mighty work in their hearts right now."

All of a sudden she'd turned from wanting to eat to wanting to pray.

Ruby bowed her head, and I did the same. I clasped my hands underneath my chin and closed my eyes even before the minister asked everyone to do so.

"Whether you accepted Jesus Christ as your personal Savior fifty years ago, or whether this is the first time you're inviting Him into your heart, I want everyone to repeat this prayer with me."

So I did. I repeated the words he recited. I'd heard a variation of what Ace's old pastor used to called the "sinner's prayer" before, but had never in my life said it. Felt it. It seemed to come with too much responsibility to live the perfect life. I hadn't been ready for it then. I wasn't sure I was ready for it now, but it was like I couldn't stop myself from repeating those words. Feeling those words. Crying because of those words.

For a minute I forgot where I was. It was hard to explain. Joy rose in my heart, crowding out my worries. Peace evicted the chaos that had been plaguing my mind. I'd heard a woman at Ace's old church once say that it was "well with her soul." I wasn't totally sure what that meant, but I thought I was feeling something like it. It *was* well with my soul . . . until my cell phone rang.

Chapter 3

That stupid thing was supposed to be on vibrate. Instead the ringtone of one of the R&B hotties interrupted my beautiful experience. I think it was the first time I'd truly felt God, or at least I thought it was Him. But some "drop it like it's hot" music had taken it all away.

I snatched the phone out of the inside pocket of my purse and silenced it, but not before a few people whipped their heads around like they were set to throw daggers.

To make the situation worse, Ruby had the audacity to whisper, "I hope it's Jesus calling."

I stood up, kept my body low and my head down—humped over like the hunchback of Notre Dame—and bolted through the back doors and out into the foyer. The soldiers guarding them didn't have time to react.

I ran right into my admirer. Actually, I rammed the door into his side. I'd bolted out the double doors without putting the brakes on my three-inch pumps and nearly knocked him out. My ankle twisted to the side, and he grabbed me to help me regain my balance.

"My mama always said women would fall for me," he said.

I let him hold my hand while I balanced on one foot then the other to pull off my high heels.

"That was a sorry pick-up line," I said. "Did you think of that all by yourself?"

He looked at me like I was a chilled glass of water in the middle of the Sahara Desert. I knew I'd walked out of the door looking like a million bucks, but his admiration upped my ante to about a billion.

"I'm not trying to pick you up," he said. "I'm trying to sweep you off your feet."

I grinned and playfully rolled my eyes at him. I played the sheepish schoolgirl part, slyly looking away from him. That's when I noticed his shoes. They were brown, dusty, and in need of a good old-fashioned buffing from one of the old men who manned the shoeshine chairs at the Atlanta airport. In fact, those shoes needed to be dropped in the nearest donation bin as soon as possible.

"So are you going to give me a chance . . ." He paused, leaving a fill-in-the-blank kind of look so I would insert my name.

I rerouted his intentions while I thought of what to tell him. "Are you a friend of the bride or groom?"

"Lynette is my cousin. Our mamas are sisters." He reached for my hand and clasped it gently. "Reggie."

"Nice to meet you, Reggie. You can call me Marcelle."

"That's what I can call you, but is that your name?"

"It has been for almost thirty-four years." At least I wasn't lying, although I wasn't a fan of my middle name. I'm not sure what my mother was thinking when she named me after a woman who won the showcase showdown at the end of the original *Price is Right* game show. I think it's because she was secretly in love with Bob Barker.

"Well, Marcelle," Reggie said. "It looks like you're in a rush, so I should probably go ahead and get your number so we can talk later." He unclipped his cell phone from the holder on his hip.

"I guess I can give you my number, since you're so sure of yourself," I said, choosing to ignore his pitiful excuse for a pair of shoes.

Broke-down shoes usually meant a broke man, but I challenged that theory lately because although everything I wore from head to toe was expensive, I currently didn't have enough money in my bank account to buy one heel off of one of my shoes.

He dialed my number from his cell and that "drop it like it's hot ringtone" played again as his call came through.

"You can tell a lot about a woman from the music she likes," he said, clearly amused as I scrambled to silence the phone again.

This time I double-checked to make sure my cell was on vibrate.

"I only listen to Mahalia Jackson," I said with a smirk. Thanks to Mama, she was the only tried and true gospel singer whose songs I knew and could sing verbatim. Mama played that same tired record every Sunday when she finally woke up around eleven o'clock to cook us our routine Sunday breakfast. Mahalia was Mama's substitute for church, and Mama sang along with her with a cigarette dangling from her lips. Every Sunday it was Mahalia, grits, corned beef hash, and scrambled eggs with onions.

I peeked through the small windows in the door, and into the sanctuary. Everyone was standing up and Ace and Lynette were gazing at each other like the figurines on a wedding cake topper. The minister was about to announce them as husband and wife, and I was about to be exposed. My senses went into overload. A horn blared from outside, intensifying my anxiety.

Cassandra was camped at the front steps in her Honda Accord, windows down and her music loud enough for the entire neighborhood to hear. I struggled to push my feet into my shoes, but it was like my size eights had ballooned to a ten in a matter of minutes.

"I've got to run," I said. Literally. "Call me," I yelled back to Reggie as I ran out of the front door barefoot.

In true Cinderella style I dropped one of my shoes as I did my best to make it down the steps in the hip-hugging skirt I'd put on this morning. I wasn't a fool. I ran back up to the first landing to get it, the heat from the concrete steps permeating the soles of my feet. I swung open the passenger door and fell into the car.

"Go," I panted.

Chapter 4

Cassandra peeled away from the curb, and I held on to the door handle to keep it from swinging open and throwing me out. My best friend and getaway driver swung her hair over her shoulder and let the oversized shades that were on her head slip down over her eyes. She defied all traffic rules while I struggled to get my seat belt from its locked position. Cassandra crossed over two lanes of traffic, then U-turned around a median nearly two and a half blocks away.

Cassandra finally slowed down. "That was like some mess out of the movies," she said. Her adrenaline was pumping so fast I could see it in her eyes. She was getting way too much enjoyment out of this, while I felt like I was about to have a heart attack.

Cassandra had U-turned to put us back on track, which meant we had to pass the church again. She slowed down like the rest of the rubberneckers and nosy people on our side of the street.

"I can see why Ace had your nose wide open. He looks even better than I remember him," she crooned and smacked her lips.

"Will you just drive, please?" I asked, looking toward the happy couple, but not really wanting to. But I couldn't pull my eyes away. Cassandra had said I'd come to one of two resolutions, and at that moment I did. I realized then that I couldn't make myself hate Ace even if I wanted to. He was where he was supposed to be and with whom he was supposed to be with. At least someone had their happily-ever-after.

We crept at the pace of a ninety-three-year-old woman past the church before I finally relaxed. Cassandra's windows were tinted, so there was no chance anyone could spot me from across the way, but I'd already had one close call too many.

I scrolled through the incoming calls on my cell phone and saw Cassandra's name. "That was you? Did you have to call my cell? It rang in the middle of the minister's prayer," I said, tossing my hat onto the back seat. It landed beside the ridiculous blonde wig Cassandra tried to persuade me to wear. Cassandra has always been about drama, and the more the better.

She swerved into the next lane without any regard for the elderly man who'd been trying to inch his way over in the merciless Saturday afternoon traffic. "Any sensible person would have their phone on vibrate," Cassandra said, smoothing down the jet black, bone-straight weave that made her look like Cher. "I was hoping you'd feel the buzz and know that I was ready to go. I have better things to do than play taxi for you on a Saturday afternoon. There's a frat convention downtown, and this sister has got to be in the mix."

The last time I checked, Cassandra already had a man, if that's what you wanted to call Frank. The crazy thing about it was that Frank used to be Lynette's old flame. I don't think their relationship ever grew past a flicker because evidently Lynette has just as much common sense as she does book sense.

Frank went from one extreme to the other with those two

women. On a ghetto scale from one to ten, Cassandra was a seven, and Lynette was a negative eight. I still couldn't figure out Frank's scheme, but I guess that wasn't for me to worry about.

After years of dealing with low-down, dirty scoundrels, I thought Cassandra had finally upgraded from her previous relationships. Frank was a landscape engineer with aspirations to become a household name as an artist. He seemed so deep, too. All of his works of art were titled based on Scriptures. The picture he'd painted of his life seemed perfect enough until the true man surfaced. I'd once heard it said that even the Devil knows Scripture. Frank proved that cliché to be true. And to think, I used to be jealous of them.

Cassandra inched up to the traffic line at the stoplight. She idled, then patted the gas pedal like we were at the starting line of the Indy 500.

"Sheila, girl, you remember when we went to that party at the Omega house in our freshman year?" And thus the stories began.

Cassandra reminded me of some of our former escapades that I'd rather forget. Thankfully, the proof of my ignorance from years ago was only relegated to our memories and hadn't been documented by digital photos and online viral videos like they would be today.

"You gave that boy a run for his money," Cassandra said, still entertaining herself.

The light turned green, and she raced to the next stop light. She hadn't even bothered to ask how I was feeling. Cassandra's only concern was about getting lost in a sea of men wearing purple and gold. I was supposed to be her best friend, and she was absolutely clueless.

"If you promise me you can get ready in less than thirty minutes, I'll swing by the house so you can take off your mourning clothes," Cassandra said. "You just need to roll out with me for a while. When I get finished, Ace will be the last man on your mind."

"I pass." I interjected before she continued with her plans. I'd had enough of her bright ideas for one day. Right now I craved some peace and quiet more than I did biceps and triceps. Being alone was a rarity since I'd moved in with Cassandra six months ago. If she wasn't prancing around the house, it was Frank. She'd given him a key to come and go as he pleased, and he took full advantage of the offer. But Frank was out of town this weekend—hence Cassandra's weekend escapade. I wanted to be by myself to think, and to try and recapture that peace I'd experienced at the church.

"I thought you wanted to . . ."

"No, *you* thought I wanted to flaunt myself in front of men like I'm a piece of meat. That's your job, not mine. Just take me home," I said, already regretting that I'd taken an unnecessary stab at Cassandra. My emotions were awry.

"Excuuuuuse me," Cassandra said. "Next time I find out some critical information that might benefit you, I'll keep it to myself. I never would've told you about the wedding if I knew it would put you in such a nasty mood."

She said the word "nasty" like she'd swallowed a tablespoon of vinegar.

"Get over it," Cassandra said. "Ace has moved on. Forever. Get a life."

I couldn't believe my ears. "First of all, I have moved on," I said. "Second, you're the one who suggested I go to the stupid wedding. Or recommitment ceremony. Whatever it was."

"Well, you don't have to listen to everything I say. As a matter of fact, it's evident that you don't. If you'd been fulfilling Ace's manly needs on a regular basis, you probably wouldn't be in this situation. I mean if a man isn't supposed to be free to enjoy sex as much as he wants to, then God wouldn't have designed them to want it so much."

The traffic light changed, and Cassandra floored it to the next light again. At this rate it was going to take forever to get home. If only I could have clicked my ruby red slippers and disappeared. Some days Cassandra was easier to handle. You'd think after being friends for over half our lives that she wouldn't be able to get to me the way she did. But today, she was pushing all of my hot buttons.

I bit down on my lip so hard that I just knew I was going to draw blood at any minute. I closed my eyes and tried to transport myself back into the place of peace. Ruby's chubby hand of comfort. The minister's prayer. But I couldn't get there with somebody on the radio rapping about money, diamonds, and oversized rims on his unpaid-for car.

I opened my eyes and decided to address Cassandra's comments as calmly as I could.

"This situation has nothing to do with fulfilling Ace's needs. Evidently God has someone else for me. Ace is where he's supposed to be. It wasn't God's will for us to be together. And there's absolutely nothing I can do about it."

Cassandra pulled out a tube of mascara and pumped the wand in and out of the pink tube. She layered a thick coat of jet black mascara on her fake lashes.

"Ace is where he's *supposed* to be or where *you* pushed him? Personally, I think people take this God's will stuff too far. There is such a thing as free will, you know. Two people withholding themselves from each other ain't natural. I think it builds up toxins in your system. Maybe that's what's wrong with you. You're full of toxins. Where's God's will in that?"

I'd had it. I forced my swollen feet into my shoes, then checked the rearview mirror before I flung open the passenger door. For one thing, I wanted to be out of the hitting range of the lightning bolt when it came to strike Cassandra's car. For another, I was just plain sick and tired of Cassandra's mouth.

"What are you doing?" Cassandra said, tossing her makeup case onto the back seat. You're going to get my car door knocked off. Either that or some crucial body part you might need one day is going to be laying in the middle of the street."

"I'll get a ride," I said, slamming the car door at the exact moment the traffic light turned green. I didn't know when. Or how. Not with only twenty dollars to my name, maxed-out credit cards, and wearing three-inch heels.

Cassandra let down the passenger's window. "If I drive off, I'm not turning around," she warned. "I'm serious. I've got things to do. Men to see."

I waited for an approaching car to pass, but it slowed down instead. The driver of a freshly washed convertible came to a slow halt. A line of irritated drivers with blaring horns tried to persuade the driver to move, but he didn't budge. So I did.

I swung my purse over my shoulder and hoped a car wouldn't swerve around him and make Cassandra's warning a reality. I needed all of my body parts, even the ones I hadn't used in a while.

"Hey, baby doll. If you need a ride, we can take you anywhere you need to go," the driver said.

I ignored him, although it was hard to do with his flawless set of thirty-twos and the way one of his eyebrows arched higher than the other—like he was up to something. He cruised forward a few feet like he was on exhibit at one of those classic car shows that my uncle used to attend. The driver probably spent his morning spit-shining his rims.

Since he was trying to be the center of attraction, I walked around to the rear of his car so that I could safely cross the street. I didn't have time for the nonsense. I hope he didn't think his Lexus was supposed to impress me. *I've got my own*, I wanted to tell him. It was sitting in the parking lot of Cassandra's apartment complex in need of a transmission and a laundry list of other repairs that I couldn't afford to pay for.

"You don't want to fool with her right now," I heard Cassandra say. She was butting in my business as usual. "She's got issues," she had the nerve to add. For the duration of me and Cassandra's friendship, "issues" had been her middle name.

Both the driver and passenger seemed to be amused, and if I hadn't decided to be the bigger woman, I would've told Cassandra who I *really* thought had the issues.

"Why you gon' put your girl on front street like that?" I heard one of them ask.

I didn't care to hear the answer. In fact, I did a cute speed-walk the rest of the way to the sidewalk so I couldn't. I fought to look better than I felt. With the heat and an empty stomach, I was already starting to feel faint, and I knew that my silk blouse was destined to cling to my back any second because June heat in Atlanta didn't show mercy to any man or woman.

I'd let my emotions get the best of me, and unfortunately life didn't have a rewind button. I needed more than that—like a complete restart button. God knows I would've pushed it a long time ago.

I marched down the sidewalk like it had been my plan since this morning to get out of Cassandra's car with absolutely no destination in mind. I couldn't think about restarting life right now because I had other things to do. Like finding a place to stay in case she kicked me out.

Chapter 5

The options for keeping a roof over my head were few and far between. Living with Mama and my brother, Devin, wasn't an option. Like Mama used to be, Devin was a chain smoker, and a single whiff of smoke gave me a headache now, even though I'd grown up breathing secondhand smoke daily. On top of that, I didn't trust Devin. My own blood had stolen from me before, and he'd probably do it again if given the chance. He was so desperate that even if I didn't have much money, he'd steal my dreams.

Thinking about Devin and all the drama he'd brought into my life only made me get more worked up. It was ten minutes before I spotted a cab and was able to flag it down. The driver did a 360-degree turn in the middle of the parking lot and pulled up to where I was standing.

I didn't move. I don't know why.

The cab driver put down the back window and leaned over the seat until he could see me.

"Hey dere lady. Me not a chauffeur. You be getting in or not?"

I rolled my eyes, muscled open the rusty door, and got in.

"Take me as far as ten dollars will go," I told the cab driver, even though I only had twenty dollars in my purse. Twenty dollars in a Louis Vuitton purse. How did I get to this point? I thought I'd only have to spend three dollars or so to catch the bus, but I'd soon learned from a gas station attendant that they'd cut the bus routes that serviced this part of the community. Even the city was broke.

The grey fake leather seat in the back of the taxicab had rips from one end to the next. The seat's upholstery stuffing stuck through the split leather, like it had been slashed with a pocket knife. I hovered as close to the back door as I could without risking my life if the rickety thing fell off its hinges

"'Dis is it, ma'am," the cab driver said after a few minutes.

I wouldn't have known which island to attribute his accent to if he hadn't been so proud of his heritage. He'd taped a small replica of the Jamaican flag to the roof of the cab and a flag the size of a hand towel draped over the middle armrest.

I'd been daydreaming out the window, but now I looked at the meter.

"I just got in here. There's no way you've driven me far enough," I protested.

Even though the cab's seats were in bad condition, the AC was blowing like an Arctic wind. I tried to delay walking back into Hot-lanta's summer swelter. "Your meter is broken," I insisted and tried to get him to admit his hustle.

"Da meter don't lie, ma'am." He tapped the black box on the dash. "It works perfectly fine."

I wasn't sure of that, but I couldn't figure out how to prove that he'd rigged that little ticking machine.

I took inventory of the surroundings outside. Mr. Jamaica had pulled up under the awning of a dilapidated gas station. Two of the three gas pump handles were covered with red plastic bags, yet the lot was still a hub of activity. A woman wearing a turban and a dashiki sat in a lawn chair in front of a van selling ten pairs of socks for five dollars. On the other end of the lot was a man selling imitation Oriental rugs and rugs with animal prints.

The driver was waiting for my ten dollars, but instead I gave him puppy dog eyes. If I had to play the damsel in distress, so be it. For years the same role had helped me pay for things that my paychecks couldn't.

"Can you at least take me to the shopping center at the next light?" When he looked at the meter, I rushed to say, "Without letting the meter run?"

The cab driver propped his arm across the span of the front seat, looked at me, then down at my purse.

"Are you trying to pull de fast one on me? Is dat how you can walk around wit ya fancy stuff? Because you get over on hard workers like me? Ya need to be around de Jamaican women. They can show ya what it means to be beautiful *and* work hard."

There was a time when I would've given him a piece of my mind, but seeing that I was at his mercy, I humbled myself.

"Sir, I wouldn't be asking you if I didn't really need the favor. The only thing I can promise you is that if you're a blessing to me, I'll make it my business to be a blessing to someone else. You know—pay it forward."

He turned around and looked out the window, then acknowledged another cab driver with a nod of his head. "Goodness. Why do I get all of de charity cases?" he mumbled, then turned back to look at me. "I'm a reasonable man. How can I say no to a pretty woman when ya ask me like dat?"

It's been proven that not too many men can say no to me, I thought.

Chapter 6

N₀."

It was worth asking, even though I didn't really think Mr. Jamaica would actually let me walk away without giving him a dime. We'd pulled into the shopping center parking lot and I'd asked the cab driver if the fare was on the house.

I flipped him two five dollar bills and thought maybe God would miraculously speak to him so he'd give it back to me. He didn't.

"God bless you," he said.

"Thank you. I'll take all the blessings I can get," I said as I forced my swelling feet back into my heels. My mother used to soak her feet in Epsom salts after working and walking for hours on her feet. What I wouldn't do for some salts and a plastic bin right now. Beauty had even more of a price now that I couldn't indulge in my regular pedicure.

I stepped out into the swelter, and it didn't waste any time putting my deodorant to the test. I was thankful that I'd layered on one of my favorite scented lotions, added the body cream, and topped it with a splash of the same fragrance. Mama taught me that trick, and I had faithfully practiced with the drug store perfumes and scented powders that used to cover her dresser.

And like Mama used to do, this morning I'd flipped my nearly-empty lotion bottle upside down like it was ketchup. I couldn't remember the last time I'd had to do that. Money—or the lack thereof—had a way of shifting your priorities. My favorite lotion and cream set wasn't a priority.

I strolled down the sidewalk of the shopping center. It didn't have much to offer. Big Papa's Pizza and Wings. A boutique specializing in eyebrows. Superior Dry Cleaners. Eden's Gates Bookstore and Gift Shop, and beside it a store that sold natural herbs and vitamins.

Even though I was starving, the fact that the door to the pizza joint was propped open didn't promise a reprieve from the heat. On top of that, there were one too many flies for my liking. Besides, the last thing I needed was a nice greasy pizza stain to complete the sweat rings forming under my arms.

The bookstore seemed like the most sensible place to go. A gospel choir serenaded my entrance, and it was like walking into heaven. It made me appreciate the fact that this was the day I'd chosen to really get my life together. I wasn't going to wait until I was on a man's arm before I set foot inside of a church. Unless of course, church was where I was going to find my new man.

Chapter 7

Welcome to Eden's Gates."

I heard a woman's voice but didn't see her. When she appeared from around a bookshelf corner, I saw why. I was five seven in my bare feet, so I guessed she was about five feet one. Maybe two, but even that extra inch was pushing it. She wore flat thong sandals with a huge fake flower in the middle that nearly hid her miniature feet. They weren't the cutest, in my opinion, but were undoubtedly more comfortable than what I was wearing.

"Are you looking for anything in particular?" she asked. She ran her fingers through a forest of thick burgundy-dyed tresses that were styled in small twists, puffing them out even more. Now they framed her face like a burst of sunshine, and her smile was just as brilliant.

"No, just browsing," I said and picked up a book from the shelf closest to me. When I realized it was about sex and the marriage bed, I slid it back into its spot and walked over to a section labeled Women's Interests. Dating Ace had taught me a few things about me and celibacy. If you don't want a fire to burn you, don't do anything to set it ablaze.

"If you need anything, let me know," the woman said. "My name is Eden."

"Sheila," I said. "And this must be your store?"

"For the last six years," she stated proudly. "It's not a huge money maker, but it's a dream fulfilled. You can't pay for that." She ran her hand through the crown again. The tint of her hair reminded me of the hair color kit I used to buy for Mama when she wanted to spruce up her look. Back then the color didn't have a name, only a number.

Eden hoisted the stack of books she was carrying over to her left hip. I hoped she wouldn't tip over.

"I'll be right over there if you need me," she said and left me to browse the shelves.

I was glad Eden didn't hover over me like she was desperate for a sale. If she was looking for a big spender today, I wasn't her woman. I still wasn't sure how I was going to survive on ten dollars for the next six days, until my unemployment benefits were direct-deposited into my checking account.

I chose a women's devotional book off the shelves because there were three ladies on the cover who looked like me on my best day. Brown skinned. Hopeful. Then I picked up a book that had a blurb on the back cover about being happy in singleness. I didn't want God to get any notion that I was content with being single forever, so I put it back.

I spotted an oversized love seat near the rear of the store. The entire area was staged like an intimate living room, and I imagined that Eden's house probably looked a lot like it. An arrangement of silk flowers—that were almost identical to the ones on her sandals—decorated a center coffee table. In the corner near a small curio, sat three columns at varying heights. On each was a plant with leaves that twined down to the rug. The rug was burgundy—just like Eden's hair.

Eden was singing along with the gospel choir and not paying much attention to me, so I settled back into the cushions of the couch. I opened the devotional first and didn't expect for it to suck me in the way that it did. I surprised myself when I actually jotted a few notes down, because it was almost like I was having a personal—and free—counseling session.

Nearly twenty minutes passed before I knew it, and I told myself that I was going to have to sacrifice at least five dollars for a greasy piece of cheese pizza with a drink. Then the closest thing that I'd had to a miracle all day happened. Eden appeared holding a tray of crackers, chicken salad, and cucumber finger sandwiches. I could've kissed her—right after I finished eating.

"Can I offer you something to eat?" Eden asked, setting the tray down on the coffee table.

I tried to keep myself from jumping on top of the table and stuffing food in my mouth and hiding some down my blouse for later.

"You're right on time," I said. "I would like a little something. Thank you so much." My stomach grumbled, telling Eden that I needed more than a little. I patted my midsection. "Stomachs don't lie, do they?"

"Eat all you'd like," she said. "And there's more where this came from." Eden scurried away.

I stood up and arched my back in a full stretch. I hadn't had a full-body massage since the day I had been laid off from my job at J. Morrow, a recruiting firm. After they had hand-delivered my separation package, I had finished packing my belongings in a box and made my coworker Clive escort me to the car. On the way out to the parking garage, I had thought I'd call the spa for an immediate appointment, figuring I might as well treat myself while I still had a few bucks to spare.

Clive loaded my box in my trunk, and through the side mirror I saw him pull out his wallet. He walked up to my window and held out a hundred dollar bill.

"I couldn't control where the ax fell," he said. Clive was part of J. Morrow's upper echelon. He would probably always be clear of the gauntlet.

"I know," I said, looking at the money but still not taking it. "So the money is a way to say you feel sorry for me."

"No. The money is so you won't spend yours on a massage. It's kind of tight out there right now."

"I'm a big girl," I said, though I slid the money out of his hand anyway. "I can take care of myself. But thank you for the gift."

That was over eight months ago, and my finances weren't only tight, they were strangling me. My life had been in a chokehold. I'd had a stint of unemployment before, but never for this long.

I was massaging a crick in my neck when I saw someone come into the bookstore who looked like my pew partner, Ruby. But Ruby was probably still at the reception shoveling down stuffed mushrooms or some other fancy cuisine, and trying her best to electric slide her way over to Reggie.

"Come on girls. We have to hurry so we can get back to the reception," the woman yelled over her shoulder. I guess she got tired of waiting for whoever she was fussing at, because she let the door close behind her.

"Welcome to Eden's Gates," I heard Eden's voice call out.

That's when I saw the woman in clear view, and she didn't just look like Ruby. She *was* Ruby.

Chapter 8

I dropped down low like I was in military training. I didn't want Ruby to see me and come at me with a barrage of a million and one questions. Thankfully there were plenty of bookshelves where I could take cover if necessary. The back sitting area was in such a wide, open space that Ruby was sure to see me if she came to the rear of the store.

I grabbed my purse and tiptoed over to the area with the tallest display cases. Angels were lined up on each of the shelves. A placard sitting in front of one of the angels had the words, "The Guardian," on it. If I *did* have a guardian angel, he or she needed to be on the job and cause either me or Ruby to disappear. I peeked around the display case to see if I was safe in my current location, or if I needed to plan a quick exit and come back once Ruby took her behind back to Ace and Lynette's reception.

The bookstore door opened again. I had to keep my knees

from giving out when Carmen and Jada walked in. This had to be some kind of joke. I'd finally said the sinner's prayer, and the Devil was already playing tricks on me.

Think, think, think, I told myself. I crouched down like I was examining items on the bottom shelf, and for the first time realized that I didn't have my shoes on. I'd tucked them under the coffee table when I'd had the nerve to make myself *too* comfortable in Eden's Gates.

"These are my cousin's children," I heard Ruby say. "I brought them to the bookstore to find them something to keep their minds occupied when they're with their grandparents while their parents go on their honeymoon."

"That's nice of you."

"Oh, I'm a retired librarian," Ruby said. "Kids think these television shows are so good, but they don't do anything but feed your head with a bunch of mess. That's why they need a book to read. And I'm not talking about none of that vampire and erotic stuff."

"You won't find any of that here," Eden said.

"I don't even mind if they find a good novel or something about girls their age and relationships with boys. You can't shelter children from everything, but you can give them what they need so they'll make better decisions."

"I've got the perfect series for them," Eden said.

Their voices were getting closer to where I was hiding.

"Shoot," I whispered.

Ruby went on and on, telling her business and theirs. "Their parents got remarried today after being divorced almost five years. My cousin—Ace—he married his first wife again."

"Mama was Daddy's only wife, not just the first wife."

That was Carmen. Always the one to be quick on her feet, and most of the time a little too grown for her own good. Of both girls, she had been the one who really didn't like me. When we'd been in each other's presence—which had been rare—she had tolerated me for Ace's sake.

"Anyway," Ruby continued, "I think I cried through the entire ceremony. This lady sitting beside me did, too." Ruby grunted. "Then she got a call from Jesus and had to leave. Ran straight out of the church."

"That was strange," Eden said.

"It's some strange people in this world," Ruby said.

Ruby was probably strutting around the store like she owned the world. Why did she have to talk about me, of all people? Ruby hadn't bothered to tell Eden that even though she was married to her third husband, she was trying to be flirtatious with another man.

My knees were getting stiff from being stooped down for so long. It was no wonder my back felt strained, because I'd been humped over most of the day. Thankfully I noticed a restroom tucked in a tiny nook, so I quietly stood up, and in less than five seconds I slipped into the hiding place. I exhaled a long stream of air so that my heart would stop thumping so hard against my chest cavity.

I'd give them ten minutes before I dared to peek out to see if they were gone. I sat on top of the toilet seat and thought about whether I should call Cassandra. She'd probably long been swallowed up in the sea of purple and gold, and the last thing she would be listening for was her cell phone ringing. If she did hear it, I know she'd see the call was from me and ignore my ringing plea for help.

I pushed my ego aside and called anyway. The call went straight to voice mail. I didn't have a long time to feel defeated, because someone knocked on the door.

I froze. There was only one toilet in the restroom, so I knew whoever it was wasn't going to go away anytime soon. Then the door knob jiggled.

"Yes?" I said, trying to disguise my voice.

"Sorry. I'll wait."

It was Jada. She was the more loving and patient teenager of the two, and I knew she wasn't going anywhere. She was the kind of person who, if I waited too long to come out, would ask me if I needed extra toilet tissue or offer to get someone else to help.

I knew there was nothing else I could do, so after a few moments I flushed the toilet, turned on the faucet like I was washing my hands, and then opened the door.

Jada was leaning against the wall flipping through a book. She was still wearing her dress from earlier, but had exchanged her dressy sandals for a pair of hot pink flip flops. Her toenails were painted the same color, which I knew was a stretch for her. Jada was one hundred percent tomboy and probably would've preferred to be in basketball shorts and tennis shoes.

I thought I could slip past her before she looked up from her book.

"Ms. Sheila?" she said. Jada squinted like I was a figment of her imagination.

I tossed my hair back dramatically so that it would sway across my shoulders. "Jada?" I said, trying to put just as much astonishment in my voice. "What a surprise. How have you been?" I shot a glance around the store and saw that Eden had Ruby and Carmen's full attention.

"I've been doing good," Jada said. "Everybody's doing really good," she added, then seemed to recoil like she shouldn't have made such a sensitive statement. Unlike her older, self-absorbed sister, she was more mindful of other people's feelings. "Mama and Daddy got married again." She said it softly, like she'd been the one who had to break the news to me. "Today."

I choked the words out. "That's great. I'm happy for you guys."

She fumbled with the bodice of her sundress, then said, "You look nice. Not that it's a surprise. You always looked nice. I mean I'm not a fashionista like Carmen, but I know a stylish woman when I see one," she complimented me. "You were always dressed like a celebrity." She frowned when she noticed I wasn't wearing shoes, but she didn't mention it.

I didn't either. I was trying to ignore the fact that she was talking about me in past tense.

"How sweet of you," I said.

"Where did you go today?" Jada asked. I don't think she really cared, but was merely making pleasant conversation.

"Doing my thing with the girls," I said, silently rebuking myself. I'd asked Jesus into my heart, and I hadn't gone two hours without telling a flat-out lie. But what was I supposed to say? *I was at the church to see your parents get married. You didn't see me in the back pew?*

"I better hurry up so we can get back to the church," Jada said. "If I don't come out soon, Cousin Ruby will come looking for me, and trust me, I don't want that to happen."

Neither do I.

To my surprise, Jada reached out and gave me an awkward hug. "It was good seeing you, Ms. Sheila. Take care of yourself."

"I plan to," I said. I felt like I wanted to cry. That hug—it was so final. I already knew the only way Ace could be mine was in my dreams, but the pain flared up again nonetheless.

I headed for the door. I didn't care if I wasn't wearing shoes, because they would only slow me down anyway. Before the door closed behind me, I looked back. My eyes made direct contact with Carmen. I pushed a smile through my pain, but Carmen rolled her eyes. I wasn't surprised.

Carmen tapped Ruby on the shoulder and whispered something in her ear.

I don't know what she said or how Ruby responded, because I sprinted into the natural herb shop next door.

Chapter 9

W e're about to close, ma'am," the woman inside the herb store yelled out. She had her hands on her hips, but it wasn't because she was happy to see me. She needed to take some customer service lessons from Eden.

"Can you give me time to look for something?" I asked.

"Five minutes. That's it." She looked down at my feet, rolled her eyes, then disappeared behind a black curtain in the back.

I poked around the store until I saw Ruby, Carmen, and Jada drive away in a silver Cadillac. Eden acted like all was well when I finally walked back in the store. I knew that Ruby and the girls had probably put two and two together. I could only imagine the opinions Ruby shared, and Carmen would've relished the opportunity to make it seem like I was a desperate soul.

I found my shoes, squeezed them on my feet, then went to stand up front at the large picture window. I called Cassandra again. This time it rang, but like I figured, she didn't answer.

"Are you leaving me?" Eden asked.

"Not exactly," I said.

"I never did get the chance to help you find anything." She was holding the books I'd left on the coffee table.

"Sorry about that," I said.

Eden flicked her hand in the air. "No big deal." She looked at her watch. "I'll be closing shortly. I close early on Saturdays."

My eyes were getting misty. I knew that if I looked at Eden, tears would slide down my cheeks and I wouldn't be able to stop them.

Eden touched my shoulder gently. "Are you all right? I know you don't know me, but I can still be a listening ear. Sometimes that's all you need. A chance to dump it all out."

I watched the community hustling outside. "There may not be much I can say that your last customers didn't tell you."

Eden didn't respond for a moment, so I knew my suspicion had been right.

Then she said, "There's always two sides to every story. Sometimes three or four sides."

I stared out of the window and thought about everything that had transpired in my life over the last year or so. Things could've been worse, but at the same time, they could've been much better, too.

"As far as my side of the story is concerned, I've turned the page. I've closed this chapter of my life and I'm moving on."

Eden grasped her arms like she was giving herself a hug. "You know there's a Scripture that came to my mind when you said that. I'm paraphrasing, but it talks about forgetting the things that are behind you and reaching forward to the things that are ahead."

"I like that," I said.

Eden flipped the door sign over to read *Closed. Come Back Again.* "I like it, too. Trust me, there are plenty of things in my past that I was happy to forget."

Eden shuffled around for the next few minutes, tidying up the store and getting her odds and ends together. It looked like I was going to have to call Mama to come from across town and take me back to Cassandra's. The three other times I'd had to call for help, she had been at work and Devin had had the car. Of course, he had been nowhere to be found, and had he been, he would've been begging me for gas money.

I called Mama's house, and nobody answered the phone. Her cell phone had been recently disconnected because my sorry brother had used all of her daytime minutes, then run up the bill to over three hundred dollars.

All of a sudden the bookstore was silent, except for the soft hum of the air conditioning unit. Eden had turned off the background gospel music, so I knew she was ready to leave and enjoy the rest of the day.

I opened the door for her. "You have a beautiful store. I hope I can come back soon. Next time I promise I'll buy something."

"Well I'd love to have you back. Come back anytime, and bring your friends, too."

Cassandra would never appreciate a bookstore like Eden's Gates.

Eden turned to walk away, then stopped. "I didn't want to be in your business at first, but do you have a place to go?"

"I do have a place to go. Hopefully. It probably doesn't help that it's not where I want to be," I admitted, though I still skated around the real dilemma.

Eden chuckled like she'd been in the same predicament before. Then she asked, "Well do you have a way to *get* to where you don't want to go?"

I sighed. I thought about lying, thought about how foolish it would be.

"I don't," I said. The two words relieved me of such a burden.

"Come on," she said. "Now you do."

"It's not very close. It's probably at least a thirty-minute ride."

"That's fine. I wasn't about to do anything but go home and sit on my behind anyway."

"Are you sure you don't mind?" I had to speed-walk to keep up with her. Her legs were short, but she almost trotted when she walked.

Eden had to be a real woman of faith if she was offering a ride to a complete stranger. Didn't she know this was Atlanta? It's not like the city topped the nation's crime statistics, but I wouldn't even pick up a toddler who was thumbing a ride. I could hear Mama's voice chastising me for getting into a stranger's car, but I was out of options. I slid into the passenger side of Eden's Yukon. It was practically the size of a school bus, but Eden muscled it around with her small arms.

This woman isn't as fragile as she looks. What if I'm the crazy one for taking the ride? I kept my hand on the door in case I had to dive out of the passenger's side and stop, drop, and roll. Neither my thirty-four-year-old body or my designer suit was meant to hit the pavement at highway speed, but a woman had to do what she had to do.

I relaxed when I felt I wasn't going to end up blindfolded and stuck in the back of the trunk.

"You're an angel," I told Eden while I slid my feet out of my shoes again. Eden was pumping the air conditioner on the highest setting, and it felt like I might have frostbitten toes before I was dropped off. I considered the alternative of standing on the corner with heat so thick around me that I could see it in waves bouncing off the paved parking lot. I'd suffer through it.

"It's no problem," Eden said.

It didn't take much to see that Eden was a carefree woman. She probably didn't let things rattle her peace, and from the way she'd gone out of her way for me in the last few hours, she was one of those people who was a natural giver. Helping other people probably made her happy. I was glad I could contribute to her joy today.

I looked over at Eden. She was having a personal party and singing along with the song on the gospel radio station. I didn't know the words, but it was definitely a cross-over song. I'd heard it on the R&B station during the last ten minutes of the weekday morning show, where they got all spiritual and read a two-minute devotion for the day.

We merged off the exit, and I directed Eden the rest of the way to Cassandra's apartment.

Of course I hadn't expected Cassandra to be there, but seeing her empty parking space gave me relief. And since Frank was out of town, I didn't have to worry about him either.

"Safe and sound," Eden said, turning down the radio. She parked in one of the front visitor spaces and let the car idle. Eden wrote two phone numbers on the back of a business card and handed it to me.

"I'll come back and see you soon," I promised. "There's a book or two I want to buy once I get a couple of other things in order." My broke-down Lexus parked in the end space was one of those things.

"Speaking of books," Eden said, reaching down between the driver's seat and door. She handed me the devotional I'd been reading. I accepted it with a smile and hugged it to my chest like it was the first black Barbie doll I'd ever gotten—on my fifth birthday. "I'm not going to act like I don't want it," I said, "so I'll just say thank you."

"You're welcome." Eden slid the wooden bangles she was wearing up and down her thin arm. "So is everything good?"

"Yes, definitely," I said, sliding her card into my wallet.

I would be fast asleep by the time Cassandra came home. Tomorrow would be a new day, and by morning both of us would be able to talk to each other like we had some sense. I wasn't above apologizing for my actions. Cassandra would accept, we'd laugh it off, and life would move on. At least that's what I hoped.

Chapter 10

Silence had never sounded so good. I closed the door behind me, and the motion-activated room deodorizer near the front door spritzed the aroma of what was supposed to be linen hanging in a summer breeze. It did nothing, however, to mask the stench of whatever had been burnt in the kitchen.

Cassandra had probably rushed home to change into something scanty and then made herself something to eat before disappearing into the chaos downtown. She'd left the fan light on over the kitchen stove, which meant she planned on making it a long night—or an early morning—out.

I went into the guest bedroom that Cassandra had used as an office and a small den before I moved in. We'd taken her futon and lamps into her main bedroom, but left her desk and computer, since they were too much trouble to manage. It could be a bother when she wanted to surf the Internet late at night, but since I was basically staying rent free (with help toward the utilities), it wasn't about my comfort and convenience.

I shed my clothes in the corner of room, then added them to the growing laundry bag of items that needed to be dry-cleaned. Unfortunately most of my clothes were marked with what I now considered an infamous tag, *Dry Clean Only*. When desperate times had called for budgeted measures, I'd attempted to wash one of my spring sweaters, and it had come out looking like a mangled puppy.

In less than fifteen minutes I'd showered and settled onto the couch with three rubbery microwaved chicken fajitas, a copy of my résumé, and a bin to soak my feet. I'd popped one migraine-strength acetaminophen for the headache pressure building up behind my eyes and tried to focus on editing my resume for the umpteenth time. I'd been a recruiter when I worked at J. Morrow, so I knew all of the key résumé words. Yet somehow I hadn't made myself attractive enough on paper to get a single interview in the last three months.

I wiggled my toes in the mixture of warm water, salts, and the last of a rose petal foot soak I'd been saving in case of a foot emergency. This was definitely a 9-1-1. Once my pains dissolved from head to toe, this was going to be a great night.

I closed my eyes and tried to escape my surroundings. I'd gotten over Cassandra's questionable taste in home décor even though I always felt like I was reclining in the African jungle whenever I kicked back on the couch. I tossed the zebra print throw on the floor and tried to focus on something positive, like a time when worry and lack weren't constant companions. The Scripture that Eden had talked about came to mind ... *don't focus on the past, look at the future.*

When I heard Cassandra fumbling outside of the door with her keys, I stood up to gather my things, then decided against it. I could be the bigger woman, and I didn't have to wait until the morning—like I'd expected—to do it.

I lifted my feet out of the water, dried my soles, then stood up to face her, making sure the expression on my face was as pleasant as possible.

Only it wasn't Cassandra. It was Frank.

"Frank?" I yanked the zebra throw off the floor and used it to shield my exposed thighs. From the smirk on his face I guess Frank had already gotten an eyeful, and he didn't mind saying so.

"Best-looking thing I've seen all day."

"Number one, keep your eyes to yourself," I said.

"You put it out there for me to see."

He can't be serious, I thought. "You know good and well I didn't know you were coming over here, which leads to point number two. What *are* you doing here? I thought you were supposed to be out of town."

Frank closed the door and turned the lock. A lump rose in my throat.

"My plans changed. I wanted to get back and hang with some of my frat."

"Can't you go to your own house?"

"I could. But I'm not. Can't you go to yours?" he asked, sarcastically, amusing only himself.

Frank opened the refrigerator and popped the tab off one of my energy drinks. It was the last can of pick-me-up that I had stashed in the fridge, and I watched him gulp it down his throat like a tidal wave.

I shook my head and kept every thought running around in my head to myself. *Look at the future, Sheila. Like when you've moved out of here,* I told myself.

I pulled the throw more tightly around my waist and snatched up my leather portfolio. It felt like Frank was peering through my clothes.

"Lock the door when you leave," I told him. He was scavenging around in the pantry to eat some food that he hadn't bought or contributed a dime to.

"Call me if you need me," he yelled out. "I mean *really* need me."

"No chance at that," I said, slamming the bedroom door. It shook, and my hands trembled. I looked down at my shaking hands and had to take deliberate breaths to contain myself. I jammed my toe against one of the many cardboard boxes stacked against the walls. I punched one of the boxes, but that only added to my list of body parts in pain. I was mad at the world. I was even angry at the stupid boxes because they were packed with the designer label clothes that I'd maxed out my credit cards to buy.

"I can't be in this house tonight," I screamed.

Frank was at my door in two seconds flat. "You calling me? I knew you couldn't resist."

I swung open the door and stepped in his face. "You know what? You are crass, evil, and disrespectful. Do you honestly have nothing else to do with your life other than hit on your girlfriend's best friend?"

Frank stepped back, wiped off the corner of his lip, where my spit of rage had showered him, then looked me over.

"It's even better with an angry woman."

I slammed the door in his face and then locked it. I yanked a pair of black jeans off their hanger and put them on with an off-the-shoulder black shirt. Somebody had to get me out of here, and preferably someone who would offer to treat me to a late-night dinner. My two-day-old leftover Mexican food hadn't done it for me.

Back in the day I owned a little pink book, my version of the infamous little black book where men kept their pursuits. During college I could flip to any letter of the alphabet and find a man who could fulfill my current need. A good dinner. An expensive night on the town. Comic relief. A snuggle and a smooch. A slamming new outfit for Homecoming weekend. A past-due telephone bill or rent for an apartment I couldn't afford in the first place.

Tonight I needed an escape, some food, and a wallet full of cash. And I knew just who to call.

Chapter 11

I'd learned something from dating Ace, who was eight years my senior. The older men were the ones with the real money. Most of them had gotten over blowing their cash on material items, at least until they reached their mid-life crises.

Three months ago I'd met a guy named Patrick who was four years younger than me, and the only thing he had to offer was embarrassment when he tried to pay for our dinner with a credit card that came back denied. What sense did it make for me to hook up with a person who had the same problem I did? I'd spent years spending money that I didn't have, and where had it left me? Jobless with no savings, no means to pay my harassing creditors, designer shoes in a cardboard banana box, and hungry.

I scrolled through the contacts in my cell phone. The bill was an expense I couldn't afford, but I needed the only line I had to the outside world in case someone called me for an interview. I wasn't about to chance anyone leaving messages on Cassandra's home voice mail.

I found Clive's cell phone number, knowing that he'd take the bait like a starving piranha. My mind wasn't functioning earlier because I should've called Clive this afternoon.

"Clive Alston." He answered the phone like he was at work instead of relishing his weekend time away from the corner office at work.

"Mr. Alston. So good to hear your voice," I teased.

"You've been playing hide-and-seek for a few days," Clive said. "I called you last Saturday."

"I know. It was too late to call you back when I realized I'd missed the call. Then I forgot. Charge it to my head, not my heart." I purposefully let a tease drip off of my words when I told him, "But I'm available now. Are you?"

Clive snagged the line quicker than I thought he would. "If you want me to be."

"I'm trying to get out of the house for a while. You know, experience a little of the mature side of the Atlanta life," I said, holding a pair of silver hoop earrings up to my lobes. I ended up settling on the gold chandelier ones. It cranked up my all black attire another notch.

"I take it you're tired of fooling with those young bucks," Clive said. "I've been telling you they're nothing but talk."

"Like I told you a million times, it doesn't matter if they're all talk because you have nothing to do with my relationships. You're like a daddy trying to dig in his grown daughter's business," I said.

"A sugar daddy is more like it," Clive said with a laugh.

I could picture him twirling that ridiculously expensive diamond pinkie ring. If I could slide that thing off his finger without him knowing, I bet I could pay off all of my debt and have money to spare. I might not know much about the Bible, but I know that "Thou shalt not steal," is right up there on the list of things I shouldn't do. God had probably already marked a strike against me for lying today.

"Sugar daddy, huh? Keep your day job," I said. "You're not as funny as you think."

"Speaking of jobs, have you found one yet? I thought maybe that was the reason I hadn't heard from you. I thought luck was finally on your side."

Luck couldn't help me. I needed God to take care of some serious business right now. And what did Clive know about luck? He'd been promoted two weeks before I'd been laid off. Even if Clive was familiar with Lady Luck, he also knew and rubbed elbows with some people higher on the totem pole.

"No job yet," I said. "I think I need cheering up." I was willing to accept any and all of Clive's pity.

"I'll be there at eight. Be ready," Clive said. He loved giving orders.

He had no idea how ready I was. Since I was already dressed in everything except my shoes, I logged onto Cassandra's computer and caught up on some senseless Hollywood gossip on a few blog sites. I liked reading about people who had more problems than I did. Of all the things I was dealing with now, at least I didn't have a cheating spouse, wasn't serving jail and/or probation time, and didn't have anyone accusing me of being a home wrecker.

Frank was howling from Cassandra's master bedroom—his version of singing. He might have been gifted at bringing art to life on canvas, but he was murdering whatever he was singing.

I turned on my radio to drown him out.

Being at Eden's inspired me to turn on some gospel music. Since I didn't own the tried and true Mahalia, I pulled out the only three gospel CDs I owned—all of which Ace had given me. Ace's grandmother loved quartet music, so consequently it had rubbed off on him. I don't know what possessed him to think I wanted to listen to a group of blind men from Alabama. Needless to say, it was still sealed in the plastic. The other two were contemporary gospel jazz CDs with selections of spiritual classics that had been given a modern twist. I'd actually grooved to it quite a few times in the last few months.

Today the melodies stroked my soul like a well-needed massage on tense shoulders.

I stared in the mirror on the back of the closet door. On the outside, the woman looking back at me had it all together. She looked like she owned the world. The woman on the inside sometimes felt like she had the weight of the world on her shoulders. She's the woman who cried at night.

But not tonight, I told myself.

Then there were three hurried—almost frantic—knocks on the bedroom door. I ignored Frank. He could bang on the door all he wanted, but I wasn't opening it until an hour and a half from now when Clive came to pick me up.

"Open up, it's me."

I hadn't even known Cassandra was home. I could tell from her voice that she was riled up. So much for us cooling off while away from each other until the morning. I turned the lock and Cassandra rammed in like a bull.

Chapter 12

We need to talk," Cassandra said.

I slowly set down a bottle of moisturizer I was shaking. I didn't want to make any sudden movement because Cassandra looked ready to pounce on me and swing for all it was worth.

"Did you hear me?"

"I can't help but hear you," I said. "Go ahead, I'm listening."

After all of the unnecessary ruckus, the only thing she did was stare at me. She tapped her foot. One. Two. Three times.

I think her anger had been defused. I decided to speak first instead.

"I never meant for things to escalate like they did today," I said. "I apologize for anything I might have said to offend you, but I think we're both adults, and there's no reason why —"

"There's no reason why you should be parading yourself around half-naked when my man is here," she said, cocking her neck back and forth with each word.

"What? You've got to be kidding me. Whatever Frank said is a lie."

"Why would he lie?"

"Why would *I* lie? I've known you since seventh grade and there has never been an issue of disrespect between me and anybody you were seeing. I don't have a reason to make an advance at Frank, if that's what you're trying to say."

"The man of your dreams just married another woman today, so yes, you have a reason to try and push up on Frank, which means, yes, you have a reason to lie."

That was low, real low.

"Trust me. If I was trying to make a move on a man, Frank would be the last person I'd approach. You need to talk to *your* man about why he's trying to make advances at *me*. In case you've forgotten, I was the one sitting behind a closed and locked door."

I crossed my arms, ready for Cassandra's next retaliation. She was just staring me down again. I knew I'd made her think.

"You know what? You stepped up for me when I needed help, so I'll be the bigger woman and not put you out. And since you're going through your issues, I'm going to chalk this little incident up as you being slightly out of your mind. We've all been there," she said. "I'm going to let everything that happened today slide and not say what I really want to say."

Cassandra wasn't the only one who was going to hold her tongue. The only reason I could contain myself was because I was under *her* roof. She hadn't asked me to contribute to the rent, but that was rightfully so. She'd been in the same predicament almost two years ago, and she'd stayed with me rent *and* utility free. At least I contributed to the bills and put food in the refrigerator.

I stood up, shook moisturizer into my hand, and acted like Cassandra standing there was the least of my concerns.

"Me and my issues will be moving out as soon as we can," I said.

Cassandra turned and walked away without saying another word. This time, *she* slammed the door. There was a time I would've followed her and brewed up another argument, but I stayed in my room, minding my own business until 8:03, when Clive called and told me he was waiting downstairs.

Chapter 13

Clive's ego swallowed up a room. I wasn't surprised that we skipped the waiting line at the front of the lounge and were immediately led by the hostess to the back corner of the room. He was obviously a regular.

The hostess wore all black, so it was easy to lose sight of her in the dark room. That's the only reason I let Clive take my hand and guide me through the maze of people. Call me naïve, but I never realized people in the fifty-and-over club found pleasure in hanging out in dimly lit clubs and hitting on people they barely knew. I could tell by the salacious looks on the men's faces and the irritated expressions of the women that there was a whole lot of that going on.

Clive had said he was taking me somewhere I'd have a nice time. I'd pictured Ray's on the River or one of the trendy downtown bistros.

I slid into the red leather booth and knew that a filet mignon entrée wasn't going to be an option. That was too bad, because I was hungry enough to order a five-course meal and take home a doggy bag of leftovers for the rest of the week. I flipped the menu open and began considering my options. Anything was better than an empty stomach.

"Can you at least act like you're interested in being with me instead of the food? I know your mama taught you how to act on a date," Clive said.

I rolled my eyes. Clive was always trying to start or say something to get a reaction out of me. "Please. You and I both know that this is *not* a date. You're simply a friend treating me to dinner."

It had never been a secret to me. Clive was naughty. He'd tried to come on to me several times, but in the past I'd only played him to the point that I needed him. We both knew the game, and he'd played it as much as I had.

No woman could deny that Clive was a fine brother. The only thing that could make him look ugly every now and then was when his confidence spilled over as cockiness.

"You know what I've figured out about you?" Clive said to me. "You'll say anything to make it look like you're the innocent good girl."

"Look like?" I asked him. I closed the menu, already having decided that I was going to order the mozzarella cheese sticks for an appetizer and the blackened catfish and pasta for my main meal.

"I might have made a few mistakes in my past, but nothing more than you or anybody else in here," I said. From the looks of how some of these people were acting, they might still be making them. "Besides," I said, thinking about the best part of my day, "I had a life-changing experience this morning. God really touched my life. There are some changes coming for me. I can feel it."

"That's probably gas, baby girl," he said.

Clive lifted his finger, and a waitress seemed to appear out of nowhere. Even a regular customer didn't get waited on hand and foot like this. She placed a coaster on the table, then set down a glass with a short, red straw in it, though Clive hadn't ordered anything. We gave her our order, and I noticed she didn't even write it down. Impressive. I remembered my stint as a waitress when I was a freshman in college. Even with a notepad, I goofed up orders on a regular basis.

"Like I was saying," Clive said, tinkling the ice in his glass. "You probably ate too many beans yesterday."

Although I'd had tacos for the last two days, I knew the difference between a touch from God and pinto beans. Clive had no idea what he was talking about. In all of my life, I'd never felt the peace of God like that, and I refused to let someone downplay my experience. "If you'd felt what I did you wouldn't be saying things like that," I said.

"So God came in your bedroom and saved your wretched soul?"

I didn't like the way Clive was being sarcastic, so I just said, "It wasn't actually in my room. It was at church."

Clive stirred with the straw in his glass and sipped some of his beverage. "You went to church on a Saturday? You barely go on Sundays."

"You don't know what I do on Sundays, as if it's any of your business anyway." I would never tell Clive the true reason for my church attendance. He would never let me live it down.

"So now you're saved and sanctified?" He waved his hands in the air like he was a woman with a wide-brimmed hat sitting on the front pew in church. "Praise the Lord, Sister Sheila," he mocked.

I didn't want to laugh, but Clive was so amused at his own antics that I couldn't help but smile. Even with a smirk on my face, I threw little daggers with my eyes. I don't know why I thought I could share anything about a conversion experience with Clive.

The waitress returned to slip a piece of paper in his hand, then sat a bowl of limes on the table. He hadn't asked for those either.

"So do you plan on telling me why you have somebody waiting on you hand and foot?"

"It's the women. They can't help it." He cupped a lime in his hand and squeezed it over his drink.

I poured some water into the syrupy sweet tea the waitress had brought me. "You wish. Your wife would never let that happen."

"Soon-to-be ex-wife." Clive rubbed the stubble on his chin. I knew that he must've taken some days off from work, because he was always clean shaven when he went into the office.

"Well, until the court system releases you, you're still married."

"That means you're out with a married man, Sister Sheila," he said. "There's got to be something in the Good Book that speaks against that."

"Whatever, Clive. Don't try to flip the script." His comments did make me feel a little guilty, but at least I knew that I didn't look at Clive in that way. I'd never crossed the line into adultery, and that wasn't going to change now. I knew that he was married, that his marriage had been on rocky ground for years, and that currently he and his wife didn't live together. I wouldn't even be sitting across from Clive if he had a happy home.

The waitress returned in record speed with our meal. Two booths of folks seated next to us looked perturbed that their order was still being held up in the kitchen, and one of the men stopped the waitress to express his disapproval. I couldn't hear the waitress's remarks, but whatever she said made the heads of everyone at the table turn in our direction.

Clive noticed, and he ate it up. He lifted his hand at them, and the man returned a nod.

"It pays to be the boss," Clive said. He twirled that pinkie ring.

"So you own this place?" I finally asked.

"This and a couple of other businesses," he admitted.

"I never knew."

"You never had a reason to. Still don't, actually. But since we're no longer colleagues, it won't hurt you to see that you've always got to have more than one hustle. If one dries up, there's another stream to feed you."

Clive continued, and for once he gave me a reason to listen to him without thinking he was going to say something sarcastic or inappropriate.

"That's where you messed up, baby girl. You banked all of your hopes, dreams, and spending habits on one paycheck. And you should never let one person have that much control over what's in your bank account. If the one river you have dries up, you'll die of thirst."

I'd almost lost my appetite thinking of how I'd not only banked on my nine-to-five job, but I'd banked on being Mrs. Ace Bowers. *My* plan had turned its back on me.

"But no fear, baby girl. You'll get back on your feet," Clive said. He stuffed his mouth until it looked like the food would explode from his cheeks. He wiped the corners of his mouth, then rubbed the napkin across the manicured cuticles on his hand.

I took a sulking bite of my pasta.

"Cheer up," Clive said. He tinkled the ice around in his glass. "I have a proposition for you that'll help you take care of some stuff until you find a job."

Although it was dark, I noticed a woman wearing a black cat-suit slink by near the back of the room. She wore her hair in a high ponytail on top of her head, and the length of it danced at the top of her waist. She opened and closed one of the rear doors quickly, but not before I saw the soft red light emanating from inside. It had to be a VIP.

"I'm not the waitress type," I said, turning my attention back to Clive. "Sorry. I know I should be grateful for the opportunity, but that would be like taking a step backward."

There was no way I was going to wear black every day or subject myself to old men with roaming eyes and roving hands. I was starting to feel that I didn't even belong here tonight. It was dark, the music was too loud, and I wasn't exactly thrilled at watching the people on the dance floor crowd gyrate against each other when the DJ played the slow jams.

Clive leaned forward so that I could hear him. "I never said anything about working *here*," he clarified.

"Then where?" I asked.

A cheer started from the other end of the club and rumbled across the room. The people who were on the dance floor raised their hands above their heads, and those who weren't on the dance floor scurried to find a tight place to sway their hips. So many people had entered the lounge at this point, that I was sure there was a risk of some kind of fire code violation. Clive didn't seem the least bit concerned. It was like I could see the dollar signs in his eyes.

I moved to the other side of the booth and slid in beside Clive. Our heads touched as I asked him again, "Then where?"

He didn't have the chance to answer.

Chapter 14

A ren't you all cute?" a woman said to Clive. "I shouldn't be surprised that you've picked yourself up a tenderoni."

She talked to Clive, but was looking at me. I silently prayed that this woman wasn't the violent type. She was overdressed for the setting in an ivory silk blouse with a high ruffled neck, like the kind Queen Elizabeth or anyone who sat on a throne would wear. Her silver pants cinched her midsection like a corset and then flared out to a wide-leg cut. This woman was used to calling the shots.

"At least you're cute," she said to me. "You've definitely got the assets afforded to a younger woman, but don't worry, gravity will take its course sooner or later, and you'll need some help—like most of these women in here—holding things up in place." She gave half a smile, like an invisible puppeteer had turned up one corner of her lip.

I was frozen, unsure of how to handle her presence, especially since Clive hadn't uttered a single word. In fact he'd reached across the table and was helping himself to one of my mozzarella sticks. He wasn't fazed.

"Don't make a scene, Gina," Clive finally said and squeezed another lime into his second drink. "It's not a good thing for the owners to cut the fool in front of their employees."

Gina. As in Gina Alston. As in Clive's wife.

The last time I'd seen her was at the corporate Christmas party about two and a half years ago. Her hair was longer then with straight bangs across the front. Now it was a chin length bob, cut from ear to ear with a deep part on one side. The midnight black color of her hair made the angles on her face sharp. Tense. Intimidating.

Gina was a powerful attorney, so she could probably make me disappear off the face of the earth and then represent herself as part of the defense. And regardless of the fact that Clive boasted that his divorce was on the horizon, she still wore a substantial diamond on her ring finger. So as not to have her right hand feel left out, she had a princess cut-emerald set in diamonds on the middle finger.

"I don't have to make a scene to draw attention," Gina said. "The lips were already flapping by the time I got here. I walked in on a conversation in the break room. One of your little hostesses was flapping her lips about you being here with your girlfriend." Gina crossed her arms. "I sent her home for the night. Now she can spend the rest of the night wondering whether or not she has a job."

Clive shook his head.

I was still stunned that she'd referred to me as Clive's girlfriend. I stood up and tried to excuse myself to go to the restroom, but Gina was posted in front of me like a three-ton boulder. If I tried to push past her, things might have gotten ugly. So far, she'd only bared her fangs at me. I didn't want to feel her bite. I felt Clive's hand on the side of my hips. He tugged slightly on the waist of my jeans, and I took it as a hint that I might want to sit down. So I did.

"I thought you were out of town until at least Wednesday," Clive said to Gina.

Is he serious? I know he's not about to carry on a conversation right now.

Gina talked over me like I wasn't there.

"I had to cut my vacation short to take care of an emergency with a client. A very good-paying client," she emphasized.

Evidently without Clive, Gina still had deep pockets. She picked up the menus that our waitress had failed to take from the table, tucked them under her arm, then looked at her Movado watch. I knew the brand well because I owned one almost exactly like it, but hadn't worn it for over a month because it needed a battery. I'd wanted one so badly and had spent a ton of time at the jewelry store until I broke down and charged it. Gina probably owned hers free and clear while I'd probably paid for mine ten times over in interest.

"I need to be going. I've got plans with a few of the girls," Gina said. She stopped a waitress and handed her the menus. Sarcasm dripped from her remarks when she said, "We have some cradles to rob ourselves. Being a cougar is in these days."

Gina's face changed when she looked at me. It's like she transformed from Attila the Hun to June Cleaver. "I'm sorry, I don't believe I caught your name."

"Friend and former coworker," Clive said for me. "Sheila."

I thought I'd have to kick-start my heart to get it beating again. I had no idea why he wanted to make that point, and I especially didn't know why he had to tell her my name. I'd planned to lie and ask God's forgiveness later.

"Sheila Rushmore," Clive added.

His hands were at the top of my shoulders, near my neck. His firm grasp kneaded into my tense body. He didn't need to massage my shoulders; he needed to reach in like a surgeon and massage my heart so it would start beating again. I shrugged my shoulders back so that he'd stop using me as the pawn in this game he was playing with his wife.

"Sheila Rushmore," Gina repeated. I could see her imprinting my name in her memory. "That's right. I remember you from one of those awfully boring office parties. It's been some time ago."

What was she expecting me to say? Nice to see you? Not a chance. Instead I said, "Yes. It's been a while."

My mouth was as dry as cotton. I reached over for my tea—which was still too syrupy sweet—and drank it until I could get a taste back into my mouth. When I looked back up, Gina had her hand extended to me. Either this was a peace offering or we were going to shake hands, go to our corners, and come out fighting.

Gina grasped my hand with a force like she wanted to dislocate my wrist. I don't care what Clive said, his wife isn't as ready to get a divorce as he is. If Gina wanted Clive, she could have him. I wasn't going to fight for a man—especially one that's not *mine* to begin with.

That Attila face was back.

"Well, nice to see you again," she said, though she didn't mean it.

Growing up, I used to get in trouble because Mama said my facial expressions "talked" too much. Gina's expression basically cursed out me, my mama, and all of my future children. She turned and walked away.

Clive turned up his glass, and I went back to my side of the booth.

"What a nice way to show me the *mature* Atlanta life," I said. Maybe it was nerves, but all of a sudden I was ravenous. I ate the last mozzarella stick Clive left on my plate, then started in on my pasta.

"You handled yourself like a lady. That says something about you."

"And you tried to play like we were together. What does that say about you?"

Clive didn't answer.

"And then you told her my first *and* last name. You might as well have given her my social security number, too."

"Please, baby girl. Gina could care less about you or anyone I'm with. She likes to try and intimidate people, and you were fresh meat for her. She might be crazy, but she ain't *that* crazy."

"That's what they all say," I said.

Clive laughed. Loud and long.

"You owe me one, Clive. You shouldn't have put me out there like that."

"You put yourself out there when *you* called *me* tonight."

Clive's comment reminded me of the other reason I'd called him. Before I could think of how to approach the subject of money, Clive made the offer himself.

"Since you want to pout, I'll make it up to you. Whatever you need let me know."

"Since you asked," I said, "you *can* help me with something."

Cliché or from the Bible, I wasn't sure, but I'd heard it said before: *You have not because you ask not.* And although money might not make a person happy, it can definitely get a broke-down vehicle back on the road.

Chapter 15

I used to hate Mondays, but I think that Monday might have changed all of that. I stood at the window and watched my car being hoisted, locked into place, and pulled away by Kenny's Towing and Recovery.

Clive had called one of his own mechanics to tow my car to the shop and take care of the transmission and whatever else had kept my poor baby from getting its roll on. I wanted to wave at my precious red Lexus—aka Lexie—as it was pulled away. It was a wonder that my car was being towed in for repairs and not to be repossessed.

That was one less monkey on my back, and I'd promised God that once I got my car back, I wouldn't miss a Sunday in church. I was a regular member at Bedside Baptist, but I knew I needed to actually go to church more, especially after Saturday.

I was still on some sort of spiritual high after watching a televangelist yesterday. Cassandra had gone with her lying boyfriend back over to his house, so my Sunday couldn't have been better.

I was awake by nine o'clock and channel-surfed past the calm, poised kind of ministers and to the good old southern preachers.

One of my favorite TV preachers moaned into the microphone. "The Bible is full of God's promises, but you've got to get up and go after them. You've got to believe He's got the best of everything waiting for you."

He was shaking his head so fast that sweat and spit were flying everywhere. I know the people in the front pew had been sprayed with one or the other because the camera accidentally landed on a woman who was dabbing her face with a handkerchief and had looked over at the man beside her in disgust. The preacher, however, didn't care about who or what was in his way.

"He's got the best for you," he repeated. "Now act like it's already yours." He revved his voice like he was a stalled car. That sent him and all of the rest of the saints in the pews into a frenzy. He told the band sitting in the orchestra pit to give him a "praise break," and praise they did. I sat my bowl of corn flakes down on the kitchen table and joined in the celebration. I looked more like I was dancing at the club, but there wasn't anybody there to judge me so I didn't care. I decided it might be a good idea to practice some more conservative moves in case I ever "caught the Spirit" in church.

Club dancing or not, I still had that praise when I woke up this morning, walked hand-in-hand with it to the bus stop, and planned to ride with it on the MARTA transit system on my way to downtown Atlanta.

I had a fierce pair of black heels tucked away in my bag because I'd learned my lesson about trying to be fashionable and cover ample ground at the same time. I walked the block from Cassandra's place to the bus stop alongside a boy who seemed to be caught in the eighties. Instead of most commuters, who had ear buds from their iPods and other mp3 players stuffed in their ears, he was carrying a radio. He'd tied a belt through the radio handle so he could hook it across his shoulders.

Thankfully the bus came as soon as I arrived at the crowded stop, and I filed onto the bus with everybody else.

I took the first available aisle seat and said, "Good morning," to the teenager sitting at the window. She looked at me but didn't crack her lips to speak. I wanted to grab her neck and shake some respect into her, but I figured that wouldn't be indicative of the new woman I'd become. Or at least was *trying* to become.

I opened up my new devotional and picked a random page to read. The bus ride wasn't as bad as I remembered. I'd ridden the bus plenty of times with Mama, and during college it was the primary mode of transportation for me and my friends when we couldn't bum a ride with somebody lucky enough to have a car on campus. Public transportation wasn't beneath me, but having the option to ride on leather seats with nobody knocking you in your head with their backpack or stepping on your toes was a nice upgrade to have.

For the first few minutes my ride was uneventful—then a bunch of nonsense took place right beside me. Why? All I wanted to do was read my devotional and try to get a little Jesus in me. Was that too much to ask?

I hadn't done a Chinese split since my early days as a middle school cheerleader, but the young man who'd walked behind me on the way to the bus stop was *way* too flexible. If anything, I would've expected him to pull out a piece of cardboard, drop down, and spin on his back. In this case that would've been too normal. He stretched his lanky arms to reach his radio, cranked up the volume, and preceded to perform some kind of liturgical dance number. He looked like a butterfly wrestling out of a cocoon, especially when he ended up on his tippy-toes with his hand stretched above his head in an arch. Okay, maybe I shouldn't have laughed. Perhaps

I should have clapped and encouraged his dream. I wasn't the only one laughing, but since I was closest, he chose to attack *me*.

"What's so funny?"

Is that a rhetorical question? I tried to ignore him, with no success.

He pulled a handkerchief out of his back pocket and swiped it across his glistening forehead. Everyone was looking at me. I widened my eyes at a guy who was wearing a city-issued blue uniform and who was three times the size of the average man. My eyes asked, *Do you plan on stepping in here? Now would be a good time.*

"I bet you don't have a man, do you?" Mr. Black Butterfly was berating me now. "Evidently not, because you don't know how to support a brother's dreams. What would make you laugh at somebody you don't even know?"

I was trying to put some Jesus in me, but old boy was trying to make the Devil come out. "I guess the same thing that made me laugh is the same thing that would make you perform 'The Dance of the Butterfly' in the middle of a bus aisle. People don't always *think* before they do something crazy."

For the first time during the entire bus ride, the girl beside me smiled. Then she burst out laughing. The people sitting around us did, too, but their reaction didn't make me feel any better. That wasn't exactly the godly thing to do, and I didn't have to grow up behind the four walls of a church to know that. The bus screeched to a stop, and the aspiring dancer was one of the first to dash off the bus, with his radio bouncing behind him.

Even though I'd asked God into my heart, I'm not sure that even He knew what He was getting into.

Chapter 16

When I stepped off of the bus and into the center of downtown Atlanta, I still didn't know exactly where I was going. Peachtree Street was the hub of activity—for wanderers, college students, and the corporate world. It was one of few places in Atlanta where social classes crossed paths. I walked past Woodruff Park and the ever-present scene of men playing checkers at the outdoor tables. I stopped at the corner and waited for the crosswalk sign to change.

"Ms. Tenderoni." I heard the voice, but I didn't immediately turn. While out in public I answered to *Sheila, Ms. Rushmore,* or other variations of my name. Not nicknames. Not a hiss or a whistle from a man trying to get my attention.

"Clive."

I don't know why I turned at the sound of Clive's name, but I did. At first I looked behind me to see if he was trying to sneak up on me. I was only a few blocks away from the skyrise that housed the offices of my former job, so it wasn't a far reach to think that he was strolling in my direction.

"This way," the voice said. I turned, then remembered the voice from Saturday night that had called me tenderoni. It was the cougar herself, Gina. How appropriate that she was wearing some type of animal print blouse and huge black sunglasses like she was a celebrity.

"Do you need a ride?" Gina asked me. She said it so sweetly that I almost believed she didn't have plans to invite me into the front seat, then somehow bind and strap me into the trunk.

"No, thank you," I said, "but thanks for the offer."

"I would say 'anytime,' but I'm not always in this good of a mood," she confessed

At least she was honest.

Gina did a slow finger wave at me—showing me her claws—and eased into the intersection, looking at me the entire time.

I'd never been so glad to see a traffic light turn green. I was green, too. Green with envy as I watched her weave down Peachtree Street in a sky blue convertible Benz. The customized white leather interior was monogrammed with her initials. It made me wonder how many commas were actually on the balance lines of her bank accounts.

As soon as Gina was out of my sight—and hopefully me out of hers—I headed back toward the MARTA station. I'd stroll through downtown Atlanta another day.

I'd always been drawn to downtown because I've always thought it was the epitome of high living. Being part of the Buckhead bourgeoisie was part of my dream. For so many years, me and Cassandra had called it the "good life." For many it probably was, but for me, everything I'd chased for all of these years had basically amounted to nothing.

I marched across the crosswalk like a woman on a mission and noticed my steps became synchronized with those of a lady in a well-worn grey business suit. Parts of it shone like it had been over-washed and over-ironed at home, ignoring the dry-clean-only tag on the inside. I wondered how long she'd been chasing her dream . . . if she'd ever attained it, then lost it . . . if like me she ever wondered what kind of life she was truly going to live.

The commuter crowd had thinned as I boarded the MARTA train and headed east. I didn't encounter any aspiring dancers, but a self-proclaimed minister of the gospel was feeling free to practice his sermons. He pulled on the tail of his electric blue suit coat, then snatched a black handkerchief from his pocket. He looked at me like he expected me to throw dollar bills at his scuffed black gators. I put my purse out of his immediate reach in case he felt the urge to snatch it and run. I clutched it tighter when he started talking about *Moses* walking on water. If Moses had walked on water, I'd never heard of it.

Chapter 17

I thought I wouldn't make the trek to the other side of town until I had my car back, but I found myself headed toward Eden's Gates again. Once I'd traveled as far as the city transit system would take me, I was able to flag down a cab parked in front of a grocery store. Thankfully this cab driver had better seats, safer driving skills, and a friendlier attitude.

Eden's cheery voice welcomed me again. It seemed she was always hiding behind bookshelves, although I don't believe it was on purpose. Anyone her height didn't have much of a choice when she lived in a world designed for people over five feet, seven inches tall.

"Hi, Eden," I called out. "It's Sheila."

"Something good must be coming your way," Eden sang from somewhere in the store. "I was thinking about you last night. Praying for you, too."

Eden appeared from around the corner wearing a bright neon

yellow dress in stark contrast to her bright burgundy hair. Any other time—and with any other person—I might've gawked at the gaudiness of it all, but Eden pulled it off with confidence. Better her than me.

Eden was looking at me in a strange way—like she was trying to see through my eyes and into my soul or something.

It was no sense wondering, so I asked, "Why are you looking at me like that?" I lifted my tote bag up on the counter. Those heels definitely wouldn't make it to my feet today.

"Like what?" Eden asked.

"I don't know. You've been praying about me, so I thought maybe God might've given you the inside scoop about me."

"Nothing in particular," she said. "But I know I'm supposed to be praying for you, so I put your name on my list with the others and stuck it in my Bible."

I realize I don't know Eden from Eve, but knowing someone was praying for me made me feel loved. Besides Ace, I'm not sure anyone had ever said anything to God about me unless they were telling Him to strike me down.

"I need all the prayer I can get," I told Eden.

"If you do your part and I do mine, I think you'll be all right," Eden said. She used her key to slit open a small box on the counter, then began unpacking and sorting a shipment of bookmarks. I followed her lead.

"By the way, you were right about something good coming my way. My car is in the shop, so I should be up and rolling by the end of the week. It's been a long three months without transportation."

"See? See what can happen when you trust God?"

I merely nodded. I wasn't going to confess to Eden that it wasn't exactly God who I'd trusted. Clive was powerful, but he wasn't anywhere close to being God.

"Trusting God will keep you from worrying about a lot of things," Eden said. "I've been walking with Him for over twenty-five years, and He's always stretching me to trust Him more."

"After twenty-five years?" I asked. In my mind that made Eden a saint. If God was still working on her after that long, then it was going to take a lifetime for me to get it right.

"Yes," Eden said. "I can't speak for anybody else, but I think God challenges me to keep me on my toes and down on my knees."

I came across a bookmark that said, *I'm not perfect, just forgiven.* I put it aside so I could buy it before I left. Two days ago I only had ten dollars to my name, but thanks to Clive's generosity, I now had two hundred and ten.

"I guess as I grow in my relationship with God, that'll come easier," I said. "I'm taking baby steps. I just started my walk with God on Saturday. Literally." I felt like I could open up to Eden, so I did. "I've gone to church every now and then, but even that was because of a man and not because of my own desire."

"Been there, done that," Eden confessed. "And then some more."

"You, too?"

Eden stopped working with the bookmarks and leaned over the edge of the countertop, listening like she had nothing else better to do in the world. Her demeanor and inviting warmth made me comfortable enough to come clean.

"Since you've already heard one side of the story, let me tell you mine," I said. "On Saturday, I went to my ex's wedding. Uninvited, of course."

I paused. I guess I was waiting for Eden to look at me like I'd grown an extra head or sound off about why a woman would be stupid enough to do such a thing. But she didn't. In fact, her facial expression didn't change a bit. I continued.

"My best friend found out about it and thought I should go to get closure on Ace and the abrupt end to our relationship. To this day I don't know how she knew about the ceremony, but Cassandra's always been that way. For whatever reason, she always finds out about things. This time—like a dummy—I let her convince me to sneak into the wedding. Do you think I'm crazy yet?"

Eden laughed. "Crazy used to be my middle name. Trust me, I've done bigger things than that. Now if you had stood up in the back, confessed your undying love, and tried to drag him out of the church, *then* I'd file you in the crazy category."

I thought about Ruby. She was a robust woman, and she *had* said that she'd buried one of her husbands. She never said if he died from natural causes or by her hands. Ruby would've taken me down like one of those wrestlers on the WWF matches Devin used to force me to watch on Saturday mornings. I could picture her unleashing that "Russian sickle" move across my neck when I least expected it.

"I never would've made it to the front of the altar," I said. "You saw that woman Ruby on Saturday? I was sitting beside her the entire time."

I guess an image of Ruby flashed before Eden's eyes. She shook her head and frowned like she could physically feel the pain of one of Ruby's tackles. "You're right. You wouldn't have gotten very far."

I could laugh about the situation now, but on Saturday it had only brought me pain. Truthfully, it still did, only it wasn't as much.

"I went to the ceremony to close a door, and I feel like God opened my heart to Him."

"Now that's a salvation story if I've ever heard one. A man will truly drive you to Jesus one way or the other."

"Isn't that the truth?" I agreed.

We chatted for a few minutes more until Eden excused herself to take a phone call. I wandered back to my favorite spot and settled in for a while. I was like a stray cat Eden had fed that wouldn't go away.

Even though it was a little after eleven in the morning, Eden returned with a small tray of assorted fruit and cheese cubes. Evidently I wasn't the only one who considered me a stray. She produced a coaster then set down a glass of lemonade large enough to quench my thirst until next week.

Eden sat down on the love seat beside me and curled her feet under her sundress.

I remembered that I'd written a thank you note to her and pulled it out of my bag. I wished I had a small gift to go along with it, but Eden seemed like the kind of woman who'd appreciate my words from the heart more than anything.

"This is for you," I said to Eden.

"How sweet of you," she said, rubbing her hand over my initials that were embossed on the flap of the envelope. "And so classy. A woman with exquisite taste."

"Thank you," I said. If she knew the kind of debt I'd amassed with my so-called exquisite taste, she wouldn't be so impressed.

"I see you came to your senses and wore flats today," Eden said, pointing down at my feet.

I held up my tote bag. "Don't worry. I've got my trusty three-inch heels in here. But unless a New York model scout decides to grace our presence today, you won't see them on my feet."

"I gave up on heels a long time ago. When you put a size six foot in a pair of heels, half of the time you end up looking like a little girl trying to be too grown, wearing her Mama's shoes. And then there are those awful corns I used to get on my little toe. My feet have been a whole lot happier since flats became my best friends."

Thanks to regular pedicure and spa treatments in the past, I'd never seen the likes of corns or calluses, and if I had anything to do with it, I never would. The therapists at my favorite spot had made foot massages a science, and just thinking about their skilled hands made me want to call and make an appointment. After two months of doing my own pedicures, I deserved to treat myself. Now that I didn't have to think about getting my car repaired, I could spare the money. I looked at my fingernails. I might as well treat them to a fresh coat of that peachy shade I loved. A Georgia peach might as well look sweet.

I heard the doorbell announce a customer's arrival and wondered if this was going to be another visitor who would cause me to crawl around the store.

Eden yelled out her customary greeting: "Welcome to Eden's Gates." She stood up to welcome her guest, then moved toward the front with urgency. I stood up so that I could see what had rattled her usually calm demeanor.

The man was wearing brown from head to toe, except for the soiled grey backpack harnessed across his shoulders and buckled in front of his chest. It was one of those oversized canvas bags that hikers carried, but it didn't seem to have much in it. The hair on his head and his face was overgrown, dusty, and slightly matted. I didn't know the reason for his visit—but I doubt it was to purchase the latest bestseller.

For Eden's safety and mine, I wasn't about to take my eyes off him.

Chapter 18

Eden hugged the man. She wrapped her bony arms around him like he'd just stepped out of the shower and smelled like mountain-scented soap and deodorant. Obviously, there was nothing to fear, but I still found it strange when she kissed his cheek. When he pulled away and turned his head, I saw that he wasn't as old as I had assumed. He was probably my age—give or take a couple of years. A good trip to the barber would work wonders on him.

He was fidgety and looked like he was anxious to leave as quickly as he'd come. I could tell Eden was trying to convince him of something, because he continuously shook his head. I guess she realized that she wasn't going to break through to him. I watched her go behind the counter and open the register. Even the brightness of her neon yellow dress couldn't hide the gloom that had washed over her face as she folded up some money and pressed it into his hand.

Then my cell phone rang. My stupid cell phone was disrupting things again. The man turned to look in my direction, and I ducked out of his sight.

I didn't recognize the number, but I answered it anyway in case it was a job opportunity. The last thing I needed was to miss a chance to be gainfully employed again.

"Hello, this is Sheila," I answered in my professional voice.

"Sheila? I must have the wrong number."

"Wait," I rushed to say. The voice was alluring and sounded like it belonged on the late night, quiet storm hour on the radio. "Who is this?"

"Reggie."

I connected the name with the voice. Reggie!

"Reggie who I met at Ace and Lynette's wedding," I said. "This is Marcelle. But call me Sheila."

"So you gave me an alias?"

"No, it wasn't an alias. Sheila Marcelle is really my name."

"Well, long time, no see, Sheila Marcelle," Reggie said.

"I wouldn't exactly say, 'Long time, no see.'"

"One day is too long for me," he said.

"Is trying to be charismatic your full-time job or something you do on the side?" I asked him.

"You're quick, you know that?"

"I try to be."

"Look, did I catch you at a bad time?"

"Not really a bad time, but if you could call me back later this evening, it would be better."

"Talk to you tonight," he said.

For some reason, I hadn't expected Reggie to call. In fact, I hadn't thought about him at all, since I had so many other things plaguing my mind. I settled back onto the sofa and pulled out my devotional so that I'd have something else to do besides be in Eden's business. I read an entry about God's compassion, mercy, and forgiveness.

Although I can admit to ulterior motives when I'd gone to church with Ace, I had still gotten something out of the sermons every now and then. I knew God was forgiving, but it still amazed me that He gave me a clean slate every time. I guess that's why *He* was God, and I wasn't. I could forgive; it was the forgetting I had a hard time doing.

I stood up to see if Eden was still dealing with her visitor. He was gone, but Eden had opened another box and was sorting through sets of figurines. Good. I could relax.

I tucked a round throw pillow behind my head and closed my eyes. There was plenty in my past that I wished I'd never done. But the verse Eden had shared with me popped up in my mind like it had done so many times over the past two days. *Forget the past, look at the future.*

I was focused so much on the future that I'd fallen asleep, and I woke up to a soft nudge on my shoulder.

"Wake up, sleeping beauty," Eden said. Her voice was as soothing as the alto voice serenading the store.

I sat up and felt that the right corner of my mouth was wet. No one can look cute wiping slobber off her mouth, but I played it off. A little sleep and slobber was a trait that ran down the bloodline of women in my family and usually reared its ugly head when I was exhausted.

"I'm so embarrassed," I said. I smoothed out the book's pages that had bent after being crunched between my hip and the sofa.

"For what?" Eden chuckled. "For getting some rest? It looked like you were thoroughly enjoying it."

"It was good," I admitted. I fingered my hair to make sure it was in place and stood up to straighten my clothes.

"I'm going next door to get some wings," Eden said. "I only eat fried foods once a month, and I'm having a down-home Southern craving. Would you like to join me?"

The best thing about being laid off was that I'd dropped off ten pounds, weight that I once couldn't have paid to leave me. Stress wasn't something that I wanted to deal with on a regular basis, but it had done some things that a diet of chicken caesar salads hadn't. An order of wings and fries wouldn't eat up too much of my money, but tonight I was going to make an effort to plan some meals and go to the grocery store.

"Wings sound good to me," I said. "Who's going to watch the store?"

"Oh I shut down every day at lunchtime and close early on Wednesdays so I can go to mid-week Bible study. Some things you have to do for your health and sanity. You know what I mean?"

"I'll be thirty-four in a few months, and there are plenty of things I'm just now learning."

I followed Eden to the front door, and she offered to lock my tote bag in the drawer up front behind the counter.

"Learning is a lifelong pursuit. I once heard someone say life gives you the test first, then the answers later. Just wait until you get to be fifty-three years old like me, when you have more life behind you than you do ahead of you."

"I hope you're not offended by this comment, but you don't look like you're that old. Well," I said, sidestepping, "maybe I should use the word 'seasoned' instead of 'old'."

"It is what it is," Eden said. She taped a note on the door that said she was out to lunch. "Whatever you call it, I'm flattered. In my opinion I look more vibrant now than I did when I was in my twenties."

I looked out across the parking lot while she locked the door. This must've been Mr. Jamaica's hot spot because I saw his cab illegally parked in a handicapped spot. There was a towel draped on his head to shield him from the sun. He wiped his forehead with it, set it back on top like a tent, then went back to chatting with his fellow cab driver. He looked in my direction, and then paused like he recognized me.

Eden slid her set of keys on her wrist and shook the door to make sure it was secure. "I had a bad smoking habit, could turn up beers like a sailor, and was addicted to an abusive man. Then I gave my life to Christ, and I haven't been the same since."

"I never would've thought you'd been down that road," I said, smiling at a man who was holding the door open for me and Eden. He was on his way out with a Styrofoam container of wings that were sure to torch his tongue. They were so hot and spicy, I could smell them. Practically made my eyes water. The old Sheila would've asked if I could join him for lunch. He was that handsome.

Both Eden and I thanked him for his chivalry. Eden already had her eyes targeted on the menu board at the counter, but I'd done a double-take on the brother. Mr. Jamaica had pulled his cab to the curb, and the cutie opened the door. I sighed. The last thing I needed was to have my eyes on a man without a ride. I was days from getting my own car back and didn't plan on chauffeuring a brother around, even if he was the finest thing who'd caught my attention for a while.

"Believe me when I say what you put in your body is reflected on the outside," Eden was saying, though I'd zoned out of the conversation. "But when I quit smoking and drinking and those toxins were cleansed from my body, the age lines around my lips and the dark circles under my eyes disappeared. I was cleansed from the inside out. You can't get better plastic surgery than when God puts His hands on you."

"Uh-huh," I said absentmindedly.

Any other time I would've been wrapped up in wondering about Eden's past, but I was still watching the brother who'd captured my attention. It turned out that he was holding the door open for an elderly man. As I figured he would, he turned around to see if I was watching, then headed back toward the resturant.

I consciously sucked in my stomach and wished I'd bothered to put my heels on to make me look even more like the diva that I am.

"Travis," he said, not wasting any time at all.

I shook his hand. "Sheila."

"Since you were staring me down, I thought I'd be a gentle-man and come back and speak to you."

I felt myself blush. "I was getting a good look in. I can admit that."

Eden was busy catching up on everything that had been happening with the cashier's family and convincing the woman that she needed to start selling slices of her red velvet cake again.

"I need to get back to work, but I'd like to call you later if you don't mind," Travis said.

"I don't mind at all," I said.

Just like with Reggie, I told him my number and he logged it into his cell.

I had the chance to analyze Travis from head to toe. When it came to doing a quick once-over, I was probably as bad as a man checking out a woman. Travis wore a pair of heavily starched khaki pants and a polo shirt with the logo of one of the national cell phone providers embroidered on the pocket. I'd seen people wearing the same attire when I went into the store to pay my overdue cell bill.

Basically, that meant Travis spent the majority of his day behind a counter and not supervising behind a desk. There was a time in my life when that would've severely impeded Travis's chances of even getting my number, but at least he had a job. That's more than what I could say.

"Talk to you tonight," Travis said, grabbing one of the community newspapers from the windowsill as he left.

"All right, little lady, you ready to order?" the snaggle-toothed cook yelled from behind the counter. He wiped his hands on the front of his apron and picked up a container of red sauce. He shook it above his head. "I've got barbeque, lemon pepper, mild, medium, hot, and shut-yo-mouth hot. However you want 'em, I got 'em."

"I definitely like them hot," I said, and I wasn't just talking about the wings.

Chapter 19

It was never my intention for Eden to take me home again, but she refused to let me take the hour and a half return ride on the public transportation system when she said she could get me home in less than thirty minutes.

I held on to the door handle while Eden floored it through the yellow lights and let her monstrous vehicle hug the curb. We made it to Cassandra's place in one piece, but I would've rather endured the male ballerina and bootleg preacher than have Eden see what was happening out in front of Cassandra's building.

Cassandra and Frank looked like they were about to have an all-out brawl. Eden gripped the steering wheel and pulled up so close to the edge of the sidewalk that I thought she was going to jump the curb. She picked up her cell phone from the middle console and flipped it open.

"I'm calling 9-1-1," she warned. "I know domestic violence when I see it."

I put my hand on Eden's. "Hold on one minute," I said. If Cassandra thought I was connected in any way to the police showing up, it would only mean more drama for me. Until I got on my feet and moved into my own place, I planned to lie low.

"Do you know them?" Eden asked.

"It's my roommate, Cassandra, and her boyfriend."

Cassandra was so close to Frank's face that she could probably smell what he'd eaten for the past week. Cassandra didn't cower, and I could tell that she was pushing Frank to his breaking point. His face was twisted in rage, and although I could never justify a man hitting a woman, she was pushing the button to send him over the edge.

"Lord Jesus, help that girl," Eden said. Concern blanketed her face like she'd slipped down memory lane. "If you don't want me to call the police, then you might want to try and get them calmed down. I don't mind involving the law when it's necessary."

I hopped out of the car, ready to make them stop this embarrassing display. I slowed my gait, realizing that if I ran up on them like I was looking for a fight, then one or both of them might turn on me.

People returning from work moved from the sidewalk and onto the grass to avoid Cassandra and Frank's altercation. Cell phones were glued to the ears of most who walked by, and if the past actions of her neighbors was any indication, they'd already beat Eden to calling the police. Cassandra's neighbors were quiet, middle-income professionals, and they called the police if they even smelled what they thought might be a disturbance.

I was composed and used the tone of voice Eden would've used. "Cassandra, let's go ahead and go inside," I coaxed. "You don't want to do this out here."

"Yes, I do," she retorted. Cassandra didn't back out of Frank's personal space. "Because he needs to tell me why he had the nerve to spend the night at his baby mama's house."

"I already told you one time. You need to back out of my face, Cassandra. You need to respect me."

"Respect you? Respect you?" Cassandra retreated physically, but her verbal lashing continued. "Respect with no check? You have tons of paintings lining the walls at your house, and you can't get a decent showing anywhere. And when you do, nobody buys a thing. Is that what you want me to respect, Frank?"

"It's all about the money with you," Frank roared.

The fury in Frank's voice shook my insides. He wasn't the man that I'd first met, but given a little time, all wolves exposed their fangs. Frank was pounding his fist into his hand. His fingertips were covered in paint like he'd spent the day creating masterpieces.

"All you want is for somebody to take care of you and go broke on a high-maintenance woman from the hood."

I tried to ignore the small group of women congregated at the other end of the parking lot. The scene had turned into a public spectacle. When I noticed the apartment security guard making his way over from the rental office on the other side of the complex, I knew I had to get Cassandra inside. At this rate, we might all end up homeless.

"Let's go inside, Cassandra," I said, gently gripping her shoulders.

Frank turned his anger toward me, which didn't surprise me. I was attempting to be the peacemaker, but he called me everything but a daughter of God. Now *he* was pushing *my* buttons, igniting the fight in me. I wasn't as bold as Cassandra, but I could hold my own when necessary.

"You should get your own man and your own life," he spat.

I was so angry that I couldn't get the words out. I hated that the words for the lashing I wanted to give Frank had escaped me. But he had plenty of words, and I stood there dumbfounded as Cassandra shrank away from us—attempting to make herself invisible.

The only weapon I had against Frank was my pair of heels in Eden's car, but three inches on a pump was as good a weapon as any.

"You're just like your crazy friend. Looking for a millionaire to rescue you so you can play house, shop with all of his hard-earned money, and make a reputation for yourself on the social scene."

The sound of Eden slamming her car door made all of us turn around. She stomped toward us like her weight could quake the ground.

"The police are on the way," she said.

Her announcement must've calmed the fears of the three women frozen in the parking lot, because they scurried past us and into the safety of one of the first floor apartments. Yet and still, their curiosity pulled them onto the patio where they had front row seats like we were shooting an episode of *Cops*.

Frank left, but he cursed me, Cassandra, *and* Eden out in the process. He ripped out of the parking lot, leaving skid marks behind with his dramatic exit. He wasn't as adept at handling his big machine as Eden was at handling hers, because his SUV jumped the curb and ran through the bushes before he pulled out onto the street.

Cassandra stormed inside the building and left me standing outside like a fool. The security guard seemed to assess the situation, then decided to head back to the rental office.

"I'm sorry you had to see all of that," I said, walking back over to Eden.

She shrugged. "It happens. I'm sorry that you have to live in the midst of it."

"I keep reminding myself that it's temporary," I said. "Cassandra has been my friend since middle school, and I've never seen her so strung out over a man. She used to trade men like baseball cards, but Frank has really got a hold on her. I don't know what she sees in him."

"Soul tie," Eden said. "Some are stronger than others."

I wasn't sure what a soul tie was, but I wasn't going to worry Eden about giving me a Bible lesson when she had a husband to get home to.

"I guess I should get inside and check on Cassandra," I said, going back to the passenger's side and getting my things. "Thanks for another peaceful day at the bookstore," I said. "If it wasn't for you, I wouldn't have had a place to escape the drama over the last couple of days."

"Eden's Gates is your place to be, if you're looking to be drama free," she sang. She seemed impressed with her impromptu slogan.

"I don't know about that one, Eden," I said. "Maybe I can help you think of something else," I joked.

Eden hoisted herself up into the truck. "If you really want to help me with something, I could use some help with inventory tomorrow if you're free. It's nice to have you around. Being around young people keeps me vibrant."

"I'm not sure if I told you, but not only am I homeless and man-less, I'm also jobless," I told her. "I have nothing but time on my hands."

If God was on my side, the whole man-less thing was about to change. I should've put closure on my relationship with Ace a long time ago if it meant I was going to have my choice of men. Reggie. Travis. I was open for one more if it was true that the third time's a charm.

"Great," Eden said. "I'll be out here to pick you up at—"

"I can ride the bus over. Really, it's no problem."

"Eight. I'll be here at eight o'clock," Eden said. "And bring something to freshen up and change into later, because we're going to Bible study in the evening."

I like how Eden nicely told me I'd be going to church instead of extending me the offer. I guess she figured with everything I'd had to deal with—and the people I had to deal with—there was no way I'd object. She was right.

"Thanks, Eden. For everything. Yet again."

Eden waved at me and at the girls still posted on the porch. "Show's over," she said loud enough for me to hear but nobody else. "And for the record," Eden said, "I didn't actually call the police. I said it to scare that creep off. No man I know wants his portfolio updated with a mug shot. Now get inside and take care of your friend. We sisters need each other during times like these."

It was a slow walk from the parking lot to Cassandra's apartment door. Intentionally. I had no way of knowing if I was about to enter a lion's den and be unable to escape without getting my head bitten off.

Chapter 20

Cassandra didn't want my comfort or advice. In all our years of friendship, we'd never been mushy. We typically didn't cry on each other's shoulder about issues with the opposite sex or anything else for that matter. The same was true in my household growing up. Mama worked two jobs, so she when she was at home, she rarely offered a shoulder to cry on. As a single parent, her main concern was providing for us, but that didn't always include our emotional needs.

I put my arm around Cassandra's shoulder. It was awkward for both of us. She shrugged my embrace from around her and yanked open the refrigerator.

"Whatever you have to say, I don't want to hear it," she said.

"Actually I wasn't going to offer any advice. I'm here as a friend. In case you need to talk."

"Good. I'm a grown woman and don't need your advice unless I ask for it anyway."

I had no idea what she was looking for in the refrigerator, and I don't think she knew either. She took out a half-empty jar of sweet relish, put it back, then took the top off of a container holding a leftover stuffed mushroom that she'd cooked last week.

She looked at me and rolled her eyes. "Go ahead and say something. You know you want to."

"Sometimes when you're in a situation, it's hard to see how wrong it is for you," I said matter-of-factly.

"So now Frank is wrong for me? It doesn't mean people are wrong for each other because they get into it."

"You're right. But I think you're settling with Frank."

Cassandra fell silent, and I knew she was at least thinking about what I'd said. She walked out of the kitchen and locked herself in her bedroom. I didn't hear her come out until about nine thirty that night when she let Frank into the apartment. I guess he was waiting until he was back in her good graces before he started using his own key again.

I'd decided to let Cassandra be the pilot of her own relationship. If she crashed, that would be her business. My business was with Reggie and Travis, since both of them had called. I was going out with Reggie on Thursday night, and Travis had claimed my Friday. Even though Clive wasn't officially in the running for my love, he was going to find himself up against much younger competition.

Chapter 21

Eden was waiting outside at exactly eight the next morning. I'd planned to be ready by the time she arrived, but ended up keeping her waiting for ten minutes while I decided what would be appropriate to wear. Doing inventory at a bookstore wasn't anything I'd done before, but I imagined it would probably entail pushing and lifting some heavy cardboard boxes, or doing a lot of bending and squatting. I'd been trying to persuade my body to cooperate with my mind's desire to exercise, and it looked like today my body was going to be broken in.

I finally put on a pair of jeans and a light grey V-neck knit shirt, even though I thought it showed a little too much cleavage. I camouflaged it with a beaded necklace that cascaded down like a waterfall, then picked up the garment bag that held my clothes for Bible study.

I didn't expect to see Frank sitting at the bistro table in

Cassandra's kitchenette when I walked out. As usual she'd left for work about thirty minutes before, but she'd left him behind. He was humped over a drawing pad, and an array of colored pencils and chalks were strewn across the glass tabletop. Cassandra would flip if she saw the chalk dust everywhere.

"I bet you thought you'd gotten rid of me," Frank said. His eyes were heavy like he hadn't gotten much sleep, but that didn't stop him from spouting a bunch of junk. He stood like he had something to show off, and that's when I noticed he was in his boxers.

I walked out the door, ignoring him.

I thought I heard him mutter another smart aleck remark before I pulled the door closed, but anything he had to say wasn't something I wanted to hear—unless he was saying that I'd never see him again.

"Sorry I kept you waiting," I apologized, pulling myself up into the car.

"Do you have to look like a celebrity every time I see you?" Eden leaned over, taking a good look at me.

"I'm wearing jeans," I said.

"Designer jeans. Just too cute. If I had a daughter I'd make her keep me up to date. I absolutely live in sundresses and sandals in the summertime," she said. "I need a personal stylist or somebody to keep me up to par."

"You've got your own style. Your own flair," I said, though her attire was tamer today— she wore white from head to toe. "Not many women can rock your hair color and get away with it. Trust me. I've seen some attempts that looked disastrous."

"Does your mama want to put you up for sale?" Eden asked, shifting into reverse. "I'd benefit from all the hard work she put in while you were growing up."

Eden made me think about Mama. From the day I left home for college, our lives went in two different directions. Mama was content with the life she lived and never saw more for herself than working a ten-hour workday, having enough money to pay the bills, and buying something nice for herself every now and then. But I dreamt about more and figured that there was no reason why I couldn't have anything and everything that I wanted. Regardless of our contrasting views of life, Mama was Mama. And I needed to see her.

Eden turned down the commercials that interrupted the morning gospel praise on the radio station. "You remind me of a young lady at my church who's probably about your age. You said you're in your early thirties, right?"

"Thirty-three," I reminded her.

"Sherri's probably around that age, too. Petite little thing who can wear the heaven out of some clothes. She makes most of her own pieces and the cutest outfits for her daughter, Faith."

I held on to the side of the door when Eden accelerated so she could merge into the highway traffic. I stomped on the imaginary brake pedal on my side when she came breathtakingly close to the bumper of a Volkswagen Beetle.

Eden glanced over at me and laughed. "My husband always tells me I drive like I'm on a race track. He never lets me behind the wheel when we're together—which is fine by me."

"As long as you get me to church tonight," I said.

Eden slowed down to the speed limit and merged into the right lane—probably to calm my nerves.

"Rest assured that tonight you'll be safe and in the place," Eden said.

I was definitely going to feel the effects of pushing, pulling, and lifting things at the bookstore. Eden packed more muscle in her petite body than I expected, and besides our lunch break, we worked nonstop until the task was done. I only hoped my body wouldn't go stiff at church and the ushers would have to carry me out on a board and dump me into the back seat of Eden's SUV.

"Here we are," Eden said, opening the front door of her home. "The first time you're a guest and we'll cater to you, but the next time you're on your own," she said.

I followed Eden and placed my things on the living room couch.

My favorite spot of serenity in Eden's Gates turned out to be a small replica of the style and warmth of her home. I could tell she'd considered every purchased piece so that it reflected who she was—inside and out. Eden favored oversized floor pillows that were strategically placed around the room, usually near a basket of books. Display shelves framed the fireplace in the middle of the room. One side showcased a collection of hand-sewn African-American dolls, and the other side was lined with family pictures and miniature-sized China tea sets.

"I can definitely tell the bookstore is an extension of your home. I wouldn't be surprised if I started hearing harps playing in here and angels flying around," I jested.

Eden chuckled. "Come back when me and my husband are having an argument. I guarantee you, if there are angels in here, we'd run them straight out."

I followed Eden through an arched doorway that led from the den to a spacious kitchen, where there was a huge man towering over the kitchen counter. He was peering into a pot on the stove and looked like he could have eaten the pot and all of its contents in a single gulp.

"Speaking of *my* angel," Eden said, walking up behind the monstrosity of a man and wrapping her arms around his midsection. She looked like a jockey trying to tackle a defensive linebacker.

"Sheila, this is my husband, Bear. His mama named him James Mayfield, but she's the only one who still calls him that."

Bear's nickname was befitting. I don't recall ever seeing a man who was as massive as he was. He was solid like a brick wall from one side to the other, and it looked like the circumference of his arm was twice the size of that of an average man.

"Nice to meet you," I said and took a seat on one of the red cushioned stools at the bar.

"Pardon me for not shaking your hand," he said and turned the knob on the kitchen sink with his wrist. "I'm all floured up from trying to cook some fried chicken for my wife before we leave for Bible study."

Eden had her hands on her hips. "Now how can you sit and tell a lie like that? I told you this morning that I had my fried item for the month yesterday when me and Sheila grabbed some wings. These are for *you*," she fussed, then opened the lid of the pot on the stove. "You know what I want," she said.

When he smiled, he wasn't as intimidating as he had seemed. His bright white teeth actually made him look more like a cartoon bear—like Smokey—instead of a grizzly.

"I think she loves my red beans and rice more than she loves me," Bear said to me.

Eden opened a kitchen cabinet and pulled out three dinner plates. "I'm too hungry to make an intelligent response to that. I've also got a healthy, but hefty salad in the fridge with grilled chicken and all of the fixings, Sheila," Eden offered. "But of course you're welcome to the chef's special fried chicken."

"I'll have what you're having," I said.

Eden made all of our plates, and then joined me and Bear at the dining room table to say grace. Their relationship was so Claire and Cliff Huxtable-like, minus the house full of children. It was the life that I'd envisioned for me and Ace once upon a time. He would've arrived home in his pilot's uniform, and I would have met him at the door with a greeting suitable for a man who'd been away from his loving wife for three days. I would have served him dinner in the kitchen and dessert in the bedroom.

I had to arrest my thoughts. I was about to go to church, and

I was sitting at Eden's table daydreaming about somebody else's husband. I don't know how I was going to live for God if I couldn't even stop the sinful thoughts from getting in my mind.

Bear shifted in the chair, but no matter how he positioned himself, his body spilled over the edge. His seat was the only one at the round table that had a high back that curved around on either side like a throne.

"So, Sheila"—he waited until he finished a mouthful of beans and rice—"you don't know how much you helped me by going to the bookstore today. Working with Eden stresses me out, and it's the last thing I wanted to deal with this Saturday. Now I can go golfing like I planned in the first place."

"You get stressed out?" Eden stared at him like she was in disbelief. "I have to go back and reshelve most of what you do because you throw the books up on the shelves how *you* think they should go, then try to explain the method behind the madness."

"She still keeps asking me to help," Bear said, ripping the meat off a chicken leg. "So it must not be too bad."

"No. I just keep praying that one day you'll get it right, and it's all really because I like to have you around."

"See, now. That's the real reason," Bear said. He reached over and pulled his wife into a hug. If I was a stranger watching them on the street, I might have rushed to save Eden from suffocation—being buried under his immense arms. But Eden's only struggle was probably trying to contain herself from being too intimate with her husband in front of me.

After a fulfilling dinner, Eden showed me upstairs to the guest bathroom where I freshened up and then went into the bedroom to change into a pair of light grey cotton slacks and a soft yellow shirt that tied at the hip. While I strapped on my shoes, my phone rang. I didn't recognize the number and thought it must be Travis or Reggie since I hadn't saved either of their numbers in my phone yet.

"Hello?"

"Yes, is Sheila Rushmore available?"

The creditors didn't care that it was six o'clock, and I was trying to get ready for church. I'd been with Eden all day with gospel music piping in my ears, so I guess that helped me be on my best behavior. Since this morning I'd been inspired and rejuvenated, and I wasn't about to ruin it by using any choice words with this woman. I'd already written out a list of who was going to get paid this month. If this woman's company wasn't on the list, she'd have to wait until next month's round.

"How can I help you?" I said.

"This is Debbie Stallworth calling from Mapp Career Consultants. I apologize for contacting you so late in the evening, but we recently reviewed your résumé, and I was hoping I could schedule you for an interview tomorrow morning."

I was so glad I'd kept my calm.

"Sure, that would be great," I said.

I didn't remember when I'd applied to Mapp Career Consultants or what the position was. The only thing I knew was that it had to be in the human resources area. I'd figure out the rest later when I looked at the spreadsheet I'd made to keep track of all the jobs I'd been applying for.

There was a notepad and pens on the guestroom nightstand so I jotted down the address and the landmarks she gave. First the car, now the job interview. I looked up and imagined God looking down at me. *This must be what it feels like to have God smile down on you.* I couldn't wait to tell Eden.

I repacked my garment and toiletry bag and headed downstairs. I could see straight into the den from the bottom of the stairs. I saw Eden and Bear engaged in a conversation that didn't look like it was as polite and loving as the one at dinner.

"If he wants money, he needs to find a job," Bear was saying. He'd turned his back to Eden and was looking out the living room bay window.

"Sometimes that's easier said than done," Eden said. Her voice was shaky, like she'd been crying and had pleaded this case before hundreds of times. "Every now and then—"

"It's not every now and then. It's all the time. You can't keep financing an addict. You're helping him more than hurting him."

"He needs to eat."

"Is that what you think he's using the money for, Eden?"

I tiptoed back upstairs, then waited for a few minutes before I came down. This time I made sure I made enough noise to announce my arrival.

"Sorry to keep you waiting," I said. They were on opposite ends of the room now—Eden curled up in a chair reading her Bible and Bear still staring out of the window. I saw Eden brush a tear from her cheek before she stood up.

"Perfect timing," Eden said. "Just let me get my purse."

Bear walked out the front door without saying a word and waited for us in Eden's truck. The ride to church started off quietly, and I acted like the tension in the car didn't exist. But by the time we arrived at church, I noticed how Bear had slid his monstrous arm to the armrest between the seats, and he and Eden were holding hands.

I guess after twenty-five years of being together, sometimes it didn't take words to resolve an argument.

Chapter 22

It shouldn't have surprised me that Eden's church members were just as loving as she was. Maybe they poured out the extra love and courtesy for me because she kept introducing me as her guest, but it was refreshing nonetheless.

I had connected with the energy and feel of the church already, and I hadn't heard the choir sing one note or the pastor preach one word. The ushers passed a stack of papers down each row for people who wanted to take notes. The words "How This Lesson Applies to My Life" were at the top of the page, followed by a list of Scriptures.

I couldn't quote a single verse from any of the Scriptures. Truth be told, I didn't know where to find them, either. I usually steered away from the front half of the Bible. It was like reading a foreign language, with all the unpronounceable names and places. I knew Adam and Eve were kicked out of the garden of Eden in Genesis, but after that I was basically clueless.

I'd expected to experience a spiritual uplifting during service, but I hadn't thought I was going to cry most of the time. Despite my tears, I was still refreshed. I used Eden's entire pack of tissues until she finally had to confiscate Bear's handkerchief.

"I look a mess, don't I?" I asked Eden when the service was over.

"Actually you don't," Eden said, giving me a tight squeeze. She'd given me quite a few of them during the service. "That's a miracle in and of itself," she teased. "After all those tears, you still look beautiful. I'd have a big old swollen nose and puffy eyes."

I laughed and hoped that I really looked as cute as Eden had said. First impressions were everything, and I had one to leave on the man walking in our direction. I could tell he was headed toward Bear and hoped Bear would be so kind as to introduce me.

Thank you God, I said to myself when I noticed he wasn't wearing a wedding band. He might be my third bachelor in the running. I'd felt the pain of watching Ace get married, but every day my relationship prospects were increasing.

I sat down in the pew and tried to be patient waiting for Bear (and the man he was talking with) to acknowledge me. Eden had been pulled away by a woman with a young child. Eden stroked the young child's ponytails, which fell all the way to her shoulders, even though they were pulled high to the top of her head. The woman's face seemed a bit stressed, but by the time the conversation with Eden ended, she seemed more relaxed. She came with Eden to where I was sitting like a lady-in-waiting.

"Sheila, I'd like you to meet Sherri." Eden patted the little girl's shoulder. "And this is her daughter, Faith."

I stood up to shake her hand, but Sherri leaned in for a hug. Everyone at the church was always hugging. I guessed a good old handshake had long grown out of style here. Even little Faith reached up for a snuggle from me.

"I'm five and a half," Faith proudly announced. I remembered those days when it was important to add that half at the end of your age.

"Welcome to Grace Worship Center," Sherri said. "Did you enjoy the service?"

"More than enjoyed it," I said. I quickly glanced to see if Bear's friend had gone, but to my relief they were still engaged in conversation. "I'll definitely be back Sunday," I assured them.

Clive had sent me a text during service, though I didn't see it until church was dismissed. My car would be ready in the morning. I hadn't forgotten my promise to God. Whenever they opened the doors of the church, barring any emergency, I'd be there.

"There's Anisha," Sherri said to Eden and waved over a slim woman from across the sanctuary. Sherri's daughter was rubbing the sleeve of my blouse.

"I like your shirt," Faith said. "Is it silk?"

That was the last question I expected to hear from a five-year-old.

"You have to excuse her," Sherri said. "That's what happens when you have a daughter who's always in fabric stores and around a sewing machine." She pinched her daughter's cheek. "I design clothes," she told me.

"She does more than design clothes," Eden said. "She owns a boutique, too. At the beginning of the season I have Sherri sew up tons of sundresses. I choose the fabrics, and she goes to work." Eden snapped her fingers. "She whips them up just like that—in less than a week."

"Eden," Sherri said, "it's basically one piece of fabric with some bunching. You're my easiest client."

Sherri was the same height as Eden, but Sherri had more in the trunk and under the hood, so to speak. It didn't surprise me that she was a designer. She was rocking a pair of capris and a matching cropped jacket that was perfectly shaped to her proportions. Faith was wearing a spaghetti-strapped sundress of the same fabric, with a scripted letter *F* embroidered on the bodice.

I could coordinate an eye-turning ensemble with clothes off the rack at any department store, but it was evident that Sherri could take customized to the next level.

"You two should get together sometime," Eden suggested, as if she were reading my mind.

I've only known Sheila for a short time," she said to Sherri, "but she looks impeccable in even the simplest things. I'm telling you, a T-shirt and jeans are like couture on this woman."

Eden was layering her compliments like a thick peanut butter and jelly sandwich, but I didn't mind.

"I promise I didn't pay her to say that," I said. I glanced in Bear's direction. He was still talking to the fine specimen, and I was still waiting for my big moment.

In the meantime the slender woman, Anisha, whom Sherri had called over, joined us. I hadn't even noticed she was pregnant from across the room, but she was carrying a pregnancy bump under one of those loose-fitting maternity shirts. I wonder if she knew she could easily transform that blouse into an after-pregnancy outfit with a belt and the perfect pair of jeans.

Anisha massaged her midsection like she was already cradling her newborn in her arms. Some things in life aren't fair when it comes to being a pregnant woman. This was one of them. She glowed with flawless skin, didn't have swollen ankles and feet stuffed into shoes that were too small, and her pregnant nose didn't cover half of her face.

I already knew that wasn't going to be my luck. DNA had a way of showing up when you didn't want it to. I'd seen Mama in pictures when she was pregnant with me, and to be honest, she always looked like she was uncomfortable and having a hot flash.

It didn't take long for me to find out that Anisha and that pregnant belly of hers "belonged" to Tyson Randall, the man I'd been eyeing as he was talking with Bear. I wasn't going to claim fault for looking at a married man. He should've been wearing his wedding band.

"So you met my beautiful wife and my baby?" Tyson asked me, rubbing Anisha's stomach. I had to admit, it was ridiculously cute the way he doted over his wife. I admired them, trying not to be envious. If God could bless Anisha with it, He could bless me, too. There were still Reggie and Travis in the running. Now it was only a matter of which one of them could handle me.

Chapter 23

I gripped the steering wheel of my pride and joy, then laid my forehead against it. "Thank you, God. And thank you, Clive," I added.

It felt so good to be behind the wheel of my car again that I wanted to sleep in it. If I had dark-as-night tinted windows I may have seriously considered it.

Clive walked around from the back of the auto shop with the mechanic. It was obvious he was talking about me because they simultaneously looked in my direction. I was wearing a pair of sunglasses so I acted like I didn't see them. There was no telling what exaggerated story Clive was feeding the man, but it was the least of my worries. I knew the truth.

I tooted the horn to warn Clive that he only had a few more minutes to make me wait before I pulled out onto the street and pressed the pedal to the metal. The shop had also washed and detailed the car until it shone like a trophy, and that morning I'd taken the time to look like a prize, too.

I felt fantastic today. A fine woman who was getting her life right with God, driving a sleek machine, on her way to a job interview, and looking forward to being wined and dined over the weekend. With blessings flowing like this, it would be no time before I landed a high-paying job and found happiness in love again.

Clive walked toward me with an unnecessary swagger. I could tell he was putting on a show for the mechanics that'd already taken a break to salivate over his spanking new Benz. He'd left them to ogle over the upgraded features and probably talk about what a big spender Clive was.

Clive liked the feeling of taking care of a woman. I could see it on his face. Smell it exuding out of his pores.

"You're a little anxious to get your baby on the road, I see," Clive said, stepping back to admire the high-gloss wax job.

"It's been a long time coming," I said. "I feel like I've been shipwrecked on an abandoned island."

"Glad to be able to save you," he said, drumming the hood of the car with his fingertips.

I wanted to tell him not to put his fingerprint smudges on my hood, but he was the reason why my car looked—and drove—the way it did. I kept my grateful mouth closed.

"And since I threw out the life jacket, I know you'll make time to have lunch with me," Clive said. "I told them I'd be out of the office for a little while."

"Actually I'm on my way to an interview," I said, crossing my fingers.

Clive walked around to the passenger side of the car and got in. If he was about twelve to fifteen years younger—and, most importantly, single—I would've kept him on my radar. Besides the difference in age, he encompassed everything that I looked for in a man. Clive didn't mind making sure a woman had what she needed, he believed in career advancement, and he was well traveled. No man was perfect, but Clive was close to it. The biggest adjustment he needed was a strong and confident woman who could tame his cocky side.

"Call me when you get finished," he suggested. "Maybe we can catch a late lunch. And depending on what happens with this job, I have something for you that can tide you over until you can find something permanent."

"I have a feeling I'll be getting hired for this position, so I doubt I'll need your side gig," I said, more confident than ever. I'd said a special prayer this morning and even read and highlighted the Scriptures that the pastor had referenced in Bible study last night. "And as far as calling you later, I'm going to go by and see Mama."

I'd tried calling to tell Mama I was coming by, but now her home phone was disconnected, too. The only way I'd ever get in contact with her was if I went over there myself.

"A man gets your car fixed and you kick him to the curb before you pull off the lot," Clive said, getting out of the car.

I ignored Clive's attempt to hold his good deed over my head. He was at the top of my list of creditors to pay back. He'd get his money sooner or later.

I shifted Lexie into drive and left Clive wishing that he had a woman as beautiful, hopeful, and faith-filled as me.

Chapter 24

The job was in the bag. I was sure of it. It was only a matter of time before I'd receive that much anticipated phone call offering me a ticket back into the corporate world. One with some funds attached to it.

It didn't hurt that my interviewer, Debbie, was as into fashion as I was. We immediately connected when she complimented me on the lines and tailoring of my suit. From what I'd seen, Debbie was one of a handful of women in the office, and I didn't doubt that she had to beat off the single men with a stick. Maybe even some of the married ones. I could give a beautiful woman her props—and Debbie deserved her props.

At the end of our twenty-minute interview, Debbie scheduled me for another interview in the morning with her supervisor. Then she quizzed me on my shoe expertise. I lassoed her in with my knowledge of the hot shoe spots in Atlanta, and she told me about two high-end consignments where she found her treasures. I could defintely relate to *Debbie's* shoe obsession.

But it was *Mama's* obsession that I couldn't deal with.

I shook my head when I pulled into the driveway behind Mama's beat-up Camry. I bet it was Devin who'd "repaired" her busted right taillight by covering it with red electrical tape.

Mama's tendency to collect things was spilling out onto the front porch of my small childhood house. Mama called it collecting; I called it hoarding. The last time I'd come to visit Mama was two weeks before Lexie had broken down and left me stranded at the mall.

Not having my car was a good reason to not endure the claustrophobic feeling I'd get while squeezing through the tight spaces in Mama's house. At our last visit she'd left me at home for a quick trip to the corner store to buy a liter of ginger ale to nurse Devin's nauseated stomach. I had ended up downing a glass myself. I had felt queasy looking at all that stuff.

When Mama had returned, I had been rummaging through a box of small kitchen appliances in the corner of the front room. I had had every intention to sneak the box to my car trunk and dump it, or either bag the appliances and stow them in the garbage can for the next day's pick-up. But Mama had caught me red-handed—or should I say green-handed—because I was examining a horrid green electric can opener straight from the seventies.

"What are you doing with my stuff?" she'd fussed.

"I'm helping you clear some things out so you can get around a little better."

"No, thanks," Mama had said.

I could tell she was trying to sound pleasant instead of agitated. She had snatched the rusty can opener out of my hands, shoved it back into the box, and kicked the box to the corner into its place beside a shopping bag full of old *Ebony* magazines.

"Devin's going to fix those appliances so I can take them down to the flea market and set up a table. They're antiques," she had justified.

Antiques? I'd thought. *Is she serious?*

The same box of "antiques" from my last visit was in the same corner when Devin opened the door. The house reeked of smoke, and I knew I'd have to take the time to soak in a bath and then wash my hair tonight, or else risk carrying the smell of cigarette smoke into my interview the next morning.

"Hey," I said to Devin. He let the screen door slam behind him, and I nearly jumped out of my heels.

He seemed amused by the whole thing. "Dag, girl. You think there's a drive-by shooting going down or something? You been staying in those gated communities too long."

Devin picked up a brown bottle from the coffee table and took a swig from it. That's when I knew Mama wasn't at home and probably wouldn't be back anytime soon. She was adamant about people not drinking alcohol in her house.

"Where's Mama?" I asked.

Devin opened one of the kitchen cabinets and slammed it shut when he saw there was only a small canister of coffee and some cans of vegetables inside.

"She went out of town this morning with Pearl to some kind of church service or something. She's supposed to be back tonight."

If Mama was going to church and it wasn't a funeral or a holiday, then I knew something was going on. Maybe we were going through our spiritual awakenings at the same time. God truly did work in mysterious ways.

"Really? That's nice," I said, attempting to make small talk despite the headache I felt creeping up.

Before we hit double digits in age, me and Devin used to be close. We'd have video game competitions on the Atari we shared and take turns making dinner for each other if Mama had to work late—which was most of the time. Devin's favorite was beans and franks, and mine was a tuna casserole concoction Mama taught me how to make. I'd eaten so much of the stuff that by the time I reached high school I'd sworn off both of the dishes.

Now Devin was opening the tops of a stack of Styrofoam containers he'd pulled from the fridge. The smell itself should've been enough to keep him from eating any of it, but he shoved something in his mouth without even heating it in the microwave.

I slid over a container of unopened rice—no doubt bought in bulk by my mother because of a special at the grocery store—and sat down on the couch. There was a brown slipcover tucked over it now, but I knew the old paisley stained couch was hiding under it.

"So what's been up with you?" I asked Devin.

From the looks of him, nothing much. The left half of his hair was braided in cornrows and the other half looked like it hadn't seen a comb all week. I assumed Devin definitely wasn't up to being employed.

"Just doin' what I do," Devin said.

That was his answer for everything.

"It looks like you're making it happen," he said. "You're still rolling in your Lexus and dressing top dollar." He pulled a raggedy wallet out of his back pocket and opened it up so I could see it. "Nothing," he said, flapping it in the air. "Little sis, you got about two-fifty I can hold?"

"Two-fifty what?"

"Two hundred fifty dollars. Something to help me take care of some things until I get on my feet."

"I can't help you this time," I said.

I thought about the money from Clive that was still in my purse. My unemployment check had been deposited, but by the time the checks I'd written last night posted, my balance would be teetering close to zero again. I'd spent just under seventy-five dollars at the grocery store and only had four bags in my hands when I walked out. Money didn't go very far these days. And now that

Lexie was rolling again, gas was an expense I'd have to think about. No. I wasn't giving a dime to Devin only to have him smoke or drink it away.

"I just can't help you," I said.

He looked at me like he didn't believe me. He gave me at least three sob stories about his failed business ventures, and how it was hard for a black man to make it in America. I finally broke down so he would shut up.

"I can give you twenty dollars," I whined. "Have you forgotten that I haven't worked in months, Devin?"

He looked insulted that I'd only offered him twenty dollars, but he could take the Andrew Jackson or nothing at all.

"I'll give it to you before I leave," I said. I didn't want to risk Devin seeing a wad of cash in my wallet, because I knew he'd be looking over my shoulder as soon as I cracked open my purse.

I loved my older brother, but over the years he'd given me fewer reasons to trust him. Time healed all wounds, but it didn't do much for my memory. When I was in college he'd opened some of my student loan mail that was still being sent to the house. He stole my social security number then applied for a gas card. Of all things, a gas card. Mama sat down for an intervention between us in order to get us back on speaking terms, but it was a long time before we were cordial again.

I'd decided to settle in for a visit with Devin when a loud bang hit the front door—so loud that it shook the wall, too. And my heart. Whoever it was, wasn't just mad. They were furious.

Chapter 25

W ho is that?" I whispered.

Devin didn't have to answer.

"Open the door, Devin," a woman's voice screamed. "I mean it. Right now, or I'll bust this door down with this bat. I ain't playing."

I was slightly relieved to hear that it was a woman acting this way, but nevertheless it was not where I wanted to be. Devin could deal with his problem alone.

"Be a man, Devin," the woman screamed again. "I know you've got a chick up in there because Meka saw her when she pulled up."

Chick? I guess she was talking about me. And what business was it of Meka—whoever she was—to announce who was going in and out of Mama's house?

Devin was acting like there was absolutely nothing going on. He pulled up his sagging pants and fingered the end of one of his braids.

"That ain't nobody but Shakira," Devin said to me, sucking his teeth and using a toothpick to dislodge a piece of meat.

"Shakira or Sha-crazy. I don't care who it is." I peeked in my purse and fished out a twenty and slapped it on the kitchen table. Devin snatched it up before my hand left the table. "I'm out of here."

When I threw open the door I was standing face to face with a girl who under normal, peaceful circumstances I would've considered nice looking. She looked to be in her early twenties—too young for Devin's thirty-eight-year-old behind in my opinion. Too young for Devin, and too old for this nonsense. Her doe-like eyes and high cheekbones could attract boys her own age, but a little bit of crazy on the most attractive face could make a whole lot of ugly.

"Who are you?" Shakira yelled at me and threw a few curse words in my direction.

This girl needed prayer, but I wanted to smack her instead.

"Calm down, Shakira. Don't disrespect my mama's house," I said. I could tell I'd thrown her off by saying her name. "You might want to get yourself together before you come up in here like that. Devin is my *brother*, not my man."

A bit of the anger drained from her face, but she was still wearing a scowl. She looked at Devin as if to confirm my statement. "Your *sister*?"

"His *sister*." I answered for Devin, since he was still playing dental hygienist.

"Devin never told me he had a sister," Shakira said, leaning on the bat she'd been wielding. It had dents and pieces of wood chipped off of it like she and the bat had a history.

"Devin probably hasn't told you a lot of things," I said and laughed as I walked out of the door and to my car.

With all of this drama I believed I deserved to treat myself to a manicure and pedicure. It was too beautiful of a day to spend it sitting behind closed doors at Cassandra's place. There were a few other errands I wanted to run before going to meet Clive at his downtown condo. After leaving the interview at Mapp Consultants, I'd decided it might not be a bad idea to have some extra cash on the side so I could catch up on my bills—and feed my shopping fetish when necessary. Having Debbie in the office was going to keep me on top of my fashion game.

At Clive's suggestion, I'd stopped by his office to pick up a spare key to his place so that I could let myself in if he ended up working longer than he expected. I had made him meet me in the parking garage instead of going up to my old stomping grounds. I had no desire whatsoever to see any of my former colleagues.

I was about to have new colleagues, anyway.

Chapter 26

Is dinner ready, sweetheart?"

Clive wasted no time making jokes when he walked in the door. He dropped his briefcase at the entryway and threw his keys in the ceramic bowl that held his pocket change, a couple of fountain pens, and some business cards.

I was sitting at his high-top bar in the kitchen eating a cold-cut sandwich. "You wish you had a woman as fine as me waiting for you when you got home."

"I can't say you're lying about that," he said, removing his cufflinks. Clive also took off his Italian tie and unbuttoned the first few buttons of his heavily starched dress shirt.

I held up my hand before he got too comfortable. "Don't go there," I said. "Keep your clothes on."

"This is what I always do when I get home from work," he said.

Clive started to unbuckle his belt, and I immediately stood up and stuffed my sandwich back into the plastic bag.

"Calm your nerves," he said. "I'm playing with you. Can't an old man have a little fun?"

"No. I'm not here for fun," I said, wiping my mouth and hands. "I'm here to hear about your business proposition, remember?"

Clive opened the refrigerator and twisted the cap off of a bottle of seltzer water. "I like a woman who's all about business. And speaking of business, how was your interview?"

I followed Clive down the hall. "Just a matter of time. I'm going in for a second interview in the morning."

"You sound pretty sure of yourself," he said.

"I am," I said, enjoying the feel of the carpet under my toes. It was so thick it felt like I was walking across a cloud. Cloud nine.

The open floor plan and high ceilings made the condo seem larger than it actually was. I'd already done all of my gawking while examining the rooms before Clive arrived. Surely he didn't expect me to let myself in and not do a little exploring. I knew Clive had money, but I didn't realize he was banking like this. No doubt J. Morrow paid him well, but it must've been his other business ventures that helped him finance his extravagant lifestyle. The arched hallway led back to his office and a grand master bedroom suite. Clive's impeccable taste in clothing flowed over into his interior decorating, and vice versa. Classic, clean straight lines. Expensive.

"I'm a stickler for organization," Clive was saying as he clicked on the overhead light and the desk lamps in his office. "Unfortunately I haven't been able to stay on top of the filing and some of the other administrative tasks for my businesses. Gina and I used to have an assistant who came to our house and kept things in order, but Gina became fast friends with her. She didn't know how to stay out of our private lives."

"So you fired her?" I asked.

"I prefer to say I let her seek other opportunities. Which is why I need you."

Clive walked me through his filing system and recordkeeping software. Before certain papers were filed, the data had to be input into spreadsheets, printed, and placed in labeled notebooks. Clive was particular and meticulous.

"I'm impressed," I said, taking notes and soaking it all in. "You've got your stuff together."

"Prosperity has a way of binding itself to people who do. You can bet money on that."

I rolled myself up to a cherry wood desk that was as nice as any furniture I'd seen in a corporate office. "Consider me hired, but of course it'll only be part-time after I start my new job. How often do you want me to come by?"

"Once a week. You can keep that key you have, and I'll set a personal alarm code for you."

"Works for me," I said, standing up. I checked my watch, grateful that I'd finally been able to get a battery for it. "I better get going. It's been a long day." But not so long that I couldn't meet Reggie tonight.

Clive unbuttoned the rest of his shirt. "If you don't mind, let yourself out and lock the door. The Jacuzzi is calling me."

It wouldn't surprise me if Clive had hired a woman to wait in the bathroom and fan him with oversized palm leaves and feed him grapes. Amusing.

"Why are you standing there smiling?" Clive asked.

"Hmm? Just thinking," I said. "I'll talk to you later."

Things were finally getting better. I could see a light at the end of the tunnel. Yes. There was plenty to smile about.

Chapter 27

I pulled into Cassandra's complex. Frank's truck was nowhere in sight, and I couldn't have been happier. The sight of him had a way of souring my good mood. I unlocked the front door, expecting to see Cassandra lounging on the couch and watching one of her favorite reality shows. Cassandra was a night owl and could stay up watching senseless drama, then wake up early the next morning for work. Back in college, I pulled the same thing between partying and schoolwork, but those days are over. I rarely see eleven o'clock come and go.

Cassandra's bedroom door was closed, but I could hear the slight sound of music from the end of the hall. She must've been calling it an early night.

I took my toiletry bag into the hall bathroom and showered, but decided not to wash my hair. I was too tired to deal with it before I got ready for my late date with Reggie.

Since I had some time to spare, I focused my attention on finding the perfect outfit to wear for my second interview. This one was going to seal the deal, so I had to not only talk the part, but also look the part. I chose a suit that stopped traffic when I wore it and paired it with a fuchsia blouse to give it a little signature Sheila flavor. I hung it on my closet door and decided to do a little Internet surfing. While I was booting up my laptop, there was a knock on my door.

"Come in," I said.

The door eased open and Cassandra's hand stuck through the crack holding a Krispy Kreme doughnut wrapped in a napkin. I could tell by the glistening glaze that she'd microwaved it for nine seconds, just like I liked it.

"A peace offering," Cassandra said from behind the partially open bedroom door.

I took the doughnut from her hand then opened the door the rest of the way. "Peace offering?" I asked, taking a bite of the doughnut.

"Okay, so it's no secret. Things have been kind of strained between me and you," she said.

"True," I said.

"And I miss the old Sheila," Cassandra said. "We used to kick it and have a good time."

She leaned against the doorframe and ran her fingers through her new hair. I call it new hair because just the other day it was midnight black and down to her shoulder, but now it was cut in an asymmetrical bob and brown with a few honey blond highlights to frame her face. The look softened the sharp angles of her facial features. I left the wigs and the weaves to Cassandra, but I could definitely use an updated summer look myself. I'd have my hair stylist, Takiyah, hook me up for my first day on the job.

"We've definitely had our good times," I admitted. "And some worth forgetting."

Cassandra was doing what she always did when we were having

talks—going through my closet. If she hoped to discover some new finds since her last browse, she was going to be disappointed.

"We should go out Friday," Cassandra said. "They're having a mixer for the grown and sexy at the Blue Lounge tomorrow night. I think we qualify for that."

"I'm supposed to be going out with this guy I met," I said. "Reggie tonight and Travis tomorrow night."

"Good for you," Cassandra said. "It's about time."

"Tell me about it," I said. "I know you and Frank will manage to have a good time without me."

Cassandra pulled out a pair of jeans and held them up to her waist. Her waist was teeny, but there was no way she was going to get her hips into my pants. She had the kind of hips that were passed down from generation to generation.

Cassandra looked at me, and I shook my head. She put them back.

"I haven't talked to Frank since yesterday," she said. "He needs to take care of his issues with his baby's mama. I can't deal with it right now. Tangela wants him back. I know she wants him back, but he refuses to see it. But what can I do about it? They have to talk to each other because they have a son. As much as little black boys need their daddies these days, I'm not mad about that. But his baby mama still ticks me off."

I'd become an impromptu counselor. Cassandra kept shuffling through my closet like she was going to find an answer to her relationship problems in there. Believe me, if there was one, I would've dug it out for *myself* already.

"That's why I want to get out, so I can take my mind off of Frank."

I thought about how Eden had been there for me and reached out to me during a time of need. How could I do any less for a woman I'd been friends with since our double-dutch jump rope days?

"Anyway," she said, snapping back from the far-away look in

her eyes. "Maybe I can catch somebody with my new look. How do you like it?" She flipped her hair over her shoulder.

"Very becoming," I said. "I *love* it."

"And I love you too, girl. Even when we act crazy," she said, holding out a floral print halter top.

I almost fainted when I heard her say the words "I love you." Cassandra was admiring herself in the mirror and acted like she hadn't said a word. She tilted her head to the side.

"Can you still fit into this?" she asked. "It might be a little small for you now. You've put on a few pounds since then."

"Your eyes are going bad," I said, standing up. I pinched my waist. "I've lost weight. At least ten pounds."

"It must've all dropped off below your waist," Cassandra said, convincingly.

It made me assess my body again. I looked at my silhouette in the mirror. I disagreed, but Cassandra would probably say anything to get that top.

"Take it," I said.

"Really?"

"No, not like *take it forever*. I mean take it to wear when you go out. I want my shirt back. Don't make me put out an APB for it," I said.

She tossed the top across her shoulder. "Don't forget to tell me all the juicy details about your dates," she said.

I didn't know how juicy the details would be, but I hoped they would be nights to remember.

Chapter 28

Reggie may not have cared much about his dress shoes, but it wouldn't surprise me if he cleaned his tennis shoes with a toothbrush. I guess athletic gear was his thing because he was coordinated in blue and yellow from head to toe. I felt overdressed in slacks and a lacy camisole, but I was willing to make the best of the night.

I tried not to stare at how shiny his face looked, but I think he'd slathered a layer of petroleum jelly across his forehead instead of investing in some moisturizer. As hot as it was outside, I hoped his face wouldn't start to sizzle.

"Would you like to sit outside on the deck, or eat inside?" the hostess asked us.

"Inside is fine," I said. I wasn't up to going to the hospital for the second-degree burns that might pop up on Reggie's face.

Despite his fondness for hip-hop gear and his method of

moisturizing, the man was finer than I don't know what. That was his saving grace. I'd even arrived early, staked out the restaurant's parking lot so I could see him before he saw me. Emotions can skew your view about situations and people, so I had wanted to make sure the pity I'd felt for myself at Ace's wedding hadn't made Reggie seem more handsome than he actually was.

I'd been so wrapped up in perfecting my makeup I hadn't seen Reggie pull up in his car, but I did see him walking into the restaurant.

"So tell me about Sheila Marcelle," Reggie said.

We'd already had this discussion the first time we talked on the phone, so I'm not sure what new information he was looking for me to divulge. And I wished he'd stop calling me by my first and middle names.

"What do you want to know?" I asked.

"Anything," he said, rearing back on the back legs of the chair.

"I'm hungry," I said. It wasn't an exaggeration, even though I'd eaten the cold cut sandwiches at Clive's.

"Let's get the lady some food," Reggie said, standing up to flag over a waiter. "I'm all about keeping the ladies happy." He sat down, satisfied with himself, like he'd done some brave feat like rescue me from a burning building.

I'd already perused the menu and decided that the owners of this place were trying to send everyone to an early grave. Everything was fried food, or you could opt for a colossal burger with pounds of meat and homemade sauces. I ended up ordering a caesar salad without the crispy chicken.

"Have you talked to Ace since he and Lynette got back from the honeymoon?" Reggie asked me after we placed our order.

I wasn't about to let our conversation lean toward Ace and Lynette. I was bound to have to lie, so I'd rather commit a sin of omission. If he couldn't ask me, then I wasn't obliged to tell him.

"Are we here to talk about them or find out more about each other?" I asked.

Reggie turned the brim of his hat to the back of his head. "I like a straightforward woman," he said. "That turns me on."

"You might want to turn yourself off," I said. "It's not going down like that."

Reggie laughed, then guzzled down nearly half a bottle of beer before coming up for air. I wasn't a fan of men who drank, because I couldn't stand the smell of beer in my face.

"Do you drink a lot?" I asked him.

"Only when I go out," he said. Reggie tilted back the bottle and finished it off.

"How often do you go out?" I asked.

"Shouldn't you be asking me the crucial questions like, 'Am I married? Do I have baby mama drama? Do I have benefits?'"

"I'll get to that, too," I said. Reggie was dodging the question.

A man up front had approached a microphone, set up on a stage. He was short, spindly, and at first glance seemed to be extremely shy. Then he grabbed the microphone and the confidence in his spoken word skills made him seem two feet taller. He recited a powerful piece about politics, love, and facing the man in the mirror.

After everyone in the restaurant gave him a standing ovation, he retreated back into his shell and went to eat at a table alone.

"That brother was bad," Reggie said.

"Definitely," I agreed. "Now getting back to my question. How often do you go out?"

"About four days out of the week."

"That's a lot," I said. From my experience a man who had that much time on his hands to hang out and drink beers at the bar wasn't doing much with his life. I think Reggie sensed my judgment.

"I'm single with no children," Reggie said unapologetically. "I'm going to enjoy my freedom as long as I can. Until I meet and fall in love with a woman who makes me want to lay it all down. When I find her, you'll never see me in another bar."

That was a fair answer. From that point on conversation flowed easily between me and Reggie. He was highly opinionated and had a great sense of humor. It ended up being a nice date after all, and I was anxious to know when we'd see each other again.

Then things started on a slippery slope downhill.

"Would you mind taking me home?" he asked me when we got up to leave. "My friend had to use my car, so I let him drop me off."

"So you assumed I wouldn't mind?"

"I only live ten minutes away. I didn't think it would be a problem."

I chose to believe his story about his friend needing to use his car, even though it sounded far-fetched. Being without a car wasn't an easy thing.

Reggie kept me entertained on the ride to his house by doing bad impressions of celebrities. When we pulled into the driveway, I had a gut feeling that Reggie didn't live here alone. There were too many hanging fern baskets and other potted plants for a man's taste. Reggie didn't seem like the kind of man with a green thumb.

"You're into plants," I said.

"That's my mama's doing," Reggie said.

Something made me ask, "So your mama lives here?"

Reggie shifted in the seat and opened the door. I guess he'd had enough of my questions for one night. "As Mama got older, she didn't want to live alone, so I told her she could live with me," he said.

Or was it the other way around?

"That woman's my heart," Reggie said, pounding his chest.

Headlights shone through the back window as a car pulled into the driveway behind mine.

"Is there something else I should know?" I asked him.

"That's just Mama. Probably coming back from shopping again. She met some new friend at the wedding and now she can't get rid of the woman".

Reggie's mama's face was pressed against my driver's side window before Reggie and I had the chance to say good-bye. I'd been eyeing his lips all night and had already imagined how they'd feel against mine. I wasn't going to find out tonight.

She tapped on the window, and I rolled it down.

"It looks like I'm seeing more and more of you," Reggie's mother said. "Is your son feeling better?"

It was obviously a case of mistaken identity.

"I don't have a son," I said.

"Mama, this is Sheila," Reggie said. "We met at Ace and Lynette's wedding."

"Oh. So you're like family," she crooned. She had a handful of shopping bags looped on her arms, and Reggie came around the car to take them from her. She yelled back to the car behind me. "Ruby, come and meet Sheila. She's just as cute as she wants to be."

Ruby? Did she say Ruby?

I looked out the rearview mirror at the dark shadow approaching the car. I'd recognize that waddle anywhere. I knew I couldn't get away by trying to maneuver in reverse past the car behind me, blocking my exit. I hated to ruin the manicured yard, but since it may have been a matter of life and death I cut the steering wheel to a hard left and barreled over the yard figurines and the curb.

So much for Reggie. He'd never hear from Sheila Marcelle again.

Chapter 29

No one was answering the phone. Not Eden. Not Mama, who I'd already called twice. I even tried to call Travis. Reggie was the only person who'd reached out to me this morning, and that was probably because he thought he could sucker me into another date with him. And his Mama. And Ruby. Not going to happen.

It was funny how when I was working, I wished I wasn't. And now that I wasn't working, finding a job consumed most of my thoughts. Even though I was still asleep when Debbie called around ten this morning, I answered the phone like I'd been awake since sunrise.

"Hi, Sheila?" Debbie had said when I answered the phone.

"This is she," I said, ready to accept her offer and all the benefits that would come with it. I'd calculated my possible take-home pay about a million times.

"I wanted to call you personally and thank you for coming in for the interview," she said.

Her first sentence told me it wasn't going to be the news I expected.

"We were impressed with your skills and what you could potentially bring to the company, but . . ."

Don't say it.

". . . we found someone who would be a better match for us."

I paused and got myself together. "Thank you for the opportunity," I said. "I hope you'll consider me if you have any openings in the near future."

"I definitely will," Debbie said. "And I'll call you if I happen upon any great shoe sales."

Yeah, right. And what money did she think I was going to use to buy them?

"You do that," I said. "Have a good one."

That's when I started making calls to find someone who could help me lick my wounds. Travis was the first to finally return my call. I'd decided to drag myself out of bed even though I wanted to roll around in pity all day. I felt better once I was dressed. I played one of my gospel CDs and let the psalmists sing me into a better mood. I even listened to the quartet for the first—and last—time.

"I was just thinking about you," Travis said.

I was smiling already. Blushing, really. "And what were you thinking?"

"About how I wanted to do something special with you tomorrow."

"Tomorrow?" I said confused. "I thought we were going out tonight. Unless you plan on wining and dining me the entire weekend."

"Actually," Travis said, "I need to cancel for tonight."

"Oh. So that's why the word 'special' was added to the equation," I joked, but I was clearly disappointed. I noticed how my body seemed to respond to his comments. My shoulders slumped.

I thrust my shoulders back and acted like Travis could see me.

"Hello, Sheila?"

"I'm here," I answered.

"I thought you'd hung up on me."

"No. Just wondering why any man would want to postpone seeing *me* for another day," I said. "But I understand. I'll hold out for my Saturday night special."

"Perfect," Travis said. "Call you Saturday morning."

I let myself sulk for about twenty more minutes then tried to think of something worthwhile to get into tonight. Something worthwhile and worth my gas.

I wouldn't mind spending time with Clive—perhaps catch a movie. But there was no way he was getting a call from me tonight. I liked my head and didn't want to see it being served on a silver platter by Gina.

So I called Cassandra at work and told her that I'd be ready for a good time tonight. One thing about Cassandra was that she'd make herself have a good time, despite what may have been going on in her life. Her relationship with Frank might have been going downhill, but you'd never know by looking at her. By nine o'clock that night she was ready to pull me out the door.

"Girl, how much longer are you going to be?" she asked me through the closed bedroom door. "If you want to get in free, you need to hurry up so we can get there by ten."

"Fifteen minutes, tops," I said, pulling on a pair of black jeans that could've doubled for slacks if you didn't see them up close, and an irresistible black shirt I'd purchased on a trip to the mall for retail therapy. It was short sleeved and cinched at the waist so it gave me an hourglass figure. I added a gold link belt and gold accessories, including a pair of strappy gold stilettos. I hoped we'd have somewhere to sit, because the last thing I wanted to do was suffer standing on my feet all night.

Takiyah had fit me in for a last-minute hair appointment, although I had to beg her for a Friday afternoon slot. She was pregnant with her first child and was scheduling only a few appointments each day so that she could stay off her swollen feet as much as possible. After seeing those feet up close and personal today, I empathized with her. It looked like someone had over inflated them with an air pump. Poor thing. But I didn't feel bad enough for her to give up my appointment. She may have lost her ability to stand for long periods of time, but she was still a magician with some scissors and a bottle of permanent hair color.

She gave me a trendy cut with flirty bangs and long layers. She'd convinced me to streak my hair with more than one color, but I'd warned her that I was still trying to secure a job in the corporate world and I didn't want a look that was too young and trendy to keep me from being a serious candidate.

"So I see you do still have a little diva in you," Cassandra said when I walked into the living room. She was painting the toenail of the one toe you could see peeking out from the front of her shoe.

"What do you mean by that? Still?"

"I was afraid you had gone all church missionary on me or something," she said. "For a while I thought you were going to stay cooped up in the house listening to that same tired gospel CD you've been playing over and over for the past week. I know it's jazzy and all contemporary, but please."

Cassandra fanned her hand over her toes and blew on them like she was trying to put out flames.

"And last time I asked you how you'd spent your day, you were talking about helping that lady at the bookstore with some inventory. You know. The one who was going to call the police on me," Cassandra said as if she needed to remind me.

I corrected her. "Actually, she was going to call the police on Frank."

"Same difference," Cassandra said. "I probably should've let her so they could've arrested him for being stupid."

That same night we'd talked about Eden, I'd shared with Cassandra about my spiritual experience at the wedding. She thought I'd been caught up in the moment and had let my emotions get the best of me. Since she had made several references to my "issues," I had stopped wasting my time trying to convince her that what I'd felt was real.

I picked around in the junk drawer in the kitchen until I found a pack of spearmint gum that I'd stashed in there.

"Just so you know, Eden is not all that old," I said. "And like I said before, since when is it against the law for a diva to try and have a relationship with God?"

Cassandra looked at me like I'd grown another head. "And like *I* said before . . . since it's you. It doesn't even fit your personality. I told you, you're going through a phase. But that phase will end tonight." She stood up and swiveled her hips.

Cassandra's words stung. I knew the changes in my life were real. And like my bookmark said, I wasn't perfect. But at least I was forgiven.

I filed Cassandra's comments away with my job search disappointment, because nothing was going to spoil my night. Cassandra would probably always be Cassandra. She had a habit of speaking before thinking, but at least you didn't have to worry whether she was telling you what she felt.

Cassandra walked out the door chattering, like she hadn't just burst my bubble. "It's going down tonight," she said, throwing her hands in the air. "We're going to have a good time. For old time's sake," she said.

I locked the door behind me and wondered if I'd had a temporary case of insanity.

Chapter 30

Cassandra was right. It *was* just like old times. I watched the clusters of women who were zeroing in on the professional men who were—of course—much fewer in number. As always, it seemed that the men would have an ongoing night of meeting more than their share of the opposite sex, while the women would resort to dancing with each other in small groups and pretending like they were having a good time being out with their girlfriends.

The owners had tried to make the place seem more mature by calling it a lounge. But a club was still a club, no matter what fancy name you tried to attach to it. Since the last time I'd been, the place had been completely renovated. The cheap vinyl booths had been replaced with chocolate brown leather, and the tacky overhead lights were now chandeliers.

I surveyed the prospects and the environment. I already knew this wasn't the way I was going to meet my knight in shining armor.

But I was here, and I was going to make the best of it...until midnight at the latest...and after that I was headed out.

"I'm glad I ate something before I came," Cassandra said, flipping over the menu. "How can they charge twelve dollars for a plate of eight chicken wings and some celery?"

"Well, I didn't eat," I said. I was either going to order the overpriced wings or the ridiculously high-priced crab cakes.

It was another fifteen minutes before a waitress took my order then squeezed back through the crowd that was starting to overtake the dance floor. Men were trickling in now. I assume they waited to arrive after ten when they knew a sea of women would be here.

Cassandra excused herself to go to the ladies' room.

I noticed a guy two booths over trying to make eye contact with me. I ignored him, which is why I didn't see him approach our table. He wasn't bad looking, but I knew without standing up that he was shorter than me. He already had one strike against him, and he hadn't uttered a word.

"How are you doing?" he asked.

"Good," I answered. I tried not to stare at the braces that covered so much of his miniature-sized teeth. Although I shouldn't have judged him for wanting to boost his confidence by straightening his smile, I had to give him another strike. His parents should've helped him straighten his teeth when he was in high school.

"Do you dance?" he asked me. "I was hoping you'd join me on the dance floor."

"I don't even know your name," I said, stalling so I could think of a kind way to turn him down and let him walk back to his booth with his pride intact.

"Willie," he said.

Strike three, I wanted to say. He was country. "What name did your mother give you?" I asked him.

"William," he said.

"Well, William. I'm waiting for my food to arrive, and crab cakes aren't the same when they're cold. Can I get a rain check for later in the evening?"

"You can. And I'm going to hold you to it," he said.

Cassandra reappeared out of nowhere. I was hoping Willie would disappear before she returned, but I had no such luck.

"Hold her to what?" Cassandra asked, sliding into the booth. "I know she didn't turn you down for a dance. You have to excuse her. She hasn't been out in a while. We may have to teach her how to have a good time."

Willie stuck his hands in his pockets and reared back on the heels of his cheap-looking black shoes. "Don't worry. I'll be back to drag her out onto the dance floor later."

"When you come to get her, make sure you bring someone for me to dance with," she said. "I'd hate to be left over here alone."

"I've got my boy here with me," Willie said.

His name is probably John Boy, I thought.

Cassandra leaned out of the booth so she could get a clear view of Willie's friend. "Never mind," she said.

I almost spit out the water I was drinking. I would've crawled under the table in embarrassment if I thought I could fit without scuffing up my knees and elbows. I could tell Willie didn't know what to say either, so he walked away. Poor Willie. Now I was definitely going to have to take him up on his offer later.

"I'm going to pray for you," I said to Cassandra. "That was just downright mean."

"Why waste my time or his?" Cassandra said, already scoping out more options.

My crab cakes arrived, and I scarfed them down. Cassandra and I engaged in a little small talk, but all of a sudden it was like pulling teeth. We weren't interested in the same things anymore, and I could sense that Cassandra was as frustrated as I was. In a way I wished that Willie would hurry and come rescue me. The problem was that he *was* on the dance floor, just not with me.

Cassandra turned down a few men who came over and asked her to dance, and I knew it was because they looked like they didn't fit her physical standard and their clothes seemed like they'd seen better days. In Cassandra's eyes, that meant they were lacking in the financial department. In the past I'd heard one too many of her and Frank's arguments about his financial instability. That's why I didn't understand why she stayed with him, when all the years before Cassandra had walked around with dollar signs in her eyes.

My own eyes didn't have dollar signs in them at the moment, but they definitely had shock. I was checking out the couples on the dance floor when I saw a familiar face—a face that looked a little too much like Frank's. I tried to get a better look without being so obvious, but it was hard to see with the dim lighting.

They always say everyone in the world has a twin, so I hoped I was looking at Frank's. I guessed it was also a coincidence that Frank's "twin" was wearing the exact outfit that Cassandra had bought for Frank's birthday three weeks earlier. There was no use trying to fool myself. Even from the back I knew it was Frank—and his birthday shirt—with a set of woman's hands clawing and rubbing his back.

I didn't have time to say a quick prayer that Cassandra wouldn't see her estranged boyfriend. He was supposedly getting things straight with his son's mother, but unless that was her, he'd found someone else to take up his time during the interim.

"Please tell me that isn't Frank," Cassandra said, though she already knew the answer. She slammed down her glass of water. I was glad she put it down; otherwise it might've ended up dumped on Frank's head or thrown in his face.

"Sheila, please tell me that my eyes are deceiving me," she yelled over the music. "I *must* be seeing things. I *better* be seeing things."

I didn't want to look again, and I didn't want to say anything that would push Cassandra over the top.

"That *looks* like him," I said.

It was him. We both knew that.

"But who cares if it is? It's ladies' night, and Frank's the last person you should care about."

Cassandra stood up. This wasn't going to be good. "I *do* care if it's him. He's got it all wrong if he thinks he can disrespect me like this."

"Frank doesn't even know you're here."

"Which is exactly why it's disrespectful. Even more so."

I tugged at Cassandra's elbow to try and stop her without making a scene. Cassandra was already talking loud enough to get the attention of the booths on either side of us.

"Don't worry," she told me. "They're not going to put a news story in the church bulletin. Your newfound angelic reputation is secure."

The night was turning out to be just as bad as my morning had been, and all I wanted to do was go home.

I tried to meditate on the Scripture that I'd read this morning during my devotion time, but with an old school Bobby Brown song playing in the background, I couldn't remember the Scripture or the book of the Bible it was in.

I closed my eyes and tried to mentally transport myself out of this lounge. Who knows how long they had been closed before I felt a tap on the shoulder? I'd been zoned out so long that I didn't know if I'd actually fallen asleep. I hoped it wasn't Willie.

I was disappointed to see Cassandra hanging onto Frank like one of those little clip-on trolls I used to clamp on my pencils in middle school. She detached herself from his arm and bent down to whisper in my ear.

"It's all good. It was an old high school classmate. She's nice enough, but I don't want any woman who looks that good hanging all over my man."

"Oh, okay." That's all I could say. Now was not the time for me to tell Cassandra she was being naïve.

"He's straightened everything out with Tangela. We're back in business."

"So you're dumping me for Frank?" I said. I hoped she was. It would give me a reason to leave even sooner.

"You won't be mad at me, will you?"

"Not at all," I assured. "Go ahead do your thing. I'm heading home."

I got up and let Frank and Cassandra take over the booth. Frank hadn't made eye contact with me once since walking up to the table. Liars and cheaters can never look you in the eyes.

"Hi, Frank," I said, deciding to be the adult.

Maybe he ignored me, but I chose to believe that he couldn't hear me over the bass music pounding in all of our ears.

As soon as I walked outside to the parking lot and away from all of the distractions, the Scripture I'd read this morning tumbled into my mind. The exact words didn't come back to me, but it talked about trusting in the Lord with all of my heart and not relying on my understanding. If I did that, God would make my paths straight.

I was so caught up in my own thoughts that I stepped off of the curb with no regard for traffic. A blaring horn jolted me back to reality. I clutched my chest. I wanted to know God, but I didn't want to see Him face-to-face tonight.

"Oh, God," I prayed. My hands and legs were shaking.

"Don't go killing yourself before you get my office in order."

"Clive?"

"In the flesh."

"What are you doing here?" I opened the passenger's side door, then made myself comfortable on the soft leather interior. It had that fresh brand-new-car smell. I inhaled. I loved the smell of money.

Clive turned into a front reserved parking space and looked at me.

"Are you serious?" I said, "Don't tell me you own this club, too."

"Okay, I won't tell you."

"I still can't believe I worked with you for over two years and never knew this side of you."

Clive put down the driver's side window and propped his elbow on it. The security guard standing near the front door acknowledged his boss then pulled the brim of his black cap down lower over his brow.

"You came out alone tonight?" he asked me.

"With Cassandra. But she's been duped and in love, so now I'm leaving by myself."

"I'll only be here a few minutes, then I'm going home. We can grab a movie and go back to the condo, if you don't feel like being by yourself."

Funny how a movie with Clive was just the thing I'd wanted earlier, but now I was too sleepy to enjoy it. I was also too tired to fight off any advances that I knew Clive would make toward me once we were at his place and supposedly caught up in a movie. I'd always had a rule about not dating anyone at my place of employment, especially the boss. And right now, Clive was the only boss I had.

"Thanks for the offer, but before I nearly killed myself, I was headed home."

"So you want *me* to join *you*." He said it like a statement and not a question. "I can do that."

"You never give up do you, Clive?"

"I wouldn't be myself if I did. My mama didn't raise a quitter. What kind of woman did *your* mama raise?"

I thought about it for a minute. Watched two women trying to flirt their way into the overcrowded club, but with his boss watching, the security guard had already given them more than one rejection. Not even their skintight dresses or waist-length, bone-straight hair was going to help.

What kind of woman did my mama raise? No one had ever asked me that question. Leave it to Clive—of all people—to make me think.

"I don't think I was raised, in the true sense of the word," I said. "No fault of my mother's," I added. "As a single parent she did what she had to do to make sure we had our basic needs, which meant she had to work all the time. Most of what I learned—good and bad—I learned by myself or from the other latch-key kids in my neighborhood."

"So let me guess. Because you didn't have what you wanted when you were growing up, you vowed you wouldn't live your life like that when you were old enough to do for yourself."

"Bingo. Isn't that the story of every little girl whose mama couldn't afford the trends and designer labels?"

"I don't know your Mama, but I can bet you one thing. She did the best she could with what she had and what she knew. That's enough for you to honor her."

"When I had the means, I was always buying Mama something. I've never had a problem with that."

Mama hadn't really realized the value of most of the gifts I'd given her over the years, but at least I knew she had appreciated them.

"I said, 'Honor her,'" Clive said again. "Buying her things isn't necessarily honoring her, even though it's a nice gesture. Parents don't want your stuff as much as they want your time. You'll always be your mama's baby no matter how old you are."

"You must be a mama's boy."

"And proud of it," Clive said.

I imagine that Clive would've made a good father, but despite my belief that most men wanted a son to carry on their legacy, Clive had told me once that he never wanted children. He said it had been like finding a needle in a haystack when he met Gina and soon found out that she didn't want children, either. They'd married with shared beliefs in the importance of building their careers, but I suppose they hadn't spent as much time building their marriage.

After more than twenty years together, it seemed they should have been able to find some common ground to rebuild upon. If I were either of them, I wouldn't want the hassle of starting over.

Clive took the key out of the ignition, a sign that he was ready to deal with his business so he could call it quits for the night. "My offer still stands," he said.

"And so does my objection," I said, getting out of the car. "See you next week, boss."

I started to walk away but turned back around when Clive called me.

"I didn't mention how nice you look," Clive said.

"Thank you," I said. I was glad somebody noticed besides Willie.

"I guess you took some of that money and got yourself a new hairdo, too. If I knew a young buck worth having you, I'd hook you up."

"So you go from hitting on me one minute, to trying to find somebody for me the next."

"Somebody should reap the benefits," he said. "I'm not a selfish man, and I know a good thing when I see it. And you're a good thing, Sheila. Get that in your head."

"Thanks, Dad," I said. Clive knew I was harping on our age difference.

Clive rubbed the hairs of his goatee. "I told you. If you call me anything, call me 'Sugar Daddy.'"

Chapter 31

I forced my eyes open when I heard my cell phone ring. I knew by the ringtone that it was Mama or Devin. I guess she'd gotten the house phone turned back on. Maybe Devin had donated the twenty dollars I'd given him to the cause. Even at almost two o'clock in the morning I couldn't help being sarcastic.

I fought my way out of two layers of sheets. Cassandra had the air conditioner temperature dropped so low that I assumed she was dealing with the hot flashes she sometimes claimed to have.

I contemplated not answering, because I knew the reason for the call. Devin had probably gotten himself into some trouble, and Mama was stressing herself trying to figure out how to get him out of it. *My* purse was usually the answer.

"Hey, Mama," I said, so sleepy that my eyes hurt. I'd been asleep less than thirty minutes, because I'd gotten caught up in a romance movie on television. Being the hopeless romantic that I am, I couldn't fall asleep until I knew the couple got their happily-ever-after.

Mama's voice quivered. "Sheila, I hate to call you so late, but Devin needs your help. *I* need your help."

Mama had a way of taking on Devin's evils and trying to make me feel sorry for *her*, instead of angry at my brother's poor choices. Ace had helped me see that I was helping my mother enable Devin's behavior. As long as there was someone to swoop down and rescue him, he wasn't going to change. Maybe Mama figured that since Ace was out of my life, I would change my response. He'd helped me stand up for myself when Mama and Devin called for money.

"What happened, Mama?" I asked.

"I was hoping you had some money I could borrow so I could help Devin with a situation he's gotten himself into."

"Borrow" in my family's dictionary actually meant, "give." For the life of me, I didn't see why Mama couldn't exercise a little tough love with her beloved son. He wasn't doing anything for her except running her to an early grave.

I huffed. "The money I *do* have is not going to be used to get Devin out of trouble, yet again. Let him figure out his own problems and pay his own debts. It won't kill him. It might actually do him some good this time."

Devin was going to get money out of me any way he could. I was sure he'd concocted a story to scare Mama into action.

"I can't believe you'd do your brother like this," Mama said.

She was trying to sound so sorrowful, but I wasn't falling for her game this time. Mama sat in silence, probably hoping that her attempt to guilt me had worked.

"No, Ma. Not this time."

More silence.

"I'm sleepy, Mama. I'm going to bed now, okay? I'll be over Sunday afternoon after church. Unless you want me to come pick you up to come to church with me."

"Not this time. I'll be here Sunday afternoon," she said, with no excitement in her voice. "And I pray Devin will be, too."

Mama hung up without saying good-bye. She might've been upset with me at the moment, but by Sunday she'd be on to the next thing. That was Mama.

I couldn't fall back into a blissful sleep because Frank and Cassandra had returned from their night of reconciliation. I could tell Cassandra was trying to keep her voice low, but Frank had no problem being loud and inconsiderate.

"If she doesn't want to hear what I have to say, then she needs to find some place else to stay. I'm a grown man. I don't have to lower my voice for nobody."

They'd moved into the kitchen, where Cassandra was probably trying to find something to eat. If I knew tightwad Frank, he hadn't bought her those twelve-dollar chicken wings.

"If we're going to be together, you're gonna have to trust me. We have a child together, so Tangela will always be around. Nothing you can do can change that. Nothing."

"That may be true, but you don't have to jump through every hoop Tangela sets up for you. It's ridiculous. If you're going to do all of that, then you might as well be with her."

"Maybe I will," Frank retorted.

The next sound I heard was Cassandra's door slamming. So much for her attempt to keep things quiet so I could sleep. The door opened and shut again, and the muffled—but still loud—screaming bout began.

"God, I can't live like this," I said. "Please help me get a job so I can get out of here. Please help Cassandra. And Frank," I added, although I said his name with slight reluctance.

I couldn't go to sleep until I heard their fighting stop.

My eyelids got heavy, and I tried to forget about Devin and my roommate's relationship problems. I tried to imagine, instead, the surprise Travis had in store for me. Anything would be better than Reggie's sorry excuse for a date.

Chapter 32

Are you sure my car will be okay here?" I asked Travis as we walked into the twenty-four-hour discount superstore.

"It's not like your precious car is going to be out here alone. He's got plenty of automobiles to keep him company."

"It's a she, not a he," I corrected him. "Lexie. I told you, she just got out of major surgery, so she needs to be in a place where she can recuperate safely."

"Would you rather stay here with your car, then?" Travis said, wandering over to the fruits and vegetables. He picked up a carton of strawberries and a couple of peaches. "I'm biased toward Georgia peaches," he said.

"Well, I'm born and bred here, so you couldn't have picked a better woman," I said. I watched him drop the peaches in a plastic bag and head off toward the apples. "Is there going to be some place to wash that stuff off?" I asked.

He thought about it then picked up a tray of prewashed and precut fruit instead.

Travis looked even cuter than I remembered. His hair was freshly cut and the lines of his facial hair so precise that I knew he'd probably been to the barber just hours before.

Travis checked me out, too. He complimented me on my new haircut and said I looked like "one of those Brazilian women" because of the way my canary yellow sundress complemented my skin. Eden's style had inspired me to rummage through four unpacked bins to find it, but it was worth it. I was accessorized in gold from head to toe—hoop earrings, bangles, even a toe ring. I looked like a sparkling gold trophy, and Travis acted like he knew he'd won a prize.

"I was thinking about grabbing a bottle of wine, too," he said.

"Wine? I'm not drinking, and since you're the sole driver, you're not either."

"So you've never had a glass of wine?"

"I didn't say that."

"You must be a church girl or something. I should've asked you that."

"And how would that have changed things?" I asked, grabbing a bag of trail mix. Travis said he'd packed a picnic basket with some things he'd thrown together. For all I knew that could've been some molding leftovers from his refrigerator. He hadn't even thought about how he was going to wash those strawberries and peaches.

"I guess it probably wouldn't have changed much," Travis said. "After a while, church girls always end up doing things they say they wouldn't. You just have to wait them out."

"I don't know what kind of 'things' you're referring to, but don't lump me in that group. I may not be your typical church girl, but I know how to hold my own."

"Didn't mean to push any buttons," Travis said, wrapping an arm around me. He tried to slide his arm all the way down my back, but I slapped his hand off. A woman passing us laughed and shook her head.

"I was just testing you," he said.

I smacked my lips and walked ahead of him. "Don't play games with me," I said over my shoulder. "You'll never win."

Travis and I waited at least ten minutes in line. We were in the line for purchasing less than twenty items, but it seemed like everybody in Atlanta had come to the same store at the same time. I hoped we weren't going to be late for this secret night Travis had planned. I was the one who'd forced him to come inside so it wouldn't look so obvious that he was picking me up and leaving my car behind. I typically didn't let men drive me on a first date, but Travis talked me into it, since he said we'd be taking a trip to the other side of town.

Travis paid for our groceries, and then we wandered around the parking lot looking for his car. He kept grabbing my hand and touching whatever other body part was within his reach. He was a touchy-feely kind of man, and I must admit that once I knew a man, I was a touchy-feely kind of woman.

If me and Travis ended up having a relationship, I could see how that was going to be a problem. I'd had a hard enough time keeping myself contained with Ace, who *wanted* to be celibate. From what I could tell and by our past conversations, Travis had no intention of walking that path.

We finally found the car when we were close enough for Travis to trip off the panic alarm with his keychain. I was glad he'd left the windows cracked, so it wasn't as blazing hot as it could've been on the leather seats.

"So you're really not going to tell me where we're going?" I asked, buckling my seat belt.

"You'll enjoy yourself, don't worry," Travis said. He reached into the back seat and retrieved a ridiculous-looking hat that reminded me of something my uncle Remo would wear.

"What?" he said, running his palms along the brim and shaping it to his head. I guess he noticed the questioning look on my face. "You don't like my hat?"

He turned toward me so that I could get a front view, then modeled his profile. Surprisingly, it didn't look all that bad, but he still looked like Uncle Remo.

"It works for you," I said. I could tell he wanted me to pour on the compliments about how fine and irresistible he looked. That was what he was probably used to hearing. But he wasn't going to get it from me today, even if it was true. If I pumped his head up too much it might not fit into that hat.

Before long we were rolling down I-285, and Travis was serenading me with every song that came on the old school station. And *every* was no exaggeration. Travis was to music what I was to fashion. He knew them all, and the boy could sing. Make that *sang*.

Travis had a tenor voice that could soar to notes fit for an alto, but still drop deep like he'd been professionally trained to do it, from his diaphragm. I remembered that much from fifth and sixth grade chorus.

When we exited at Roswell Road, I knew where we were going. Chastain Park was synonymous with great concerts in a relaxing atmosphere. Travis dealt with the inevitable traffic and parking issues until we found a lot where we wouldn't have to trek from too far away.

"Was this surprise for me or for you?" I asked.

He grinned—still wearing Uncle Remo's hat—lifted a blue cooler from the trunk, then handed me two small citronella candles.

"For mosquitoes," he told me. Winked. Gave me a crooked smile that showcased the one deep dimple in his left cheek.

I hadn't been to a concert in ages. "I'm impressed. This is going to be worth the extra day's wait."

"You're not dealing with an amateur," he said.

On any other day my phone would never ring, but I could hear it vibrating inside my purse as I followed Travis to our plaza table. The calls kept coming back to back, so I checked it out once we got settled and Travis disappeared to find a bathroom.

Eden, Clive, and Cassandra. All phone calls that could wait. Like Mama used to say when she was at work and me and Devin were at home alone, "If it's an emergency, you need to be calling 9-1-1 or Jesus, not me."

I knew this was supposed to be Travis' surprise, but I took it upon myself to set our table with the spread of his food selection, even the flameless citronella candles. I felt sorry for the table next to ours, with two couples who looked like they'd fished out a stained plastic table cover from their last barbecue. The women seemed disgusted, but the men looked like they couldn't have cared less.

I spotted Travis from afar and watched him hurry back to our table. While we waited for the concert to start, we relaxed and enjoyed each other's company and the comfortable weather. Being there took us back to our high school days and our first concert experiences. Like every other teenage girl, I had been in love with Al B. Sure and almost every member of New Edition. Nobody could have convinced me that Al or Ralph wasn't going to fall madly in love with me once one of them spotted me from the ninety-ninth row at their concert.

Travis slid his chair closer to mine, and we zoned out everyone else around us. We were all into each other until our conversation was interrupted. Rudely.

Chapter 33

I was about tired of these pop-up approaches. There's nothing like being caught off guard by a woman—or in this case, *women*—who looked like they wanted to snatch off the head of the person you're with. First Clive, now Travis.

"I knew that was you. I can spot that head of yours and that walk from five miles away," one of the ladies said.

She had a purse on her shoulder and was carrying a cooler in one hand and a thermos in the other. All of them were potential weapons. I scooted my chair over so I'd be out of the line of fire.

The lady wielding the possible "weapons" had a sidekick who was posted with her arms crossed. Her wide hips sat on a pair of legs shaped like drumsticks, and she was tapping her foot like she was counting down the seconds until she'd explode. It looked like the words she wanted to say were stuck behind her clenched lips, and I was thankful. I guarantee that I didn't want to hear them if she ever got it together.

Travis was trying to act like he didn't know they were talking to or about him. He looked at them blankly, like he was watching a bad television show. Not once did he look my way.

"Oh, so you're deaf now?"

"Ananda, you need to stop tripping," he finally said.

"Are you serious?" She turned to her accomplice. "Is he serious?"

"He's not serious. He's busted," her partner finally said.

The sidekick yanked out a cell phone and aimed it in our direction. She took a picture, maybe one or two, as evidence. This was unbelievable. I couldn't think of one Scripture right now that could help me relax in the middle of this madness.

Lips were already flapping around us, and I saw a girl from two tables over laughing with her friends. Her phone was aimed in our direction, too. I turned away from her, praying this fiasco wasn't about to become a YouTube phenomenon.

Ananda turned to me, not looking mad at all. I think she knew I was an innocent victim. "I'm sorry to have to subject you to this, but I feel it's only fair for you to know that your date here is engaged. To our best friend."

The sidekick finally put away her phone. "Yes, and while she has gotten pulled away at the last minute by her job to stand in on a business trip, *he* is out with *you* enjoying *their* tickets. The ones *she* bought as a gift to *him*. But don't worry. She'll be back tonight and get the full update."

"You can rest assured that I had no idea—"

"Sheila, you don't have to explain yourself to them," Travis said.

Why does my name always come up during these little confrontations? I might as well start handing out copies of my driver's license.

"Well then, maybe *you* should explain yourself to me," I said to Travis.

Silence. Sometimes it takes a while to come up with a believable lie. But there wasn't much Travis could say to dig his way out of this one.

Ananda and company weren't going to let up on Travis, standing over him like two hens pecking at a weak rooster. He finally lost his cool and all respect from me. Travis looked at his fiancée's friends like they were the Devil in heels, then got up and walked away.

Finally, the show at my table ended, right before the real show on the stage started. When Travis came back, I would demand that he take me home. It was going to be a long, quiet trip.

Chapter 34

The featured performers were on their fourth song, and Travis still hadn't returned. I'd taken the liberty to eat the spread he'd packed. Since I figured I was being jilted, I might as well do it on a full stomach. I munched on my trail mix, actually enjoying the time alone and watching the scenery more than watching the concert.

By the seventh song I decided to leave. In this situation I knew there was only one person I could call. Clive. I'd never hear the end of it, but it was better than being stranded.

Then again maybe it wasn't.

"I don't want to hear it, Clive. Just take me to get my car."

"Dumped again by another man you met at a restaurant. I told you one time —"

I held up my hand as close to his face as I could without obstructing his view. "Please. Not tonight. Save it for another day." I shook my head. "As a matter of fact, I never want to hear about this night again. Ever. I'm erasing it from my mind right now as I speak, so you should, too."

"Okay, baby girl. Have it your way."

"Thank you," I said, staring out of the window. I never should've taken that second look that day when I'd gone to get lunch with Eden. Needless to say I'd brought this drama on myself. I hoped Travis hadn't brought anything he desperately needed to the park with him, because I'd left everything behind except those two flameless candles. I didn't want the night to be a total loss.

Clive didn't bother me for a while, which was a relief because I had plenty to think about. In the middle of everything else I had rolling around in my head, my phone kept beeping to alert me of new text messages. I checked the text messages and could've hurled the phone through the windshield when I saw that it was Travis. I had no intention of ever speaking to him again anyway, but the fact that he chose to text me instead of call revealed how much of a coward he was.

He texted: *Wasn't like it seemed. Can we talk later?*

I didn't respond to his text. In fact, I deleted it and any memory of him.

About twenty minutes into the silence Clive asked me, "Can I say something now, or am I banned from talking for this entire ride?"

"I guess I can allow you to say a few words, since I inconvenienced you tonight," I said.

"Thanks for your permission," he said.

Clive opened the sunroof. It was a cloudless night sky, and if things had panned out the way I'd dreamed, it would've been the perfect night.

"I need a favor," Clive said.

"I think I owe you a couple."

"Can you housesit for me for two weeks?"

"And you'll be gone, right? For an entire two weeks?"

"Yep. I'm headed to the Atlantis for a little rest and relaxation. I was admiring myself in the mirror a couple of weeks ago and noticed some new strands of grey coming in at my temples. That's a sign to me I need to use some of this vacation time I've got stockpiled."

"The Atlantis? That sounds like a trip for lovers," I said. "This wouldn't happen to be a reconciliation vacation to the Bahamas with Gina, would it?"

"No," he said quickly. "I'm treating a few of my fellas so we can get away for some much-needed rounds of golf and a change in the nightlife. See some things that the Bahamian women have to offer."

"Sounds like you're going to the Bahamas to get in trouble. You can do that here."

"In trouble? You can't get in trouble if you don't have anybody to answer to."

"We all have somebody to answer to, whether we want to acknowledge it or not."

"That's right, Sister Sheila." Clive made his voice spooky, like he was narrating a horror movie. "God's eyes are always watching."

Here we go again. Clive didn't have much reverence for God. I hadn't always acknowledged God, but I always knew there were consequences for my actions. I'd hope for the best and cross my fingers that they would never be too much for me to handle or think my way out of.

"So are you down for it?" Clive asked me.

"Sure. It's going to help me more than it's going to help you." I patted Clive roughly on his back and shook his shoulder. "You know, Sugar Daddy, you sure have a way of coming through right on time."

Clive might have been going on a vacation, but I was going to be on a stay-cation. His condo was as nice as any high-end hotel suite and I was going to take advantage of all of the amenities the building had to offer. Any opportunity to get away from Cassandra's place for a while was as good as a trip to the Bahamas.

Chapter 35

I'd promised God that I wouldn't miss a Sunday service once my car was repaired, but I hadn't promised that I wouldn't be late. Thank goodness. I rode through the front parking lot of Grace Worship Center, even though I knew the chances of finding a close space were slim to none. I'd always thought churches were more packed during the summer because the winter hibernators came out of their caves once the hot weather settled in.

In the wintry months it had been hard for me to convince my body that it wanted to crawl from under my down comforter so that I could go to church. Now, I don't think a blizzard would keep me from being there. I'd ski to church if I had to. After the Travis fiasco I needed to get my mind and actions on track.

I parked Lexie then strapped on my heels. That's when I noticed Eden a few rows away. She was talking into a car that had made its own parking space in the grassy area off to the side. She wore a grimace that made me want to watch—wait and see if she was okay. I wondered what had made her so upset. The driver's side door opened, and I didn't have to guess any longer.

Although Eden hadn't said a word to me about the man I'd first noticed at the bookstore, I knew he had to be her son. I knew a mother's unconditional love for a son when I saw it, because I'd seen it in Mama's love for Devin.

His face and hair looked like they'd been recently washed and groomed, but his clothes still needed some tender loving care. Eden tried to pull him down so she could give him a strong embrace, like her hug would transform him into the loving son she had once known before he had been snatched by whatever had a hold on him.

His arms hung limply by his side, but Eden didn't let him go. After a moment, he let his arms rest on her back. His head drooped. His shoulders bowed. Then he pulled away.

Eden had a handkerchief in her hand. She used it to blot her cheeks, and then wiped it across his forehead. Down both of his cheeks. Across his chin. Her son got back into the car and rolled down the window, but he wouldn't let Eden kiss his head. He gently grabbed her wrists as if her touch and prayers were torturing him.

My eyes welled with tears. Watching them made me understand why my mother tolerated Devin. I didn't like it . . . couldn't support it . . . but I understood it.

Eden stood in the parking lot and watched the car until it pulled out onto the main street. Her lips were moving, and I knew she was praying for her own strength and for her son's. I didn't want to intrude on her moment so I waited until she turned and started heading back toward the church before I opened my door.

I nearly had to run to catch up with her.

"Eden," I called.

She didn't answer until I called her name a third time.

She smiled when she saw me. "Say you forgive me. I didn't get a chance to call you back until last night."

"I saw that you called, but I was on one of the most horrific dates of my life," I said, giving her a hug. "More about that later. Or maybe not."

She laughed, and her eyes widened with hopefulness. "So when do you start your new job? Tell me all about it."

"Still yet to be determined," I said. "I didn't get the job I just interviewed for, but I'm keeping the faith that I'll have one soon."

Eden was visibly disappointed, but in her encouraging way she rushed to brighten things up. "Look at it as interview practice for the real job."

"Somebody needs to bottle your encouragement and sell it."

"I'll make my millions any legal way I can," Eden said. She quickened her stride. "We better get inside to the sanctuary before Pastor Armstrong starts preaching. Our ushers don't play about disrupting the sermon."

I could relate. The usher who manned the doors on the side of the church where I'd entered the second time I visited had been as sweet as strawberry pie *before* and *after* service, but when she was at her post, she had taken her position seriously—like God Himself was giving her a weekly paycheck. She hadn't been about to let you save a seat, and she hadn't let latecomers disrupt the service by prancing around looking for a seat close to the front.

"I'll see you after service," Eden whispered as she headed up front. I watched her slide onto the pew beside Bear, then nearly disappear from sight when he stretched his arm out across the pew behind her. He'd probably assumed Eden had tiptoed out to go to the restroom, never thinking that his son had been on the church grounds. Not knowing that his wife had added more tears to the millions she'd probably already cried.

The Queen Bee usher saw me standing in the back and motioned for me to take a seat on a pew two rows from the back. It was a pleasant surprise to see it was beside Sherri. Her daughter, Faith, was nestled in the crook of her arm.

"Hey, girl," I said, leaning over. We air-kissed and touched cheek to cheek.

"I see you had a hard time getting out of the house on time, too," Sherri said.

"Turned off the alarm and told myself I was getting up in five minutes." I shook my head. "Ended up being thirty-five minutes."

Sherri tapped me on the leg, and I followed her gaze. The Queen Bee had her eyes on us, and she didn't look happy.

Sherri whispered without moving her lips, "You're gonna get kicked out of church."

"No, *we* are going to get kicked out of church," I said when the usher turned her head for a second. She finally took her seat after one of the ministers stood up to give the church announcements.

I watched Faith play the role of personal stylist with her black Barbie doll. She switched her from a black jean outfit to a red sequined ball gown. One of the doll's stiff rubber arms was above her head, and Faith was twirling her around on her perfectly arched feet.

Pastor Armstrong took his place at the podium, and I bent down to get my Bible out of my purse. That's when I noticed Travis sitting at the end of my row.

Chapter 36

Travis shouldn't have come to church. Not because I was here, but because it was disrespectful and rude for him to sit there like he was watching paint dry. He was visibly bored, and even had the nerve to pull out a phone and send a text message or check his email. Whatever he was doing was inappropriate. It looked like it had been a long night for him and like the woman beside him had dragged him to church so that God could wash away his sins and his stupidity.

His fiancée—at least that's who I assumed she was—was wearing a respectably sized engagement ring. If she'd been sitting in the front row, one of the old church mothers probably would've thrown a large lacy handkerchief over her lap. Her skirt rose to the upper part of her thighs, showcasing a pair of well-toned legs. Her calf muscles bulged, like she could split a wooden board with a single karate kick. Travis was probably scared to leave her for fear that she'd break him into two pieces. But even her strong-looking physique hadn't kept Travis from throwing out his net to see who he could catch.

I leaned back against the pew and told myself that I wouldn't look at them. My curiosity got the best of me, and every now and then I'd peek at the end of the row. She was leaning against Travis and attempted to share her Bible. He yawned, his mouth stretched wide like a roaring lion.

I looked back at Pastor Armstrong and tried to focus on the sermon. I hadn't heard a word or taken one note. Travis was a distraction. Instead of listening to words to uplift me, I was wondering why Travis had thought I was the kind of woman he could play. What had he seen in me that made it okay to take me out on a date, even though he was engaged to be married?

Travis's fiancée flipped through her Bible in search of Pastor Armstrong's Scripture references, but Travis seemed more interested in seeing what everybody else around him was doing. He looked toward the end of the pew. I could've easily leaned back and ducked out of his sight, but I didn't.

Travis got fidgety. He bounced his leg like he was gearing up for a takeoff. I watched him squirm. He unbuttoned the top of his shirt like it was choking him. His fiancée looked my way. Paused. She looked at Travis, then back at me. Surely, her girlfriends had sent her the pictures they'd taken of us with their cellphones. "Evidence," one of the friends had called it.

I prayed she was a woman with class who wouldn't approach me at church. If the worst-case scenario should arise, I knew Eden and Sherri had my back. Or at least I hoped so. Eden and Sherri might just stand there and pray for the girl to release her hands from around my neck.

When he could no longer handle the pressure, Travis stepped around his fiancée and made the exit he'd been waiting for. Two minutes later his woman was out the door behind him.

"You all right?" Sherri asked, running her hands across Faith's braids. She was asleep, flopped over her mother's lap, yet still clutching her doll.

"I'm good," I said.

Once Travis and his fiancée left, I was actually able to pay attention to Pastor Armstrong. Granted it was the last ten minutes of his sermon, but I heard what I needed. I wrote one sentence in my notepad. *There's a purpose and a season for everything.*

After church I waited at the information kiosk while Sherri registered Faith for cheerleading with the church's youth football league. I read through brochures of the classes available to members. One named *Financial Authority* caught my eye, so I signed up for the Thursday night class. It was about time I ruled my money instead of my money ruling me.

"Faith, be careful," Sherri said.

I turned in time to see Sherri's purse tumble from the counter and the contents spill on the floor. I picked up two tubes of lipstick that had rolled near my shoe, then helped her shove the rest back in her bag.

"Time to clean out this thing," Sherri said. She straightened a handful of receipts then stuffed them into her wallet.

"You live out of your bag, don't you?" I said, handing her a plastic spoon and sandwich bag of baby wipes.

"Wait until you have children," she said. "You'd be surprised what'll end up in your purse." She took the spoon. "I need that for Faith's fruit cup snack later."

Faith wasn't worried about a fruit cup because she was too busy gathering up loose change. She was stacking rows of pennies, dimes, and nickels on the back of a book. I helped Faith dump the change in her ladybug-shaped purse, then flipped over the back of the novel.

"This sounds good," I told Sherri.

"It is. I always keep something to read in my purse. This is

Atlanta. There are always traffic accidents, two-mile delays, long lines. When I'm not moving, I'm reading. Eden asked me to start a book club at her store a couple of years ago, but I didn't have the time. Now that Faith is a little older, I've been thinking about bringing it up to her."

"You should," I said. "And I'll help you."

"Only if you won't start off with it, then abandon me."

"I won't," I promised. "If you knew what happened to me over the last couple of days, you'd beg me to be around some people who are strong in the faith," I said, handing her novel back to her. "I'm not going to act like I can walk this journey alone. I feel like sometimes I'm on the path, and sometimes I'm on the side of the road."

"You're not the only one," Sherri said. "When I veered off the path I ended up with quite a surprise," she said, patting the top of Faith's head. Faith looked up and smiled, her lips smeared with a thick coat of grape-flavored lip balm. "Thank God He works all things out for our good. I've had those words from Romans 8:28 tacked up all around my house for about two years."

That sounded like a Scripture I needed. I wrote it down.

Sherri had to dig through the mess in her purse to find a piece of tissue. "So it's a done deal," she said, cleaning around Faith's lips. "We'll talk to Eden and get the ball rolling for the book club."

"That'll work," I said, noticing Eden. "No time like the present."

Eden was back to her bubbly self and was latched onto Bear's arm. She had a lightweight shawl draped over her shoulders. She waved us over.

"I was looking for you girls to see if you wanted to come over for dinner. Me and Bear decided to grill some meat and vegetables, maybe make a few shish kabobs. We'd love to have you."

My stomach wanted to go to Eden's, but I'd promised Mama that I'd stop by.

"I'll have to take a rain check this time," I said. "I'm going to my mom's house."

"Me and Faith will come by," Sherri said quickly, like Eden was going to retract the offer. "I haven't even thought about what we were going to eat. We'll run home and change clothes, then come right over."

"Perfect," Eden said. "Where's Anisha?"

"Home with swollen feet, but I'll call her. Since she's been pregnant, she's never passed up a meal."

"Go by and pick her up," Eden suggested. "I have the perfect treatment for her. A little something my grandmother taught me to cure ailing feet."

I picked up the receipt for the class I'd registered for. "You guys have fun. I'm headed over to my mom's house."

"You'll have to invite your mother to visit us," Eden said. "Family and Friends Day should be coming up soon. We do it every year."

Mama and I hadn't been to church together since before I had left for college. She never admitted it, but I think the only reason she made me go that particular Sunday was because the church down the street from our house was having a drawing for some dorm room items for new college freshmen. Mama had hoped I'd win the small refrigerator, but my name had been drawn for an ironing board. Mama still had that thing propped against the wall in her room. The cover was permanently stained from where I'd used it as a food tray.

"I'll definitely ask Mama to come. Maybe I'll even be able to get Cassandra to come with me," I said.

Pastor Armstrong had said there was a season for everything. Maybe this was the season I could show Mama, Devin, and Cassandra a new me.

Chapter 37

I was on my way to Mama's house with three pieces of luggage in the trunk. I'd swung by Cassandra's place to get my things and left her a note that I was housesitting at Clive's place for the next two weeks. I told her to call my cell if she needed me, but I imagined that she needed a break from my presence as much as I needed a break from hers.

Summer storm clouds rolled over the cityscape of Atlanta's downtown area as I flew down Interstate 20. The skies may have looked gloomy, but I tried to look at it the way Eden would. She'd probably say it was an indication of the blessings that were about to rain down on me. I had new living arrangements (two weeks were better than nothing). And I'd had some interview practice for my real job, as Eden had so appropriately put it. My love life was still lacking, but I didn't fret over that, because men are like buses. Another one was bound to come around sooner or later. I just had to make sure I chose the right one. One that was actually going somewhere.

Lexie hugged the curb as I pulled onto Mama's street.

"You look like a million dollars," Mama said, walking out onto the front porch.

I'd just opened the door, and already she was comparing my looks to money. I hope this wasn't another segue into asking me for money for Devin.

"Good genes, Mama," I said, unhooking a dry cleaner's bag from the hook behind the seat. "I brought you a few of my things that I know you'd look better in than me."

"So you're giving me your hand-me-downs?" Mama asked. She took them anyway, despite her smart-aleck remark.

"Consider them hand-me-ups," I said, eyeing Mama's outfit. There was one thing I could say about my mother. Despite the clutter stuffed in the house, she prided herself on keeping up her appearance. Her clothes were always clean and pressed, even if they weren't fashionable. I didn't even know they still sold jeans with pleats in the front like the ones she was wearing. This bagful of blessings was right on time for her.

Looking at Mama, I thought that the clothes I'd brought over might slip right off her frame. Maybe all of the walking to the bus stop she'd had to do over the last couple of weeks was causing her to lose weight. Then there was her skin. It looked dry and paler than I'd ever seen it—like the color of the ashes she used to flick from the end of her cigarette.

I hugged my mother—tried to give her a little of my over-flowing peace—and she returned the embrace weakly. I didn't want to dampen our time together by talking about the things that may have been wrong in her life, so I opened up the conversation with her visit to church.

"So Devin told me you went to a revival service or something with Ms. Pearl last week. How was it?"

"It was nice, but I was about starved by the time we got out of service. You talking about some people who don't mind praising the Lord all night. And I do mean *all* night."

I laughed and followed her inside, stepping around a cardboard box of candles in assorted colors and sizes. I didn't ask. I'd rather think that my mother was being proactive in stockpiling items in case of an emergency blackout or ice storm in Atlanta.

"What made you go to church with Ms. Pearl?" I probed.

"Sometimes when things happen in your life, you have to seek help from the Almighty."

"Tell me about it," I said, wondering what specific circumstance of hers was driving her to the church doors.

Back in the day—on Sundays—after we finished listening to Mahalia and eating breakfast, Mama took advantage of her time off to rest. Me and Devin wasted most of the day doing whatever we wanted. Mama lay on the couch and watched old black and white movies, Devin hung in the streets with his no good friends, who he was still hanging with to this day, and I kicked it with my friends on the front porch. We'd gossip about the boys we had crushes on at school and the life we were going to live after we grew up and married them. Thankfully those juvenile dreams didn't come true. I'd heard through the grapevine that my childhood crush had served several stints behind bars for domestic abuse.

Me and Mama went into the kitchen, which right now was probably the cleanest room in the entire house. It was still cluttered, but at least it was organized clutter, and all of the cooking and eating surfaces were wiped clean. She was burning a vanilla-scented votive candle in the corner, and that's when I noticed the smell of cigarette smoke wasn't as heavy in the house as usual. I wasn't sure, but perhaps Devin had to enjoy the lovely accommodations provided by the Fulton County jail. I didn't ask, and Mama didn't tell.

"I've been going to church, too, Mama," I said.

171

"I knew something was going on with you. I can tell there's something different."

"You can?" I asked, sitting down in the high-backed wooden chair at the kitchen table.

"Yes. You look like a new woman or something. It's hard to put it in words, but I can tell."

"That's a good thing."

"Real good. Keep it up. You don't want to get to the end of your life and regret not having God and strong faith in your life. I've seen the people who trust in God, and I've seen the ones who couldn't care less. Trust me. The ones with God in their lives always have more peace, even in trying times," Mama said. "I should've learned more about God and taught y'all better."

Mama let out a long sigh, then tried to force a smile when she saw me staring at her. Something was wrong.

"So what has *you* going to church?" Mama asked. "Don't tell me it's some man there that you've got your eye on."

"No. But I have to admit it was a man who drove me to the church in the first place."

"I knew it. Tell me about it. I hope he doesn't have an ex-wife and kids lurking in the background to steal him away, because you don't need another Ace holding up your life and stringing you along. That whole situation was a mess."

The last thing I wanted to do was get Mama started about Ace.

"I'm learning that God can bring a good thing out of your messes, too," I said, calming her down a bit. I still told her the entire story about how I snuck into Ace's recommitment ceremony and then felt God's presence overtake me. Excitement spilled over in me the more I talked and I shared with her about the devotional I'd been reading and Pastor Armstrong's last two sermons. I told her about how Eden had taken me under her wing in a way. And that's when I saw what I thought was a hint of hurt in Mama's eyes.

"Eden sounds like a nice woman," she said. "I'm sure she can teach you a lot of things that I didn't. It's never too late to learn some things as a woman."

"I hope you don't think I'm trying to replace you or something, Mama," I said, because I know how Mama thinks.

"No, I don't think that," she lied. "I'm just telling you to keep women like Eden in your life. I won't always be around."

"Mama, you and Eden are probably around the same age. Next weekend, I'll come by and get you so I can take you to her bookstore. I bet you two will hit it off. She's spunky like you," I said, thinking about the Mama I used to know and not the aged one sitting in front of me.

"I don't have as much spunk as I used to," she said. "I'm sick, Sheila."

She said it like she'd commented on the weather. Time stopped. And for a moment, my world stopped spinning.

"Mama, what are you talking about? What kind of sick?"

"The doctor diagnosed me with emphysema."

"And you're just now telling me? How long have you known?"

"About four months."

"And why didn't you tell me?"

"What's the sense in worrying you? You have too much on your mind as it is. Besides there's nothing you can do about it."

"There's always something that can be done. We can look into the treatments, even holistic options, and we—"

"Who's going to pay for it?" she asked. "My insurance barely covers routine doctor's appointments, and you don't have a job. You can't spare any money to help Devin. How do you think you can find the mountains of money it takes to pay doctor bills? You know how I feel about medical treatments and stuff like that. It seems like as soon as doctors start poking around in people and filling them with medicine they get sicker." Mama let out another long sigh. "If you really want to do something for me, pray."

I couldn't get my mind calm enough to pray, because I was

mad. I was mad at Mama for getting caught up in being a smoker all of those years, even though it had been five years since she'd kicked the habit. But my real problem was with Devin for being a chain smoker and tainting Mama's lungs with secondhand smoke even more than she'd done to herself. Even though she hadn't told me, I knew she'd told Devin.

"Why do you continue to let Devin smoke in the house, Mama? Some things just don't make sense to me."

"Quitting is hard, Sheila," she said. "You don't know about having an addiction. Addictions can steal your will power to say no."

I got up and stormed down the hallway—pushing stray boxes against the walls—and burst into Devin's room. It reeked, which made me even madder. It took a lot for me to get my emotions under control, but after I calmly counted to ten, I started collecting every pack of cigarettes I saw. I even scoped his dresser and discovered an entire unopened case in the bottom drawer. I bet my twenty dollars had financed his habit.

"Don't do that, Sheila," Mama said. She watched me from the door but didn't make any moves to stop me. "Devin's going to be furious when he gets home."

"I don't care about Devin. I'm worried about *you*."

Clive had reminded me to honor my mother, and this was my way of doing it. I couldn't sit back and be an accomplice to her killer.

I took the confiscated cigarette packs, stuffed them in a plastic grocery bag that I found on the side of the fridge, then walked outside and threw them in the trunk. I was going to throw them away as far from Mama's house as possible.

When I walked back inside, Mama walked over and hugged me. For the first time in a long while, she really hugged me, for a reason other than to greet me. I held Mama and prayed. Not out loud, but in my mind. Mama didn't hear me, but I know that God did.

I felt both Mama's pain *and* her love, and I cried. We cried. And when the clouds opened over Atlanta, heaven cried with us.

Chapter 38

Sheets of rain hit my windshield so hard that the wipers were useless. I followed suit with the other cautious drivers on the road and pulled over to the right emergency lane with my hazard lights blinking. The rain had subsided to a drizzle when I'd left Mama's house to go to Clive's, but now it was a full-fledged storm again. I'd gone too far to turn around and go back to Mama's, so I crept along at a snail's pace with the other drivers who'd been caught off guard. It took me an additional twenty minutes and a bunch of twisted nerves before arriving at Clive's.

Even though I had an umbrella, my feet and the hem of my slacks were drenched. I pulled off my shoes and dropped them in the foyer as soon as Clive opened the front door.

Before he had a chance to say anything, I sent him outside to get my luggage from the trunk.

"Dang, little woman. You pack like you're coming on the trip with me. Do you actually need all of this?"

"I don't plan on going back to Cassandra's unless it's absolutely necessary," I said. "You're not the only one who needs this vacation time." I took the dripping umbrella from him and slid it in the umbrella holder. He'd definitely had a woman's help with decorating. The men I know don't think of those kinds of details.

"Don't get too comfortable," he joked. "You've still got work to do."

"No need to crack the whip. I know how to handle business," I said, looking at my watch. "Am I supposed to be taking you to the airport?"

"I've got a car coming to get me. You can stay inside and keep dry and pretty."

"Perfect," I said.

The sooner I could be alone in this lap of luxury, the better. I'm sure God was more than adept at handling my needs, but I needed a job that wouldn't require me to live on canned vegetables and frozen dinners. I was still training my brain to look at the future, and if Clive's place was a foretaste of things to come, life sure tasted good.

"I'm going to get my bags," Clive said.

I never understood how men could pack most of their life in one suitcase. When Clive rolled his bag out of his room and to the front foyer, I marveled at how he could make it through a two-week stay in Nassau, Bahamas, with only one suitcase and a carry-on. The storm clouds were refusing to travel past the downtown area, so I sat in the living room with my devotional, my journal, and a Bible, reading and writing by the light from the end table lamp.

Clive sat down on the love seat across from me and perched his laptop on his knees. I imagined he was probably making transactions or business decisions of some sort that were putting thousands of dollars in his bank account with each keystroke.

After a few minutes clicking around on his laptop and the other technological gadgets around him, Clive closed the laptop cover and slid it in his carry-on attaché.

"My flight's been delayed," he said. "It's leaving three hours later, so I changed my pick-up time with the driver." He walked over and stood behind me. "What are you writing?"

I closed my journal. "You're nosy."

"I prefer 'inquisitive.'"

"If you must know, I'm journaling."

"Crying on paper, in other words," Clive said.

"That is *not* what journaling is." I defended myself and everybody else who found solace in pouring their feelings out on paper. It felt good to journal again. I hadn't realized how much I'd missed it since I'd stopped journaling back in high school. After Devin had gotten a hold of my most private thoughts and I had become the object of ridicule for him and his friends, I had decided not to have any written proof of my thoughts. Now I was in a season where I was reconnecting with the simple things that made me happy.

His ringing cell phone pulled Clive's attention away. He looked at the phone like he was deciding whether to answer it.

"You might get struck by lightning if you answer that thing," I said with a smirk.

"I'll take my chances," he said, answering his cell. After he said hello, he listened intently to whoever was on the other line. He hung up without ever saying a word. I wanted to be nosy now, wondering if it was some forlorn lover leaving him a threatening message.

"That was the airline's automated system," he said. "My flight's been postponed until tomorrow morning." He stood up and walked over to the balcony window. "I'm not surprised. It's nasty out there. Looks like midnight, and it's not even eight o'clock yet."

I stuck my pen in my journal and closed the cover. "So you're staying here tonight?" I asked.

"It is my place," he said.

I didn't need a reminder. I was just caught off guard. A streak of lightning lit up the room, then a rumble of thunder shook the walls. Having a landscape view of the city was a lot more relaxing when there weren't dark clouds hovering outside. There was no way I could leave right then. Clive read my mind.

"It's too dangerous for you to go out in the middle of a monsoon," he said. He chuckled before he added, "You're safe here with me. I can see the wheels in your head turning."

"I wouldn't want anybody to get the wrong idea," I said.

"Anybody like who? You have some spies I don't know about?"

"It just doesn't feel right spending the night with you."

"You trying to tell me you've never spent the night with a man who wasn't your husband?"

"What's my past got to do with anything? I'm talking about right here. Right now."

"You're trying to go from sinner to saint overnight, baby girl," he said. "And even a saint will tell you that you've got to use common sense. It's too bad out there for you to leave, so you're stuck here. With me. Relax. I'll take good care of you."

The sky lit up again. "I guess you're right," I said, standing up and stretching. "I'm going to go change into something more comfortable."

"That's what I'm talking about," Clive said.

My hands didn't have time to make it to my hips before he said, "Calm your nerves. I'm playing with you." Clive pulled the sheer panels across the floor-to-ceiling balcony windows. "Call me if you need me. I'm headed to bed."

"You need your beauty rest?" I teased.

"Getting rested up for the Bahamian women."

"You're so pitiful," I said, following him down the hall toward the bedrooms with my bags.

Clive stopped in front of his bedroom door. I looked at Clive. He looked at me.

Clive was still staring at me like he was waiting for me to say something or make a move. So I did. I went into the guest bedroom —alone—and closed the door behind me.

Chapter 39

The knock on the door was so light that it barely stirred me out of my dream. The rain had lulled me into a peaceful sleep. *There is no way it could be morning already,* I thought.

I fluttered my eyes open and immediately noticed it was unusually dark. I could sense Clive's presence in the room even though I couldn't see him.

"The power's out. I heard a huge bang. Lightning must've struck a generator," he said.

Clive moved through the room. His weight shifted the bed when he sat down.

"You okay?" he asked, moving the covers back off my shoulders.

I yawned. "I'm a big girl. I'm not afraid of the dark."

"I am."

I felt Clive slide one of his legs under the sheets, then the other. He smelled like a man. There was no other way to describe it. It wasn't like a man who'd just finished hooping on the basketball court. Or one who'd been power lifting in the gym. It was just a manly scent.

Having Clive beside me heightened all of my senses.

His breath warmed the back of my neck and tickled the hairs at the top of my shoulders. He'd gargled before he came into the room. I could smell the mint.

I knew I shouldn't be here with Clive. He was a married man, and I was trying to walk the straight and narrow. Everything about this path right now *was* so crooked. But everything about it *felt* so right.

Clive rested his arm across my midsection and paused like he was assessing the rise and fall of my body to see if I was breathing. "Gina and I are over. We've been over for years," he whispered. "It's just a matter of paperwork."

"It's still wrong, Clive. You're more of a friend. A mentor," I said, searching for a reason to stop this madness.

"Well, I *can* teach you some things," Clive said.

He was rubbing the fabric of my nightgown. It was pink satin, and I'd packed it along with three other negligees in black, powder blue, and a flowery pattern. They'd been meant for my eyes, and my eyes only. Now I wondered if it would've been better if I'd slept in a turtleneck and long johns.

"You think everything is so funny, don't you?" I tried to lighten the mood, more for myself than for Clive. My body ignored my silent plea for it to get itself under control.

"You deserve the best, Sheila," Clive said. His lips brushed my ear lobes, then traveled to my neck. "Every day I live the kind of life you dream about. You've got a chance to make those dreams come true."

Clive was speaking my language, especially my body language. I had an "on" switch, and he'd flipped it to overdrive. It had been a long time. Too long. Maybe Cassandra was right. I had toxins built up in my system.

God was forgiving, and I wasn't perfect, right?

Just this one time, I told myself.

I was lying in the dark. My eyes finally adjusted to my surroundings, and my mind began to grasp what I'd done. One decision had forever changed my relationship with Clive. He would never look at me the same; and I would also see him through different eyes.

After a flicker, the lights came back on. Clive opened his eyes and leaned over me to see the flashing digital alarm clock.

"I better get up and see what time it is," he said, though he didn't make an immediate effort to move.

I was confused. I wanted him to leave. And I wanted him to stay.

"I can send the fellas off without me if you'll give me a good reason to stay."

I pulled the covers off him and used my foot to coax him off the bed.

"No. You better get ready. I'm sure it's getting close to time for you to head out. I imagine it's going to be crazy at the airport with all the delays."

I rolled over and closed my eyes so that I wouldn't have to look at Clive. "Call me when you get there so I know you're safe."

The words were a familiar part of my vocabulary. I used to tell Ace that all the time, because even though he took international flights on a regular basis, I always worried about him.

"Sleep tight," he said. "I'll leave some money on the bar in case something comes up," he said.

"All right," I said. "I know how to take care of everything."

Clive pulled the door closed after he said, "That you do."

Chapter 40

I'd been waiting for this date all week long. I'd spent the entire week going above and beyond the call of duty on my work for Clive. It was my gift to him for asking me to stay at his place. I also felt like I owed it to him in some way since I'd shown him a side of me that I'd never intended to. One day I'm preaching to him about how God touched my life, and two weeks later I've shared the most intimate parts of myself.

This little light of mine was growing dim. That's why I had to cheer myself up.

I'd fought the urge to go shopping even though Clive had left three hundred dollars in case of a house emergency and another five hundred to pay me for housesitting. I'm not sure housesitting was all he'd paid me for.

I pinned my hair in an upsweep and stuck in a pair of earrings that grazed my shoulders. Dramatic. I liked it. I'd flipped through some old magazines in Clive's bathroom and noticed some ways to rework some individual pieces of clothing that I'd brought with me. I knew there'd be a reason for three suitcases of clothing. I'd given myself a makeover, and I didn't have to deal with an ounce of buyer's remorse.

Since my accessories were so bold, I opted for a natural look for my face. I was wearing an all-white ensemble and had to admit that I looked kind of angelic. That was on purpose, for the devilish thing I'd done.

That's why I needed to get as close to God as I could. Since Monday I'd gotten up every morning before eight. The more I read my Bible, the more I was able to understand. Granted, I'd only been reading Proverbs, but I had to start somewhere.

I was praying now, too. The first day my prayers lasted less than a minute, but by the end of the week, I'd worked up to nearly five minutes. I felt closer to God already. He wasn't only at church or in Eden's bookstore. God was right *here* inside of me.

So tonight it was all about me and Him. I had to show myself I didn't need to be on a man's arm in order to enjoy a night out. Eden had shared a Scripture with me yesterday when I went to help her at the bookstore. It fit me so perfectly that I'd written it down: *I will praise you, for I am fearfully and wonderfully made.* And tonight I *absolutely* looked wonderful.

"You've come a long way, girlfriend," I told my reflection. I'd spent more quality time with God this week than I had in my entire life.

I couldn't help but wonder what Ace would think if he knew about the changes I was making. What would've happened between us if I'd been this woman when we were together? Would we have been able to work things out?

The devotional I'd been reading answered a lot of questions about living like a woman of faith, but there were some questions I guessed I'd never have answers to. Yet and still, my devotional had become like a best friend. I carried it everywhere I went and treasured the nuggets I found between the pages. I'd yet to read the novel Sherri had told me about, because I was so engrossed in the little pink book that was changing my life.

My second week at Clive's passed too soon. Every day I felt like this walk wasn't as hard as I'd once thought it to be. In three days, Clive would return home to take over as king of his castle. It had been good to feel like the queen, but my reign was coming to an end. At Cassandra's house I'd felt more like a pauper, and I imagined I was going to have to do some serious praying—more than five minutes—if I wanted to keep my peace.

I'd found a shade tree at Piedmont Park and spent the first part of the morning writing in my journal. Dreaming. Putting on paper everything that I didn't have the courage to share with anyone yet.

Afterward I spent the rest of the afternoon at Eden's bookstore. At one time I would've thought about Cassandra's opinion about it. She'd say something cynical, like I was going to start getting the senior citizen's discount when I went out if I kept spending time with Eden. But I'd gotten to the point that I didn't care what Cassandra thought. I'd spent too much time letting her opinions affect my life.

I genuinely enjoyed spending time with Eden. No one had ever taken the time to teach me about God or show me how to grow in my faith. Eden was like a bucket of water, and I was like a sponge. I could tell how she'd been pushing me to do things on my own. I used to ask questions about the Bible that she'd readily answer. Now she was starting to give me books so I could look things up for myself.

Today was also the second time this week Eden had left me alone to man the store for a couple of hours while she ran errands. Eden had a number of regular customers from the office building across the street who dropped in a couple times a week. Then there was Kenyatta from the wing shop next door, who stopped in for her daily visit near closing time.

Kenyatta was so full of stories and gossip that I couldn't tell the difference between the truth and her exaggeration of events. But there was one thing I did know was true. Kenyatta had been hurt many times—and most deeply by her former church. She wouldn't give the details of what happened, only that she'd been so ridiculed and scorned by church members that she had ended up leaving. Although Kenyatta wouldn't attend church anymore, she *would* come to Eden's bookstore. Like me, she found solace there.

Before I left, Eden taught me how to count down the register, set the alarm, and lock up the store. I'd told her that I could be her relief worker if she ever needed to take a day off to handle business—and Bear was included in that business. She told me how he'd been complaining that he missed spending quality time with her because she was exhausted by the time she got home in the evening.

I wanted to thank Eden for all she'd done for me, so I volunteered to help her. Eden wouldn't hear of it, and said that anyone who put in a day's work for her would be paid fairly. I wasn't going to argue with her. I'd prayed for a way to make some money, so I considered it an answered prayer.

The next prayer I'd say tonight was the grace over my food. I'd left a dinner of pot roast, potatoes, and carrots cooking this morning in the slow cooker I'd found buried at the bottom of Clive's cabinet.

As tantalizing as it smelled, I wanted to shower first. The high-powered massage head in Clive's master bathroom always beckoned me to his shower. Clive had told me to make myself comfortable, and it had become easier to do every day. I'd claimed a corner of the shower for all of my toiletries and had set Clive's shower radio to my favorite station.

I pulled off my clothes and stepped into the shower. Fifteen minutes later I was walking down the hallway swaddled in one of Clive's robes and with food on my mind.

A woman's voice stopped me in my tracks. Before I had time to react, Gina walked out of the office. She looked like she had the same reaction as I had. Shock. I noticed how quickly she replaced her stunned expression with a sneer. They must've taught her that in law school.

"Playing house, I see," Gina said. She tucked a stack of manila folders under her arm. I hoped it wasn't something Clive wanted to keep from her, because I wasn't about to fight this woman.

"Actually I'm helping Clive catch up on some work," I said.

She looked at my bare feet, the only body part not covered by Clive's plush robe. Suddenly I felt a chill, and it wasn't because the air conditioner was set at seventy-five degrees.

"It makes me wonder what kind of 'work' you've been helping Clive with," Gina said. "He must've started a new endeavor, because none of *our* businesses have employees who work without their clothes."

The way she said the word "our" made me think Gina still considered them a couple. I was stunned, like a deer caught in headlights. This was one of the times I needed Cassandra to have my back, because she could attack a person quickly and where it hurt the most. Cassandra's mouth was a lethal weapon. I, on the other hand, only shot blanks. I had no idea what to say.

Gina was still staring me down.

I looked guilty even though I was innocent. To make matters worse, the front door opened.

Chapter 41

Papa Bear is home," Clive yelled from the foyer. He'd picked the wrong time to be funny, and definitely the wrong time to return home early from vacation.

"There's nothing like coming home to a hot meal," he said. I assumed he'd eyed my dinner and the table for one that I'd set for myself.

"He's been out of town," I said quickly to Gina. "For two weeks, and suddenly he shows up."

Gina wasn't listening to me grappling with my words.

She touched her finger to her chin like she'd just had a revelation. "He's Papa Bear, so you must be Mama Bear. Is there a Baby Bear coming in the picture? Is that where this whole thing is coming from?"

If Gina really wanted to make comparisons to children's stories I'd dub her the Big Bad Wolf. Not like I would ever tell her that.

Instead I said, "Trust me, it's not the way it looks."

Clive finally appeared around the corner and saw us. He didn't flinch. I didn't understand that man's ability to stay cool under uncomfortable circumstances.

"She's right," Clive said. He walked over and had the nerve to try and kiss both of us on the cheek. It was like I was living in a drama-filled reality TV show. I pulled away and so did Gina.

"Nigel's mother-in-law died," Clive said. "We didn't want to send him back alone."

I think he'd just noticed that I was wearing his robe. He smiled then looked at Gina. His eyebrows lifted. He saw how this entire scenario looked suspicious.

"I know why Sheila is here, but what are you doing here?" he asked Gina.

"I tried calling you a thousand times yesterday and today, but it kept going to voice mail. I didn't know whether to be nervous or angry."

"Oh, so you still care about me?" Clive chuckled.

Gina snarled.

I felt like I was an intruder in a private moment.

"No. I needed the last quarterly report for the lounge," she said, waving the folder in his face.

I excused myself and went back into the guest room. I don't remember a time when I'd changed clothes so fast. I threw all of my clothes into my luggage as quickly as I could without stuffing them in like they were worthless rags. Designer labels deserved to be treated with respect.

When I rolled my baggage to the front door, Clive and Gina were sitting at the bar with papers spread across the marble countertop. Gina revealed more of her legs than was necessary and was swishing red wine around in a crystal flute. She looked content—like she'd just won a monumental case.

I accepted Clive's help to carry my luggage downstairs.

"Good seeing you again, Gina," I said.

She looked at me like I'd lost my mind, but said anyway, "Have a good one, Mama Bear."

I started in on Clive as soon as we were in the parking lot. "You could've called and told me you were coming home early."

"I don't see why I need to call to let someone know I'm coming home early to *my* house," he said matter-of-factly.

"I was put in an uncomfortable position. Again." I said, popping the trunk. "And I don't appreciate it."

Clive was usually gentle in how he handled me, but I could hear the irritation in his voice.

"What do you mean you don't appreciate it? I didn't know Gina was going to show up. She hasn't been to the condo since we separated. We used to use it as our getaway, but now it's my bachelor pad. That's why she's refused to come over."

Clive took my attaché out of my hand. "It's not that big of a deal," he said, making sure my bags were secure. "And by the way, that robe looked nice on you."

I got in the car and nearly ran Clive over when I backed out. Some things don't deserve a response. I'm not sure why I thought he would've forgotten about our encounter by the time he returned from the Bahamas.

Then there was me. I couldn't make sense of my feelings, because although I wanted Clive to move forward from what had happened between us, I couldn't help but question whether his conversation with Gina was going to move from the kitchen to the bedroom.

I was falling from the cloud I'd been walking on for almost two weeks. I thought I needed a Scripture to help me fight through this. I wiped away tears. And I needed it fast.

Chapter 42

I'd planned on spending a relaxing night alone with God and my pot roast, but instead I was pulling into the church parking lot. It was probably where I should've been tonight in the first place. I'd learned some things over the last few weeks. God has a way of pre-empting your plans—even the ones with the best intentions. I'd told Him I wouldn't miss church. He'd held me to it.

I'd left Clive's and stopped by Cassandra's. As usual she was home with Frank. They were all lovey-dovey tonight. I didn't want to spend too much time there and disrupt their couch cuddling, so I'd rolled all of my bags inside and dropped them in my room. When I arrived at church, I realized I'd forgotten my Bible and prayer journal on the bed.

I was seeing more and more familiar faces with every visit, and I ran into Sherri again. I'd written in my journal this morning about how I wanted God to give me friends who shared my beliefs and could help me grow stronger in my faith. I knew my season of friendship with Cassandra was coming to an end; I just didn't know how to tell her. If I should tell her. And if so, when? I'm not stupid. Telling a person that you've outgrown their friendship isn't something you do when you're staying in their home. I'd poured my prayers on paper, hoping God would answer them.

"What's up, girl?" Sherri said. "Have you been reading the book?"

"I'm not yet, but I will be soon," I promised her. Sherri was starting to take the whole book club thing seriously. By the time I saw her again, I'd be finished. If it was as good as the blurb on the back cover made it sound, I could finish it in one day.

Sherri and I walked into the sanctuary together. It was at least another ten minutes until the start of the empowerment service. *Empower me, God. Give me just what I need today,* I prayed as I slid into the pew beside Sherri.

I wasn't living an authentic life.

Once again Pastor Armstrong's sermon left me taking a look in the mirror. *Who am I really?* I asked myself throughout the entire sermon. I'd gotten one of those note sheets again that said, "How Does This Apply to My Life?" at the top. There wasn't a blank space left on the page.

"You've spent all of your life living for other people," Pastor Armstrong had said.

It looked like he was looking directly at me, so I pretended to be taking notes until he walked over to the other side of the sanctuary.

"You think you know who you are, but you only know the counterfeit you. You know the person that people want you to be, or what *another* person fashioned you to be. But what about who God says you are?"

Pastor Armstrong kept walking back and forth among the pews, and I kept praying he'd go back to his podium and read his notes or something. But something told me he wasn't preaching from notes. God was probably talking directly to that man…or, more accurately, to me, but only using Pastor Armstrong's voice.

"I'd say that ninety percent of you aren't living the life God has for you because you're too busy lugging around old baggage."

One of the ministers pulled out a larger-than-life navy blue suitcase that was hidden behind one of the high-backed pulpit chairs. Pastor Armstrong dragged the suitcase around with him as he continued preaching.

"Oh, everything looks good from the outside," he said, unzipping the suitcase. "But if people could really see inside of your life—the areas that only God may know about—they would see that you've got some unresolved issues."

Issues. I am familiar with that word, I thought. Cassandra would have appreciated this sermon. I'm sure she could outline *my* issues better than she could her own.

One by one Pastor Armstrong held up bricks that had words painted on them. *Heartache. Abortion. Laziness. Debt. Insecurity.*

Pastor Armstrong might as well have taped a bull's-eye on my forehead and thrown the bricks straight at me. He was right on target with some of the issues and demons lurking in my past.

"One of the most freeing experiences you'll have is addressing the person or thing that left those issues in your life," Pastor Armstrong said. "Some of you can do it in your heart, but there are some of you who need to have some face-to-face conversations so you can close some doors. It's time to move on. God's word says that eye hasn't seen and ear hasn't heard, and it hasn't even entered into the heart of man about the things God has for you. Don't let your unresolved issues keep you from stepping into the good life."

I'd walked into a lot of situations over time, but never once stepped into the good life. It was high time.

I went up front to the altar when the associate minister called for people desiring church membership. Wednesday night empowerment service typically didn't have as many people as Sunday worship services, and I almost considered waiting until Sunday so I could be lost in the crowd. *That's insecurity,* I told myself and found the boldness to be the first one out of the pews and walking down the aisle. They made it seem like I was walking the red carpet. I was glad I was looking as cute as I was.

After completing some preliminary paperwork and getting a schedule of classes they liked new members to take, I was anxious to get home and write in my journal.

When I walked out from the back, Eden, Bear, and Sherri greeted me.

"Welcome to the family," Sherri was the first to say.

"I had a feeling you were joining tonight," Eden said. "I'm always having these thoughts about you."

My prayers had been answered right before my eyes. Who would've thought a crazy idea like sneaking into Ace's wedding would be such a blessing?

I promised Eden I'd help her at the bookstore the next morning, said good-bye to everyone else, then walked outside with Sherri. Our cars were parked near each other, and I ended up sitting in the car with her for another hour talking about life.

"Excuse me," she said, stifling a yawn. "I've been burning the candle at both ends. I think it's starting to catch up with me."

"Working on some new pieces?" I asked.

"Nothing original. A last-minute request to do some bridesmaids' dresses for a party of twelve."

"Twelve?" I said. "She must have a lot of girlfriends or sisters."

"I think she just has a problem saying no. You heard what Pastor Armstrong was saying about trying to meet everyone's expectations," Sherri said. "At any rate, the extra money won't hurt, so I decided to help her out. I figure the bride probably has enough on her plate with such a large wedding party."

"I'm far from being a seamstress, but if you need my help, just let me know. I can at least cut patterns. I was a pro at that in home economics class in high school. You should've seen that pillow I made," I bragged.

"I'll take you up on that offer," Sherri said. "Is your Friday evening free? I don't want to ruin any of your plans for a hot date you may have lined up."

"Please," I said. "The only things I have lined up on Friday night are the books on my nightstand. I'd love to help you out."

"Great," Sherri said. "That way Faith will be with her dad and we can work without interruption."

We exchanged numbers, then I headed home. I'd recaptured that peaceful feeling. Life for me was about to change. I just didn't know it was going to happen when I opened the door at Cassandra's.

Chapter 43

An eviction notice was on Cassandra's living room coffee table. It wasn't something written and signed by Cassandra. It was my journal. It was opened, and to my horror, parts of some of the pages had been highlighted. I picked it up. Cassandra had highlighted every section where I mentioned her name.

"Who do you think you are?" She stormed into the room before I had time to think about how to explain.

"Cassandra, you probably misunderstood some things I wrote," I said.

Cassandra snatched the journal out of my hand. "How do you misunderstand this?" she said, then read my personal prayers and private thoughts aloud.

"'My prayer is for new friends,'" she read. "'I need people around me who know You and want to live for You. Cassandra's not one of those people. Eden is. I even think Sherri would be better for me. Pastor talked about people being in your life for a reason, a season, or a lifetime. I'm beginning to feel like the season of my friendship with Cassandra has come to an end.'" Cassandra screamed the words with an intensity and anger that wasn't meant for them.

"I'm concerned for you, Cassandra," I said. "I want God's best for you, that's all."

"What? Don't put God in it. What you want is for me to be unhappy like you."

"You're wrong. Because I'm happier than I've been in a long time."

"You have no man, no job—and consequently very little money. Which means you can't shop and shower yourself with expensive gifts that you can't afford. So no, you are not happy. I know you."

"No. You know the *old* me."

"Oh," she said, flipping through the pages of my journal, which she was still holding.

Now I was becoming furious as I thought about how she'd invaded my private thoughts.

"So it's the *new* you who realizes that—and I quote—'God, if You want to bless me, give me a job so I can get out of here. Cassandra and Frank are crazy. I'm convinced of it.'"

She slammed the journal on the coffee table. I picked it up.

"You don't have a right to go through my things. I don't care if it's your place or not, there's still such a thing as privacy and respect," I said, trying to walk past her to the bedroom. I surprised myself that I could stay so calm. If I didn't aggravate the situation, Cassandra would calm down by morning. She'd realize I didn't mean any harm.

Cassandra followed me and leaned her weight against the bedroom door to prevent me from closing it.

"You need to leave. Tonight. Why wait for this so-called season to come to an end? There's no time like the present."

Cassandra's breathing was quick and heavy. My heart was

probably racing twice as fast as hers, but I did my best to keep my reactions under control. If I responded the way my emotions were pushing me to do, it would be like throwing a log onto an already raging fire.

"I mean it," Cassandra said. "You're not going to talk trash about me and lay up in my house. Not going to happen."

Cassandra slammed the bedroom door.

My luggage was leaning against the foot of the bed like I'd left it. My forgotten Bible was also on the bed and so was the halter-top I'd let Cassandra borrow. She must've come into the room to bring back the top or to use her computer. Either way, she'd seen my journal and her innate curiosity drove her to open it in hopes of finding something juicy.

All of that . . . had led to this.

I let myself cry because there was no sense in acting like the feeling of my world caving in around me didn't hurt. Even through the tears I pressed my way to unpack my dirty clothes and replace them with clean ones. I stuffed my bags until I had to sit on them to zip them shut. There was no way I'd be able to take all of my belongings with me that night. I knew it, and Cassandra knew it. I tried not to think about how and when I was going to get the rest of my things. I had one immediate concern. Where was I going to stay?

Being broke limits your options. I couldn't see myself using the money Clive had given me to stay in a hotel. I needed to hold on to every dime I had. It was already almost eleven o'clock at night, and even a late checkout time would only let me stay until one o'clock the next day. The other option would be cheap motel, but I wouldn't get a wink of sleep thinking about my safety and the crawling creatures in the bed. I'd stayed at a motel like that twice in my life, and both times were in college. I shuddered when I remembered why I'd been there in the first place.

I pulled into the parking lot of the twenty-four-hour store; the same one where I'd left my car the night I went out with Travis. I had to think my way out of this.

I wasn't going back to Clive's, and the clutter and smoke that clung to everything at Mama's house crossed that option off my list. A person should always be able to count on family, and I could. But tonight, it just wasn't going to be my biological one.

I called Eden. Maybe she'd already had a feeling that we'd see each other again tonight.

I'd seen tons of those license plates that said *God is my co-pilot*. Here I was in front of Eden's house, and I knew for sure that God had been my *head* pilot. I didn't remember the trip there at all. After I'd called Eden and blubbered and cried my way through the story, I zoned out.

I could feel the trail of dried tears on my face. I thought I'd cried myself dry until Eden opened the door. I knew she'd been watching out for me. She'd burn the midnight oil for somebody else's crisis. I considered myself to be in crisis.

Eden turned off the patio light as I got closer to the steps, so that the moths flying around wouldn't follow me inside.

Eden calmed me with an embrace. She hugged me, and her petite arms felt like they were as huge as Bear's. She let me cry like a baby, then we sat down in the den. We shared a love seat with cushions set so deep and wide that our feet didn't touch the ground. I couldn't believe I was here, reaching out to a woman I'd known for less time than anyone else in my life.

"It may not seem like it now," Eden said in nearly a whisper, "but things will get better."

I had to believe. That's what faith meant to me. Why read about it if I wasn't going to believe it?

"Have you ever felt like you were knocked flat on your back,"

I said, "and then someone put their foot on your throat so you couldn't get up? So you couldn't breathe? That's how I feel right now."

Eden smiled. "Keep living. You're liable to feel this way again. But I bet you've been through something before when you thought you'd die or felt like you'd never get over it. But you did. Look at where you were this time last year. Remember when you told me you felt there was no reason to go on? Well, look at you. You went on. You made it. And you're stronger. And you'll grow stronger once this storm passes, too."

I hugged my shoulders. "I thought living for God was going to keep me from this drama."

"Living for God doesn't shield you from what life throws at you," Eden said. "But it does give you a peace and a reassurance that others may not have."

Eden picked up a Bible lying open on the back of the love seat. She flipped through a few pages, then read, "And we know that in all things God works for the good of those who love Him, who are called according to His purpose."

She set the Bible on her lap. "All things. Not some. Your unemployment. Your financial troubles. Trials strengthen your faith. You're going to learn something from all of this."

"Even Mama's illness? She waited four months before she told me about her emphysema."

Eden put her hand on mine. "I'm sorry. I had no idea," she said. "But yes. Even that."

"I didn't say anything initially because Mama used to always tell us that what goes on in our house is no one else's business. I guess I was still holding on to that. But I can't carry all of these burdens alone. Not anymore," I said.

I couldn't bring myself to tell Eden that I'd slept with Clive. She said all things worked together, but I wondered if that indiscretion fell into that category, too.

"You don't have to carry your burdens alone," Eden assured me. "You've got God. You've got me and Bear. Sherri. Your church friends and family."

"Is it too much for me to want to be happy? Is it too much for me to not have drama for once?"

Eden laughed. "Believe me. Everyone's got drama. You don't know what goes on behind closed doors. You know how they say this world is a stage? That should tell you right there that there's going to be drama. Sometimes a comedy, sometimes a tragedy, sometimes a romance."

"I'll take the romance," I said, wiping my face. I covered my eyes and exhaled a long, cleansing breath. "A romance."

"I do know someone you'd fall utterly and completely head-over-heels in love with."

"How soon can I meet him?" I asked and laughed.

It was a shame how the mention of a man had changed my entire attitude. Hopeless romantics can't help it. But I didn't need to find a man. I needed to find somewhere to live.

Chapter 44

The sunrise welcomed me and Eden the next morning. We'd been lost in conversation with no regard for time and didn't realize we'd been up all night. The last time I'd been up all night was from stress and worry. Of course my situation hadn't changed, but Eden had helped lift some of the worry off of my mind. As always, she'd given me a Scripture to help, and I wrote it down: *Finally, brothers and sisters, whatever is true, whatever is noble, whatever is right, whatever is pure, whatever is lovely, whatever is admirable—if anything is excellent or praiseworthy—think about such things.*

I went to sleep thinking about the good things that had recently happened in my life, instead of dwelling on the bad.

Eden still had to be at the bookstore this morning, but she'd told me to sleep in as long as I wanted, then suggested I get out and spend time enjoying God's new day. Despite having so little sleep, I was wide-awake by ten o'clock. I called Mama and was happy to hear that she had the day off. I was glad she was getting the much-needed rest to help her body take care of itself. The last thing she needed was extra stress.

I was going to take advantage of my time of unemployment. I liked what Eden called it better—*transition*. I could be there for Mama as much as she'd allow me. Mama hated to be fussed over, so I knew I had to ease into lending her a hand.

I wanted her to at least be open to treatment alternatives, since she wasn't one for medical intervention. Whenever I was sick with menstrual cramps or other trivial illnesses, she'd tell me that I didn't need all of that medicine in my body and that it would heal itself when it was time. I don't know how many times I snuck an ibuprofen or two when that time of the month came around. I didn't ascribe to my mother's medicine-free philosophy, and I didn't think her philosophy was going to help her this time either.

I looked out of the window of the guest bedroom that faced the front of the house and saw that both Bear's and Eden's cars were gone. That was strange, because I thought I heard someone talking downstairs. With a closer listen I figured out it was the radio tuned to the gospel station. Eden didn't play. She made sure God's presence was all up in everything. That's probably why her house was so peaceful. As soon as I got my own place again, I was going to do the same thing.

I sat down at the breakfast bar in the kitchen with my Bible and journal.

Eden had written a note for me and slid it under a glass bowl of fruit.

This is the day that the Lord has made. Rejoice and be glad in it. Help yourself to anything in the fridge or anything else in the house . . . except me and Bear's room. That's for grown folks.
Above all, have a great day, but don't come by the bookstore! I mean it! Go see your Mama!

I found some blueberry yogurt in the refrigerator and ate it while I had some devotion time. Afterward I took Pastor Armstrong's sermon to heart and wrote down the names of some people who had left some baggage in my life, as well as a few whom I had wronged. In some cases, my hands had been just as dirty as the next person's. There was no way I'd be able to contact them all, but the act of releasing them to God and asking for forgiveness did something for me. Mama, Devin, Ace, Cassandra, Clive. The list grew.

Mama was first on the list. Our relationship wasn't full of strife, but it could be strained at times. We had more good days than bad. Yet in the past it seemed that the less time we spent together, the better we got along. That seems backward, especially since the more time I spend with God, the deeper in love I fall.

I'd been so focused on leaving the life that I'd grown up in, that I'd left behind Mama, too. But I was going to make it right. With her and the rest of my list.

Chapter 45

Mama seemed a little winded when she opened the door. She had to nearly crawl over an obstacle course of boxes and bags to get to it, so I'm sure that didn't help.

"Hey, Mama," I said.

I'm not going to focus on the mess, I told myself. It looked like Mama had tried to push some of the stuff over onto the couch so we could have room to sit and talk, but we ended up at the kitchen table again. We always had our talks at the kitchen table. Back in the day, Mama had called them family meetings. Me and Devin thought things should be a democracy; Mama didn't see it that way. She was the queen of the castle.

"So what brings you here to spend time with *me?*" Mama asked.

She'd decided to take some time off from work, something Mama had rarely done over the years. There was a pan of store-bought rolls and a box of oats on the counter. Mama didn't think microwave oatmeal compared to the slowly simmered kind she preferred.

"There's no law about when a daughter can spend time with her mama," I said.

"You're right about that," she said. "I think losing your job has been a good thing for you," she said. "I haven't seen you this much in a long time. You might be broke, but at least you seem happy."

"Hopefully being broke won't last, but being happy will," I said.

"It's all in what you want," Mama said. "If you want happy, it'll come to you."

Sometimes Mama could drop some wisdom without even thinking about it. Eden had shared a similar verse with me. *As a man thinks, so he is.* Or something like that.

"What makes me happy right now is spending time with you," I said.

I don't think I've ever been so sentimental with Mama. We loved each other but rarely expressed it through words. It was strange for me to say them and probably even stranger for Mama to hear. We usually only said, "Love you," out of habit. It was the same as saying "Good-bye," or "Talk to you soon."

"Until I find a job, I can come over and help you with the house or run you on some errands."

"Devin's around," Mama said.

Surely she wasn't serious. How did she think he was going to ride her around? On bike handlebars?

"Well if you don't want to bother Devin, call me," I said, not pushing the point.

Mama started fiddling with the end of a placemat on her side of the table. I knew something was coming up that I didn't want to hear. Mama always fiddled with things when she didn't want to tackle a situation head on. I waited for her to get up the courage to tell me. I waited for *me* to get up the courage to hear it.

"You don't need to bother yourself with helping around the house," Mama said. "There's not much around here that needs to be done unless you want to cook something now and then."

She gave me a little smirk. My cooking skills—or lack thereof—were no secret.

"I might surprise you with a gourmet meal," I teased, keeping things light until she could tell me the real thing plaguing her mind. "I can fix a succulent pot roast in a Crock Pot."

"Succulent, huh? And I *do* know what succulent means," she said.

"I never thought you didn't, Mama," I said, trying not to get irritated.

Mama always thought I talked down to her after I left for college. But that was then and this was now. I'd thought I was the one carrying baggage and issues that Mama had given me, but it was apparent that I'd left her dragging some suitcases as well.

Mama got up and washed two dishes that were in the sink, then sat back down at the table and pretended like she was looking for a recipe. The loose pages were falling out of the cookbook. Like me. I was barely keeping myself together waiting for the bomb to drop. Then she dropped it.

"I've decided I won't be going back to any doctor's appointments," she said. She didn't look up at me. She stopped on a recipe for bread pudding.

"What do you mean you're not going?"

"I started taking some of the medicines they gave me at first, but they make me feel funny. I know they're doing something to my body that's not right."

"No, Ma. The *emphysema* is doing something to your body that's not right. This isn't some minor illness that you can fix with a home remedy," I cried. "This is serious. It might be a matter of life and death."

"And if I live, I live. If I die, I die."

I took a deep breath. I wasn't going to be ruled by Mama's temporary insanity. I couldn't imagine the emotional wreck she was experiencing inside. Half of the battle was with her body, and the other half was going to be with her mind.

"I think we should research all of the options we have available," I said, trying to keep my mind on hopeful things. "Then we'll make the decision."

"This is not a decision for *we*," Mama said. "It's a decision for *me*. I'm not changing my mind."

Mama was on her throne, and she wasn't getting down. She was stubborn. I believed every word she said, but that didn't mean I wasn't going to fight her about it.

"I think if I change my eating habits and eat foods that aren't so processed then that will help my body build some kinds of cells or immunity on its own," she said. "I can help my lungs rebuild and repair themselves if I take vitamins and herbs."

Mama sounded so sure that she almost convinced me it was the route to go. Almost. Now wasn't the time for breaking out home remedies.

"You're a woman of faith now, aren't you, Sheila?" Mama asked me.

"Yes."

"Well then you should know that when it's all said and done, God controls everything. He has the right to decide whether I'll live or die."

I don't know what Ms. Pearl had been feeding Mama or what the pastor at that revival she'd attended a few weeks ago had said. I just hoped she hadn't been brainwashed into some kind of cult thinking.

"There's nothing wrong with combining faith and medication," I said.

"It doesn't make sense to me," Mama said, shaking her head. "It's like putting some toxins in your body so you can get some toxins out."

"I'm not a medical professional," I said. "I only want you to get better, and there's nothing wrong with medication. Plenty of people take medication and do perfectly fine."

"Well, I'm not plenty of people. For every patient that does fine, there's probably someone who gets worse from taking that stuff. I'm not going to be that person."

I sighed heavily. I could talk until my face was blue and Mama's was purple. There was nothing I could say to change her mind. She would have to change it on her own. And I would pray that she would.

Mama started going on and on about other things—giving me updates about what was happening with people in my old neighborhood. Since it was summertime, some of my childhood friends had dropped off their children to spend part of their summer vacation with their grandparents . . . mainly the grandmothers. After a while I knew where the conversation was leading. Mama was about to sing the "I wish I had grandchildren" song.

"I just knew I was next in line for grandbabies," she said. "I know you and Ace would've made some beautiful babies. Especially if you'd had a boy. He probably would've looked just like his daddy and been real smart, too. He would've been a pilot, too."

"It's never too late," I said.

"Tell your eggs it's not too late," Mama said. "Them things don't last forever."

"My eggs function just fine," I said, standing up. "Let's talk in my room," I suggested.

I walked down the hall before Mama had a chance to object. I already knew that I'd only have a small passage that led from the doorway to the small twin bed in the room. Mama followed behind me with excuses about when she was going to organize her garage sale finds that were piled against the walls.

Mama sat at the foot of the bed while I slid out a plastic bin that had been under the bed for years. It was sealed tightly with memories that flooded me as soon as I popped off the top. There was my senior memory book, some Polaroid pictures of me and Devin when we were younger and actually friends, and another stack of pictures that me and Cassandra had taken. We'd taken some shots outside under a tree and also staged some shots inside that we planned to send to a modeling agency. Both of our faces were overdone with makeup in an attempt to look sophisticated, but we looked more like clowns.

"You and Cassandra were always chasing the big life," Mama said. She shook her head as she looked at the pictures. "Oh excuse me," she corrected. "Y'all called it the *good* life."

"Funny how definitions of success change after you live life a little," I said.

"How is Cassandra doing anyway? Tell her she ain't too grown to come and see me."

Cassandra rarely ventured to this side of town anymore. After her grandmother died, she saw little reason to return to the part of town that reminded her of a lifestyle she tried so hard to escape.

"Cassandra doesn't want to hear anything I have to say right now," I told Mama, sliding our pictures back into a plastic sandwich bag. "As a matter of fact, she put me out."

"What do you mean she put you out?"

I told Mama the story, even though it was a situation I didn't particularly want to think about. Eden was being gracious enough to let me stay at her home, but I wasn't going to take advantage of her kindness. And there was absolutely no way I would survive living in a house that looked more like a flea market than a home. No offense to Mama, but the truth was the truth.

"I can see how Cassandra was hurt by what she read, but she had no business reading your personal stuff in the first place," Mama said. "When you do that, you're asking for trouble."

"What's done is done," I said, shuffling through more pictures. I tossed a few in an old grocery store bag because I intended to throw them away. I could tell Mama was about to have a conniption, but since it was my stuff, there wasn't much she could say. Or at least I thought.

"Devin might want to see those," she said, reaching for the bag. I moved it out of her reach. "He'll be fine," I assured her. "He hasn't thought about them in all this time, so he won't miss them. Trust me."

Mama pulled a different stack out of the plastic bin and started flipping through them like playing cards.

"I remember when I bought you that Polaroid camera. You were taking pictures of everything. Every time you earned a little money you were running to buy some film."

Despite her diagnosis, Mama seemed to be in a happy place. She was more peaceful than I think I would've been if I were in her shoes. She caught me staring at her. Her lips curled up into a grin.

"Don't worry about me," Mama said. Her eyes were soft, pleading. "Keep on living for God, and He'll take care of you. I've never been a religious kind of woman, but I believe if I leave you and Devin in God's hands, you'll be all right."

"Mama, don't talk like that. Emphysema is not a death sentence. It just needs to be properly managed."

Mama held her hand up to silence me. "I've read up on it. I know that. But if anything were to ever happen to me for any reason, I'm depending on you to watch after Devin. He hasn't made the best decisions in life, and that's why he's where he is. But remember the good times and how close y'all used to be when you were little." She held up one of the pictures in her hand. "Like these times."

I took the picture. Our small front yard used to be the hangout spot for the neighborhood, since our home was near the end of the cul-de-sac. I'd called Mama outside to take a picture of all of us with big cheesy smiles after coming back from swimming at the public pool. The sun had dried us on the ride back, but all of the girls' hair was a sight. We had our arms draped around each other like we were depending on each other to hold ourselves up. There were about nine of us, but in the front row were me, Devin, and his good friend, Fontaine. That was when my friendship with Fontaine had been innocent.

I looked at Mama. I think she knew what I was thinking. She didn't say a word when I tossed the picture in the trash.

Chapter 46

A lot of other memories found their way to the trash, too. Mama sat in silence and watched me purge three boxes. By the end of the process I'd let her keep three pictures for herself, and I had five pictures that I wanted to keep. I cherished the time to connect. Me and Mama chatted about much of nothing—until there was a bang, like someone kicking down the front door.

Mama didn't look unnerved at all. She arose slowly, like her house being knocked off the slab was a daily occurrence.

"It's probably Devin's lady friend," Mama said.

"Shakira? I met her one time before when I was over. I see she still wants to be crazy. I wonder what it is this time?"

Mama moved a cardboard box filled with batteries out of her way. "I was talking about Tyesha. They met when she was pregnant with somebody else's baby. I think she thought that Devin was going to step in and take care of the baby like it was his."

"She thought wrong. Devin doesn't even take care of himself."
I regretted the words as soon as I said them. Me and Mama
were doing good. She didn't respond, and I knew that meant her
wall was going up.

"I'm sorry, Ma," I said, trying to save the time we had spent together today.

Mama peeked out of the window beside the front door. She
huffed, shook her head, and rolled her eyes all in one disgusted
motion.

"Devin needs to stop playing with these girls. I can tell she's all
up in arms about something."

"Evidently so. She nearly knocked the door off the frame," I
said, trying to get a look out of the window myself. I couldn't see
her clearly because her back was turned.

Mama unlocked the deadbolt, and I stood behind her with my
arms crossed.

The chick watered down her anger when she saw Mama. She
was probably expecting Devin to open the door. To make things
worse, she was carrying a baby—plump, with his neck covered in
baby powder. The baby giggled, and slobber dribbled from his juicy
bottom lip. He was enjoying his mid-morning snack of his knuck-
les shoved into his mouth.

I was going to pray for the adorable fellow, because if episodes
like this were any indication of the things he'd see in life, his childhood was going to be full of drama.

"Ms. Rushmore. I'm sorry. I knocked a few times but nobody
answered." She averted her eyes, a sure sign that she was lying.
Mama didn't call her out, but her expression said it all. The girl
swatted a fly buzzing around her head.

"Devin's not here, Tyesha," Mama said.

"Myesha," she corrected. "Do you know when he'll be back?""

"You can never tell," Mama said.

I know when Mama feels sorry for somebody. She stares at

them like she's walked in their shoes—and with Mama's history and upbringing, she undoubtedly has. Mama may have been concerned about Myesha and her son, but I was looking outside to make sure that Shakira's lookout wasn't sending her a signal again that there was another woman on Devin's doorstep.

Mama said to Myesha, "You should live your life and not worry about Devin. Most times a woman cares about a man more than that man cares about her. Listen to what I'm telling you."

Myesha looked past Mama and peered at me like it was the first time she'd noticed me.

"I'm his sister," I told her. She probably didn't know about me either, like I was the hidden shame of the family. "I agree with Mama," I said. "Moving on is the best thing you can do for yourself and your son."

I wanted to pinch his cheek, but I wasn't much for baby fluids—from either end.

Myesha sighed, and I think, inwardly, me and Mama did, too. Myesha would have to make the decision to do it on her own. Nothing me and Mama said was going to convince her. She wasn't sick and tired of being sick and tired yet.

"Can you tell Devin I came by? Please."

"I'll tell him," Mama said.

Myesha retreated from the porch, or should I say, stumbled. She tripped over an empty clay flowerpot on the bottom step.

"Be careful with that baby," Mama warned, like Myesha had tripped over her own two feet. "I hope she heeds my advice," she added.

"About the baby or about Devin?"

Mama slapped my shoulder.

"You're gonna mess around and hurt somebody who comes to visit you," I said. I wanted so badly to dump the other withered, dead plants dangling above Mama's head. I remembered a time when her ferns and azaleas flourished around the porch, and we actually had room to sit there and eat sherbert Push-ups or Rocket Pops from the ice cream man.

Me and Mama stood on the porch and watched Myesha walk away. The baby's fingers clutched her shoulders as he bounced at her side.

"Devin is just like your daddy. A rolling stone. I'm surprised he doesn't have a baby by now."

"Thank God he doesn't." And I didn't say it to be sarcastic. "These days you can end up with more than a baby. And some stuff can't be cured with creams or a three-day pill."

Mama picked dead leaves off a plant that was struggling to stay alive. She didn't say a word.

Standing on the porch watching cars go by made me think about Daddy. He was on my list to forgive, and one of the people I knew I'd never talk to in order to get my closure.

I was fourteen the last time I saw him. We passed by each other at the mall, and I don't think he even recognized me because I wasn't the seven-year-old girl he'd last visited. Puberty had changed me physically and mentally. The physical changes were obvious—what happens to every girl—but mentally I'd erased his existence from my memory. It was easier to act like I'd never known him than to try and justify his disappearing act.

Daddy had never lived with us. We were never the Huxtables —but then again I could count on one hand the number of people I knew from two-parent households. All of my friends had drop-in daddies. Drop in on birthdays. Drop in at Christmas. Then drop out of your life.

No matter what, Daddy always smelled like Egyptian musk oil. That's how I had known it was him when he walked by that day. I stood on the porch and released my bitterness toward him.

"What's got you thinking?" Mama asked.

"Life," I said. I didn't want to get her started on Daddy.

"I think about my life all the time."

Mama sat down on the top step, and I joined her. We watched the neighbor across the street sweep his front porch. His body was humped over like a lower case *n*.

"I've got more life behind me than I do ahead of me."

"Nobody knows how much life they have left," I said. "That's why we have to live and enjoy each day. Tell people you love them while we still have them."

I leaned over and kissed Mama on the cheek. "Love you, Ma."

"I love you, too, baby."

Clive was right. No matter how old I got, I would always be Mama's baby.

Chapter 47

For almost seven months, I'd been distracted by finding a job. Now it was more important for me to find myself. I knew there were bills to be paid—but I didn't miss bumper-to-bumper commutes, rushed lunch hours, or evenings that were my employer's instead of my own.

I'd found another Scripture that I'd written in my journal. I read it every night before I fell into another peaceful night's sleep at Eden's. *Therefore do not worry about tomorrow, for tomorrow will worry about itself. Each day has enough trouble of its own.*

For the last two days I'd spent my mornings with God, my afternoons helping Eden at the bookstore, and let my evenings flow where they may. Tonight I'd flowed over to Sherri's boutique.

Sherri's tailoring and design skills were impeccable. I'd been in her quaint boutique for nearly an hour, and I was still admiring her work. In the middle of showing me her favorite custom-designed pieces, two clients had come in with requests for attire for a special event. It was evident that her work was more than just a job. It was her passion.

I, on the other hand, had no idea what my life's calling was. I had a degree in business and had worked in human resources and workplace recruitment for years, but it didn't fulfill me. Other than that, most of my adult life had been spent keeping up with the Joneses. I wondered if being a shopaholic accounted for anything.

"You're in high demand," I said, once her client had finally decided on the look she wanted Sherri to create.

"It took a while to get here," Sherri said, closing her sketchbook. "But I'm glad I stuck with it."

Sherri stifled a yawn. "I'm glad we decided not to finish cutting those patterns tonight. It'll be nice to kick back and do nothing for a change."

Sherri went to a back closet and pulled out three pairs of slacks. She hung them on a hook behind the counter. "I have one last client that I'm waiting for, and I'll close up," she said.

"Well, I'm not in a hurry," I said.

"For the sake of my purse, neither am I," Sherri said. "This client is extremely particular, but she pays me enough money to be so I don't complain. She even likes for me to embroider her initials at the top of the waistband on her slacks. GA. And only in red thread."

"That must be her signature thing. You know, like celebrities who only wear white, or like that financial guru woman whose signature accessory is the same pair of gold earrings she wears whenever she's on air."

"But embroidered only in red? No matter what?" Sherri asked.

I'd read about the psychology of colors once when I was choosing some furniture and home décor.

"Red is an emotionally intense color," I remembered. "It can be intimidating when you wear it, so maybe it's her small signal to other people that she can be intimidating."

I was building a picture of this woman before she came in. I wanted to see how close my assessment would be.

"What does she do for a living?" I asked.

"She's an attorney. And probably a cutthroat one," Sherri laughed. "That red is probably for the blood she draws."

I liked Sherri. She had a sense of humor that I didn't expect her to have. I used to think that all church-going women who were serious about God needed to be at least somebody's grandma's age or they were wasting their life by following a bunch of religious rules and traditions. It wasn't like that at all. It wasn't even all about going to church, even though I knew I should. It was about my relationship with God. And God didn't mind a woman serving Him yet still having ambition, fun, and a sense of style.

I was trying on some bracelets from the jewelry display, and Sherri was talking to her little girl, Faith, on the phone. Sherri had explained that since Anisha had gotten pregnant, she'd been feeling all motherly and wanted to spend more time with Faith. She'd volunteered to babysit Faith two afternoons a week so that Sherri could work at the boutique freely. From what I could tell listening to one side of the conversation, Faith was working her mother's patience about going to spend time with her daddy this weekend.

We both instinctively turned when the door chime announced the client's arrival.

Sherri met her with a warm smile, but I nearly had to pick my mouth up off the floor.

Chapter 48

Get yourself together, girl. Gina hadn't noticed me yet over in the corner. It was almost like I was trying not to breathe so that she wouldn't turn my way. If her fangs were out today, she was sure to draw blood at my expense. Just like Sherri had said. Yep...the red was psychologically doing its job. I was experiencing some intense emotions. I had to get myself together because for whatever reason, Gina was always crossing my path when I least expected it.

"Sheila. Come over and meet Gina Alston," Sherri called out.

I took a deep breath and hoped that Gina would be in a hurry and have to rush out of the door without making my acquaintance.

"Sheila is a corporate woman who's in transition right now," I heard Sherri tell Gina. That was her nice way of saying I didn't have a job. "Maybe you have some contacts you can point her to."

There was no sense delaying the inevitable. I walked to the front counter and into firing range.

"Oh," Gina said. "We've met before. More than once."

She extended her hand and I accepted it. Maybe it was a peace offering. On any given day she might have crushed it in her grasp, but today she didn't have any fight in her at all. I could sense something was different, and there was almost an aura of sadness. I wondered if it was about Clive, not that it was any of my business. Once I worked off my debt to Clive, I was going to be out of his business . . . and *theirs* . . . if there was any. I'd been ignoring Clive's phone calls and texts for the past two days.

Gina paid Sherri and left.

"That's the first time she hasn't had anything to say," Sherri said as we watched Gina get in her car. "She's usually running off at the mouth about some big case." Sherri picked up her sketchbook and some other papers on the counter.

"So how do you know Gina?" Sherri asked me.

"I used to work with her husband," I explained.

That was all I was giving. What was I supposed to say? Oh yeah, I slept with her husband, and then stayed at his house for two weeks. Two days ago she walked in on me freshly showered and wearing his robe. And then before that, I went out to the club with her husband to have dinner and she walked up on us.

That didn't exactly paint an innocent picture of me.

"Oh, okay," Sherri said. She was half distracted by counting down her register and filling out a business deposit slip, so she didn't ask anything else. Thank God.

But despite how Gina usually intimidated me, I couldn't help thinking about her. Even after we picked up Faith from Anisha's house, I was still thinking about Gina, so instead of just wondering what was going on with her, I prayed for her. That's when I knew for sure that I'd been changed.

Chapter 49

It just as easily could've been me. We were parked in front of a drugstore waiting for Faith's dad to come and pick her up. Faith was jumping up and down on the seat in the back. She couldn't contain her excitement about spending the weekend with her dad.

"She acts like her dad is God," Sherri whispered.

Sherri was rolling through text messages on her phone and I could tell she was trying not to chastise Faith for being a little over the top. In a perfect world, mothers should be excited that their daughters want to spend time with their fathers. But also in a perfect world, there would be a mother, father, two point five children in the home, and a picket fence.

Sherri kept the conversation up with empty chatter, but I could tell she, like Faith, was growing restless. She checked her watch again and kept looking in the rearview and side mirrors for a sign of Faith's dad.

"How much longer before Daddy comes?" Faith whined. She'd started to unpack one of the two bags that were with her in the back seat. One was filled with her clothes, and the other with coloring books and dolls. Another ten minutes passed, and she grew tired of perfecting her juvenile cosmetology skills on her favorite doll. It was flipped upside down on the seat beside her with a colorful assortment of hair bows clipped to her bangs.

"I promise he's coming," Sherri said. "He's just a little late, that's all." She whispered under her breath, "As always."

"You know she loves you just as much, if not more," I felt the need to say to Sherri. "I can tell she's a mama's girl, but you should be happy that she actually loves her father and proud of yourself for making it easy for her to do. There are plenty of single moms who talk so much trash about their children's fathers that the children feel guilty for loving them. Believe me. I know."

"I can't get mad at her about it," Sherri said. "I chose her father for her. She didn't do it." She was speaking quietly and had adjusted the radio to the back speakers so she could drown out her voice for Faith. "When I went with my hormones and not with my head, I made the decision." She shook her head. "I just wish Xavier would do right. We're never going to be together. I never thought we would. But I wish he would live his life right. She goes with him for two days, and it takes me a week to deprogram her."

Sherri genuinely smiled for the first time since she'd been in the car that evening.

"A five year old shouldn't know how to drop it like it's hot. Not better than her mama."

Even in stress Sherri's since of humor couldn't help but show itself.

"She'll be okay. She's got a good mama. A good praying mama," I said. I wanted to say that she probably had some aunties and uncles that would beat the daddy down if need be, but I'd wait until Faith was out of the car. That was a conversation for grown women.

Faith sat on the edge of the back seat so she could see between the front seats.

"Ms. Sheila, do you know my dad?"

"I haven't had the pleasure of meeting him yet," I said and winked at Sherri. "But if he's as nice as you, then he's pretty cool."

"And he's handsome, too," Faith said. "Women always think so because their smiles go from here to here when he's talking to them," she said, sweeping her finger from her right ear to the left one.

"Deprogram," Sherri mouthed.

Faith wasn't paying any attention to her mother because she was about ten inches from my face. Children didn't care anything about personal space. With Faith I didn't mind. I could tell her hair had been freshly shampooed, and she smelled like baby lotion.

"Your breath smells good," Faith told me.

"Thank you," I said. I pushed the peppermint I was sucking up between my teeth so she could see it.

"Can I have a piece?" she asked.

"No, you may not," Sherri answered for her. "No candy."

Faith dropped down on the seat in a huff and crossed her arms over her chest. Sherri shot her a look, and she sucked in her bottom lip like she'd been warned about pouting and knew what to do.

"Daddy lets me eat candy," Faith said in a meek voice.

"Sometimes daddies don't worry about dentist bills and stuff like that," Sherri said. She rubbed her hand down the side of Faith's face, a gentle gesture of a mother's love.

Watching Sherri with Faith made me wonder what kind of mother I would've been. My life might've been drastically different if I hadn't made the decision to have an abortion. Really, the decision had been made for me. Maybe I would've been more careful about the things I'd done and said if I'd had someone else to consider. I smiled at Faith's round cheeks. If there were a face like that helping to guide my life, maybe I would've been a better person—sooner.

Out of the blue, Faith leaned over and kissed my cheek. It was as soft as a butterfly brushing against me. I knew it was God's kiss to me. I took it as a sign from God. I'd prayed last night for God to release me from the pain I'd been harboring toward Fontaine. I'd pushed it so far down in my psyche that I didn't know it was there. But the list of people to forgive, baggage to drop, and issues to address had grown to three pages.

"You're such a sweetie," I said to Faith. "One day I hope I'll have a little girl just like you."

"When?" Faith asked.

I laughed out loud. So did Sherri. "As soon as I have a husband. And I really don't have much control over that," I admitted.

"I'll ask God to send you one," Faith said.

"Please do," I said.

Sherri pointed to the line of cars at the stoplight in front of the drugstore. "There's your dad," she told Faith, then looked at me. "Pray for a sista."

Chapter 50

No sex before marriage. Every Christian woman knows the rules.

But men like Xavier might make that hard to do. He wore a bald head like it was a designer suit and was driving a car suitable for his swagger. A black Mustang. Seeing him proved one thing. Even the finest man had his issues. I was learning that good looks don't mean much if there was no integrity to match it. Of course I'd only heard one side of the story, but Sherri didn't seem like the kind of woman who brought more drama and trauma to her life than necessary.

Xavier stepped out of his car dressed like he was spending his time tonight with a grown woman with benefits and not playing dolls with a kindergartner.

Sherri was standing on the sidewalk clutching Faith's hand and her extra duffel bag of clothes. I could tell it was paining her to let Faith leave for the weekend, even though it was a bi-monthly routine.

I knew Sherri wasn't playing when she asked me to pray, so I did. Right up until the time she opened the door and slid back into the driver's seat.

"I could feel your prayers, girl," she said, buckling up. "I usually go ahead and buckle Faith in his car, then close the car doors so I can have it out with Xavier. We usually have a ten-minute tit-for-tat before he drives off. This time, nothing."

"God's got you. You know that."

"That's true," Sherri said, backing out of the space. We headed back in the direction of her apartment, but less than two minutes into the short ride, she must've needed to let loose. She hit the steering wheel.

"Can I take off my spiritual hat for a minute?" she said. "I need to vent."

"All ears," I said.

"For the life of me I can't see why Xavier constantly complains about his court-appointed child support payments, but last month he bought a brand spanking new car. Not a used car. As far as I know, his other Mustang was working perfectly fine."

I wasn't sure if she wanted me to respond, so I didn't say a word. I actually didn't want her to ask my opinion, because it was probably something that she didn't want to hear. But then she asked me. So I had to tell her.

"Isn't that crazy to you?"

I sighed. I didn't want to say anything to ground a friendship that was just starting to take off.

"I want the truth. You don't have to dress things up for me."

Since she insisted, I gave it to her. "The truth is that he doesn't owe you an explanation if he wants to buy a car off the used or the new car lot. It's his prerogative, and it's his money. You share a child, not a bank account. As long as he's making his child support payments, let it go."

"You've got some sass in you, Sheila," Sherri said.

"More than you know," I said. I smoothed out my pant leg. "I haven't always been this put together."

Sherri looked thoughtful. "My main concern should be about Faith's safety. Xavier's parental monitor is virtually nonexistent. I mean he has no regard about the kinds of movies and music that are appropriate for a child. I feel like I spend ninety percent of my time praying when Faith is away with Xavier."

"So if nothing else, Xavier has increased your prayer life," I said. I was doing one of Eden's moves, trying to find the best in everything.

"I can tell Eden's starting to rub off on you," Sherri said, like she was reading my mind.

"That's a good thing to know," I said.

"Next thing you know, God will send you a man ten times your size."

"Hey, if that's the way God wants to do it, then I'll take it. I'm not locked into getting six feet, a six pack, and six figures." I looked out the window. "Anymore." I paused.

"Throw some of your prayer on me again, then," Sherri said. "Because I'm still stuck there."

"Girl, at this point in life, we need to be praying for each other," I said. My cell phone rang, and I saw that it was Cassandra. I almost ignored her call, but since she was the kind of person who would call and tell me that my belongings were sitting on the street, I answered.

"Hey, Sheila. I need your help."

It was the first time we'd talked since she'd kicked me out, and she didn't ask how I was doing or if I was all right. I decided to steer the conversation and get us off to a better start.

"Hi, Cassandra. How you doing?"

"Not good. That's why I need your help," she said.

Some things were a waste of time. Trying to get Cassandra to be polite and considerate of others was one of them.

"Frank left Eric here because someone called him and wanted to meet last minute about an art showing. If it hadn't been for the fact that this could mean some serious money for him, I would've said no. But money for him means money for me, if you know what I'm saying."

"I guess," I said.

"Anyway, he's stuck across town, which means I need to meet Eric's mama to drop him off. We got outside, and my car won't start. It won't even jump start."

"So what are you asking me?" I said.

"To pick us up so I can get Eric to his mama. This boy is getting on my last nerve."

Cassandra had kicked me out of her house without a second thought, and now she was pleading for my help. I could've hung up in her face. I thought about doing it. Then I decided to be the bigger woman.

"I'll be there as soon as I can," I said.

When I hung up the phone, Sherri said, "It sounds like you have new plans."

"Yes. I have to take a rain check. I hope you and Anisha don't mind. I feel bad about it."

We were supposed to be headed back over to Anisha's for Chinese takeout and a movie while Sherri updated Anisha on the baby shower plans.

"Are you sure I didn't run you away with my baby daddy drama?" Sherri asked.

"Trust me. I've seen worse. Way worse. I just need to help Cassandra."

Sherri's eyebrows lifted in question. I'd filled her in on the turn of events.

"If that's the case, I won't hold you hostage," she said, she rerouted our direction so I could go back to Sherri's boutique and pick up my car.

Think on the positive things, I reminded myself on the drive over to Cassandra's. At least I could pick up a few more of my things.

I couldn't imagine what the evening had in store. I'd said I was going to let my evenings flow. I just hoped the current wasn't pulling me into rough waters.

Chapter 51

I don't want to kill the woman, but I wouldn't mind hurting her real bad," Cassandra said. "I'll do whatever it takes to keep me out of one of those orange prisoner's suits, but I'll let her know she's messing with the wrong one."

I turned around to look at Frank's son, Eric, in the back seat. It was a good thing his headphones were blocking his ears from Cassandra's comments. He was so entranced by one of those portable games that he probably didn't know the car was stopped. I'd never known Cassandra to play surrogate mother to anybody's child.

Cassandra was tapping her nails on the door handle and mumbling more trash under her breath. *Has she always been this crazy?* I thought. *Yes, she has,* I decided. And if the saying was true that birds of a feather flock together, then I probably had some dormant craziness in my system, too. Crazy was the only thing that would've gotten me into this situation. Maybe I *should* have ignored Cassandra's call. I'd rather be talking about one of those silly baby shower games or discussing colors of streamers and balloons.

But I had a front row seat to some foolishness.

Cassandra was seething. "That woman gets on my nerves," she said, rolling her eyes. "Tangela's late just to spite me."

"She's only ten minutes late. This is Atlanta. Traffic can change anybody's schedule."

"Whose side are you on?" Cassandra looked at me like I'd slapped her. "Whenever Frank is one second late with anything concerning Eric, she's blowing up his phone like it's a world crisis."

This was the second episode of baby mama/daddy drama that I'd endured over the past hour. If God was trying to tell me something, His voice was speaking loud and clear. Keep myself pure until I'm married so I can cut down the probability of all of this drama happening to me.

Cassandra had stopped fussing and was reapplying a coat of lip gloss. I knew why. She was making it a point to look better than the woman she considered her competition. Why else would she have changed out of perfectly presentable yoga pants and a baby doll tee, and into a pair of black hip hugging jeans and a blouse with a plunging neckline?

"I don't know how I'm going to get her yet, but she's not going to be the last one standing in this bout. I'll guarantee that." Cassandra puckered her lips and kissed at herself in the visor mirror. "I thought I'd almost met my match, then I reached down further in my guts and found some more arsenal."

I looked at my watch to see how long it would be before I could escape. "One day you're going to have to stand before God and be accountable for your actions."

"My goodness, Sheila," Cassandra huffed. "One day is not *today*. My grandma used to talk about Jesus coming back one day soon, and she was still waiting the day she died."

"I'm just saying maybe you should replace your crazy with prayer."

"Girl, who are you?" She pinched my arm. "Is this a clone? Bring my girl back. Bring my ride-or-die chick back. We're supposed to take over the world. I can't do that with a missionary as a sidekick."

"This is the new and improved me," I said.

"'New' is right. But I don't know about 'improved.'"

I thought about the things I could say. But then I thought about where an argument with Cassandra might take me. I was supposed be showing her the light, trying to be an example so she would want to experience the love I had. I kept my mouth shut.

"Finally," Cassandra said when an older model Jeep Cherokee pulled up beside us. The navy blue paint job had faded, and I could tell by the smoke puffing out of the back tailpipe that it had seen better days.

"My mama," Eric screamed. Cassandra seemed annoyed by his excitement to see his own mother, but she still couldn't wait to see him go. She hit the automatic door lock and, instead of getting out of the car to help him with his things, let down the back window and told his mother, "The rest of his stuff is in the trunk."

I heard the trunk latch pop, and Eric's mother unloaded a week's worth of clothes, toys, and odds and ends before dumping them back into her own trunk.

"Ready to go, babe?" she asked Eric.

Tangela and Cassandra hadn't exchanged cordial pleasantries. Only scowls. But her face transformed when it came to her son. She picked him up and squeezed him like he was a six-month-old baby.

"Daddy said he's coming to spend the night tomorrow," Eric announced.

My mouth dropped. I knew it was about to be on.

"Yes. He told me. And we're going to have soooo much fun," she emphasized, cutting her eyes at Cassandra. She'd just delivered her enemy a blind uppercut, and she knew it. "Get in the car, baby. I think we'll have pizza tonight for dinner."

"I know that little boy just didn't say what I think he said." Cassandra was still recovering. "Please tell me, he didn't say—"

"Yes, he said it," I confirmed. "And you don't have to let Frank do you like that."

Cassandra was ignoring my affirmations. She probably couldn't see me because I swear I saw smoke puffing from her nose like a raging bull. She got out of the car, and I put up all of the windows to shut out the drama.

Chapter 52

There was a key on the bed in the guestroom when I arrived back at Eden's. She'd told me that she and Bear wouldn't be there tonight because she was forcing him to go to a play at the Rialto Theater. He struggled through watching stage plays about as much as she struggled through watching golf on Sundays, she'd said. Eden said she plugged her ears with an audio book while she watched television, but I imagine there wasn't much poor Bear could do from front row seats.

I'd watched my own drama that evening and I was relieved the show was over. Tangela had finally gotten in her car and driven away, leaving Cassandra seething and still cursing after her. She had jumped in the car like we were about to go on police highway pursuit, but then she realized that I was the driver, thus in control. As soon as I dropped her off, she'd stomped into the house without saying much else.

I picked up the note on the bed.

You can stay here as long as you need, but if you need your own piece of space you're welcome to stay at our family home. Rent free, of course. It's waiting for you if you want it. Feel free to ride by tonight or I can take you on Monday.

Eden had written the address and directions on the back of the page. I was floored. Eden has such a kind heart. Of course it was an offer I hadn't expected, and I was trying to fight off the voice telling me that I was being a burden. I thought it would be best if I waited for Eden to go to the home with me, so I settled downstairs with the novel that Sherri wanted to present during our first book club meet-and-greet.

Before I read the first sentence, Clive called. It looked like he wasn't going to let up until he talked to me. Cassandra said he'd popped up at her place yesterday afternoon when Frank happened to be there. Of course Frank had told Clive that I'd been kicked out, and I could imagine he added his own mix of lies and exaggerations to the story.

I admit it. I was running from Clive. It wasn't about the money. It was about *that* night.

I answered the call, since I'd eventually have to face Clive anyway.

"You had me worried," he said.

"I don't believe you."

"You don't have to believe me for it to be true."

"I'm fine," I said. "Great is more like it."

"So where are you staying?"

"With a friend."

Clive paused. "A friend?"

"Yes," I said. It wasn't his business who. I imagine his mind was going a million different places.

"You know you can always stay with me," Clive said.

"I won't be staying there again," I said. "And what happened between us . . . will *never* happen again."

"You sound so sure."

"I am. *Never* again."

"I've learned to never say never," Clive said.

I wasn't open to taking any of his advice any more. In fact, as soon as I'd done a sufficient amount of work for him, I planned on staying as far away from Clive as possible in case my hormones found a way to influence my better judgment.

"Don't worry. I'm not going to run away from our deal," I said. "I'll help you until my debt to you is settled."

Clive chuckled like I'd insulted him with my effort to repay the money I owed.

"I'm not worried about that," he said. "I've got bigger things to take up my time and thoughts. Much bigger things."

Chapter 53

Silk pajamas. On Monday morning Clive came to the door wearing doggone blue silk pajamas that were embroidered with his initials on the shirt pocket. He and Gina were two peas in a pod. They were made for each other whether Clive wanted to admit it or not.

"What are you doing here?" I asked. "Shouldn't you be at work?"

"I am at work," he said.

He was definitely doing something. There were papers spread on the floor in front of the television, and a paper plate on the coffee table with bread crusts and the remains of what looked like an omelet.

Clive eyed me from head to toe. I crossed my arms and eyed him right back. If he knew what was good for him, he'd take a longer, harder look. He was about to be history in my life, and there wouldn't be too many chances to take all of *this* in.

"I had my own business to take care of this morning before I went to go work for the man," Clive said. "I'll be out of here before lunch time," he said, kneeling down to clean up his mess.

I would, too. Eden was taking me to see the house when she closed the bookstore for lunch. I went to Clive's office and tuned the radio to the gospel station. The DJ was playing yet another great hit by Mary Mary, and I was feeling this one.

"How are you gonna get down like that to some church music?" Clive asked as he passed by the office.

"I'm getting my praise on. Leave me alone," I said, shooing him away. I threw my hands above my head and started clapping.

"I'll leave you to your church service." Clive was practically screaming now because I'd turned up the music to run him out. I cranked out two hours of uninterrupted work and still hadn't heard a peep from Clive.

All of the lights were turned off throughout the house, but Clive had opened up all of the window treatments to let the natural light inside. From the hallway I could hear his muffled voice in his bedroom. I walked back to let Clive know I was leaving.

I hesitantly knocked on the door, hoping that he wouldn't open it and be standing in all of his glory. After a few moments, the door swung open. I instinctively turned my head in case Clive was, in fact, in his birthday suit. I wouldn't put it past him.

"I wanted to let you know I was leaving," I said. I turned to look at him once I could see out of my peripheral vision that he was fully clothed. He was on the phone. He nodded at me and followed me down the hall. His voice sounded drained.

"You're the one who's confused. You don't know if you want to be with me because you love me, or because you think I'm with somebody else. I know you, Gina. You've always kept tally of your victories. I'm not one of your legal cases."

When I reached for the door Clive put a hand on my shoulder to stop me. He paced around in the living room then sat on the arm of the couch. I could tell he'd been in the process of getting ready for work before he took the phone call. Only half of his beard was shaven. He rubbed his fingers across the stubbly side.

"We turned into business partners, not lovers," Clive said. "How long did you think we were going to last like that?"

I felt like I shouldn't be hearing this conversation. If Gina knew I was here, it would probably crush a heart that was already aching. Now I knew why she'd seemed so solemn that day at Sherri's boutique. She wanted her husband back, and she thought I had him. I'd felt the pull so strong for her that day, because she was at the place where I'd once been with Ace. Wanting more of a man than he was willing to give.

Clive huffed. "Look, I'll call you back later." Pause. "No. That's not a good idea." Pause. "I will." Pause. "Don't worry about that. I'll make sure we're covered."

He hung up the phone without saying good-bye. I hate it when men do that.

I doubt Clive is the kind of man to cry over a woman, but I could tell that Gina was wearing on him emotionally.

"Tell me you don't love her," I said to Clive. It wasn't my place to intrude, but he'd brought me into the conversation. "Tell me you don't love Gina, and I'll tell you that you *might* have a justifiable reason not to try again. But if you still love her, you can make it work."

Miraculously, I was giving Clive advice from a situation that had caused *me* pain. Ace and Lynette had made it work after being divorced for four years. Clive and Gina's divorce wasn't even final.

"Since when did you become Gina's advocate?" Clive asked.

My hand was still holding the door. It was like I needed the knob for moral support. I didn't want to leave his house thinking about what I should've said. Sometimes comments never seem to have the same impact once you've kept them to yourself for so long. I could tell God was pushing me forward. I preferred to stay out of Clive and Gina's business, but God wouldn't let me keep my lips sealed.

"My pastor was talking one night at Bible study about having faith that's the size of a mustard seed. That can move mountains. Don't you think love that's the size of a mustard seed might be able to move mountains, too?" I don't know if that analogy made biblical sense, but I think I got my point across.

"Maybe."

That's all Clive said. I'd said all I needed to say, too.

"I'll finish up what's left tomorrow and then come back twice a week for three more weeks," I said matter-of-factly. "Can we call it even after that?"

"Yes," he said, though I don't think Clive was completely listening to me. Maybe his conscience was talking to him. I bet it sounded a lot like God's voice.

Chapter 54

Eden opened the front door to her family home and stepped back so that I could walk in first. I think she wanted me to feel the impact of the house. To breathe in everything that it represented. To assure me that this indeed would be a place of peace for me, and not just somewhere that she was dumping me so that she and Bear wouldn't have to deal with my company.

Love lived here. I could tell that it had worked in that very kitchen. I could tell it must've had intimate conversations on the couches or lit freshly chopped wood in the well-used fireplace. One entire wall was like looking through the pages of a family scrap-book. Most of the pictures had a familiar backdrop—the front porch of this very home.

"There have always been pictures taken of the family and friends who've visited here over the years," Eden explained. "Whether they were just passing through or given a place to lay their head, everyone has become a part of this home. Now it's your turn."

"I haven't even known you long enough for you to do something like this for me," I said. I felt the need to try and rationalize her generosity. "You don't even know me."

"But I know God's voice when He speaks to me," Eden said, gently touching her hand to her heart. "Sometimes the way God connects people can transcend the time they've known each other. The morning you left to go to Ace's wedding, did you have any idea that we would meet the way we did?"

"No, of course not," I said.

"You didn't, but God did. So just sit back and let Him do His work. You're in a season of transition in your life, and there's no sense trying to fight it." She refolded a quilt that was stuffed in a huge wicker basket beside the sofa. "I once heard a wise preacher say that crisis is change trying to take place. You may in fact be in a crisis in your life, but you better believe you're being changed, too."

"Stop trying to make me cry," I said. "I think you like seeing me slobber like a baby."

"No," Eden said, "but I do like seeing you cleansed and set free."

I followed Eden back through the rest of the house. The hallway that fed off of the living room led to three bedrooms. The house looked deceivingly small from the outside, but it was longer than it was wide. The high ceilings, wooden baseboards, and crown molding gave it that much more flavor.

"You can use this as your master room," she said, pushing back the door of the largest room. And the other rooms you can use for storage so you don't have to keep paying fees for the public storage unit."

"I have tons of stuff," I said, thinking about my storage unit, which was packed to maximum capacity.

"Then it's a good thing we have plenty of space. You can close the door to those spare rooms, and no one will even know what's in there," Eden said. "And before you start to worry about it, I've already asked Bear to help get your things moved. He and a few other men from the church do this sort of thing all the time," she said. "They need to get some use out of their trucks besides washing and waxing them all the time."

Bear had told me the story of how he and his friends all ended up buying double-cab trucks after their wives refused to let them buy motorcycles.

"Do you know how ridiculous Bear would look on a motorcycle?" Eden had asked. "Like a grizzly riding a scooter."

When we walked out onto the back deck, one of the neighbors peeked his head between some stalks of corn in his garden and waved at Eden.

"How are you doing there, Eden?" he said. He used his forearm to brush the sweat from his brow, then set a shovel against the gate beside his other garden tools.

"Hi, Mr. Barron," Eden said. "Even as hot as it is today, I'm not surprised to see you out here."

I followed her down the side steps. That's when I noticed another oasis hidden under the red stained deck—an alcove of sorts. There was a stand-hammock on one end, and in the middle of the layout there was a table with a set of chairs. By now I knew Eden's taste when I saw it.

Mr. Barron came into the yard and stomped some of the dirt off his feet. "The wife kicks me out early every morning so she can enjoy her cup of coffee and watch her favorite preacher lady on television," he said. "I've got to do something with my time until the sun goes down and she unlocks the door to let me back in," he joked.

"I think it's a good thing she locks you out," Eden said. "Look at your garden. Tomatoes. Cucumbers. Corn. And I know I saw some watermelons. How would we eat if she didn't put you out the house?"

"I've been able to do a little something with this Georgia clay," Mr. Barron said, though his chest was puffed out from the compliment.

Eden turned toward me. "Sorry for being so rude," she said. "Sheila, this is Mr. Barron. Mr. Barron, Sheila will be staying here for a while. I know you'll keep an eye out for her."

"I knew it was about time to have another guest," Mr. Barron said with a crooked smile.

He was missing two teeth—one in the top left corner of his mouth and another in the bottom right.

"If you need anything, don't hesitate to come ask me," Mr. Barron said. "This neighborhood is relatively quiet, but we always look out for each other. Make sure you let me and the missus have all of your numbers in case we see something strange at the house. I ain't nosy, but I do a whole lot of watchin'," he said.

We all laughed. All of this felt so right to me. Eden and I walked over to admire Mr. Barron's garden. I was tempted ask him about his interesting choices for flower pots, but thought I'd better wait until we knew a little more about each other. For the life of me I couldn't figure out why he had a set of three white toilets lined up with daffodils, begonias, and another yellow flower with huge petals in them. He told me everything about the flowers, but nothing about the toilets. Eden didn't either. She was probably so used to seeing them by now that she didn't notice them anymore.

It was easy to overlook things that you were used to.

Mama could probably attest to that. I think her junk was multiplying. I went to her house after leaving Eden and Mr. Barron behind.

"Don't you look nice today," I said to Mama. She'd actually put together an outfit that I would've chosen for her. Now that I think about it, it was one of the outfits I'd gotten for her.

246

"I knew you were coming over, so I wanted to look my best. You know how you turn your nose up when I wear some of my clothes."

"Not all of them," I said. "Just the ones that need to be in the trash."

Mama rolled her eyes. "Are you hungry?" she asked. "I ate some rotisserie chicken and some fruit that Devin bought for me from the grocery store. Can you believe he did a little shopping?"

I nearly fell over. Devin rarely contributed anything to the household.

"Really? Is he working now?"

"Him and Fontaine took some things down to the flea market this past weekend," she said. "I told you we had plans for this stuff." Mama pointed to her priceless collections. I had to eat a piece of humble pie, though. Devin—for once—had proved me wrong.

"He's taking those boxes on Saturday," she said, pointing at a stack in the hallway.

I assumed she meant the leaning tower that was threatening the life of her little toe.

But right now I could care less about those boxes. The name Fontaine brought some buried feelings back up to the surface. It was clear that I hadn't totally dealt with them.

But I'd get the chance today. Devin pushed open the screen door and walked in. With Fontaine behind him.

Chapter 55

The hood girl from seventh grade almost rose up in me. Fontaine tried to hug me like he'd found his long-lost sister. I wanted to smack him. But I was sophisticated now, and Jesus lived in me. I don't think God would approve of me smacking his pitted cheek with all the strength I could muster.

Fontaine used to be nice looking, but his looks had slid down like mud on a hill. Of course youthfulness can only carry a person so far, but old age hadn't caused Fontaine's downward spiral. Smoking and drinking had. I could smell the residue of both on his clothes and on his breath.

I blocked Fontaine's embrace with my forearm and put the force of a NFL linebacker against his chest.

"Dang, girl. You got some guns," he said, pushing on my biceps. "You straight blocked a brother from getting some love."

I put out my hand for him to shake. He took it, but I could tell he was expecting me to break out at any minute and tell him I was joking. No chance of that.

"Long time, no see," I said.

"Too long," Fontaine said. "Looking like a million dollars. Life must be treating you right. Rolling in a big baller Lexus and what not. Fresh, def, like a million bucks. Isn't that what that rapper used to say?"

"God's good," I said, spouting a religious cliché.

"All right. All right. Got God up in your life, too. Ain't nothing wrong with that." Fontaine threw his hands up in the air and cocked his head skyward. "Amen, saints," he said.

He and Devin laughed at his foolishness. I wasn't amused.

"Stop acting up, boy," Mama said. "Sheila is not in the mood to be playing with you."

Actually I was in a spectacular mood, but at least Mama had stepped in to get Fontaine off my back.

Devin added his two cents. "Sheila's always got something wrong with her," he had the nerve to say.

I ignored Devin. He was probably still bitter that I'd let him roast in jail until Mama came up with some money. I had never asked where she got the money. I didn't want to know.

"So what's really been going on with you, Sheila?" Fontaine asked.

He ignored the family tension. He'd been around it so much that he was oblivious to me and Devin's sibling spats. He had two older brothers of his own, so I knew he was used to it.

"I thought you'd be married by now," Fontaine said. "The last I heard you were seeing some pilot or something."

"Old boy flew out of her life," Devin answered.

"That means there's room for me," Fontaine said. He stretched his arms out like he was a prize package.

"Not in your dreams," I said.

I didn't want to crack a grin at him, but Fontaine was standing there looking so goofy that I couldn't help it.

"I'm waiting for a real man who knows how to handle his business, knows how to treat a queen, and first and foremost loves God. If you don't have all three of those—in the least—then you need not apply," I said.

"Excuse me, Queen Sheila," Fontaine said.

He removed his baseball cap, wrapped an arm around his midsection, and bowed as close to the ground as his inflexible body would allow. He stumbled to the side, and Devin caught his arm before he fell onto a stack of Mama's "historical" magazines.

"Got the blood rushing to my head, girl," he said, steadying himself.

"It's something rushing to your head all right," I said. "But it ain't blood."

I didn't even notice that Mama had disappeared from the kitchen. Devin started directing Fontaine to some boxes that he wanted him to load in his truck, while my brother hoisted some others from the hallway and took them out. Even though it wasn't quite what I wanted Devin to do with his time, at least he had a *legal* hustle. There were a few times in his life when I knew his money was questionable, but me and Mama had turned a blind eye to them.

I'd prayed for God to light a match under Devin's behind, but it wasn't up to me how that was going to be done. I also would've chosen a different business partner for him, but God has a reason for everything. Maybe the sole reason was for me and Fontaine to cross paths so that I could dump another piece of baggage.

I peeked in on Mama, who was taking a nap in her bedroom. Devin had disappeared into the bathroom, and since he'd been gone for at least five minutes, I knew I had some time to confront Fontaine.

I found him outside smoking a cigarette and leaning up against a rusty pickup truck that was just as run down as he. When I saw the faded silhouette of some downtown Atlanta skyscrapers painted across the bottom, I realized it was the same truck he'd driven in high school. My Lexus, freshly washed and waxed—compliments of Bear—was parked beside it. No wonder he thought I was a "big baller." But looks were deceiving. Fontaine's ride was paid for, and he didn't have to worry about the repo man.

Fontaine snuffed out his cigarette on the bottom of his shoe when he noticed me. He blew smoke rings into the air and took a sip from the soda can sitting on the hood. I started right in on him before he had a chance to try and be a stand-up comedian or something.

"I'm at a point in my life where I'm assessing my past mistakes," I explained. "I've been looking at the things—and people—in the past that have shaped my life for the better or for the worse." I took a deep breath. "You were one of the people who shaped me for the worse. You scarred me, and I tried to move on without ever forgiving you."

Fontaine tried to say something. I felt like he was going to try and justify what he had done. Tell me that it had been a mutual decision and that we were hormonal teenagers looking for the same thing. Who knows? At that time, maybe I actually had been looking for love, but I had wanted to give it willfully, not have it taken away.

"We both know what really happened. But today I choose to leave the past behind. To give it over to God and pray that one day you'll take this journey that I'm on, too."

I turned around when the patio door squeaked open. Devin walked out with a hand towel sitting on top of his head. "And that's all I have to say," I said, going back inside to get my purse and say good-bye to Mama.

Fontaine was standing there with a blank look on his face, but I, on the other hand, was smiling. There's nothing like being free.

Chapter 56

I loved waking up weekday mornings and going to work—although being at Eden's bookstore wasn't work for me. It was life. I'd been at Eden's Gates all week after Bear convinced Eden to spend some time with him this week doing absolutely nothing. For handing over the reins to the bookstore, Eden made Bear promise that he'd indulge her with a country-style breakfast on her days off, and take her shoe shopping. He'd agreed.

I printed out flyers and an interest sheet for people who wanted to sign up for our book club's meet-and-greet. Sherri and I had decided the best thing to do for the book club would be to get everyone's input on the book selections, and then we'd also have a chance to feel out each other's personalities. It seemed simple enough to me. Eden was going to provide her specialty lemonade and give us freedom to use the bookstore whenever we needed. And for our first meeting, Sherri and I were going to chip in on the light hors d'oeuvres.

I counted down the register, completed doing the required paperwork, then walked to the back room so I could lock the safe. I yawned loudly and drew it out, the way my grandma used to do after the late-night news and she was headed to bed. Mr. Sandman had first tapped on my shoulder at four o'clock, but now at almost seven o'clock, he was riding on my back.

The clock on the microwave in the back office said it was 6:49 p.m. I never left a minute before it was time because I owed Eden a full day's work. I waited until the last chord of what had become one of my favorite Be Be and Ce Ce Winans' songs faded out before I turned off the overhead radio system. It was an upgrade, Bear's gift to replace the ancient radio that Eden used to hide behind a plant in the music section.

I walked out from the back, caught up in my version of the Winans' song. It might have been a joyful noise to God's ears, but that was the only person who would've enjoyed it.

Then I froze.

I'd already locked the back office, and I knew there was no way for me to fumble through Eden's circle of keys in time to barricade myself in the room. Not the way my hands trembled.

Eden's son was behind the counter, and I could tell he was surprised to see me instead of his mama. He turned away from me and frantically hit the buttons on the cash register. When it didn't open, he beat the side of it with his fist. Cursed at it. He turned back to me with an expression of desperation. I didn't like the look in his eyes. The hairs on the back of my neck stood up.

Think. I made myself think. This wasn't the time to freeze.

When I saw him come from behind the cash register like he was going to block the door, I hurried toward the front of the store and the full wall of windows so I could put myself in the sight of others. People were always strolling by on their way to eat wings or drop off clothes at the dry cleaners, although now not a single person was to be found.

But me. And him.

"Good evening," my voice quivered. "Can I help you?" Stupid. That was a stupid thing to say.

"Where's my ma? Eden Mayfield," he said.

"I assume she's at home right now, but she'll be here tomorrow," I said. "Maybe you can come back then."

"I can't wait until tomorrow." He was standing in front of me before I had the chance to react. "I need money now."

"Eden will be here. Tomorrow. I'm sure she—"

He yanked at my purse, but it was strapped securely around my neck so that it hung across my shoulders and by my side. I'd paid good money for this purse. It was going to take a team of horses to snap the strap. He pulled at it again, and I snatched it back.

"No," I screamed. I probably bared fangs because I was up for a fight. I knew all of the rules. You should give up your purse. Give up the keys to your car. But I didn't see any signs of a weapon, so the worst I could get was bruised up. Bruises could heal before an empty wallet could. I still had some of the money Clive had given me for housesitting because I'd procrastinated about going to the bank.

We played tug-of-war with my purse until I caught him off guard and I muscled enough strength to sling him into the door. Adrenaline was on my side. He fell into the door with a thud. It was like one of the climax scenes in an action movie. I was impressed with my skills. And I was out of breath.

And just like the movie villain, he found the strength and drive he needed to pull himself up and lunge toward me again.

Chapter 57

Evidently his drugged-up stupor had impaired his judgment and agility because I easily dodged him and he slammed into the front counter. He grabbed his head, and I bolted for the door. I was running out just as Kenyatta from next door was coming in. I pushed her outside and pushed the glass door closed.

"Help me hold the door," I screamed. I miraculously put the right key in the lock on the first try and dead-bolted Eden's son inside. At least that's who I'd been assuming he was.

"Sheila, what in the world?" Kenyatta said, her back against the door and her feet soundly planted on the sidewalk.

Kenyatta was the kind of person you need on your side in the event of an emergency. She didn't try to get all of the facts; she just did what she was told.

"It's Eden's son," I said, catching my breath. "He's gone crazy. He tried to break into the cash register, and then he tried to steal my purse."

"Don't just stand there," Kenyatta said. "Call the police."

"Call the police?"

"Call the police!" she insisted. She pushed her face against the window and shielded her eyes so that she could see inside. "Yes, that's him. That's Romando. You should've let him have the purse. He could've hurt you. You could've replaced everything in there."

"I wasn't thinking rationally."

"Got that right," Kenyatta said.

The dispatcher said the police were on the way. I hated having to make the call. If Eden put me out for calling the law on her son—before I had the chance to even move in—I was going to make Kenyatta put a mat for me on her living room floor.

Romando hammered on the windows and door like he was a wild animal.

"As soon as things look like they're turning around for that boy, things take a turn for the worse," Kenyatta said. "Eden has sacrificed so much for Romando."

Romando. Now I had a name to put with the face. Kenyatta was looking through the window at him like he was a human art exhibit, but I was busy calling Eden.

Two teenage boys who were walking by slowed down in front of the bookstore.

"Mind your business," Kenyatta told them and held her arms out like the span of her two arms was going to prevent them from seeing in.

"Eden," I said. "There's been a situation at the store with your son. You might want to come up here."

"Uh-oh," Kenyatta said. "This is going to be a bad day for Romando. He better pray Bear doesn't come."

Romando had stopped beating the window. I take it he was smart enough to know that his actions were only drawing attention to himself and that there was nothing he could do about the situation he'd gotten himself in. On top of that, I believe he was straining to hear what me and Kenyatta were saying.

Fifteen minutes after I called, Bear and Eden arrived at the bookstore, where me and Kenyatta were still waiting for the police. Eden opened the door before their car was barely at a complete stop.

"You don't know how sorry I am," Eden said. "This is truly embarrassing, and this is not the way Romando was raised. Not only did he try to steal from me, but he tried to rob you?" She placed her palm across her forehead like the reality of it all had brought on a migraine. I could tell she'd already been crying.

When I handed Eden the key, Bear stepped out of the car. He was moving slowly, as if he were calculating each step—calming himself before he did or said something that he'd regret later.

Romando was no longer in plain sight. Maybe he'd done like everybody else who loved the store, and gone to take a nap on the sofa in the back.

I didn't want to stay, but I knew the police would want to talk to me.

"If Sheila wants to press charges it might help us get Romando into mandatory rehab. We've got to do something, Eden."

Eden looked ready to break down in tears.

"I'm not going to press charges," I said. I didn't know if I could, seeing that Romando hadn't actually gotten away with anything. On top of that, I didn't want to see Eden wilt before my eyes.

Eden walked over to me and picked up my hands, held them inside of hers. "You're still moving into the home Saturday, right? I don't want you to think our family is so dysfunctional and you'll be in danger if you're around us."

"I don't think that at all," I assured her. "Every family is dysfunctional in their own way. Half of us just don't want to admit it. If I told you about my family, you wouldn't feel so bad."

"I *know* my family is dysfunctional," Kenyatta chimed in. "I don't even claim half of them because they're so crazy."

The after-work crowd would be coming soon, and I was sure there was something Kenyatta could do to help the cook dice, slice, or prepare. Drop some wings. Season the fries. Anything but watch Eden and her family like they were a soap opera.

"I think I need a slice of red velvet cake to go with my wings," I said to Kenyatta. I hooked my arm through hers and led her back to the wing shop. I could wait there until the police arrived and while Eden and Bear dealt with their son.

Eden finally unlocked the door, and Bear walked in behind her. I heard the lock click.

"Bear is probably going to beat that boy like he's a child instead of a grown man."

"Mind your business, Kenyatta," I said, even though I snickered.

"Beat him straight down to the altar, I bet," Kenyatta said.

I didn't leave for Cassandra's until an hour later. The policeman tried to use his scare tactics to whip Romando into shape, but I had a feeling he'd heard it all before. At any rate, Romando still left with his parents, and I went to pack and prep my boxes for the move on Saturday. Eden assured me that Romando wasn't coming to their home until after I moved out. Bear looked like he wouldn't have cared if the boy were chained to a fence somewhere.

I wanted everything organized so that all Bear and the other men had to do was pick up the boxes and load them onto their trucks. When I had called to make sure I wasn't disrupting any of Cassandra's plans, she'd informed me that she was going to an after-work mixer with some colleagues from the job. Maybe this time she'd truly moved on from Frank—but I hoped for her sake that she didn't walk back into a revolving door of relationships.

"By the way," I had said to her, "we're having Family and Friends Day at the church in a couple of weeks. I'd love it if you'd come join me."

"Now you know I'm not a holy roller."

"Neither am I," I had said.

"Not yet, but you may well be on your way."

"I guess if you had to call me something, a holy roller isn't so bad. There are plenty of things worse than that you could call me."

Cassandra had laughed. "I might have called you those things, too. Just not to your face."

"I can always count on you to tell me the truth," I had said.

"The truth and nothing but the truth, so help me God."

"Oh," I had said, "so you admit that you do need God's help. That's why you need to come to church with me."

"Quick thinker," Cassandra had said. "But it's not going to work. I have too much of my life to live for me to settle down with a bunch of religious rules and hypocrites."

I had heard noises in the background like Cassandra was opening and closing cabinet doors in the kitchen. If I knew Cassandra, she had been fixing her own cocktails to enjoy before she actually arrived at the mixer.

"Will you at least consider it?" I had asked her, giving it one more try. I didn't want to belabor the point and turn her off completely.

"Are there any cute men there? I mean manly men. You know what I mean."

"A lot of them," I had said. That wasn't the feature that I wanted her to focus on, but if it got her in the doors, God would do the rest.

"Well, I'll consider it then. Call and remind me." Cassandra had added quickly, "But I'm not making any promises."

By the time I arrived at Cassandra's, she was already gone. I took the liberty to write a reminder about Family and Friends Day and post it on her refrigerator. Every time she opened the door for a snack, she'd see my bright red reminder on the piece of yellow legal paper. If she thought she was living good now, just wait until God was in her life.

Chapter 58

I felt like Mama. Maybe I was a hoarder, too and had never realized it. I didn't remember having so much stuff. I'd already purged a lot of things when I'd moved from my condo to Cassandra's apartment, but it still looked like so much.

Bear and the other two men from the church had been working most of the morning to move my furniture from the storage unit and into the house. It was the solid, heavy furniture that required brute and brawn to lift. There were two things I believed were worth money well spent—clothes and furniture. With both, you got what you paid for.

"I hope you have some muscle rub in one of these boxes," Bear joked. They'd carefully and skillfully maneuvered my chest of drawers through the front door without a single scratch on my furniture or on the doorframe.

"I don't think so, but I'll be happy to run to the drugstore if you need me to," I said. I'd already been thinking that the men were going to need some of that or a good alcohol rubdown before it was over.

Sherri came outside carrying some bottles of cold water. She'd ask Anisha to watch both her boutique and Faith this morning so that she could help me organize and unpack some of my things. I'd already wanted to take a break at least three times, but Sherri kept the assignment moving forward.

"Bear, I think you're going to need prayer more than some muscle rub," Sherri said.

Bear downed his entire bottle of water without coming up for air. "What we need are some men with younger minds and younger bodies to join our moving team," he told everybody. "My nephew was going to try and help us if he could. It was my fault for calling him at the last minute," Bear said, huffing. Sherri tossed him another bottle of water. "He worked part time for a moving company when he was in college. He knows all the tricks of the trade."

After he caught his breath, Bear stood up and twisted to each side to crack his back. "Up and at 'em fellas. We can take two of the trucks and finish this off."

He picked up two more water bottles and strolled to the truck. I didn't think he had a limp before, but now he was favoring his right side when he walked. He was going to return home to Eden injured, and it was all my fault.

I felt bad. I actually might have to pick up some Ben-Gay and a bottle of ibuprofen before they get back. They left in Bear's truck and one of the other men's, and Sherri shooed me back inside.

"If you get the bedroom in order, you'll feel and rest a lot better," she instructed.

Since there was already a queen-sized bed in the room, I merely changed the sheets to one of my personal sets. I always feel better rolling around on my own linens.

I knew the next task at hand because Sherri was staring at the wall of shoeboxes. "You can't be serious about having this many shoes." She flipped open a few box tops. "A pair of black sandals with three straps. Black gladiator-style sandals. A black sandal with a kitten heel."

"What? A girl needs options."

"This many options?" she said, laughing. "I used to think I was bad, but you have me beat by a long shot. You're in another league, girlfriend."

Shoes have always made me feel like a wealthy woman. I bought shoes to celebrate. I bought shoes to comfort an aching heart. I even bought shoes the day I received the lay-off notice from my last job.

"I'd tell you that you could borrow some anytime, but your foot is miniature compared to mine," I said to Sherri.

"Borrow? Girl, you don't need to let anybody borrow these shoes. You need to let them buy them. I know you've said things are a little tight for you right now, but you have no reason to be broke."

"What are you saying?" I asked.

I could identify most of my shoes and the occasion for which I bought them simply by looking at the box. I picked up a shiny red box. It was a four-inch gold stiletto with a peek-a-boo toe that I'd gotten the week after Ace told me he was leaving me for Lynette. There was a matching purse somewhere.

"What I'm saying," Sherri continued, "is that you need to sell some of your things."

She must be crazy. "Do you know how much I paid for most of these shoes?"

"No," she said. "But you've given me hints about how much you owe. That would be enough to make me a saleswoman," she said. She crossed her arms. Looked at the wall of shoes. Looked at me.

That's what I get for telling people my personal business. Now

Sherri was trying to be my financial consultant. I didn't need her to remind me about my bills. Calls from collection agencies had already done that this morning. Even on Saturdays they didn't let up.

"So I'm supposed to line up my shoes on folding tables under the trees outside and post a yard sale sign at the street? I don't think so."

Sherri rolled her eyes at me. I know I was talking crazy, but she was, too.

"You can get a fair price for your babies if you take them to a high-end consignment shop. Or try posting them for sale on an Internet site. You'd be surprised. People love to click and order these days. You'll have some money in your pocket and knock out your debt in no time. Or at least it'll be a start."

She had a point, but I still wasn't trying to hear it. Parting with my shoes would be like parting with a close friend.

"You've been talking about being free and dumping your old baggage," Sherri said. "Girlfriend, debt is baggage. What's that Scripture? 'Owe man nothing but love.'"

"Throw a Scripture on me." I laughed. "You're not playing fair. Clothes make a good impression, and you of all people know it. Clothes make the woman."

"Not if the woman is broke."

I had to give her that one. "I'll think about it," I said as the front doorbell rang.

I know the men hadn't returned that quickly with my last load. I imagined it was one of my neighbors. Mrs. Barron had already stopped by after her morning stroll to admire some of my belongings that were lined up on the lawn before they'd been brought into the house. Me and Sherri had to listen to a story about her family heirloom desk. Then again it could be another one of the community children coming to peddle some chocolate bars for their summer camp fundraiser. I was like the new meat on the street, and had already been solicited three times this morning.

It was neither, and I was glad. I would have preferred to see the face I was looking at over theirs any day. *Lord, let this be one of my neighbors. The Neighborhood Watch president. Anything.*

Chapter 59

I'd been praying God would send me a man. Or maybe it was the innocent prayer from a child that had done it. Faith had definitely asked God to send her mommy's new friend a husband. And he was standing on my doorstep.

I'm not one to open the door for a stranger, but I found myself unlocking the latch to open up the barrier between me and the statue of chocolate on the porch. *Maybe I should invite him inside. In case he melts.*

"Would you happen to be Sheila?"

I would happen to be anybody you want me to be.

I chastised myself. I had to keep my thoughts under control. God probably wasn't thrilled with me right now, but there shouldn't be anything wrong with me admiring His creation. I'd been having a lot of success taming my thoughts and my tongue lately. Then he came along and messed it all up.

"Yes, I'm Sheila," I said. "Can I help you?"

He pointed a finger at me like a lightbulb had just gone off in his head. "Do I know you?"

"I'm not sure," I said. "I'm sure I'd remember your face."

His eyes brightened. "From Mount Pisgah. You used to come with Ace Bowers, didn't you?"

"Wow, good memory. Too good," I said, not wanting him to equate me with Ace. "Ace and I have been going about our separate ways for some time now. Living single. Not sure if you can relate to that." *Translation: I'm single and available. Are you?*

"I'm familiar with the single lifestyle," he said in response to my blatant attempt to know which marital status box he'd checked on the census survey.

"I was supposed to meet my uncle Bear here earlier, but my meeting ran over. Have they finished moving your things?"

"Are you going to tell me your name?" I asked.

"Lee Mayfield."

"Nice to meet you, Lee. Bear and the others went to pick up the last load. They should be back in about an hour if you'd like to wait for them." *Please say yes.*

"I think I'll go grab a bite to eat and come back. Can I get you something?"

"No. I'm fine." I'd already eaten some chicken wraps courtesy of Sherri.

"All right then. I'll see you in a while."

I watched Lee get into his car, back out of the driveway. I think I've seen him in my dreams before.

Sherri surprised me. "You are such a flirt," she said. "Hitting on a man of the cloth like that. You should be ashamed."

"He's a minister?"

"I've only met him once, but if I recall correctly, he's a minister at his church."

266

"Don't strike me down, Lord," I said, clasping my hands under my chin.

"Girl, please. Ministers want a woman just as much as anybody else."

I sniffed the armpit of my shirt. I hope I hadn't smelled offensive. I didn't know Sherri would be slaving me like she had. At least I knew Lee had seen me in something other than moving clothes, and obviously I'd made an impression. Whenever I was on Ace's arm at church, I made sure to look like I deserved to be there.

"Lee's coming back," I said. "Would it be too obvious if I changed?"

"The only thing you need to change is your mind," Sherri said. "Get your mind off the man, back on getting the house together and thinking about what you want to do with your mountain of shoes. I just remembered a shoe consignment boutique that one of my clients told me about. I think it will be the perfect place for you."

"You don't have to stay here and help me anymore, you know." I cleaned off the kitchen table in case Lee came back to eat his food.

"Stop trying to run me off," Sherri said. "Anisha is taking care of everything until tonight. We still have to finish up here and meet Eden at the bookstore. We have work to do."

I closed and locked the front door. "Eden had to postpone. Family emergency," I said, leaving out the details.

"Is everything all right? Bear didn't say anything about it," Sherri said, looking perplexed.

"It's probably fine, that's why Bear didn't mention it."

I clasped my hands and rubbed them together. I didn't want to think about anything that had gone down between me and Romando or the aftermath that may have happened at the Mayfield's house. "Come help me go through these shoes," I said, before I realized what had come out of my mouth.

Sherri walked back to the bedroom like she'd been rejuvenated with an extra spurt of energy.

"If you thought you looked good stepping out in these shoes before, wait until you're stepping out on faith," Sherri said.

I loved the sound of that.

Chapter 60

Lee didn't come back over to the house. Before he had a chance to, Bear called him and told him that they had everything under control. When I heard Bear saying those words, I wanted to rip the phone out of his hand. Bear used to be one of my favorite people. Right then, that wasn't the case.

I was lying in bed staring at a stack of shoeboxes that Sherri had helped me sort through. It was like forcing a woman to choose which of her children she wanted to keep and which she wanted to sell. Maybe it wasn't that drastic to the average person, but to me it was an emotional experience. I'd worked so hard the day before that I had a dream about some of my shoes crying to be rescued.

Eden had awakened me before my alarm clock had the chance. Even though I heard the phone, it took me a moment to realize where I was, and that it was actually my phone ringing.

"Hello?" I said.

"Did I wake you?" Eden asked. She was talking low, almost whispering. "I thought you might be up getting ready for church."

"Eden? No, it's fine. It's almost time for me to get up anyway."

"I hate to do this to you, Sheila, but I was calling to see if you could take over running the bookstore for a few weeks."

"I hope everything is okay," I said, sitting up.

"It's going to be," Eden said.

I could hear both weariness and hope in her voice. I pushed myself up against the back of the headboard. Sleepiness left me, and concern entered in.

"It's Romando. He needs his mama right now, and I've been praying for God to bring him home. He's come back before and asked for help getting his life right, but every time he'd sneak out before the sun came up."

Eden paused as if she expected me to say something.

"I peeked in the guest room this morning. He's still here," she said. "And I need to stay here for him."

Eden wept softly. And I prayed. It was becoming easier for me to talk to God like a friend. Like a Father.

"I know I've never talked that much about Romando, but that's because I only wanted to keep my mind on the man that I know he is and not the darkness he's fallen into. But he's clawing his way out now." She paused. Thoughtful. "And I'm going to hold his hand until he makes it to the top."

"You're a strong woman, Eden. He's blessed to have you for a mama."

"Thank you."

We sat in comfortable silence. I think we were thinking about our lives and the journey God had each of us on.

"I don't want to pressure you about being at the bookstore every day. It can be a lot to handle," Eden said. "If you can't help, just let me know. It's no problem for me to close the store down for a few weeks. Family first. And I asked my cousin to take over on the weekends so you can have some days off. And don't worry, I'll pay you well."

"Eden, please." I had to snap her out of it.

"I tend to get worked up," she said.

"You've got enough on your plate. However long you need me will be fine."

We planned to meet after church so I could pick up the keys to the bookstore and so Eden could go over a few things she thought she'd neglected to tell me before. I dressed in jeans and a casual top, since Pastor Armstrong had declared it Casual Sunday for the rest of the summer. It was a good thing; I was running low on church-appropriate attire. I'd never realized how many low-cut blouses and form-fitting clothes I owned. I think I had a justifiable reason to pray for God to give me a fashion budget.

By the time I met Sherri at church, she'd already signed Faith into the children's service and I could hear the music from the band—lovingly called "The Posse" by Pastor Armstrong—striking up one of the praise and worship songs that I finally knew the words to.

Immediately following praise and worship, Pastor Armstrong told us to circle up in groups of three so we could pray for one another and then for people who we wanted God to especially bless. A list of folks ran through my head like credits at the end of a movie, most of them from my "baggage list."

Then I added an epilogue to my prayer—some words from my heart especially for God's ears.

God, this has been one of the scariest, most exhilarating, and faith-building walks in my life. I don't want this to be a temporary thing. I don't think it is. Now that I've been with You, I can't imagine being without You.

I didn't realize the tears were falling so fast—and so freely—until the woman beside me pushed a tissue into my hand. After all the years I'd cried tears of regret and sorrow, I finally had a reason to weep tears of joy.

I opened my eyes to see that most of the people in the church were sitting down and there were only a handful of us who were so caught up in the presence of God that we hadn't noticed. I sat down on the pew and fished my compact out of my purse. I popped it open so that I could take a look at my face, never expecting to see a reflection of Lee's face behind me.

Chapter 61

It might have been vain for me to think about, but I still hoped I'd been worshiping God with a pretty face. I'd seen some people caught up in a personal experience with God who had some contortionist kind of expressions on their face. Then there were those with pleasant smiles, like they could see angels playing harps. I prayed I was one of those people.

I turned slightly and nodded to Lee. He put his hands on my shoulders and patted the sides of them to silently say "hello." I wondered what he was doing at this church today, since he was a minister at another church across town. I'd already stolen a glance on either side of him to see if he may have been attending with someone, but the ladies on either side of him were too old to be his love interest. Unless he was into cougars.

"You look well rested," he told me after church was over. "Did you get everything moved?"

Looking well rested in my language meant I'd done an impeccable job applying my concealer to mask the dark shadows and bags under my eyes.

"Everything is moved in," I said. "Now it's just a matter of putting things in place in a way that makes sense."

"It'll get it done sooner or later," he said, shifting his Bible to his other hand. "So Aunt Eden told me you were going to take over for her at the bookstore. I'm glad she has someone dependable to step in."

"With everything she's done for me, it's my pleasure."

"I'm not sure if you know it or not, but you've done a lot for her, too. She's been talking a lot about you for the last few weeks," Lee revealed. "With everything going on with Romando, she needed someone to nurture. She needed to know that she could get through to someone. You were that person."

"Thank you for sharing that."

I picked up my things, and we walked to the side of the church where parents could pick up their children. Lee seemed to be a familiar face at the church, so I guess he hadn't come this morning just to search for me.

"So what are you up to this afternoon?"

"Sherri and I are going to run a couple of errands if she's still up to it," I said, leaving it open so Lee would know I'd willingly change my plans if he had a better offer.

A woman with two young boys interrupted us. She came over to tell Lee about her sons' miraculous change in attitude since she'd gotten them involved in a mentoring program. I thought for a moment Lee had forgotten I was there, but I wasn't going anywhere. If I had to, I'd wait for him until they turned off all the lights in church.

Lee was wearing jeans and a long-sleeved dress shirt. His jeans were hard pressed with starch, like his grandmother had schooled him on how to put a crease in his pants that would last forever.

"Sorry about that," Lee said once he'd finished his conversation and given the boys some advice. "Where were we?"

"You were asking me what I was doing this afternoon."

"Right. I was going to ask you if you played racquetball. I'm going to play with Tyson and some other friends. You know Tyson, right? Anisha's husband?"

"Yes, I know the proud future papa," I said. "But no, I don't play racquetball."

I'd attempted to take tennis lessons once upon a time, but dropped out after two lessons. I hadn't touched a racquet since.

"I'm going to go pick up Tyson so he can play off some of his stress. You know, beat him down a couple of rounds."

"I don't know if that'll lower his stress level or not," I said. Men are so competitive.

"He'll get me back on the basketball court, trust me. He's got ups."

Lee told me how he and Tyson had first connected when Bear introduced them about four years ago. Tyson had been looking for some more men to help with the mentoring program for boys that he operated in the inner city, and Bear knew Lee had worked with a few big brother programs in the past. They'd been acquaintances ever since.

The cell phone on Lee's hip vibrated. He unclipped it and read the text message, shaking his head.

"Tyson said Anisha wants to do a yard sale this coming Saturday. He wants me to hurry up and rescue him."

I shrugged. "When duty calls, the husband has to step up," I said. "Isn't that the rule?"

"If you want a happy home, it is," he replied.

Sherri appeared out of nowhere, clutching her cell phone in one hand and Faith with the other. "This is going to be a good week for you," she said. "Anisha is having a yard sale on Saturday. Can you say money, money, money?" She looked over at Lee. "Good to see you again, Lee."

"You, too," he said.

Sherri shifted the tone of the conversation, which was exactly what I wanted her to do. I didn't want Lee to think I was in desperate need of money. Being broke didn't look good on anybody.

"Are you ready to go?" Sherri asked, cautiously. I think she was trying to figure out if she'd interrupted some kind of blooming romantic exchange.

"Ready whenever you are," I said.

"Let me get your number, Sheila," Lee said. "I'll give you a call. Maybe we'll see each other at the yard sale. Tyson will probably put me on duty."

All of a sudden I had an urge to sell some things.

Chapter 62

Sherri probably thought I was exaggerating. The intensity of the emotions I was feeling had frozen me in my footsteps. And on top of that, we were standing in the middle of shoe heaven.

Sherri shook my shoulder, and I held my arms out by my side to steady my wobbly knees.

"Do you need a paper bag or something?" she asked me. "You look like you're about to hyperventilate."

"A paper bag is a joke. I might need an oxygen mask."

Sherri picked up a pink leather pump and held it out to examine it. I wanted to snatch it out of her hand and run out of this shoe paradise, escaping with it and the rest of my twenty-three boxes of shoes that were in the trunk.

"It's like dropping off your children to someone you don't even know," I said.

"You might not know the owner, but you'll know the presidents on those green dollar bills that you'll be getting back. Remember the goal. Stay focused," Sherri urged.

I'd gathered thirty-two pairs of shoes and put them by the door this morning before I left for church, but I'd only had the courage to bring twenty-three of them with me.

"Baby steps," I'd told her. If I weren't in dire need of this money, I'd be acting like a baby, kicking and screaming until she dragged me out of the store.

A stick-thin woman with skin the color of a porcelain China doll came from around one of the jewelry cases. "Are one of you Sheila Rushmore?" she asked us.

"Me," I said.

"Welcome. I'm Karli." She extended a hand so fragile and tender-looking that I was almost afraid to shake it, lest it shatter in my grip. "You're my only appointment for the day, so if you'll follow me, we can get some minor paperwork done and then I can take a look at your shoes," she said. "Sundays are my slow days. This is actually the last Sunday I'll be open. From now on I'll just be open Tuesday through Saturday."

"See how God worked that out?" Sherri said, pinching my elbow.

I smacked my lips. "Don't try to get deep on me now."

Karli swept through the store like she was a ballerina. She was light on her feet and her movements were so fluid. Mr. Black Butterfly from the MARTA bus could take some hints from her.

"Can I offer you some mineral water?" Karli said.

"Yes, please," Sherri answered for me. "I think she's having shoe separation anxiety."

"Don't worry, you're not the first one," Karli said. "I love shoes so much that I left the banking industry so I could be around them all of the time."

"Now that's stepping out on faith."

"Yes, definitely on faith. And my husband's wallet, too. But

278

God has been good to us, so I can't complain. He works everything out for your good, and I can say that because I've seen it in my own life."

Sherri winked at me. We were probably thinking the same thing. You can't judge a person's relationship with God by their looks, because I definitely wouldn't have pointed her out as someone who'd publicly testify to God's goodness. I felt better about parting with my shoes now. It was like they were being adopted into a loving Christian home. After I filled out the profile and payment agreements, the three of us unloaded the boxes out of the back of my trunk.

"These are the kind of shoes that'll make a woman sell her possessions to buy," Karli said. She handled my footwear like they were pieces of heirloom wedding china. I liked her. She knew quality when she saw it.

While Karli inspected and priced the shoes, Sherri and I went outside and walked along the upscale shopping strip.

"This is good for you," Sherri said.

"I'm glad you think so."

"And after the yard sale this weekend, you're going to see just how good. I'm telling you, at one time I thought I'd never get my head above water, because I thought all single mothers who didn't have the fathers of their children actively involved were doomed to poverty or close to it. That's why you have to put your faith and trust in God and not in man."

"That's becoming more of a reality for me every day," I admitted.

Sherri shared her rise from a struggling entrepreneur to a booming business owner. She'd completely transformed her life in five years, and although being a single parent had its share of struggles, she admitted not being able to imagine her life without Faith. Most of the time, it had been her daughter that made her press even further when she felt like giving up.

We were about to pass a stationery and gift shop when the glass door swung open.

"Sherri, I thought that was you. What are you doing on this side of town?"

"Hi, Lenora. Can't I leave the east side every now and then?"

She exchanged air kisses with a woman who was teetering in a pair of three-inch heels. Without them I knew she would be just as short as Sherri.

"Of course, you can broaden your Atlanta horizons," Lenora said. "Every now and then you need to diversify," she said, lifting her eyebrows in two perfect arches when she said "diversify." "You know what I mean."

"Lenora meet Sheila. Sheila—Lenora. Sheila recently joined Grace."

"Welcome to the family," Lenora said, hugging me. She smelled like mango lotion. "Our family just keeps on growing." Lenora beamed.

She gave me one of those ear-to-ear smiles that our greeters at church give when you arrive at church. I know that has to be a God-given gift. There's no way I could stand up and smile that long

Lenora was holding an intricately wrapped box. It was covered in a lime green embellished paper that had a glittery gold sheen to it. Instead of a bow on top there, was an arrangement of silk tulips attached to it. I wondered what was inside, and Sherri voiced the same question I had.

"What's inside the box? You must have another event to attend." Sherri put her hand on Lenora's shoulder. "She's the socialite of the city."

"Oh, is that what you call it? I think people just invite me because they're trying to get close to my husband." She waved her hand in the air. "I take it for what it is." Lenora picked at the tips of one of the silk tulip petals with her fingernail. "This is a little wedding token for my great-niece. Some stationery printed with her new initials. She's getting married this evening. First Sunday wedding I've ever been to."

"If the stationery is anything like the wrapping paper, then I can imagine how beautiful it is," I said, all the while thinking what role her husband had that people wanted to get close to him.

"Sherri knows me. I like everything over the top."

"Yes, she does," Sherri said. "I try to reel her back in every now and then, but it never works. Let's just say the things I've designed for her are true conversation starters."

"Speaking of which, I need something for an awards banquet. The hubby is getting recognized, so I can't go in just any little old thing, honey. It's in two weeks, and I totally neglected to put it on my calendar."

"Two weeks is pushing it," Sherri said. "I'd love to squeeze you in, but I don't think I can do it."

Lenora tried to give Sherri a pitiful look, but Sherri didn't budge. On top of everything else on her plate, I knew she had a lot to do to get Faith prepared for kindergarten.

"Then do you know of *anyone* who can do some personal shopping for me? I've got way too much to do right now."

"Well . . ." Sherri looked in my direction.

Initially I was nervous and was going to act like I didn't know who in the world Sherri was referring to, but then I figured that was my chance. An opportunity not only to earn some money but to step out into a passion I'd always had. Buying fine clothes, but using someone else's money to do it. If Eden, Sherri, and Karli could turn their passions into profit, so could I.

"Since we're family and all," I said. "I'd love to offer you my services."

Lenora eyed me from head to toe like she was taking inventory of whether my image could meet her expectations.

"Trust me," Sherri said. "You won't be disappointed, and I'll put my word on that."

Lenora fished inside her purse and pulled out her keys and a monogrammed business card holder. "How can I not consider a recommendation like that one?" She flipped a business card toward me like it was a prized possession.

"Can you call me tomorrow? Maybe we can schedule time for you to come by the house so you can get an idea of my taste and my budget." She threw her head back and laughed. "What am I talking about? There won't be a budget. All I have to do is massage my husband's shoulders, call him 'Judge,' and he forgets everything about those spending restrictions he tries to put on me. Spare no expense, sweetheart. And don't worry, I pay well."

"I'll definitely give you a call tomorrow evening," I said. "I should be available after seven o'clock."

"Perfect."

Lenora left us standing on the sidewalk, and she walked to her car like the entire world was watching.

"You've officially become an entrepreneur," Sherri said. "Doesn't it feel good?"

"I'm actually going to get paid for shopping. You can't beat that. It's the best thing that's happened to me since I snuck into my ex-boyfriend's wedding."

"You did what?"

"Don't even ask," I said, opening the door to the stationery shop.

"So what? Now you've been inspired to look at paper?"

"No. I'm sure they do business cards. I'm envisioning something in light coral with my name imprinted in gold metallic and an embossed stiletto on the right side."

Sherri held up her hand. "Wait a minute, hold up." She stepped in front of me.

I was starting to hate that I'd told Sherri to hold me accountable. I know it was best for me, but she was starting to take the job too seriously.

"You have one client. Let's start off with some free cards off the Internet. You only have to pay shipping and handling. I had the free ones for two years and they worked perfectly fine while building my business. You can upgrade later."

I let the door to the stationery shop float closed.

"You'll thank me later," Sherri sang.

Even though I'd have to update my business cards later, Karli had upgraded my bank account. She forked over two thousand, eight hundred and seventy-five dollars for my shoes. Money talks. Sherri didn't have to waste another word trying to convince me to bring in my other nine pairs. Nearly three thousand dollars wasn't bad for shoes that hadn't seen the light of day in a while. My shoes had finally seen the light, and I had, too!

Chapter 63

I abhor people who wake up at the crack of dawn to mow their lawns, especially on Saturday mornings. Maybe *abhor* was too strong of a word to put on Mr. Barron, because in every other aspect he was such a kind and respectable man. But I knew it was him, Mr. Green Thumb himself.

I should've taped a note to his door to let him know that I hadn't closed my eyes until almost two o'clock that morning because I'd had to tag and box my items for Anisha's yard sale today. Yard sales were meant to be for quick and easy money, but I was ready for some negotiations. There were things like my extra set of living room end tables and two white-cushioned wingback chairs that I refused to let go for pennies on the dollar. I'd suggested they call it an "estate sale," since we had high-ticket items, but Anisha didn't want to scare off the majority of potential customers. It was her sale, and she was the pregnant woman; hence what she says, goes.

I kicked the sheets to the end of the bed and let the air from the ceiling fan awaken my body and get me moving. I would've drifted back off to a deep sleep if the roar and buzz from the lawn mower hadn't been close enough to rattle the windowpanes. Mr. Barron must've felt sorry for the overgrown yard and decided to lend a neighborly hand.

I looked out the window, expecting to see him in his regular long-sleeved plaid shirt, khaki pants, grass-stained shoes, and that ridiculous hat that makes him look like he's on an African safari. But it wasn't Mr. Barron. The shoulders were too broad, and I'd never seen Mr. Barron wearing a baseball cap. It took me a moment to make out who was riding on the back of one of those self-propelled mowers, zipping across the side of the yard.

The man and his machine whipped around a bush and headed back in my direction, making perfect lines on the yard. When he rode close enough, I realized it was Lee.

I let the blinds snap shut. There was no way he could've seen me and the silk scarf tied around my head, but I moved away from the window anyway.

Until yesterday evening, Lee hadn't called me at all. Even then he'd contacted me at the bookstore instead of on my cell. Just like he'd said, Tyson had put him to work. Tyson had asked Lee to pick up my heavier items on the back of his small pickup truck and take them over to the yard sale. I think it was more of Sherri's suggestion and planning than it was Tyson's, but I wasn't complaining. At any rate, I hadn't been expecting him for at least another forty-five minutes.

I'd taken a shower before I'd gotten into bed so that I could squeeze every ounce of sleep out of the few hours I had to rest. I prayed while I dressed, then went to greet Lee. He was outside pushing the lawnmower into the small shed at the back of the yard. I waved at him from the back deck.

Lee rinsed his hands off under the outside faucet then trudged up the back steps. He smelled like sweat and grass, but he still looked fine as I don't know what, even through all of that dirt and grime.

"You started the day off early," I said. I'd poured him a glass of orange juice and offered him a banana to go with it. I guess the women back in the day would've had a full breakfast cooked, but today he was going to have to take what he could get.

"I'm an early riser," Lee said. He took my meager breakfast offering. "Appreciate it." Lee used a bandana hanging out of his jeans pocket to wipe his face. "So you all set?"

"Tagged and ready."

Lee handed me back the empty glass. "I guess I better keep it moving. Show me what to load up and I'll be on the way."

I parked at the end of the cul-de-sac and walked toward Anisha and Tyson's place. I wondered what was left inside of their home, because it looked like the house had been tipped over and all of their belongings had slid out into the front yard. It was like walking through a home décor store.

I had to keep my mind on the goal: to make money, not spend it. There was a set of matching gold leaf vases calling my name, but I ignored their taunting and set my eyes on the two tables where most of my things were already set up. Even though I insisted I could bring the lighter boxes on my own, Lee had brought over everything that could fit in the back of his truck and still have room for the treadmill he was going to try and sell. That left me with my purse and a small cooler of water and some other snacks I'd packed to make sure we'd stay hydrated and energized. In the meantime, Lee had gone to his house around the corner to shower.

Sherri walked out the front door dressed and accessorized for business. She was wearing a sun visor decorated with fake paper money and a fanny pack for stashing cash. She looked like Mama wearing that ridiculous thing around her waist.

"Don't look at me like that," Sherri said. She bit into a perfectly ripened Georgia peach and handed me one. "I mean business today."

"You're not the only one," I said, gesturing at the packed front yard. "Is there anything left in the house?"

"Of course. The carpet is still in there," Sherri joked. "At least for now."

"This has got to be a result of hormones," I said.

"Anisha is doing some serious nesting. Getting things ready for the baby and clearing the clutter."

I followed behind Sherri, and we hammered a yard sign attached to a wooden stake into the grass at the corner of the driveway. At Anisha's request, Sherri had bought a bundle of balloons to attach to the sign to draw more shoppers to her yard of treasures.

"Where's Anisha now?" I asked.

"She's inside lying down and watching cartoons with Faith. Tyson gave her strict orders not to get up until he got back from the grocery store, because she said she'd been having Braxton Hicks contractions since late last night. I'm supposed to be on the lookout to make sure Anisha doesn't move, but I told Tyson I couldn't promise that she wouldn't escape and bind me to the stairwell or something."

"Anisha will be fine. Our job is to keep her happy and safe."

"And to keep me and Tyson sane. I don't know who's more ready for this baby to come—me, her, or Tyson," Sherri said, opening the storm door. "I'll be back. Do you need anything?"

"More money," I said. "Let's get this party started."

"No hyperventilating this morning?" Sherri asked.

"If I can get rid of my shoes," I said, unpacking the last bit of trinkets out of a box, "I can get rid of this stuff."

Sherri had only been gone ten minutes, but the eager yard sale shoppers were already swarming around the yard like bees around a hive. One minute there were two or three stragglers, and the next minute there were at least twelve or thirteen people milling around the grass. Since we'd all set up our tables separately so we could keep an accurate count of our own money, I was doing my best to keep watch on everyone's belongings. Although these were items we wanted to get rid of, we didn't plan on letting them go for free. We were in a nice neighborhood, but that didn't mean some of these people didn't have sticky fingers.

Sherri walked out of Anisha's house like a woman on a mission. "Tyson called and said he should be back in about fifteen minutes. Lee should be back so he can help load the heavier items if somebody buys them."

I accepted three dollars from a woman who bought a punch bowl that had barely been used. I'd gotten it during the short stint when I planned to throw the ultimate dinner and cocktail parties so I could build my own brand image as a young black socialite. Fantasy world. I'd been watching too much television. Hosting parties was more trouble—and work—than I was interested in.

"Lee's so helpful," I said.

Sherri mocked me in a little girl voice, "'Lee's so helpful.' You're crushing on him hard."

"Yes, I am," I admitted. "But he hasn't taken a second look at me. He didn't call me until last night and that was only to tell me he was picking up my stuff for the yard sale. He's probably looking for someone more reserved and conservative."

Sherri waved off my comment. "Don't let the white collar fool you."

"What do you know about him? Spill it," I said.

We walked out into the yard and stood in the center of the action. Some of these folks meant serious business. One woman had brought a red wagon along to collect her items.

Sherri stopped to give change for a set of placemats.

"Actually, I don't know that much about Lee," Sherri said. "We only cross paths every now and then because he's cool with Tyson."

"And you never checked him out for yourself?" I found it hard to believe that Tyson hadn't tried to hook them up. Married couples were always trying to "sell" their single friends to one another.

"Not my type," Sherri said.

I didn't see how Lee wasn't *every* woman's type, but I guessed it was good that Sherri hadn't named him and claimed him.

Sherri accepted money from a lady who'd already claimed the two gold leaf vases I had my eyes on earlier.

It seemed like everyone had gotten out of bed at the same time to come to the yard sale. It was a while before Sherri could give me the lowdown on Lee.

"From what I know, his last serious relationship lasted a little over a year," Sherri said. "I think they were talking about marriage at one point, but before he had a chance to buy a ring, she ended their relationship. Supposedly the ex-girlfriend didn't think their lives were going in the same direction, but a month later she upped and moved to Miami. If you ask me, she had another man in the picture."

Lee was probably over it by now. Men bounced back much faster than women.

Still, when I saw Lee park his truck and walk across the lawn scrubbed fresh and clean, I wanted to run up and give him a sympathetic hug. We'd both walked in the same shoes . . . as the one who was dumped.

Faith ran out the door holding a purple Popsicle in her hand.

"What are you doing?" Sherri asked. "You're supposed to be upstairs keeping Auntie Anisha company."

"Auntie Anisha told me to come and tell you that she broke water all over the bed."

"What do you mean she broke water on the bed?" Sherri said, dropping some change in the fanny pack around her waist. "Did you spill that water I gave you? Get some towels out of the bathroom and help Auntie Anisha clean it up."

"No," Faith said, shaking her head and stomping her foot. "Auntie *Anisha* broke water. Not me."

I paused. Thought about the fact that there was a pregnant woman upstairs. My mouth dropped; heart raced.

I grabbed Sherri's arm. "Anisha's water broke!"

Chapter 64

The US Olympic relay track team needs me and Sherri. From the way we moved, you'd think a gold medal was in our future. We took the steps going up to Anisha's bedroom three at a time. Sure enough, Anisha was there in obvious, back-wrenching pain.

"My water broke. Out of nowhere." Anisha huffed. Then her face grimaced in pain.

Sherri threw all of Faith's toys and the snacks she'd spread out on the bed onto the floor. Chips and gummy fruit snacks were everywhere.

"Call 9-1-1!" she yelled at me. She was frantic. I was hoping she'd be the calm once, since out of the three of us, she was the one who'd been through this before. If anyone was supposed to be about to jump off the deep end, it should've been Anisha. I'm sure she'd expected all of this to be happening at the hospital. Not at her house with a bunch of strangers walking through her yard.

I prayed to calm myself down, even after the several rings it took for the dispatcher to answer.

"9-1-1. What is your emergency?"

"My friend is having a baby," I told the operator. "Right now. Her water broke, and we're upstairs in her bedroom. I don't think we can make it to a hospital."

"Ma'am, what is your location?"

I had no idea. It was written down in my car but that didn't do me any good. Didn't do Anisha any good.

"Sherri, what's the address?"

"What?" Sherri was trying to listen to me and Anisha at the same time. Anisha's plea's were more urgent.

"Ma'am, what's your location?" the operator calmly asked me again. Thank goodness she was trained not to get frenzied in emergencies because now I was shaking like a leaf. *Pull yourself together, Sheila,* I told myself. *Pull yourself together.*

Anisha managed to rattle off her address, and I repeated it to the operator.

"You have *got* to be kidding me," Sherri gasped. Then I saw the reason for Sherri's urgency—the baby's head was in full view.

"Ma'am, I see the head," I told the operator. I'd regained my composure. I tried not to look—respect Anisha's privacy—but it was a sight like I'd never experienced. And although I realized this was all God's creation and His way of bringing babies into the world, I couldn't help but think that I might have to find another option, should I ever have kids.

"Ma'am," the operator snapped me back into the emergency at hand. "How is Mom doing?"

"How is she doing?" I couldn't believe she'd asked that question. "She's having her first baby without any drugs and with her friends here and not a doctor. How do you think she's doing?"

"Put the operator on speaker," Sherri called.

Tears streamed down Anisha's face, but she was relatively calm considering the situation.

"Place your hand in front of the baby's head so it won't come out too fast," the operator instructed.

I heard someone running up the steps. It was Lee. "Hey, guys. I need some help out here. It's getting crazy."

He stepped into the doorway holding Faith in his arms. "Whoa!" He disappeared.

I crawled up on the bed and held Anisha's hand. "I just want my baby to be safe," she whimpered. I guess another contraction hit, because her entire body tensed as straight as a board.

"Do your best to keep Mommy relaxed," the operator said.

I rubbed Anisha's head. "Your baby is going to be fine. And you are too."

Anisha was panting. "You promise?" she asked, strengthening her grip on my hand.

"God promises," I answered.

Anisha squeezed her eyes shut. "It's coming. Another contrac—"

I prayed. Anisha bore her chin down to her chest and pushed. Sherri played obstetrician with the dispatcher's help. And right before my eyes a life plopped out onto Anisha's king-sized bed. Anisha reached down and picked up her son. She pulled him into her chest and gently wiped his head with the top of her shirt. The baby was shaking so I snatched open all the dresser drawers until I found a clean white T-shirt of Tyson's.

I retracted the thoughts I'd had earlier—that I didn't want to have a child. Anisha cried and stared at her son like she'd hadn't experienced one ounce of pain. It was like everything she'd felt had been replaced with love.

Sherri yanked the laces out of her tennis shoes and followed the dispatcher's directions for tying off the umbilical cord. The baby was so tiny that I would've been scared to touch him, but the way

Anisha handled him, I could tell her motherly instincts had already kicked in. The baby hadn't cried yet, but was sucking his middle two fingers like it had been his pastime the entire time he'd been in the womb.

Sherri's wits came back to her, and she led us in prayer, thanking God for the safe delivery and for her godson.

"Amen," we chimed together once she finished praying. Then we heard the distant shrill of the ambulance.

Chapter 65

I still couldn't believe what happened, and neither could any of Anisha and Tyson's family and friends who were calling the home phone and Tyson's cell phone hoping to hear the full story. He usually ended up handing the phone to me, and I did my best to give a replay to everyone who called.

No matter how many times I repeated it, I never imagined this was how my day would unfold.

The yard sale junkies had watched in astonishment as the paramedics cleared a path to bring out Anisha and the baby. But once they knew the two were fine and had been safely loaded into the ambulance to be transported to the hospital, the yard-sale-aholics went back to business as usual.

After repeated calls to Tyson, he finally arrived two minutes before the ambulance pulled off with his wife and newborn son. We were all glad that Tyson *hadn't* been there after all. I thought the paramedics were going to have to administer oxygen to *him* so he wouldn't faint.

Lee and I were left in charge of the yard sale. I might've thought before that I was the last person on Lee's mind, but after spending all day with him, I think that might have been the furthest thing from the truth.

"Eventful day, huh?" Lee said.

"To say the least," I said.

We were taking the last few packed boxes inside. The yard sale had brought in some major bucks for all of us. Even Lee, who only had his treadmill to sell, had made a fair price off of it. I think the drama had drawn more people, and it ended up working in our favor.

"We make a good team," Lee said.

"I couldn't agree more."

If Sherri were there she would've said I was flirting. And I would've agreed.

We sat in Tyson and Anisha's breakfast nook and took a rest, since the sun had sucked out most of our energy. I watched Lee shell and eat sunflower seeds. He offered me some, but I didn't think I could crack and eat them and still look cute, so I passed. I'd already decided that I was going to enjoy a take-out dinner from the Chinese restaurant I'd seen on the way over this morning.

"Is your evening going to be as exciting as our day has been?" I asked Lee.

"I don't think anything can top the baby coming a month early, but I was going to go out tonight and play a little bit."

Play a little bit? I almost didn't want to ask, because I had an ideal image in my head of what a minister should be like, and Lee's admission might shatter it all.

"What's that look about?" Lee asked me.

I still hadn't mastered my facial expressions. "Honestly, I'm wondering what kind of *playing* you had on your schedule."

"You can always come with me and find out for yourself."

I lifted my eyebrows. My curiosity was piqued, but I was still leery about accepting the offer. I knew I couldn't be perfect, but if I was going to take a fall, it wasn't going to be with a minister.

Lee got up and dumped his sunflower seed shells in the trash. "What's the matter? Don't you trust me?"

"I don't know you enough to trust you," I said.

"Well trust the God in me," Lee said. "You'll be fine. If I do anything to hurt or harm you, you can always call Uncle Bear."

"That sounds fair," I said. That was enough to convince me that I was in good hands for the night.

We locked up the house and went our separate ways, planning to get together at eight o'clock. That gave me three hours—minus travel time—to eat then get myself together. Lee was picking me up. I broke my normal rules, because it wasn't like he didn't know where I lived anyway.

Clive called while I was getting ready to go and "play," but I didn't answer the phone. He'd probably finally opened the check I'd mailed to him, paying off the rest of what I owed him.

I listened to his message. "Call me. We need to talk. Thanks for the check, but I ripped it up. Keep your money. You need it more than I do. Praise the Lord, Sister Sheila." Then he hung up.

I saved the message so that later I could figure out a way to record it and keep it permanently. In case Clive and Gina ever reconciled, I didn't want her to come after me and say that I'd borrowed money and never repaid it. I know she'd been down the last time we'd seen each other, but that didn't mean she wouldn't rise again with more venom than she'd had before.

I wasn't sure yet if I'd ever call Clive back. It was a door that needed to be closed.

Chapter 66

Lee said what he meant. We'd come out to play a little bit. Actually a lot.

The things that caught my attention as soon as we walked into the hotel's banquet room were the human-sized game boards. I'd been transported back into my childhood. It was like being a kid in a candy store. Literally. One part of the room was decorated with huge lollipops and gumballs suspended with wire from the ceiling.

"You never expected this, did you?" Lee asked.

He'd bought two bags of cotton candy from the vendor as soon as he walked in and was already stuffing his mouth with the air-whipped sugar. He'd handed me a bag of pink cotton candy, and he ate the blue one.

"I didn't know what to expect," I said, "but I'm glad I came."

"I'm glad you did, too," Lee said. "Come on, let's get in on the Scrabble table."

"Scrabble? That's a game for nerds," I joked. I pointed to another corner. "What about that?"

He laughed, shook his head and backed up like I'd just shown him a fire pit. "Back in the day, I would've been over there, but *Minister* Lee can't play Twister with a bunch of grown men and women. Everybody *ain't* just having fun."

I laughed. "I see what you mean." He probably thought I was some kind of freak, but I brushed my negative thoughts off and looked for something else to play. I spotted an empty table in the area where couples were playing on jumbo checkerboards.

"Is checkers safe?" I asked, walking over to the table. "It'll help get my brain warmed up before I take you on in Scrabble."

"Fair enough," Lee said, pulling out my chair before taking his seat.

It had been a long time since I'd had this much fun, and even longer since I felt like I could completely be myself without feeling like I was being judged. I didn't consider this a date—and I doubt Lee did either—but I did consider this a trial run of whether we'd actually like to spend more time together. Lee was easy to be with, and I could tell that the only expectation he'd have at the end of the night was to see that I was home safely. I remembered that Eden had said there was someone she wanted me to spend some time with. She'd never mentioned Lee's name specifically, but I wouldn't doubt if it was him.

Lee was the perfect gentleman the entire night, even up until the moment he walked me to the front door. I knew a kiss might ignite fires that didn't need to be ignited. I knew a kiss could lead to other things between a grown man and a grown woman. But I still wanted Lee to kiss me.

And he did.

On my left cheek—like I was his little sister.

I touched my cheek when Lee left; let my hand linger for a moment like it would keep him there. I could tell there was

Someone bigger than Bear who influenced how Lee treated ladies. And I was glad.

Chapter 67

My cell phone rang. It was Mama. I knew she'd be excited to hear about my non-date with Lee tonight. I hadn't been by her house in over a week, but I called in to check on her at least every other day. Come to think of it, I hadn't talked to her in three days, because I'd been so busy at the bookstore and helping Lenora become the fashionable talk of the awards banquet.

After Lenora modeled and nitpicked over the five final outfits I'd taken to her house, she had finally settled on a red ensemble because she wanted to stand out from everyone else as much as possible. I needed to give Mama that update, too. She'd be glad to hear that my taste in clothes had finally yielded some profits for me.

Yes, I definitely needed some time with Mama. The last time we talked she told me she'd actually cleared out some space for me so that we can sit in the rockers on the porch. Baby steps were better than none at all.

"Hi, Ma," I said.

"Sheila. It's Devin." He sounded out of breath. Nervous.

"What's up?"

"It's Mama," he said. "She doesn't sound too good. She sounds like she's coughing up her insides."

"What?" I tried to stay calm for the second time that day. "What happened?"

I could hear Mama gagging in the background. Devin was right. She sounded like she was coughing up nearly everything in her body.

"Ain't nothing happened. She's been walking around here coughing all day, but she took some cough medicine and said she'd be all right. Tonight it got worse, and she won't let me call the ambulance."

"What do you mean she won't *let* you? She doesn't have an option. Can you be a man and make the right decision for once?" I yelled.

"Will you shut up?" Devin hissed. "Just shut up and stop thinking you know everything."

"Devin," I said in a voice that calmed both of us. We didn't need to argue. It would only make matters worse with Mama. "Hang up and call 9-1-1. I'm on my way."

Devin didn't operate well under pressure. If I knew Devin he was about to punch the wall or do something else destructive. He'd never handled stress well. There are patched holes all around Mama's house to prove it.

"Mama's not going to be happy," he said, anxiety still in his voice.

"Would you rather that Mama be mad or dead?" I asked him.

He hung up the phone. I knew that had spurred him into action.

When I pulled up at Mama's twenty minutes later, half of the neighborhood was standing in the yard. So was Devin, and unfortunately he was smoking a cigarette. He snuffed it out on the bottom of his shoe when he noticed me run up.

"Is Mama all right?" I asked as he followed me into the house. I pushed past the paramedic standing in the doorway. There was another one sitting on the corner of the couch, monitoring Mama as she breathed into an oxygen mask.

She took the mask off of her face. I leaned down to hug her and the paramedic let me sit in the space beside her.

"I thought I was goin' to die," Mama said. "I couldn't catch my breath for nothing."

"Mama, you've got to go to the doctor. You can't help emphysema with cough medicine."

She shook her head. "I didn't think it would ever get this bad, but it's like things flared up out of the blue. I tell you one thing. I don't want to die anytime soon. It's an awful thing when you can't catch your breath."

"You're not going to die, Mama. Not if I have anything to do with it."

Mama put the mask back on her face and took four deep breaths. She took it back off and then said, "I'm not sure you *do* have anything to do with it. But if you can convince God to keep me here long enough for me to see and spend time with some grandchildren, be my guest."

I took one of Mama's hands in mine. "I will Mama. Maybe I can talk Him into keeping you here until we're both real old and grey."

"Old, maybe. But I'll never go grey. Not as long as hair color exists."

Since Mama's breathing had regulated, the paramedics felt confident that she would be fine until she went to the doctor's office on Monday morning. I assured them that I would personally take her in and seek appropriate treatment for her emphysema. Mama didn't object, so I knew it would be a willing ride to see the specialist.

Devin came inside once all of the neighbors had retreated into their own homes. I'd peeked outside once and seen both of Devin's lady friends posted on either side of the yard like they were in their boxing corners. The next time I looked out, both of them were gone. Devin had probably sent them home with their tails tucked between their legs.

I was looking at the December 1974 issue of *Ebony* magazine with all of the Jackson family on the front of it when Devin pulled up a chair from the kitchen table. He sat it in front of us, but didn't say a word for a while.

"Go ahead and say it," he said to me.

I closed the magazine and turned my attention to him. "What are you talking about it?"

"I know I need to stop smoking. You think I caused Mama's episode tonight, don't you?"

I crossed my legs and picked at the hem of my jeans. Then I looked up at Devin. Stared him straight in his eyes. They were tired. The whites of his eyes were slightly yellowed. Devin wasn't the man that he could be, but like Eden had done for Romando, I had to look past that to the man he could become. If God could change me, He could change anybody.

"You know what you need to do. Make the best decision for Mama. And for yourself."

He traced the shape of his mustache and his goatee. I'd been too panicked to notice before, but he'd cut off his cornrows.

"Nice cut," I said. "You look handsome."

He seemed surprised by my compliment. I guess it had been a while since I'd given him a compliment instead of an insult.

Mama set down the glass of room temperature water she'd been sipping. "He does look nice, doesn't he? If you take off his facial hair, he looks just like his kindergarten picture."

"Mama's baby boy," I said. I leaned over like I was going to rub his cheek, but then playfully slapped the side of his face.

He punched back at me, but I was too quick for him. "You always messing with somebody."

We enjoyed the silence of being around each other. Mama started tapping her feet, and I could hear a low hum of a familiar song. The melody grew progressively louder. She was humming "Amazing Grace."

"I could use me some good church singing right now," Mama said. "I bet it'll work better than anything the doctors can give me."

I sat forward. "Now, Mama—"

"Don't get yourself all worked up," she said, without moving a muscle or raising her voice. "I'm still going to the doctor, and I'm going to take my medicine. Don't worry about that. I just wish I had my old Mahalia Jackson record."

I stood up and turned on the ceiling fan. "But if you want to hear some good gospel music, you should come with me to church next Sunday. It's Family and Friends Day. You *and* Devin."

Devin reached his hands up to his head like he'd forgotten that his locks had been buzzed off.

"I don't know, man," he said. "I ain't gon' promise you nothing. I ain't one for church."

He sounded like Cassandra.

Mama stood up and walked into the kitchen. "Don't act like you ain't never been to church, boy."

"How long ago was that, Mama?" he asked. "Too many years to count."

I stood up and grabbed my purse. It had been an exhausting day, and I could barely keep my eyes open. "Any day is a good day for change," I said.

Devin stood. "Wait a minute," he said. "Let me get something for you." He went into his room, and I suspected he was going to go get some cartons of cigarettes. I'd happily take them, even though I wasn't sure if he'd survive one night going cold turkey. Mama had weaned herself off of them, so she could give Devin some advice on how to break his nicotine addiction.

"Hand me my remote," Mama said. "It looks like they've busted another one of those clubs."

Women were scurrying past the television cameras with their faces covered. Microphones were being pushed into their faces, but not one stopped to address the allegations that they were providing illegal services to businessmen in the back of the lounge. The women were dressed identically in tight black catsuits and had long ponytails that reached their waists.

It gave me an unsettling feeling in my stomach that only intensified when the camera caught Clive coming out of the rear door and trying to make it to his car without being seen. Like the women who'd run out, he tried to conceal his face.

"I don't see why these people think they can get away with stuff. They've been taking these illegal businesses down one by one," Mama said. "See, these investigative reporters are smart. They lay low until people think they're gone, then they show up when you least expect them ... with hidden cameras and all kinds of stuff. That man is going down."

The only thing I could do was thank God that I hadn't gotten caught up with Clive any more than I had. Not only was I going to close the door to our relationship, I was going to dead-bolt it.

Devin returned and handed me some money. I counted out the bills. Sixty-eight dollars. "What's this for?" I asked. "Did you sell some of my stuff at the flea market?"

He reached for those nonexistent cornrows again. "Nah. I kinda borrowed some money the last time you were here. A hundred dollars, but that's all I have left. Man, I felt bad spending it."

"How did you—?

"You were outside talking to Fontaine."

"I thought you were—" I stopped myself. "It doesn't even matter. Thank you for *my* money," I said and put it in my pocket. "But you still owe me thirty-two dollars."

I kissed Mama good-bye again, then slapped Devin on the head on the way out. He'd stolen my money, but there was still something to be thankful for. The change in me had caused a change in him.

Chapter 68

Eden couldn't have looked any more brilliant. She was wearing a two-piece daffodil yellow pantsuit and her burgundy tresses were twisted into natural coils. Although we'd talked frequently, I hadn't seen her since the Sunday I'd picked up the keys to the bookstore. I knew the reason her smile couldn't be erased—her arm was looped through Romando's, and he looked like he was just as proud to have Eden as a mother as she was to have him as a son.

Romando was cleanly shaven, and he looked like Eden had been stuffing him with meat and potatoes. His body looked strengthened, but being around Eden, I know his spirit had received just as much nourishment.

"I've missed seeing you so much," I said. She embraced me so tightly that she didn't have to use words to tell me she felt the same.

"You look different," Eden said. "What's going on with you?"

"I've been spending time with God. Loving life. Living life. Being free."

"Oh, girlfriend, I can tell," she said. "God looks good on you."

Eden pulled Romando up beside her. I hope he didn't think he could hide himself behind his miniature-sized mother. He looked embarrassed because of our first encounter, but I knew that I wasn't looking at the same man. Inside or out.

"You all have never been officially introduced," Eden said. "Sheila, this is my only child, Romando."

We shook hands. He wasn't about all that hugging. Not yet.

"Sorry we had to meet under those . . . um . . . circumstances," he mumbled.

"Let's not look backward. Only forward," I said. "It's all good."

He looked a little more relieved, but I could imagine that he wasn't settled with the fact that someone who he'd attacked could see him as anything but a criminal or addict.

Once Romando left his mother's side to go help Bear unload back-to-school supplies with some of the other men, Eden gave me her family update and I gave her mine.

"So I finally get to meet your mama?" Eden said.

"Finally," I said.

I was anxiously waiting for Mama and Devin to arrive, but now I was wondering if I should've trusted that my brother would bring her. Fontaine had repaired Mama's car this week, but she'd insisted that she was going to make Devin bring her to church. She'd said if he did, she was more likely to be able to convince Devin to stay for service.

"So, I hear you and Lee went out last Saturday," Eden said.

"Who told you that?" I asked. The only other people I'd told were Mama and Sherri. "Sherri spilled the beans, didn't she?"

"No. Lee told Bear. And of course Bear told me."

"So Lee was the man you wanted me to spend time with, wasn't he? Remember the night I came boo-hooing over to your house?"

"Lee?" Eden laughed and shook her head. "No. I wanted you to spend time with God. I knew if you'd begin to know Him, that everything else would work itself out."

"I've got a long way to go," I said.

"But you're not where you used to be," Eden said. "And just because you'd want to know, Lee had nothing but good things to say about you. I was going to introduce you two eventually to see if you'd hit it off, but Lee beat me to the punch. And I'm glad he did."

"Me, too," I said.

I saw Mama's car pull into the entrance at the far end of the parking lot. Clouds of black smoke were puffing out of the back tailpipe, but at least they'd made it. Devin pulled into the circular drop-off at the front door. The way Mama's car engine sounded, I doubted the car was permanently repaired, but Fontaine had done enough to get her rolling until we could figure out the rest.

Devin came around and opened the passenger's door for Mama. She stepped out wearing one of the suits I'd given her.

"I know that's your mama," Eden said. "She looks just like you. Fashionable like you, too."

"Yes," I said. This time I was the one with my chest puffed out. "That's my mama."

I went outside to meet Mama as Devin and the car puffed away.

"Couldn't get Devin to stay, huh?" I said, disappointed. At least Mama was here.

"He's staying," she said. "He's going to park the car."

I thought somebody might have to come and pick me up off the sidewalk.

"Any day is a good day for change," Mama said. "Isn't that what you said?"

Mama was carrying a huge large print Bible with a cracked leather cover. I'd seen it inside her nightstand before, but I'd never seen her take it out of the house. It looked like she'd tried to buff the front with petroleum jelly. Only Mama.

When we walked back inside, Eden was still buzzing around like a bumblebee, talking and hugging everyone in her path like it had been years since she'd seen them.

"Ms. Sheila, Ms. Sheila," Faith kept calling my name even after she ran and jumped into my arms. "Ms. Sheila, did you know I have a baby godbrother? His name is Joshua, and he's itsy-bitsy small just like this." She held her hands about twelve inches apart.

"I know. I was there—remember? I can't wait to go to your Auntie Anisha's house so I can see him again."

"I'll tell my mommy to call and let her know."

"Thank you," I told her, kissing her forehead. "I'd appreciate that."

I introduced Faith to Mama and they became fast buddies. As usual, Faith was firing about twenty questions a minute and Mama was patiently entertaining her. I'd noticed earlier that Sherri had looked to see that Faith was safely with me, but now she had her back turned, talking to a woman near the stone statue of Samson that was in the west wing of the church.

"Ms. Sheila, can I go back with Mommy and Ms. Gina?"

"Ms. Gina?"

"Yes. Ms. Gina came with me and Mommy to church today. She's our family-and-friend visitor."

Sherri and Gina spoke to Eden before they made it over to me, but that still didn't give me the time I needed to get my thoughts together. I had no idea what to say. Thankfully Eden had enough to say for everybody.

"I think this is the best Sunday I've had all year," Eden said. She beamed at Mama, Gina, and Devin, who'd just walked up behind us. "I hope this won't be the last Sunday you come to visit. I hope you see and feel that we're one big happy family. God's family."

I think Eden missed her calling as head of the greeting committee.

I walked over to Gina and got up the nerve to speak. It was

still an uncomfortable situation, but not acknowledging her at all would make it even more uncomfortable. I didn't want anything to stand between Gina and anything that God might speak to heart.

"Good to see you again, Gina. Especially under these circumstances and not any other."

"Thank you," she said. "Sherri's always been so sweet and accommodating to me that I couldn't turn down her invitation."

I could tell she wanted to say more. That we were both skating around circumstances that needed to be cleared up.

"Can I talk to you for a moment?" she asked. "Privately?"

"Sure," I said.

I felt safer because we were in the church. And on top of that, Mama was here. She was acting dignified now, but Mama would take off her earrings if she had to. We stepped away so the others couldn't hear us.

"I have one question," Gina said. "Were you ever in a relationship with Clive?" Her face showed no emotion, and her voice was even, but firm. I imagined that was how she drilled witnesses in court.

"No," I answered truthfully. "I considered Clive a friend, but we were never in a relationship."

I hoped Gina didn't ask anything else. I'd already settled everything else with God—asked for His forgiveness. God would forgive and forget, but I didn't know what Gina would do.

"I'm not sure if you saw the news report or not," she said.

"I saw it."

"Of course the news will swing a story in whatever way will get them the most viewers."

"I don't doubt that," I said.

"Regardless of that, Clive is still *my* husband. Until the divorce decree is signed, *I'm* going to stand by him. He hasn't signed the papers yet. That says a lot." Gina was talking like she thought I'd lied to her, but it wasn't my job to convince her.

"It does."

"Me and Clive were at the point of divorce seven years ago, but he came back home. And he *always* will," she said.

"And he should," I said. "Enjoy the service."

I walked away when it was evident that the chip on her shoulder toward me had returned. Gina was Sherri's guest, not mine. I wasn't going to let that ruin my day. I looked at Devin. He'd put on a tie. I don't think I'd seen him in a tie since Mama forced him to wear one to my college graduation dinner.

"You clean up nice," I told him.

"That's what the ladies say," he said. I pulled him to me and made him hug me—partly because I wanted to see if he smelled like smoke. I did a quick sniff check.

"You think you're slick," Devin said. "I know what you're trying to do. I ain't had a cigarette since last night." He pulled a fistful of peppermints and other assorted hard candies out of his pocket. "I'll probably eat all of this before this church service is out. I hope your pastor won't have me up in here all day."

Mama walked up to us like she thought we were having an argument.

"I know y'all ain't acting up in God's house."

Devin shook his head. "Calm down, Mama. We don't need you starting to wheeze and carrying on."

"Did you take your medicine?" I asked her.

"I told you—you're not going to worry me about that medicine. I'm going to take it every day and do exactly what the doctor tells me to do."

I waved my hands in the air. "Prayer works," I said.

Devin shook his head. "Next thing you know, Mama, your daughter is going to be preaching."

"I don't know about all of that," I said.

I walked with my family into the sanctuary—my biological one and my God-sent one. Eden had asked me to work at the bookstore for another two months, and I jumped at the opportunity. Most days I didn't know what tomorrow would hold, but I'd learned more every day that God's Word was true. Everything *was* working together for my good. And after thirty-three years, I was finally . . . finally . . . steppin' into the good life.

Epilogue

I don't even read books," Cassandra said. "I'm just here for the food."

She dipped a carrot stick in ranch dressing. Even though me and Sherri hadn't finished making the food trays for our book club's first meet-and-greet, Cassandra had taken it upon herself to make a plate. And a full one at that. I stopped her when I saw her eyeing the petit fours.

Cassandra had called the night after our Family and Friends Day at church. She claimed she'd had every intention of coming, but had come down with a stomach virus or some sort of food poisoning. I told her she could make it up to me, so I invited her to join us at the bookstore, hoping to introduce her to some women of faith, but not thinking she'd actually come.

She'd shown up early.

I told her it was a meet-and-greet at a *Christian* bookstore, but with how she was dressed, she must've somehow confused it with one of those after-work mixers she liked to attend. Cassandra had been boasting to Eden and Sherri most of the morning about how she'd been attracting professional men since she'd finally sent sorry Frank on his way and packing.

"I don't need a man who's chasing his dream. I need one who's already caught it," Cassandra had told them.

"I can tell your life must've been pretty interesting with Cassandra as your bestie," Sherri said when she'd gotten me alone.

"More than you'll *ever* know," I said.

Eden had gone up front to help the customers that were browsing through the store. She'd been handing out flyers all morning and talking about the book club to everyone who came in. She told me she'd even convinced a lady and her husband to return. Although her husband had stayed buried in the theological section, his wife was looking for a lighter read.

"This lemonade is tart," Cassandra complained. "Y'all got some more sugar?"

"Cassandra," I said. "Put the lemonade down and make yourself useful. Can you go ask Sherri where she put the name badges?"

"Okay. And I'll ask her where the sugar is, too."

My cell chimed, alerting me that I had a text. It was Lee.

Movie tonight?

I texted him back: *Of course. Call you later.*

It didn't even seem like I was talking to a minister when I talked to Lee. I guess I'd always thought ministers were supposed to be stuffy and talk about getting to heaven all the time. That wasn't the case with Lee.

Cassandra walked back into the office, holding the name badges and a black permanent marker. "Your bookworms are starting to show up," she said. "And Ace is out there, too."

"Chase who?" I asked.

"No. Ace," she said louder. "As in 'ace of spades.' As in 'ace in the hole.' As in Ace . . . *your* ex-man."

316

"Stop lying," I said, sitting down to write names on the badges.

"Do you think I'd lie?"

I smacked my lips and gave her *that* look.

"Okay, don't answer that question. Do you think I'd lie about *that*? Go look for yourself."

I peeped out the door and sure enough Ace was the first person I saw. And Lynette was with him.

"Maybe he'll leave in a minute," I said, not wanting to put any of us in an uncomfortable situation. "I'll go out when they're gone."

"You're going to be back here until after the meeting's over then, because they're here for the book club. I heard 'em say so. So what are you gonna do?"

There wasn't much of an option. "It's a meet-and-greet, so that's what I'm going out to do," I said.

"This should be interesting," Cassandra said, following me out on the back of my heels.

I turned around. Faced Cassandra so close that our noses touched.

"I am not about the drama anymore, Cassandra. And you aren't coming out here to embarrass me or make anybody uncomfortable. If you can't behave yourself and act like you've got some sense, you need to leave."

"Look at you with a backbone and what not," Cassandra said. She picked up one of the veggie trays and put on a perfect, innocent smile. "I'm officially minding my own business," she said. "I promise."

Ace and Lynette weren't the only people waiting for the meet-and-greet to start. I knew we'd had twelve people to sign up on the interest sheets, but there were at least twenty people in all. Sherri and Eden were already buzzing around to introduce themselves to people, and hand out the bookmarks and welcome packets Eden had supplied.

I immediately went up to Ace and Lynette.

"Uh . . . hi," I said. Their backs were turned to me, but even if they'd tried, they couldn't have re-created the looks they had on their faces when they saw it was me. Lynette was the first to recover.

"Small world," Lynette said.

"It is," I said. "I would've never thought this would be the place where I'd see you two again." I cleared my throat. "Congratulations, by the way."

Then I realized I'd given myself away.

"So you *were* there," Ace said.

I didn't know what to say. I was embarrassed, but there was nothing I could do about the past except try not to repeat my mistakes.

"That was me," I said. "I was right there beside Cousin Ruby."

"I thought the girls had concocted that story," Ace said.

Lynette looked at him like she'd believed her daughters from the beginning. "I told you," she said to him.

Ace was as attractive as he'd always been to me, but my heart didn't skip a beat the way it had done since the very first time I'd laid eyes on him in the Atlanta airport. God had erased my desire to be with Ace and even the pain that had lingered when I used to think about him.

"So you went out with Reggie, too, didn't you?" Lynette asked.

"I did," I said.

"Well, don't do it again," she said. "I love my cousin, but I wouldn't wish him on my worst enemy."

If there was any uneasiness between us, it was gone now.

"It was wrong. I shouldn't have intruded on your family moment," I admitted. "But I met a Man there that changed my life. And it wasn't Reggie," I was quick to say. "I let God into my heart that day."

I turned to Ace. "You were in my life for a reason. And for a season. But God . . . He's in my life for a lifetime."

"Amen to that," Cassandra said.

She'd finished putting out the trays and had made her way close enough to us to hear our conversation. She chomped down on a piece of broccoli like she was watching a stage play and we were the main actors.

"That's Cassandra for you," Ace said.

"Yep. That's Cassandra."

Lynette handed back the welcome packet and bookmark. "I think it's best if me and Ace find another activity to enjoy as a couple," she said.

"Agreed," Ace said to Lynette. "Regardless of what happened between us," he said to me, "I always wanted the best for you. I'm glad you found it."

I escorted them to the front of the bookstore, and Ace and Lynette walked out of Eden's Gates hand in hand. And just like God had promised, I was able to close the door. Forever.

Reading Group Guide

Dear Readers:

These questions are provided to help facilitate an entertaining and thoughtful exchange about the issues and characters in *Steppin' Into the Good Life*. If you'd like to arrange for Tia McCollors to join your book club discussion or visit your organization, she can be reached at Tia@TiaMcCollors.com. She also welcomes readers to visit her website (**www.TiaMcCollors.com**) and to follow her via her blog (**www.TiasPen.blogspot.com**), Facebook, or Twitter.

QUESTIONS

What are the most memorable scenes in the book?

What character(s) could you relate most closely to?

What lessons did you learn from the characters in *Steppin' Into the Good Life*?

What were the characters' flaws? What were their redeeming qualities?

Fiction often imitates life. Did the characters or situations in *Steppin' Into the Good Life* remind you of your life or the life of anyone you know?

How does your current life situation compare to what you used to envision? How could it be better?

What steps have you recently taken to fulfill your dreams/goals? What's holding you back? What helps to propel you forward?

SCRIPTURAL REFERENCES

* Romans 8:28 * Philippians 3:13–14 * Philippians 4:8
* Psalm 139:14 * 2 Corinthians 5:7

Lift Every Voice Books

Lift every voice and sing
Till earth and heaven ring,
Ring with the harmonies of Liberty;
Let our rejoicing rise
High as the listening skies,
Let it resound loud as the rolling sea.
Sing a song full of the faith that the dark past has taught us,
Sing a song full of the hope that the present has brought us,
Facing the rising sun of our new day begun
Let us march on till victory is won.

The Black National Anthem, written by James Weldon Johnson in 1900, captures the essence of Lift Every Voice Books. Lift Every Voice Books is an imprint of Moody Publishers that celebrates a rich culture and great heritage of faith, based on the foundation of eternal truth—God's Word. We endeavor to restore the fabric of the African-American soul and reclaim the indomitable spirit that kept our forefathers true to God in spite of insurmountable odds.

We are Lift Every Voice Books—Christ-centered books and resources for restoring the African-American soul.

For more information on other books and products
written and produced from a biblical perspective, go to
www.lifteveryvoicebooks.com or write to:

Lift Every Voice Books
820 N. LaSalle Boulevard
Chicago, IL 60610
www.lifteveryvoicebooks.com

The Last Woman Standing

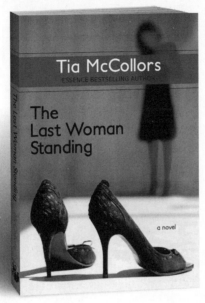

ISBN-13: 978-0-8024-9863-2

After being married to their careers instead of each other for ten years, "Ace" and Lynette Bowers ended their marriage. Four years later however, it seems as though their love never ended—to both their surprise and denial. Sheila Rushmore is Ace's current girlfriend and a woman who is used to getting what she wants—all except Ace's commitment to marriage. When Sheila realizes Lynette may be the cause, she launches a plan to play the hand of God, instead of allowing God to bring the love they all desire in His way.

LiftEveryVoiceBooks.com

Other titles by Tia McCollors

A Heart of Devotion

With life crumbling around her, Anisha is faced with choices she was sure she'd never have to make. An inspiring and emotional journey through adversity and spiritual self-discovery.

ISBN-13: 978-0-8024-5913-8

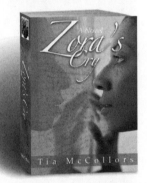

Zora's Cry

Zora Bridgeforth is twenty-nine and grappling with identity issues. To find an outlet for her feelings, she joins a multi-church women's discipleship group. God's hand works through their fellowship.

ISBN-13: 978-0-8024-9861-8

The Truth About Love

In the anticipated sequel to Zora's Cry, revisit the lives of the four women from the P.O.W.E.R. discipleship group. The women confirm the truth about love: that it never fails.

ISBN-13: 978-0-8024-9862-5

LEVB
LIFT EVERY VOICE BOOKS

LiftEveryVoiceBooks.com